Praise for Claire Lorrimer's novels:

Frost in the Sun

'Passion in the bloody battlefields of the Spanish Civil War . . . a huge and powerful novel'
Evening Standard

'A magnificent international historical saga'
Bookseller

'A sizzling read . . . exciting to the end'
Woman's Realm

'[The] setting is sheer glamour'   *Evening Telegraph*

Last Year's Nightingale

'Matchless storytelling . . . a fine historical saga'
Yorkshire Post

'Unashamedly romantic'   *Evening Telegraph*

'Gripping, vivid . . . a stirring tale'   *Bookseller*

The Silver Link

'Lovers of romantic fiction will love this book'
Bookseller

'Yet another successful historical family saga – perfect holiday read'   *Yorkshire Post*

Claire Lorrimer wrote her first book at the age of twelve, encouraged by her mother, the bestselling author Denise Robins. After the Second World War, during which Claire served in the WAAF on secret duties, she started her career as a romantic novelist under her maiden name, Patricia Robins. In 1970 she began writing her magnificent family sagas and thrillers under the name Claire Lorrimer. She is currently at work on her seventy-first book. Claire lives in Kent.

Find out more about Claire: www.clairelorrimer.co.uk

Also by Claire Lorrimer and available from Hodder

In ebook and paperback
Georgia
Last Year's Nightingale
The Silver Link
Frost in the Sun

Available in ebook
Second Chance
The Secret of Quarry House
The Shadow Falls
Troubled Waters
A Voice in the Dark
The Woven Thread
Variations
The Garden
You Never Know
Deception
Beneath the Sun

For Always
Relentless Storm
The Spinning Wheel
Dead Centre
An Open Door
The Reunion
Over My Dead Body
Connie's Daughter
Never Say Goodbye
The Search for Love
House of Tomorrow
Truth to Tell
Infatuation
Dead Reckoning
The Faithful Heart
The Reckoning
Emotions

CLAIRE LORRIMER

ORTOLANS

HODDER

First published in Great Britain in 1990
by Bantam Press
a division of Transworld Publishers Ltd.

This edition published in 2015
by Hodder & Stoughton
An Hachette UK company

1

A CIP catalogue record for this title is available from the British Library

Paperback ISBN 978 1 473 61304 1
eBook ISBN 978 1 444 75053 9

Typeset by Sabon LT Std by Palimpsest Book Production Ltd,
Falkirk, Stirlingshire

Printed and bound by Clays Ltd, St Ives plc

Hodder & Stoughton policy is to use papers that are natural, renewable
and recyclable products and made from wood grown in sustainable
forests. The logging and manufacturing processes are expected to conform to
the environmental regulations of the country of origin.

Hodder & Stoughton Ltd
338 Euston Road
London NW1 3BH

www.hodder.co.uk

For my cousin and dear friend Phyllis Calverley, in
grateful thanks for her steadfast encouragement,
and not least for her generosity in allowing me
access to her family's historic diaries in order
to create this work of fiction.

ACKNOWLEDGEMENTS

I would like to thank Mr and Mrs Bellière, who allowed me to use their lovely house as the inspiration for Ortolans; Amanda Willett for her help with the media research; Peter Chadwick for his help in the creation of the fresco; and the following people who have assisted me with the research necessary for this book: Iain Clark; the Victoria and Albert Museum; English Heritage; the National Trust; Kent County Council Listed Buildings Department; the *Mid Sussex Times* and Edenbridge and East Grinstead libraries.

In particular, I would like to thank my editor, Diane Pearson, and my secretary, Penrose Scott, for their unstinting support; and lastly my family for their patience and encouragement.

CL
1989

ACKNOWLEDGEMENTS

PROLOGUE

1588

In a tall oak tree overhanging the banks of a gently flowing river in the county of Sussex, an osprey was devouring the small carp it had caught in the shallows. The white feathers of its head and lower part of its body were dappled by rays of fierce June sunlight filtering through the green leaves. At frequent intervals, the bird lifted its head, listening to the unaccustomed noises that drifted across the still hot air. The sound of hammering was intermittent and disturbed the osprey more than did the steady rasping of a wood saw.

Down in the valley, the silvery tones of the Detcham village church clock chimed the midday hour and the disturbing noises ceased. The osprey settled, preening itself to the familiar sounds of running water, of sheep calling to their lambs and the metallic chatter of the ortolans nesting in the meadows.

''Tis lamentable hot!' sighed Master Pylbeam, the carpenter, as he, too, heard the midday chimes and, wiping the sweat from his forehead, settled himself in the shade cast by the north wall of the house. John, his eldest son, and young Tom sprawled beside him, leaving room for Master Merrymore, whose team of oxen, unhitched from their wagon, were grazing on the lush grass not far from the load of oak tree trunks they had carted this morning from the forest.

The two lads watched whilst their father unwound the cloth in which their mother had packed the midday repast – slices of pickled pork, corn bread and chunks of hard cheese. Near to hand stood a brown earthenware jug of ale. The youths had been working beside their father since an hour after daybreak and they were too concerned with the hunger gnawing at their stomachs to notice the leisurely approach of a stranger.

Master Hicks, the mason, was first to espy the young man strolling towards the half-built house upon which they had all been working. The stranger had a leather bag strung over one shoulder and his doublet was draped loosely over his other arm. It was obvious from the cut and style of his garments that this was no farm labourer; but curiously he was not mounted as a gentleman travelling across country would be.

'Good-day to you!' he said as he drew near enough for speech. Beneath his fringe of fair, curling hair, his green eyes smiled pleasantly at the group of workmen who were rising to their feet at the sound of his educated voice. 'No, please be seated. I have no wish to disturb you. On the contrary, I shall join you if I may.'

He sprawled in the grass beside them, perfectly at ease where they were not.

'I will introduce myself to you – Michael Darwin, at your service.'

'This be Master Pylbeam, the carpenter and they two do be his sons, Tom and John. I be Alfred Hicks, master mason and he be Merrymore, the carter.'

'It is my pleasure to meet you,' said the young man. He nodded his head in the direction of the building. 'I see that you are indeed master craftsmen. 'Tis a truly beautiful house in the making. I envy you your skills!'

There was such genuine admiration in his tone that the workmen relaxed and Tom, the youngest, grinned.

'It be hot for walking, Sir, surelye,' he said.

'And that is for certain,' said Michael Darwin. 'I was told in the village that there is a river nearby where I intended to slake my thirst.'

Simultaneously, the three men pushed their flagons of ale towards the visitor. He drank eagerly and, with no pretence of reluctance, accepted the subsequent offer of food. His method of eating was fastidious and whilst remaining respectfully silent, the men were hard put to conceal their curiosity. Sensitive to their feelings, their uninvited guest proceeded to enlighten them as to the reason for his presence.

'I am an artist,' he said, adding with a smile, 'or at least, that is what I hope to be when I have mastered my trade as well as you have mastered yours, Master Pylbeam and Master Hicks. I am making my way as best I can to Italy where I hope to find a tutor to teach me. Meanwhile, I am obliged to pursue my craft as best I can.'

He gave a short, merry laugh.

'I have been following a group of travelling players, who are making their way to the south coast. Last Saturday we were at Henfield Common. Whilst the crowds gather to watch the tumblers and jugglers or the dancing bear, I draw likenesses of people in the hope that they will buy their portraits from me for a few groats. Since I am without other means of support, you might call me both artist and vagabond!'

'I were at that there occasion in Henfield!' said the carter. 'It were axcellent. I justabout did enjoy myself although there must'a been two or three hundred people a-scrouging about. My missus was queered where they all did come from!'

Michael Darwin nodded.

'There was a good crowd. I earned myself a few pence that day. Now I am on my way to Rye where the players will be performing again later in the summer.'

'Rye be near the sea!' Tom announced. 'They do say the Spanish Frencheys will be coming across the sea and we shall be burnded and bloodshedded if us doant stop 'em.'

'Spanish Frencheys?' the artist repeated. 'Surely they cannot be both!'

'Frencheys be our name for foreigners in these parts,' explained Master Pylbeam kindly. 'If there'd be Frenchmen a-coming to kill us, we'd call 'em French Frencheys!'

'I am grateful to you for the explanation,' said the visitor, a look of amusement on his face. 'I learn something new every day on my travels. It would interest me greatly to learn more about your trade, Master Hicks. I have seen many beautiful houses, but never yet in the making. You must tell me how 'tis accomplished.'

Seeing that the youth's interest was genuine, the master mason rose to his feet.

'Once the site is chosen and the plans agreed, Master Pylbeam selects the timbers for the sill plates, tie beams and bay posts. When these are in place, 'tis time for the wall plates, the purlins and rafters, then the roof. Most often we put tiles on but new squire – Sir Richard Calverley he be – chose for to have these slabs. They did come from the east side o' Sussex – from a village called Horsham where stone's quarried. They be more durable than our baked tiles but, though I'd no ought to say so, I do think the red tiles be purtier.'

'Nevertheless, the slabs blend well with the surroundings,' the young man said, viewing the roof with his artist's eye.

'The gen'leman who do be going to live here, he said justa-bout the same. He be unaccountable pleased with the house,' the carpenter proffered. 'He didn't have no fancy to live in the old Grange up on the hill though he tol' me t'was part of the gift to him from Her Majesty, the Queen. In all the four hundred acres she gifted him for some brave service he done for Her Majesty, this here dip in this here meadow is where he be choosing to live. His mistus fancied being able to sight the river yonder from the upstairs window and Squire's fancy was took by the trees and all them dratted ortolans. That's what the house is to be named – Ortolans House – after them pesky finches!'

''Tis the owner's choice since he's paying the bills!' laughed the artist. 'I dare say he is a country lover, happy, as I am, to be in this corner of Sussex far away from the big city. If he is a family man, he'll not think London a healthy place to raise children.'

'You'm come from Lunnon then?' enquired Master Pylbeam whose curiosity had finally loosened his tongue.

'I was born there!' said Michael Darwin, running his hand appreciatively over a carved oak boss waiting to be mounted over the roof intersections. 'I'd be living there now but for a disagreement with my father as to my future.'

Young Tom was staring at the artist with round eyes.

'If you been a-living in Lunnon, Sur, then mebbe you seed the Queen?' he asked.

The artist nodded. 'Several times! My father often took me with him to court. I saw Her Majesty last on my seventeenth birthday – a year ago, that was – before I had made up my mind to leave home.' He paused, noticing the boy's simple homespun jerkin and breeches, and added thoughtfully: 'I suppose it must seem strange to you that I should wish to leave a life of luxury for that of a vagabond. But my father and I were in great disharmony. He wished me to accompany him to fight the Spaniards and I – well, ever since I can remember, I have wanted nothing else but to be a great painter.'

'Can you not be a great painter in Lunnon, then?' asked the carpenter.

'England is not the country in which to learn my trade,' Michael Darwin said. 'I need to go to Italy where painters like Signor Leonardo da Vinci and Raphael Santi lived. But the Pope lives in Italy and many Italians are Roman Catholics so my father would not hear of my going there. Thus I must make my own way, and since he would give me no money to pay my passage, I am obliged to earn it for myself.'

''Tis a strange way for a young gen'leman to earn a living!' said John Merrymore. 'Me – I'd leastways be building things that'll be standing, surelye, long after I be in graveyard.'

'Paintings last, too,' argued Michael Darwin gently. 'In our separate ways, we are both creators – or such I hope to be,' he added modestly.

Across the meadows came the sound of the church clock chiming the hour.

''Tis time we was at work!' said Master Pylbeam firmly.

'Plasterer comes in marnin' and we'll not be ready for him this road.'

'Perhaps I can be of some help?' suggested the visitor, but the men would not hear of it. For all the young man called himself a vagabond, he was no labourer and his hands were white and smooth. It would not seem fit that he should even assist John who was already back at work applying the wet wadges of wattle and daub between the studs. Tom, the youngster, was mixing the dung, horsehair and clay for his elder brother to apply.

'Then since you will not allow me to repay your hospitality with my labour, I will draw your likenesses for your amusement – and to pass the time!' said Michael Darwin.

He opened the leather satchel he had flung on the ground and withdrew some sticks of charcoal and several sheets of rough white paper. Sitting himself on one of the tree trunks, he became engrossed in his drawings.

By the time the men paused for a rest, he had done a fair likeness of Master Pylbeam facing up a length of oak with his adze, the carpenter's skill in the handling of this hoe-like implement such that the timber shone with a beautiful smoothness, the grain of the wood visible in flowing lines. He had drawn Tom and his brother; and the mason, who had been fixing the studs on either side of the gabled window-frames, making them ready to receive the wattle and daub. He had drawn John Merrymore, harnessing his oxen back between the heavy wooden shafts of the empty cart.

Each man in turn stared at his own likeness and that of the others in admiration. Their uncritical pleasure in the sketches was enhanced by the assurance of the artist that the portraits were theirs and might be taken home to show their families and to keep. The boy, Tom, quickly found his voice.

'You be clever enough, surelye, to draw the Queen!' he said, goggle-eyed.

'Alas, I have had no such opportunity!' smiled the artist,

'although I have painted a picture once of Hampton Court – which is one of her palaces.'

'Have you drawed Lunnon, then?' persisted Tom. 'I allus did want to go to Lunnon. My Dad was up at Smiffle Show adunnamany years ago, afore I were born, but I never did see Lunnon, nor never will I doubt!'

''Tis a big place!' said Michael Darwin. 'If I had more paper to spare, I could draw London for you. Then you could see how it looks.'

'Can you not draw on the wall?' Tom said eagerly. 'Plasterer will be covering it in marnin and t'wouldn't do no harm.'

'You shouldn't ought to be pestering the young gen'leman,' broke in his father, giving the lad a none-too-gentle clip over his ear, but at the same time leading the way back into the house. 'I doant see as how it would do no harm,' he muttered, 'leastways not if you've a fancy to make a drawing, Mr Darwin, Sir? But t'will be sundown soon and like as not ye've got to be going on your way?'

'I'm in no hurry, Master Pylbeam, other than that I must find a roof under which I can sleep this night.' The young man glanced at the pile of wood shavings in a corner of the room and his face broke into a smile.

'We could come to an arrangement, Master Pylbeam. If you will allow me to stay here for the night, by morning, I will have young Tom's picture of London completed for him. T'would save me the cost of a night's lodging at an inn, and with the weather so warm, I'll not be cold.'

The men were uneasy at the thought of this strange youth, who they did not doubt was of gentle birth, sleeping rough in the half-completed house. But by sundown, they had given way to persuasion and young Tom had been sent home to fetch food, a lantern and a blanket. The boy would have liked to remain with the artist but he was not permitted. Nevertheless he was awake at the sound of the first cock's crow and, for once forgoing his breakfast of porridge, ran the two miles to the new house to see how his picture was progressing.

Michael Darwin had covered a section of one wall with dark bold lines. He greeted the boy with a sigh.

"Tis not as I'd hoped, Tom. The surface is too bumpy. See here, the surface of the river – that's the Thames by the way – it should be smooth, with ripples only where there is a wake from the boats and barges.' Shaking his head, he pointed out the uneven lines of towers, the curves of the bridge where none should be.

'Oh, but 'tis a prime picture, surelye!' gasped Tom.

'Perhaps . . . if I had had a good surface and my paints . . .'

'Plasterer comes today. He'll make you a prime surface. He be sing'lar good at plastering, so my dad says. If master mason tells him to do it, he'll do as he's tolt.'

Michael Darwin looked longingly at his pigskin pack. Within were his treasured sable paintbrushes, his chamois-leather pouches of pigments. He needed but a few yolks of raw eggs to make paints and he would dearly love to feel the brushes in his hand again. When he had left home with only a sovereign in his pocket, he had believed, on his journey to the south coast, he might find a burgher or squire who would commission him to paint his wife or child, and in such manner, earn his passage to Italy. With little knowledge of the world beyond the protected environment of his home, he had discovered that work was not so easily come by for an eighteen-year-old, untrained, unknown artist. After several weeks, he had realized that if he were to provide himself with no more than victuals, he had no alternative but to join the travelling players and earn what little he could with his charcoal sticks. There had been no single opportunity to paint.

Now, despite the handicaps of the roughly applied daub and wattle, his picture had begun to take shape not only on the wall but in rich colours in his head – the lapis-lazuli blue he would mix with a pinch or two of black-lamp pigment to dull it for the sky; the malachite green toned with raw umber for the meadows leading down to the south banks of the Thames, yellow ochre for London Bridge and for the stonework of the Tower of London and the Palace of Westminster.

He pulled himself up sharply. Pigments were expensive to buy and once his meagre supply was used, he knew of no other place than London where he could renew his stock, even if he could afford to. He had vowed never to return to London until after he had made his way to Italy; that when next he saw his family, he would be a famous painter. There would be no opportunity to purchase further pigments until he reached Italy.

'Well, young Tom, if Master Hicks agrees to allow me a little piece of wall to work on, and if you can bring me a fowl's egg or two, I will paint you a small part of this drawing – the river, perhaps and London Bridge, the rooftops and spires of the city.'

At first, all the men were doubtful. What if the Squire were to visit them unexpectedly and find the plasterer wasting his time; and it would be wasted because, so the artist told them, he must apply his paint whilst the plaster was still wet and once dry, would remain there for ever. They could all lose their jobs and their reputations for such foolery . . . and foolery it was since the painting was for no better reason than to let young Tom see London town as it was.

Nevertheless, it was finally agreed that a small section of wall between two beams could be freshly plastered for the artist, since this room was to be the library when it was completed and all its walls wood panelled. No one, lest it be an unexpected visitor, would ever know the plaster behind the panelling had been painted.

By sundown, a second section of wall had been plastered. To please the child, the artist had painted in a tiny figure of Tom on the south bank of the Thames and now all the men wished to be included in the painting. They had watched with fascination the manner in which the young painter had carefully separated the white from the yolk of the eggs Tom had fetched for him, drying each yolk by passing it from one hand to the

other until there was no trace of albumen left. On the surface
of the smooth piece of board Master Pylbeam had provided,
Michael Darwin had mixed the precious pigments painstakingly into the yolk, sometimes merging the resulting colours
together to obtain a new shade of green or red or blue. They
had watched, neglecting their own work, how easily and with
such concentration he applied the paint to the damp plaster
and with it, created a world he knew and which they were
coming to know.

'And ye'll stay another night and put *me* in the picture
tomorrow?' each one pleaded. 'The mistus, too, she askt to
be put in. She did say to tell 'ee she'd be wearing her pink
Sunday gown in London and if t'was hot like today, her'd be
carrying her pink sunshade with the white tassles what
belonged to her gurt-granny.'

The days became a week and then another week. Whenever
the artist had completed a section of wall, the plasterer came
from whichever room he was working in to prepare another.
Mistress Pylbeam, accompanied by three little children, came
to see the wall, bringing cherries, pastries, a bowl of curdy
cheese and fresh-baked bread, and a further supply of hens'
eggs, so that the three toddlers could be in the picture.

Beyond caring now about his fast-dwindling supply of
pigments, Michael Darwin worked all the daylight hours on
his first fresco. He was happy as he had not been in months,
and Italy, with its promise for the future, was momentarily
forgotten. With cheerful compliance, he added even the carter's
oxen dragging a load of timber across the meadows leading
down to the wharf at South Warke. He painted the Queen
being carried to the Palace of Whitehall in the royal barge,
waving her handkerchief to Mistress Pylbeam clothed in her
pink Sunday dress. He painted Sir Francis Drake, mounted on
a big white horse, tossing a gold sovereign into young John's
buttoned-back felt cap.

'And that is you, Master Armitage,' he told the plasterer as
he painted a tiny figure high up on the ramparts of the Tower

of London, 'when you were chosen by the Lord Chamberlain to repair the east tower!'

Finally, to please young Tom, he added his own figure standing on the prow of a large sailing-ship heading down the Thames, 't'wards Italy!' as Tom insisted.

But even Michael Darwin's wall fresco ceased to be the topic of conversation the night bonfires were lit high up on the South Downs. News reached the village and from thence the artist that well over a hundred Spanish ships had been sighted off Plymouth and that English ships had sailed under Sir Francis Drake's command to intercept them.

For several days rumours were rife until finally by the end of the month, facts were confirmed by the vicar from his pulpit that the Spanish armada had been driven into the North Sea and the threat of invasion was over.

It was the moment, Michael Darwin decided, that he must move on if he were to reach Rye on foot to rejoin the group of travelling players. It would be safe now to cross the English Channel and although the beautiful house had almost come to feel his own, he had exhausted his supply of pigments and could paint no more.

It was of little consequence to him that he must leave his work behind him and that Master Pylbeam had already begun to cut the oak panels that would hide his painting from others' gaze. His pleasure had come from the creating and he knew that he had not wasted his time. He had discovered how much he needed to learn if he were to be more than a simple amateur; that talent was not enough on its own to meet the standards he had set himself.

It was his fellow craftsmen – the master mason, the carpenter, the plasterer and finally the newly-arrived wood-carver – who were saddened, not by the young gentleman's departure, although they liked him well and wished him well, but by the necessity to cover over the charming London scene in which they themselves had been immortalized.

''Tis hidden now!' Master Pylbeam said to his sons as they

fixed the last of the wood panels between the beams. 'But doant you never disremember it's there, young Tom.' He noted the wistful expression in the boy's eyes and added with a grin: 'And you beant be lying if you tells your gran'chillun' as how once you was pictured standing on the banks of the Thames awaving to the Queen!'

'That I was, surelye!' said young Tom, his face slowly resuming its customary grin.

PART ONE

1788–92

CHAPTER ONE

1788

Lady Calverley pulled the bell rope and summoned the footman.

'Find out if the child is awake yet, Harry!' she ordered. 'If she is, tell Dora to bring her down to see me.'

'Yes, milady! Dora asked for breakfast for the young lady an hour ago, but Cook said the tray came back untouched.'

Lady Calverley sighed.

'Then tell Dora I want to see her before she brings Miss Eleanor down.'

As the footman departed, the elderly woman straightened her lace mob-cap and turned to regard her husband whose head was buried in the *Morning Post*.

'I do hope the poor child is not ill, Walter!' she exclaimed. 'That long journey down from Scotland may have proved too much for her. She looks so thin and frail!'

'Country air will put some colour into her cheeks!' muttered Sir Walter, who had not greeted with enthusiasm his wife's arrangement to have her unknown godchild to stay with them at Ortolans for six months. He had glimpsed the girl in the hallway when their neighbours, the Howells, had delivered her last night. Half-hidden by an over-large black travelling cloak, the child had looked scared out of her wits as she bobbed him a curtsy and scuttled upstairs after the maid.

Frequently bored and frustrated by the infirmities of old age, Sir Walter had become something of a recluse since their only surviving daughter had married a Frenchman and gone to live abroad. Their only son, William, was absent on a prolonged

Grand Tour. At least the house was peaceful, he told himself, and he had his wife's undiluted attentions. Now he was obliged to put up with a strange child around the place!

'As soon as Eleanor is well enough, I must have her fitted for some new clothes!' his wife was saying. 'I know the McCores are strict Calvinists but really, Walter, you would have been as horrified as I to see the garments Dora unpacked last night. All Eleanor's dresses are shapeless and made in some horrible black, grey or dark brown colour – and the child only fifteen!'

'Didn't look it! Skinny little scarecrow!' her husband grunted, returning to his newspaper.

There was a knock on the door and the young girl Lady Calverley had hired to look after her visiting god-daughter came into the drawing-room. Only two years older than her new charge, Dora Pylbeam was nevertheless the eldest daughter in a family of thirteen, and well accustomed to children. She was rosy-cheeked, cheerful, plump and good-natured, and Lady Calverley thought her the right choice as maid for Eleanor since, being so close in age, she could also serve as companion to her. For the past month, her own maid, Molly, had been training Dora in her duties.

'Well, Dora, I understand Miss Eleanor has not eaten her breakfast. Is she not well?'

''Tis my opinion she's no more'n queered, milady!'

Lady Calverley, who was familiar with the Sussex dialect, concealed a smile.

'What has she to be frightened of, Dora? You've not been telling her the house is haunted, I hope!'

'No, milady, I've not done no such thing. Her be just finding things a bit strange, surelye. She ain't had no maid afore – and the bed, she'd not never seen a four-poster. Seems as how all her can say is: "Oh, look! Dora!" at this and that, admiring like. I thought as how she were sleepin' but when I went in, she was in that twill nightshirt kneeling on the winder-seat, a-lookin' out at the garden.'

'No harm in that, Dora!' Lady Calverley said gently.

'No, milady, 'ceptin' her could catch her death of cold, but though her hops back into bed fast as ever I tolt her, her kept askin' me: "What are those blue flowers called, Dora?" And when I tells her thems bluebells and if'n the sun stays shining, we can go down to the wood and pick as many as her wants, you'd have thought as how it was Christmas, milady. She were like a bairn with a golden guinea when I tolt her she could throw grain to them pesky white doves she espied on the roof! "It's all so purty, so purty!" her keeps saying.'

'You must remember, Dora, Miss Eleanor has spent nearly all her life in a city,' Lady Calverley said. 'She is unaccustomed to country life. Since she is not ill, you may bring her down as soon as she is dressed.'

Though Lady Calverley had written on many occasions to Tabitha and Hamish McCore asking if her god-daughter might come on a visit, the Scottish couple had been unwilling to make the necessary arrangements for their ward. Walter was of the opinion that they disapproved of the Calverleys who, because they had title and wealth and were not Calvinists, they probably considered to be dissolute! There was little Joan Calverley could do other than to write regularly to her god-daughter and send her gifts on her birthday and at Christmas time. She was convinced that the girl's neatly written replies were censored, for the language was stilted and the spelling too perfect for so young a child. Eleanor's day-to-day exist-ence, by all accounts, was quite unnaturally restricted – prayers, lessons, sewing, embroidery, more prayers, and her only outings were to prayer meetings at the kirk.

Although Lady Calverley went regularly to church every Sunday and on holy days, and had brought up all her children very firmly in the Christian faith, she believed that their child-hood should be as carefree and happy as circumstances allowed. It was a policy she had never regretted, more especially when three of her four daughters died prematurely – one of diphtheria in childhood, one in her twenties of consumption and the third in childbirth. Now that the fourth, Catherine, was living so far away from home, she renewed her attempts to persuade the McCores to allow little Eleanor to visit them.

Fortuitously, the Calverleys were on excellent terms with their neighbours, the Howells, who lived at The Grange up on the hill to the north of Detcham. On learning of Lady Calverley's interest in her god-daughter, they offered to bring Eleanor back with them when they next returned from their estate in Scotland. One of their children, Jane, Mrs Howell said, was of the same age as Eleanor and the two girls could enjoy each other's society during the summer.

Unable to produce any valid excuse for a further refusal of their permission, the McCores had allowed Eleanor to accept the invitation.

The door of the big drawing-room opened, and the girl came into the room. She made her curtsy and with head still bent, waited for her godmother to speak. Dressed in a drab brown shapeless garment, her fair hair scraped back in a tight bun at the back of her head, she looked like a child from the poorhouse.

'I hear from Dora that you have been admiring the garden, my dear!' Lady Calverley said encouragingly. 'I myself am a very keen gardener and so it pleases me to hear that you share my interest.'

At last, the drooped head was raised, and Lady Calverley found herself staring into a pair of violet-blue eyes which looked enormous in the pale, thin face. The girl appeared to be nearer twelve than fifteen – and was far too thin, she thought anxiously.

'There are so *many* flowers, ma'am!' the girl murmured. 'They are even growing on the house!'

Lady Calverley smiled.

'That is because I like the scent of roses at my bedroom window. Now you must call me Godmother, my dear, and this is your Uncle Walter who you met last night.'

The eager expression was gone as once again, the girl's head drooped as she curtsyed.

'Now, my dear, I want you to enjoy your little holiday with us. You are therefore to do exactly as you please except that I shall insist upon you eating properly. You are far too thin! When you have had something to eat, you shall choose how you will spend this afternoon.'

There would be time enough for the dressmaker another day, Lady Calverley thought, guessing instinctively that this child needed time to settle down. She rang the bell and told Harry to have Cook send in a dish of scrambled eggs and a glass of cold milk.

'You shall go down to the farm with Dora and collect some eggs for Cook,' she suggested as she motioned Eleanor into a chair. 'Perhaps you would also like to watch the cows being milked?'

Once again, the huge eyes were raised with an expression of pleasure, followed by anxiety.

'You don't have to go if you don't wish it,' Lady Calverley said, patting the girl's arm.

'Oh, it isn't that, ma'am – I mean, Godmother. It's just that . . . that . . . could I see the house first?' She looked round the room and murmured: 'It is all so pretty – like a doll's house I once saw in a shop – only big instead of small. I have never seen a house like it!'

'Ortolans was built a long time ago, during the reign of Queen Elizabeth. That was when the first Calverley came to live here. You can read about it in the journal your Uncle Walter is writing which tells the history of Ortolans. But first, tell me about your house – your guardian's house – in Edinburgh. Is that not quite large?'

Gradually, Lady Calverley prised from her god-daughter a description of the gaunt, grey stone mansion on the outskirts of Edinburgh in which Eleanor had been incarcerated. Since the untimely death of her parents in the West Indies when she was eight years old – and having no other relatives – she had been despatched to Scotland to live with her elderly aunt and uncle who were childless. In this grim, cold environment, the

lonely little girl had grown up unloved, harshly disciplined
and subjected to the parsimonious restrictions of her strict
Calvinist relatives. It was small wonder, Lady Calverley thought
as she pieced together the halting replies to her questions, that
Eleanor looked such a frightened waif!

Despite the emotional and physical privations of the past
seven years, Eleanor's spirit had not been entirely subdued,
her godmother realized. The tray of food brought in by Harry
was slowly consumed and true to her promise, Lady Calverley
took the girl on a tour of the house, herself deriving great
pleasure in Eleanor's rapt fascination with everything she saw.
Slowly the apprehensive expression in her face gave way to
one of eager delight, and her questions and exclamations, at
first hesitant, became increasingly spontaneous. Were all the
portraits in the dining-room of the Calverley ancestors? How
prettily the panelling shone on the walls – it must be quite a
lot of work keeping it all so beautifully polished!

Lady Calverley smiled.

'We are fortunate in having all the labour we need!' she
explained. 'The women and girls come up daily from the village
so we are not dependent upon the living-in staff. Cook, the two
footmen, the butler and grooms live over the stables which
you shall see presently. Do you ride, my dear?'

She might as well have asked if Eleanor had ever flown to
the moon! But the violet-blue eyes were sparkling with
excitement.

'I would very much like to do so!' she said in an awed
whisper as Lady Calverley led the way out of the dining-room
and along the passage to the library.

After a moment of staring wide-eyed at the book-lined
walls, Eleanor looked tentatively at her godmother.

'May I touch the books?' she asked shyly. 'I have never
seen so many!'

Lady Calverley smiled.

'But of course, my dear. Sir Walter and I have always
encouraged our children to read. I will look out some suitable

titles for you. Now, do you see on the desktop that big leather book? That is my husband's hobby now that he can no longer enjoy his former sporting activities.'

Eleanor took a step towards the desk and gently touched the cover.

'*The Calverley Journal*,' she read, '*1588 to* . . . But there is no final date!'

'Because it is our hope that there will be future generations of Calverleys for many years to come!' Lady Calverley said. 'We are waiting for our son, William, to return from abroad and, hopefully, to marry and settle down to providing Sir Walter with an heir. The house and estate are entailed, you see, and may not be passed to the distaff members of the family.'

With Eleanor at her side exclaiming at the low height of the ceilings which she could touch quite easily if she stood on tiptoe, Lady Calverley went back into the hall and pointed to yet another portrait.

'That is my son, William!' she said proudly.

Eleanor stood gazing at the picture of a young man leaning nonchalantly against a pillar. He was wearing court dress, and the blue velvet coat – full-skirted – was open to reveal an elaborately embroidered pink waistcoat. The white breeches and stockings were in sharp contrast to the black of his Spanish leather pumps with their blue rosettes.

'He is very handsome!' the girl said softly as she admired the somewhat aquiline features which were softened by gentle blue eyes. Beneath his rounded chin was an intricately folded, white silk neckcloth.

'Of course, William is much older now; that was painted over fourteen years ago!' Lady Calverley said. 'His father and I miss him quite dreadfully, but according to his letters, he is enjoying himself so vastly on his travels round Europe and the Middle East that we cannot be sure when we may expect him home.'

Her voice was wistful and at once the girl responded.

'I shall pray that your son will soon come back!' she said simply, wanting to please this kindly woman who she knew already she was going to love. Her Aunt Tabitha, she had long ago decided, did not have a heart, or else it was too deeply encased in that drab, rigid body to be touched. Her only concerns in life, so often repeated to Eleanor, were to do her duty and observe all the tenets of her Calvinist teaching. Eleanor, as she followed her godmother up the oak staircase to the upstairs landing, noting the soft deep-piled rugs and pretty curtaining hanging in all the leaded light casement-windows, was astonished to find that Lady Calverley did not share her aunt's belief that any form of luxury was a sin! There was, too, she discovered to her delight, an enchanting informality about this old house. Rooms led off each other, some with quaint, sloping ceilings and cupboards built under the eaves; others with wide, uneven floorboards, all made of beautifully polished oak.

Her godmother's room was in the east wing, Uncle Walter's dressing-room adjoining. Another door led to a tiny room for the maid, Molly, who, Dora had told her this morning, was like herself a member of the Pylbeam family and Dora's aunt. Eleanor already knew every inch of her own bedroom with its three-sided window-seat and exciting four-poster bed; but the old nursery adjoining, to which her godmother now took her, was a fresh revelation.

'I have left most of my children's favourite toys untouched!' Lady Calverley said as she pointed to the big wooden grey-and-white rocking horse and the shelf full of dolls. '. . . for the time when I have grandchildren to enjoy them!' she added with a smile. 'Those regiments of lead soldiers belonged to my husband when he was a boy, and William treasures them.'

Seeing Eleanor's glance at the big oblong scrubbed deal table, she explained that this day nursery was also the school-room, and that the Calverley children had done their lessons here with a governess or tutor to teach them. There were four large, upholstered armchairs by the window which looked well-worn but comfortable.

'If you have little Jane Howell to visit, you may wish to entertain her here,' said Lady Calverley, 'although hopefully we shall have a fine, hot summer and you can spend a great deal of time out of doors.'

As she took her young protégée out on to the landing, she pointed to a small narrow staircase leading sharply upwards.

'There are several attics up there,' she announced. 'Sir Walter and I have often thought of having them converted into bedrooms for the servants, but now that the children have left home and we have so many spare rooms, there seems little point in it. We use them only as storerooms.'

She linked her arm through Eleanor's and together they descended the main staircase. From a table in the downstairs hall, she picked up a wide-brimmed, straw hat and placed it on her head. Taking Eleanor's hand she led her through a garden door into the warm sunshine.

'Should I not wear a bonnet?' the girl asked in a puzzled voice.

Lady Calverley paused.

'But of course, if you wish, dear, but do you not like to feel the breeze in your hair and the sun on your cheeks? I really do not think the rays are strong enough to harm your complexion!' Seeing Eleanor's look of astonishment, she added thoughtfully: 'I am sure it is necessary in a city to behave more conventionally when you go out. Down here in the heart of the country, we tend to do as we please!'

There seemed to be almost a tangible relaxation of Eleanor's body as, side by side, they crossed the terrace, and walked down the brick path between the borders of forget-me-nots and lavender bushes. Lady Calverley paused as they reached the big walnut tree at the end of the path, around which was a circular oak bench.

'It is such a pretty view of the house from here,' she said. 'I often come to sit here on a summer's evening. From the other side of the tree, one can see the river.'

Eleanor was standing unmoving as her eyes followed the

old lady's pointing finger. The sight of the house lying sleepily in the afternoon sunshine brought a lump to her throat. Clusters of creamy pink rosebuds covered the close-studded walls. Swallows were darting to and fro, building their nests under the eaves of one of the cross wings. A cluster of white doves were preening themselves on the great stone slabs of the roof. As Eleanor watched, one of the swallows swooped down in an arc over the mirror-like surface of an ornamental lily pond, snatching at an insect before flying back to its nest.

Mistaking the expression on the girl's face, Lady Calverley said gently:

'I expect everything will seem a little strange at first, my dear, but it will not be long, I hope, before you feel quite at home with us.'

She was unprepared for the vehemence of Eleanor's reply – her voice raised for the first time – as she said:

'Everything is very different, but not strange, Godmother. I feel somehow as if this is my real home. I love your house. I love your garden and I'm so very, very happy to be here!'

'Oh, my dear, I am so pleased!' Lady Calverley said. 'I only wish you could have come to visit us before. But let us not waste this lovely day with regrets. We will go back to the house and summon Dora, and she shall walk with you down to the Home Farm. That will give you an appetite for dinner!'

'But I have done no work today, Godmother. You have not yet told me my duties!'

Lady Calverley regarded Eleanor in astonishment.

'But my dear, you are not a servant!' she said gently.

The girl looked on the point of tears.

'But I must do my duty and assist in any way I can!' Her voice broke as she added forlornly: 'I have never worked on a farm!'

Lady Calverley was shocked. Although she was fully aware of the Calvinist dogma that through work alone one could obtain salvation, she had not anticipated that her god-daughter would be so deeply indoctrinated. She had never met the

Scottish couple who, she now suspected, had taken on the guardianship of the orphan as a matter of duty rather than love.

'You will find our ways very different here in England,' she said, putting an arm round the girl's drooping shoulders. 'You must not worry about work – we have many servants to do what is needed. You are here on holiday and if you wish to please me, you will do so merely by being happy.'

She was rewarded by the look of amazement followed by relief on Eleanor's face. The child could be quite pretty given new clothes and a ribbon in her hair, she thought as she noted the radiance in her god-daughter's eyes. It was going to afford her the greatest pleasure to effect the transition she now envisaged. She would be like the fairy godmother in the French tale of Cendrillon, and she could not wait for the time when she could surprise Walter. He had always enjoyed it when Catherine had had her young friends for an afternoon, especially if they were pretty girls. Being a mere, unimaginative male, he would not be prepared for the transformation of this drab little cygnet into a swan!

Eleanor was no less surprised than her uncle by her metamorphosis. It was as if her new, pretty appearance had changed her, too. Even the freeing of her long, fair hair from confinement had somehow freed her spirit, and gradually she had succumbed to her godmother's suggestion that she need not concern herself quite so often with what was right and what was the wrong thing to do. Conditioned by Aunt Tabitha's puritanical upbringing, it took a little time before she had felt able to run across the grass instead of walk; to laugh instead of pray; to pick wild flowers with Dora or garden flowers with Godmother, knowing there would always be more another day. Now she could talk on any subject she wished and be certain of Lady Calverley's kindly response. She had even learned not to be afraid of Uncle Walter with whom she played backgammon or chess, and who liked it when she read the newspaper to him. Her godmother said she was the only member of the household who could put him in a good humour these days! Although he denied it, she knew it was Uncle Walter who had given permission for her to have one of the farm puppies, a big shaggy bob-tailed sheepdog she called Rex.

As one summer's day followed another, the only cloud on Eleanor's happiness was the knowledge that soon the six months of her holiday would be over, and she must return to the dreary house and company of her guardians. For this reason, she struggled ineffectually not to love too deeply her godmother, Dora, Rex, the gardens, the river, the trees – and not least Ortolans. When no one was about, she would sometimes wander from room to room, pressing her face against the mullioned panes of the windows, resting her hands on the shining, carved oak newel-posts, feeling the house opening its arms to her as if it were alive. It demanded that she love it and she tried very hard – though unsuccessfully – to prevent herself doing so.

Although she was perfectly content and well accustomed to being without the company of her contemporaries, to please her godmother, she went to tea with Jane Howell at The Grange. Surprisingly, she found herself enjoying the company of the friendly, freckle-faced girl and returned the invitation. Jane arrived with her brother, Charles, a painfully shy young man who, Jane told her later, was quite 'brainy' and expected to do very well at Oxford. He tended to blush whenever Eleanor spoke to him, and she felt ill at ease in his presence. Fortunately, the afternoon passed quite quickly with games of Pall Mall and a promenade down to the river much enjoyed by Rex whose energetic antics reduced both girls to helpless laughter. Dora, who had been instructed to accompany them, later informed Lady Calverley that the Howells' visit was a success.

''Tis my thinking, your ladyship, begging your pardon, as it were all Miss Eleanor needed to be like other girls her age.

She and Miss Jane were a-giggling and a-whispering and it were only the poor young man as was out of it like.'

Lady Calverley smiled.

'Tell Harry we'll all take refreshment on the terrace. It will be an excellent moment to impart some good news I have for Miss Eleanor. I am sure you will be pleased, too, Dora. Her guardians have agreed to my request that she remain with me for a whole year!'

Dora grinned.

'She'll be that happy, your ladyship, surelye. I reckon as how it's been keepin' her awake at night, a-worryin' she'd soon be going back to that there aunt and uncle of hern. They be that strict – always a-prayin' and Miss Eleanor not doing nothing but learn her bible and stitch the mending!'

'Yes, well, we won't discuss that, Dora. No doubt they do things differently in Scotland. Tell the children tea will be served at half-past four.'

Somehow, Lady Calverley thought as she went upstairs to tidy herself before tea, she must try to persuade the McCores to consider a change of guardianship. There could be no doubt that Eleanor was happy here at Ortolans. Her face and figure had rounded, her cheeks bloomed and it was by no means unusual to hear her singing! Walter was enchanted by the child, although he would not admit to it. As for herself, having Eleanor for company was the next best thing to having William home. Surely, she thought, it could not be long now before he returned. He had been absent nearly two whole years.

The summer turned to autumn and then to winter. Huge logs burned in all the fireplaces and at Christmas, a vast yule log was lodged in the inglenook fireplace in the drawing-room. Eleanor learned to play the spinet and practised carols which Sir Walter hummed, slightly out of tune, from behind his newspaper. The puppy, almost full grown now, was her shadow and despite Walter's half-hearted complaints, followed his young mistress from room to room.

There were visits and exchanges of gifts from freckle-faced

Jane; visits, too, from her brother, Charles, who Sir Walter now called 'The Love-Sick Swain' when in jocular mood, and he spoke of him to Eleanor. Charles was as tongue-tied and dull as ever, and despite his moderate good looks, did not cut a romantic figure in Eleanor's eyes. Secretly, when she was unobserved, she would stand gazing at the portrait of William Calverley, the unknown son and heir who one day would return from his travels. It was something she both longed for and dreaded. Although she was immensely curious to meet the handsome William, she feared his advent might mean that Godmother would no longer have need of her company, and she would have to return to her guardians, to the cold grey silent edifice on the rainswept hill in Edinburgh. Tears would come to her eyes at the thought of leaving her adored godmother, Uncle Walter, Dora, the devoted Rex – and flow down her cheeks uncontrollably as she imagined herself, trunks piled on to the carriage roof, turning to wave a last goodbye to Ortolans. Prising from her the reason for her tears, Dora did her best to comfort the girl.

'Adone-do, Miss Eleanor! Even if'n you did have to leave, her ladyship would be wanting you back on another visit, surelye. Her's that fond of you, and the Master, too. Anyroad, I doant see no purpose her ladyship sending you away just 'cos Mr William be back. My mam allus says as how it's daughters as is company when they grows up, not sons, and you be like a daughter to her ladyship, surelye!'

Reassured, Eleanor threw herself wholeheartedly into the preparations for Christmas – her first ever at Ortolans and which proved a jolly occasion. Soon it was spring again. Eleanor went down to the woods with Dora to pick armfuls of bluebells. The following month, with a sense of joyful recognition, she saw that the swallows had returned. It was the start of her second year at Ortolans and she knew exactly what would happen – the doves would start building in the dovecot, the fireplaces would be swept clean of their ashes and she would help Godmother pick flowers to stand in the empty grates. Uncle Walter would come out to sit in the garden and Albert, the carpenter handyman, would put ladders up the sides of the house and paint strong-smelling linseed oil on the wintered oak beams. The old gardener would come grumbling about the damage done by Albert to his roses and once again, the fresh, sweet smell of newly opened blooms would waft in through her bedroom windows.

She had believed herself happy, Eleanor thought, as she went in search of her godmother, but on this magical day, she knew herself happier than she had ever been in her life before.

'I'm going down to the river with Dora to see if the king-fishers are back, if you don't need me for anything, Godmother!' she said.

For once she was wearing a hat – a yellow chip bonnet – which she fastened round her neck with ribbons for no better reason than that it was so pretty. The ribbons matched the blue stripes of her full-skirted cambric dress beneath which she wore only her petticoat, for she had long since discarded the tightly binding stays Aunt Tabitha had insisted upon. As a consequence, the soft, newly developing curves of her bosom were outlined beneath the muslin tucker of her bodice.

Lady Calverley smiled, amused to see that this morning, her god-daughter was all child. There were occasions now when Eleanor could look like a young woman – and there were signs that her forecast of beauty for the child was proving correct.

'Run along then, child! I shall not need your company until this afternoon when you might care to come with me to see poor old Mrs Merrymore who is ill. I will see you at luncheon.'

Eleanor's departure was delayed however by the entrance of Harry, the junior footman. He came into the room carrying a silver salver on which lay a letter which he presented to Sir Walter with the advice that the postboy was waiting to see if there was any reply.

'Why, bless my soul – this must be from William, my dear!'

Sir Walter said as he glanced at the Italian letter heading. His face broke into a smile as, putting in his eyeglass, he scanned the writing. 'It is indeed! He is leaving Florence today and is on his way to France. He intends to spend a few weeks visiting friends in Paris and will then make his way home via Rouen where he will sojourn briefly with Catherine.'

Lady Calverley gave a little gasp of pleasure as her husband dismissed the servant.

'Then we can expect our dear boy home this summer. What wonderful news!' Excitedly she paced the room. 'Tomorrow, the servants shall begin a thorough spring-cleaning of William's room,' she said radiantly to Eleanor. 'I think we might go together to Brighthelmstone and see if we can purchase some material for new hangings. You shall help me choose something really fashionable.' Turning to her husband, she said: 'You must instruct the groom to make sure William's stallion is properly exercised, my dear. As soon as we have a more exact date of arrival from William, we will arrange a ball for him. There will be so many people anxious to see him again after so long! He is so well liked by all our neighbours, Eleanor, but you will soon see why for yourself.'

'We shall have all the scheming matrons with marriageable daughters back on our doorstep!' announced Sir Walter gruffly. 'However, 'tis time the boy took a wife. I'll not go to my Maker without the certainty that there is an heir to follow William!'

'For gracious sake, Walter, you will please not speak of your demise even in a light-hearted fashion!' Lady Calverley's frown was short-lived and she was smiling at Eleanor again, her face momentarily taking on the guise of the beautiful young woman she had once been before age overtook her. 'Even as a little boy, my William was always partial to candied fruit. Tomorrow, Cook shall make some, and I shall send to London for marchpane.'

Her happiness was infectious, and Eleanor was drawn into the feeling of excited anticipation. Several times during the following days, she went to stand by the portrait of young William Calverley and did not wonder, as she regarded his handsome features, why his parents doted upon him. Moreover, Dora had only good to speak of him.

'He be well liked in the village, Miss Eleanor, surelye! Harry just about thinks as how the sun sets on Mister William. It were he as persuaded the Master to tek Harry into service. A bootboy were Harry when he started work here but Mister William, he tekked a larmentable int'rest in our Harry and saw as how he were raised to footman. Nor 'tis only us Pylbeams as be advantaged – the Calverleys done all as ever they could for village if'n a body's ill or sore in need. Mister William, he be real primer-lookin', surelye.'

The air of expectancy prevailed throughout the month of June and into July. Now, however, it was tempered by a breath of anxiety. Word reached Sir Walter from London that there was a great deal of unrest amongst the commoners in France and particularly in the capital.

'Which is only to be expected!' pronounced Sir Walter. 'The poor are too heavily taxed and the wealthy not at all. They must pay taxes not only to the King and to the Church, but to their local lords. Consequently, a great many are starving. There is no freedom of person or speech, and arrests and imprisonments can be made without the hapless offender receiving a trial. I don't wonder that they are in revolt.'

Not a fortnight later, a further letter was received from William who was now in Paris. A vast mob had destroyed the Bastille, releasing the prisoners and massacring the garrison. William wrote:

I have spoken last night with my Host, the Duc de la Rochefoucauld-Liancourt, and he is of the Opinion that this is only the beginnings of a Revolution. On his Advice, I am curtailing my Visit and am leaving at once for Rouen. Liancourt is of the Opinion that I should bring Catherine, Philippe and their Children back to England until the Unrest

is resolved. I do not care to Worry you, but you will wish
to be Prepared for their Arrival.

Preparations began, but no further word was received from
William. The Calverleys waited anxiously for news, but such
as came to them was far from reassuring. Nobles had been
attacked in their castles and the violence was no longer confined
to Paris, but had spread to the suburbs and outlying provinces.
Reluctant though Sir Walter was to admit to the possible dangers
confronting William and their daughter, he felt the need for
some divine intervention and authorized morning family prayers
in the library, including pleas for the safety of all those across
the water, thus disrupting the well-ordered running of the house
and putting everyone behind with their daily chores.

'If mortal harm were to befall William, there would be no
Calverley to carry on the line!' Eleanor, who knew the family
tree backwards, remarked to the uncomprehending Dora. 'The
estate is entailed and can pass only down the spear side.'

'My dad says as how there's allus been more girls than boys
in the family!' Dora announced gloomily. 'My grandad said
as how once there'd been two other boys aside Sir Walter, but
them was killed in foreign parts.'

Eleanor had heard of the two brothers, Robert and Edwin,
from Sir Walter when he had been showing her the family
tree on the fly sheet of the family journal. Edwin, the younger,
his wife Jane and their two little children, but newly arrived
in Portugal, had all perished in the Lisbon earthquake twenty-
seven years ago. Time had softened Sir Walter's grief, but it
was obvious to Eleanor that he had a special fondness for his
youngest brother. There had been no such love for Robert – a
ne'er-do-well who had ignominiously escaped to the North
Americas in order to avoid his gambling debts. Sir Walter's
father had been able to buy the creditors' silence and preserve
the good name of the Calverleys. No communication had ever
been received from Robert, and the family had presumed him
dead, not without a sense of relief.

'So you see, Eleanor, every family has a black sheep if you search far enough back in its history!' Sir Walter told Eleanor. 'I thank God that William is so fine and upstanding a man.'

Living as a daughter would with William's parents, no one knew better than Eleanor the place their only son held in their hearts. No one was more aware of their distress than she, therefore, when finally a letter arrived from France, penned by one of Catherine's friends, the Comte de Valderton. William, he wrote, had arrived too late to protect his sister. The peasants had attacked their château in Rouen and although William and Catherine's husband, Philippe, had fought to protect the women and children, all but William had perished. By some stroke of good fortune or chance of fate, he had been left for dead. His valet, Dora's eldest brother, Jack, had saved his life, taking him on horseback to a physician who had been obliged to amputate one of his arms which had been cruelly pierced with a pitchfork. William was making a slow recovery in the Comte de Valderton's household and, God willing, as soon as he was well enough, one of them would escort him back to England.

When Lady Calverley recovered from the first shock and grief, she took Eleanor in her arms and said tremulously: 'I shall write to your Aunt Tabitha this very day, Eleanor. There can be no question of you returning to your guardians in the near future for I shall need you to help me nurse my poor William back to health. If your guardians will allow it, you will stay and assist me, dearest child, will you not?'

'Yes, yes, you know I will!' Eleanor cried.

That night, she begged God's forgiveness for welcoming this misfortune since it would allow her to remain indefinitely at Ortolans – the house she had prayed never to leave.

CHAPTER TWO

1789–90

For six weeks, Ortolans and its household mourned the death of Catherine and her family, and waited uneasily for William's return. Affairs in France appeared to be worsening and Sir Walter was convinced that the country was on the brink of a revolution. A number of prescient aristocratic French families, aware of the simmering bitterness within the populace, were seeking refuge in England.

Although deeply shocked by the news of Catherine's death, Eleanor could not grieve for someone unknown to her except by hearsay. She did what she could to comfort Lady Calverley, diverting her thoughts whenever possible to the imminent arrival of William and how they would assist in his convalescence. That he had almost lost his life in a heroic but vain attempt to save his sister was a matter for pride as well as sadness.

It was a beautiful if cold September day when the chaise bringing William home drew up outside Ortolans and the house sprang to life. Servants hurried to unload the second carriage filled with valises and the Comte de Valderton's servants. Maids scurried through the numerous bedrooms lighting fires and putting warming pans between the sheets, whilst William, supported by his valet, Jack, and the comte, was assisted into the house.

But for the sleeve of his caped greatcoat folded across his chest, Eleanor would not have recognized this pale, thin stranger as the William in the portrait. Though still handsome in feature, his extreme pallor and drooping air of fatigue made him look far older than his years. Tears ran down Lady

Calverley's cheeks as she settled him into a large wing chair close to the blazing fire.

'Come now, Mama!' William said with a smile. 'There is no need for this distress. I am safely home.' He regarded his father, seated opposite him, with deep affection. 'You are looking in good health, Papa,' he said. 'Now that we are comfortably seated, may I introduce my very good friend, Antoine, Comte de Valderton. I will be hard put ever to repay his hospitality and kindness to me these past weeks.'

'We are deeply indebted to you, sir,' said Sir Walter gruffly. 'From all accounts, our son owes his life to you!'

'And indeed to his servant!' the comte said graciously. 'It was Jack who brought William to us that dreadful night when we were all in fear of our lives. May I offer my sincere condolences – such a tragic and unnecessary loss of life! Catherine and Phillipe were very dear friends and I share your grief.'

'Let us not speak of it for the present!' William said as he noticed the trembling of his mother's lips. There was a timely interruption as a servant came in with a tray of refreshments. 'You have not yet introduced us to the young lady standing so silently by the window, Mama. Miss McCore, is it not?'

Lady Calverley left her position beside William's chair and hurried across the room to Eleanor.

'Forgive me, my dear, in all the excitement . . . gentlemen, may I present my beloved god-daughter, Eleanor. I cannot tell you what a great comfort the child has been to us!'

Eleanor curtsyed to the French count – a middle-aged, rotund gentleman who now gave her a courtly bow. Then she curtsyed to William and for the first time met his gaze, which was gentle and, so it seemed, admiring.

'My mother told me in her letters that you would grow up to be a great beauty!' he said with a pleasant smile. 'I think, however, that we have no need to await the future!' Seeing the colour his compliment brought rushing to Eleanor's cheeks, he added gently: 'It will not be long, young lady, before you will become quite accustomed to admiration.'

Lady Calverley laughed.

'Eleanor already has an admirer. Charles Howell is a constant caller.'

For the first time, William laughed.

'Young Charlie! I remember him as a schoolboy!'

'He's at university now,' Lady Calverley began, but broke off to look apologetically at the visitor. 'You must excuse these personal reminiscences, Monsieur le Comte. What is of far greater concern to us all is the safety of you and your family. We have read in the *Morning Post* of further terrible happenings in your country.'

The comte's face darkened with anxiety.

'I fear events may be even more grave than you know,' he said. 'The King seems to have no conception of the seriousness of the matter or of the danger to himself. Last August, the Assembly attempted to calm the situation and framed a new constitution compelling the Church, the municipalities and landowners such as ourselves to surrender our feudal rights and privileges. The riff-raff do not understand such governmental niceties and have continued to loot and burn at whim. They do not pay their taxes and it would not be an exaggeration to admit that anarchy prevails.'

Sir Walter nodded thoughtfully.

'You will be aware that our own King George has recently been too deranged to manage our country's affairs. Let us hope your sovereign has not likewise lost his wits,' he said.

'In my opinion,' said the comte gravely, 'if things continue as they are, Louis will lose his throne. I see no future in France the way matters are developing, and whilst I am in England, I shall find accommodation for my wife and family in London, as many of our friends have done already. What happened to your daughter could all too easily occur in our household despite the guards I have put upon the estate. One cannot be sure that even they can be trusted.'

'My dear Comte, it would give me great pleasure if you would allow me to put our house in Sackville Street at your disposal,' Sir Walter said eagerly. 'We closed it when William went abroad, and are unlikely to have need of it until he has fully recovered. The house is yours for as long as you require.'

The comte looked relieved.

'That is exceedingly kind of you, sir, and if I am unable to find permanent accommodation when I go to London tomorrow, I shall gratefully accept your most generous offer.'

'You were our dear Catherine's friend as well as William's saviour, and we shall always be indebted to you,' Sir Walter replied gravely.

Lady Calverley's eyes had filled with tears at this further mention of Catherine, but she would not now ask the comte for details of her daughter's tragic death lest it marred William's homecoming. There would be time for Walter to question their son at a later date.

William had turned once more towards the silent Eleanor.

'Mama wrote and told me that you are like a dear daughter to her. I hope therefore that you will look upon me as a brother, and that I may call you Eleanor?'

Before she could reply, he winced suddenly and his face paled.

'You are in pain, William!' his mother said instantly. 'I am sure Monsieur le Comte will not think it impolite if I insist that you go to your bed. All is made ready for you.'

Despite William's protests that he was not unwell, he soon allowed his mother and Jack to assist him to bed. The Frenchman turned to Sir Walter and handed him a letter.

'It is from the physician who attended William,' he explained. 'Your son has been very ill, close to death on several occasions. He has such courage that he seldom admits to any pain or weakness, but as you will see from the letter, the surgeon is far from satisfied.'

He glanced at Eleanor hesitantly. Guessing his reluctance to continue upon such a subject in her presence, Eleanor said quickly:

'My godmother has said that I am to help nurse William

back to health,' she said quietly. 'If I am to be of use, I should know the extent of his injuries.'

Sir Walter nodded approvingly.

'Eleanor is a very sensible young lady – not given to hysterics and the vapours. Pray do continue, sir.'

'Then I must tell you that William's wounds were caused by a pitchfork which – one could imagine – was none too clean. Two of the prongs pierced his arm and the third, his shoulder. When his servant brought William to us two days later, the wounds were inflamed and William had a high fever. There was no option for the surgeon but to amputate the arm, but there was nothing he could do for the shoulder wound. It has taken several weeks to heal, and even now the physician fears it could cause further trouble.'

'He shall have every care!' said Sir Walter, his voice once more gruff with emotion he was unable to conceal. 'I shall send a servant to tell our physician that he is to call and see William tomorrow. He lives near Brighthelmstone some ten miles distant. It is a most popular spa and doubtless the waters will be highly beneficial to William once he is strong enough to make the journey there.'

So began William's long convalescence. Not unnaturally, the journey from France had caused a setback and for some weeks, the Calverleys' physician would not guarantee his recovery. But both Eleanor and Lady Calverley were deter-mined that he should get well, taking it in turns to supervise the two women who were helping Jack to care for the invalid. Eleanor spent many hours in the sickroom, reading to William from his favourite books, diverting him with minutiae concerning the daily life of the household and village, and somehow always succeeding in bringing a smile to his face even when he was in pain.

As he grew better, his friends and neighbours called to see him. At the end of such visits, he would turn to Eleanor with a sigh of relief and say: 'It was delightful to see old friends again but really I'd far prefer to sit here and listen to you read to me, Eleanor. Your voice is almost as soothing as your hands when you bathe my forehead.'

Eleanor was still not able to control her blushes when he paid her compliments, but she was far more at ease with him. The romantic notions she had once entertained, during those secret moments when she had stood gazing up at his portrait, had disappeared with his arrival home. The William of today, she realized, was not the handsome, elegant youth of her imagining, but a man nearing middle age, his brow furrowed, his eyes frequently narrowed to conceal his pain.

The feeling now uppermost in her heart when she was with him was of admiration for his courage and endurance, to which was added a genuine fondness. He had become like the dear elder brother she had once longed for but never had.

Lady Calverley, however, was slowly reaching the conclusion that the feelings of her adored son for her little god-daughter were no longer those of a brother for his sister. She had noted the special tone of his voice which he used whenever he spoke to Eleanor; the way his face lit up when she came through the door; the way his eyes followed her as she moved around the room.

She reported her suspicion to her husband as the new year approached. 'William has said nothing to me, but I know him so well, I am convinced that I am not mistaken,' she said.

Sir Walter, who was reading a belated account of the mob attack upon the French king at his palace in Versailles, looked over the top of his newspaper.

'If you are right, my dear, I see no harm in it. Eleanor is a remarkably pretty girl, and you know how anxious I am that William should marry.'

Lady Calverley looked shocked.

'But there is a vast disparity in their ages, Walter. William is thirty-seven this year and Eleanor is barely seventeen – a child still!'

Sir Walter chuckled.

'Quite old enough for marriage, my dear, and it would be

a good marriage for that girl. She has no dowry to offer a husband so it is unlikely she could do better than William who, fortunately, has no need of one.'

Lady Calverley sank on to the sofa, her hand to her brow. Her emotions were perplexingly mixed. Like her husband, she longed for William to marry and, in due course, produce the heir Walter so fervently wanted; but as a woman, and as Eleanor's devoted godmother, she doubted if it were right to marry so young and inexperienced a girl to a man nearing middle age; a man, moreover, who seemed likely to suffer continual ill health as a result of his wounds. She knew that Eleanor loved Ortolans and her life here, but now she questioned whether her much-loved god-daughter harboured more than sisterly affection coupled with respect for William. Might such regard develop into something nearer love? she asked herself.

Remembering her own youth, she recalled the first time that her heart had been ensnared – by a young cavalry officer. He was exceedingly handsome and had flirted quite outrageously with her as they danced the quadrille at the Assembly Rooms. She had been convinced that she would die of a broken heart were she not allowed to marry him, but her parents had persuaded her that Walter was the most desirable of her many suitors and could offer her the comforts and lifestyle to which she was accustomed. How quickly that broken heart had mended when Walter became her affectionate and indulgent husband and they settled down to married life at Ortolans.

It would be the same for Eleanor, she thought now. One learned to love one's husband, and as Walter said, it would be a good marriage for the child. If William did declare himself, she would give the union her blessing.

Unaware that her life might soon be drastically changed, Eleanor continued to spend as much time as she could with William who was, at last, beginning to recover his health. They went for walks together, gentle perambulations down to the river where Eleanor showed him the kingfishers' nest.

Spring brought the return of the ortolans and to please Eleanor, William sent word to everyone on his estate that there would be the most severe punishment for anyone caught trapping the little birds. Like the larks trapped on the South Downs, the ortolans were caught by the hundreds and taken to market where they fetched a good price for the tables of the gentry. He also ordered at her request the removal of the mantrap their bailiff had erected in the beech woods to catch poachers.

William was kind as well as brave, Eleanor thought, and listened, silent and attentive, whilst he regaled her with exciting stories of all the countries he had visited. She longed to go to Egypt and see the Great Pyramids and the Sphynx; to Vienna to see the Lipizzaner stallions at the Hofburg Palace; to Florence to see the art galleries and most of all, to Rome to see Michelangelo's magnificent *Last Judgement* in the Sistine Chapel.

'One day, when I am fully recovered, I will take you to see these sights!' said William, as he concluded a description of the Swiss Alps. 'Would that please you, little Eleanor?'

Something in the husky tone of William's voice brought Eleanor's eyes to his face. He was gazing at her with an intensity which brought the colour rushing to her cheeks. Only recently, Jane had told her that she was certain William was enamoured of her. Convinced her friend was jesting, Eleanor had laughed and reminded Jane that William was nearing forty years of age and would have no interest in a girl still in her teens.

'Just because poor Charles dotes on me, Jane, you suppose every man must do so!' she had reasoned, 'whereas I am quite plain, as you can see for yourself! My mouth is too big, my nose upturned and I have a horrid mole on my cheek. Dora calls it a beauty spot, but I think it most disfiguring!'

'Wait and see, then,' had been Jane's retort. 'I'll wager Mr Calverley will propose before Midsummer Day.'

Recalling Jane's prophecy, Eleanor now felt a sudden urge to pick up her skirts and run back to the house . . . to safety. As if reading her mind, William said:

'I beg you not to run away, Eleanor. I have something of importance I must say to you – namely that I would be very honoured if you would consider marrying me! I am very aware of your youth and indeed, of the differences in our ages, so I do not expect you to reach any decision hastily. However, I am no longer able to conceal the fact that I love you dearly and want you to be my wife.'

It was done . . . said, Eleanor thought, wishing the declaration had never been made and that the uncomplicated friendship that had existed between them could continue. Now she would never be at ease with him again. This was her first proposal, but it brought no joy – only an awkward embarrassment. She did not know how she could reply.

'I am . . .' she struggled to find the right words '. . . quite overcome . . . by the honour you do me, but I could not marry you, William. I mean, I have given no thought to marriage. Once, a long time ago, Godmother asked me if I would like her to arrange some parties, balls, a sojourn in London with the Howells, to enable me to . . . to meet some young people of my own age. She said I must consider the future and . . . and the possibility of marriage now that I was growing up. I explained that I was quite happy here at Ortolans with her and Uncle Walter . . . and that is still true. I have been happier still since . . . since you came home . . .' The rush of words halted abruptly before she added in a near whisper: 'But I think of you as a brother . . . not . . . not . . . as I think I should feel when you speak of marriage.'

William did not appear unduly perturbed by the outburst. He was smiling as in a paternal manner, he took her hand and led her back towards the house.

'I expected no more, Eleanor. You are very young and it is natural that you should not have considered me as a husband. There is no haste in all this. Now that you know how I feel, I ask only that you give the matter serious thought. I believe I could make you happy – it would be my first purpose in life to do so. You will think about it, my dear?'

As soon as she could, she sought the sanctuary of her sunny bedroom which faced southwards across the meadows to the Downs. She went at once to the window-seat beneath the mullioned casements and curled up on the comfortable padded cushions. Rex settled himself in his usual place at her feet, his head raised to lie heavily against her knees. As Dora came into the room, she fussed and tut-tutted as she always did at the trail of hairs the dog had left on the Persian rugs.

The maid regarded her young mistress's face anxiously.

'You be looking unaccountable pale, Miss Eleanor. You'd no ought to have walked so far with Mister William.'

'Oh, Dora, I'm not in the least tired – only concerned!' Eleanor burst out, her longing to confide too great to contain any longer. There would come a time when she must discuss William's proposal with her godmother, but first she needed time to clear her thoughts.

'You ain't being sent back to Scotland, surelye?' Dora's round blue eyes narrowed with anxiety. No one knew better than she how Eleanor dreaded her eventual return to her rightful guardians, a calamity which had already been postponed on two occasions.

Eleanor shook her head.

'No, not that, Dora – although I must confess I put that possibility to the back of my mind when Aunt Tabitha said I might stay to help Godmother nurse Mr Calverley. Now that he is so much better . . .'

She broke off as the likelihood of her having to leave Ortolans in the near future filled her with dread and an unbearable sadness. This house had become her real home, and her godmother and Sir Walter like her parents. She belonged here!

Tears filled her eyes as she stared out of the window. Already the banks and flower borders were ablaze with yellow daffodils and jonquils. The first tiny, lime green buds of the beech leaves were decorating the trees, and mauve, white and yellow crocuses carpeted the lawns beneath the walnut and copper-beech

trees. Spring was touching Ortolans with its special beauty.
Soon the swallows as well as the ortolans would return from
their wintering in the hot climates and she might not be here
to welcome them.

'William has asked me to marry him!' she whispered to her
astonished maid. 'If I said "yes", then I could stay here for
ever; but I don't know if I love him as one should love one's
husband.'

One of thirteen children in a family where the wages were
barely sufficient for survival, Dora had a realistic approach to
life.

'Landsakes, Miss Eleanor!' she gasped. 'You'm not thinking
straight, surelye. Happen them poets' books you telled me of
a-turned your wits! Mister William be a good, valiant man as
would mek you a fine husband – a larmentable fine husband
– and if'n you wed to him, you be loving him, surelye.' She
paused to draw breath before adding: 'When God sees fit to
tek the Master, you'd be "Her Ladyship", if'n you was Mister
William's wife. You'd wear fine jew'lry, and purty gowns, and
have carriages, and like as not your own horse to ride,
and . . .' she added with unaccustomed subtlety '. . . as many
dogs as you've a fancy for!'

Eleanor's face softened into a smile.

'You make marriage to Mister William sound very inviting,
Dora . . . but I do believe there is a special love that can exist
between a man and woman. Shakespeare describes it many
times – the passionate love that Hermia had for Lysander, the
despairing love Juliet had for Romeo – and what of Isolde's
love for Tristan? Cleopatra's for Antony?'

'I doant count no storytellers for much!' Dora said firmly.

Eleanor's smile deepened.

'Dora, you know that is not true. What of your granny's
story about the fairies – or Pharisees as you call them – frightening the farmer, Jeems Meppom, into his grave with the curse
they put upon him? You believe that!'

''Tis a fact, surelye!' Dora said indignantly. 'T'was no story from a book, Miss Eleanor! My granny seed Jeems Meppom's tombstone in graveyard when she were a girl!'

Not wishing to accuse Dora's granny of telling fibs, Eleanor said only:

'I have read that "Love is a torment of the mind, a tempest everlasting," and I believe it could be so. How could I make poor William happy if I cannot love him as I should?'

Dora threw her apron over her head in helpless frustration. Her young mistress was so devoid of vanity that it seemed a waste of breath to point out that any full-blooded man would be only too happy to share his bed with her. Whatever Eleanor's books might say, Dora knew very well from her own family life and that of the villagers what men were seeking when they went courting. It was nature – as everyone well knew – and she could see no reason why nature should be otherwise in the households of the gentry. No doubting the look on young Mr Howell's face when he came calling! she thought as she brushed Eleanor's long fair hair. He'd taken note of Miss Eleanor's pretty figure and sweet nature! It did not surprise Dora one whit that Mister William was smitten. Even Parson had blushed and stammered when Miss Eleanor had smiled at him and complimented him on his sermon last Sunday. Pretty as a picture, she'd looked, in her green chemise gown of sarcenet and fine new bonnet decorated with field flowers! With Mister William beside her – tall, thin and military looking in his well-cut blue coat and trousers, shiny top boots and bicorne hat – they made a singularly handsome couple, Dora thought but forbore to say. It was her opinion that Miss Eleanor had been taken by surprise, not expecting Mister William's proposal of marriage, but given more time then she would forget her precious books and see the sense of it.

Lady Calverley was of the same opinion when she called Eleanor into her bedroom to talk to her privately. She was seated at her marquetry dressing-table in front of the oval mirror. Her maid, Molly, had just finished pinning her long white hair into a chignon. Dismissing Molly, the older woman turned to her god-daughter.

'You may fasten this for me, my dear!' she said, withdrawing a sapphire and pearl necklace from her jewelbox. 'It is charming, is it not? It belonged to Walter's great-grandmother.'

As Eleanor fastened the beautiful ornament round her godmother's throat, Lady Calverley added:

'William has told me of his proposal, dear child, so I am hoping that one day soon, I can fasten this around your neck where it will look far prettier than around mine!' She turned in her chair and took Eleanor's hands in hers. 'You cannot be in doubt as to the extent of the love I have grown to feel for you, dearest Eleanor. I do realize that you are still very young, but as William assures me, there is no haste to marry. With my poor dear Catherine not long departed, even a formal betrothal would not yet be proper. However, if there were to be an understanding . . .? I can think of no other I would prefer to call daughter-in-law, and your Uncle Walter feels likewise.'

With a demonstrativeness she had only been able to reveal since she had come to live in her godmother's house, Eleanor flung her arms round the elderly woman and embraced her.

'I would do anything to make you happy, dearest Godmother!' she said fervently. 'I love you dearly – and Uncle Walter – and . . . and I have grown to care very much for William. It is just that . . . that I do not know if I love him . . . as is fitting for a wife. I love him as . . . as a brother, and I am always happy in his company. I suppose because of the difference in our ages, I have never thought of him as a husband, and I believed he looked upon me as a sister.'

Lady Calverley patted Eleanor's hands.

'I am pleased to hear you say so, Eleanor, for it is proof that William has always behaved towards you with the utmost propriety, but now that he has declared himself, it would not be correct for me to allow you to be alone together. I could not permit your reputation to be tarnished by even a hint of gossip, and people are all too ready to tittle-tattle if given the opportunity!'

Eleanor's face paled and she drew in her breath sharply.

'You mean that if I were to become betrothed to William I should have to go back to Aunt Tabitha – to Scotland?'

'No, my dear, not until an engagement was formally declared. Then it would be right for you to go back to your guardians until your wedding. It need not be for long, I assure you. I will ask them if they would agree to your being married here. The expenditure would be a heavy burden that your Uncle Hamish could ill afford.'

Eleanor's expression of unease intensified as she said hesitantly: 'You are speaking as if . . . as if it is already agreed that . . . that I . . . that William and I . . .'

'Then I should not have done so, my dear!' Lady Calverley broke in quickly. 'I meant only to give you an understanding of what would be entailed. It is for you to make up your own mind according to the dictates of your heart. William has specifically begged me not to add my persuasions to his since he feels it would be wrong for so young a person as yourself to be unduly influenced.'

Eleanor felt a wave of relief – and of gratitude to William.

'He is so good and kind!' she said warmly. 'He has so many virtues. He never complains when he is in pain and is always thoughtful of those who care for him. All the servants adore him; Dora has told me so. He is well deserving of their respect and indeed, he has mine.'

Lady Calverley turned back to her mirror, her expression thoughtful as she placed a beribboned, white lace cap over her head.

'It is my belief that you already love my son as befits a wife!' she said softly.

Eleanor nodded.

'If I were to marry William, I would do everything in my power to make him happy!' she said impulsively. 'I know I have no dowry to offer him and that he does me the greatest honour in asking for my hand. I would always be grateful to him for that. I would do my best to please him.'

Lady Calverley replied shrewdly:

'To my knowledge, William has never lost his heart before. Cupid's arrow may have struck him late in life, but all the more ardently for that. You have only to smile at him to make him happy, dear child! Now run along and change for dinner else you will upset your Uncle Walter by being late – not to mention Cook who is making William's favourite salmon soufflé!'

Her godmother's reference to William's feelings did little to alleviate Eleanor's misgivings. A smile from William would not be sufficient to ensure *her* happiness, she thought as she made her way up to her bedroom. Nor had she felt Cupid's arrow in her heart, ardent or otherwise. The touch of William's hand beneath her arm did not cause her heartbeat to quicken and his frequent compliments made her unhappily self-conscious.

If only she could be certain that she would learn to love him, she thought as Dora, hearing her footsteps, opened the door to greet her. Rex bounded out to welcome her, licking her face with his damp pink tongue, his tail wagging furiously. Eleanor's frown turned to smiles as she patted him.

'You'd no ought to let that pesky varmint near you, Miss Eleanor!' Dora reproached her, shooing the dog under the bed. 'If'n I had my way, you'd get shut of him once and fer all!'

Eleanor laughed.

'I'm very well aware that you don't love him, Dora, but I do. I cannot bear the thought of having to leave him when I return to Scotland – any more than I can bear the thought of leaving this house!'

Even as she spoke the words, the thought crossed her mind that perhaps, since Godmother thought it was enough for her simply to be fond of William, she should accept his proposal, for then Ortolans would be her home for the rest of her life.

CHAPTER THREE

1790

In one lithe movement, Daniel Calverley raised himself from the soft, buxom thighs of his female companion and disentangled himself from her embrace. Her lips parted in a pout as she longingly regarded the tall, naked figure of her young lover. He had already pleasured her twice in as many hours but, as always, it seemed, to Matilda, Countess Wotherington, that she was not satiated by his lovemaking, despite his undoubted skill and vigour.

She stared up at the young man nearly fifteen years her junior and marvelled yet again at his extraordinary beauty. Tall, slim, without an ounce of excess flesh, he was undoubtedly the most attractive lover she had ever had. The prominent cheekbones and aquiline nose gave him a proud, almost haughty appearance; but the most striking of his features were his eyes – jet black, deep set, the expression in them more often than not unfathomable.

'Matty does not want her Danny to go!' she protested, holding out her plump white arms towards him. It was her custom to use this infantile method of speech to her lovers, and there had been several who had responded likewise. Daniel never did so, and she was newly uncertain as to whether he genuinely cared for her. He rarely smiled and his voice, with its curious North American intonation, gave no indication of his emotions.

She touched the almost hairless skin of his arm, intrigued as always by the unusual coppery colour. Once when she had remarked upon it, he had told her that his skin colouring was as the result of his Red Indian blood; that he was the son of an Algonquin Princess; but of course, she had not believed him. He was forever telling extraordinary stories, many of which she had discovered to be quite untrue. When she had challenged him with the truth, he had raised those strange dark eyebrows and with a half-smile, told her that he made up such tales to amuse her.

'Your husband will be returning home at any moment, madam!' he said as he pulled on his purple Florentine silk breeches and lace-frilled shirt. 'Moreover, I have an important letter that I must write tonight. You may recall my telling you that I had relatives in Sussex who I have not yet informed of my arrival in this country.'

He looked with distaste at the voluptuous figure of the middle-aged woman with whose services, he hoped fervently, he might soon dispense. He feared neither the dangers of discovery he had risked nor, indeed, did he regret the hours when he had been obliged to pleasure the woman who was so besotted with him. He accepted that whilst he might despise her, she had been of immeasurable use to him.

As Daniel brushed his black, straight hair from his high forehead, he realized that this indeed might be his last assignation with the Countess, and, as he completed his toilet, he was even more certain that the moment had finally come when he must put his years of training to the test. Born with but one winning card in his hand, he had had to acquire others with the aid of his native wit, intelligence, shrewdness; with his capacity for patience; with that will-o'-the-wisp, luck.

For the first five years of Daniel's life, he had been raised by his mother. As the daughter of a chieftain, she was a respected member of the Algonquin tribe of Red Indians whose lands lay in the Rocky Mountains of Western America. As far as Daniel was aware, his father, a white man, was readily accepted by the tribe. Robert Calverley, however, had soon tired of this primitive existence, and taking his wife and young son with him, he had returned to civilization in the vain hope of re-establishing himself in New York at the gambling tables where, six years earlier, he had lost the money his father had given him in the hope that he would make a fresh start in the New World.

Only gradually had the young Daniel begun to realize the prejudice that existed amongst the white people against redskins – and in particular against half-breeds like himself. The tales his father told of his rich relatives in England did nothing to alter their status – and only Daniel believed them. He never tired of hearing these stories of his father's childhood in the big country house in England, of the family's wealth, the luxuries, the servants, the horses, the land; of the respect that any Calverley automatically commanded.

Robert Calverley was by now in his fifties. He had become a heavy drinker and spent the little money he earned at gambling tables on alcohol. Gradually he became more violent and aggressive, losing the last shred of the refinement which his young son had once admired in him. Daniel and his mother learned to keep out of his way, and were obliged to resort to stealing to obtain the bare necessities of life.

It was a relief to both of them when Robert Calverley died, taking to the grave with him the true reason why he had been obliged in the forties to leave England – namely dishonoured gambling debts that had threatened the good name of the Calverleys. Daniel knew only that his father and grandfather had quarrelled. His mother decided to return with him to her tribe, but Daniel, now in his early twenties, had other plans. He had seen how rich men lived; the respect they commanded; the big houses they owned and not least, the beautiful horses they rode. He was intelligent as well as cunning, and none knew better than he that a half-breed, without the benefit of a good education, had little hope ever of acquiring the wealth and position in Society he wanted.

Although his father had had no contact with his family since he had come to America, Daniel was in no doubt that the Calverley relations were people of consequence in their own country. He assumed that the grandfather with whom his father had quarrelled by now would be dead, and pinned his hopes on the possibility that his two unknown uncles would have no wish to carry the quarrel into the next generation. He had but to hide the fact of his illegitimacy and his mother's race, present himself as a respectable member of the Calverley family, and it was a reasonable gamble that these affluent relatives would welcome him into the fold.

Leaving his distressed mother to find her own way back to her tribe, Daniel had scraped together his fare to England on a merchant sloop. During the voyage, he had closely observed the behaviour of an English family on board, and quickly realized that if he were ever to pass as a gentleman, he had a great deal more to learn than his dissolute father and illiterate mother had taught him. He lacked the refinement, the manners and not least of all, knowledge of the intricate etiquette surrounding the lives of such men. It was then he had decided to postpone his plan for an immediate return to his family, and take whatever time was necessary to learn what he needed to know if he were to be accepted by his relatives without dangerous questioning.

He had considered himself fortunate beyond measure to be accepted without references into a big Yorkshire family as a footman. His extreme good looks had caught the eye of the mistress of the house who had chosen to overlook his lack of training and accepted his glib explanation that being of English birth, the American family who had employed him had summarily dismissed him when the war had started.

He had spent three years in the household, quickly assimilating the manners, language and behaviour of the people he served.

Daniel's mother had filled his early years with Indian lore and had always maintained that the omens had been especially good on the night of his birth. He believed that now, at long last, the Great Spirit was indeed favouring him. In the Yorkshire household, he discovered a copy of *Correct Peerage* and from it, was able to bring himself up to date with his paternal connections. His grandfather, Sir Richard, had indeed died. So, too, had his uncle, Edwin Calverley. On the spear side, only his Uncle Walter survived, although he was now an old man. He had one surviving son, William, and since William was unmarried, he was without an heir. Daniel was barely able to conceal his excitement – or his impatience.

Well practised in the art, he now made frequent undetected thefts of money or a watch or bauble left carelessly around by one of his rich employers. Soon he had saved enough to pay his fare on the stagecoach to London. There, he took rooms befitting a gentleman at a respectable abode in Upper Grosvenor Street. He had long ago made note of his master's tailor, Weston, and now ordered the clothes he knew he required if he were to become an accepted member of Society.

When finally Daniel was properly attired, he had set about the task of establishing himself, and his chosen means of doing so was quickly effected. He bribed the doormen at various gentlemen's clubs until he discovered where his relative, Sir Walter Calverley, was a member.

From that moment on, Daniel had been obliged to plan more deviously, for he was by now all but penniless once more, and owing a large sum to his tailor. Waiting unseen in the shadows outside White's for several nights on end, he was finally able to bump into one of the members who had summoned his coach, and before the man could step into it, had removed his gold watch. There were a number of people in the street including several urchins who had been begging. He darted after one of the boys who, seeing himself followed, automatically made off for the nearest unlit side-street. As he had intended, Daniel let him escape.

Congratulating himself that he had lost none of his sleight-of-hand, he now made his way to the club member's house in Hanover Square where he introduced himself to the bewildered and slightly befuddled earl who was in residence. He explained that he had seen a pickpocket steal his gold hunter

watch and had given chase. He then returned the timepiece
to its rightful owner. The doorman, he told his astonished and
much gratified listener, had observed the whole incident, but
had not had time to alert the earl's coachman before he had
driven away.

As Daniel now descended the back staircase of the earl's
London house, tipping lavishly any servant he happened to
encounter, he recalled that evening and his first meeting with
the countess. Summoned by her husband to hear the remarkable story of Daniel's recovery of the precious timepiece,
Matilda Wotherington had sailed into the room; and as Daniel
had bowed over her hand, she had instantly succumbed to his
charms.

All his adult life, Daniel had known of the power he could
exert over women. There had been several ladies of noble birth
in the Yorkshire household who had made it plain that they
would unlock their bedroom doors if he chose to pay them a
nocturnal visit. He had known better than to risk losing his
employment, but had benefited nonetheless, for it was their
unfailing reaction to him which had given him the idea of
ingratiating himself with someone like Matilda, Countess
Wotherington.

He had allowed himself to be drawn into a secret liaison
with her and let his penurious state be known to the doting
woman. Her generosity matched her lasciviousness, and Daniel
was soon able to pay off his tailor and his rental, and begin
to enjoy the social delights of London. All the time, as a
popular guest of the earl, he was gaining entrée to the people
who mattered; who might one day be useful to him. If he
gambled too heavily at the tables or on the racecourse, he
was always able to remove some tiny object of value without
detection – an art he had learned in his childhood – pawn it
and pay off the debt.

Now, Daniel decided, as he called a chaise to take him back
to Upper Grosvenor Street, he was ready at long last to claim
his rightful heritage.

Returning to his rooms, the countess far from his thoughts, he reached for quill and paper. He had passed his apprenticeship with flying colours. Matilda's Society friends had accepted that he was a distant American relation of the Calverleys, and the earl had even offered to put his name up for membership at his club! Now was the moment so long awaited when he could proceed with his plans, so meticulously made.

20 April, 1790

Dear Uncle Walter,

Without doubt you will be Surprised to hear from me, your Nephew, Daniel. My late Father, your Brother, Robert, informed me that he had not kept in touch with the Family, but shortly before his Death, he spoke of his longing to be reunited with you and his Brother, Edwin. Regrettably he would not allow me to Write to you, fearing that his Quarrel with my Grandfather would not be forgiven.

I arrived in England several years ago from America, but have only now decided to take my Courage in both hands and make myself known to you. Perhaps I should have done so earlier, but in view of the Rift between your Father and mine, I did not wish to be an Embarrassment to you. However, I have been persuaded by our mutual Friends, the Earl and Countess Wotherington, that you might favour a Reconciliation with your Nephew, of whose existence you must be in Ignorance.

The Wotheringtons tell me you are in Ill Health and seldom come to London. Since it is not possible therefore for me to call and present myself to you at Sackville Street, I write now to your Country Address and request your Permission to pay a visit to you in Sussex.

I shall, of course, understand if the past Rift with my Father leads you to refuse this Request, in which instance I will not trouble you further. However, it has long been my very Dear Wish that time will have Healed the Wounds, and that you will retain no Harsh Feelings towards me, your Nephew, or, now that he has passed away, to my late Father's memory.

I shall await your Reply with such Patience as I can muster. As you can see, I am residing in rooms in Upper Grosvenor Street.

In the meanwhile, Sir, I remain your Humble Servant, Daniel Calverley.

He leaned back in his chair, a hint of a smile enhancing his exceptionally handsome face. He was in no doubt that it would not be long before he received Sir Walter Calverley's favourable reply.

'Upon my soul, who would have believed it!' Walter said, handing the letter to his wife. 'Robert's son, Daniel, by all accounts. It's confoundedly difficult to take in!'

Lady Calverley read the letter and returned it to her husband with a smile.

'If he is your brother's child, we must make him welcome, my dear.'

Sir Walter hurrumphed, scratching his bald pate from which he had but recently removed his wig.

'Damn near brought disgrace on the family, all the same – pardon my language!' he muttered.

Lady Calverley sighed.

'That was over forty years ago, Walter, and you are speaking of Robert, not his son. Personally I have never accepted the Bible's edict that the sins of the fathers should be visited on their children. Besides which, for all you know, Robert may have ceased to be the wicked profligate you remember and made amends for his youthful misdeeds!'

'Then he should have written and set the old man's mind at rest before he died. However, his son sounds a polite sort of fellow – nothing presumptuous about his letter.'

'He should have got in touch with us as soon as he came

to England,' Lady Calverley said. 'Poor boy! He obviously fears we might hold Robert's misbehaviour against him!'

'My brother's dead by all accounts, so we won't speak ill of him. As for his son – well, he seems anxious to renew his family connections and I've no mind to close the door to my own kith and kin. Will you write to the young fellow on my behalf, my dear, and tell him we'll be pleased to see him? Devil take it, Robert's boy!'

'I confess I am intrigued to learn that I may have a first cousin,' William said to Lady Calverley when she told him the remarkable news. 'I suppose he'll have credentials? After all, he could be an imposter, Mother.'

'We will worry about that when we meet him, my dearest!' his mother said. 'I think your papa is looking forward to the occasion, although he will not admit to it.'

As the days passed, William's curiosity about this unknown relative deepened, as did Eleanor's. He had little to say in answer to her questions about his cousin other than to reiterate that his Uncle Robert had fled the country as a young man because of dishonoured debts.

'Let us hope this is not a case of "bad blood will out"!' he said gloomily. 'However, for my mother's sake, I am trying to be charitable, and I'll give the boy the benefit of the doubt. He should have received Mama's letter by now.'

It lay newly opened on Daniel's writing-bureau.

After reading it a second time, he placed it in a drawer of his desk and closed the lid. There was an expression of quiet triumph on his face as he set off to hire a manservant and a curricle. Twenty-four hours later he was on his way to Detcham village in the county of Sussex.

It was of little concern to him that by then, he was several hundred pounds in debt.

CHAPTER FOUR

1790

Although there were times when William's shoulder wound caused him severe pain, he was beginning to regain his lost weight and to look less the invalid – improvements Lady Calverley generously attributed to the happiness Eleanor had given him when she consented to become his wife. They were now formally betrothed and the wedding date arranged for a year hence. When their neighbours, the Howells, returned to London for the summer season, Eleanor was to go with them and buy her trousseau. For the present, however, she was permitted to remain at Ortolans. The threat of temporary banishment to her guardians had mercifully been lifted on the understanding that she and William would never be alone together and must have a suitable chaperon even on their walks. Since this task invariably fell to Dora, Eleanor did not feel her former freedom was curtailed.

To the general air of elation her betrothal to William had engendered in the household, was added a further excitement. The unknown Calverley relation had that afternoon arrived at Ortolans and was even now in one of the spare bedrooms where he had retired to change from his travelling clothes.

Standing beside her godmother in the drawing-room where they were waiting to receive the visitor, Eleanor noticed the frown on William's face.

'Cousin Daniel would appear to be somewhat of a macaroni!' he commented, 'or else I have been too long abroad and am unaware of the fashions of the *ton*!'

'Come now, dearest!' Lady Calverley said quickly. 'Remember that you promised me you would make your cousin welcome!'

'A promise I intend to keep, Mama!' William replied with a smile. 'I do not, however, have to approve of his appearance.'

Unsure of the meaning of the word 'macaroni', Eleanor guessed only that it was in some way derogatory; her first impression of William's cousin as he came into the room was therefore one of surprise. She had not expected anyone so excessively handsome. Although not quite as tall as William, there was an indefinable grace about him as he bowed first over Lady Calverley's hand and then over hers. His eyes, she noticed, were a deep, liquid black, the expression in them unfathomable. The colouring of his skin beneath the white-curled peruke was strange – not gold but deeper-toned as if he had been exposed recently to tropical sunlight.

Ignorant of the meaning of William's criticism of his cousin when he had observed him in the hallway, Eleanor was in any case unfitted to judge whether Daniel Calverley's appearance was dandified or otherwise. William, his father, Charles and Mr Howell, were always clothed as any country squire might be, and she had had occasion to meet few other men. The young man to whom she had just been presented was, she realized, much more colourfully attired. Seeing his scarlet, high-collared topcoat open to reveal a black and white striped waistcoat with two rows of mother-of-pearl buttons, she assumed that this was the London fashion. His white Florentine silk breeches were fastened at the knee with scarlet rosettes, the black and white striped stockings ornamented with scarlet clocks.

To Eleanor's eyes, the visitor's manner of dress was most becoming, and not for the first time, she thought wistfully of William's colourful attire in the hall portrait. She had fallen a little in love with that elegant, handsome young man, she reflected, and although, of course, she loved the William who had finally come home to his family, it had to be accepted that he was older, more heavily jowled and his waistline had thickened. The unlined forehead was now furrowed, aggravated no doubt by the pain he bore so stoically, for despite the regular attention of the physician, he was constantly plagued by abscesses on his wounds. He often reminded her of her Uncle Walter whose kindly face was also drawn by the pain he suffered as a result of his severe attacks of gout.

Was Daniel's striking flamboyance the real reason for William's criticism, she wondered? Or was he still mistrustful of this stranger? Glancing shyly at the newcomer's handsome face, she saw no family likeness to the Calverleys, but it was not long before even this was being explained.

'My father remained unmarried for many years,' Daniel Calverley was telling Sir Walter, beside whose chair he was now seated. 'He was a young man when he first met my mother, the daughter of a Spanish émigré to Mexico. He always told me I greatly resembled her.'

'As indeed it is common for sons to take after their mothers,' said Lady Calverley. 'You made no mention of her in your letter, Daniel.'

Daniel turned to regard her sadly.

'Alas, my mother died of the fever not long after my birth. I remember little about her, and as it pained my father, who loved her dearly, to speak of her, I am sadly lacking in information about my maternal forebears. My father, however, talked incessantly about *his* family, in particular of his affection for you, Uncle Walter. His greatest treasure was this silver snuff-box which you had given him on his twenty-first birthday.'

'Upon my soul!' said Sir Walter, taking the box Daniel had extracted from his pocket and examining it closely. 'To think that poor Robert kept it all those years!'

Daniel's face remained inscrutable as he thought cynically that it was he who had kept it, hiding it from his drunken father and starving mother lest it should be sold for drink, gambling or food.

He launched into a fictitious account of his father's life, first tried out on the plump Countess Wotherington, and when it was not questioned by her, well-rehearsed in the privacy of his rooms. His father, he recounted in a soft, accented voice, had arrived penniless in America, but determined to make good. After years of hard work as a fur trader, he had finally amassed sufficient wealth to build a fine house on the prairies to the west of the Wind River mountains. He was at last able to marry the beautiful Spanish girl – Daniel's mother – with whom he had fallen in love. His happiness was not long lived, for she had died soon after Daniel's birth. Nevertheless, Daniel continued glibly, the cattle ranch flourished until the day a terrible fire had wiped out the house and, sweeping across the tinder-dry plain, had destroyed the herds of cattle into which his father had invested his wealth.

'By now he was nearly sixty years of age, and his spirit was broken,' Daniel related to his silent audience. 'I had been hoping to volunteer my services to our Army, but I could not leave poor Papa. With the little I could salvage, I was able to take him to New York, but ill health overtook him and two years ago, he died. As you know, the Americans had won their war for independence some years previously so, although I was now free to volunteer, the English had no use for me in their Army.'

He gave a rueful smile.

'Unfortunately, I had had little opportunity for education in my childhood and whilst I had become an excellent horseman and rancher, there seemed little likelihood of me obtaining suitable employment in the city. I decided to sell such possessions as my father had owned, and pay my passage to England.'

He turned towards Sir Walter and said earnestly:

'I do assure you, sir, that it is not my intention to be a burden to you. I hope merely to obtain an introduction from you to some affluent family of your acquaintance who would give me employment – as a companion, perhaps, to their young sons? As I have said, I trust without seeming immodest, I do excel as a horseman and, indeed, at other sporting pursuits. If there are salmon in a river I am fishing, they do not remain there long! I am also an excellent shot, and I do not think I would often be the loser in a bout of fisticuffs!'

'You do not give the impression of a gentleman so well versed in sports!' William said quietly, once more quizzing his colourfully attired cousin.

The hint of a smile crossed Daniel's face as he glanced briefly at his clothes which, he now realized, were more befitting a London drawing-room than his uncle's.

'I am wearing my finest attire, Cousin William!' he said, 'since I did not wish to appear before my family for the first time as the proverbial "poor relation"!'

Lady Calverley was instantly overcome by the simple honesty of Daniel's reply. She looked at William reproachfully and then at Sir Walter who, much moved by the story of his unfortunate brother, was clearing his throat.

'I do not think there is any necessity for a Calverley to take employment,' he said gruffly. 'Poverty is not to be looked down upon if it has been brought about by misfortune. We will discuss your future tomorrow, my boy. Meanwhile, I am happy to tell you that you have arrived most opportunely. Tonight we are having a little dinner party with our neighbours, the Howells, to celebrate William's betrothal. Until now, the engagement has been a family secret whilst we awaited the approval of Miss McCore's guardians.'

Daniel had risen and now inclined his head towards William and Eleanor. William was holding Eleanor's left hand, on the third finger of which shone a beautiful emerald set in a circlet of tiny diamonds.

'May I offer you both my congratulations!' Daniel said. 'May I also express my pleasure in your return to health, Cousin William. Lord Wotherington informed me of your unfortunate encounter with the French peasantry in Rouen, but he was unaware of the extent of your recovery.'

'But for the loss of my arm, I am fully recovered!' William said. Frowning, he added: 'It surprises me that the Wotheringtons are so well informed about my misfortunes. However, I suppose such matters do manage to circulate in Society!'

Sir Walter, assuming that everyone was as interested as he

in the events taking place in France, now launched into a political diatribe. Lady Calverley interrupted him.

'I do not consider this a subject of interest to Eleanor,' she said firmly. 'Moreover, I myself cannot bear to think what the people of that country did to my beloved Catherine. You are perhaps not aware, Daniel, that we lost our youngest daughter last year at the hands of that rabble! Nor can I ever forgive them for what they did to my poor William.' Her eyes filled with tears and she rose to her feet. 'It is time we retired for a rest before tonight's festivities,' she said with a courageous attempt to hide her grief. 'Come Eleanor, my child, you may accompany me upstairs!'

Eleanor was not sorry to leave. Whilst she had found the conversation quite fascinating, she had sensed the tension in the room which she attributed to William's ill-concealed mistrust of his cousin. It was most unlike him to be uncharitable. Listening to Daniel's story, she had been filled with sympathy for the poor young man who, she believed, was doing his utmost to maintain his pride.

Obeying her godmother's gentle command to lie on her bed and rest until it was time to change for dinner, she found herself newly intrigued by the Calverley cousin's past. She wondered about his Spanish mother and realized that, like herself, he too had had no mother to love him as a child. Now, of course, she had her adored godmother and when she was finally married to William, Godmother would become a true relation. She hoped very much that the orphaned Daniel, too, was now to acquire a family to love him. His presence had brought an aura of expectancy to the household, she thought as she waited impatiently for the evening to begin. She was strangely excited and quite unable to doze or even to relax.

When Dora finally arrived to dress Eleanor in her new formal dinner-gown, the little maid was forced to protest. 'A'done-do, Miss Eleanor! If you doant stop fidgeting, I won't never get these buttons fastened!'

Eleanor gazed at her reflection in the long cheval glass. There would be no need to pinch her cheeks for they were aglow with excitement. The new blue dress, tight-fitting at the waist, flattered her figure and accentuated the colour of her eyes. The full-hooped skirt was open at the front to reveal the flounces of cream silk underskirt which whispered as she moved, reminding her of the breeze in the poplars down by the river. She wanted very much to look her best on this special evening arranged by her dear godmother in her honour.

As a rule, evenings spent with William and his parents were uneventful and, she now realized, even a little dull. So, too, were the Howells who, though kindly and well-meaning, were limited in their interests. Tonight would be different. Cousin Daniel was no ordinary English country squire who spoke of little but his sporting activities or upon such dull subjects as the ceaseless arguments about Ireland which she did not understand. He must have many exciting stories to relate of his life in the wild northern regions of America.

'If'n you doant keep still, Miss Eleanor, this hair of yourn gonna look like one o' Master Green's haystacks, surelye! I never did see you in such a larmentable fidget!'

When the pearl necklace – the family heirloom Lady Calverley had given her on the day she had agreed to marry William – was fastened round Eleanor's throat, Dora stopped her complaining and stood back to admire her young mistress.

'You do be lookin' purtier than ever I seed you afore!' she said, adding with a grin: 'Reckon as how Mister William'll be justabout proud o' you, Miss Eleanor!'

For a moment, a little of Eleanor's strange euphoria vanished as she realized that everything she did now must be to please William. It was true she wanted him to be proud of her, and his happiness was paramount in her thoughts. She did love him. Everyone loved him! He was a good, kind, gentle, thoughtful man who would undoubtedly make a good husband. If only she could be certain that she would make him a good wife! The thought of marriage frightened her, not least the prospect of sharing a bed with William. Dora had hinted that things happened in the bridal bed that led to pregnancy and childbirth . . .

As always when such doubts assailed her, Eleanor put them quickly to the back of her mind. There was a whole year to be lived before her marriage and, she told herself firmly, twelve months was sufficient time for her to overcome her fears of the intimacy of married life.

Her feeling of excitement returned, and impulsively she hugged her loyal and patient little maid.

'Just wait till you see Mister William's new cousin!' she said. 'He is quite charming, Dora, and without doubt, the most handsome young man you will ever set eyes on!'

For once Dora's curiosity was not aroused. She was too busy picking up Eleanor's discarded day dress, and shooing the big dog under the bed.

As the sumptuous meal progressed, and saddle of mutton, turkey pie and veal burrhs with an oyster sauce followed soup and then poached salmon, Daniel felt the customary anger tightening his heartstrings. He should, after three years as a servant in the big Yorkshire household and a further year as a guest in the earl's household in London, have accustomed himself to these lavish banquets. Yet no matter how hard he tried, the vast dishes of food, unneeded, often unwanted, brought to mind those years as a child when he and his mother had begged for a mouldy crust of bread, a rotted piece of fruit, a stinking piece of offal, simply to keep themselves from starvation. As he grew older and more adept at thieving, they had merely been hungry.

As he watched one of the servants washing the silver cutlery in preparation for the next course, he quickly put such memories from his mind. The past was past and he was on the point of achieving the goal for which he had strived, fought and suffered for so long. His eyes went to the elderly man at the head of the table – his Uncle Walter. How different a man to his father, that drunken ne'er-do-well!, yet physically resembling him. Old, in poor health, saddened by the recent loss of his daughter, Sir Walter was easy prey to his plans. The elderly man had accepted his fictitious story without question and, as far as Daniel could see, did not doubt his legitimacy. His wife, too, was sentimentally inclined, clearly sorry for him and ready to accept him into the family.

Daniel's gaze travelled down the table to William. This cousin was more wary, and Daniel knew that he must take care what stories he told in William's hearing. He had no record of his birth, of his father's marriage – since there had never been one – nor of his mother's supposed Spanish family. It was his intention to explain that all such papers and documents had been burnt in the prairie fire – and William could not prove otherwise. Nevertheless, the Calverleys had connections, and for all Daniel knew, might have friends or relatives who had travelled to America, who could disprove his story of the cattle ranch. He must take care never to specify an exact location.

The merest hint of a smile curved Daniel's lips as his eyes turned to the elder of the two female Howells. How fortunate that he had made their acquaintance in London at one of Matilda Wotherington's soirées. The middle-aged woman had readily responded to his attentions and now, seeing his gaze upon her, was fluttering her eyelids at him. Here was one ally should he have need of one! The girl, Jane, blushed whenever he spoke to her and he knew that if he cared to attempt it, this would be a conquest easily made. The Howells were wealthy and the girl their only daughter. She would almost certainly bring a healthy dowry to a marriage. It was a possibility he would consider once he had established himself more securely as a member of the Calverley family.

Almost unwillingly, Daniel allowed himself finally to look at Eleanor. He should, he knew, be filled with resentment for her untimely intrusion into the family. She had not been part of the plan he had been formulating ever since he had learned that William, a bachelor, was the only surviving Calverley heir. Supposing that his cousin were to remain unmarried, Daniel's ultimate claim to the Calverley fortune would have been unopposed. If William were to have died – through illness or by accident, as indeed it transpired he so nearly had – he, Daniel, would have inherited. Now it was all too likely that this young girl would beget a legitimate heir, and therefore was his enemy.

In all the twenty-eight years of his life, Daniel had never let his heart rule his head. Nothing had been allowed to interfere with that cold, calculating reason which he knew to be his biggest asset; for of what use were his powers over females if he could not put them to good use! Now, for the first time in his life, Daniel felt something more than lust as he looked into Eleanor's eyes. He wanted her for his woman – wanted her more than he had ever wanted anything in his life. There was a fire inside him which would not be quenched until he possessed her. His cousin William had claimed her for his bride, but it was he, Daniel, to whom she belonged.

Seeing Daniel's dark, intent gaze once more centred upon her, Eleanor looked quickly down at her plate. There was nothing impertinent, flirtatious or improper in his glance and yet she found it deeply disturbing. So, too, was the hollow ache in the pit of her stomach which she attributed to nerves and which throughout the meal had been destroying her appetite.

No matter how earnestly Eleanor had engaged in conversation with Jane or William or the voluble Mrs Howell, her mind had been hopelessly wayward, she thought as she toyed with her food. Her thoughts kept returning to the look on Cousin Daniel's face when she had descended the stairs; to the warmth of his hand beneath her elbow when he had moved forward to assist her. His touch had been momentary, for William had come into the hall, tucked his arm through hers and in his quiet, adoring voice, told her that he had never before seen her looking so beautiful. She seemed even now still to feel the tingling of her skin where Daniel's hand had touched her.

I have no cause to be afraid of him! she thought, yet she feared to look in his direction lest she found his eyes once more searching hers.

At least William seemed in more friendly mood towards his cousin, she decided as he invited Daniel to go riding with him in the morning. William's cheeks were flushed, and he looked frequently in Eleanor's direction. Lady Calverley, too, smiled at her constantly.

'You have made my son the happiest man on earth!' she said to Eleanor when finally the last toast to the engaged couple had been drunk and they withdrew, leaving the men to enjoy their brandy and more masculine conversation. 'I have never seen William so overjoyed! Your betrothal has also brought your Uncle Walter and me great happiness, my dear, and it is most agreeable that Daniel should have appeared in time to share our family celebrations.' She pressed Eleanor's arm affectionately as they walked through to the drawing-room. 'Your uncle was very attached to both his brothers during their childhood,' she continued confidentially, 'and now that he knows poor Robert finally vindicated himself, it has taken a great load off his mind. What a charming young man Robert's son has turned out to be! He has had a hard life it would seem, but your Uncle Walter is determined to help him. He thinks it most laudable that Daniel should have contemplated employment in preference to asking his family for financial assistance. We must take care not to injure his pride which, it would seem, is all the poor boy possesses!'

There was no opportunity for further such confidences since they were interrupted by Jane and her mother who had been attending to life's necessities – a task made far simpler for the men who had a chamberpot in the cupboard of the dining-room sideboard at hand for such requirements.

'We must congratulate you on a magnificent repast,' said Mrs Howell graciously as she came into the room. She smiled in kindly manner at Eleanor.

'How pretty you look, child. It will be a pleasure to assist you in the choosing of your trousseau, for I can see that whatever we select, you will look charming in it.'

'Poor Charles will be devastated when he receives my letter telling him of your betrothal, Eleanor,' Jane said. 'When he was last home for the holidays, we told him it was quite likely you would marry William, did we not, Mama? But he declared that if he cannot marry you, he will remain a bachelor for the rest of his life!'

'I despair of both my children!' Mrs Howell said with mock seriousness as, fanning her face, she addressed her hostess. 'Jane has two suitors, both quite acceptable to her father and to me, but will not choose between them. Is that not most contrary?'

'Only because I love neither one nor the other!' said Jane, laughing. 'I have told you, Mama, that I am waiting for a tall, dark stranger who, with one burning look, will capture my heart!'

'For gracious sake, what nonsense you do talk, Jane,' said her mother as Lady Calverley laughed. 'What have I done to deserve two such addle-pated children!'

Jane turned to Eleanor, her expression still mischievous.

'*You* understand, do you not, dearest? Do you recall that tale we invented of a mysterious highwayman who stopped our coach and demanded not our jewellery but our virtue? Of course we were so pleased when eventually he proved to be a nobleman in disguise, but we never agreed which one of us he would choose!'

Whilst the two older women engaged in conversation about Eleanor's trousseau, the girls moved away, their arms linked.

'Tell me how it feels to be betrothed!' Jane whispered. 'Do you tremble when William touches you? What does it feel like to have a man love you as William does? He reminds me of Charles the way he dotes upon you. Do you love him very dearly, Eleanor? What does it feel like to love?'

'So many questions!' Eleanor prevaricated. 'But of course I love William dearly. As to how it feels . . . I cannot explain. As to when he touches my hand . . .'

She broke off the sentence, realizing with a frightening certainty that the strange, burning, tingling sensation she had felt was at the touch of Daniel's, not William's, hand upon her arm. From across the room, she could hear her godmother's voice telling Mrs Howell that Daniel was to remain at Ortolans for as long as he wished.

'It is, after all, his home,' Lady Calverley was saying. 'He has had a singularly sad life, poor boy, and Sir Walter and I want to make up to him for his unhappy childhood. Such an interesting young man, do you not agree?'

Eleanor caught her breath. With one half of her, she wished that Daniel Calverley would leave Ortolans as soon as the weekend was over; that they could all return to their quiet, uneventful day-to-day lives without the disturbing presence of this new cousin. Yet there was another part of her – a part she had never known existed – which trembled with expectation and dragged her gaze continually to the doorway. Inexplicably, it seemed as if she both longed for and dreaded the moment when Daniel Calverley came back into the room and she saw once more those black, burning eyes.

CHAPTER FIVE

1790

'Most excellent entertainment – top notch!' said Mr Bannel as the coach conducting his party back to their London house in Burlington Street bumped over the rutted road, narrowly missing two bedraggled old women who were on their way to one of the gin houses.

His wife nodded her agreement.

'Mrs Siddons' clothes were quite delightful – so original, do you not agree, Verity, my dear?'

The gentle pale-faced girl, seated beside her mother, smiled.

'Richard has told me that the producer, Mr John Kemble, insists upon costumes in keeping with the era of the plays.'

Verity Bannel glanced at her fiancé, the dreamy expression of her face momentarily animated as she looked at the handsome man facing her. Like herself, he was blue-eyed, but where she was tiny, delicate and the epitome of femininity, Richard was tall, broad-shouldered and essentially masculine. Everyone considered they perfectly complemented one another, and had it not been for the sad death of Richard's mother during the Christmas festivities of 1789, she and Richard would now be man and wife. Out of respect for his late mother and at the request of Richard's heartbroken father, Sir Greville Mascal, they had delayed their wedding for a year.

The coachman turned the horses' heads into Burlington Street and drew them to a halt outside the big, three-storeyed house. The branches of the plane trees were bare, and stood eerily outlined by the carriage lamps.

'You will come in and join us in a nightcap, won't you,

m'boy?' Mr Bannel asked, for he enjoyed the company of his prospective son-in-law. Richard was well informed on most topics and, not unnaturally since he was the son of an author, very well read.

Richard shook his head.

'I do not like to leave my father too long in his own company,' he said. 'But I thank you nonetheless.'

As the butler opened the big front door, Richard bowed over Mrs Bannel's hand and then, as the young girl removed one small gloved hand from her large velvet muff, he touched it with his lips.

'I will see you before long, my dearest!' he said in a low voice.

'Bingham shall drive you back to your house in my equipage!' stated his future father-in-law. 'Our thanks once again, dear boy. A most commendable evening, but then Shakespeare never fails to please.'

Coriolanus was not one of Richard's favourite plays, but it had been a pleasant evening in pleasant company. If it had not been for the overshadowing grief of his mother's recent death, he might have enjoyed the occasion more. He had not wanted to leave his father alone, but the old man had insisted that he should spend this evening with Verity who, poor girl, had seen nothing of him since the funeral and must be finding life excessively tedious at home.

As he expected, he found his father waiting for him in the library, a book unopened on his lap. A decanter of brandy was on the sofa table and Sir Greville instructed the attendant footman to serve Richard with a drink before he dismissed the servant.

When Richard was seated opposite him, he reached forward and poked at the big coal fire, stirring the glowing embers into flames.

'Deuced cold, eh?' he muttered. 'Or perhaps I am just feeling my age. Damned if I can get warm tonight!'

Richard looked at his father anxiously.

'You are not unwell, Father?'

The older man removed his reading spectacles and drew a deep sigh.

'I'm well enough in my body, Richard. It is my mind which is ailing!'

'Come now, Father, your mind is keener than mine.' There was a hint of amusement now in Richard's blue eyes as he said mischievously: 'What you are really trying to tell me is that your new book is not flowing as it should!'

Sir Greville did not return the smile.

'I wish that were the case!' he said quietly. 'I regret to say that what troubles me is not a story of fiction, but a story of fact.'

Richard leant back in his chair and crossed his long legs.

'You wish to tell me this story?' he asked gently for his father's mood was strange and curiously uneasy.

'I do not want to tell you, my boy, but I feel it is my duty to do so, more especially as you are soon to be married.'

'Not for many months yet, Father!' Richard said quickly. 'Moreover, I will not marry at all if you do not wish it, whatever the reason.'

'No, no, Richard, I am devoted to little Verity, and the Bannels are a worthy family.' He paused for a moment, sipping his brandy thoughtfully. Then he said: 'I *must* tell you this story, Richard – and in my own way. Bear with me if you do not at first see why I am doing so.'

Richard remained silent, his own sense of uneasiness now matching his father's.

'It begins in the year 1760,' Sir Greville said slowly. 'Your dear mother and I were travelling – I, as usual, in search of material for my new book. We travelled a great deal; not just for my purposes, but because your dear mother was barren and, so we realized after many years of marriage, likely to remain so. It was a cause of great grief to her, and our sojourns abroad took her mind off her condition and afforded her other things to think about.'

Since Richard, unlike his many friends, had no brothers and sisters, he already knew these facts from his mother to whom he had been devoted. She had also let him know that since his arrival, she had felt totally fulfilled and needed no other child.

'As I said, it was 1760,' continued Sir Greville. 'We were touring in Spain when for no reason I can recall, we decided to travel on to Portugal. Five years previously, Lisbon had suffered an earthquake of catastrophic proportions. The city was being rebuilt having been all but razed to the ground, and I suppose I may have thought at the time that there was a story to be had if I spoke to those who had survived.'

He paused to glance up at the portrait of Richard's mother that hung over the mantelshelf.

'Had it once crossed my mind that such a tragedy could occur a second time, I would never have laid your dear mother open to danger. It was during the following year when we were still some distance from Lisbon, that another earthquake occurred. I learned subsequently that it was of three times greater velocity than that of fifty-five. Many lives were lost. I myself wished to return at once to England, but your mother would not hear of it. She was convinced that there must be great need of young, healthy people to assist in the relief of the population and would brook no argument from me. Afterwards she always insisted that it was the hand of God which was directing her. Who knows but she was right!'

This was an account of his parents' past of which Richard had heard nothing. He tried to imagine the mother he had known – an invalid since the days of his childhood when she had contracted smallpox – with the young, healthy woman his father was describing.

'Several weeks after the quake, we arrived in Lisbon. We managed to make our way to the British Embassy where your dear mother bravely volunteered our services. The Consul would not hear of it. Typhoid and other such deadly diseases were rife. He insisted that we leave on the next boat for England with a number of other Europeans who had gathered in one of the still upstanding hotels. It was there we met an Austrian baroness who had taken it upon herself to care for two English children – identical twins to be exact, who had been orphaned in the earthquake.'

Sir Greville glanced briefly at Richard and held out his brandy glass to be refilled. When Richard had accomplished the task, he resumed his story.

'These children were two years of age, or thereabouts. They spoke only a few infantile English words and could neither identify themselves nor their parents. According to the baroness a young Portuguese girl, who had been a servant in the pension where the English family were residing, had brought the children to the British Consul after the earthquake which had totally destroyed the pension. As far as the girl knew, she and the twin boys were the only survivors, unharmed because she had been taking them for a walk in the gardens when the quake occurred. No records of the pension's guests were discovered. All the Portuguese servant knew was that the family had but newly arrived in Lisbon and her services had been enlisted for an hour or two whilst the children's mother made enquiries about engaging a temporary nurse for them, their own nurse being indisposed.'

'I can see why you have travelled abroad so frequently for inspiration for your adventure stories!' Richard said smiling. 'Do continue, sir!'

Sir Greville did not return his smile.

'This is no story of fiction, Richard, nor am I finding the telling of it easy. I will try to keep to facts. The baroness and her husband had a small son the same age as the two orphans. A charitable woman, she was prepared to take one of the boys back to Vienna with her as a companion to her own child, but her husband would not agree to take both. Your mother immediately volunteered to adopt the other twin. The British Consul was only too glad to have the problem of the children so easily resolved and agreed to this arrangement. The child your mother and I brought home to England was you, Richard.'

Richard sprang to his feet; his face paled and then flushed a dark, angry red as the impact of his father's confession turned disbelief into a bitter credulity.

'Why were these facts not told to me before? Surely I had a right to know that I am not . . . not who I have been led to believe. Who am I, sir? You tell me now that I have a twin brother. Where is he? This should have been told to me if not as a young child, then at very least when I came of age!'

Sir Greville looked up and met his son's accusing eyes.

'I think I can understand how you feel, Richard, but I beg you, be reseated and hear me out. Your mother had been childless for many years. You were the child she had always wanted. She loved you with a devotion more intense than that of most other mothers with natural children. We had been abroad so long that, when we returned to England with you, no one doubted you were our natural son. Perhaps I should not have allowed her to perpetrate this lie, but my dear Elizabeth was so happy and fulfilled, I did not have the heart to confess the truth to our friends and families.'

He turned to stare into the dying fire and, his voice filled with emotion, he said brokenly:

'I do not regret it, although it has always been on my conscience since you grew to manhood. However, I had given your mother my promise that I would never speak out and only now . . . now that your poor dear mother is no longer with us . . . do I feel released from this promise. Perhaps I should not have told you, my boy, but you are soon to be married and . . . well, 'tis said and cannot be unsaid.'

It was some moments before Richard could bring himself to speak. A little of the bitterness towards his father evaporated for none knew better than he how devotedly his parents had loved one another. Nor could he deny the love they had always shown to him – his mother in particular. He had adored her.

'How could Mama have imagined I might love her the less had I known the truth!' he burst out. 'For twenty-eight years

I have believed myself to be your son, Richard Mascal. Who am I really? What is my real name?'

'If I knew the answers to your questions, I would tell you, my boy. Both the baron and I made as many enquiries as we could that fateful week we remained in Lisbon, but they came to nought. We were able to ascertain nothing beyond the fact that you were English and of gentle birth. The clothes you were wearing were of fine quality and according to the Portuguese maid, your parents had two English servants with them, a valet and an elderly woman, your nurse, who was ill with a fever. That is all the information I can give you.'

Richard was trying to visualize his unknown parents and, more importantly, the brother who might well be still alive.

'The Austrian baroness – you must have known her name?'

Sir Greville sighed.

'It was a name I could not get my tongue to – all C's and Z's – Hungarian I think. I made note of it at the time although your mother and the baroness had agreed that since you and your brother were identical twins, we must never meet again. I had expected to find the name in your mother's records of the event amongst her papers, but I fear she must have destroyed them all. You must realize, Richard, that she wanted to think of you as her child – her natural child.'

'And you remember nothing, sir – nothing at all? It would not be right to withhold this information now that you have revealed so much.'

'This past week, I have done little else but attempt to recall the name. Perhaps, like your mother, I did not wish to think of you as other than my true son; or perhaps it is due to my advancing years, but I remember nothing other than that the baron and baroness came from Vienna.'

Seeing the look of distress on Richard's face, he added quickly: 'I realize now that your mother and I were – remiss in our deception. Every man has a right to know his heritage, his ancestry. I wish I could do something to put matters right, but alas, I can think of no way to do so. There is one small link with your past, though it can be of no consequence to you. You will find it in the top drawer of my bureau.'

Feeling both excited and apprehensive for he knew not what reason, Richard went slowly across the room to the bureau and withdrew from it a small, beautifully carved wooden horse.

'It was the only plaything the children had with them,' Sir Greville said as Richard stood examining the miniature work of art. 'The son of the baroness had several toys which could be shared with the child she was adopting, so she insisted that your mother should retain that one for you. It being a reminder of your origins, your mother put it away as soon as we arrived home and could purchase others for you.'

Richard did not return to his chair but remained standing by the bureau, his hands fingering the lines of the carved animal as if by some magic they could feel back through time to hidden memories.

'I shall be obliged to confess these facts to the Bannels!' he said, as much to himself as to his father.

'My dear boy, I see no reason for you to do any such thing. To all intents and purposes, you are my son and when I die, you will inherit from me.'

Richard appeared not to have heard his comment for he continued his own train of thought.

'So, I am a foundling like any other! I can claim no right to my name – your name,' he corrected himself. 'I do not even have the dubious claims of a bastard.'

Suddenly aware of the unhappiness of the old man who had, without question, been a magnificent father to him, Richard hurried to his side and put his hand on Sir Greville's shoulder.

'You must not think me ungrateful,' he said quietly but forcefully. 'No man could have had better parents than I, and but for you and Mama, who knows what might have become of me! Nevertheless, Papa . . .' unconsciously he used his childish name for his father '. . . I feel this desperate need to

know who I really am. I cannot explain it . . . and if I can
no longer feel myself to be Richard Mascal, I must face the
fact that Verity might feel equally uncertain as to who her
future husband is.'

He was still clasping the wooden horse and, gazing at it
once more, he had the strange feeling that its contours were
familiar to him. The smooth polished grain felt velvety beneath
his touch, except beneath the little animal's belly. Upturning
it, he noticed some tiny characters which, on closer inspection,
spelled out the word PYLBEAM. Silently, he handed the plaything to his father.

'It is too neatly carved to have been accomplished by the
owner,' Sir Greville said, guessing Richard's hopes. 'I'll wager
this is the name of the carver – a master craftsman without
doubt.'

Disappointed, but still curious, Richard took up the horse
once more in his long, sensitive hands.

'It is an unusual name,' he said thoughtfully. 'If I could
trace the likely whereabouts of men with such a surname,
perhaps . . .' He broke off and turned back to his father.

'Would it pain you, sir, if I make this one attempt to discover
my true forebears? Though the chances are so slim that I do
not expect to succeed, I give you my word that were it to do
so, no man could ever replace you in my affections, nor seem
more a true father to me. From the story you gave me, it
is more than likely that both my natural parents died in the
quake, but I have a twin brother – an identical twin. If it is
possible, I should like to be reunited with him.'

Sir Greville rose stiffly from his chair and laid both hands
on his son's shoulders.

'The existence of your brother is the only thing that has
troubled me all these years,' he confessed. 'I have heard that
there is a special affinity between identical twins and if this
is so, then perhaps it was wrong to part you. Your mother
would happily have taken you both, but the baroness was
determined upon keeping your brother as a companion for

her child and could not be dissuaded. Go find him if you can, Richard. If he is even half as fine a man as you, I shall welcome him.'

He walked towards the door where he paused for one last comment.

'On the matter of your fiancée, I would caution you to think twice before you speak of these matters to her or to her parents. The Bannels are charming people, but a trifle pretentious – narrow-minded. They could persuade the girl to look elsewhere for a husband and she's pretty enough to find one!'

Richard's blue eyes seemed to darken in colour as he said proudly: 'Then she cannot truly love me; certainly not . . .' he added with a smile returning to his handsome countenance '. . . as Mama loved you.'

'Or you, m'boy!' Sir Greville said gruffly. He banged on the polished floor with his stick and a footman came hurrying in. 'Tell that confounded valet of mine that I am ready for my bed. Goodnight to you, Richard, my boy.'

Richard bowed to his father and stood at the foot of the stairs watching the elderly man ascend on the arm of his servant. He had, Richard thought, aged a great deal in the month since his wife had died. He had never before thought of his father as anything but ageless and now it pained him to note the difference in him. Throughout Richard's childhood, Sir Greville had been his tutor, mentor and unusual companion. He had imbued in Richard his own love of books, and enlivened every aspect of his life with his vivid and lively imagination. His adventure stories had been read and enjoyed by hundreds, young and old, and were now by way of being classics. Richard loved, revered and respected this man whose characteristics he had hoped with maturity to emulate. He had even written a book about the origins of the slave trade – an industry the member of Parliament, Mr Wilberforce, was trying so hard to abolish. The book was to be published in the autumn and to Richard's astonishment and delight, Mr Wilberforce had promised to write a foreword to it. To become an acknowledged author like his father had been his dearest ambition.

Richard returned to the fireside, his long, lean face – which could appear autocratic until he smiled – looking suddenly youthful and vulnerable. His father's words of warning regarding his engagement to Miss Verity Bannel had disturbed him more than he had first realized. As Sir Greville had said, her parents were conventional to a degree and ambitious for their only daughter. Sir Greville's popularity as an author had been an important factor in their decision to allow the betrothal. They had hoped to marry Verity to a title and Sir Greville had recently been knighted, although the title was not hereditary.

As for Verity, his pretty, innocent, accomplished betrothed – Richard could not be certain as to the depth of her declared affection for him. He sensed a lack of the undoubted passion he felt when he took her arm or kissed her hand. Despite her youth, she always appeared calm, unflustered and in control of herself. He had hoped their betrothal might reveal greater fires within, awaiting only their marriage to materialize.

He heard a sudden slight movement beyond the closed door and knew instantly who it was. Peter, his Negro servant, had stationed himself outside despite Richard's instruction that he could retire to bed. This reminder of his black servant recalled another aspect of his fiancée's character which disturbed him. She had made clear the fact that she would not tolerate the Negro in their marital home.

Peter, in his early childhood, had been bought from a slave trader to be trained as a pageboy for a countess. When he was about eleven years of age, his mistress, who had doted upon him for he was a handsome child, decided that he had grown too tall and manly in appearance to remain as a page, and had sold him to a banker who owned a big house in the City. This man had not only treated the black youth most cruelly, but had approached him for unnatural pleasures of a criminal nature. Peter, like so many black servants who were

indentured to cruel employers, had run away. The usual adver-
tisements had appeared in the newspapers offering a reward
of a guinea or two for the recapture of such unfortunates. As
often as not, they were discovered and returned to their owners,
for all wore silver collars about their necks on which was
inscribed the name and address of the man whose servant they
had become.

Several years ago, one of Richard's own servants had discovered Peter, a runaway, hiding in the stables. Upon questioning
him, Richard had learned his story and was horrified. He was
further impressed because the blackamoor, now full grown
and of magnificent stature, still retained a measure of pride
despite his bedraggled, starving condition. He would prefer,
he informed Richard, to die rather than be subjected ever
again to his master's unnatural, animal appetites.

Realizing that the servant was intelligent, and had greatly
benefited from the refined conditions he had enjoyed as a child
in the households of the countess, Richard decided not to turn
him in, as was strictly his duty. He offered to give him employment in his own household, but first, he paid a visit to the
degenerate banker from whom the unfortunate fellow had
escaped. He offered to buy Peter from him, and when this
offer was refused, let the pervert know that he, Richard, was
aware of his predilections and threatened to expose the truth
if Peter were not freed from his indenture. The man had
immediately agreed to release him.

It was a decision Richard had never regretted. Although sometimes he was irked by Peter's silent but ever-present shadow – the
man had appointed himself Richard's bodyguard – he had become
accustomed to his devotion. Indeed, Peter had saved his life when
once, on his way to the British Museum, he had been attacked
by a lunatic who had escaped from Bedlam. The attendant who
came to their assistance informed Richard apologetically that
normally the lunatic was docile and harmless, but that he was
apt to become dangerously violent when allowed into the en-
closure where the public watched the antics of the inmates.

Richard knew of this way of entertainment, but he himself took no pleasure in observing these miserable unfortunates.

Peter proved to be an excellent servant, often anticipating Richard's requirements even before his master was himself aware of them. Yet it was Peter who was responsible for the only serious disagreement Richard had ever had with Verity. Like her father, she was not in favour of the abolition of the slave trade. She was frightened of these black Africans and considered them little superior to animals, fitted only for work in the colonies and other foreign countries. She would not permit Richard to bring Peter into the house, and he was always obliged to wait in the stables when Richard visited the Bannels. She refused to read Richard's book upon the plight of slaves, and preferred that he did not discuss the subject, despite its recent prominence in Parliament.

Richard had told himself that the young girl was unduly influenced by her parents' opinions, and tried to convince himself that once married to her, he could alter her attitude. They had not yet resolved the problem of what was to be done with Peter after their marriage. Richard would not part with him and Verity insisted that she would not have him in her house.

Richard looked now at the wooden horse still clasped in his hands. Was this small relic of his infancy going to prove of far more importance than that of a mere memento of his past? Would it, with his father's revelation of the truth, now bring to an end his betrothal to Verity? He was no longer sure his love for her would withstand the several differences in their attitudes to which he had so far turned a blind eye.

Richard was by no means without experience of the feminine sex. His manly figure had always attracted the attention of women as well as young girls like Verity, and his cheerful, kindly nature had led several of his more mature paramours to confess themselves hopelessly enamoured of him. Whilst no philanderer, he had enjoyed numerous affairs since he had become adult and he possessed any normal, healthy young man's need for a desirable female. For a while, he had kept a mistress, a stage actress, of whom he was genuinely fond, preferring the easiness of such a relationship to the ties and responsibilities of marriage. His mistress had finally found a wealthy wool merchant willing to marry her, and at the same time, he, Richard, had been introduced to Verity.

Her tiny, delicate figure had fascinated him, bringing out all that was most chivalrous and protective in his nature. When she had smiled at him so demurely from her huge, pale blue eyes, he had felt his body stir with familiar longing. Her proximity became a torture to him for he could think of little else but stripping her of her pretty clothes and stirring that composed little face into an agony of desire equal to his own. Her virginity, her composure, challenged him, and he had taken up the challenge. That he had frequently found her conversation and her narrow-minded attitudes boring, he had conveniently ignored, allowing the demands of his body to overrule his misgivings.

Suddenly, Richard knew what he wanted now from his life. He was no longer impatient for marriage. He had more urgent matters to occupy him – he wanted to discover who his forebears were; and most of all, he wanted to find his twin brother. He would use his foundling status as an excuse to extricate himself from an engagement he was no longer sure he wanted. If Verity truly loved him, she would wait for him. For the present, he would remain a free man, free to search for the truth.

'Pylbeam!' He spoke the name aloud. In what county of England was this strange-sounding name prolific? Tomorrow he would go to the British Museum, to Lambeth Palace Library, even to Oxford perhaps to the Bodleian; to any place where he could find out where in England the name was a common one. Then his search could begin even if he had to visit every Pylbeam in the country! Although it was all of twenty-five years since the woodcarver had fashioned the little horse, the man might yet be living; or if not, his sons might recall when he had carved the plaything and, most important of all, for whom.

Richard summoned his servant and looked up into the face of the black man, who despite his own six feet of height, still towered above him.

'You recall our discussion concerning your future when I marry Miss Bannel?' he said, and for once ignored the look of dismay in Peter's dark eyes. 'You can forget that I ever contemplated finding you a new master. In all probability, I shall not be marrying Miss Bannel and I give you my word that, unless you commit some serious misdemeanour, you shall remain in my service until one or other of us is dead.'

Two rows of gleaming white teeth were revealed as the man's full lips widened in a smile, partly of relief and partly in joy.

'You saved my life, Peter, and you look after me well.' Richard gave his sudden quick smile as he added: 'Nor do you gossip as do my white-skinned servants. If, at some later date, I decide to find myself a wife, she will have to appreciate my indebtedness to you since you risked your own life to save mine.'

'Master, I am glad!' said the man simply, his expression indicating his relief.

Richard patted his servant affectionately on the shoulder. He, too, felt as if a heavy load had been lifted from his heart. The news his father had imparted had been a great shock and knocked him momentarily off his balance. Now he felt ready to face the truth and to accept it. Somewhere in the world he had a twin brother, and he would find him, just as he would find the name of his true ancestors.

'To bed, Peter,' he said. 'The hour is late and I must rise early for I have much to do.'

Tomorrow, he thought as the servant held open the door for him, his all-important quest would begin.

CHAPTER SIX

1790

The same thought was in the minds of every member of the Ortolans household, though none spoke it – Sir Walter Calverley's condition was fast deteriorating. Despite the advent of an eminent London physician, neither he nor the family's own physician seemed able to diagnose the exact nature of his illness.

It was not long after Daniel's introduction to the family that Sir Walter had complained of feeling unwell and been confined to his bed. He was unable to contain food and vomited continuously. Within a few days, his skin and the whites of his eyes had turned yellow. The family physician had declared that his patient was jaundiced, dosed him with calomel to purge him and when still Sir Walter showed no sign of improvement, professed himself ignorant as to the disease causing the jaundiced condition. When, after six weary weeks, he was still no better, a London physician had finally been called in to give a more learned opinion. He was equally nonplussed.

'Sir Humphrey will return next week to see if Father has developed further symptoms which might give him new insight into this unknown disease,' William now stated, having seen the physician depart for London. 'Poor Mama is quite distraught and has retired to her room.'

Eleanor, who had been waiting anxiously in the drawing-room with Daniel, hurried across to William's side.

'I am so sorry!' she said. 'Shall I go to your mother, William?'

He shook his head.

'Thank you, Eleanor, but Mama has said she wishes to be alone. I have promised Father I will go back to the sickroom as he has matters of importance he wishes to discuss. I shall not, therefore, be able to accompany you to the village, my dearest!'

'You must not concern yourself on my account,' Eleanor said quickly. 'I have much to do, not least pen my thank-you letter to dear Mrs Howell for all her kindnesses to me these past two months.'

Eleanor had but newly returned from her sojourn in London which, whilst she had enjoyed the sightseeing and Jane's cheerful companionship, had nevertheless proved an exhausting round of shopping and fittings for her trousseau. The smoke, grime and noise of the city had not been to her liking and she had been looking forward eagerly to her return to the country and to Ortolans. The matter of poor Uncle Walter's ill health, and her beloved godmother's concern for him, were serious blows to the joy of her homecoming.

The discovery of Daniel's presence in the household was a further unwelcome surprise for he had expressed his intention to return to London shortly after his first visit to his family, to settle his affairs. Sir William had told him that he might occupy the Calverleys' London house in Sackville Street now that the Comte de Valderton and his family had removed to Battersea, preferring the country life for their children.

Daniel had made several formal calls upon the Howells in London during Eleanor's visit with them. He had accompanied them on one occasion to see the launching of a hot air balloon at St George's Fields, and on another, obtained tickets for an evening's entertainment at Covent Garden. On neither occasion had he told her that he was still residing at Ortolans and that these were only fleeting visits to London.

Jane had confessed to Eleanor that she was living in hope that she was the object of Daniel's interest, professing him to be the most fascinating man of her acquaintance. Eleanor, however, was uneasy on Jane's behalf. She had been unable to ignore the fact that whenever she had turned her head, it was to find Daniel's eyes upon herself. As always, she had felt self-conscious and ill at ease in his presence.

William, however, seemed delighted to have his cousin's company at Ortolans and now, as Daniel offered to give Eleanor her first riding lesson and so occupy her afternoon, he looked at him gratefully.

'It is excellent weather to be out of doors and most kind of you, cousin. Besides which, that new little mare I bought Eleanor needs exercise. Run along, Eleanor, and change your clothes. I will see you at dinner.'

Eleanor felt a stab of irritation. William had addressed her as if he were a father, she a child. Suppose she had not wished to go riding? He had not even asked if she did so! But she was being unfair to dear William, she reproved herself quickly. He was quite right in thinking her eager to be out in the autumn sunshine and, after all this time, to learn to ride horseback.

She turned to Daniel to tell him she would be changed into her riding habit and in the stable courtyard within a quarter of an hour. His expression was, as usual, unfathomable, but his eyes seemed to shine like wet coals, staring into hers as if he had some private message for her. It unnerved her – made her feel gauche and uncomfortable – yet excited her, too.

Fortunately, Dora seemed for once to have other thoughts on her mind than Mr Daniel Calverley to whom, without cause, she had taken an ill-masked dislike. Like all the servants, she was deeply concerned about Sir Walter's ill health and now plied Eleanor with questions regarding the London physician's visit.

'He be nobbut a money-making quack!' she pronounced sourly when Eleanor said there was nothing new to report. 'The Mistress should hearken to my gran. She knows more'n all them apothecaries, surelye. Gran says there's two certain ways to cure the yellow disease.'

She lifted Eleanor's spotted day-dress over her head and

took out the new, emerald green, corded silk riding habit from the wardrobe.

'You mun hardboil a hen's egg in Master's own water furst, then prick it with a pin or the like and bury her in an anthill; and if'n that doant do the trick nohow, then Master mun eat nine live lice each marnin'. Gran says one or t'other allus cures the yellows. Mrs Green, carter's wife, she did have it and Master Mason's lad, Billy, and my gran cured 'em.'

Eleanor did not entirely discredit these old wives' tales. There was one old woman in the village who successfully cured most of the livestock with her home-made potions and balms. Rex, when still a puppy, had developed a weeping sore on one of his pads and the old woman's poultice had healed it in less than a week. Nevertheless, neither of Dora's suggested remedies for poor Uncle Walter sounded as if they would be effective and were not very pleasant, either.

'Harry says as how the Master's wasted to a spindle!' Dora continued. 'Cook says if'n he doant keep no victuals in his belly, he'll not live to Christmas!' she added lugubriously.

'Dora!' Eleanor protested. 'I've told you before I'll not listen to such gossip. Cook has no idea what she is talking about. Now fasten the buttons at my wrists please, and tie my cravat.'

Her anger was born partly of fear. She loved her uncle who was near to being a father to her, having none of her own, and his appearance had frightened her when she had returned from London. The bones of his face seemed to protrude through the discoloured skin and his hands, plucking at the bedsheets, were like those of a skeleton. She would not – could not – bear to think of him dying.

She ran downstairs and out into the garden, hurrying past the herbaceous borders, through the walled kitchen garden and into the cobbled courtyard. The summer sunshine warmed her cheeks, and her natural feeling of well-being returned as Rex came bounding towards her. The air was redolent with the smell of the horses, their heads turned inquisitively towards her over the top of their stable doors.

She drew closer to the two men standing by a big grey – one of the family's six carriage horses. Daniel was running a hand down the animal's foreleg.

'That's no sprain, you numskull!' Daniel was saying. 'Liniment is the very last thing you should be using. He's pulled a tendon, poor fellow. His hock is red hot. What in devil's name have you been doing with him?'

The groom – a young lad not long in the Calverleys' employment – looked sheepish.

'I only took 'im for a canter up on Downs, sir!' he said. ''Ee likes it up there!'

'Don't lie to me, boy. He wouldn't get a leg like this unless you'd been galloping him. Moreover, you should know better than to take him up on those chalk hills. The ground's bone hard after this hot summer. Where's the head groom?'

'Tasker, sir – he be foaling Starlight, sir. She be having a hard time, surelye!'

'Then I suppose you'll just have to manage, you dunderhead. Now get this horse's leg into that water trough – and keep it there for at least a half-hour. Can you not see the poor brute is in pain? His leg's boiling hot. Now get on with it!'

As the abject lad led the limping horse across the yard, Daniel turned and saw Eleanor.

'My apologies, Miss McCore. I was not aware you were there!'

Eleanor smiled.

'You seem to know a great deal about horses, Mr Calverley. I am very impressed, although I must confess I did feel a little sorry for poor Jem. I hope you will not tell William, else the boy will surely be dismissed.'

Daniel did not return her smile.

'He should know better if he's to work with horses!' he said. 'However, if it pleases you, I will keep quiet about this particular incident.'

'He's still young,' Eleanor pleaded. 'I'm sure he will never make the same mistake again.'

Daniel took a step towards her so that their bodies were almost touching.

'Are you as compassionate as it would seem to everyone around you? Is that why you have agreed to marry Cousin William? You feel pity for him because he lost an arm?'

Eleanor flushed an angry red. She was deeply shocked.

'You have no right to say such a thing!' she protested. 'It is none of your business why I am marrying William – but since you choose to raise the subject, perhaps it will conclude the conversation if I tell you that I love William very dearly. That is why I shall marry him.'

Daniel's dark eyes were narrowed, but their glance never wavered.

'You would tell me I was impertinent were I to declare that is no nearer the truth than that boy's fibbing, so I will hold my tongue. Let us put our minds to pleasanter things than your marriage to my cousin. Your mare is ready saddled in her stable. Since Jem is otherwise occupied, I will get her for you.'

It was on the tip of Eleanor's tongue to say that she had changed her mind and no longer wished to go riding. Had Daniel not momentarily disappeared, she might have done so. Her heart was racing furiously with anger. He had no excuse for raising so personal a subject! Moreover, his conjectures were, she now realized with dismay, far nearer the truth than she cared to admit even to herself.

During those long weeks in William's sickroom prior to their engagement, pity had indeed been the strongest of her emotions. He had borne the pain so courageously and although he made light of the amputation, she knew that he fretted over the indignities caused by his physical handicap. Besides, she admired his stoicism, she told herself furiously, and what did Daniel Calverley know about pity or love? She would not take the trouble to dispute his accusation lest he thought that she took his opinion seriously. Far better to treat it as the nonsense it was.

When he returned, leading the little roan mare William had

given her, Eleanor's head was held high and the tone of her voice was deliberately inconsequential as she said:

'William has already shown me how to be seated and how to hold the reins. He says I have a natural balance and should make a good horsewoman.'

Daniel made no reply as he put his hands beneath her foot and hoisted her into the saddle. Still silent, he adjusted the tightness of the girth and in doing so, his dark, uncovered head leant momentarily against her thigh. Eleanor felt herself begin to tremble and she tried ineffectually to keep her hands still as Daniel readjusted her grip on the reins. As if sensing her tension, the little mare shifted uneasily and as Eleanor swayed in the saddle, Daniel reached up and put both hands about her waist.

'You must not be afraid!' he said quietly. 'The horse senses it and that is why she is uneasy. You have nothing to fear!'

From the mare or from him, Eleanor thought as she subdued a gasp.

'I am perfectly all right!' she declared with what she hoped was the correct degree of haughtiness. 'Are we riding or not, Mr Calverley?'

For the first time, she saw him smile – not a full smile, but a slow curving of his mouth. Her eyes were drawn now to his face, recognizing this man's extraordinary beauty, most noticeable when his features softened as they now had. For one long moment, their eyes were locked. Eleanor's heart was beating so forcefully that she was terrified lest the man standing so close to her could hear. Then the mare whinnied, Daniel took a pace backwards, and the spell was broken.

Daniel now disappeared into one of the stables and came out leading William's black hunter, Jason. It was spirited, moving restlessly whilst Daniel mounted and, leaning over, took hold of the mare's leading rein. Surprisingly, the hunter quietened the moment Daniel was in the saddle.

'We'll go down across the meadows to the river,' he said. 'I rode there yesterday and I think you will find it very pleasant.'

Eleanor glanced at the stable lad who was still engaged in bathing the grey's leg in the trough as Daniel had ordered.

'But who will go with us, Mr Calverley?' she said, for she knew that it would be quite improper for her to go riding alone with a man.

Daniel gave an imperceptible shrug of his shoulders.

'Are you doubting my capacity to take care of you, Miss McCore?' he asked. 'Or are you concerned that you have no chaperon? I hardly think we need bother with such niceties since Cousin William himself gave permission for you to ride with me.'

It was on the tip of Eleanor's tongue to protest that William would have taken it for granted that they would be accompanied by one of the grooms, but fearing that Daniel might think her priggish, she made no demur.

Daniel was silent as they rode out of the courtyard and into the meadow, the horses moving at a gentle walking pace. He glanced frequently at Eleanor and spoke only once to tell her that William had judged her potential as a horsewoman accurately. Eleanor's initial nervousness gave way to delight and a total lack of fear. When Daniel suggested that they should trot, she nodded eagerly. It was several minutes before she was able to time the rise and fall of her body to that of the mare beneath her. Occasionally she mistimed her movements and bobbed like a cork in a river.

'You are managing very well for a beginner,' Daniel said as she laughed at her mistakes. 'You would find it easier were you able to sit astride your horse. It is also easier when you canter.'

Eleanor was now filled with excitement.

'May we do so, Mr Calverley? I am not frightened. Please say we may.'

Daniel knew himself to be completely in control of the big hunter and the mare was clearly a gentle, docile animal. Since Eleanor could keep her seat so well in a trot, there should be little danger in a gentle canter.

'Very well, but you must promise not to tell Cousin William I allowed it!' he said. 'He would not approve of my putting you at risk, and were you to fall off . . .'

'But I will not, I promise!' Eleanor cried. 'And I promise I will not tell William!'

As the hunter broke into a canter, the mare stretched her legs and Eleanor felt herself gliding forward in a delightful, undulating movement, so pleasing that she wished it to continue for ever. She was conscious of the wind trying to lift her cocked hat and tangle her hair; of the thin white ribbon of the river on their right rushing by; of the hindquarters of the big black horse in front of her, Daniel seemingly a part of him. Then, without warning, her mare tripped in an unseen rabbit hole. Eleanor was barely aware that she was falling before she hit the ground, her hat flying from her head and her riding crop disappearing into the branches of a young rowan tree. The breath was knocked from her and she lay gasping, staring up at the blue sky before she drifted into unconsciousness.

She came to her senses to discover herself still lying in the soft grass, but cradled in Daniel's arms. For a moment, she lay still, trying to gather her wits and recall why she was in this extraordinary position. She was not aware of any pain although her head throbbed. She tried to make sense of the words Daniel was saying – something to do with thanking 'the great spirit' – which she did not comprehend. He looked shocked and very concerned. She attempted a smile, whereupon his arms tightened around her and he said:

'Tell me you are not hurt! I shall never forgive myself. You have not broken any limbs? Please say something, Eleanor!'

In her state of confusion, Eleanor was not aware of his use of her Christian name, but she knew that she could not continue lying here in his arms. She struggled into a sitting position, fighting the momentary giddiness the action evoked.

'Lean your head against my shoulder!' Daniel's words were almost a command and automatically she obeyed him.

'I fear I fell off!' she said stupidly. 'The horse stumbled and . . .'

'Hush, do not talk. Just rest!' With one arm still supporting her, he ran his other down both her arms, feeling for broken bones. Now fully conscious and aware that if she did not prevent it, he might feel for broken bones in her legs, Eleanor attempted to struggle free.

'I do assure you, I am unharmed, Mr Calverley. Please let me go!'

It was a full minute before he obeyed her and releasing his hold upon her, he stood up. Then his hands were once more upon her, clasping her waist as he drew her to her feet. Another wave of giddiness assailed her and she swayed in his arms, her eyes closed. Her whole body was trembling, the reason for which, she now told herself, being the effects of her fall; but at the same time, she could feel the warmth of Daniel's face so close to hers that for one brief moment of insanity, she thought he was about to kiss her. Lifting her lids quickly, she found herself staring into the big dark pools of his eyes in which she could see mirrored her own reflection. She could hear his hurried breathing as she struggled to get her own breath. Suddenly she was conscious of his vice-like hold upon her and she gasped: 'Let me go, you are hurting me!'

He seemed not to hear her for he made no move to obey her command.

'Mr Calverley . . . !' Her protest was the fiercer for the fact that she was now filled with unreasonable fear. She had the frightening feeling that this dark-eyed, silent man was a stranger, an enemy who was seeking to keep her a prisoner, who would harm her if she could not free herself.

Without warning, his arms dropped to his sides and in a soft voice quite without threat, he said:

'Even in disarray, you are the most beautiful woman I have ever seen!'

Eleanor was deeply shocked. Even allowing for the fact that this cousin of William's had grown up in a different country where doubtless, the conventions were also very different, he must be aware that to make so personal a comment, however flattering, was unpardonable.

Watching the expression on Eleanor's face, a faint smile touched Daniel's lips as he said:

'Has Cousin William not told you this many times? Surely you have no cause to look so startled! Was I wrong to say what I think?'

Was he mocking her? Eleanor thought. Was he right and she outmoded in thinking he was ill-mannered, presumptuous and unjustifiably familiar? It was certainly childish of her to be afraid of him – for what harm could he possibly do her? Holding her as he had was a natural thing to do believing her giddy and liable to faint after her fall.

'It is best if we say nothing of this to William . . . or my godmother!' she spoke her thoughts aloud. 'You were in no way to blame for my fall, Mr Calverley, and thankfully, I am none the worse for it. Shall we remount?'

Daniel bowed, his expression once more unreadable. He moved easily and gracefully towards the two horses who, unperturbed, were quietly cropping the grass which had grown in since the haymaking. Taking up their reins, he led them back to the waiting girl.

'I should not have allowed you to canter so soon,' he said as he retrieved her hat and assisted her back into the saddle. 'We will walk the horses home. Please tell me at once if you feel faint. You could ride behind me if you would feel safer.'

'No, no, I am quite able to ride by myself!' Eleanor said quickly, having no wish to sit behind this man with her arms clasped about his waist in the manner she had seen done by the farmer's sons during haymaking. 'Let us be on our way, Mr Calverley, lest William is worrying for my safety.'

She thought privately that it was unlikely he would be watching his timepiece for her return. Since Uncle Walter's illness, he had been engrossed in the affairs of the estate which he was now handling for his father. If he were not in the library poring over papers and writing letters, he was out with the estate manager, touring round the farms or going through game books with his gamekeeper. There were many days when, Eleanor knew, his shoulder wound pained him and on two occasions, the Brighthelmstone physician had had to cleanse the wound which developed abscesses. By the time the evening meal was over, he looked pale and drawn and, excusing himself, would retire early to bed.

As a consequence, Eleanor saw far less of him since their betrothal than she had in the days when she had sat by his bedside in the sickroom. He always spoke to her affectionately, asked after her health and well-being, and reassured himself that her time was occupied before hurrying off to pursue his own duties. Of course, she told Jane on one of their regular exchanges of visits, it would be different once they were married! There would be occasion in the privacy of their bedroom to discuss the books Eleanor loved to read; the plays, operas and sights she had seen during her sojourn in London with the Howells. They would be good companions as well as lovers.

Somehow, Eleanor always had difficulty in casting William in the role of a lover. He was not an emotional man and although from time to time, he still looked at her in that searching fashion which she had once found so disturbing, and quite often told her when she appeared at the breakfast table that she looked 'charming' and even 'captivating', he had certainly never gone so far as to call her 'beautiful'.

She became conscious once more of the man riding beside her. Had he intended to embarrass her with his compliment? Was it simply because he really thought her beautiful that he was forever staring at her in the manner she found so unsettling? With one half of her, she had hoped that Daniel would not be at Ortolans when she returned from London, yet she had felt relief, excitement, aliveness as well as apprehension when he had stepped into the hall to greet her.

The gentle movement of the horses as they ambled at slow

pace towards the house was strangely soothing. Eleanor felt her body relaxing as she caught sight of her godmother, waving a handkerchief from her bedroom window. How silly she, Eleanor, was to be frightened by her companion when her godmother thought so well of him! He was always unfailingly chivalrous towards Lady Calverley, attentive to her every need and the first to offer her his arm. He had charmed her completely when she had remarked that Cook had warned her they were perilously short of her favourite Hyson's tea, and without giving notice of his intent, had ridden the ten miles into Brighthelmstone and somehow managed to obtain a supply of this tea from the Duke of Cumberland's provisioners. He had furthermore bought a cask of water from the Chalybeate Springs in the hope that they might benefit Uncle Walter. Eleanor herself had not been forgotten and he had presented her with a spray of artificial flowers to add to her box of furbelows.

As they rode side by side into the courtyard, Eleanor's mood changed yet again, for hurrying out to meet them was William. He had been thinking of her after all, she thought, which was a clear indication of his love for her. Despite the empty sleeve pinned across his chest, he was a tall, manly figure, reminding her unexpectedly of the portrait in the hall which she had so often admired when first she had come to live at Ortolans.

Grey wisps of smoke were curling into the air from one of the four chimneys. Harry must have lit the fire in the sickroom, she supposed, for poor Uncle Walter complained continually that he was chilled. The mullioned windows were reflecting the rosy rays of the sun and it seemed to Eleanor as if the house itself were waiting to welcome her. She smiled as William came hurrying towards them, but the smile died on her lips as he drew close and she saw the gravity of his expression.

'Papa has had a convulsion!' he said without preamble. 'Poor Mama has sent for the physician. He is very weak and we fear for his life. He has asked to see you, dearest.'

'I will come this instant!' Eleanor said as William lifted her down from the saddle.

'Is there anything I can do, cousin?' Daniel asked as he jumped easily to the ground and handed the reins of his horse to the waiting boy.

'No, no, I thank you, Daniel. It is Eleanor he wishes to see.'

Eleanor followed William into the house, feeling at once the tension as servants went hurrying from room to room. Lady Calverley stood outside the sickroom door, her face lined and deathly pale. As Eleanor ran forward to comfort her, Lady Calverley wiped the tears from her eyes and clasping Eleanor in her arms, she said softly:

'Your uncle is not in any pain, my dear, and if anything he is a little better. He is talking quite coherently, but his mind is not at rest.'

She glanced briefly at William who nodded as if to encourage her to continue.

'He believes it will not be long before the Almighty takes him to his bosom!' she said brokenly. 'He is prepared for the call but wants only one thing before he leaves us . . . to see you and William married.'

Seeing his mother's distress, William continued for her.

'Papa thinks it unlikely he will see the year out, my dear. Mama and I think we should obtain a special licence and then it would pose no problem for Parson Dicker to perform the marriage rites here at Ortolans – that is if you would not mind too greatly forgoing the wedding we had planned. It is this my poor father wishes to discuss with you.'

'When . . . when would the wedding take place?' Eleanor forced the question from her lips.

'A week or two, perhaps . . . just as soon as it can be arranged, dearest. We do not know how long Papa has left. I will write at once to your guardians.'

Eleanor looked at the closed door of Sir Walter's room, her mind in a panic. Her instinct was to cry out: 'No, no, I am not ready for marriage to you, William. I need more time . . .'

but as she saw the look of appeal in her dear godmother's eyes, she knew that time was the one thing they did not have. She turned her eyes to William who now gently pressed her hand.

'Is this too much to ask of you, dearest? It would make Papa so happy!'

Unable to do more than nod her assent, Eleanor turned and opened her uncle's door. Her eyes went to the high four-poster where he lay, his valet stationed on one side, one of the women who had been engaged to nurse him on the other. At first she thought he was sleeping but his eyes, still yellow with the jaundice, opened as she approached the bed.

'Eleanor, dear child! William said you would be coming to see me. Did he tell you of my request? You are not unwilling?'

'Not if it is what you want, Uncle Walter!' Eleanor whispered. She was unprepared for her uncle's words, spoken now in a loud, clear voice.

'I want to be certain that there is another generation of Calverleys to follow William!' he said. 'You are young and healthy and I have no doubt whatever that you will beget him a son. Next spring is too far in the future. We none of us know what the good Lord has in store for us.'

He beckoned one claw-like hand towards Eleanor.

'Ever since those dastardly Frenchies killed my Catherine and so nearly killed my only son, I have thought about William marrying and giving me a grandson. It should have been done years ago. But I am not sorry he waited. You are a good girl, Eleanor, and will make him a good wife.' He paused to sip from the glass of cordial the nurse held out to him and then said:

'There have been Calverleys around since Doomsday, Eleanor. Did you know that? There have been Calverleys living in this house for the past two hundred years. I would not want Ortolans to pass into the hands of strangers.'

Eleanor spoke out loud.

'I understand how you feel, Uncle Walter,' she said truthfully.

'But have you not forgotten your nephew, Daniel? He is a Calverley – your brother's son – and William and I may not . . .'

'You will beget him a son,' Sir Walter broke in. 'I am determined upon it. I have nothing against Robert's boy, but he was not raised to love this place as William has been. We Calverleys have a responsibility towards the parish, to our tenants, to our employees, to Detcham itself. Moreover this house needs someone who cares for it, Eleanor. People think of houses as dead things – wood, plaster, bricks – but houses have souls. There are good ones and bad ones and they can influence the families who live in them. You must see to it that your son and William's understands this as you do, child. You *do* understand what I am saying?'

Unable to speak for the lump that had risen to her throat, Eleanor could but nod her head. It was as if her uncle were handing the house into her hands to love and to cherish and to protect for future generations. In such altruistic light, she was no longer frightened by the thought of marrying William and begetting his son.

CHAPTER SEVEN

1790

If only someone had warned her what her marital duties entailed, Eleanor thought as tears dripped down her cheeks. Someone should have told her about the pain, the indignity, the fearful intimacy involved.

Beside her, William was fast asleep. To add to her misery, he was snoring. At least he had turned on his side and his arm no longer lay across her body, imprisoning her.

'I am a prisoner!' she thought as the tears flowed faster. She was trapped for the rest of her life in marriage to a man whose physical proximity appalled her. She had not felt this way when he had kissed her cheek or her hand; but those kisses had borne no resemblance to the pressure of his moist mouth on hers as his hand searched beneath the thin lawn of her night chemise, fastened on her breasts and then her thighs . . .

She squeezed her eyes shut as if this irrelevant gesture could stop her from remembering the worst part of all – the great throbbing organ being thrust into her, not once but again and again, each time adding to her pain and humiliation.

On the night before her wedding, she had begged Dora to pass on whatever knowledge she might have – but Dora was unmarried and she could not expect her to be an authority on the subject. Dora had said comfortingly:

'You doant need to know what's what, Miss Eleanor. All you be needin' to know is lettin' Mister William have his pleasure howsoever he wants it. That's what my mam tolt our Doris when she were getting wed.'

The advice left Eleanor none the wiser. As Dora had helped

her into her bridal gown, she herself had forgotten her concern about her wedding night as the formalities of the simple ceremony had run their course in the drawing-room at Ortolans. Uncle Walter seemed to have rallied a little for the occasion and so, with all the servants present, Jane as her single bridesmaid, and Lady Calverley and a scowling Cousin Daniel as witnesses, Eleanor's marriage to William had taken place. With Uncle Walter too weak to officiate, it had fallen to Mr Howell to give Eleanor away. Daniel had acted as William's best man. That he had outshone William in the magnificence of his attire seemed to go unnoticed by everyone but Eleanor.

The big bedroom in Sackville Street where she now lay was in darkness. Its unknown contours and the strange noises from the street outside added to her sense of isolation and loneliness. She wished William had not agreed with his mother that since they could not have a full honeymoon away from Ortolans because of Uncle Walter's decline, they could at least have a week alone together in London. More than anything in the world at this moment, she wished herself back in her own bed, in her own room at Ortolans.

Perhaps I am just overtired after all the excitement, Eleanor told herself as she moved a fraction of an inch further from William's intrusive body. Perhaps all brides felt as she did on their wedding night, but in time became accustomed to their husband's presence. Somehow she doubted that she would ever be able to endure the repetition of the last half-hour's activities.

Most of all, Eleanor thought, she wanted to call Dora, ask her to fill the big tin bath with scalding hot water so that she could wash herself, soak away all evidence and, if it were only possible, all memory of the ordeal. Although Dora was in fact within calling distance, unlike the other servants who slept in the attics of the big house, Eleanor dared not move lest she wake William and she would be obliged, as Dora had advised her, to pleasure him again.

Slowly, the salt tears dried. She lay wide-eyed and tense. How was it possible that she, in her ignorance, had allowed herself to put her whole future in jeopardy? When Uncle Walter had fallen so ill and her godmother and William had pleaded with her to allow the wedding to be brought forward, she had barely hesitated in her acquiescence. It was not that either of them had put unfair pressure on her. She could still have told them she needed more time to get to know William. On the other hand, what use would 'more time' have been to her? She would have been no wiser in the spring as to what marriage entailed than she had been two days ago. The fact was she should never have agreed to marry William suspecting as she did that her love for him was inadequate, based as it was on the desire to please her godmother and William, and on the less worthy motive that it meant she would never have to leave Ortolans!

Her tears fell once more and she wiped them with the edge of the linen sheet. Even now, given the choice of going back to live with Aunt Tabitha and Uncle Hamish or submitting to William's desires, she supposed she would make the same decision. One could become accustomed to anything in time, and William, before falling asleep, had assured her that it would all be less painful in the future; that it was inevitably uncomfortable for any young girl when her maidenhead was broken.

Eleanor had not even been aware of this part of her anatomy, or what purpose it served. Dora had once spoken of a servant girl at The Grange who had lost her maidenhead to the butcher's delivery boy, and as a consequence, was disgraced and likely to end up in the parish workhouse. When Eleanor had requested an explanation, Dora had blushed and told her such things were not fitting for a young lady's ears.

Why was there no one to explain life, love, marriage, or even why 'love was a torment, a tempest everlasting', as the poet said? Did that poet have in mind the kind of torment she had suffered this night? Or was the 'tempest' the strange wild feeling she had experienced when she had fallen from her horse and lain in Daniel's arms?

This memory of William's cousin was followed swiftly by another – of Daniel's expression when William had told him that same evening at supper that he and Eleanor were to be married in two weeks' time. It was the first occasion Eleanor had ever seen Daniel at a loss for words. His mouth had gaped and he had stared at her almost accusingly, certainly disbelievingly. Gradually, he succeeded in bringing his lips into a twisted smile, and murmured something about it probably being for the best with Uncle Walter so ill. Could Daniel possibly have known that she did not truly love William? she asked herself now. Or, since at last she was being totally honest with herself, was it that Daniel disliked the prospect of her marriage to William because he wanted her himself?

Thankful for the darkness, Eleanor buried her hot, flushed cheeks in the cool, lace-edged pillow. She was ashamed of her thoughts – and most of all, ashamed of the disgraceful thought that had it been Daniel lying here beside her, she would not be feeling violated but violently excited. How furiously her heart had beaten when he had touched her face, her arms, her body! How she had trembled when he had pressed his head against her thighs! How disturbing she had always found those dark, enigmatic eyes; how inviting the soft, golden glow of his skin and the movements of his lithe, graceful body!

Yet withal, she did not like him – had never liked him. She was, she admitted, frightened of him, aware deep within her that he threatened her in some way. Despite everything that had happened, she did not fear William, and if she no longer respected him quite as she had used to do, it was not his fault that she found his white, thin body, hairy chest and limbs repulsive. He was still far from being a healthy man and not unnaturally, the sedentary life he had been forced to lead these past fourteen months had allowed his muscles to degenerate into a flabbiness that had seemed to smother her as he lay atop her. It was not his fault that he had had to hurt her. He had afterwards apologized, as indeed he had apologized constantly for his clumsy one-armed embraces. He was kind, good, everything that was desirable in a husband if only . . .

There was no escape. Eleanor faced the fact and determined never again to allow self-pity to take hold of her. Tomorrow, she and William were to visit the Comte de Valderton and his family in Battersea Village. She would wear one of her new trousseau day gowns – the sky blue silk with the blue velvet, fur-trimmed pelise – since she was certain that the Comtesse, being French, would be very fashionable. In the evening, William had taken a box at the theatre to hear Madame Mara, the wonderful German soprano who was to sing in *The Marriage of Figaro*. William had told her she was quite likely to see the Prince of Wales and, quite certainly, a number of distinguished people to whom he could proudly introduce his wife. She would never be Eleanor McCore again and must accustom herself to being addressed as Mrs William Calverley.

'I shall always be indebted to you, Eleanor,' he had said in the carriage taking them to London after the wedding. 'You have made Papa and Mama very happy and I shall do everything in my power to make you happy, my dear.'

She knew that he meant it; that her life with William would be happy if only they could resume the relationship they had previously enjoyed, affectionate, considerate, companionable; if only her marriage vows had not included those promises she did not wish to keep! How readily she had given her promise 'to serve and obey' her husband, not knowing then what William's demands entailed – demands to which she now knew she could never happily submit.

'I am not over partial to the French as a race!' William commented as they drove home along the King's Road, leaving the Thames and the trees and fields of Battersea behind them. 'However, I think Antoine de Valderton and his wife a most delightful couple, do you not agree?'

Eleanor nodded.

'I do hope they will come and visit us at Ortolans once Uncle Walter is better. He *will* recover, will he not, William?'

William patted her hand, aware that Eleanor herself had little more faith in his father's recovery than had he.

'The Valdertons were most complimentary about you, my dear,' he said, ignoring her question. 'They consider you have grown into a very beautiful young woman – and I have to say, I agree!'

He squeezed her hand and smiled paternally as he saw the colour rush into her cheeks.

'We shall be home within the hour,' he added, his voice suddenly deepening. 'That means we will have time alone together before we leave for the theatre.'

Mistaking her silence for a natural shyness about such matters, he was unperturbed by her lack of response. Desperately seeking to change the line of William's thoughts, Eleanor said:

'Look William, it has started to rain!'

He continued to stare at her, but Eleanor was now able to gaze out of the carriage window, showing an interest in the weather she did not really have. It was she, therefore, who first noticed that there was some kind of congestion further along the street. As the carriage slowed, the coachman bent down from his seat and informed them that a cart had over-turned and was entangled with a brewer's dray travelling in the opposite direction. A crowd had gathered and it appeared one of the horses was lying in the road.

'Confound it!' William said, anxious now to be home in good time. 'Can you turn our horses round, Whelks?'

The coachman did his best to obey these instructions but by now, other vehicles had drawn to a halt behind them. Their carriage was now sideways across the road and Eleanor could see the grisly scene quite clearly. A carthorse was lying between the shafts of a farmer's wagon. The contents – a load of Brussels sprouts – were spread across the muddy surface of the road whilst the farmer, red-faced, was attempting by means of a whip to urge the miserable animal to its feet. More skin and bone than flesh, the wretched beast was whinnying as the blows struck it about the head. It was obviously unable to struggle to its feet.

White-faced, she turned to William.

'We must do something quickly,' she gasped. 'The poor thing is on the point of death. Please, William . . .'

William glanced briefly across her shoulder to the mêlée outside and then tried to draw her back from the window.

'It is better not to interfere!' he cautioned. 'There are quite enough people trying to assist as it is!'

Eleanor gripped the edge of the window, unable to disassociate herself from the drama. As she watched in horrified silence, a huge black man stepped out of the crowd and, obtaining a precarious foothold on the side of the farm cart, reached up to wrest the whip from the irate farmer's hand.

'Oh, well done, well done!' she whispered in relief, but now the farmer was expending his wrath on the blackamoor. He brought the stinging thong of the whip down across the man's face in an obvious attempt to dislodge him. Blood poured down the dark face, dripping on to his pale blue livery as further blows rained down on him. The sight of the blood now acted as a stimulant to the watching crowd. The mood was against the blackamoor, who they felt had no right to interfere with the farmer whose horse was his beast of burden to chastise as he thought fit. One or two of the braver men in the crowd moved forward, avoiding the flailing whip end in an attempt to drag the black man from the cart.

'William, they will lynch him!' Eleanor cried. 'We must stop them!'

William tried once more to draw her back from the window.

'This is London, Eleanor, and these things happen. Besides, I cannot leave you unprotected, and as you can see, it is all poor Whelks can do to calm the horses!'

Before he had begun to grasp her intention, Eleanor opened

the carriage door and holding up her skirts, jumped to the ground.

'Let me pass! Move aside!' she commanded in her most authoritative tone.

Slowly, the men and women parted to let her through. Astonished to see so grand a lady in their midst, they automatically obeyed her. One or two wondered if by chance the blackamoor was her servant, speculating that if this were the case, the farmer could find himself in trouble for striking him. They waited, suddenly silent, to see what would happen.

Their silence brought Eleanor to her senses. She realized that she had quite possibly placed herself in real danger, but her concern for the man – and indeed the horse – would not allow her to give in to her fear. She walked boldly up to the cart.

'Stop it this minute!' she called up to the farmer. 'Can't you see, you stupid numskull, that your horse is dying? As for this man, he was seeking only to prevent you hastening it to its death. Now put down that whip this instant!'

A costermonger in colourful yellow waistcoat, chocolate and yellow spotted neckerchief, brown thickset breeches and leather spatterdashes stepped forward, a grin on his pockmarked face.

''Er Ladyship's right an' all!' he shouted. 'No good flogging a dead 'oss, eh?'

His quip changed the mood of the others, defusing their lust for blood and changing it now to laughter.

'Yer nag'll fetch a bob or two at knackers yard!' shouted a woman evoking another burst of laughter. Although the farmer had now ceased wielding his whip, he was still fired with anger at his misfortune. A broken cart, a dead horse and the loss of his crop of vegetables could mean starvation this coming winter for him and his family. He jumped down from the cart and grabbed the black man, now lying in the muddy road, by his collar.

'Weren't nought wrong wi me 'oss till you comes by!' he

shouted. 'Put a spell on 'im, you did, you black savage! Witchcraft – that's what it was!'

Yet again the mood of the crowd changed. All were superstitious and the huge bloodied black man was an awesome sight – one who might well have brought supernatural powers out of the jungle.

Eleanor guessed their intent as they surged forward. Reaching down, she helped the man regain his feet. As she did so, she heard William's voice beside her.

'For the love of God, will you cease this madness!' he said in a low voice. 'Come back to the coach this minute, Eleanor.'

She struggled against the pressure of his arm.

'We cannot leave him!' she said. 'They might kill him, William!'

Seeing that he would have extreme difficulty in persuading her out of the determined stand she had taken, William turned to the farmer.

'These will compensate you for your losses!' he said, taking some guineas from his waistcoat pocket. 'As for the servant, I'll take him with me before he can do you further harm!' He threw another handful of coins into the crowd. 'Give the poor fellow a hand with his cart. There'll be more if you move it out of the way speedily. It's delaying our passage.'

He took Eleanor's arm and motioned the black man to get up beside Whelks. The crowd were too busy scrabbling for the coins he had tossed amongst them to impede their movements.

It was a further five minutes before the crowd had shifted the broken cart to the side of the road and dragged the now dead beast into the gutter. William turned to Eleanor with a sigh of relief as their coach was at last able to move forward.

'I do beg you, my dear, never to do anything so foolhardy again!' he said. 'I admire your courage but no matter what the circumstances, it can never be right for a lady to intervene. Now promise me you will never do such a thing again.'

Eleanor nodded, the aftermath of her fear making itself felt.

'Fellow says he lives in Dover Street, sir!' called down Whelks. 'Shall we drop him off there, sir? 'T'is on our way!'

Ten minutes later, their coach drew to a halt outside one of the big residential houses in Dover Street and the black man, the blood now congealing on the side of his face and livery, leaned down to the window on William's side of their carriage.

'You and the lady saved my life, sir, for which I thank you. My master . . .'

'Just try and keep out of trouble in the future!' William cut short his thanks. 'Be off with you!'

As Whelks turned the horses' heads into Bond Street, William took out his timepiece. The delay meant that they would barely have time to change their clothes before leaving for the theatre, which he thought was a pity in the light of the fact that his young wife was now holding his arm in a most affectionate way. She looked happy – and very beautiful.

'It was a splendid idea to take that poor man with us, William,' she said. 'I should have been so worried had we left him to that mob.' She smiled up at him. 'Did it not surprise you how well spoken he was when he thanked us? Do many people have black servants? I have never seen one before!'

'It is not unusual,' William replied briefly, resenting her train of thought which he would far prefer to have been centred upon himself. 'Now let's forget the whole unpleasant interlude. I will explain about the black slaves some other time.'

It was on the tip of Eleanor's tongue to advise William that she had been closely following in Uncle Walter's newspapers Mr Wilberforce's horrifying accounts of the slave trade, but by now they had arrived home. In the excitement of the theatre and the subsequent mortification of a second night enduring her husband's ardent attentions, she gave no further thought to the black man until the following day.

It was mid-morning when she received an unexpected caller. She was seated at the escritoire in the morning-room writing a letter to her aunt and uncle in Scotland. They had not attended the wedding but had sent a canteen of cutlery as a gift, together with a letter which was so worded as to indicate that they were more than happy to relinquish their guardianship into William's care. Knowing that it was unlikely she would see them again, Eleanor was striving to find words to express an affection she could not feel, when the butler came into the room.

'There is a gentleman asking to see you and the master, madam,' he said. 'I told him the master was at his tailors, but he said he was leaving London after luncheon and since he could not return, would you be so good as to see him yourself, madam?'

'Is he a friend of the family, Bates?' Eleanor enquired, uncertain whether it was proper for her to receive a gentleman alone.

'No, madam, I do not think so. He gave his name as Mr Richard Mascal. He seemed . . . very respectable, madam!'

Eleanor concealed a smile, realizing that this was Bates's way of letting her know that there would be nothing amiss in her receiving the stranger.

The tall, well-built man who Bates now showed into the room was younger than William, Eleanor thought as he bowed to her. He had a very pleasing, open countenance and blue eyes fringed unexpectedly with dark lashes. His voice was deep and pleasingly toned.

'It is exceedingly kind of you to receive me at such short notice, Mrs Calverley. May I introduce myself to you – Richard Mascal, at your service.' He gave another slight bow.

'Please be seated, Mr Mascal,' Eleanor said, hoping that she was behaving as a married lady should. 'I regret that my husband is not at home. Can I be of assistance to you?'

'Madam, you have already been of such assistance that I find myself at a loss for words which adequately express my gratitude.' Obedient to her command, he seated himself in the lyre-back chair facing her. 'Yesterday afternoon, you rescued my servant, Peter, from possible death and certainly greater injury. Peter has described your bravery and now that I have met you, I am even more astonished. I had imagined that . . .'

He broke off in mid-sentence, aware that his impulsiveness was leading him to pass a most personal remark. He had indeed imagined that the courageous lady of Peter's description was a great deal older – an imperious lady accustomed to having her commands obeyed – a socialite, in all probability. The young girl seated opposite him looked no older than Verity and he suspected that she was attempting to appear far more mature than she was. She had a girl's slim figure, and if not as tiny as Verity, was fine boned and slender. Her eyes, he decided, were her most remarkable feature – a deep violet blue that accentuated the pallor of her face.

To fill the awkwardness of the silence that had fallen, Eleanor said with genuine interest:

'Please tell me that your servant is none the worse for that cruel whipping? My husband and I were concerned for the poor fellow. He was in no way to blame.'

Richard forgot his momentary embarrassment and said eagerly:

'A few stitches were necessary, but he makes light of his injuries. He is too relieved not to be in the hands of the Bow Street Runners. Had they been called to the fracas and you had not been there to speak for him, he would almost certainly have been flung into gaol and press-ganged into the Navy.'

'I have heard of this practice. It struck me as not dissimilar to slavery,' Eleanor said, forgetting her shyness in the presence of this charming visitor. 'I am one of those who, like Mr Wilberforce, is much opposed to the trade in human beings. Even the most lowly are still men and women, not animals, are they not, Mr Mascal?'

'If those poor devils – pardon my language, madam – behave like animals as some do, it is because we have robbed them of all dignity. One has but to learn the mind of someone such as Peter to realize that their feelings are no different from our own.'

Seeing the look of genuine interest on Eleanor's face, he continued to express his opinions.

'It is interesting, I think, to ponder what governs human behaviour. I have noted that the ignorant and ill-educated will often derive satisfaction – indeed, pleasure – in attacking that which they fear. Our national pastimes such as bear-baiting, bull-baiting, dog-fighting are but examples. Pepper will sometimes be blown up a bull's nostrils to exacerbate his fury; an ape may be tied to the back of a pony so that in his terror he will prance and rear up thus exciting the dogs to attack him with greater ferocity. It is quite remarkable that the more gory, the more pain inflicted, the more violent such spectacles, the happier is the crowd. But perchance you have seen such sights yourself, Mrs Calverley?'

Eleanor shook her head. 'I have been only once before to London and although my hostess had arranged for us to go one Sunday to the bear garden in Southwark, the weather was too inclement and the outing was cancelled. I was quite pleased, for I cannot tolerate the sight of animals in pain.'

'Or people!' Richard said. 'Peter told me it was but a few minutes before you went to his defence. A mob will always turn against those who are not one of themselves, and many look upon the Negroes as little better than apes. As it happens, Peter's childhood was spent as a pageboy to a titled lady with the consequence that he is well spoken, well mannered and without doubt in this case, a deal more civilized than his attackers! He is a good man and I owe him my life. But that is another story. He is most anxious that I should thank you adequately for saving his life, Mrs Calverley. And your husband, of course!'

Ever since Peter had arrived home in his sorry state and Richard had been given an account of the disaster which had befallen him, he had puzzled why it had been the lady and not the gentleman who had first come to Peter's rescue. Later, when Peter recalled that the gentleman had but one arm and in any event, had been more concerned with rescuing his wife than himself, Richard had felt more kindly disposed towards William. Upon hearing that the coachman had identified his master to Peter, Richard had been determined to call in person to express his gratitude.

'I leave for the country later today,' he said. 'I shall not therefore be able to thank Mr Calverley, and I would greatly appreciate it if you would do so on my behalf.'

'William . . . my husband . . . will be sorry not to have made your acquaintance,' Eleanor replied. 'Perhaps there will be another occasion when you can meet him.'

'I hope so!' Richard said quietly, knowing that he very much wanted to see this girl again. It seemed to him as if she had far more depth and intelligence than most of the young women he met – mainly Verity's friends whose sole topics of conversation were their entertainments, their attire or how the newest fashions would suit their personal appearances. 'I fear I shall be out of town for some time, though not out of the country. Silly as it must sound to you, I am going in search of a man of whom I know nothing more than his name!' He gave a sudden smile which lit up his face and caused Eleanor to notice for the first time that her visitor was an exceptionally handsome man. He reminded her of the young William in the Romney portrait at Ortolans.

The smile left Richard's face as he added gravely:

'However hopeless my quest may look to be, I must nevertheless pursue it since my past as well as my future depend upon my obtaining information which only he can give me.'

'Then I can but hope that you find him!' Eleanor said as Richard stood up to take his leave.

After Bates had shown the visitor to the door, she returned to her escritoire, but despite the quill she held poised over the paper, she was unable to concentrate on her half-finished letter to Aunt Tabitha. She was consumed with curiosity about her visitor and longed for William's return so that she could question if he knew of the Mascals. They had talked for nearly half an hour and yet not one word had they spoken about themselves. Was he married? she wondered, as one of the footmen brought in a glass of cordial for her. Surely so personable a man would have a great many female admirers and been long since persuaded into marriage? Or had he, perchance, like William, been adventuring abroad? He had spoken most mysteriously of his past as well as suggesting that his future was at stake, in which case he could be in trouble of some kind. She could not believe that he was other than a good upright person. He did not give the impression of a dishonourable man – yet had not Aunt Tabitha so often warned her that 'the devil always went disguised!'

With an effort of concentration, Eleanor finally returned to her letter. Only later, when William finally returned home for luncheon, did her curiosity about her visitor return. It was not shared, however, by William. As one of the footmen cut up his slices of braised venison into small portions he could manage single handed – a necessary service which invariably irritated him since it highlighted his handicap – William's replies to her questions were short.

'Met a fellow called Greville Mascal once – author, I believe, but well into his fifties. Could have been a son, I suppose. Whoever he was, he'd no right to bother you, my dear. He could have written a note if he felt compelled to offer his thanks, though why he should make such a to-do about one of his servants, I cannot for the life of me think.'

'I believe the man once saved Mr Mascal's life,' Eleanor said gently.

'That explains it, I suppose!' William said disinterestedly. The fact was he was feeling far from well. His shoulder wound was paining him again and had throbbed unmercifully whilst he had stood patiently being measured by his tailor. He suspected that yet another abscess might be forming and the very last thing he wanted was to be confined to bed with a fever on his honeymoon.

He glanced down the length of the mahogany table at Eleanor and a little of his good humour returned. Since marriage and an heir had become important to his family, he had been fortunate in finding so pretty and accommodating a wife. He had been gratified to note how impressed the Valdertons were by Eleanor's contributions to the conversation at the luncheon. She had shown herself well versed in French literature and art, and he had been proud of her. It was of no consequence that she was virtually penniless – the Calverley estates and investments were flourishing. His father had been able to give young Daniel a reasonable allowance without the slightest hardship to anyone. A fine horseman, his cousin, he thought now, always willing to give praise where he believed it to be due . . . be an asset on the hunting field once he'd learned the ropes as well as being a fine shot – in short, a cousin he would be proud to introduce to their neighbours when Father was better and they could resume their social life at Ortolans.

William's good spirits were only momentarily restored. For the second time that day, the newly-weds received a visitor. This time it was Daniel, dust-stained from his unbroken, six-hour ride to London bringing the news that Walter Calverley had, in the early hours of the morning, died in his sleep.

CHAPTER EIGHT

1791

'You are such a comfort to me, Daniel! I do not know how poor William, Eleanor and I would have maintained our spirits had you not been here to divert us!'

Daniel smiled at the frail, white-haired old lady he now called Aunt Joan, and assisted her to the arbour where the branches of a chestnut tree provided shade from the hot August sunshine. The strong, sweet scent from the honeysuckle which had entwined itself in the branches drifted through the cool shadows.

'I wish there was something more positive I could do,' he said. 'It has been such a worrying time for us all!'

Lady Calverley had aged a great deal since her husband's death the previous summer, and undoubtedly she still mourned him although William's decline in health that Christmas had, to some extent, diverted her attention from her grief.

Daniel moved surreptitiously from her side as she dozed, so that he was seated in the entrance where the burning rays of the sun could fall on his face. Beyond the rose beds, a gardener was scything the grass; another, following behind with his horse, whose hoofs were padded with woollen mufflers, was guiding the roller.

Daniel's gaze, however, was not on this halcyon scene. He was looking beyond the lawn to the meadow, watching for Eleanor's return. Despite the heat, she had walked down to the river with her maid to look for the kingfishers. When she had announced her intention, he had at once offered to accompany her but, to his intense irritation, she had turned to him and said: 'Oh, but Cousin Daniel, I had thought you would keep Godmother company. She so likes to have you to herself!'

He had had no alternative but to pretend his willingness to do as she wished but now, as he waited impatiently for her return, his frustration mounted. He was convinced that she was deliberately avoiding him. Either she was in the sickroom with William or busying herself with the domestic duties she had taken over from Lady Calverley. It was the more frustrating because he knew she was not indifferent to him. He had but to stare at her long enough and the colour would rush to her cheeks. It was the same if he could find an occasion to touch her hand or move his body close to her. His desire to possess her had become an obsession which he was finding increasingly difficult to control.

How much longer, Daniel wondered, would it be before his cousin finally succumbed to his wounds and left him heir not only to the Calverley fortunes but to his wife? The uncertainty kept him awake at night when it had become his habit to go out in the darkness and walk until he was exhausted. There was not a corner of Ortolans with which he was unfamiliar as a result of these nocturnal excursions. Even on moonless nights, he could find his way about, moving by smell from the syringa bush to the lime tree, from lavender-bordered path to the bed of scented stocks; to the kitchen garden where great clumps of verbena, mint and thyme gave off their heady odours as he crushed them underfoot.

He would stand motionless, staring at the dark shape of the house visible in the moonlight, and marvel at its mysterious beauty. It was unlike any house he had ever seen in his native country, yet it had a strange familiarity. It was as if he had found his home, his birthright. He sensed that it was resisting him – just as Eleanor did – but that like her, it was waiting to be wooed into submission. It belonged to him. The Great Spirit had ordained that. He had but to break down their resistance and both the objects of his desire would be his.

Daniel's Algonquin ancestry ran deep in his blood and

already he had discovered the healing properties of Ortolans's wild plants and herbs and the poisonous properties of deadly nightshade and the death cap fungus. He had first thought of using such a poison last autumn when he had discovered himself deeply resenting Eleanor's passionate adoration for her dog. It was like a physical pain each time he saw her reach out one small white hand and fondle the dog's head, or permit the brute to rest a great paw on her lap. He resented the animal even more than he resented William, whose betrothal to her he had still hoped to jeopardize. Their accelerated wedding had been an untold shock to him.

It was not long, however, before Daniel saw that Eleanor might not after all be irretrievably lost to him. When the newly-weds returned to Ortolans for Uncle Walter's funeral and the physician had had once more to be called from Brighthelmstone to treat William's suppurating wound, he realized that if William were, like his father, to die, Eleanor as well as the Calverley estates would be his.

Having dried out several death cap fungi by stringing them up in one of the disused attic rooms, Daniel powdered the plants into a fine, grey-white dust, and using Rex as an exemplar, experimented with the dosage required to kill a man. In November, the dog died twelve hours after he had administered the powder. Its vomiting, diarrhoea and thirst were followed by paralysis and no one was in doubt that it had been poisoned, it being thought most likely to have picked up some rat poison put down in the stables. Daniel was reassured that he could dispense with William as easily, for his cousin was frequently sickly and fevered, and no one would be greatly surprised if he expired.

As Lady Calverley gave a gentle snore, Daniel saw his opportunity to leave the arbour and walk down to meet Eleanor. The mere sight of her was enough now to fire his blood, and he had constantly to control his need to touch her. At times, his desire became unbearable and then he would leave the house, travel up to London and relieve his frustration with the ever-willing Matilda. The middle-aged countess had lost none of her interest in him since learning that he had been united with his Sussex relatives, and always made him welcome.

Such visits, however, afforded Daniel no permanent relief, and his resolve to kill William hardened. Unfortunately, the opportunity to carry out his decision was baulked, and, to Daniel's biting fury, by a mere servant. Jack Pylbeam, William's valet, appeared to have made it his personal responsibility never to leave his master alone.

Daniel knew from his childhood days in his mother's tribe that it was possible for a man to divine another's intent. The medicine man would accurately foretell a forthcoming battle, a man's success on a hunting trip, a man's death. He was forced now to concede that whilst this servant, although having no standing or title to indicate his powers, nevertheless possessed them. Each time he, Daniel, went to William's room, the valet remained on some pretext or other, his eyes following Daniel's every movement.

It did not occur to him that Jack, William's valet of some thirty years, needed no supernatural power to suspect Daniel's intent. Although his master and indeed, Sir Walter and Lady Calverley, had trusted the stranger who had come into their lives, Jack did not. His instinct told him that the man's story somehow did not ring true. There were other ever more numerous reasons to doubt him – the oversolicitous manner in which Mr Daniel Calverley fawned upon Her Ladyship; the way his eyes devoured Miss Eleanor; the way he avoided a direct answer when he was questioned about his childhood years.

After a lifetime spent interpreting his employer's humours, Jack recognized very easily when a man was angry, at ease, frustrated, saddened, antagonistic, satisfied, befuddled, excited. He sensed Daniel's antipathy towards the man he called cousin in so affectionate a manner. It was not difficult for Jack to put two and two together although he could only suspect that they made four. If Mister Daniel wanted young Lady Calverley, or indeed, to be master in the Calverley household, he thought, only Sir William stood in his way.

It was two years now since his master had contracted his wounds in France, during which time he had survived repeated relapses. Jack had heard with his own ears the physician state that there was no reason why Sir William might not continue to overcome the recurring infections for many years to come. Even allowing for the fact that following Sir Walter's funeral, he had been confined to bed for several weeks with fever, his condition was not deteriorating and there were days when his master had felt well enough to go downstairs; even out into the garden.

Of course, there was no question of his resuming the more intimate aspects of married life. Lady William – as he now thought of Miss Eleanor – had returned to her own bedroom. It was almost as if the two had never been wed, except that Lady William spent a large part of her time during the day and every evening reading to the invalid, playing backgammon or chess with him or, if he were tired, sitting quietly by his bedside, embroidering a handkerchief or working on her tapestry. It was not an entertaining life for a young woman of quality and yet Jack had never heard her complain; nor, indeed, was she ever anything but scrupulously correct in her behaviour towards Mister Daniel. If anything, she seemed to avoid him when she could and when Mister Daniel was away in London, she appeared more relaxed. He, himself, would never relax his vigil. His master was a thoughtful, generous man and Jack's loyalty was total. With nothing more pressing to do, he stood at an upstairs window as Daniel made his way across the lawn towards Lady William and Dora who had just come into view.

Deliberately, Daniel slowed his pace as he, too, caught sight of them. Above all, he did not want to frighten Eleanor by making his attentions too obvious. He sensed her nervousness in his presence and knew that he must not give his feelings away now that he had made up his mind to dispose of William. Gentleness and subtlety were required. He must be content with the fact that he knew she was not indifferent to him; that her young healthy body must be as ready as his for coupling, the more so since she was no longer a virgin. She had known what it was to feel a man's hands on her breasts, her thighs; to be kissed and coaxed and stroked to a delirium. She had known the aftermath of sweet contentment which followed the climax of love. Aware that she no longer shared William's bed, Daniel assumed that she was as avid for these pleasures as poor, fat Matilda who could not get him into her bed fast enough!

Pretending to gather a few flowers for a nosegay for Lady Calverley, Daniel allowed his thoughts to concentrate once more upon William's valet. He had already sown the first seeds of his plan – skilfully removing small objects from William's dressing-room. He was so adept a thief that even the vigilant Jack had not observed him. As an added precaution, he secreted the objects in one of the disused attics, thus obviating any risk of them being discovered in his room by a servant. Tomorrow, he would purloin the silver inkwell from William's desk, and when there was a sufficient quantity of valuables, he would find a way to cast blame upon the valet. With Jack dismissed from the household, he would have no difficulty in administering a lethal dose of poison to his worthy cousin without suspicion being cast upon himself.

Eleanor pressed her body closer to the near side of the chaise, aware that she was trembling, and fearful lest Daniel, sitting so close to her, might hear the rapid beating of her heart. She wished now that they had travelled to Brighthelmstone in the large Vidler coach whose more spacious interior would have enabled her to suggest that Daniel sat opposite her. Glancing out of the window, she saw that darkness had fallen, and by the slowing of the chaise, realized that they were climbing the south side of the Downs. She could no longer see the postillion astride the nearside horse, and her feeling of being trapped increased. With the thundering of the horses' hoofs and the crunch of the wheels over the chalky road, she doubted if the coachman would hear her if she cried out to him to stop.

With an effort, Eleanor attempted to quell her anxiety.

Throughout the evening, Daniel had given her no cause for her misgivings. Nevertheless, she wished desperately that William had been well enough to go with them. When the invitation from the Earl and Countess Wotherington to join them for an evening at the theatre in Brighthelmstone had first arrived, William had insisted that Eleanor should accept. She had been too long confined at Ortolans, he said, and deserved this pleasant diversion. Cousin Daniel, via whom the invitation had been sent, could escort her since unfortunately he, William, was not well enough to undertake the journey. It would be good for her to meet Cousin Daniel's friends who had taken a house in the fashionable coastal spa for the summer season.

Daniel had added his persuasions, explaining that the countess was on excellent terms with the Prince of Wales who now spent the entire summer in Brighthelmstone where he was building a luxurious Palladian villa. Nearly all the most influential members of society had followed him to the seaside and the theatrical performance would undoubtedly be a gala occasion.

'I insist that you go, my dearest!' William declared when Eleanor had demurred. 'You will enjoy it and I shall feel responsible for denying you this pleasure if you refuse.'

'It will be quite in order, dear child!' Godmother had added her persuasions. 'You are a married woman now and dear Daniel, being a relative, can chaperon you.'

Now, as a pothole in the road caused the chaise to bounce alarmingly, Daniel was pressed close against her.

'You are not cold, cousin?' he asked, taking one of her hands from her muff and holding it.

Without wishing to appear apprehensive, Eleanor nevertheless withdrew her hand as quickly as she could.

'You did enjoy the performance?' Daniel enquired, his tone casual although his body was still touching hers. 'You must give me your opinion of the countess. She was very taken with you.'

Eleanor could not return the compliment for she had thought the countess over-painted and at times, embarrassingly flirtatious. Nor did she believe that the older woman was so 'taken' with her. Eleanor had had the impression that she was far more interested in Daniel whose attention she had constantly demanded, leaving Eleanor to the mercy of the elderly earl who did little else but ogle her through his quizzing glass and pat her hand.

She wished fervently that Daniel would move back to his own side of the chaise, but he made no attempt to do so. On the contrary, he placed his arm behind her head, suggesting that she might be more comfortable if he could cushion the jolts in this manner.

'The countess seemed very . . . fond of you, Cousin Daniel!' she remarked by way of conversation.

'Oh, she is quite devoted – the poor old dear!' Daniel replied smoothly. 'She took me under her wing when first I arrived in London and I suppose you could say she has been like a mother to me.'

'I did not think her attentions were exactly maternal!' Eleanor replied impulsively and was furious with herself for doing so as Daniel smiled and said:

'You were observing her then? Perhaps she is a trifle excessive at times! But you should not be critical of her, Cousin Eleanor. She was exceedingly complimentary about you.'

When Eleanor made no reply, he said in a low voice: 'During supper, she chided me most severely for having delayed so long in introducing myself to my family.'

'Why so?' asked Eleanor, not understanding the connection with his prior remark.

'Lady Wotherington has been trying to persuade me into marriage for some time. She thinks you would have made the perfect wife for me, and that had I made myself known at Ortolans earlier, I could have made my proposal before Cousin William thought of doing so.'

'You should not say such a thing!' Eleanor protested, aghast.

'And why not, if I speak the truth? I consider Cousin William to be the most fortunate of men and I see no reason to conceal my envy. I have no doubts as to *his* satisfaction in the choice of a wife; but what of you, Eleanor? You are very young and tied for life to a semi-invalid who cannot possibly love you as you deserve. Do you not long to be held in the arms of a man who would die for you, adore you, fight for you, oblige your deepest needs and open the world of loving to you? Does William's gratitude, generosity, worthiness, make up for all you are forgoing? I think not!'

Eleanor's heart was thudding and, she told herself, she was furiously angry. She was also deeply shocked. Daniel had seen into the very core of her being, had assessed only too accurately her secret belief that true love was as he had described. His statement made it all the harder for her to pretend that she was happy in her marriage. No matter how content the days spent at Ortolans, at night when she lay in her bed, her heart and body had craved so much more than William could give her.

She felt a fresh wave of anger at Daniel who owed so much to William and his parents, and yet could be disloyal enough to declare himself – for that was what he had done with those wild words. She knew without any shadow of a doubt that were she to give him the slightest encouragement, he would take her in his arms, kiss her . . .

'I love William! I love him dearly. If you speak one word more, Cousin Daniel, we will cease to be friends. I will tell my husband that I do not care to have you stay at Ortolans – and, if necessary, why – and you will be obliged to leave.'

To her dismay, Daniel laughed – a deep husky laugh that offered no apology.

'You are only afraid of me because you are afraid of yourself!' he said. 'Your eyes, your voice, your body betray you too often. You avoid me because you fear that I will make a movement in an unguarded moment and without time to raise your defences, you will succumb. Why try to hide the truth? Were it possible without dishonour, you would welcome me in your bed, knowing as you do how it would be for us.'

'If you do not desist, I will get out of this chaise and leave you to explain to William why I did so!' Eleanor cried. 'How dare you even speak of honour! Have you forgotten that I am a married woman?'

Again, Daniel laughed.

'Are you really so innocent that you are unaware that a great many married ladies have liaisons, some with their husbands' compliance? At least three of the ladies you met tonight have lovers.'

'And that, I suppose, includes your friend, the countess!' said Eleanor before she could stop to think.

'I dare say!' Daniel answered vaguely. 'I do assure you, it is quite recognized in Society. Once a wife has produced a male heir, she may do as she pleases provided she does it discreetly. However, you have no cause to fear my advances, Cousin Eleanor. Now you are aware how I feel, I shall do nothing to embarrass you. It will be for you to advise me once you have made up your mind to set aside your quite unworldly moralizing. You are flesh and blood as I am, Eleanor, and one day you will be mine!'

Before she realized his intent, he took her face between his hands and, turning her to him, pressed his mouth upon hers. They were travelling now uphill and the coachman had slowed the horses to a walk. It seemed to Eleanor as if time had stopped and only her heart was racing, racing, carrying her into an abyss from which there might be no return. Every nerve in her body was alive, on fire and demanding something more than a kiss, however searching, however prolonged. Only a part of her was struggling to break free, her innermost self urging her to submit to the strange, wild longing that was consuming her.

There was a sudden, fierce jolt, a violent crack and the chaise lurched sideways, throwing its two occupants apart. Almost immediately, the coachman's head appeared through the window.

'One of the straps as holds a spring is broke, sir!' he said. 'I reckons 't'were that big pothole a few leagues back, surelye. Doant know as I can fix it, sir.'

Daniel opened the door and climbed out into the darkness. They were now on the summit of the Downs, and a short distance away, he could see the winking lights of the village of Pyecombe.

'Can you not make a temporary repair?' he asked. 'There'll be an inn over there where we can get assistance. If not, you'll have to ride there and bring back help.'

The coachman's mouth tightened. Whilst not considering risking his job in any way whatever, he was in no mind to please Mister Daniel Calverley. It was this man who had berated his young son, the stable lad Jem, and as near as nothing got him dismissed. As it was, the boy had been docked a month's pay and those few shillings were sorely needed at home where there were twelve more mouths to feed. The boy had done wrong, for sure, but the responsibility was Tasker's, the head groom, who should have made it clear to the lad that he was not to ride on the Downs. None of the servants liked Mister Daniel. It was not so much that he was thoughtless for their welfare – gentlemen often were, keeping them up till all hours or leaving a fellow like himself hanging around in the pouring rain – but they didn't swear at them the way Mister Daniel did if there was no one around; and most of them tipped well. At the same time, like all the servants, he was devoted to his young mistress and did not want her sitting out in the dark catching her death of cold.

'I've me leather belt, sir,' he said grudgingly. 'Mayhap that would hold as far as village.'

With Daniel holding the horses' heads, the man fastened his breeches with a frayed piece of string and finally managed with some difficulty to attach the makeshift strap to the spring. The chaise was put back on an even keel and cautiously, they moved at walking pace towards the lights.

'We'll not reach Ortolans like this,' Daniel told the silent Eleanor. 'Hopefully, there'll be an ostler at the next inn we pass who can help us.'

A quarter of an hour later, they reached the Plough Inn, a somewhat seedy alehouse which Eleanor regarded with apprehension. It could not be too dreadful, she thought as she saw a stagecoach in the yard. There were also several curricles, whiskeys and gigs.

Daniel helped her down from the chaise and, as they walked towards the door of the parlour, two drunken yokels staggered past them, jostling her.

Daniel raised his arm and sent one man flying into the straw and muck of the yard.

'Lay one of your dirty paws on this lady and I will do the same for you!' he said to the other.

'Please, Daniel, they do not intend any harm. Let us go in, please!'

As he pushed open the door, Eleanor wished she had not been so precipitate. A wave of foul-smelling air assailed their nostrils – an odious mixture of ale, cabbage, woodsmoke and unwashed bodies.

'Can I not wait outside, Cousin Daniel?' she whispered. Every one of the high-back wooden benches appeared to be occupied by travellers. Many were finishing a meal and the tables were littered with empty soup bowls and plates containing the remains of turkey legs and rabbit stew. These were clearly stagecoach passengers enjoying a late supper.

At the bar stood a dozen or more young bloods, their wigs in disarray, their frockcoats open and their waistcoats unbuttoned. Their faces were flushed with an over-abundance of punch which stood steaming in a big bowl before them. One of them had his arm round a buxom serving girl who, Eleanor presumed, was the landlord's daughter. All were laughing raucously at the glimpse of the girl's bare thighs revealed above her red and white knee-length striped stockings as she bent to pick up a fallen pewter beer mug.

Daniel was uncertain whether he could leave Eleanor alone in such company. However, he had little alternative for he knew the coachman might have difficulty in obtaining assistance with the inn so busy and the servants so occupied. He espied a plump, matronly figure – a tradesman's wife by the look of her – holding a small child by the arm.

'You will be safe enough with her,' he said when the woman nodded her willingness to have so fine a young lady sit beside her. She moved up the settle and patted the space beside her. The child, its face and clothes dirty, its nose running, stared at Eleanor with huge, round eyes.

'We been t' races at Kemptown, missus!' the woman said cheerfully. 'Missed the last two stages so we 'ad to wait for this 'un. Made two bob, I did and me ole man – 'ee backed two winners, God bless 'im.'

'I am glad you had a good day,' Eleanor said, not wishing to appear too grand to talk to this good-natured woman. She saw the child eyeing the bunch of artificial violets pinned to her pearl grey gown and with a smile, unpinned them and handed them to the toddler. But before either the astonished recipient or its beaming mother could express their thanks, the stagecoach horn sounded its unmistakable message.

The woman straightened her huge balloon hat of black sarcanet, puffed up its satin bows and, grabbing the child and a piece of cold ham pie, bobbed a curtsy to Eleanor and pushed her way out to find her husband.

Within minutes, the room had emptied, leaving only Eleanor and the young men. She looked anxiously at the door, hoping to see Daniel who had been gone this past five minutes. One of the young men sauntered across the room and made an elaborate leg.

'Your shervant, ma'am. May I offer you a little of our punsshh?'

By the slurring of his voice, Eleanor realized that he was very drunk.

'Thank you, no!' she said. 'I shall be leaving in a minute!'

'She's leaving ush – the beautiful lady ish leaving ush! What've we done to desherve such mishfortune!' cried her would-be host.

''Tis you, Armitage – you have but to look at a lady to frighten the wits out of her,' called another, sauntering across the room to join his friend. He, too, made a leg and then went down on one knee.

'I beg you, dear lady, take pity on a lonely youth who is quite devastated by your beauty. Allow me to offer you some refreshment!'

This theatrical performance elicited a loud laugh from another of his friends.

'Confound it, Carstairs. You think that jush becaush your father's an earl, the ladies will dishregard your ugly vishage. Not bad, that, eh? Fishes. That's what you are, old fellow, a fish-fache!'

He, too, came to join them, walking slowly and carefully, steadying himself on the tables as he approached.

'Ma'am,' he said, 'my friends are totally lacking in good manners, let alone finesse. I hope I can make up for their . . . their . . .' He was unable to find the word he wanted. 'It is of no import. I wish to introdush myshelf – the Honourable Alfred Courtney, at your shervish!'

The landlady's daughter, who had made her escape, now re-entered the room, laden with a huge tray of cold ham and home-made bread, which she placed on one of the tables. As she bent over, one of the young bloods gave her a hearty smack on her plump buttocks. She seemed not to mind and grinned at her customers.

''Reckon as 'ow you gen'lemen justabout did enjoy yourseln at the prize fight!' she said as she spread out knives, forks and plates. 'Right merry you be, surelye!'

'Thash right, Rosie, ole girl – we be right merry gen'lemen, God resht us, and this be a right merry young lady who is going to share our repast. Ish that not sho, ma'am?'

He took a step nearer as if to assist Eleanor from her seat.

'Join us, join us!' his friends were calling, beckoning her and waving their punch glasses in her direction, oblivious to the contents which splashed their clothes and slopped on to the floor. One broke into a chorus of 'God rest ye, merry gentlemen!' but was silenced by another who tipped a glass of punch over his head.

Eleanor knew that she must somehow extricate herself before their vocal entreaties became physical.

'I have already eaten, gentlemen,' she said quietly. 'I trust you will enjoy your meal. I fear I must leave you to your own company!'

'We are not taking no for an answer, are we, fellows? If a lady says no, often as not she meansh yesh. Ish that not sho, madame? Allow me to give you my arm?'

As he leant towards her, his balance far from steady, the door of the parlour opened. This surely must be Daniel, Eleanor thought, but to her dismay, she saw that the new arrival was a stranger. Then she gave a small cry of relief as she rose to her feet and hurried towards him.

'Mr Mascal, is it not? Do you remember, we met last year in London? I am Eleanor Calverley! I . . . I would greatly appreciate your help.'

Richard turned towards her and his face widened into a delighted smile.

'Why, Mrs Calverley, what a very pleasant surprise . . .' He glanced at the young men, one of whom was now quite openly bussing the serving wench, and his smile vanished. 'You should not be here alone,' he said, taking her arm and leading her out of the room into the lobby. 'Are you in trouble? Please tell me how I can help you?'

Close to tears, Eleanor related the accident to their chaise.

'Cousin Daniel, my husband's cousin who was escorting me, has gone to see if our coach can be repaired,' she said. 'I cannot think what has happened to him. We have been to the theatre in Brighthelmstone and were on our way to our country house in Detcham.'

'Then it is my lucky day even if it has not proved to be yours!' Richard said, his voice calming her, for he could see that she had been severely frightened by the inebriated youths. 'I only stopped here by chance on my way to Ditchling. I had thought to take the route over Devil's Dyke but decided not to risk meeting old Nick!'

Glad that he had managed to elicit a smile, he said:

'I have my phaeton outside. If you will permit me, I shall be only too happy to drive you home. We can go together to advise your cousin that help is at hand.'

Eleanor drew a great sigh of relief. Not only was she rescued from the drunken young men, but now she need not face an hour's drive in the back of the chaise alone with Daniel. His conversation and attentions had frightened her almost as much as the behaviour of the men.

'It is most kind of you, Mr Mascal. If you are quite certain it will not take you too far out of your way, I shall be eternally grateful.'

'But you have forgotten, Mrs Calverley – it is I who am eternally grateful to you.'

'Then we shall each have done the other a service!' Eleanor said, smiling once more. She had quite forgotten how charming this man was, and, she was convinced, perfectly trustworthy. William might not approve of her driving with a stranger, but Richard Mascal did not seem like a stranger.

'You do not have your black shadow with you, sir?' she asked as he despatched a stable boy to go in search of Daniel.

Richard laughed.

'But to be sure, I do! Peter has charge of my horse. Since there will be no room for him in the phaeton, he can ride back with your cousin. I can assure you, I am as safe a driver as your coachman!'

For the first time since she had left Ortolans with Daniel to set off for Brighthelmstone, Eleanor laughed.

'I do not doubt it!' she said. 'I trust you absolutely, Mr Mascal!'

If only she could trust Daniel with that same confidence, she thought as she followed her rescuer into the night . . . and trust herself when she was alone with Daniel. His kisses had totally undermined her and the embers of the fire he had lit within her still burned, despite the unexpected coldness of the night.

CHAPTER NINE

1791

William had a high fever and was in continual pain, relieved only by the doses of laudanum the physician had prescribed. Despite the soft, down pillows, he was unable to sit or lie comfortably in his bed, and his suppurating shoulder wound was red with inflammation. As if this was not sufficient to distress Eleanor, his stoicism had given way to resignation.

'I have sent word to Mr Endicote, my dear,' he told her as she approached his bedside two days after the accident to the chaise. 'I wish to see him without delay!'

Eleanor's face paled. The family lawyer had been a frequent visitor following upon Uncle Walter's death and she knew that William had been in constant communication with him settling his father's affairs. She herself had written many letters on William's behalf, and she knew that the final details had been concluded. There could, therefore, be but one reason now for William's desire to have his lawyer at his bedside.

'Is it really necessary, dearest?' she enquired as she sat down in the chair by her husband's bed and took his hand in her own.

He gave her a searching look and then drew a deep sigh.

'We must face facts, my dear. Poor Mama is not strong enough to do so, so I must rely upon you to be strong. My condition may deteriorate still further and if I go into a delirium, I want Mr Endicote to know of my wishes and for you to speak on my behalf.'

Tears filled Eleanor's eyes.

'You are going to get better. This is only a temporary set-back, I am convinced of it. Please . . .'

'It would be irresponsible of me to assume I shall recover,' William interrupted her gently. 'I have questioned both physicians and albeit reluctantly, they have admitted that following upon the amputation of my arm, it is quite possible that the bones have become infected. I have perhaps been fortunate that my former good health and strength have kept me from succumbing to my injuries for so long.'

'I cannot bear to hear you talk like this!' Eleanor cried.

'You are very young!' William said inconsequentially. 'However, I believe you have greater strength than many women of such tender years. For my peace of mind, my dear, lend me your strength now.'

'I will do anything, dearest William!' Eleanor said huskily, fighting against her tears. 'You have but to ask me.'

William lay back against his pillows, wincing with pain as he did so.

'Then I will speak my mind openly since there is a great deal which concerns me. My first concern is, of course, that we have no son to inherit. I had hoped . . . my father had hoped . . . but notwithstanding, I am grateful for our early marriage. We enjoyed a few days of happiness, did we not, before poor Father's death curtailed our honeymonth?'

As Eleanor nodded, he continued in a stronger voice:

'We must thank the good Lord for bringing Cousin Daniel back into the family. He, of course, will now inherit if I die. I have already addressed this matter to Mr Endicote who has said, quite rightly, that Daniel must produce some legal evidence of his claim to be a Calverley. This could prove difficult for him since all his family's documents were destroyed in that prairie fire, but Daniel assures me he can obtain verification of his parents' marriage from his mother's family, although this may take time.'

He looked directly into Eleanor's shocked face and said:

'It is a matter of great relief to me that Cousin Daniel will be here to look after Mama, you, Ortolans. He is devoted to you and well capable of looking after your interests. To be

frank, Eleanor, it has even crossed my mind that you might
one day consider marriage to Daniel. I would like to think
that since they cannot be mine, the Calverley heirs might yet
be yours!'

Eleanor was on her feet, her face now flushed a deep pink.

'I will not listen to such talk!' she cried, 'not even to please
you.'

'Very well, my dear, if it distresses you, but please be seated.
I have much more I wish to discuss. There is a very serious
matter concerning Jack.'

'Jack!' Eleanor repeated as she sat down once more, her
pallor returning. 'What of him?'

'There is a possibility that he has . . . well, that he has been
thieving!'

The suggestion was so totally unexpected that Eleanor rose
once more to her feet.

'I do not believe it, William. I cannot think how you could
doubt him. He has been your valet for twenty, thirty – how
many years? And he saved your life in France. No, I do not
believe it!'

William sighed.

'Quite frankly, Eleanor, I too find it hard to credit, but
someone in this household has removed my silver inkwell,
Father's snuffbox and Mama's étui.'

'I was aware Godmother had lost her étui, but you know
how forgetful she has become since poor Uncle Walter passed
away. She thinks she may have lost it in the garden where, as
you know, she quite often takes her sewing.'

'Yes, yes, I said as much to Cousin Daniel, but he said that
unfortunately there is little doubt about the inkwell. On the
morning following upon your mishap with the chaise, he was
in the library writing letters and knew therefore that the inkwell
was on the bureau. He was obliged to leave the room for a
few minutes. When he returned, Jack was coming out of the
room and that was when Daniel noticed the inkwell had
disappeared.'

'But why . . . I do not understand this!' Eleanor protested. Jack was Dora's brother and had been in service to the Calverleys since he was a boy of fourteen. Like all the Pylbeams, he was totally trustworthy; besides which, his employment was secured for life and to risk so much for a few items of silver, which he would surely have difficulty in selling, was sheer lunacy. Were he caught, it would mean hanging – or perhaps transportation.

'No!' she said emphatically. 'Not Jack! Cousin Daniel must have been mistaken!'

'So said I!' William acknowledged, 'but whilst Daniel agreed that one of the other servants might have slipped in and out of the library in his absence, there remains the enigma of my snuffbox. As you know, that resides here by my bedside and Jack is the only servant who comes in here.'

'The maids who clean the room . . .' Eleanor suggested.

'Jack remains here in the room – he would have seen them, besides which they would instantly have been suspect.'

Eleanor was effectively silenced but no nearer believing William's valet had suddenly, in his mid-years, become a thief!

William interpreted her expression and gave another sigh.

'When Cousin Daniel told me he wished to speak to me alone, I sent Jack out of the room. As you know, he chooses always to remain within call in case I am in need, and only leaves if you or Mama are here. On this occasion, he was quite noticeably unwilling to do as he was bade. I had to order him twice before he would depart. As soon as Cousin Daniel voiced his fears, I requested that he search the room most thoroughly – the box is small and could have become dislodged from my bedtable. It was not to be found.'

'That is still no proof that Jack is guilty,' Eleanor said quietly. 'Have you questioned him, William?'

'I have found myself quite unequal to the task. After all these years . . . it is most distressing, Eleanor, and as I told Daniel, I prefer to give Jack the benefit of the doubt until there is more direct proof. Daniel has kindly offered to keep an eye on him, for if Jack has been stealing, he may do so again, and these objects must be somewhere concealed since the man can scarcely dispose of them in Detcham!'

'We shall find he is innocent. I am convinced of it!' Eleanor said.

William nodded.

'I trust you are right, my dear. Meanwhile, you must say nothing of this to Dora lest she alert her brother. It is a dreadful business . . . the Pylbeams have served our family for over two hundred years. The disgrace to the family is unthinkable.'

'Then let us not even think of it further,' Eleanor said quickly. 'Cousin Daniel should not have troubled you whilst you are ill.'

William shook his head.

'He was quite right to do so. As he pointed out, we Calverleys are all very lenient with the servants, unlike many households he has been in. It is human nature to take advantage. If Jack thinks I am shortly to leave this world, he may fear for his future and be trying to feather his nest.'

'You do not believe that,' Eleanor said. 'It is Cousin Daniel who has put such thoughts into your head – and you cannot be sure that you can trust *him*, William. We have known him little more than a year.'

'You astonish me, Eleanor!' William said with a hint of reproach in his voice. 'I had thought both you and Mama found him very likeable and most considerate for your welfare. He is certainly devoted to you, my dear, and no one could have been more remorseful that he had allowed you to travel home late at night with a stranger two evenings ago.'

'You mean Mr Mascal? But he was not a stranger, William, as you know. He could not have behaved with greater decorum; although I know it was not Cousin Daniel's fault that I was deeply embarrassed by the occupants of that horrible wayside inn, Mr Mascal rescued me from them, as it happened. I insisted upon travelling home with him despite Cousin Daniel's objections.'

'Mr Mascal proved to be a very pleasant fellow, I agree,' William said, 'although I must confess I was somewhat confused by his story of a search for his ancestors! However, his father, being a writer, is doubtless an eccentric and I suppose the son likewise has his head filled with strange notions! I was touched, nonetheless, by Daniel's concern for you, and for your reputation.'

Eleanor rose to her feet.

'You are tired, my dearest, and I think it best if I leave you now to rest. I will return as soon as you wish when we can talk further.'

But not about Daniel, she thought as she made her way slowly downstairs. Sadly, she noted the absence of her dog. Even now, almost nine months after he had eaten some rat poison left lying in the stables, she still missed the animal and despite William's offer to do so, had felt unable to replace him.

Daniel, she knew, had taken Lady Calverley for a ride in the whiskey to Detcham village. As always when he was absent from the house, she felt a sense of relief. It was almost as if the house itself took a deep breath and whispered: 'Now we can be ourselves again!' She knew such fantasies were ridiculous and spoke of them to no one. Not even to Dora, her former confidante, could she speak of her fears regarding Daniel. The threat he seemed to pose had been nameless until the night of their return from the theatre. Since then, she could no longer pretend an ignorance of his feelings, so shockingly confessed. Even more shocking was her awakening to the knowledge of her own feelings. She had wanted Daniel to kiss her, hold her, touch her. She craved that sweet, trembling excitement which set her whole body alight whenever he was near her. Most deeply shocking of all were the strange dreams she had had these past two nights – dreams in which she had lain in the big marital bed in Sackville Street, not cringing in her husband's arms, but eagerly responding to Daniel's advances; craving more and more intimacies which never took place. Each night she had woken before that pinnacle of delight she had known must come, sobbing, incomplete, and filled with a terrible sense first of loss and then of guilt.

Lying awake in the darkness, she had been unable to keep from pondering Daniel's suggestion that most married ladies had liaisons and that there was nothing to prevent her enjoying a similar liaison with him. They were not even cousins, except by marriage . . . and William had been too ill these past six months to make any demands upon her. Yet she knew it was wrong, evil, even to think of lying with another man, let alone a man who her husband trusted. William believed Daniel's concern for her was that of a family relative. She longed to be able to tell William that his cousin was very far from being his friend; that Daniel had no regard for gentlemanly behaviour and was using every opportunity to try to persuade her to betray her husband. Several times she had been on the point of confession but had not yet found the courage to disillusion him. Not only was he greatly attached to Daniel but she feared that in his weakened state of health, the shock of discovery of the truth might undermine his longed for recovery.

Thus there was no reason for him to suspect that Daniel's anger at her acceptance of Mr Mascal's offer to drive her home was caused by jealousy; that he had not been in the least concerned for her reputation, or even her safety.

Richard Mascal was a very personable man, a bachelor, a gentleman. Undoubtedly Daniel had been jealous and he had scarcely spoken to her since. Quite unfairly, he had made several derogatory remarks to Godmother regarding Mr Mascal's black servant, Peter. In America, he said, such men would not be permitted in a white man's home except as the most lowly servant; they were fit only to be slaves, yet Eleanor's fine knight errant had seemed as much concerned for the man's welfare as his own.

Without conscious intent, Eleanor's feet now took her into the library. It was a beautiful room, overlooking the front garden, and in the afternoons – if the servants had not drawn the curtains – was filled with warm, golden sunshine. The walls were panelled in a soft brown oak, beautifully carved by one of Dora's ancestors. His initials were carved into one of the vast oak beams supporting the floor above, and sometimes Eleanor would run her fingers over the grooved letters thinking how strange it was that two hundred years after the master carpenter had put his name to his labours, it had survived the time as if he had done so yesterday.

Across the west wall were shelves of books, not often read by William, nor had they been by Uncle Walter, but which had doubtless been purchased by an earlier, more scholarly Calverley. Many were illustrated with coloured prints, carefully preserved by sheets of tissue paper. On winter evenings, Eleanor loved to take down one of these big tomes, look at the beautiful paintings of rare, tropical butterflies and birds; of crustaceans and vegetations from under the seas. There was a Bible, the text illuminated by some long-dead monk; a history of England which even mentioned the name of Detcham where, in Saxon times, a battle had been fought, the river – her river – lying between the two armies.

Those winter afternoons, curled up in front of the huge log fire, Uncle Walter in one chair and Godmother opposite him in another, belonged to the days of her childhood, Eleanor thought, and she was filled with sadness. Life was so transient – and now there was the unthinkable prospect of William dying. She was far from sure if she would be strong enough to bear such a sorrow, although she knew in her heart that it would be even more devastating to poor Lady Calverley.

'If I had borne William a son . . . !' The thought lingered as she stood staring with unseeing eyes across the garden. William had voiced a suggestion that one day she might marry Daniel and beget his children. She was still young – not yet nineteen – and if she did not remarry, when Lady Calverley died she would be alone in the world. It was not a prospect which frightened her so long as she could live here, at Ortolans, where she had never known anything but love and kindness, and a certain inner peace which she felt nowhere else in the world. But Ortolans would belong to Daniel and other than as William's widow, she had no rights to this house she felt was her home.

Eleanor could not bring herself to contemplate marriage to Daniel. No matter how her dreams might oblige her to betray William, she never did so whilst she was awake. She loved William and if that love was more befitting a father or brother than a husband, it was nonetheless real. It had never been 'a torment of the mind, a tempest everlasting', but she was no longer sure that she wanted such a love. The words made her think of Daniel who was, without doubt, 'a torment to her mind'. She would be happier, she thought now, if Daniel were to leave Ortolans and never return. Yet even as the idea came to mind, her body leapt to life as she turned to see him standing in the doorway.

'Aunt Joan said you might be here. She sent me to find you!'

'I am glad to have this chance to talk to you alone,' she said curtly. 'It concerns William.'

As Daniel took a step towards her, a half-smile on his lips, she took a step backwards and would have fallen but for the support of the bookcase behind her.

'It is a matter of great seriousness, Cousin Daniel!' she said in as firm a voice as she could manage. 'I fear he is very ill and I will not have him worried unduly. He tells me you have been casting suspicions upon Jack. I myself do not give them the slightest credence, but if you have further cause for worry, I would be obliged if you would first tell me. William is devoted to his valet and I will not have him distressed unless there is positive proof of Jack's guilt.'

Daniel's dark eyes narrowed imperceptibly.

'If this is your wish, I shall do as you ask. As you know, my sole purpose in life is to please you, to make you happy.'

His voice was low, intense and his meaning obvious.

'Then you will cease making impertinent remarks of a personal nature!' she said with genuine anger. 'They can do nothing but distress me, as well you know!'

Daniel did not move towards her but his smile deepened.

'The truth should never be a matter for distress, my beautiful Eleanor.' With slow, studied gestures, he took out his snuff-box, took a pinch of the powder and held it to his nostrils. 'I think I prefer this mode of address to *cousin* since the latter places you in the category of family – and we are not related except by marriage, are we? What think you of this?'

Eleanor was shocked into wordlessness. Her heart was thudding and the palms of her hands were wet.

'If you had any real concern for my happiness, you would not talk to me as if . . . as if . . .' Once again, she sought desperately for words. They finally burst from her as tears of mortification sprang to her eyes. 'I wish you would go away – far away, at least whilst William is so ill. I do not want you here in this house. I want you to go away!'

Daniel gave the barest lift of his shoulders.

'Aunt Joan has this very afternoon told me that I have become like a second son to her and begged me not to return to London whilst poor William is at death's door. Am I then to please her and remain, or please you and leave? It is for you to decide.'

Eleanor felt the tension leave her body as suddenly as it had taken hold upon her. She did not have the power to fight this man. It was as if he knew what lay in her mind; knew that part of her did not want him to go.

'If Godmother relies upon you, then you must stay!' she said quietly. 'But I ask you once more, Cousin Daniel, please leave me alone. I do not wish your company, your conversation or your intimate mode of address; and now will you be so good as to tell my godmother that I have a slight headache from the sun this morning and have gone to my room to lie down.'

Keeping as great a distance as she could, she gathered up

her skirts and swept past him to the door. Daniel stood perfectly still, the same smile of quiet satisfaction curving his lips. Eleanor's anger was a denial of indifference. He had no doubt whatever that she was as physically aware of his presence as he was of hers.

If nothing else, the years had taught Daniel patience, and he was content now to wait, knowing that it could not be long before he claimed what was his – this girl and the Calverley estates. William's condition was giving serious cause for alarm. It would not take much to bring his life to an end, but to do so, he must be rid of the servant. Eleanor might champion the valet, declaring him honest and trustworthy, but William was uncertain. He, Daniel, had but to provide one irrefutable proof of guilt for the man to be dismissed. That Jack might be hanged despite his true innocence did not concern him. He had stood many times outside Newgate prison watching the public hangings, mingling unnoticed amongst the crowds who always turned out for such spectacles. He found them exciting and they stirred in him half-forgotten memories of tortures inflicted on his tribal enemies. Once the watchdog valet was swinging from the end of a rope, he could bring Cousin William's irritating existence to a speedy end. Then . . . then . . . Eleanor would be freed from her prudish ideas of marital duty and faithfulness, and would be eager to give herself to him.

He was jolted from his thoughts by the entrance of Lady Calverley's personal maid, Molly.

'Her ladyship sent me to ask what had become of you, sir!' she said, bobbing a curtsy. Unlike the other servants, she approved of Daniel who was always polite and agreeable to her and as kind as could be to her ladyship. She did not share their view that he was sweet on Miss Eleanor since, as she stoutly defended him, he was that attentive to her mistress she knew it was just his natural way to be charming to ladies. As she said to Dora, she had no truck with kitchen staff – they always gossiped more than was good for them. At least none thought anything but good of Miss Eleanor. They might have gossiped about her turning up late last Thursday night with a strange gentleman, but they never doubted she had good cause, as turned out to be the case. Besides, the blackamoor had given them enough to chatter about, none but Jack ever having seen a darkie before!

As Daniel went past her on his way to the drawing-room, Molly's mind remained on Jack Pylbeam. It was strange how such a quiet, sensible man should have took against Mr Daniel, she thought. Dora could not understand it either.

But Dora's brother was a taciturn chap and would not discuss Mr Daniel even with Dora. Folk were funny sometimes, Molly decided, as she went to the servants' dining-room for her tea. For herself, she had a soft spot for the master's dark, handsome cousin. He made her poor ladyship smile and, as she said to Cook, there was 'no doubt whatsumdever' but he had lessened her grief at Sir Walter's passing. That was good enough for Molly whose love for her mistress was no less than Jack's for the sickly man upstairs.

Richard Mascal removed his wig and ran his hands through his fair hair.

''Tis a deal too warm for this confounded peruke!' he commented to Peter. 'I've a mind to cast my lot in with the fashion setters and dispense with the wretched thing!'

He loosened the white, lace-edged cravat at his throat and glanced at his timepiece.

'Almost three o'clock,' he commented. 'Time for some refreshment, Peter. Since we are almost in Detcham, we may as well stop at the first inn we see and trust to Providence they have something edible to offer us!'

He glanced at a dusty lane leading off to their left, and a smile lit his face.

'Bedamn me if that is not the road leading to the Calverleys' house! I recognize that huge oak. Lady Calverley told me to watch for it lest I miss the turning!' He grinned at Peter who was slowing the horses to a walk. 'Do you think we might risk an uninvited call? Perhaps not with the master of the house ill . . .'

The smile left his eyes as he pictured the face of the beautiful young girl he had escorted home little more than a week past. She had seldom been out of his thoughts, intruding with irritating frequency, like the refrain of a song one only half-remembered. It was not simply a matter of her appearance, though undoubtedly he had thought her beautiful, but there was an unusual intelligence in her expression, and an innocence which caught his imagination and haunted him. He wanted very much to see her again – yet he knew to do so would merely aggravate his interest, and at the end of the day, she was a married woman, for all she looked like a girl! Besides, he reminded himself, he had more urgent business to attend to. In Falmer, where they had been the previous night, he had been told there was a master carpenter in Detcham who went by the name of Pylbeam – and of excellent reputation. Since he had resolved to visit every craftsman of that name – a formidable task that might take him many years! – he could not afford to indulge in time-consuming diversions, however attractive they might be.

'Drive on, Peter!' he instructed. 'I have no business there!'

''Tis as well, master!' the man said as he urged the horses forward. 'There is evil in that house!'

'What in the name of Heaven makes you say such a thing?' Richard remarked. 'I thought the place very comfortable and pleasing, and the occupants charming. Were you ill treated in the kitchens?'

'No, sir. They stared as they always do as haven't seen a black man before. It was the dark-haired young gentleman. He is evil, master!'

Richard regarded his servant in astonishment. As far as he could remember, he had never heard Peter express an opinion without first being asked for it, still less make so slanderous a comment.

'Evil! That is a harsh word, Peter. The little I saw of Mr Daniel Calverley, I found harmless enough. I think he may have resented my interference that night at the inn near Pyecombe, but that was understandable since he was made to appear at fault for leaving the hapless lady at the mercy of those drunken dolts. Explain yourself!'

'He robbed me, master!'

'Robbed you!' Richard repeated, on the point of laughter. 'Come now, Peter, the sun must have scorched your wits. How so, robbed you?'

Peter's black face remained inscrutable although his mouth tightened.

'That guinea which I keep always in my waistcoat pocket – it had gone before we reached the house that night.'

'My good fellow, it is as well you are not given to prattling, for you could be hanged for saying such things about a gentleman. You have just accused Mr Calverley of being a common pickpocket, and lenient though I may be, I'll not stand for such calumny. The Calverleys are a highly respected family.'

'Yes, sir, but that gentleman is but newly come to the family from America, so the valet told me. He said I was not to think he come from the same stable as his master who was a good man, a real gentleman. He told me that this Mr Daniel Calverley had poisoned the lady's dog.'

'This is servants' gossip, Peter, and you should know better than to listen to it. I consider it very disloyal for any one of the staff to speak as they did to a stranger. I am most surprised – and disturbed. I trust you made no mention of the lost guinea?'

'No, master, I kept my mouth shut.'

'And did not even tell me until now!' Richard said nonplussed.

'I had no proof, sir, and as I myself had found it hard to credit, I did not think you would believe me.'

Richard sighed.

'No more I do, Peter. The coin must have fallen into the

road or some such thing. Now pull up, man! This looks a
likely hostelry, and if I do not get a pint of ale down me soon,
I shall perish of thirst!'

Peter's fantasies were forgotten as over a delicious meal of
potted tongue and braised beef with forcemeat dumplings,
followed by a generous helping of mulberry pie and jelly,
Richard quizzed the landlord about the Pylbeam family.

'Master Pylbeam be an axcellent carpenter, sir,' the landlord waxed loquacious. 'Master Thomas, that be. Young
Bert, he be Master Pylbeam's eldest. He be a valiant man,
surelye; won the prize for fisticuffs, he did, for Detcham
village this summer. He be a woodcarver. Young Joshua,
now, he be a lear, miserable, skinny-looking lad if ever I
seed one but knowledgeable. Poor fellow allus got his head
in a book. He be sittin' by inglenook over there, sir. If'n
you be wanting Master Pylbeam, he'll tell 'ee where to find
him, surelye.'

'Give the fellow a drink and ask him to wait for me,'
Richard said. 'I'll have a word with him as soon as I have
finished this excellent meal. My congratulations to your good
wife, landlord!'

As soon as he had completed his repast, Richard sent Peter
to bring in his portmanteau from the phaeton. From it, he took
the carved wooden horse which he now carried over to the
youth who was enjoying his free tankard of ale. He stood up
as Richard approached and touched his forelock.

'Thank you kindly, sir. Landlord said you be wantin' to
talk to me?'

'Sit down – Joshua, is it not? I doubt if I shall keep you
long.' Richard handed the plaything to the youth, upending
it so that the signature was visible. 'Can you tell me if anyone
in your family might have made this?'

The lad took it and ran his hands gently over the surface.

'It be axcellent work,' he muttered, as much to himself as
to Richard. 'I doant mind my dad nor my brother carvin' this.
I'd not disremember if'n I'd seed it afore!'

Richard was too well accustomed to disappointment after eighteen months of fruitless searching to be discouraged.

'I expected no less, but you see, this must have been made many years ago, possibly even before your father was born. I was hoping that amongst your forebears, there might have been a carpenter who made his living from fashioning animals – or indeed, any plaything of a similar nature.'

The youth appeared to grasp his point.

'Most carpenters, hereabouts anyroads, meks furniture or houses. There ain't no call for such as this, 'ceptin' a man might carve a whistle or a peg doll for his own chillun'. I mind my dad tellin' me his dad once made a rocking horse for big house down by t'river. Squire's house, that is. It were a mighty fine thing, near as big as a billy goat and Squire gifted him a hectare o' land for his pains he were that pleased. Land be ourn to this day.'

Richard's breath caught in his throat. This was the nearest he had yet come to a possible clue. Might he, by some miracle, have discovered the right Pylbeam? The dates were about right, and if Joshua's grandfather made one plaything, why not another? He had been well rewarded!

'Can you tell me the name of this squire?' he asked eagerly. 'He has not parted with his land? He may well be able to help. It is of singular importance to me.' He took out a coin from his pocket and handed it to the surprised lad. 'The squire's name, boy. You must know it.'

'I mind it well enough, sir!' Joshua Pylbeam said grinning. 'He be Sir William Calverley of Ortolans House.' He pocketed the coin quickly before Richard might change his mind. 'He be a gurt squire though some do say he be larmentable ill. He be . . .'

He broke off, realizing that his audience was no longer listening. Richard was already on his way through the door.

CHAPTER TEN

1791–92

Daniel was riding round the estate with William's bailiff. He had wanted Eleanor to accompany him but she had resolutely declined, using as an excuse – untruthful though it was – that she had been frightened by her fall and did not wish to ride again until she had recovered her confidence. Thus it was Eleanor who received Richard Mascal when he called late one afternoon.

'It seems as if you are destined to make do with my company each time you ask to see my husband!' she said as she invited him to be seated. As he returned her smile, she was surprised once more at how greatly it enhanced his looks. It was a warm, friendly smile, unstilted and informal. 'I am sorry to say that my husband is not well enough to receive visitors. May I be of any help to you?'

Reminding himself sharply that this beautiful young woman was another man's wife and that he should not be considering how greatly her face and figure and voice appealed to him, Richard cleared his throat and said:

'Since I cannot disturb Sir William, whose indisposition I very much regret, would it be possible for you to approach him on my behalf? It is not a matter which should concern him in any way, but it is of utmost importance to me.'

His blue eyes seemed to darken with the urgency of his voice.

'This little horse, Lady Calverley,' he said, handing it to her. 'It is the only clue I have to my parentage. I believe it was carved by a man called Pylbeam – the carpenter I have been searching for this past eighteen months.'

As briefly as he could, he related its history, concluding his story with an apologetic smile.

'I know that I am in all probability chasing shadows. Although I do know my parents were of English nationality, I do not know for certain even if they once lived in this country. I can but assume it since the boat that took them to Lisbon had come from England.'

Fascinated by the story he had just related of the Lisbon earthquake and its far-reaching consequences, Eleanor leant forward in her chair, one hand on her forehead as if to aid her memory.

'You must not set store by this, but I think I can recall Uncle Walter – my husband's father – telling me that his youngest brother – Edward, no Edwin, I think – had been killed in an earthquake. I believe it was in Mexico although it might have been elsewhere. Lady Calverley will remember . . .'

She hesitated, realizing from the expectant expression on her visitor's face how much hope she was raising, perhaps only to be dashed.

'It is only a slim chance . . .' she said gently.

'But the nearest I have yet come even to a single clue!' Richard broke in. 'The names Edward, Edwin mean nothing to me since I am unaware of my father's Christian name, or indeed of my mother's. I know only that I had a twin brother, and that we were in that earthquake.'

Eleanor's face paled and for a moment, she believed she might faint. Was it possible, she asked herself, that Daniel might be the twin this man was trying so hard to find? No, she told herself as her heart steadied. There was not even a slight family resemblance between the two men, and Richard Mascal had stated that he and his brother were identical twins.

'My mother-in-law is very frail these days and tires quickly, but I will take you to her and we can but hope that her memory will be of assistance. Like many old people, her recall of things long past is better than of yesterday's events.'

As Eleanor led the way to the library, Richard, despite the intensity of his excitement, was yet again struck by the beauty of this house. The young woman he was following seemed strangely to be almost a part of it, as if it belonged to her and her to it.

Lady Calverley woke from a light doze as they came into the room.

'Why, William, dear boy. You are feeling better!' she said, her mind still confused as she stared up at Richard.

'No, Godmother, this is a gentleman you have not yet met – Mr Richard Mascal. He wants to talk to you!'

Lady Calverley smiled as Eleanor bent to kiss her cheek.

'I always enjoy talking to handsome young men!' she said, her voice so youthful and coquettish that both Eleanor and Richard smiled. He kissed the old lady's hand and said gallantly:

'And I always enjoy talking to beautiful young women!'

Lady Calverley patted his hand with her fan.

'That may have been true once, young man, but that was a long time ago. I think I was at my best the day I married my dear Walter. I was nineteen, and . . .'

'Godmother, you are so good at remembering things,' Eleanor interrupted gently. 'Can you perhaps help Mr Mascal by telling him a little of those days . . . when you were first married to Uncle Walter? He had two brothers, did he not?'

'Indeed, yes! Edwin was his best man – so handsome he looked, and there was I with your uncle on one hand and poor dear Edwin on the other – such a pretty bride!'

'What happened to Edwin, Godmother?' Eleanor persisted. 'Did he ever marry?'

Lady Calverley straightened her black lace mob-cap and said at once:

'Oh, yes, indeed! He married that young girl from The Grange – what was her name? – Margaret, I think. They had two dear little baby boys – Matthew and Mark – alike as two peas in a pod, so you could not tell one from the other. So sad . . . so very sad . . .'

Eleanor glanced swiftly at Richard and back again to the elderly woman in the armchair.

'What was so sad, Godmother? What happened to them?'

'I am afraid I forget quite why, my dear, but Edwin decided to go abroad. Something to do with importing brandy – or was it port? Edwin had no money, you see, and as he did not fancy the Army or the Church, he thought he would try to make his fortune overseas. Poor Walter blamed himself for allowing it, although I doubt if he could have stopped Edwin who was very strong-willed. Then that dreadful earthquake . . . those poor sweet little boys . . .'

'It was a long time ago and you must not let it distress you now, Lady Calverley,' Richard said. 'Let us think of happier times. Does *this* bring back any memories?'

Gently, he placed the wooden horse in her hands. For a moment, she looked at it in bewilderment and then suddenly, her face lit up and once again, she looked momentarily like a young girl.

'Why, yes, of course! I had Thomas carve this little horse for the elder of the twins, and a dog for the other child. I thought, you see, that so long as they each carried their own toy, I should be able to identify the twins correctly. Just fancy that! Wherever did you find it?'

Not wishing to shock her with the whole answer but still needing a last verification, Richard said:

'You told us someone called Thomas carved this, Lady Calverley. Was that his surname?'

'Oh, no, I am talking of Thomas Pylbeam. Let me see now, that would be Dora's grandfather, would it not, Eleanor? I do wish people would not give all their generations the same Christian names – so confusing! I did not call my son Walter or my girls Joan for that very reason. My poor Catherine . . . she died, you know, in France. Have you heard, Mr Mascal, what terrible things are happening there? They are using that dreadful guillotine to massacre the aristocracy – quite barbaric, is it not? William does not like me to read the newspaper but

I make Molly retrieve his copy for me when he has finished with it!'

She smiled again like a mischievous child.

Eleanor turned to Richard.

'It would seem as if you have all the answers you wanted!' she said quietly. 'In the circumstances, I think you should see my husband. It does look, does it not, as if you may well be a member of this family . . . the second, you know, who has turned up out of the blue heavens. Cousin Daniel, who you met recently, is also a newly discovered relative. His father, Robert Calverley, was your father's brother. He disappeared in America over forty years ago and no one was aware he had had a son until Cousin Daniel appeared from the New World.'

Richard made no comment until they had left Lady Calverley who, with the aptitude of the old, had dropped off to sleep as Eleanor was talking. As he followed Eleanor up the polished oak staircase, he said:

'When I came here this afternoon, I never really expected to discover the truth. Even now, I am finding it hard to believe that I have come to the end of my search – that I am quite probably Richard Calverley; that Lady Calverley and your husband are my blood relatives; that my real father was almost certainly born in this house! It does not seem credible!'

Sensing his confusion, Eleanor paused and turned to look at the personable young man beside her.

'There seems very little doubt about it, Mr Mascal,' she said. 'Godmother recognized the little horse at once and even recalls that it was a Thomas Pylbeam who carved it. It would be too coincidental, would it not, if it had found its way into the hands of some other English child during that earthquake?'

Richard nodded.

'My father said it was the only possession I had when he and my mother adopted me. Now it remains for me to find my brother and verify that I have an identical twin.'

'If you succeed and discover that he, too, was adopted at

the time of the earthquake in Lisbon, that surely will be all the proof you need of your identity,' Eleanor said. She turned as a figure stepped out of the shadows of the landing.

'Ah, Jack, is the master sleeping? I have a visitor for him.'

'The master is awake, milady, and a little better since this morning.'

'Then we will go in to see him,' Eleanor said. 'I think he will be greatly cheered by your presence, Mr Mascal. The family is and always has been of great importance to him.'

As the valet opened the door for them, Richard paused on the threshold, trying to compose his emotions. He was standing here in the house which in all probability was his ancestral home.

I am a Calverley! was the thought uppermost in his mind. At long last, he had discovered his true identity and knew who he really was. The strange thing was that he did not feel any different from the person he had always been.

'I am sorry, Mr Calverley, but the matter is not quite as simple as you think.'

Mr Alfred Endicote, the family lawyer, looked at Daniel over the top of his spectacles and tried to curb his irritation. The tiresome fellow had been pestering him for months to establish his claim to the family estate which, of course, included the title, but it was not proving easy. In point of fact, he now added as he looked at young Lady Calverley, it was proving exceedingly difficult.

'Why so? I can see no difficulty,' Daniel said, curbing his anger with difficulty.

'You must understand,' the lawyer said firmly to Daniel, 'that neither you nor I have any record of your date of birth, or indeed of your father's marriage. I am sorry if this distresses you, but in legal terms you have no proof of your existence – let alone your legitimacy. To compound the difficulties this poses, Mr Richard Mascal is also without documented proof of his birth. It is also suggested – and Lady Joan Calverley has raised this point – that if Mr Mascal is a Calverley, he has a twin brother and although her ladyship believes Mr Mascal to be the elder, we have no legal proof of it. There are therefore three possible heirs, of which you are only one.'

Eleanor, seated beside Daniel in the lawyer's dusty London chambers in Lincoln's Inn, sensed the barely controlled tension in Daniel's body. On the journey to London, he had openly voiced his disapproval of the worthy Mr Endicote who, he declared, was 'a senile incompetent with the speed of a tortoise and the intelligence of a halfwit'. Eleanor had tried to defend the old man who was, unarguably, in his seventies, and on his own admission, somewhat out of his depth. At the same time, she knew that William had always thought highly of the lawyer and had nominated him a trustee in his will.

'You make matters no clearer, sir!' Daniel said forcibly. 'The late Sir Walter Calverley never questioned my claim to be his nephew nor, so far as I am aware, did my cousin, William, doubt our relationship. I cannot see why you or anyone else should do so now. My father was Sir Walter's elder brother and the law cannot dispute that I am next in line.'

Mr Endicote cleared his throat and shuffled the papers on his desk. But for the presence of young Lady Calverley for whom he had a special regard, he might have told the furious man facing him that he should hold his tongue since he clearly had no knowledge of the law. Instead, he said carefully:

'Unfortunately, your late cousin died within two weeks of Mr Richard Mascal's introduction to the family, and was too ill when last I saw him to do more than instruct me to look into the whole affair. As his trustee, I am under a legal obligation to ascertain the truth, and as his lawyer, it is my duty. Perhaps if you could expedite your search for documentation of some kind, Mr Calverley, I could arrive at a satisfactory conclusion. I understand Mr Mascal has gone to Vienna in search of further proof of his identity. Perhaps you, also, could return to your country of birth for the same purpose?'

Daniel's eyes narrowed.

'That, sir, would mean my absence from Ortolans for a minimum of three months, and my cousin would not have approved the suggestion. He begged me with his dying breath to take care of Aunt Joan and Lady Calverley and there are no circumstances in which I would abnegate my duty.'

'Cousin Daniel has been ensuring the smooth running of the estate since before . . . before my husband passed away,' Eleanor explained, sadness at the memory of William's death in August momentarily overwhelming her. 'I do not know how we would have managed without him. However, if it is necessary for Cousin Daniel to go to America, I . . .'

'No, no, my dear Lady Calverley,' Mr Endicote said gently. 'I am sure the documentation can be sent by ship once it is found. It was simply that Mr Calverley wished a speedy conclusion and I was suggesting a way in which that was most likely to be achieved.'

On their way to Curzon Street where she and Daniel were to spend the night with the Howells before driving back to Sussex, Eleanor tried to soften Daniel's mood. He was tight-lipped and had not spoken one word since they had left the lawyer. Since William's death, he had been so immensely kind and thoughtful that it distressed her to see him so upset.

'I am sure Mr Endicote is doing all he can to help us sort out this confusion,' she said gently. 'When you consider it, Cousin Daniel, it *is* his duty to take every legal precaution. We must not condemn him for doing so.'

'There can be no question but that I am the rightful heir,' Daniel declared in a low, angry voice. 'Your Mr Mascal has no claim even if he proves himself a Calverley which, by the sound of it, I doubt he can. He is the son of your father-in-law's youngest brother, Edwin, and inheritance passes through the *elder* brother, my father, Robert Calverley.'

'He is not exactly "my" Mr Mascal!' Eleanor said gently. 'I do not know why you have taken such a dislike to him, Cousin Daniel. I thought it quite remarkably commendable of him to suggest that even if he proved to be the legal heir,

he would hand over to you any part of the estate or investments that were not entailed. He was most sympathetic to
your impoverished state, and promised that since he is more
than amply provided for by Sir Greville Mascal, he would
make no claim for benefit of any kind. He wishes only to
establish his true identity – nothing more.'

'So he professes!' Daniel muttered ungraciously. 'We shall
see if he means it!'

'You cannot think ill of him!' Eleanor protested. 'After all,
what would have become of poor Jack had Mr Mascal not
offered to take him to Europe and hopefully find him employment there! We are in his debt, are we not?'

Daniel's scowl deepened. He had wanted Jack hanged, which
would have ensured that the valet could never again protest
his innocence. The man was no fool and he suspected the
truth – that Daniel himself had removed the valuables. It was
an accusation the servant had not dared to make since he had
no proof. For a moment, Daniel's mood lightened as he recalled
how simple a matter it had been to slip the silver vinaigrette
into the valet's coat pocket and then, in William's presence,
demand a search. Poor Cousin William had been so distressed,
he had nearly expired on the spot! Daniel's one mistake, he
soon realized, was to have carried this scenario to its finale
whilst Mascal was a guest in the house. The fellow had been
present when Eleanor, with tears in her eyes, had kneeled at
Lady Calverley's feet and begged her to be merciful with the
valet. Jack, she had pleaded, was Dora's brother, and
the maid, like every other member of the Pylbeam family,
would share Jack's disgrace.

Cousin William had delegated the decision to his mother,
who appeared deeply shocked. Had he, Daniel, been alone
with the old lady, he might have persuaded her it was her
duty to have the man apprehended and punished for his crimes,
but Mascal had intervened, adding his persuasions for clem-
ency. He had pointed out that it was the Pylbeam family which
had been responsible for reuniting him with his relations; that

as a consequence he felt obliged to support Eleanor in her plea for leniency. The confounded fellow then pointed out that since no one really wanted the valet hanged and since mere dismissal without references was inadequate punishment for so serious a crime, he personally would escort Jack out of the country, effectively banishing him as permanently as if he were transported to the colonies.

Daniel had felt it wiser not to argue for the death penalty. He had, after all, achieved what he wanted – the valet no longer a watchdog outside Cousin William's bedroom door. Within days of Jack's departure with Mr Mascal, he had been able to proceed with his plan to bring William's life to a speedy conclusion. The poisonous fungi had been as effective upon his cousin as upon the dog, and within a few hours after its administration in a glass of sweetened cordial, William was dead.

Eleanor's grief was genuine, and she was deeply shocked by her husband's death, even whilst it was not, in the circumstances of his long illness, entirely unexpected. Astute enough to realize this – and long versed in the art of patience – Daniel made no more personal advances, and behaved with the utmost circumspection towards her. He was sympathetic, a tower of strength throughout the funeral and subsequently when friends and neighbours called. He assisted her in replying to the many letters of condolence. At the same time, he took every opportunity to divert old Lady Calverley who, when she was not too confused, was heartbroken by the death of her last remaining child. It was he, Daniel, who had seen to the disposal of William's clothes, generously donating them to the village poor when he might have kept them for himself; and whenever the old lady or Eleanor needed his assistance or advice, he was at their elbows.

Daniel's face twisted in an expression that was in part a grimace but in part an ironic smile. By establishing himself with the right to be in William's room to sort out his cousin's belongings, he had been able to keep at bay immediate disaster.

Although unnerved by the story Richard Mascal had told of his possible connection to the Calverley family, Daniel could see little likelihood of the man being able to trace either his twin or the unnamed Austrian baron who had adopted him. Mascal's claim to the title was no more valid than his own.

Or so he had believed that afternoon in William's bedroom when he had discovered the key to the iron strongbox that stood almost unnoticed in a recess by the fireplace. Daniel had found a key in William's bedside cabinet and in the expectation that he might find something of considerable value in the strongbox, he had inspected the contents. At first, he had been disappointed by the discovery that it contained no more than carefully tied parcels of letters addressed to Sir Walter or his father; but as he sifted through them, he saw his own father's name on one of the bundles.

Daniel was unsurprised by the few letters concerning the youthful Robert. Most were letters demanding payment of enclosed notes of hand. One contained a threat of legal action and attached to it was another, thanking Sir Walter for payment of the debt and for the assurance that Robert was to be despatched to the New World within the week.

With a shrug of his shoulders, Daniel had put them aside and opened another small bundle on which was written the name 'EDWIN CALVERLEY'. There were letters concerning his marriage, the birth of his twin sons, his decision to go abroad – none of interest to Daniel until he came upon a single page dated 1761, with the heading 'The *Maria Luiza*, Brest harbour'.

We have berthed here to take on fresh provisions and will proceed through the Bay of Biscay tomorrow. The Captain tells us we should arrive in Lisbon by the end of the week.

Margaret and I are both well and have not so far suffered from mal de mer. Little Matthew, however, took a nasty tumble from his bunk soon after we left Liverpool and sustained a severe cut above his wrist. The First Officer stitched the Wound and has assured us that with the aid of salt Sea Air, it will be healed before we reach our Destination, although the poor Child will undoubtedly retain a Scar. My Dear Margaret has not blamed the nurse who, poor soul, is most unwell.

Please give our Fondest Love to Mama and Papa and tell them to rest assured that I will write again as soon as we Arrive.

I remain

Your Devoted Brother, Edwin

Daniel had been aghast for his quick eye had noted the long white scar above the joint of Mascal's right wrist when the ruffle of his shirt had fallen back as he took a pinch of snuff from the box Daniel had proffered him.

With a sickening jolt, Daniel had realized that here was irrefutable proof of Mascal's identity, and he knew he must destroy the letter instantly. As luck would have it, Eleanor had chosen that very moment to enter the room to inform him that her godmother was asking him to join them in the garden.

Unable to hide the letter from her, Daniel could do nothing but replace it in the chest.

'There seems little of interest to anyone here,' he had said, rising to his feet and quickly turning the key in the lock. 'Just some old documents belonging to Sir Walter. I will put the box in the attic and perhaps when Aunt Joan feels up to it, she will look through them.'

'How thoughtful of you, Cousin Daniel!' Eleanor said. 'If it is safely locked, I will put the key with the others Godmother keeps. You must not overwork yourself. Perhaps we might take a walk and enjoy some fresh air.'

Daniel had carried the box to the attic where it still reposed. He had removed the valuables he had stored there. Now that he had ample financial means, there was little point in risking their sale in a London pawn shop, so reluctantly, he had thrown them in the river. If any were found, he had but to suggest that Jack had been frightened into ridding himself of them in such fashion. The strongbox, however, could not be similarly secreted without his being observed. Nor could he force the lock with a crowbar without danger of being overheard. Somehow, he thought, he must arrange matters so that he had the house to himself. He knew there was little hope of stealing the key from Lady Calverley's key ring. Her maid slept on a truckle bed in her room and was as close a watchdog to her mistress as Jack had been to his master.

Aware that Eleanor's attitude to him had softened considerably in recent weeks, he continued to make himself as indispensable to her as possible. Grateful for his support, she had agreed to go to London with him to see Mr Endicote. Ignorant of legal affairs, he hoped her presence might influence the old man into believing that the family had personally acknowledged his claim to be the rightful heir. With Mascal abroad and unable to make any counterclaim, the lawyer might decide that the matter of inheritance had been in abeyance too long and sign the necessary documents in Daniel's favour.

He had been furious when Endicote had stubbornly refused to sign any document without written proof.

At least Eleanor had acknowledged to the tiresome lawyer that she and Lady Calverley could not have managed without him, he thought, as the carriage drew to a halt outside the Howells' London house. He had successfully assumed the role of master of Ortolans, and no one but that punctilious lawyer questioned his right to do so. There seemed little doubt now that he would have to forge the necessary documents. He would have to go down to the less reputable area of the City, perhaps bribe some seedy lawyer or clerk of the court to supply him with the names of convicted forgers. At least there was no shortage of money for bribery, or for any other requirement he might have. Before his death, Cousin William had given him power of attorney and he could acquire unlimited credit.

A year or two ago, Daniel reflected wryly, that would have been enough to realize his wildest dreams. Now, however, he wanted more. He wanted the title and estate; he wanted to be the squire, the respected Lord of the Manor, the acknowledged owner of Ortolans – and most of all, he wanted Eleanor.

For the first time since, at the age of fifteen, she had gone to live at Ortolans, Eleanor was not happy there. By the spring, an awareness of the finality of William's death distressed her more than her immediate grief had done. Although they had never been true lovers, she had loved him, and she missed his presence. The atmosphere in the house was oppressive. The servants never smiled or sang, and went about their duties with closed, drawn faces. Although the windows were no longer curtained, every member of the household was still in mourning and William's portrait and all the mirrors were still draped in black. Cousin Daniel made every effort to cheer the household, but there was no stemming Godmother's tears, nor indeed those of Dora and the other Pylbeam servants. The dreadful affair of Jack's treachery hung heavily on all their shoulders, and by unspoken consent, his name was never mentioned.

No, it was not a happy house any more, she thought, as she joined Lady Calverley at breakfast. Daniel was out riding and a boy from the village had just delivered the post, including a letter with a foreign franking. Momentarily, her spirits lifted.

'Here is a letter from Mr Mascal, Godmother,' she said, opening the seal with her knife. 'You remember him, do you not? He was the nice-looking man who called you a beautiful young lady, and who we think may be your nephew.'

'I think I do, dear. I get so confused these days. William is late for breakfast again, naughty boy!'

'Yes, Godmother, I'll speak to him about it,' Eleanor said, a lump rising in her throat and threatening tears. There were days when Lady Calverley was unaware that William had left them; days when she could not remember who Daniel was, although she always appeared to recognize Eleanor.

'Godmother, listen to this!' she cried, and read aloud from the letter:

After many weeks of inquiry, I have at last had the astonishing good fortune to discover the name of the Austrian baroness who adopted my brother. It came about in this fashion. I was walking across Michaelplatz on my way to Dehn's, a delightful pastry house where it is the custom here to meet in mid-morning and drink large glasses of hot chocolate topped with whipped cream! I was suddenly approached by a gentleman of my own age who greeted me most warmly, slapping me across the shoulders and addressing me as Johann. When I looked at him uncomprehendingly, he laughed and accused me of indulging in the childish prank of pretending I did not know him. I replied in English that I really had not met him before and seeing his genuine disbelief, the possible explanation occurred to me – the man he called Johann might be my twin!

We took coffee together and I told this stranger my story, whereupon he informed me that Johann was one of two sons of the Baron and Baroness Valschintzky – Johann, fair-haired like me, and the other, Karl, dark like his parents. The Valschintzkys own a big Schloss in Wachau on the banks of the Danube where they are currently residing, and my new friend does not expect them to return to Vienna until the end of November.

My first instinct was to jump into my carriage and drive to Wachau. On second thought, I have decided to await their return to Vienna when my new friend has promised to alert my brother to my presence, thus avoiding too great a shock for him and, more importantly, for his adoptive parents. They may have reasons for wishing to keep the secret of Johann's adoption and it would be wrong of me to cause them distress were this the case.

You can imagine, dear Lady Calverley, how impatient I am to meet my brother, a truly identical twin according to my new friend. He tells me that he would have gone to the gallows swearing that I was Johann! I doubt I would have convinced him I was not had it not been for my execrable German accent which, he agreed, could only come from an Englishman!

Perhaps you will be kind enough to explain all this to Lady Calverley as she may wish to know that almost certainly, she now has two more nephews. I would also greatly appreciate it if you would pay a call upon my father, Sir Greville Mascal, if ever you are in London. I hear he is not too well and I know he has been most anxious to make your acquaintance ever since learning that I may in all probability be a member of the Calverley family. I can but hope now that the Baron and Baroness Valschintzky will be similarly understanding if Johann proves to be my brother

. . .

The letter ended with the customary good wishes for their health and well-being and in addition, there was a postscript which Eleanor did not read aloud to Lady Calverley. Jack, he wrote, had obtained employment with a Viennese cellist who did not seem in the least concerned by his lack of references having discovered that Jack could smooth-iron the satin lining of his opera cloak without causing it to wrinkle – as had his last valet! Jack, poor fellow, was still protesting his innocence, and he had asked Richard to remember him to all the members of his family.

Eleanor put down the letter with a smile as she thought of the relief this news of her brother would afford poor Dora. It was pleasurable, too, to contemplate the mood of excited anticipation in which Richard's letter had been penned. Even Mr Endicote, she thought, could not question Richard's claim to be a Calverley if now he had discovered the existence of his identical twin.

Her smile vanished as she recalled the last meeting with Mr Endicote and Daniel. Unlike that of Richard, Daniel's

situation was no nearer being resolved. Yet again there was
no letter for him from America in today's post and he would
be newly downcast, as always, by the lack of replies to the
many requests for information he had sent to officials there.
He had been so good to her and to Godmother that she longed
for him to be happy. She was no longer afraid of him, for,
although frequently she still found him staring at her with
those dark, unusual eyes, he had long ceased making the
personal remarks which had once so disturbed her. He behaved
always with the utmost propriety, never touching her unless
circumstances demanded he help her into a carriage or give
her his arm on a pavement or stairway.

Eleanor did not try to deny to herself that she was still very
aware of his presence in a room or carriage. She had but to
meet his gaze to feel the colour warming her cheeks and for
her heart to beat more swiftly. There were nights when she
still dreamt and awoke ashamed of the content of those dreams;
but now she was able to push such anxieties to the back of
her mind. For the present, she grieved for William and did
what she could to comfort Lady Calverley. The future, she
told herself, could take care of itself, and in the meanwhile,
Daniel posed no threat.

She folded Richard's letter and put it away in her escritoire.
Its contents would not afford Daniel much comfort and
Richard's progress might exacerbate his failure to prove his
identity. On several occasions recently, Daniel had made the
suggestion that they should close Ortolans for the summer
and repair to Sackville Street. The change of scenery and
lifestyle would be good for her – and for Lady Calverley, he
believed. The Ortolans servants who did not go with them
could be given a holiday, for they, too, were downcast, and a
caretaker left to ensure that the house was kept aired.

Eleanor had pleaded for time to consider the proposal. It
was many years since Lady Calverley had gone to London,
she argued, and the journey might be too much for her.
Moreover, they were all still in mourning and it would be out

of the question that they should participate in the summer seasonal events. Now, suddenly, she felt as if the house itself was urging her to go. It was as if it knew that she could no longer feel at peace here.

Breakfast over, Eleanor wandered from room to room, trying to understand why or quite how the atmosphere had changed. Once the very walls had seemed to embrace her, and now she felt no unseen hands holding her, warming her heart.

I am becoming fanciful and quite absurdly whimsical! she told herself as she heard the sound of the hoofs of Daniel's black stallion clattering on the cobbles in the stableyard below. Daniel is quite right. I need a change of scene – to get away from this house of sorrow!

Slowly, she went downstairs to meet him.

'Subject to Godmother's approval, I am agreed that we should go to London for a month or two,' she said, and was rewarded by Daniel's instant look of delight.

At last, he thought triumphantly, he would regain control of his destiny. Ortolans would be devoid of watchful servants and their prying eyes. He might not yet be able to produce the proof of his identity, but now he could at least destroy Mascal's.

Old Fred Pylbeam, Jack's uncle, shuffled his way along the upstairs landing in his carpet slippers, muttering to himself as he went from room to room. His inspection was routine before he retired to the kitchen for the night. He shielded his candle with one bony hand, gnarled by rheumatism, from the faint breeze that always seemed to whisper along the dark landing.

'I'll tweat ye, ye liddle rascals!' he muttered, for he had no doubt that Pharisees came creeping into the house when the family were away. Deaf as he was, he could hear their voices 'tweating' him and he knew if he did not keep an eye out for them, they would get up to mischief. Sometimes they outwitted him, and he would find a book fallen from the bookshelf, or an ornament knocked off a windowsill. Although his grandmother had seen them often enough, dancing on the grass in circles that remained a darker green next day for all to see, he had not yet met one face to face. But he knew they were there.

He glanced up the rickety wooden stairway to the attics – the low-roofed rooms beneath the eaves – and gave a quiet chuckle.

'T'aint them dratted Pharisees been up there!' he muttered knowingly. 'Better not, neither, if'n they knows what's gurt for 'em!'

He turned and went slowly down the main staircase, and paused outside the library. A chink of light showed beneath the closed door. He knocked on it and shuffled his way in.

'If'n you doant need nuffin more, sir, I do be turnin' in!'

'Be off with you then!' Daniel said as he continued to eat the salt pork and pickled onions the old man had managed to unearth for him. He should have stopped for a meal at an inn on the journey down from London, he thought, as he pushed the half-eaten meal away from him. For all its smoking, he was convinced the meat had turned in the summer heat.

As the sound of the caretaker's shuffle disappeared in the direction of the kitchen, he went across to the sideboard and poured himself a liberal glass of brandy. Despite his displeasure with his food, there was a look of quiet satisfaction on his face although his body was tense, as it always was before action.

He waited a further half-hour before he put down his glass and took up his candle and the heavy iron poker from the fireplace. How easy it all had been, he told himself as he made his way without sound up the main staircase. Yesterday, he had given a most excellent forgery of the registration of his birth to Mr Endicote who had peered at it, scrutinized it, read it twice and queried the strange name of the North American outpost where he had supposedly been baptized. Finally, he had pronounced it adequate proof and accepted that Daniel was Robert Calverley's legitimate son.

Damned old fool was none too pleased by it! Daniel thought, well aware that the lawyer had always mistrusted him. Now that he was Sir Daniel Calverley – well, almost titled but for the formalities – he would get rid of the man and choose someone more to his liking for the family lawyer; someone who would never question him about anything.

As the old caretaker had done but an hour previously, he paused on the landing, shielding his candle as he held it aloft so that the light fell on the attic stairs. He had but one last task to perform, Daniel thought – the destruction of the letter establishing Mascal's right to call himself a Calverley. Were the fellow in possession of such proof, he might seek to discredit the forgery. There was a great deal at stake and Mascal might consider it well worth a journey to North America, as would he if their positions were reversed.

Now that he had achieved everything he wanted, Daniel was not going to leave any loophole that could unseat him.

As he started to ascend the stairs, he thought how simple it had been to convince the guileless Eleanor that he must come back to Ortolans for a day or two to ensure that the unreliable stable lad was taking proper care of his hunter, and that the bailiff was taking adequate care of the estate.

A cobweb brushed his forehead when he was almost at the top of the steep uncarpeted stairway, and he paused to brush it away. This house was never as clean as he would like it – as he would have it, he thought. He would wait until Eleanor was his wife and then he would sack all the Pylbeam servants and some of the others as well. They did not like him. He sensed their enmity and it made him uneasy. Sometimes, he felt the house was his enemy too, beautiful but mistrustful.

A faint smile twisted Daniel's lips. Eleanor was beautiful but she, at last, was beginning to trust him. Only a little longer and he would be able to crush that moist red mouth, tear the fine clothes from her body and claim what was his.

Two more steps to go to reach the attic door – but Daniel never reached the top one. The worm-eaten oak boarding gave way beneath his weight, broke in jagged halves and sent him crashing to the landing below.

At the far end of the passage, old Fred Pylbeam shuffled towards the crumpled figure and bent stiffly to quench the flame of the still burning candle between wetted fingers. Holding his own candle aloft, he crouched for a moment, watching for a heartbeat as blood seeped from a gaping wound in the man's head. Slowly, he straightened up, a smile spreading over his wrinkled face.

'Dratted Pharisees!' he said, glancing up at the broken stair tread with a grin. 'Whosoever'd s'pose them liddle piskies 'ud do a thing like that!'

CHAPTER ELEVEN

Extracts from The Calverley Journal 1793–1876

5 MAY, 1793. *Eleanor and I were married on this, her twentieth birthday. The vicar was much confused by Johann's likeness to me, and my darling Eleanor may well have found herself married to the Best Man. A joyous occasion at which my much loved, adoptive father, the Valschintzkys, and many of our friends were happily present. We shall honeymoon in the Baron's schloss in Wachau.*

JULY, 1793. *We are home once more. It is doubtful if any couple could be more happily married than are we.*

AUGUST, 1793. *I have spoken to old Fred Pylbeam, and I am obliged to agree with Eleanor that he may well have tampered with the stair which caused Daniel's death. He knew of Jack's fears that Daniel intended to harm William. Jack was undoubtedly innocent. I can see no purpose in calling for a public enquiry. Daniel deserved his death and none of us would wish to see old Fred hanged as his executioner. I believe justice has been done.*

1 JULY, 1794. *The thatchers have arrived to re-roof the stables, coach house, barn and the oxen stalls. It is fortunate the weather remains dry. They will have completed their task before Johann and Karl visit us. They will travel via Bavaria and Westphalia to avoid the Revolution in France. Eleanor cannot bear to read the accounts in the newspapers of the daily massacres at the guillotine.*

AUGUST, 1794. *Father is enjoying this wonderful summer which he is spending with us. For much of the time, he is in the garden composing his new novel. Old Lady Calverley, who is now rising eighty, is his constant companion, but she is a little confused at times and calls my father, William.*

12 DECEMBER, 1794. *Eleanor and I returned to the peace of Ortolans having been in London this past week following my father's death. A great many of his literary friends attended his funeral. I shall sell Father's house in Dover Street as Ortolans has become my true home and we have Sackville Street for our sojourns in London.*

MARCH, 1795. *I have given Eleanor half an acre of Barn Field adjoining the orchard to make the herb garden she so much wants. The area is to be surrounded with a twelve-feet-high brick wall, and we shall have an iron gate leading into it from the stable courtyard.*

APRIL, 1796. *I joined the men fishing the meadow lake for pike. It proved most excellent sport and we caught two, one of 26lbs and one of 32lbs. I shall now be able to restock the lake with carp and tench which I shall buy from Parson Gould.*

10 JUNE, 1796. *We have been blessed with a son. Lady Calverley dotes on the baby who we shall call George. Johann is to be a godfather. Eleanor is in excellent health.*

OCTOBER, 1797. *At long last I have been able to build the cellars beneath the house and now have adequate storage for my wines. The Pylbeams have done an excellent job. Eleanor and Cook are delighted with the new pantry and still-room. The ceiling had to be reinforced with cross members of oak to support the heavy dining-room and library floors.*

AUGUST, 1798. *Great news indeed. Nelson achieved a resounding victory over the French on 1 August in Aboukir Bay. I have little doubt that this battle will take a well-deserved place in the annals of naval history. Now perhaps England will be able to restore her position in the Mediterranean.*

DECEMBER, 1798. *I am happy to record that Eleanor has quite recovered from the miscarriage she suffered last month. Little George has also recovered. He had been laid low these past weeks with the whooping cough, although this was not the cause of his prolonged indisposition. Eleanor discovered that Dora had been treating him with her mother's old cure – an unsavoury recipe of mice cooked and crumbled to a powder and fed to the child night and morning. Dora has been severely reprimanded and instructed by Doctor Poole that no matter how good her intentions, she is never again to assume his role. George might have been dangerously poisoned.*

21 MAY, 1801. *I gave permission today for Daisy to be buried in the saw-pit in Bluebell Wood. She was thirty-five years old. Meppom was close to tears when he asked me to break with tradition and allow him to have his faithful old carthorse buried in her skin, which I have agreed.*

3 MARCH, 1802. *Eleanor was safely delivered of our second son, Thomas. During her lying-in, I have hung the new French tapestries in the drawing-room and removed the portraits to the dining-room and gallery where they look very fine.*

MAY, 1803. *We are at war with France once more despite the Treaty signed last year at Amiens. Is there no end to Bonaparte's ambitions?*

AUGUST, 1804. *Spain has declared war against us. It would seem we are never to have peace in Europe!*

23 OCTOBER, 1805. *We are in mourning for dear Lady Calverley who died peacefully in her sleep this morning. We cannot therefore join in the celebrations for Lord Nelson's brilliant victory over the French fleet. We shall mourn his death, too. This is a sad day indeed.*

30 NOVEMBER, 1805. *I had not thought so soon to be mourning yet another death, but I received word this morning that my twin, Johann, was mortally wounded fighting Napoleon's hordes when they swept into Vienna. Would that I could comfort the Valschintzkys, but Napoleon seems set on adding most of Europe to his empire, and Eleanor will not hear of me going there.*

AUGUST, 1806. *We have finally found time to renew the apple and pear trees in the orchard. I have also planted a number of filbert trees as Eleanor is so fond of the nuts. Eleanor is teaching Thomas his alphabet. He is now four years old. The physician thinks it unlikely she will carry further children full term and so she dotes upon the boys, as indeed, do I.*

25 MARCH, 1807. *The bill for which I have campaigned so vigorously has been passed by Parliament. The slave trade is to be abolished in the British Empire. Our rejoicings are nevertheless tempered by the thought that my devoted negro, Peter, did not live to see his dream accomplished. Twenty-seven was too young to die, but his breed were not fashioned easily to withstand the bitter cold of our English winters. Eleanor placed flowers on his grave on Sunday.*

MAY, 1807. *Eleanor and I have decided to gift part of Prior's Mead where it abounds the churchyard, for the building of*

*a new brick rectory. Pylbeam estimates this will cost £182
or thereabouts. When the new incumbent is installed, I shall
retire Reverend Dicker who can continue to live in the Old
Parsonage in East Street.*

JUNE, 1808. *George's twelfth birthday which, but for the
timely intervention and courage of his tutor, John Pridmore,
might well have been his last. To mark the day, we had
made an expedition to Brighton to sample the sea bathing
so much enjoyed by our Prince. I had not realized the extent
of the swell, and the boy and I were carried away from the
bathing machine by the pull of the tide. I had inhaled such
quantities of water I was in no condition to assist my son,
but Pridmore, God bless him, plunged fully clothed into
the water and dragged George to safety. I shall reward him
suitably for his courage. Neither George's health nor his
enthusiasm have suffered, and I have praised him for his
manly attitude to this misfortune.*

FEBRUARY, 1812. *As if it were not enough to be fighting
endlessly in Europe, it seems we are now having to fight
our own kind. An organization of workmen who call themselves Luddites are burning and looting in the Midlands in
an attempt to disallow the new industrial machinery. They
seem unaware of the prosperity this could bring to the
country and think only of their loss of employment.*

OCTOBER, 1812. *The French are in retreat from Moscow.
It is rumoured that Napoleon's Grand army has been
destroyed. Is the self-styled Emperor's reign finally to topple?*

5 APRIL, 1813. *My darling Eleanor has confounded the
physicians and proved them wrong in their prognosis. In
her fortieth year she has given me my heart's desire, not
just one daughter but two. The twins are identical and
neither Eleanor nor the nurse can tell them apart. What*

cause for celebration! The church bells are already ringing from dawn till dusk for the defeat of Napoleon by Wellington. The King will almost certainly make him a duke. This is a happy day. We feel the church bells are also ringing for us.

DECEMBER, 1814. *What a magnificent year this has been – Wellington's victory at Toulouse, the abdication of Napoleon and the crown of France restored to Louis XVIII. Order is at last being restored in Europe.*

7 FEBRUARY, 1815. *Pridmore took George and Thomas to a prize-fight in Lewes where, to their gratification, young Bert Pylbeam won a splendid victory over his opponent.*

OCTOBER, 1815. *Mercifully, Napoleon's escape from the island of Elba has proved short-lived. He has been sent to St Helena, a lonely isle in the south Atlantic, 1200 miles off the coast of West Africa. It is doubtful if he will escape again.*

5 JANUARY, 1816. *Thomas shot his first otter today on the river close by the ford. The animal was well covered, doubtless having banqueted this winter on our salmon trout. I must ask the Howells to bring their otter-hounds, as these poachers will soon be breeding.*

29 JANUARY, 1820. *I hereby record the death of our Sovereign George III. I have disputed with Parson Gould that we should mourn the passing of His Majesty other than to observe the conventions as a mark of respect. His death cannot be looked upon as anything but a release following so many years of sickness. Grief in such circumstances can be no less than hypocritical.*

JUNE, 1821. *The newspapers have finally given an account of the death of Napoleon on St Helena on 5 May.*

1 JANUARY, 1823. *Thomas departed today for India where he will serve in the East India army. Eleanor was very brave when we saw him off at Tilbury. It is fortunate that George is content with our quiet life here in the country, and of course, the twins, little Georgie and Nellie, are a great comfort to her.*

SEPTEMBER, 1824. *Charles X has succeeded to the throne of France. I cannot believe he will make a good monarch.*

AUGUST, 1825. *Pylbeam has been busy this summer underpinning the great barn and the buttery. Joshua has replastered the wash-house. The gardens are particularly beautiful this year and I was pleased that Johann's son, Nikolas, should see Ortolans at its best when he visited us in July. Georgie and Nellie were charmed by the miniature of Nikolas's two-year-old son, Karl, and pleaded with their poor mother to give them a baby brother.*

JANUARY, 1830. *I am once more confined to my bed with dropsy of the chest, and was therefore unable to conduct the household to the church service in Detcham to mark the passing of the King. This is my second attack and Eleanor fusses. I have assured her that I shall make a full recovery as I did last time. The cold has been bitter since Christmas.*

SUMMER, 1830. *Thomas's home leave coincided with the coronation of William, our new King. Thomas remains a bachelor as does George, but tells us he has his eye on the young daughter of his colonel. It is to be hoped that one of our sons will marry soon as Ortolans needs an heir.*

There were no further entries in the journal until those made by Georgina and Eleanor Calverley.

JULY, 1863. *Young Mr Endicote has reminded us that now dearest George has passed away, it our duty to sort the papers in Grandfather's desk. This evening, after the last of the funeral guests departed, Nellie and I commenced the task and came upon this book,* The Calverley Journal. *It is thirty years since we lost dear Papa, so Nellie and I shall attempt this winter to fill in the many gaps in our family history. We shall try to be as accurate as possible for the future generations, as we still hope that before long, Thomas's wife Patience will produce a healthy child.*

In 1833, our father, Richard Calverley died aged seventy-five. Darling Mother joined him a year later. We knew that is what she wanted which lessened our grief. When King William died in 1837, we left for Africa and therefore missed the coronation of his young niece, Victoria. Georgie and I felt sorry for the child, burdened with such responsibility at so tender an age; but she has subsequently proved herself most capable and is much loved by her subjects. She still mourns the death of her beloved Albert two years ago.

1850 – Nellie and I went to India for the occasion of Thomas's marriage. His wife, Patience, has since had three children, all stillborn. So sad for her and Thomas.

In '51, Mother's faithful maid, Dora Pylbeam, died at the remarkable age of eighty-one.

As the Valschintzkys are distant relatives of ours, we feel we should record the birth of Karl Valschintzky's son and heir, Konrad, in 1857. In that same year we were much concerned for Thomas when we read in the newspaper accounts of the mutiny of the native troops throughout India and the horrifying massacre of British residents. Mercifully, Thomas was unscathed and was Mentioned in Dispatches for bravery in action. Peace was restored the following year and Georgie and I travelled once more to India. Our dear Thomas had been promoted to Colonel.

Sadly, Patience was recovering from a miscarriage. We brought home some magnificent specimens for our butterfly and moth collection.

In 1860, while Georgie and I were in Egypt, George had a water-closet installed by the scullery. A large cesspool was dug in the stable yard. He also had earth closets installed in the guest bedrooms. These are welcome additions. At the same time he had the kitchen and scullery walls tiled, and Joshua Pylbeam installed a new iron range. We also had a new stone sink to replace the copper in the wash-house together with an internal iron pump.

In June 1863 our dear brother, George, passed away. The physician gave the cause of death as Angina Pectoris. He told us that George had suffered lesser attacks of the heart for some time past, but had bravely withheld the information from us lest we made an invalid of him and forbade him his enjoyment of his shooting and other outdoor activities. We have cabled to Thomas.

SEPTEMBER, 1863. *Thomas has been home on compassionate leave although, of course, he arrived too late for poor George's funeral. Georgie and I have agreed to curtail our travels and remain here at Ortolans in order to manage the estate with the aid of our new bailiff, Rogers, who is very capable. Young Mr Endicote will take care of the financial management, Thomas himself being reluctant to give up his army career. As we have now entered our fifty-first year, it is perhaps not such a hardship for us to remain at home.*

APRIL, 1865. *We have said special prayers this morning for the poor American President, Mr Lincoln, whose assassination last week has shocked us all.*

JUNE, 1865. *We have had a visit from Baroness Theresa Valschintzky, with her little son, Konrad. The child is now eight, and following her late husband's wishes, the baroness is here to make arrangements for the boy to be educated at Eton. When he is old enough, he will return to enter the Austro-Hungarian army. Such a pretty child, who showed great interest in our butterfly collection. We think he is our first cousin twice removed.*

MAY, 1868. *The work on the new conservatory has been completed. How sad that George is not here to see his design materialized so effectively. Nellie and I have been in London this past week to visit Kew Gardens in order to list the names of tropical plants we shall put in the new room. Mr Endicote took tea with us at Browns Hotel and did not seem disturbed by our expenditure on the conservatory.*

20 JUNE, 1870. *Thomas has written to tell us that Patience is once more with child and that their physician is hopeful for a successful delivery this time. Georgie and I pray that it will survive and that it will be a boy. Thomas is no longer a young man and there will be no Calverley to inherit should he die without an heir.*

MARCH, 1871. *Joshua has completed the plastering of the brewhouse and has made a fine job of pargeting with a design of barley stalks and hops. The stone flags are a great improvement.*

We have received two cablegrams from Thomas, the first to announce the birth of a daughter who has been baptized Sophia; the second contained the sad news that poor dear Patience passed away three days later having succumbed to the puerperal fever. This is indeed a sad day. We shall sail at the earliest opportunity for India. Our journey will be mercifully shortened by our passage through the new Suez Canal.

10 MARCH, 1872. *Georgie and I arrived home last week. It is always a joy to come back to Ortolans, but we were both in tears when we said goodbye to Thomas and his dear little girl. We would gladly have brought her back to England to take care of her here, but Thomas will not be parted from her as she is his last link with poor dear Patience. He has an excellent Scottish nurse and an Indian amah, so the child is well cared for. Thomas has promised to bring her with him on his next home leave.*

15 JUNE, 1873. *Harry Pylbeam has used nearly all the pretty elm boards that came originally from Four-Acre Wood to face the walls of the stables. It is a big improvement. On Monday he will reline the loose boxes with chestnut and then Joshua can replaster Albert's quarters above.*

18 APRIL, 1874. *Nellie and I made the journey to London in order to attend the burial of that great missionary, the Reverend Livingstone, at Westminster Abbey. We shall reread his magnificent books on our beloved Africa.*

6 JULY, 1875. *We received a visit today from a gentleman from the War Office who broke the news to us of the death of our brother Thomas. Thomas had contracted enteric fever from which he did not recover. Our visitor will very kindly be making arrangements for little Sophia to be brought home to England in the care of the wife of one of Thomas's fellow officers. Her nurse will accompany her on the voyage, but will then be retiring to her home in Scotland.*

SEPTEMBER, 1875. *Georgie and I have arranged for Ada Pylbeam to take charge of the child when she arrives. Harry is redecorating the nurseries and a bed has been brought down from the attic for Ada to sleep in the room adjoining Sophia's. I have found a number of our old dolls and toys and the boys' old rocking-horse which Harry is to repaint. We must do everything we can to make sure our little orphaned niece will be happy here. Saddened though we are by the loss of our brother, we are very excited at the prospect of having the little girl to lighten our lives. Ada is a motherly soul, and we shall give Sophia all the love we once thought to give our own children. May God grant her a safe journey home.*

PART TWO

1888–90

CHAPTER TWELVE

1888

'We have decided that it is time you found a husband, Sophia!' said Aunt Georgie.

'A nice good-looking young man who will take care of you!' amplified Aunt Nellie.

'So we've accepted an invitation for you to attend the Lamberhills' Hunt Ball next month,' continued Aunt Georgie.

'We wrote yesterday!' said Aunt Nellie.

Sophia's hazel-green eyes widened as she stared partly in disbelief and partly in amusement at each of her aunts as they made their statements.

'But I don't want to get married!' she said. 'I'm perfectly happy as I am!'

Her two maiden aunts were identical twins, Georgie the elder by five minutes and therefore usually the first to speak. Both wore identical black dresses, black lace caps and high button boots, and were indistinguishable except by Sophia whose keen musical ear could detect a very slightly higher pitch to Aunt Nellie's voice. Even the family retainers could not tell one from the other and simply addressed either one as 'Miss Calverley' since their orders or wishes were likewise identical.

'We're gratified to hear it, my dear,' said Aunt Georgie, speaking for both of them. 'Nevertheless, we've realized we must look to your future.'

'Long-term future!' agreed Aunt Nellie. 'We're seventy-five years old, Sophia, and although the Good Lord has seen fit to bless us with excellent health, we cannot live for ever.'

'And then who would look after you? No, we must find you a husband.'

Sophia was shocked into a thoughtful silence. Her adored aunts had seemed immortal. She had been five years old when she had arrived at Ortolans House after the sudden death of her father in India. Standing in the front hall, her hand in that of the kindly housekeeper, she had watched with trepidation the two plump little women as they walked across the hall. Seeing them encased in their black bombazine dresses, she had wondered anxiously if they might be witches.

Prompted by the housekeeper, she had attempted a curtsy, but before her trembling legs could straighten, they had descended upon her with hugs, kisses and little cries of approval.

'What a pretty little girl!'

'Such beautiful curls . . .'

'Just like those horse chestnuts we used to collect!'

'And she has the Calverley eyes . . .'

'So like her poor papa!'

They had swept her into the drawing-room, each holding a hand, and Sophia had known she was loved by and would love these strange new relatives for ever and ever.

Until this very moment, she had never given a thought to the fact that there was no such thing as 'ever' – that one day they would die. Her childhood had been idyllic. The aunts were fanatical lepidopterists and Sophia's summers were filled with sunny days on the South Downs, in the hayfields and woods and lanes, chasing the butterflies and moths the two aunts collected. On cold wet days, the three of them would sit in the heated conservatory among the green ferns and pin out their specimens on trays which were placed in the drawers of the large cabinets Sophia could look at but, when she was still very young, never touch. How she had resented the long mornings in the old nursery at the top of the house when she was obliged to do her lessons with the elderly tutor the aunts had engaged for her, unmindful of the opinion of their neighbours that the little girl should have a governess rather than a man to instruct her.

'Nonsense!' Aunt Georgie had declared. 'We shared our brother's tutor and actually had a proper education.'

'The same as if we had been boys,' agreed Aunt Nellie.

'The child can have piano and singing lessons from the vicar's daughter!'

'Mabel Longhurst – although I don't approve of the way she races through the hymns . . .'

'And always has a drip on the end of her nose, poor thing!'

Sophia looked across the breakfast table at the two aunts with an almost unbearable rush of affection. Aunt Georgie was sitting at one end of the long oak refectory table beneath the portrait of her great-great-uncle, Sir Walter Calverley; Aunt Nellie was on her right, seated beneath the portrait of his son, William. Sophia took her place opposite Aunt Nellie beneath the portrait of her grandmother, Eleanor. Despite the sombre effect of the oak panelled walls, these pictures of her Calverley forebears, beautifully painted by talented artists, lent the room colour and an aura of historic continuity which even as a young child she had found reassuring. Even on a cold November morning such as this, an atmosphere of happiness pervaded.

Perhaps it was the aunts who took happiness with them into any room they entered, Sophia thought fondly. They were not only kind but great fun, seeing the humorous side of life and never regretting what could not be theirs. There were miniatures of them painted when they were young and they had been remarkably pretty girls. Despite this, neither had married although, they explained carefully to Sophia, this was not for lack of suitors. The difficulty had lain in the fact that since they could not be told apart, the young men had never been sure to whom they were proposing.

'They were in love with both of us!' Aunt Georgie explained.

'We did once consider tossing a coin to decide which of us would say "yes",' Aunt Nellie told the intrigued Sophia, 'but neither of us was willing to leave the other. So we both said "no"!'

'Perhaps we would have married if we had been wooed by twins!' Aunt Georgie had acknowledged.

'Because we did think it would be nice to have a husband, and we both wanted children.'

'But you have made up for that, Sophia.'

'Completely!' agreed Aunt Nellie.

Aunt Georgie rang the bell for the maid to bring some more tea. She smiled encouragingly at her niece.

'Anyone would think we were suggesting a prison sentence! And we thought you would be pleased, my dear.'

'We have written to the dressmaker in Brighton asking her to bring some materials.'

'To make you a beautiful ball gown . . .'

'And some fashionable day dresses. You'll meet a lot of young people of your own age so you will need some pretty clothes. Your Aunt Nellie and I feel very guilty that we have neglected you for so long.'

'We should have thought about your future years ago, but the time has passed so quickly! It seems only the other day you were still in short petticoats.'

'We should have kept on the London house instead of leasing it when our dear parents and then your Uncle George died; but because we have always been country girls and disliked city life, we selfishly kept you here at Ortolans with us.'

Sophia looked from one crestfallen countenance to the other and hurried round the table to hug each of them in turn.

'Of course you were not selfish. You know how I love Ortolans! There is nowhere else in the whole world I'd rather be, and I'm sure I would have hated London life. No one could have had a happier childhood and as to making friends – I have never needed other companions. I love you and I love this house and I never want to leave my home – *never*!'

The aunts glanced at one another uneasily. Sophia now was

standing at the open window, calling out across the garden
an instruction to the gardener who was not trimming the edges
of the lawn to her satisfaction. They were aware that, like all
the servants, indoor and out, old Jake adored Sophia, and
although it was unusual for the men to take orders from a
young, unmarried girl, they respected her judgement and the
natural air of authority with which she had slowly but surely
taken over the running of the estate as she grew up. Ever since
she had been quite small, if they did not comprehend what
exactly it was she wished them to do, she was well capable
of hitching up her petticoats and showing them how to do it!
But for all her bossy ways, when the well-being of the estate
was involved, Sophia's love for Ortolans, the fields, the woods,
the river and, not least, the villagers themselves, was never in
doubt.

'Oh dear!' Aunt Georgie murmured, repeating the familiar
regret. 'If only she had been born a boy!'

'She doesn't seem to realize . . .'

'We must remind her!' Aunt Georgie completed the sentence.
'Sophia, my dear, will you please return to the table. We have
something we must talk to you about.'

She waited whilst Sophia reseated herself opposite them.

'About Lady Lamberhill's ball where I must find myself a
husband?' she asked with a mischievous smile.

'No, dear, not quite that!' said Aunt Nellie.

'It's about the house, dear, being your home, I mean. Of
course, it is so for the present, but we mustn't forget Ortolans
does not belong to us.'

'We have been most fortunate that the real owner is a
foreigner who has no use for his English estate. We told you
long ago that . . .'

'Oh, I know all about the Austrian baron who inherited
when Papa died,' Sophia broke in, 'but he's hardly likely to
want Ortolans after all these years . . .'

Her voice trailed into silence as a horrifying thought struck
her. The baron had never seen Ortolans, and were he to do

so, it was all too probable he would fall under its spell. Without doubt, she thought, it was the most beautiful house in the whole world – a little demanding at times because, being so old and built in Elizabethan times, there were dark crannies and corners where the dust and cobwebs gathered, draughty passages and creaking stairs; but as if to compensate for its antiquity, it shone, glowed and smiled beneath the attentive care of the servants. Members of the Pylbeam family had cared for the house since the first Calverley had come to live here three hundred years ago.

It was the same outside the house. Ada's father, Dick Pylbeam, was forever coming up from the village to linseed oil the beams, to mend a leaded light, replace a lintel; it was sometimes weeks before he sent in his bill, and Sophia, who kept the household accounts, had frequently to remind him to do so. She was in little doubt he worked as much for love as for a living. He was always receptive to her ideas for enhancing the house. When she expressed a wish to enlarge the conservatory built by his father for her late uncle George, in order to make a sunny, sheltered winter garden for her aunts, he had transmitted her ideas so well that the new addition looked an integral part of the old building.

For the past four years the aunts had allowed Sophia to take over more and more of the running of Ortolans and the estate. Whilst they approved of her management of the house, they had been obliged to overcome their conventional objections to a young girl taking over the management of the land. As a child, Sophia had looked upon Rogers, the bailiff, as her best friend. Riding his cob beside her pony, he would listen gravely to her suggestions that the fallow ground to the south side of Bluebell Wood could if fenced in, be useful grubbing ground for Farmer Merrymore's pigs; that the planting of two weeping willows on the banks of the river would enhance the view from the house. He would discuss her suggestions seriously and as often as not, implement her ideas. In recent years, he had come to defer to her as if she were the squire.

Sophia kept the account books, the game books, and dealt with all the estate correspondence, and when thus engaged, remembered gratefully her tutor's lessons in mathematics and English. Although it was the aunts, as senior members of the household, who signed the letters and dealt personally with the family lawyers, Messrs Endicote and Endicote, it was to Sophia that any member of the staff came if they had a problem.

As the footman came into the dining-room with a rack of fresh toast, Sophia turned to look at the two old ladies, her green eyes thoughtful.

'I see no reason why the owner should want to interfere with the present arrangement. We run the estate very efficiently – the lawyer said so – and the baron receives a very handsome income from it.'

'Yes, I know, dear, but it isn't quite right to refer to Ortolans as *your* home.'

'Besides—' Aunt Nellie added quickly as she saw the tell-tale tightening of Sophia's mouth – always a sign that she was about to argue a point – 'when you marry, you will be living in the home your husband provides for you.'

Sophia was on her feet.

'I'm perfectly willing to find a husband if that is what you both want,' she said, 'but he will have to love me well enough to agree to live here. No one will make me leave Ortolans – no one!'

The idea of leaving this house which meant more to her than anything in the world was beyond contemplation. It was not simply a matter of Ortolans being a beautiful building – it was her home, her refuge, her friend. However unhappy she might be because of some trifling disappointment or mishap, she had but to walk through the quiet restful rooms or curl up on the window-seat in her bedroom and stare across the gardens and the river to the soft sweep of the South Downs, and her mood would become peaceful once more, her heart full of well-being. How was it possible, she wondered, that it had never before crossed her mind that she would not always live here? Now, in the space of five minutes, the aunts, who professed to love her, had propounded two ways by which she might be obliged to leave her home. I won't go, I'll never leave Ortolans, she vowed silently. Shocked beyond speech, she ran from the room before the aunts could see the threatening tears.

'Oh, dear, if only the child was more . . .'

'. . . More equable! said Aunt Nellie. 'She has always been very determined.'

'And far too impulsive!'

'Of course, she is still very young. Maybe we should not worry too much about the future.'

'If she falls in love, then the house won't seem nearly so important to her.'

Aunt Nellie nodded, relieved by this likely possibility. 'You do think she will attend Maud Lamberhill's ball?'

'Of course she will! Have you not noticed how she is growing up? When Ada can make her pay attention to her appearance, she is really quite lovely! I saw her looking at herself in that long mirror in the gallery last week when she thought herself unobserved!'

'Perhaps we have been at fault, allowing her to run wild the way we have.'

'Wearing those dreadful boy's breeches!'

'And riding astride her horse!'

'All by herself! We must be more strict with her in future, Nellie!'

'Yes, indeed!'

'It would be wrong to curb her too strictly!' Aunt Georgie murmured. 'She is such a happy child!'

'And she imparts so much happiness. They have been very happy years for us as well as for Sophia.'

The aunts were momentarily silent, remembering the picnics by the river; the jolly games of French cricket on the lawn; teaching Sophia to skate on the frozen village pond; decorating the house for Christmas; picking blackberries and rose-hips for Cook's jam; and always the exciting hunt for butterflies new to their collection; identifying them in the big encyclopedia and cataloguing them in the Record Book.

The door opened and Sophia came hurrying back into the room.

The brief time she had spent alone in the library had completely transformed her mood. By some extraordinary coincidence, the family journal she had been updating the previous evening had lain open at an entry made by her grandfather, Richard Calverley:

December 1794. Eleanor and I returned to the peace of Ortolans having been in London this past week following my father's death. A great many of his literary friends attended his funeral. I shall sell Father's house in Dover Street as Ortolans has become my true home and we have Sackville Street for our sojourns in London.

If her grandfather preferred Ortolans to his own home, she had but to find a husband who would do likewise. Seated at her grandfather's large oak desk, Sophia's eyes had lit with excitement mingled with relief. She could still fulfil the aunts' wishes to safeguard her future. As to this Austrian baron – it was inconceivable that after fourteen years he was suddenly going to appear, and even were he to do so, improbable that he, a foreigner, would want to bury himself in a remote village in England.

'I did not mean to upset you, truly I didn't!' she said, planting a kiss on each of the old ladies' cheeks. 'You must not worry about me, either of you. There really is no need. After all, can you imagine any suitor I might inveigle into marriage who would not of his own accord want to live here? It will all work out right, you'll see!'

The aunts looked relieved.

'Then you do understand, dear, that because of our advanced

years, it is our duty to look to the future,' Georgie said firmly. 'We are most fortunate that Maud Lamberhill is our neighbour. She says in her letter that Delia has quite refused to be presented. I think the poor child is going to turn out to be a bluestocking. Young men do not take to clever girls, however pretty they may be.'

'We were never wallflowers, were we, Georgie? Nevertheless, some unfortunate girls were never asked for a dance unless a young man was pushed to the invitation by his hostess. You're so pretty, Sophia, you'll never lack for partners!'

'Am I pretty, really pretty?' Sophia asked curiously. 'You're probably both biased because you are fond of me.'

'You're as beautiful as your dear grandmother!' said Aunt Georgie firmly. 'You have her colouring, Sophia. Of course, your father took after her, too. Poor Thomas's eyes were the self-same green. So sad to think that you were too young when he passed away that you cannot recall him.'

Since Sophia had only the barest memory of her father and none of her mother, she could not share her aunts' regrets. She had seen photographs in the family album – her mother in a beautiful lace wedding-gown with her father in full dress uniform looking every inch the military officer, standing ramrod stiff beside her. There was another sepia coloured, faded photograph of her father holding her – a tiny baby whose appearance was swamped by a trailing, floor-length christening gown. Sometimes Sophia felt guilty that she had only the haziest recollection of him. Both her parents had been buried in India, so their names were not on the family vault in the village graveyard – only on a brass memorial plaque inside the little Norman church where she and the aunts placed fresh flowers every Sunday. Her aunts had also had an elder brother, George, who had lived with them at Ortolans until his death several years before Sophia was born.

It was Uncle George who had ploughed up Stony Meadow adjacent to Bluebell Wood and planted kale as a habitat for the partridges he reared for his shoot. They now leased the shoot to the Lamberhills, although their own gamekeeper, Hutchins, was responsible for its welfare.

This unknown Uncle George's portrait showed him as fat and florid and Sophia was glad to learn that she resembled her handsome father.

Sophia, who knew practically every word of *The Calverley Journal* by heart, now recalled a further entry in her grandfather's neat, copperplate script:

> George and Thomas are so much enjoying the ha-ha with which I have replaced the row of laurel bushes where the garden joins Home Farm field. It affords us a perfect vista of the river. The boys and their friends play endless games of soldiers, jumping out of the ditch and scaring the life out of poor Dora when she takes the twins for a walk. Eleanor loves the sound of their laughter and insists that I built the ha-ha for the children's pleasure!

Sophia suddenly foresaw herself living at Ortolans with a medley of babies and nursemaids filling the large empty rooms and gardens with childish laughter and activity. The aunts loved children and the highlight of their year was the annual Christmas party they gave for the village children, planning the jellies and gingerbread men, the presents, the conjuror who came each year from Brighton, the games of 'Blind Man's Buff' and 'Pass the Parcel'. The aunts were in their element. When the carol singers called, they were always invited in, given lemonade and cinnamon cake and shiny threepenny pieces.

Sophia's friend, Delia Lamberhill, whose family lived in the nearby village of Newtimber, always spoke of her visits to Ortolans House with envy.

'You don't know how lucky you are!' she had said so many times that Sophia had long since ceased arguing the matter. There were thirteen Lamberhill children of varying ages, of which Delia was the second eldest daughter. 'I can never enjoy

a moment's peace and quiet as you do here, Sophia,' she said
enviously.

As she had grown older, Sophia realized there was another
reason why Delia envied her. Lady Lamberhill was a dictatorial, autocratic woman who dominated her large family and
all those who came into her orbit, including Delia's father, Sir
Sydney. Poor Delia could not be in her mother's presence for
more than a few minutes without some criticism being levelled
at her, not least because her head was always buried in a book.
Had Delia been able to ordain her own life, she would have
studied to become a great scholar.

But instead of having a tutor like Sophia's Mr Deakin, her
mother had sent her away to a boarding school where she
learned to sew and paint watercolours but little else. Sophia
was obliged to list for Delia every book Mr Deakin recommended her to read, and if it were not in the Lamberhills'
library, secretly to lend it to Delia.

Despite her lack of education Delia's avid consumption of
books, together with Sophia's assistance from Mr Deakin,
resulted in her becoming a scholar despite her mother's intentions. Now, it seemed, poor Delia like herself was to be found
a husband – and if Lady Lamberhill had her way, it would
mean someone titled. Lady Lamberhill was a social snob and
did little to hide her disappointment with her husband who
was perfectly content with a mere baronetcy. He, as much as
Delia, hated the social round they were obliged to live in
London during the Season and, given a choice in the matter,
would have stayed permanently in Sussex with his gun dogs
and fishing rods and gardens.

As a child, Sophia had loved her visits to Lamberhill Court
which usually took place when Delia's brothers were away at
boarding school. Elizabeth, Delia's elder sister, lived in London.
She had left home when she had come of age, and having
refused several proposals of marriage, now enjoyed a bachelor
existence, shocking her poor mother by running a refuge for
children of the poor.

Whilst the nanny and nursemaid took the five youngest Lamberhills for their afternoon perambulations round the estate, the two little girls had been left to enjoy each other's company in the care of Sophia's nursemaid, Ada Pylbeam. Sir Sydney, who knew of the aunts' passion for lepidoptera, would escort Sophia round the garden with her butterfly net, pointing out the clusters of red admirals on the buddleia bushes; the yellow underwing moths hiding under the leaves of the strawberry plants; or a solitary hummingbird moth hovering near the geraniums. Quite often, he would drive Sophia home in his gig, partly to exchange notes with the aunts but also to escape from his wife's vociferous criticisms. Comparing the atmosphere in Delia's house with that of Ortolans, Sophia gradually realized that it was the aunts' contented, loving natures which made people feel happy under their roof. Even Delia relaxed when she visited Ortolans and a grin would replace the scowl that so often marred her pretty features.

'Will I stay overnight at Lamberhill Court?' Sophia now questioned her aunts. 'Will you be coming with me?'

'Nothing has yet been arranged, my dear!' said Aunt Georgie, picking up Lady Lamberhill's letter. 'We are to drive over there this afternoon and discuss the details!'

'Such a wonderful opportunity,' murmured Aunt Nellie. 'They know so many people and your aunt and I have quite shamefully neglected to keep up with our family connections.'

Sophia was aware once more of their underlying anxiety and her better nature instantly resurfaced. There was nothing she would not do to prevent them worrying – even if it meant finding a husband!

'I'll ask Delia to lend us some of her mother's fashion journals,' she said. 'It'll be great fun choosing dresses. Will I have to put my hair up? Miss Longhurst said that the polka and the waltz are most popular dances. I shall have to practise the steps.'

The aunts beamed. They had feared that Sophia might not really want to come out, and yet their sense of duty to her was uppermost. Now it seemed as if she were becoming quite excited at the prospect of the Hunt Ball and a wardrobe of new clothes.

'Our darling Sophia has been a chrysallis long enough!' Aunt Nellie declared. 'It is time she emerged and became the loveliest butterfly of all.'

CHAPTER THIRTEEN

1888

'I know it is only a small victory,' Delia said wryly, 'but it's the first time I've stood up to Mama and she has given way!'

The two girls were in the music-room of the Lamberhills' London house in Grosvenor Square where they were awaiting the arrival of the woman who was supervising their deportment lessons. For the next half-hour they would be walking round the room with books balanced on their heads, and if they dropped one, it would mean a further five minutes added to the ordeal. The next half-hour would be spent practising curtsys after which would come an interval whilst they changed into their ball gowns and practised rising gracefully from chairs. Miss Bloomfield, their teacher, assumed the role of their prospective dancing partner and watched them with a beady eye whilst they inclined their heads in assent to her invitation to dance and then rose to do so. Her assumption of a deep male voice invariably reduced both Delia and Sophia to helpless giggles, made worse by her total lack of a sense of humour.

'You mean about not being presented?' Sophia asked now as she refastened the coil of thick chestnut hair into the nape of her neck.

Delia nodded.

'Not just that – about refusing to go through all this stupid "training to behave like a grown-up". I told Mama I would only obey her with good grace if you were with me.'

'Since you hate it all so much, it was not very kind of you to insist that I share the ordeal!' Sophia teased.

'But there's some point to it for you, dearest!' Delia said, sighing. 'You've got to find a husband and get married and have children. But I do not intend to. Papa told me last night that when I am thirty, I shall inherit a sum of money from my grandmother. Then I shall go to Girton and study for a degree. I certainly do not want a husband or children prohibiting me.'

Would a marriage curtail the life *she* wanted? Sophia asked herself. If she could have her way, it would continue exactly as it was, but a husband might expect to take over her unofficial role as controller of the estate. Ada was forever reminding her that it was quite improper for a young lady to be concerning herself with such matters. If she had a husband, Sophia thought, she could no longer counter such disapproval with the irrefutable argument that there was no-one else to do so.

A husband might also demand changes within the house, and this was something Sophia could not tolerate. She wanted Ortolans to remain exactly as it was for ever and ever – or at least until she died!

If she was to consider a husband, he would have to be no more than a loving companion. On the other hand, secretly she was looking forward to the Hunt Ball. This past year she had been occupied reading the romantic novels of Emily and Charlotte Brontë and consequently envisaged herself at the side of an exciting Heathcliff or an adoring Rochester. Such imaginary lovers haunted her dreams. The beautiful new frocks, for which she was enduring eternal fittings, now added to her anticipatory excitement. According to the dressmaker, she had the perfect figure – a tiny waist and a becoming bosom – not too large, but sufficiently rounded to do justice to the off-the-shoulder necklines. Delia's maid spent patient hours with the tongs coaxing the girls' hair into fashionable curls; but Delia showed little interest in the results.

'And with good reason!' she said to Sophia. 'If I should attract a suitor, Mama will fasten on to the poor young man like a leech and there will be endless hours of nagging if I do not accept a proposal. Poor Mama – she will see it as a positive disgrace if her second daughter remains a spinster like her first!'

'We must think of a suitable way of thanking Lady Lamberhill,' Aunt Georgie said when Sophia returned to the country.

'We are so indebted to her!' agreed Aunt Nellie. 'We would never have been able to launch you ourselves.'

Sophia laughed.

'I think Lady Lamberhill is more than happy to oblige you both,' she said. 'She tells her friends that she has taken me on as her protégée and in the next breath, adds that you are distantly related to one of our Queen's Ladies of the Bedchamber!'

'Goodness me!' said Aunt Georgie. 'She must be referring to your Great-Aunt Marjorie; her husband was second cousin to a Canning. We must look at the family tree, Nellie. However did Maud Lamberhill come by that information!'

'Delia's mama knows the family trees of all the nobility in the country,' Sophia said, smiling. 'She's a fearful snob. Delia says it is because she came from quite a humble background, and only married Sir Sydney because he had a title.'

'How very sad!' said Aunt Nellie.

'You must marry for love, Sophia!' said Aunt Georgie. 'It must be quite dreadful living with someone you don't care for. Our dear Queen set such an admirable example of happy family life. She still mourns her beloved Albert.'

'Yes, my dear, you must marry for love!' agreed Aunt Nellie.

But would she recognize love if she found it, Sophia wondered. She continued to wonder until the night of the Hunt Ball when Delia presented her eldest brother, Francis, to her.

'Francis quite refuses to believe that you are "the little Calverley girl",' she said laughing, and added mischievously: 'He described you as: "that untidy, tomboyish child" who came to play with me!'

'Your memory serves you well, sir!' Sophia said with a smile as she gazed into eyes that reminded her instantly of aquamarines. A brilliant, pale blue, they seemed to look right through her.

'Indeed, Miss Calverley, it does not. Will you forgive those remarks, so indiscreetly repeated by my reprehensible sister, and allow me to put my name on your dance programme?'

As Sophia handed Francis her card, which was already well marked with names, he wrote his own in one of the few remaining vacant spaces, and with a little bow, made way for her partner for the polka which had just commenced.

Over her partner's shoulder, Sophia observed the slim, fair-haired young man as he crossed the ballroom floor, and felt her heart thudding with excitement. Delia's eldest brother, she reflected, was older than most of the young men present, and must be in his early twenties. Though impeccably well-mannered and correct, the others were obviously as un-accustomed as Delia and she herself to grand occasions. Their conversation was stilted and self-conscious and consisted for the most part of apologies when they stumbled their dance steps. They were young boys, Sophia thought, whereas Francis Lamberhill was a self-confident young man, and by his manner, indicated that he found her attractive. She felt beautiful in her new silvered lace gown with her hair freshly washed and curled, and her thick chestnut ringlets securely fastened behind each ear with a jewelled clip. Her long white evening gloves were spotless, and round one wrist, she wore for the first time the lovely diamond bracelet which the aunts had told her was her grandmother's. But there were many pretty girls in the room, one especially charming brunette with sparkling brown eyes who, she noted, was flirting quite openly with Delia's handsome brother.

Hurriedly, she forced herself to listen to the music, aware that she had twice missed her step and caused her poor perspiring partner to stumble. He was still apologizing as he led her back to her chair adjoining that of one of Delia's elderly relatives who was present as a chaperon.

She was barely seated before Francis Lamberhill appeared at her side.

'I am sure you would like a cool drink, Miss Calverley!'

he said easily. 'If you will permit me, Mrs Amsoft, I will take this young lady to find some refreshment.'

Sophia was immediately conscious of the pressure of his gloved hand beneath her arm as he led her towards the dining-room.

'I make no apology for seeking to monopolize you,' he said in an undertone. He took two glasses of fruit punch from a passing lackey and as he handed one to her, she was once again conscious of the penetrating blue eyes gazing into hers. 'Delia told me you would be present tonight and that I would find you much changed, but she did not inform me that you had grown up to be so beautiful!'

The band was now playing a waltz and as Sophia glanced at her programme, he said:

'This is my dance, I think. Shall we sit it out and become better acquainted? I'm not the best of dancers, I fear.'

Taking her agreement for granted, he led her to a relatively quiet corner at the far end of the room.

'I am hoping shortly to make up a party to go to Brighton races,' he said. 'Delia informs me that you have never attended a race meeting. Would you care to join us?'

'Oh, I'd love to go!' Sophia said eagerly. 'That is, if my aunts will give their permission.'

'Did you know that your eyes glow when you are excited? I have been trying to fathom whether they are green or hazel.'

'Both!' laughed Sophia happily. She was no longer in any doubt that she had made a conquest and was gratified to realize that she had the attention of the best-looking man in the room. 'My aunts call them angel-shades – because they are the same mix of colours as in the wings of the angel-shade moth.'

She detailed her aunts' hobby and Francis said at once:

'Then I shall call upon these two delightful ladies and ask if I may see their rare collection.'

This feeling of excitement she now felt could well be the beginnings of love, Sophia thought, and how happy the aunts would be to receive this handsome young man at Ortolans!

As she expected, the aunts were delighted when, two days later, Francis Lamberhill paid them a call. Within minutes, he charmed them with his interest in their hobby and, more importantly, impressed them by the respectful yet obvious interest he showed in Sophia.

'His eyes followed you wherever you went, dear child!' said Aunt Georgie after he had left.

'Completely smitten!' agreed Aunt Nellie with a sigh. 'And *so* handsome, Sophia.'

'And eligible,' continued Aunt Georgie. 'The Lamberhills made a fortune from investment in the railways, and this young man is the eldest son.'

Delia, too, gave grudging approval. She had come to spend an afternoon with Sophia. The heavy rain had made it impossible for the two girls to go out and they had automatically repaired to the childhood den they had created in the attic. The aunts had allowed them to make use of the sagging old *chaise-longue* with its broken springs and worn purple velvet cover, and the rosewood whatnot with a missing leg which they had discovered in the storeroom in the cellar. The aunts had not allowed them to remove the Indian memorabilia belonging to Sophia's father which had been temptingly stacked on the stone shelves. The attic had been a perfect setting for their dolls' tea parties and games of make-believe. Now that they were older, it had become a place for the exchange of confidences.

'I suppose if you must marry anyone,' Delia said, 'Francis will make as good a husband as any, and we'd become sisters-in-law. More importantly, you wouldn't have to move miles away from home . . . at least, I imagine Francis would buy a house not too far from Lamberhill Court.'

Sophia's heart missed a beat.

'Francis would not have to buy a house,' she said abruptly. 'We could live at Ortolans. I could not possibly leave the aunts on their own!'

'I suppose not!' agreed Delia. 'But Francis might want his own home!'

Sophia's chin lifted.

'I'll worry about that when and if your brother proposes!' she said evasively. 'He might not – and anyway, it is much too soon for me to know if I really love him.'

'Well, he certainly loves you!' Delia said as she prepared to leave. 'He talks of nothing else to the point where we are all becoming wearied of your name!'

As soon as Delia had departed, Sophia went to her room and, with the assistance of her disapproving maid, Ada, she changed into her riding clothes. She had, in her early teens, abandoned the full-skirted habit, silk hat and veil, and on her rides round the estate, worn the boy's corduroy breeches and shirt she had discovered in a tin trunk in the attic. She had, furthermore, discarded the side saddle and rode astride her horse. The grooms and estate workers had long since become accustomed to seeing her thus mounted and unconventionally attired. Avoiding the village or roads where she might be recognized by their neighbours, Sophia could give vent to the physical energy with which good health had blessed her, and rode fast or ambled through the countryside as the mood took her.

As always, Ada protested.

'T'aint right, Miss Sophia. Supposin' Mr Lamberhill were to see you!'

Sophia laughed as she pulled on a rough-spun jersey.

'I very much doubt if I could do wrong in Francis's eyes!' she boasted. 'Delia thinks he is certain to propose. She said he was terribly jealous because his friend, John Akers, is going to invite me to his family's Christmas party, and several of his other friends from university have admired me to him.'

'Pride comes before a fall, Miss Sophia. Happen you was the prettiest girl at the Lamberhills' party, but looks doant mek you a young lady nohow – not if'n you doant behave like one!'

'I don't see why I should give up what I enjoy just to please Mr Francis Lamberhill!' Sophia rejoined tartly.

But for the first time in her life, she did see the advantage of being attractive to the opposite sex. She could twist Francis round her little finger and it cost her no more than a smile. Being female did not, after all, mean she had no power to shape events as she pleased. The thought of the power her beauty might lend her was exhilarating, and one she had not before consciously realized.

'If Sir Sydney or Lady Lamberhill were to see you in them clothes,' Ada muttered anxiously, 'they'd say as how you wasn't a suitable wife for Mister Francis!'

Sophia grinned.

'Sir Sydney wouldn't mind! He's quite devoted to me.'

There was no denying it, Ada thought, as she picked up Sophia's discarded dress and petticoat from the floor. No wonder her young mistress was so headstrong. Ever since she'd been a little bit of a thing, she had charmed those around her. There was not one of the servants, estate workers or villagers who did not adore her, and indeed, respect her. They knew, as did Ada, that her interest in them was genuine. No question of: 'And how are you today, Mrs Green?' without stopping to listen to the answer – as some of the gentry were known to do. Ever since Miss Sophia had been a little girl, it had always been the same. There was the time when Bert Hutchins's youngest had been dying of consumption and Miss Sophia, who was visiting with her aunts, went straight home in the carriage and back again to give the poor child her beautiful new doll. There was the summer night she'd not slept in her bed and Ada had found her next morning in the wood nursing Merrymore's prize new ram which had got tangled up in a snare, despite she hated the brute. 'He might have died of fright all on his own,' Miss Sophia had said, 'and Master Merrymore's been counting on Billy to give his sheep more twins.' As Sophia grew older and took over some of the Mistress's household duties, she was considerate to the servants, never docking their pay if they wanted time off to nurse a sick relative or were ill themselves. She knew all their names and family histories!

Perhaps it was only Ada herself – and to a lesser degree the two Misses Calverley – who saw the other side of Sophia's nature. She could be wilful, headstrong and impulsive, never stopping to think first before she acted, and she could fly into a paddy if things weren't done the way she wanted. Ada stood at the window watching her young mistress crossing the drive, swinging her arms as she disappeared into the stable yard. It was not surprising if she were a little spoilt, Ada told herself. Naturally enough, the two old ladies doted on their niece; and she, Ada, was equally devoted, albeit she did try from time to time to put some sense of right and wrong into her pretty head. So far as Ada could see, things were right if Miss Sophia wanted it so and were wrong if she didn't!

Sophia herself was well aware that her aunts as well as Ada disapproved of her riding unaccompanied by Rogers or one of the grooms, but today was one of the days when she wished to be alone. She could see no reason why, simply because she was a girl, she must have someone to protect her. Her mare, Silver Mist, was perfectly reliable and she was hardly likely to get lost! There was not a meadow, a spinney, a copse, a footpath with which she was unfamiliar. She knew every badger's sett, every rabbit warren, fox's earth; where to look for the ospreys, the ortolans' nests, the kingfishers, the otters. This outside world was as familiar to her as was every corner of the rambling house in which she had grown up.

This afternoon, Sophia rode slowly down to the river. The flow of the water would, she knew, soothe her. A grey November mist was drifting over the surface like wisps of smoke, curling amongst the reeds on the far bank. She sensed from the cold air whipping the colour into her cheeks that there would be frost in the night, and as she dismounted, she pulled the oversize grey jersey more closely about her. Several yards further up the river, she heard the splash of an otter or a moorhen, and a grebe scuttled from the rushes by her feet. Then there was silence.

The sound of horses' hoofs broke the stillness. It was so unusual for a horseman to be seen in this private part of the Calverley estate that Sophia looked up, retaining her hold on her mare's reins as she, too, heard the unfamiliar noise. Within minutes, a large roan stallion came through the mist, astride which sat an upright figure in the conventional garb of an English gentleman. The face beneath the top hat was that of a man not yet middle-aged but long past boyhood. He had fair hair and sideburns and a neat military moustache.

He drew to a halt and stared down at Sophia.

'Am I on the right path to Ortolans House, boy? Don't stand there gaping. I'm no ghost!'

His face broke into a smile for, mistakenly, he supposed the figure looking up at him anxiously to be that of a superstitious stable boy or groom who had been startled by his appearance in so out of the way a place.

Sophia pointed in the direction of the house.

'The landlord told me this was a short cut, but I'll wager I'd have ridden far swifter by the road. Well, since you are idling your time away here, you can make yourself useful and hold my horse whilst I relieve myself.'

He slid to the ground and handed the reins to Sophia. 'Are you a deaf mute or have you just lost your tongue?' He laughed once more and, moving a few paces away, answered the call of nature against one of the big oak trees.

Aghast, Sophia turned her head back to the river whilst struggling to keep control of the two horses.

'Nice little mare you have there!' the stranger said as he returned to remount his own steed. 'Well, boy, I scarcely think you have earned it, but seeing that I am in a good humour, take this for your pains!'

Astride his horse once more, he took a sixpenny piece from his pocket and tossed it to Sophia.

Suddenly, Sophia's sense of humour overcame her dismay.

It was her own fault that she had not immediately told the stranger she was a girl and no stable lad. Grinning, she reached down, took up the coin she had failed to catch, and putting it in the pocket of her breeches, touched her cap.

'I do thank 'ee, surelye, sir!' she said in her best imitation of Ada's Sussex dialect.

'Ah, so you can talk, you young tatterdemalion! I never saw such a scarecrow! I must assume you handle horses with more efficiency than your attire would suggest. Good day to you, boy. Time I was on my way!'

Sophia fought the desire to mount her horse and outride the stranger – which would not be difficult, she thought, for although he had an excellent seat, he did not know the terrain as she did. But she curbed the temptation since she had no knowledge of the stranger's identity and the moment she rode into the stableyard, one of the grooms would be certain to address her as Miss Calverley!

She remained by the river for a further hour, by which time it was becoming so cold that she was obliged to retrace her way home. Dusk had fallen and through the misty air, she noticed that lights were burning in the drawing-room. This, she realized, must mean that the visitor was still with her aunts. Handing her mare to the groom, she used the servants' staircase to the top landing, and hurried to her room. Ada was awaiting her.

'Wheresumdever have you been, Miss Sophia!' she clucked, pulling Sophia's cap from her head and removing her damp jersey. 'You aunts is in a right pucker. I've orders to send you downstairs fast as ever I seed you.'

Sophia shook her head so that her dark red curls cascaded around her shoulders.

'If it is to meet the visitor, then I cannot do so, Ada.' Her face creased into a grimace at the memory of their encounter by the river. 'I cannot explain now, but it would be most dreadfully embarrassing.'

Ada's plump figure quivered with agitation.

'I reckon you justabout ain't got no choice, Miss Sophia. Adam says as how the gen'leman is a distant kinsman for all he be an Austrian Frenchy with a name I can't get my tongue to nohow.'

'Well, I'm not going to meet him,' Sophia said firmly, 'not even if he's the Prince of Wales! Besides, my aunts are quite capable of entertaining him, whoever he is!'

Ada threw her apron over her head and in a voice that was almost a wail, said:

'You doant unnerstand, Miss Sophia. Adam were serving 'freshments and heard him a-tellin' your aunts that he were a Calverley and that like as not, he were a-claiming Ortolans House for hisself!'

CHAPTER FOURTEEN

1888

'My dear child, whatever kept you!' said Aunt Georgie.

'We were getting worried!' said Aunt Nellie.

Sophia dropped each a curtsy and without looking at the third person in the room, she replied:

'I am so sorry. I was out riding and it took me a little time to change my clothes!'

Aunt Nellie took her hand.

'Never mind, dear, you are here now. Let me introduce you to Baron Valschintzky – our kinsman – who also has rightful claim to the name of Sir Konrad Calverley. Our niece, Sophia!'

There was no avoiding the confrontation, but Sophia kept her head dipped as she curtsyed.

'It is a trifle confusing without our family tree to guide you,' the baron said in a friendly voice. 'Your grandfather, Sir Richard Calverley, and my great-grandfather were twins, identical twins like your delightful aunts. Obviously the tendency runs in the family . . .'

He broke off in mid-sentence as reluctantly Sophia raised her head. His expression was puzzled.

'We have met one another before, Miss Calverley, have we not? I seem to recognize—'

'I doubt we have met, sir,' Sophia broke in hurriedly, the colour rushing to her cheeks. 'I have spent only a few weeks in London and as I have only just come out, we cannot have met one another socially.'

Konrad's face was no longer bewildered. Despite the refinement of Sophia's accent, he had recognized her voice – that of the scruffy stable lad by the river! But at the same moment of recognition, he recalled also that in the presumption that she was a boy, he had committed an unpardonable offence in this respectable young lady's presence.

'I must be mistaken – forgive me!' he said, and saw the look of relief flood Sophia's face. A delightfully pretty face at that! he thought. She was very young, of course, her thick coppery tresses gathered with a ribbon in as childish a style as it was charming. It was almost impossible to imagine her now in over-large breeches and stable boy's rough-spun jersey, those beautiful curls tucked into an outsize cloth cap.

The smile returned to his face, and with a mischievous desire to see the blush return to hers, he said:

'I trust you enjoyed your ride, Miss Calverley. I came by the river path which, though lonely, was quite picturesque.'

So he had certainly recognized her, Sophia thought, but he was not going to tell tales. Nor indeed was it in his own interest to do so, she told herself indignantly.

If Adam were to be believed, this man might be here to lay claim to Ortolans and must therefore be her enemy, which, she thought as she studied him covertly, was a pity because he was quite excessively handsome, especially when his brown eyes sparkled as they now did with contained laughter.

'Baron Valschintzky is sojourning in the neighbourhood, my dear,' Aunt Georgie informed her. 'His decision to visit us was made on the spur of the moment else he would have written to Mr Endicote to advise us of his plans. Although his home is in Austria, he is shortly to be married to a young lady who has half-English nationality and wishes to have a home in this country. The baron has come to tell us that he will be bringing his fiancée to meet us tomorrow when she arrives from London, and it will be for her to decide if she would like to live here.'

It was only a few months since Sophia had talked herself out of believing that the ethereal Calverley heir might suddenly put in an appearance. She had in her assessment of the odds never once thought that he might have an English wife who would want to live at Ortolans. The prospect was so horrifying that she at once rejected it.

'Not here, at Ortolans!' she protested furiously.

'But, my dear!' Aunt Georgie remonstrated quickly, 'as you know, the baron has most kindly permitted us to continue living here all these years since your poor father passed away, but naturally, the estates are his to manage as he pleases!'

'But you and Aunt Nellie and I . . .'

'I do assure you, Miss Calverley, I have no intention of rendering you homeless!' the baron said quickly. 'The house is large enough, from what I have glimpsed, to accommodate us all. My future wife and I will spend a great deal of our time abroad and in all probability, we shall reside in London for the Season. But all this we can discuss tomorrow when my fiancée is here. I am sure you will all get along very well and she is most anxious to meet you. Now I must take no more of your time. I have greatly enjoyed our meeting and only regret that I have not made your delightful acquaintance many years ago.'

He bowed to the aunts and, continental fashion, kissed their hands. As he touched his lips to Sophia's hand, he looked into her eyes and said:

'Since you are well accustomed to riding, Miss Calverley, perhaps I may encroach on your time at some future date and ask you to ride round the estate with me? Now I shall return by the road lest I lose myself by the river!'

As Adam showed the visitor to the door, Sophia collapsed into a chair.

'Such a charming young man!' Aunt Georgie said.

'And well intentioned, I am certain of it,' Aunt Nellie agreed. 'Did you not think he bears a marked resemblance to the Calverleys? He reminds me of your grandfather, Sophia.'

Sophia finally found her voice.

'It doesn't matter who he resembles,' she said. 'What matters is that he intends to come and live here – with us! Can't you see what this would mean? The house would no longer be ours!'

Aunt Georgie sighed and Aunt Nellie looked distressed.

'We would have to alter our ways, I dare say, but we will just have to adapt to the circumstances.'

'It was remiss of us not to make other provision for our old age!' said Aunt Georgie.

'We always knew this could happen, but I must say, it does come as a little bit of a shock!'

'A shock!' Sophia echoed, her voice filled once more with indignation. 'It is a catastrophe, and I think we should write at once to Mr Endicote to ascertain whether this Mr Valgrinsky is within his rights.'

'Valschintzky, dear, and he is a baron,' Aunt Nellie said gently.

'I don't care what he is!' Sophia cried. 'I don't want him spoiling our life here. Ortolans belongs to us!'

'Come now, dearest,' Aunt Georgie reproved gently. 'We must accept the inevitable, if such it turns out to be, with good grace. If it is God's will, then so be it!'

'It isn't God's will!' Sophia cried, close to tears. 'It is *his* will and I shall make sure his precious fiancée takes an instant dislike to the house. Then he'll have to change his mind!'

On the following morning, however, Sophia found herself taking an entirely opposite stance to the one she had intended. The baron arrived at midday in a hired clarence with a young woman at his side who he introduced as his fiancée. Sophia took an instant dislike to the Honourable Miss Lavinia Challinor. Although Miss Challinor's features were faultless, her appearance was marred by a downward droop of her mouth which, Sophia told herself, undoubtedly mirrored the petulance of her nature! Having complained of the dust, smoke and soot that she and her maid had been obliged to endure on the train journey from London, she declined to take cordial with Sophia and the aunts and insisted upon wasting no time in touring the house.

Sophia led her visitors first to the library – her favourite room and one which, because she so loved it, she believed the haughty Miss Challinor could not fail to approve.

As the aunts so often reminded Sophia – albeit gently – her nature was far too impulsive.

'You really must try to cultivate the habit of thinking first before you act!' Aunt Georgie would remonstrate.

'We know you would never have done such a thing if you had thought first,' Aunt Nellie would compensate.

Only as she opened the door did she remember that she did not want Miss Challinor – nor indeed the baron – to approve of anything at Ortolans; but pride now superseded common sense.

'We use this room more than any other,' she announced. 'In the evenings, my aunts sit there by the fireside where they are close to the cabinets containing their butterfly collections. I usually sit at the desk as I have work to do. It is always beautifully warm here in the winter because, as you can see, the walls are panelled.'

'I always think panelling darkens a room,' Miss Challinor said blankly.

Sophia was about to argue the point when the baron intervened:

'What a magnificent collection of books!' He walked across to one of the shelves and withdrew a well-worn, leather-bound volume. '*A Journey through Portugal* by Sir Greville Mascal,' he read aloud.

'Oh, that's one of twenty-five books written by my grand-father's father. He was an author of some repute. His publisher always made him a presentation copy of each first edition, so the set is complete,' Sophia explained.

The baron ran his hand thoughtfully over the surface of the tooled leather.

'So this is the man who adopted one of the Calverley twins. I was told the story of the earthquake many years ago, but I had forgotten the man's name. How very interesting! I must find time to read his books, this one in particular. That other twin was, I think, my great-grandfather.'

'Then it would interest you to see the portrait in the dining-room presently,' Sophia said, warming not only to this man's genuine interest, but responding to the intimacy that seemed to have sprung up between them as he nodded eagerly.

'Are we not wasting time?' Miss Challinor stated in a voice that barely disguised her irritation. 'Do not forget that we have a luncheon appointment, Konrad.'

'But of course, my dear.' But as he replaced the book on the shelf, Sophia was intrigued to see the quizzical expression on his face and the suspicion of a smile as he met her gaze.

The drawing-room seemed, at first, to be more to Miss Challinor's liking; but as she glanced round the room it was not long before she found something to criticize. She pointed to the old spinet that stood to one side of the large window with its five mullioned casements overlooking the rose garden.

'We should have to get rid of that!' she said in a disparaging tone. 'I would want to put my piano there.' She turned to address Sophia. 'My uncle is giving us a new Blüthner as a wedding present.'

'But the spinet has always stood there,' Sophia protested. 'It belonged to my grandmother, and my aunts and I still play it.' With an angry toss of her head, she lead the visitors through to the dining-room.

As they moved from room to room, Miss Lavinia Challinor's list of complaints grew. The panelling in the dining-room would have to come out and the walls must be papered; the fireplace in the drawing-room smoked and a new chimney would be required; the leaded-light windows were old-fashioned and must be replaced with modern stained glass. Even the staircase with its beautiful, well-trodden polished oak treads she declared to be quite dangerous and would require rebuilding and carpeting. Nothing, it seemed, was to her liking.

Following silently behind her, Sophia's indignation mounted. To hear her beautiful home so maligned was to hear an old, dear friend castigated. She only succeeded in holding her tongue in its defence because she was convinced that since there was so much Miss Challinor disliked, she would decide not, after all, to make Ortolans their English country residence.

To her dismay, the visitor, having finally condescended to take a glass of cordial with the aunts, announced in her loud, clear voice: 'If there is adequate stabling for my horses, this place will suit the baron and me quite well – once the alterations are completed, of course!'

It was rare for Sophia to hold her tongue when she was outraged; but on this occasion, her emotions were so profound she was rendered speechless. Anger, indignation and panic warred with a refusal to accept that the worst had happened, and that she might have lost her beloved home. With an effort she concentrated on the comments the woman she now looked upon as an intruder was making to her aunts.

'. . . it occurred to me that at your time of life, you will doubtless prefer not to be present whilst the builders are working. They make such a noise and mess, do they not? My fiancé and I were enquiring in the village and I understand there is a house to be leased not far from here – it belongs to former neighbours of yours called Howell. I am sure we could arrange for you to move in there, can we not, Konrad?'

At least the baron had the grace to look embarrassed, Sophia thought, but to her dismay, he merely nodded.

'Of course, if the Misses Calverley and their niece wish it,' he said.

For a second his eyes met Sophia's and he saw at once that the idea of removal did not appeal to her – indeed, those remarkable green eyes of hers were ablaze with anger.

'You could return when the builders leave,' he proffered, unable to stomach the look of distress now apparent on the faces of the two old ladies. 'I noticed that the east wing has a good many rooms on two floors. Perhaps we could arrange for the builders to make a private suite of rooms for you there.'

The aunts looked relieved, but Sophia was not only very

far from placated – she was appalled. Before she could speak, Miss Challinor said brusquely:

'We can decide on such particulars when the house has been made fit to live in.'

Despite his desire to please his fiancée, Konrad Valschintzky considered her comment had been most rude.

'My dear, I find it quite delightful as it is!' he said quietly. 'Now that you have finished your cordial, I think we should be on our way.' He turned to the aunts. 'We are taking luncheon with friends of Miss Challinor's in Brighton and it would be most impolite of us to be late.' He bowed to the aunts and as before, kissed their hands. 'We shall leave you in peace until the spring,' he said. 'Then we shall return to meet with the builders and see the gardens which I am sure are delightful. We will be returning to Vienna next week where, as you may know, it is our Season. Come, Lavinia, we must not disturb these kind people any longer.'

As Sophia watched their carriage disappear down the gravel drive, she let go her breath and turned to her silent aunts.

'I thought her quite horrible! And a fearful snob! She reminded me of Lady Lamberhill the way she kept saying this or that was not *bon ton* – as if we had no good taste whatever! She wants to change Ortolans and I won't let her. Not fit to live in! Modernize, indeed! It would look perfectly fiendish filled with modern monstrosities.' Her voice rose. 'Despite what that man said, I know she wants to turn us out. Well, I won't go, I won't!'

As she paused for breath, one of the aunts tapped her hand gently with her fan. The other, in whose lap Sophia had now buried her hot face, stroked her hair.

'We thought the young man very agreeable, dear, and so personable!'

'All the more reason why he should not marry a horrible woman like Miss Challinor!' Sophia replied tartly.

'I fear there is not much we can do about the situation,' Aunt Georgie vouchsafed. 'We will write to Mr Endicote, but we have always known the distaff side of the family cannot inherit.'

'Besides which, Sophia, you will not be so badly affected. If you marry your nice Mr Lamberhill in a few years' time, you would be living elsewhere in any event.'

'No, I would not!' Sophia declared. 'If Francis proposed marriage to me, it was my intention to make my acceptance conditional upon his agreeing to live here with us!'

Unaware of her aunts' astonished faces, she stood up saying: 'Even if that man does own Ortolans, I don't see why he has to live in this house. To start with, his horrible fiancée doesn't like it, and there must be hundreds of other houses she'd prefer. Since they seem to think the Howells' old house, The Grange, is fit for us, why don't they go and live there themselves? Besides, I cannot believe Papa would have countenanced such a thing. You have lived here all your lives – seventy-five years! – and you would positively hate being anywhere else. The man may be a baron, but he is no gentleman insulting us in such a way!'

'Come, come, Sophia,' Aunt Nellie said reproachfully. 'Of course you are upset – we are, too – but it would be quite wrong to condemn the young man. We must not forget that he is our kinsman and a Calverley and we know him to be your father's rightful heir.'

'And you must not accuse him of ungentlemanly behaviour, Sophia,' added Aunt Georgie. 'His manners are impeccable and I thought him charming and intelligent.'

'He was educated in England, you know,' Aunt Nellie said gently. 'That's why he speaks such faultless English. You would not know him for a foreigner.'

Aunt Georgie nodded.

'I would have no objection to sharing the house with him if that is what he wishes. We should have quite sufficient rooms in the east wing, would we not, my dear?'

Sophia jumped to her feet.

'But it wouldn't be *our* home any more. Don't you see? He

and his wife would be running it the way *they* wanted. Anyway, I couldn't bear it if I could not go into the library when I wished, or sleep in my own bedroom or . . . or . . .'

For the second time in her life, words failed Sophia. She was as greatly shocked by her aunts' apparent acceptance of the situation as by the prospect itself. One thing was now certain – she must abandon her plan to invite Francis to live at Ortolans. He could hardly be expected to welcome it now! But *she* would not abandon Ortolans . . . not for Francis, for the baron, for the aunts, for anyone!

'Please write to Mr Endicote this very minute!' she begged her aunts. 'Perhaps Papa's will has some clause that will stop the baron taking our home away. Perhaps the baron is an impostor. There was an impostor in the past who tried to claim the Calverley estate. Don't you remember?'

Momentarily diverted by this reference to family history, Aunt Georgie said:

'Yes, dear, it was a long time ago – before your aunt and I were born. Daniel, his name was. He was born out of wedlock so he wasn't a true Calverley.'

Aunt Nellie nodded.

'He died in suspicious circumstances but nothing was ever proved.'

'I know!' said Sophia. 'It's all in the family journal.'

In recent years, she had taken over from the aunts the responsibility of keeping up the journal which had been in existence for five generations. It had been started by her great-grandfather, Sir Walter Calverley, and was not simply a dry list of births and deaths but included personal comments, about the house, the weather, friends, family pets, hobbies, pastimes. Sophia was fascinated to read these revelations of long dead ancestors – their hopes, dreams, loves, despairs, griefs. She found it easy to express herself on paper and it amused her to think that one day, perhaps a hundred years hence, some future Calverley would read her thoughts! There would certainly be something to write about now, she thought furiously as she left the aunts with pen, ink and paper, composing a letter to the family lawyer. She hurried upstairs followed by Ada, who tut-tutted as her young mistress recounted the morning's events whilst pacing the floor of her bedroom.

'I doant see as how you can do aught, Miss Sophia!' the old woman said. 'Happen her'll change her mind and not come back next spring.'

'And happen she does return!' Sophia argued fiercely.

'Naught you can do, Miss Sophia 'cepting the gen'leman gits shut of that there foreigner and weds you instead!'

She had hoped to make her young charge smile, but Sophia stopped in the centre of the room, no laughter on her face.

'Ada, you are nonpareil, laudable, matchless, a walking miracle! Such an idea would not have crossed my mind. The baron is only engaged and betrothals *can* be broken . . . but suppose he truly loves her – though I don't see how he possibly can! Suppose he married her before they return to England next spring? Even if he did not, and were free to marry me, suppose he does not fancy me?'

Ada grinned.

'I doant mind telling you, Miss Sophia, you be growed to an unaccountable purty young lady when you wears your fine new dresses and puts your hair atop your head. You stole that there Mr Lamberhill's heart, surelye, and that other young gen'leman as wants to come a-calling, and I reckon you no more set your bonnet at 'em than I done.'

Sophia hurried to the mirror and stared at her reflection.

Was she really pretty enough to captivate the baron? He was quite old – in his thirties, she supposed – but then so was Francis Lamberhill. What chance had she against the sophisticated Miss Challinor who was certainly far more accomplished than herself – *and* she had a title of sorts. She was pretty, too, Sophia acknowledged grudgingly, and altogether more feminine than herself.

She ran her hand through her hair, regretting now that she had not taken the time to pin it up before going to meet the

visitors. Nor had she troubled to wear one of her fine gowns.
Seeing herself through the baron's eyes, she could imagine that
he had thought her little more than a child just out of the
schoolroom. What was more, he had seen her dressed as a
boy and . . . and . . .

'What be you larfin' for, Miss Sophia?' Ada asked, unable
to keep abreast of Sophia's sudden changes of mood.

'I cannot possibly tell you, Ada!' Sophia replied. 'But I
should not be laughing when really I ought to be quite shocked
– which, indeed, I am!' Her smile gave way to a frown. 'If
only I could see the baron again without his horrible fiancée,
perhaps I could somehow charm him. Why, oh why, did I not
take the trouble to look my best this morning?'

Ada picked up the silver-backed hairbrush from the dressing-
table and knowing that it was something which always soothed
Sophia, she began to brush her hair.

'The maid as came with the lady said as how her mistress
were a-goin' back to Lunnon this afternoon. She said as how
the gen'leman was staying on a day or two to see the village
and farms and the like. Happen you could see him by your
ownself, Miss Sophia, though I shouldn't ought to be putting
such ideas in your pretty little head.'

Sophia's green eyes widened with excitement.

'He never told us he was staying on in Pyecombe!' she said.
'My aunts would have invited him to stay here . . . but it
doesn't matter. With Miss Challinor out of the way . . . Ada,
I shall invite him to dinner with us. Tell Tommy he's to take
a note immediately to the Plough Inn and wait there until
the baron returns from Brighton. I suppose he will think the
invitation a little impromptu, to say the least, but this is too
good an opportunity to miss.'

Ada grinned.

'If'n he says he will accept, you could wear your new silk,
Miss Sophia.'

'And you could do my hair, and Adam can serve some
excellent wines and the baron will be in a mellow mood. Ada,

go this minute and tell Tommy to be ready to leave as soon as I've written the invitation. I will not ask my aunts first because they will want to know my reasons and would certainly disapprove! If the baron says he will come, I will tell some fib or other – that I chanced to meet him in the village and he all but invited himself!'

Seeing Ada's shocked face, Sophia laughed.

'There are good fibs as well as bad ones, Ada. I am trying to save my poor aunts from a perfectly horrible future – all of us, come to that! We don't know if that Miss Challinor might decide to bring her own servants and give all of you notice.'

'Adone-do, Miss Sophia!' Ada gasped, putting down the hairbrush hurriedly. 'I'll go an' tell young Tommy he's to tek your letter quick as he can.'

The baron must accept, he *must*! Sophia told herself continuously once her invitation was on its way. She would show him that she could be the perfect hostess, gracious, accomplished in the manner of Lady Lamberhill. She would talk knowledgeably of London society and let him know in some subtle way how much sought after she had been at the Hunt Ball. He would find that she was not after all the *ingénue* he supposed. She would find a way to include a word or two of French and German so that he realized she was a talented linguist, and perhaps accompany herself on the spinet and sing a Strauss *liede*. Miss Longhurst, her music teacher, had told her her voice was charming and that she had perfect tone.

Her imagination kept her spirits high for a short while, but then the practical side of her nature brought her back to reality. Even if the baron were to be smitten to the point of wishing he had chosen her in preference to Miss Challinor, a gentleman did not break his engagement to a lady without very good cause. She had read in a book in the library that a man so defaulting could be sued for Breach of Promise, and would be thought a scoundrel devoid of honour. She would have to find some way to ensure that Miss Challinor thought better of her choice of husband.

Quite how this might be accomplished, Sophia decided to think on once the first hurdle was crossed. If only she could recall how she had behaved towards Francis; what she had said in conversation that had so enchanted him! She had certainly not intended to do so. His obvious interest in her had flattered her and now restored a little of her confidence. If only her experience with the opposite sex was not so hopelessly limited, she told herself anxiously.

The baron's reply to her invitation was brief, but sufficient to send Sophia's hopes soaring once again. He would be delighted to take dinner with the Misses Calverley at eight o'clock.

Neither Aunt Nellie nor Aunt Georgie questioned Sophia's mumbled explanation as to how and where she had encountered the baron. They were more concerned that Cook, at this last minute, might not have something suitable to offer their visitor. Sophia, who had known since childhood that old Dick Weller poached pheasants from their woodlands, reassured them that she would make certain an excellent meal was provided.

For the remainder of the afternoon, Sophia flew from dining-room to kitchen, giving orders to the servants, ensuring that the best china, plate and glasses were cleaned and polished. New wax candles were put in the Georgian silver candlesticks; tablecloth and napkins were freshly starched and ironed. Ada, meanwhile, had taken a cool flat iron to Sophia's best Gros de Naples evening gown.

By six o'clock all was ready, and Sophia sank exhausted into the tin tub of water Ada and one of the housemaids had filled for her bath. The curling tongs were heating over the burner and her clothes were spread out on the bed together with her grandmother's beautiful emerald necklace.

Only one vital part of her present plan remained unresolved – namely the answer to her own question – would she be able to beguile Konrad Valschintzky as easily as she had Francis Lamberhill? As to the future – if she succeeded – she would concern herself with this hurdle when the time came.

Konrad Valschintzky put down his knife and fork and, over the rim of his wine glass, looked across the table at the young girl opposite him. He was no longer able to conjure up the memory of her in the garb of a stable lad. The transformation from scallywag to beauty was too big a leap. Given another year or two, he reflected, the girlish chatter would be subdued, the coquetry not so obvious and the ingenuous exuberance pruned to a more mature finesse.

At the age of thirty, handsome, polished and extremely wealthy, Konrad was considered by his family and friends to be the most eligible of bachelors, and like all his fellow officers in his Majesty's Imperial Austro-Hungarian army, he had had every opportunity to enjoy the favours of ladies. For many years, he had kept a Viennese opera singer as his mistress, relinquishing her regretfully only when he had become betrothed to Lavinia. Youngest daughter of Viscount Challinor who was married to an Austrian friend of Konrad's mother, Lavinia was visiting her maternal relatives who had introduced them.

Although at first Konrad had thought her pretty and amusingly different by virtue of her Englishness, he had been disconcerted by her autocratic, sometimes dictatorial manner, and thought her very spoilt. Both families, however, encouraged the association, and his mother finally had suggested to him that marriage to Lavinia could be highly advantageous to him. Although he had never troubled to pursue his English inheritance, he had always known that one day he must do so. A wife who was born to the ways of the English aristocracy would be of great assistance to him in the management of his affairs.

That the Honourable Lavinia Challinor would bring with her a substantial dowry was of little consequence to him. He was wealthy in his own right, having received lands and a baronetcy from his great-grandfather, an Englishman who had been adopted by the Valschintzkys in the far distant past. Nonetheless, it was time he settled down, his mother told him. He had sown his wild oats and should shoulder his responsibilities, in particular in regard to his English inheritance. By birth, he was a Calverley and he was not performing his duty in leaving the care of his estates to two elderly maiden aunts who might die at any minute.

With his usual good-natured willingness to appease his mother, Konrad had drifted into the betrothal, and when Lavinia and her mother were about to leave for England, he decided on the spur of the moment to accompany them.

Looking now at the identical faces of the two old ladies and the animated face of their young niece, he was immensely glad that he had finally met his relatives, and not a little plagued by guilt that he had left them to manage what after all were his affairs so long, without a masculine hand to guide them. He was enchanted by the quaint old house which seemed to be strangely suspended in time. He was reminded of a fairy-tale told him by his French governess when he was a child. It was the story of a princess who had been put under a spell and lay asleep in a castle for a hundred years whilst waiting for a prince to cut through the briars and thornbushes to kiss her and thus waken her. He could even recall the name of the French author, Charles Perrault, who had written the tale. In this case it was the house, not the princess, who slept whilst awaiting him, the prince, to stir it back to life.

The moment of whimsical fancy was shortlived as he looked once more at Miss Sophia Calverley – no sleeping princess, she, but a glowing vibrant young girl bent upon some purpose he had not yet fathomed.

He had been intrigued to learn from the loquacious innkeeper in Pyecombe that the youthful Miss Calverley was apparently quite notorious. Not only did she manage the estate

– and most efficiently, so rumour had it – but was highly esteemed for her proficiency. Despite the fact that she was a female and absurdly young, she was clearly as highly respected as had been her uncle, the late squire. Accustomed as Konrad was to the aristocratic young women of Viennese society, he had thought the landlord's tales must be greatly exaggerated. He no longer thought so. Moreover, he detected in Sophia an obsessive streak which underlay her attitude towards him – and, indeed, towards Lavinia. Ortolans was unquestionably important to her, and he suspected that she had some scheme in mind to prevent him laying claim to 'her' house.

The mystery resolved itself when, the meal over, they repaired to the drawing-room where, the aunts told Konrad kindly, he might smoke if he so wished for they greatly enjoyed the aroma of a good cigar! As Sophia seated herself beside him on the large, if slightly shabby sofa, she invited him to look through *The Calverley Journal*.

'It might help you to understand how . . . how important Ortolans is to us!' she said in a low, urgent voice. 'My aunts are too polite to tell you how deeply distressed they were when they heard they might be obliged to move. At their age . . .' she placed a hand on his arm and leant close enough for him to catch the faint delicate scent of lavender water with which she had bathed her shoulders '. . . is it really so necessary? Miss Challinor did not strike me as much taken with the house, and although we understand that it has no family associations for her, perhaps you, a Calverley, would not wish to alter its character so ruthlessly?'

So this girl judged Lavinia to be ruthless! Konrad thought, partly with amusement, but also with interest. How passionately she spoke! And how very attractive she looked as she gazed appealingly into his eyes. Was this the explanation for that totally unexpected invitation to dine here tonight? Was this little Miss Sophia's idea – to wine and dine him and then woo him into agreement with what she wanted?

A wry smile twisting the corners of his mouth, he said bluntly:

'Do I understand you would prefer that I should not take over the responsibility for this house? For my estates?'

'I said no such thing!' Sophia replied unguardedly. 'I do not question your right to be here.'

'But you would deny such a right to my future wife?'

Two spots of colour stained Sophia's cheeks. Her chin rose defiantly.

'You are mocking me, sir! What you choose to do with your life is your affair. I suppose you will point out next that I am the one without the right to live here.' Her voice suddenly became childishly close to tears. 'It is so unfair! Had I been born a boy instead of a stupid girl, Ortolans would be mine!'

'You are far from stupid, Miss Calverley!' Konrad said gently for he sensed that her distress was genuine. 'I realize that this is your home and that naturally you are attached to it. Please be assured that for as long as you wish – and you have my word on it – you shall remain here.'

Sophia bit her lip.

'Yes, but if all is changed and there is a new mistress in place of my aunts, it will no longer be the home we love.' Suddenly she recalled the role she was playing, and looked up at him from beneath her lashes. 'You belong here, Baron Valschintzky, just as we do. You do not feel like a stranger and I truly believe we could all be happy here together.'

'I do not doubt it, Miss Calverley. Bearing in mind our first encounter by the river, I am quite certain that you and I would enjoy each other's company. You are not only a very beautiful young lady, but a spirited one, and this is much to my taste. Nevertheless, as you will appreciate, I do have to consider the wishes of others – not least those of my fiancée. If it is of comfort to you, we shall not be marrying for at least a year, and during that time, I promise I will do my best to persuade Miss Challinor not to contemplate too many changes to the house. You already have my assurance that you and the Misses Calverley may continue living here.'

It was comfort of a kind, Sophia reflected after Konrad had

made his farewells, but it did not alter the fact that she had failed in her attempt to inveigle him with her charms! It was true that he had called her 'beautiful' and 'spirited' – for what that was worth – but he was almost as firmly welded to Miss Challinor as if they were already wed.

'I will not allow him to marry her!' Sophia declared to Ada as the old servant helped her prepare for bed. 'He deserves someone far pleasanter. I cannot dislike him, Ada, if the truth be told. I would be doing him a favour to rid him of the Honourable Miss Challinor!'

It was only after Ada had blown out her candle and the curtains of her four-poster bed were drawn, enclosing her in warm darkness, that Sophia admitted the whole truth had not been told. When Konrad Valschintzky had smiled at her in that particular way of his, his brown eyes crinkling and his mouth lifting at the corners, her heart had missed its beat and set her body trembling in the most extraordinary way. Francis Lamberhill had never affected her in such a manner and it occurred to her that if she were to marry either man, she would infinitely prefer it should be the baron! Of course he was much too old for her. He had told the aunts during dinner that he had recently celebrated his thirtieth birthday and that made him more than ten years older than herself.

On the point of sleep, Sophia reminded herself that it made not the slightest difference whether he were ten, twenty, thirty years older. She would marry him if he was in his dotage – if it meant she could keep Ortolans. As for his fiancée, Lavinia Challinor, she would find a way to oust her from his life. No other woman was going to become mistress of her home.

CHAPTER FIFTEEN

1889

'You be too grown up now to go riding on your ownsum, Miss Sophia!' Ada protested as reluctantly, she unlaced Sophia's corsets and helped her into her breeches. 'S'posin' Mr Lamberhill sees you! I've told you afore, he woant a-come courting a girl as wears boy's clothing, and without a chaperon!'

Sophia pulled her jersey over her head and grinned as she tucked her red curls into the over-large cloth cap.

'I don't give a fig for Mr Lamberhill's opinions. I have decided not to marry him in any case and that's the end of it.'

Ada's bosom heaved.

'Happen you got your head in the clouds, Miss Sophia. That Austrian Frenchey ain't never goin' to marry you. Now Mr Lamberhill – he's a nice suitable gen'leman and he's that sweet on you, I reckon as how if you'd any sense in that head of yourn, you'd do as your aunts want and tell him you've changed your mind.'

'Well, I have *not* changed my mind!' Sophia said firmly.

Francis Lamberhill was a regular visitor to Ortolans, liked and approved by the aunts as a suitor, but although Sophia herself liked him and enjoyed his attentions, his devotion could not deviate her from her determination somehow to capture the heart of Baron Valschintzky. It was now five months since he had announced his existence and his intention to disrupt their lives, and not a day had passed without she had thought how she might find a way to eliminate the horrid Miss Challinor so that she, Aunt Georgie, Aunt Nellie and – if he so wished – the baron, could preserve Ortolans for themselves.

All through the winter, she had pondered how she might secure their future and try as she had to find an alternative, she was forced to accept that there was only one way – marriage to the baron.

'Doant you be out too late, Miss Sophia!' Ada said anxiously as Sophia picked up her riding crop. 'And you be sure you tell Albert whichaway you's going. One of these days you'll tek a tumble, surelye, an' we woant have no knowing where-sumdever you be!'

This afternoon was one day when she most certainly would not tell Albert where she was intending to ride, Sophia thought wryly as she hurried down to the stable yard. She dared not think what her aunts would do if they learned that she was going to pay a visit to the lady who lived in the cottage that lay halfway between Detcham and Edburton. No one ever paid calls on Mrs Enid Groom who was 'not respectable'. For a long time, Delia and Sophia had pondered why the grown-ups would not answer questions about this neighbour and forbade them to mention her name. A year ago, Delia had overheard two of her brothers discussing the lady, who, apparently, they had actually visited!

As Sophia rode through the woods in the direction of Edburton, she remembered the excitement she had felt when last night she recalled the existence of the mysterious Mrs Groom and decided that here was someone who might be able to assist her.

'She was the mistress of a duke for years and years!' Delia had discovered last summer. 'He bought her the house and it is he who pays all her bills. Sometimes he drives down from London to visit her although he is married with eight children! And that is not all, Sophia. She was on the stage and gave her favours to lots and lots of men before the duke saw her and set her up in a house in St John's Wood.'

'You mean he lived with her without being married?' Sophia had exclaimed, wide-eyed.

Delia had nodded, adding in a whisper that his wife had

found out about the liaison and made such a fuss, the duke removed his paramour to the country. According to Delia's brothers, this disreputable lady had 'a fatal fascination for men' but they had not said what this meant. They had also declared her to be quite free with her favours.

Sophia was not so much shocked as intrigued by Delia's confidences. She had enquired as to what kind of favours Mrs Groom distributed.

'Married favours!' had been Delia's whispered reply. 'They can do what husbands do but without having to get married.'

The problem was, Sophia had thought at the time, neither she nor Delia knew what husbands did – only that babies arrived as a result of it. They had once seen Farmer Merrymore's big black Sussex bull climb on the back of one of his cows, and Sir Sydney, who had been driving them in the dogcart, remarked that the cow should have a fine calf next spring. But discussing it later, the two girls agreed that this could not possibly be the way men behaved with their wives – it was far too bestial and undignified. So what were these 'favours'? Sophia badly needed to know so that she could bestow them upon the baron and make him her adoring slave. Since there could be no question of asking Ada for information, still less her aunts, Sophia had decided to go to the source of the matter. Mrs Enid Groom must know the answers, and it was she who Sophia was visiting in secret this afternoon.

Apart from a group of schoolchildren who she encountered picking bunches of primroses which grew beneath the hedgerows bordering Bramble Lane, Sophia saw no one. Skirting the village, she chose a route along the foot of the Downs that led directly to Edburton. Fortunately Mrs Groom's house lay half a mile from the village, and she was able to ride up to the stables without being questioned.

'And what may you be wanting, young fellow-me-lad?' asked a groom emerging from the harness room and surveying the untidy figure with suspicion.

'I've a message for your mistress!' Sophia mutterd as she slid to the ground. 'Gotta deliver it meself, personal like!'

Her clothing and accent misleading him, the man directed her to the tradesman's entrance. A kitchen-maid opened the scullery door and when Sophia repeated her request to see the mistress of the house, referred her to the parlour-maid. Sophia was left standing by the broom cupboard whilst the prim, uniformed girl disappeared up the back stairs. The cook gave her only a cursory glance, but clearly too busy kneading bread dough, she forbore to do more than instruct Sophia to keep her muddy boots off her clean floor.

'Mistress'll see you in the morning-room. Hurry up, boy! She doesn't like to be kept waiting!' the parlour-maid said on her return.

She led the way along a stone passage and through a door into the hallway. Immediately the smell of baking bread was replaced by a waft of scent which Sophia identified as otto of Roses. The perfume was even stronger as she was shown into a room so unusual in its décor that for a moment, she did not notice the woman reclining on the *chaise-longue*. The colours predominating were red and gold. Dark red embossed paper covered the walls on which were hung a multitude of gilt-framed pictures. Scarlet, cut-velvet curtains were draped either side of the two windows and frilled cream lace curtains covered the glass. There were gilt lamp brackets on the walls and on the floor was a thick red, brown and blue Turkish carpet.

Next to the *chaise-longue*, its pink satin covering buttoned and frilled, stood a papier-mâché table supporting a stuffed bird of paradise covered by a glass dome. On a raised dais to one side of the room was a satinwood piano, inlaid and gilded, atop which were several purple velvet, framed photographs.

'Lost your tongue, boy? Speak out. I shan't bite you!'

Sophia's eyes turned to the woman who had addressed her and was now chuckling as one beringed hand reached out to take a sweetmeat from the bonbonnière beside her. Her henna'd hair, which clashed violently with the room's colour scheme and the plum-coloured satin dress she wore, hung in ringlets from beneath her lace cap. Her white-powdered face was heavily rouged and a beauty spot had been positioned high on one plump cheek. Despite the time of day, her jewellery was elaborately ornate and flashed brilliantly as she raised her large frame into a sitting position.

As Sophia took a deep breath and removed her cap, her hair tumbled to her shoulders. Now, for the first time, she saw the striking, turquoise blue eyes of the woman she had come to visit.

'I must apologize for deceiving you, madam,' she said, inclining her head since a curtsy did not seem appropriate whilst she was clad in breeches. 'My name is Sophia Calverley and I have come to ask your assistance.'

Enid Groom studied her strange visitor with interest and not a little curiosity. Despite her extraordinary attire, the girl was obviously well-bred and most certainly would not be here with her parents' permission. Suddenly, she placed her.

'You're the niece of those two Miss Calverleys over Detcham way!' she said. Her mouth curved in a smile and the blue eyes twinkled. 'Come here, child, and sit down. We might as well become acquainted. Clearly you know who I am, and I suspect you know also of my reputation. I am not usually honoured by calls from the gentry – unless they are of the masculine gender, which, despite your garb, you obviously are not. Now sit down and tell me the reason for this unexpected honour!'

To her relief, Sophia found herself not only liking this extraordinary woman who was said to be quite wicked and without any morals, but able to confide far more than she had intended. She had meant only to ask a few key questions, but now she was telling the whole story relating to her problem.

Enid Groom was middle-aged, and without bitterness or regret of any kind despite the life she had led. At the age of thirteen, she had dragged herself up from the slums like many of her contemporaries for whom starvation was often the only alternative. She had given her body to the landlord of a cheap rooming house in exchange for a job as a chambermaid. The rooms were rented to theatrical performers and by the time Enid was seventeen, she had dropped her East End accent and had obtained small parts in the theatre. Her voluptuous figure, a natural sensuousness, a quick wit and a remarkably beautiful pair of eyes and breasts had finally led to lead roles. Still not yet twenty, she had been noticed by the young blades who came to watch her perform on stage and she used them to learn how best to behave in the company of the gentry.

Enid did not consider her plan for self-education complete until she was asked to dine at the Café Royal by the Duke of Altonberry. Too sharp-witted to allow him to seduce her immediately, she had withheld her favours until in desperation, the elderly man had agreed to set her up in a house in St John's Wood as his mistress.

They settled into a life of pleasant domesticity. She entertained him and for him, and his friends enjoyed her company but, she took care, no other favours. The duke was agreeably tolerant as to how she spent her time when he was not with her provided she was discreet and no word spread that his mistress was cuckolding him. Enid's lovers, therefore, were always of a transient nature and, more often than not, a great deal younger than herself.

When finally, the duke was obliged to pension her off, she took her congé with good grace, and with her customary adaptability, settled down to life in the country. From time to time, male friends from her past would drive out from Brighton or down from London to visit her, and since she lacked for nothing she wanted or needed, she did not regret her absence from city life. Nor did she mind in the least the fact that her reputation had removed with her and that she was barred from the social activities of the surrounding ladies, whose lives she considered to be excessively dull. Not for her the planning of jam making, church attendances, good works for the poor of the parish, routine calls, and the seasonal entertaining of a husband's hunting, shooting and fishing friends. Instead, she read novels by Alexandre Dumas and Jules Verne, obtained from the lending library in Brighton; learned the latest tunes from sheet music sent to her from London to play on her piano, and indulged her fancy for cage-birds and jigsaw puzzles. These innocent pursuits were highlighted from time to time by comparatively bawdy evenings with sons of aristocratic neighbours whose mothers cut her dead if their carriages passed hers in the road.

This visit from the Calverley girl was without doubt a novelty, she thought as she pieced together Sophia's garbled story. It was in some ways a replica of her own determination to achieve what she wanted from life by using her beauty to strike where a man was most vulnerable. Like herself, this girl sensed that she was not powerless and need not inevitably surrender her needs and desires simply because she was female!

'You must help me!' Sophia concluded. 'Tell me how to make the baron do as I want.'

'I could – but I am far from sure that I should!' Enid Groom said cryptically. She drew a deep sigh. 'You are very young and quite astonishingly innocent. How can I address you in language that will not shock you – or indeed, in language that you could understand?'

Sophia's green eyes grew wider as she leaned forward eagerly.

'I promise I will not be shocked. I don't mind what you tell me. I may be young but I'm not stupid.'

'My dear, I do not think you in the least stupid, although I confess I don't altogether understand your quite obsessive love for this house which seems to mean so much to you. Your consideration for your aunts is commendable, but should not be allowed to mar your future. This young man – Francis Lamberhill? Would it not be best to follow convention and marry him? After all, your aunts are elderly and you cannot live alone at Ortolans once they have gone.'

'That's why I must marry Baron Valschintzky!' Sophia declared. She glanced down at her clothes and added quickly: 'I can look nice when I wear dresses and have my hair up. Ada says I can appear quite beautiful but, of course, she is prejudiced because she loves me. I did try to look nice when the baron came to dinner with us, but although I think he noticed me, he clearly prefers that horrible Miss Challinor.'

'And I am to help you change his mind!' said her companion as she rose to give a lump of sugar to the three canaries perched in a gilded cage by the window. 'If your baron truly loves this young woman, it may not be possible. There are two ways, you see, to a man's heart. One is love, and the other . . . it is to make him want to possess you so much that he will throw every other notion aside.'

'To possess me?' Sophia said frowning. 'You mean to own me?'

'No, child, I mean to desire you – your body. There are some women who can arouse this desire in men, some even who are not in the least beautiful. The difficulty lies in the fact that not all men desire the same physical attributes in a woman. Some are fascinated by their faces, their eyes, their mouths; some by their figure, others by bosoms, ankles; or even by a voice, an expression. Most often, it is a combination of all these. There are women who know how to pleasure a man, excite him to even greater desire. As a virgin, you cannot possibly know such things!'

Sophia's mouth tightened.

'Then I will cease to be a virgin. It cannot be difficult because Ada has often told me that the village girls lose their maidenheads all too easily, but she would not tell me what a maidenhead was.'

It was Enid Groom's first experience of a girl so totally innocent that she was ignorant even of such primary knowledge. Momentarily, she hesitated. Little Miss Calverley was no responsibility of hers and she was under no obligation to enlighten her. Despite her own lack of morals, she pondered now whether it was in Sophia's interest for her to do so. Even if she did decide to help, time was not on their side. The baron, apparently, was due back in England in a month's time. How could she teach Sophia in four short weeks what had taken her years to learn?

'Please, Mrs Groom, please help me!' Sophia said, sensing the older woman's hesitation. 'You made a duke desire you, so you must know how 'tis accomplished.'

Enid laughed.

'Not just a duke!' she said unable to resist the urge to boast. 'I could not count the number of my conquests, there have been so many.' She shrugged her ample shoulders and added abruptly. 'Stand up, my dear. Hold up your head and pretend for a moment that I am your baron. Now smile at me!'

As Sophia obeyed, Enid nodded.

'You do have something . . . something special!' she murmured. 'A hidden fire, I think – and a good figure. Your breasts are full but firm, so your bosom will look enticing in a ball gown. If you are décolleté, try to ensure that the pendant falls just in the cleavage. That takes a man's eyes to your most feminine attribute. When you can do so, dip your body forward so that his eyes will travel further than they should.'

She noted Sophia's concentration and continued:

'Similarly, if you are mounting a staircase or the step into your carriage, lift your skirts higher than is considered proper. Such things must be done without you appearing to know that you have revealed more than you should. Lean a little too close when an occasion presents itself. You must do all you can to make the man aware of your body. This is almost as important as praising him. Men like to be made to feel interesting and attractive even when they are not – more especially if they are not! Never criticize a man no matter what he does or says. Never best him in a game. Let him know you admire his appearance. You may say something on the lines of: "I so much prefer men with dark hair to those with fair hair!" or "tall men to short" or "short to tall" – whichever he may be, and quickly cover the compliment by adding as if you have done so accidentally: "I am so sorry, I had not intended to be personal!" and blush. Blushing is most becoming if you can do so at will. It implies that the man has a physical effect on you which again will boost his ego. Do you understand what I am saying?'

'Yes, I do – at least, I think I do!' Sophia said, 'but you have not yet explained to me about my maidenhead.'

The older woman nodded.

'On reflection, I do not think I should. Your innocence may well be far more advantageous to you than knowledge. Nevertheless, you should know that men are more easily aroused than women. Their desires are very basic, and a man in his prime will have frequent need to mate, just as a stallion or a bull might do. Nature intended that he should reproduce his species and as often as not, he will do so whether he loves the female or not. If his body is responsive to a certain female, he will want to mate with her, even though he may subdue his feelings and make use of another if she is not willing; or, as in the case of an unmarried girl, convention demands that he shall not. The task you have set yourself is to arouse such desires and so inflame them that his only means of obtaining what he wants is by marriage.'

'But you . . .' Sophia broke off, her cheeks flushed as she realized how impulsively she had spoken.

Enid smiled.

'My dear girl, dukes do not marry commoners such as myself. Besides, my duke was already married. I came from very humble beginnings and I never expected marriage. For you, it is essential – and you do not have my disadvantages. I am well content with my situation. I have been well rewarded for my favours!'

Sophia caught her breath.

'Would you . . . could you explain what you mean by "favours"?' she asked hesitantly.

It was Enid Groom's turn to hesitate, but there seemed little point in prevaricating now.

'That I permit a man to use my body to take his pleasure!' she said. 'If it is easier for you to understand, then I allow him to mate with me.' Seeing the shocked look on Sophia's face, she added gently: 'It is not so terrible as it sounds, my dear. There are many married ladies who take pleasure in it, albeit not always with their husbands. If the parties like and respect each other . . . but that is another subject. You will not be granting *your* baron any favours – merely urging him to want them! Does this homily help you at all?'

Sophia nodded.

'I am to play the coquette – not, alas, one of my accomplishments. My maid is forever telling me that I should have been born a boy, and to be honest, I greatly prefer wearing these clothes to petticoats. To be constantly changing dresses is such a great waste of time. But I will do as you say and try to be more feminine. I must succeed – but the baron is very personable and I suspect there have been many beautiful women who have tried to arouse his interest. He is probably accustomed to flattery.'

'You have youth and beauty and breeding on your side!' Enid said trenchantly. 'You also have tenacity . . . and courage. Not many young girls from your background would have ridden here garbed as a boy to see a wicked woman with a reputation like mine!'

Sophia returned her smile. 'Wicked or not, you're very kind!' she declared, rising to her feet. 'I wish I didn't have to visit you in secret, but my aunts . . .'

'My dear child, I understand the difficulties!' Enid interrupted gently. 'We shall not acknowledge one another should we meet in a public place. However, if ever you feel like coming to talk to me again, you can be assured of a welcome. I wish you success next month with your baron.'

As she rode home, Sophia debated whether she could relate the extraordinary meeting with Mrs Enid Groom to Ada. She decided against it – not just because she would upset her aunts were Ada to have hysterics and tittle-tattle to them, but because she realized that Mrs Groom might be blamed for receiving her. It seemed most unfair that so kind a person should be socially ostracized. Although her appearance and that of her house was undoubtedly vulgar, it did not detract from her readiness to help Sophia. Mrs Groom had offered advice without once laughing at her for her ignorance, and had pretended not to notice her embarrassment when explaining that men were compelled by their natures to mate whether they were married or not! Even now Sophia's cheeks felt hot as she recalled the unbridled urgency of the farm dogs fighting one another to climb on the back of the gamekeeper's spaniel bitch. And she thought they were playing games and wondered why her aunts had insisted she look the other way! Did women really have to submit themselves to this ungainly ritual? Was it for this they prettied themselves and tried to charm a man into a proposal of marriage? If by some miracle she were to persuade the baron to marry her, must she allow him to . . . to perform such intimacies?

She pushed these anxieties firmly to the back of her mind as during the next four weeks she practised coquetting with the ever-faithful Francis Lamberhill, who continued to call with persistent frequency. Despite the fact that his entire family were in London for the Season, he had elected to remain at home, because, he told them, he was required to keep a watchful eye on his father's estates. Even the aunts had doubted the validity of this statement.

'I cannot think it necessary!' Aunt Georgie remarked.

'Sir Sydney has an excellent bailiff!' agreed Aunt Nellie.

'Poor Mr Lamberhill cannot bear to be parted from our Sophia!'

'I never saw a young man so smitten!'

'If you are quite certain you will not marry him, you should put the poor boy out of his misery!'

At this juncture, Sophia protested:

'He has proposed marriage three times, Aunt Georgie, and each time I have refused him. It is not my fault if he won't accept the fact that I shall not change my mind.'

'Hope springs eternal . . .' Aunt Nellie quoted, sighing. 'Not that I blame Mr Lamberhill. You are looking quite enchanting these days, my dear.'

'So like your dear grandmother, our mama.'

'Is all prepared for Baron Valschintzky's visit?' Aunt Nellie enquired. 'I must admit I am quite pleased he is not bringing his fiancée with him, although naturally I regret her poor mother is indisposed.'

Sophia had no such regrets. Although Miss Challinor was to follow in two weeks' time, her immediate absence meant she, Sophia, would have the baron's undivided attention for fourteen days. This surely should be long enough to ensnare him!

Konrad Valschintzky was in excellent good humour. The unceasing round of social entertainments in Vienna over Christmas and the New Year had begun to pall, and he had returned to his beautiful schloss on the Danube to spend a quiet month with his mother. Learning of his curiosity about his Sussex estates, the widowed baroness had related in far greater detail than before the history of his English heritage. Although Konrad had always used his Austrian title and surname, he now realized the significance of his Calverley birthright. He recalled for his mother the charm of the Elizabethan house which, though tiny in comparison to the schloss, had caught his fancy, as, indeed, he told his mother, had the two quaint maiden aunts and their pretty, enigmatic niece. If there were one fly in the ointment, it was Lavinia's criticism of both house and its occupants. Konrad could not deny that all three Miss Calverleys would resist the changes Lavinia wished to make. In point of fact, he somewhat resisted them himself!

He had intended only to remain in Austria for three months. At the end of the January, however, his whole country was plunged into dismay and confusion when it became known that the Crown Prince, the Emperor's only son, had died. When

Konrad, who had known Rudolf during his army days, and his mother, who was a friend of the Empress, returned to Vienna, they found a city in deep mourning and agog with rumours as to the manner of the prince's death.

It was not until the end of May, therefore, that Konrad felt able to leave his mother. With a sense of relief he departed for England. As he and his manservant crossed the English Channel and the distinctive white cliffs of the south coast came into view, Konrad felt a surge of excitement, not lessened by Lavinia's absence. Judging by their recent letter, he knew he would receive a warm welcome from his two elderly relatives. They made no mention of the girl, but he had a clear picture of Sophia in his mind – not as she had been in her formal dinner-gown, but as he had first glimpsed her in boy's breeches by the river! Their encounter was their secret, and the memory of it caused him to grin whenever it came into his mind. Undoubtedly she was a pretty child – and a spirited one. It would not be long before she found herself a husband. It was a reassuring thought. She was obviously devoted to her aunts and quite possibly she would take them to live with her when she married – thus vacating Ortolans for himself and Lavinia.

As Konrad drove in his hired phaeton over the South Downs and saw the Sussex Weald spread out before him, he was aware of a new smell replacing the salt air of the sea. Although he could not identify it, it came from the thyme, the meadow grass, the burgeoning lime trees and pines that were warming in the spring sunshine. High overhead, larks were singing and as he approached Detcham, he detected the busy chatter of the thousands of migrating ortolans as they returned to their breeding habitat. Cowslips, bluebells and primroses decorated the hedgerows, and as he drew nearer, he saw the first swallows circling the stone slab roof of the house.

Halting the carriage, he paused to watch as Sophia came towards him across the stone terrace, a basket of freshly cut jonquils grasped in one hand, a sprig of cherry blossom in the other. Atop her chestnut curls was a straw hat, the ribbons

matching the blue of her bustled skirt, her feet encased in tan
doeskin shoes.

'You are very welcome, sir!' she said as he stepped down
from the phaeton and handed the reins to his man. 'We were
not expecting you quite so early. I had hoped to arrange these
flowers before your arrival!'

'The wind was in our favour and we docked ahead of time,
Miss Calverley!' he explained. 'I trust I am not causing you
any inconvenience . . .'

'Oh, but of course not, sir!' Sophia broke in, smiling prettily. 'I have been awaiting your arrival with impatience!'

That should flatter him, she thought, only slightly disconcerted by the knowledge that the visitor was far more
handsome than memory had allowed. Dressed in a light brown
ulster which accentuated his height, and a matching homburg,
a slight smile on his lips, he was every bit as impressive a
figure as Sir Sydney whose upright military bearing Sophia
had always much admired.

As he bent to kiss her hand which she had liberally splashed
an hour earlier with lavender water, his dark eyes looked
directly into hers. There was no need for her to simulate the
blush Mrs Groom had recommended since the baron's expression was openly admiring, as was his compliment.

'I do declare my little cousin has grown prettier than ever!'
he remarked.

Forgetting her intention only to present her most agreeable
self, Sophia detected the note of condescension of an adult
for a child, and sharply withdrew her hand.

'I am not your cousin, sir – or at least, the connection is so
distant as to be of no account.' Seeing the look of amusement
in his eyes, she was further incensed. 'In point of fact you are
my second cousin once removed. As to your manners, sir, I can
only suppose that in your country, it is not considered impolite
to make personal comments about a lady's appearance.'

'Oh, but I do assure you, if the remarks are complimentary,
the ladies in my country are only too happy to receive them.'

With an effort, Sophia curbed her temper. This was no way to go about her plan. Convinced that he was enjoying this verbal sparring, she determined to ignore it. In a honeyed voice, she said brightly:

'You must be tired after so long a journey. Pray come indoors where you can be comfortable. I have personally supervised the preparation of your room, but please tell me at once if there is anything you need. I have given your servant the room adjacent so that he is at hand.'

She preceded him through the front door, lifting her skirts daintily as she stepped over the threshold.

Konrad was nonplussed. Was this pretentious young lady, now playing hostess to him, the same person as the girl with the flashing green eyes who had been on the brink of losing her temper a moment earlier? Recalling once more her boy's garb, he was even more confused.

She turned to smile at him over her shoulder and her voice seemed to hold a genuine warmth as she said seductively:

'May I be the first to say: "Welcome home"!'

CHAPTER SIXTEEN

1889

'I have tried everything – everything you suggested!' Sophia declared in a voice not far from tears. 'I know the baron likes me. I think he may even be a little taken with me because sometimes I look up and find him staring – the way Francis Lamberhill does when he is about to say he cannot live without me. Just when I think the baron is about to show his feelings, he starts talking about *her* again!'

'Doubtless to remind himself that he is engaged to be married and has no right to be showing an interest in you, my dear!' Enid Groom said sagely. 'Has your faithful suitor proposed again?'

Sophia nodded.

'Francis has called twice in the ten days since the baron arrived. I made myself quite agreeable to him in the hope that I might make Konrad – that is the baron's Christian name by which he wishes my aunts and me to address him – a little jealous. I suppose I should have known better. After Francis had departed, Konrad made fun of him, calling him a bit of a milksop and telling me I could do much better for myself. He said he would invite me to Vienna when he was married and that he and Miss Challinor would find me a dashing young cavalry officer who would not scowl all the time like Francis and who would escort me to dances and make me laugh.'

Enid Groom regarded the downcast face of her young visitor thoughtfully. She had not expected to see Sophia again.

'You are as determined as ever upon marriage to this man?' she enquired.

Sophia nodded vigorously, and her red curls came loose from the pins which had secured them beneath her boy's cap.

'I will do anything – anything at all!' she declared. 'But what else can I do? We go riding together and he compliments me on my management of the estate; he has taken me to the theatre in Brighton and we went walking arm in arm on the Chain Pier. In the evenings, I have played the spinet to him and he has sung Viennese songs to us. We play chess together and I always allow him to win. We went to Lamberhill Court to play tennis on their new court and Konrad – who is a far better player than Francis – gave me a lesson. He has told me I am a most agreeable companion. I have introduced him to all our estate workers and to the villagers and made a list for him of the best tradespeople to employ if work is to be done at Ortolans. He even told me I was as knowledgeable as Rogers, our bailiff. Then he spoils such compliments by telling me how pleased Miss Challinor is going to be to find everything in such good order. He is forever talking of her. Sometimes I suspect he does so simply to aggravate me.'

She paused to draw breath and unaware of Enid's smile, she continued:

'When he does not talk of her, he is talking of Vienna and Wachau, where he has his castle. His widowed mother lives there and he says the schloss is just as beautiful as Ortolans but different, with orchards of apricots quite as pretty as our apple orchards, and the Danube so much bigger than our little river flowing by the bottom of the gardens. If it was so lovely there, I asked him, why did he want to live at Ortolans? "Because it is what Miss Challinor wants," he replied. Besides, he tells me, he is fast growing to love his Sussex estate seeing it now through my eyes! Oh, Mrs Groom, is there nothing I can do to separate him from his insufferable fiancée?'

The older woman sighed.

'I suppose if you are determined upon any step to achieve

your ends, then if he cannot be seduced away from her, the
only alternative is to compromise him. But that would pose
great risks to yourself, and I am far from sure if I should
advise it.'

'Compromise Konrad! In what way? How?' Sophia asked
eagerly. 'I don't mind the risks. I will do anything to keep
Ortolans. I've got to make him marry me somehow!'

'It has been done many times,' Enid said thoughtfully,
'although not by girls brought up as you have been. It is a
matter of honour, you see – or more appropriately, dishonour.
You inveigle your baron into a situation where honour obliges
him to marry you. In your case, the risk is twofold. Is he a
man who can be counted upon to do the honourable thing?
And secondly, what if he marries before he is compromised?'

'I have not the slightest doubt that Konrad is a man of
honour!' Sophia cried, jumping to her feet and all but sending
the stuffed bird flying from the table. 'But what is this compromise you speak of, Mrs Groom? Enlighten me, please!'

'It would be necessary for you to make the baron believe
he has seduced *you*. Possibly you could find a way to make
him partake too liberally of the wines at dinner so that he is
a trifle befuddled when he retires for the night. This maid of
yours – is she someone you can trust?'

Sophia nodded.

'Then you must wait an hour or so after the baron has
retired, then, wearing your night attire, go to his room and
climb into bed with him. The room must be dark so that in
his intoxicated state, he is not quite certain who you are. Then
you must put your arms around him and kiss him.'

'Kiss him!' Sophia said aghast. 'But I have never kissed a
man!'

'It is not so difficult!' Enid said with a wry smile. 'Do not
on any account draw away if he puts his arms around you.
If he does not, *you* must put your arms around *him*. There is
no need to talk – simply to touch, and if he attempts to speak,
silence him with more kisses. Meanwhile, your maid must be

stationed outside the bedroom door. When you cry out, which you will do after an appropriate time, she must come in with her candle and find you and the baron in bed together. Preferably at this juncture, she will have hysterics.'

Sophia was now staring at her counsellor, mouth agape, her green eyes wide.

'But if Ada called out, that would waken my aunts!'

'That is one of the risks you will have to take. The point is that your baron must know your maid is aware of what has happened; and in order to protect your reputation, he has no alternative but to marry you. You will insist that it was he who in his befuddled state persuaded you, an innocent young girl, to go to his room and forced you into his bed; that you had had no idea what his intentions were and had trusted him completely. You will, of course, invent some pretext by which he inveigled you into his room.'

The silence that now fell was disturbed only by the fierce mating song of the male canary. Sophia's heart was thudding as different emotions surged through her. She had the courage, but did she have the will to carry out this scheme? Was it not cheating, trickery? How could she ensure that the baron was so befuddled that he was not aware that she was lying? Suppose Ada did not come in when she called out, and Konrad were to . . . to be . . . aroused so passionately as to demand those undefined intimacies which, according to Mrs Groom, plagued men in their prime. Was there really no alternative?

'Is it really necessary for me to be found in Konrad's bed?' Sophia asked. 'Surely my reputation would be damaged sufficiently if I were to be found in his room in my nightclothes?'

'Possibly! But you would run the risk that the baron might not then feel obliged to make an honest woman of you since he had not harmed you in any way. If the idea so horrifies you, my dear, you should put it from your mind,' Enid added sardonically. 'In any event, I could not guarantee that it would work out to your advantage. You would need both courage

and guile to go through with what clearly would be an ordeal
for you. I was wrong ever to suggest it!'

'Oh, no, Mrs Groom, I assure you you were not! I said I
would do anything and I meant it. I always do what I say –
only . . . is there no other way? It is not Konrad's fault Miss
Challinor wants to live at Ortolans and does not wish my
aunts and me to remain there. If only she had chosen someone
else to marry! If it were not for her . . .'

'But she exists, my dear, and you cannot alter this fact.
Since your baron has no intention of breaking his engagement,
your only chance lies in forcing her to do so – which she is
certain to once she learns her fiancé has seduced you. Even
were she to suspect your motives, she cannot prove them, and
she cannot guarantee that you will not tell others that the
baron violated you. Her pride would not permit her to forgive
him, however broken-hearted she might be!'

'She does not have a heart to break!' Sophia replied tartly.
'She is most autocratic and overbearing, and as far as I could
judge, not the least interested in Konrad's wishes when they
conflict with her own. From what Konrad has said, I understand the marriage has been arranged by their parents. I am
sure I could make him far happier than Miss Challinor could
ever do. If I can keep Ortolans, I will do everything I can to
please him.'

'It may not be easy!' Enid said thoughtfully. 'If the baron
suspects a marriage has been forced upon him for your
purposes, he may well hate you for it. Such a beginning does
not augur well for the future. A marriage devoid of love is a
bitter burden for a woman who is tied to her home and her
children and who risks penury if she is found discovering her
pleasures elsewhere. It is easy for a man who may take a
mistress with impunity.'

'I am not seeking married bliss!' Sophia declared. 'If Konrad
Valschintzky will marry me, that is all I ask of him. He can
have as many mistresses as he pleases for all I shall care.'

'My dear child,' Mrs Groom said gently, 'you speak as

one innocent of your bodily functions. If you prove to be one of those females who find themselves eager for the excitement, the sensations, the rewards of physical passion, you will be bitter, resentful and jealous if your husband distributes his favours elsewhere and denies you your married bliss.'

'But I do not want "physical passion" from Konrad,' Sophia declared. 'All I want from him is the right to keep my home.'

'Then be sure not to fall in love with him!' Enid said wryly. 'Like you, I thought it would be enough to have the home I wanted. To be mistress of a duke was the ultimate of my ambition. I was financially secure for life and believed I had all I needed. I did not consider that I might grow to love him; that I would hate every moment he spent away from me; that I wanted his children – children he would never give me. It did not cross my mind that he would ever leave me and abandon the life we shared. Oh, he comes to visit me sometimes, but I know it is only because he has sentimental memories of the old days when we were happy. When he bought me this house, I knew that it was all over between us. If I have any regrets now, it is only that I have had to accept that he never truly loved me. Unrequited love is not an easy bedfellow, my dear. Above all other risks you may take, be very sure that you do not grow to love this man you intend to deceive.'

As she rode back to Ortolans, Sophia found herself wishing that Mrs Enid Groom had not related the story of her life or cautioned her so vehemently about the future. In three days' time, Lavinia Challinor was arriving, and Sophia needed more time to consider the present. Already Konrad had made arrangements for Dick Pylbeam to meet with him and his fiancée to discuss the alterations Miss Challinor desired. Dick Pylbeam was the best builder in Sussex and by way of being an unofficial authority on old houses. His three sons were in the business with him. There was little work they could not carry out between them, but she doubted if they would approve such drastic reconstructions to Ortolans any more than she did.

If only she had more time to consider Mrs Groom's plan, Sophia thought as she handed her mare to Albert and made her way up the servants' staircase to the upstairs landing. How could she face Konrad tonight across the dinner-table, knowing that she planned to go to his bedroom in her night-clothes – climb into his bed and . . . and kiss him! What if he called out in alarm? What if Ada would not agree to take part in this awful charade? Suppose the aunts did wake and discover the dreadful thing she had done? It was all too easy to imagine their shocked faces. It would not console them were she to declare: 'I am doing this for us – so that we can stay here at Ortolans. I am doing this to save the house from Miss Challinor.'

'Adone-do, Miss Sophia! You be all of a fidget!' Ada said crossly as she tried yet again to remove Sophia's riding boot. 'Why you wants to go galloping off dressed like this, I'll never know. What if the master seed you?'

'He isn't "the master"!' Sophia said equally crossly. 'And even if the baron does own this house, he doesn't own me. I shall do as I please!'

'Happen the Pharisees tweaked your temper, miss!' said Ada as she removed the second boot. 'The master be a gurt, know-ledgeable man and you doant have no justification to say diff'rent.'

'If you think so well of him, Ada, I suppose you would not object to my marrying him?' Sophia flashed.

Ada paused in the act of pouring another can of hot water into the bathtub.

'You do be queered, Miss Sophia!' she said anxiously. 'You'm not talking no sense whatsumdever.'

'We shall see about that!' muttered Sophia as she stepped into the hot water. Without knowing quite how, her mind seemed suddenly to be made up – she would go through with Mrs Groom's plan despite all the risks. Somehow she must find or make the opportunity to compromise Konrad Valschintzky. Then the future could take care of itself.

It was one thing to make a resolution, but quite another to carry it out! Sophia thought as she inspected the dining-room table with a critical eye. There would be eleven seated here later this evening and she was determined that nothing would be amiss and thus afford Miss Challinor an opportunity for further criticism.

A week had passed since her last visit to Mrs Enid Groom and despite her bold declaration that she lacked neither the will nor the courage to compromise Konrad Valschintzky, she had lain in bed night after night tormented by doubts as she reflected upon the situation. Was her own need to preserve Ortolans for her aunts and herself sufficient justification for so far-reaching a deception? She convinced herself that it was, and tonight, she intended to ensure that Konrad over-imbibed to the point where he would not know the truth. Unfortunately, although clearly he enjoyed his wines and after-dinner brandy as well as the several tankards of ale or cider he drank after they returned from their rides, she had never yet seen him in the slightest bit befuddled or unsteady on his feet.

Sophia's heart thudded, partly with excitement and partly with nervous anticipation, as she rearranged the position of the epergne supporting the arrangement of violet and white lilac she had earlier placed on the damask tablecloth. The time for prevarication had run out. Miss Challinor had already selected the suite of rooms in the east wing in which Sophia and the aunts were to be confined. Dick Pylbeam was due to start work next week. The servants talked of little else and, perhaps fortuitously for Sophia, were becoming increasingly nervous about their own future. Miss Challinor's maid, a superior London-born woman, had been laying down the law to Cook, of all people. None of Miss Challinor's London staff would dream of working in so old-fashioned a kitchen, she had declared, eyeing the old range with disgust. Her mistress was accustomed to what she called 'a proper hierarchy', and the servants knew their place.

'Us is nearly all Pylbeams as works here,' Ada had protested. 'How can *her* expect our Annie to truckle to Adam, he being her own brother, surelye. "A footman" her says, all high and mighty like, "should command respect from the kitchen-maid". Lawksamercy, Miss Sophia, us don't want the likes of her a-telling us how to serve the family – us as have been tekking care of the Calverleys for nigh on three hundred years!'

It was Ada's comments which had prompted Sophia to enlist Adam's help this evening, although naturally she did not tell him the reason why she wished him to ensure that the baron's glass was constantly refilled.

'You be up to something, Miss Sophia!' Ada had said astutely. 'I hope as how you knows what you're a-doing. Adam said as how you wanted the baron tipsy – and if I know you, you've something afoot.'

Delighted that Adam had correctly interpreted her instructions, Sophia grinned.

'I'll tell you what's "afoot", Ada, all in good time,' she had promised.

Sophia was glad the impromptu dinner party was keeping her too well occupied to allow time for reflection. She was not going to permit any last-minute doubts to undermine her determination to succeed in carrying out Mrs Groom's plan. The danger to her resolve lay in the fact that against her will she was growing to like Konrad Valschintzky.

Although Lavinia's arrival had curtailed the amount of time she and Konrad spent in each other's company, he was most thoughtful in ensuring that she, Sophia, did not feel an unwelcome third. Often, he supported her when she made an unguarded objection to one of Lavinia's many plans to change the interior of the house. Although in most instances, he allowed his fiancée to have her own way, he was unexpectedly on Sophia's side when she declared that it would be a dreadful mistake to remove the carved oak panelling in the library and replace it with Chinese patterned wallpaper. Nor had he agreed with Miss Challinor's wish to put wall-width Chinese carpets over the polished oak floorboards. Most importantly, he had of his own accord objected to the removal of the old mullioned casements so that they could be replaced with tall sash windows.

These occasional differences of opinion between Konrad and his fiancée were eagerly noted by Sophia. Soon after Miss Challinor's arrival at Ortolans, the older girl had decided to treat her as a confidante. Her reasons for so doing, Sophia had quickly realized, were not that she wanted a friend so much as an admirer. Whilst in public she was docile and compliant in her manner towards Konrad, in private she seldom lost an opportunity to tell Sophia that he was totally beneath her thumb.

'It is one of the reasons I have chosen to marry him,' she said airily. 'Unlike many men, my fiancé is most easy-going, and I can always get my own way. One has, of course, to know how to accomplish this and I consider I have quite perfected the art. I pretend deference to his masculine superiority so that he considers me submissive and accommodating, then, in the most docile and gentle way, I persuade him to comply with my wishes. It is a lesson you would do well to learn, Miss Calverley. I have heard you argue with him in a most unfeminine way, and although he may laugh and appear to enjoy your debates, it is clear he is quite put out when he is obliged to concede a point.'

Her voice became irritatingly patronizing. 'Of course, you are very young, and doubtless Konrad sees you as a little sister or cousin and tolerates your temper because of your youth. Direct confrontation with a man is not very subtle, my dear, but then you have had no mother to guide you, so I suppose you have had no opportunity to learn better.'

She had every reason to believe that Konrad would be far better off if he married *her*, Sophia thought as she went upstairs

to change her clothes. If for no other reason than to outshine
Lavinia Challinor, she wanted to look her best tonight. The
aunts had invited the Lamberhills to meet Konrad and his
fiancée. Not only were Sir Sydney and Lady Lamberhill to be
present, but Delia, Francis and, as a last-minute addition,
Delia's sister, Elizabeth who had arrived unexpectedly on a
brief visit to her family in company with a Mr Murray
Armitage, a publisher friend of hers. The aunts had not had
so many guests to a formal dinner at Ortolans for very many
years. Now, as when they prepared for their annual Christmas
party for the village children, they were agog with excitement.
They seemed to have forgotten that the two guests of honour,
Konrad and Lavinia, were about to oust them from the only
home they had ever known.

Sophia was determined the evening would be a success. She
had been down to the cellar with Adam to choose some of
the port and brandy which her grandfather had laid down
forty years ago for the grandsons he had hoped to have. For
the past week, the kitchen had been a hive of activity. Cook
bossed and chivvied her underlings, delighted to have the
opportunity to prepare an elaborate meal which would
demolish any idea Miss Challinor or her critical maid might
have that she was not up to it. The menu, carefully chosen
by Sophia, was to consist of soup, fillets of sole with a lobster
sauce, *timbales de foie gras* and sweetbreads stewed with
mushrooms and truffles. This would be followed by the main
dishes of roast leg of mutton, boiled turkey with oyster sauce
and roast duck and vegetables. Finally there would be a plum
pudding and Cook's especial masterpiece, *Charlotte Russe*.
After the cheese would come the savoury.

Two of the village girls had been hired to assist Cook with
the preparations, and a further two of Ada's younger sisters
to help Annie. An hour later, as Ada put the last touches to
Sophia's hair, she said admiringly:

'You look like a princess, surelye, Miss Sophia!' She fastened
an artificial white rose on top of the upswept curls, and a tiny

black velvet band about Sophia's throat from which hung a gold filigree and topaz pendant.

Nevertheless Sophia still looked anxious as she twisted to survey herself in the glass. The soft primrose silk dress clung to her slim corsetted waist and hips, and the flounces of the skirt, trimmed with old lace, fell in a small train from her bustle.

'Adone-do, Miss Sophia! You be dressed fittin' for Buckingham Palace!' Ada declared.

If Ada's compliments were not sufficient, Delia's were even more extravagant when she arrived with her family.

'You look quite dazzling, Sophia!' she whispered, 'and so grown up! Francis will not be able to take his eyes from you!'

Even Lavinia said in a loud, patronizing voice:

'I'll wager that lovely gown was not made by a country dressmaker, Miss Calverley. I was not aware you had a London modiste!'

Delia's sister, Elizabeth, elegant in a simple blue Empire dress, was also complimentary.

'Delia has never once told me how pretty you've grown, Sophia. May I present Mr Murray Armitage to you?'

'It was most kind of you and your aunts to include me on this family occasion,' said the tall, silver-haired man who was Elizabeth Lamberhill's escort, as he bowed over Sophia's hand. 'May I take advantage of my advanced years and say that I fully endorse Elizabeth's remarks? Your beauty does justice to this charming house. It is a long time since I have been so attracted by such a fine example of Elizabethan architecture.'

Elated to find someone so admiring of Ortolans, Sophia was pleased that Mr Armitage was her dinner companion. Although Francis sat on her left, she was far more interested in the publisher's conversation which now included both Konrad and Lavinia. He was by way of being an authority on English country houses and their history, and to Sophia's delight, was gently remonstrating with Lavinia with regard to her plans to alter the main structure of Ortolans.

Lavinia was resplendent in an elaborate, carnation pink gown, with a plunging, v-shaped décolletage, heavily decorated with satin ruching and velvet ribbons. The feathers in her hair were clasped with a diamond bird ornament. Her sulky expression barely succeeded in concealing her irritation, the greater because Konrad appeared to be much influenced by Mr Armitage's obvious conversance with the subject.

As dinner progressed, Sophia was aware of a pleasant hum of conversation. Apart from Lavinia and Francis – whose scowl revealed his annoyance with Sophia's concentration upon Mr Armitage – everyone else seemed to be enjoying the party. The aunts, seated either side of Sir Sydney, beamed and chattered and, as always, completed each other's sentences. Adam, she noticed, was constantly at Konrad's elbow replenishing his glass.

Konrad now became engrossed in conversation with Elizabeth Lamberhill whose somewhat serious but handsome face was turned towards him with obvious interest. Sophia felt a ridiculous tinge of envy. This past week, when there had only been herself and the aunts at the dinner table, it was she who had monopolized Konrad's attention with her conversation. Perhaps Lavinia was right and she, Sophia, had antagonized him by her arguments and he had only pretended politely that they amused him. He was, after all, a great deal older than herself and in all probability, did think of her as a child. If only she had Elizabeth Lamberhill's sophistication and poise! Elizabeth must be close to him in age – an independent woman of the world who could fascinate him as she herself had failed to do.

Sophia had no opportunity to become closer acquainted with Elizabeth despite her wish to do so. Once the ladies repaired to the drawing-room, leaving the men to their brandy and cigars, Elizabeth seated herself between the aunts and, knowing of their interest in lepidoptera, discussed moths and butterflies with them. Delia drew Sophia to a corner of the room and after remarking what a singularly attractive man she thought the baron, she wished only to speak of the young medical student she had met at the newly opened exhibition at the Royal Academy. She was hopelessly caught in the throes of love! she declared to Sophia's astonishment. Her lifelong plan to go to university had been swept to one side. All she wanted was to remain in London not too far from St George's Hospital where her beloved was doing his training. Fortunately, his background was similar to her own and her parents liked him. It would be years, of course, before they could marry, but marry him one day she would, although, she added breathlessly, they had as yet met only three times and she could not even be sure that he loved her!

Interested though Sophia was in this phenomenal change in her best friend, she would have preferred to discuss Konrad Valschintzky and to gauge Delia's reactions were she to tell her friend that she, too, had met the man she intended to marry – albeit not for the same reason of love! Love did not enter the equation, she told herself, her eyes turning again and again to the door as she watched for Konrad's return. She hoped very much that Adam was still keeping his glass refilled.

Once or twice Sophia had heard him call his fiancée '*mein kätzchen*' which appeared to delight Lavinia. Looking up the German words in the big dictionary in the library, Sophia had noted with disgust that they translated as 'my kitten'. She now badly wanted to be able to relate this to Delia so that they could both laugh together at the inappropriateness of the endearment. With her regal, nose-in-air bearing and statuesque figure, there was nothing of the kittenish in Miss Challinor . . . unless, of course, one remembered her feline inclination to play with her victim before devouring it. Could Konrad Valschintzky really be so blind as not to see that he would be hopelessly dominated if he married her?

It was almost half past nine by the time the men, full of *bonhomie*, rejoined the ladies. Mr Armitage was unrestrained in his praise to the aunts of the excellent vintage port.

'It was of such perfection that I fear the decanter may have circulated amongst us a trifle too frequently,' he said jovially as the aunts twinkled with approval. 'I trust we have not deserted your delightful company too long.'

'No, indeed, sir. We are so pleased you appreciated our father's choice,' said Aunt Georgie.

'We seldom drink it ourselves!' supplemented Aunt Nellie.

'So we are not connoisseurs!' said Aunt Georgie. 'However we are delighted to have you gentlemen back in our midst.'

'Because we had thought you might enjoy a little game of cards?'

'Only if you would like! Our father always vouchsafed that no dinner party was complete without a hand or two.'

'A most agreeable suggestion, ladies!' Mr Armitage said. 'A little loo, perhaps or bezique, whist or faro?'

The aunts looked at one another, their expressions roguish.

'You may think us very wicked, but Father . . .'

'Father liked a French game called *baccarat*.'

'Which he had learned on his travels. Although we know it is illegal to play *baccarat* in England, we thought that just amongst ourselves . . .?'

'Why not, indeed,' broke in Sir Sydney, 'since the Prince of Wales indulges at private parties.'

'Of course, Father never allowed us to gamble with money,' Aunt Nellie vouchsafed. 'We always played for counters.'

Much amused, Mr Armitage heartily seconded their suggestion. The Garrick baize-topped card table was carried in by the footmen and Mr Armitage volunteered to explain the game to the younger ladies. The counters, each one to represent a sovereign, were shared amongst the players. Six packs of cards were shuffled and placed in a container which Mr Armitage explained was called a 'shoe', because it was so shaped.

Sophia, who had been taught to play as a child by the aunts, was well versed in the rules and knew that it was not simply a matter of luck as to how the cards fell, but of assessing one's total as likely or otherwise to better that of the banker.

This required mathematical skill and a clear head, which latter the gentlemen obviously lacked.

An experimental hand or two were played amongst much confusion and laughter, and Adam further disturbed the concentration by bringing in a tray with brandy for the gentlemen and champagne or cordial for the ladies.

Although Mr Armitage declined the glass Adam offered him, Sophia was excited to note that Konrad showed no such restraint. His cheeks were flushed and he appeared in excellent good humour, but there was no other indication that he was overindulging.

Finally, the game was started. As it progressed, the pile of counters in front of Sophia grew. As she raised the stakes, those with fewer counters dropped out, and now it was Konrad alone who challenged her.

'You may not know it, Miss Calverley, but you will stand to lose quite a fortune in so-called "sovereigns" if you tempt Fate any further,' he commented, his dark eyes dancing with amusement.

'I always gamble on a winning streak of luck, sir!' Sophia replied, her eyes sparkling. 'Will you bet against me? Or are you afraid? I see you have only one "sovereign" left. You may withdraw if you wish!'

'I'll do no such thing!' said Konrad as he poured himself another brandy. 'Deal me my cards, madam!' On his right, Lavinia frowned.

'I was not aware you were so enthusiastic a gambler!' she said in a low disapproving voice only lightly offset by a smile.

'But all of life is a gamble, my dear!' Konrad replied, laughing. 'And I have always led mine to the full. Come now, I am putting up a very moderate stake compared to Sophia's.'

'Yet again Miss Calverley has correctly assessed the odds,' Mr Armitage said a few moments later, as Sophia added Konrad's counter to her own.

'Well done, Sophia!' Francis muttered as he gazed adoringly into her eyes. The by now uncountable number of glasses of brandy he had consumed were lending him spurious courage, and beneath the table, his hand touched hers.

'Have you thought further . . . about us?' he asked in a low voice. 'Can you not give me even a little hope? You know in whose keeping my heart lies!'

The fact that he only just managed to subdue a hiccough in the middle of this speech left Sophia with no more worthy sentiment than the desire to giggle. Looking up, she caught Konrad's eye and wondered if by chance he had heard Francis's declaration. There was an expression of quizzical amusement on his face and she was certain that he had. Her first reaction was one of irritation that he was enjoying her discomfiture, but her sense of humour followed quickly and she was unable to suppress a smile.

It was a moment of isolated intimacy when it seemed to Sophia as if there were only herself and Konrad in the room, even though the conversation was continuing around them. She felt a strange breathlessness and confusion, and quickly dropped her eyes.

'*Banco*!' called Aunt Nellie returning to the table.

'*Suivie*!' said Aunt Georgie who had joined them.

'I see your aunts are enjoying themselves hugely!' Konrad's voice obliged Sophia to look up. He had risen from the table and, with a glass of brandy in one hand, had come to stand behind her chair. 'They are quite nonpareil, do you not agree, Mr Lamberhill? I have not enjoyed myself so much for years! You give an excellent party, ladies. Perfect food, matchless wine and the most entertaining company.'

Sophia was aware of Konrad's hand on the back of her chair as he steadied himself. The 'matchless wine', together with the brandy, was having its effect at last, she thought as he swayed slightly. Mr Armitage was obviously similarly afflicted for when the aunts completed the coup, he stood up and said to them:

'I am afraid, dear ladies, that I, a mere male, cannot match your stamina. Elizabeth, my dear, do you think it is time we left?'

Lady Lamberhill, who had enjoyed the delightfully informal atmosphere, nodded at her husband who looked suspiciously as if he might fall asleep at any moment.

'Yes, it is time we went home. A *most* enjoyable evening, and I can well understand your liking for this card game. We shall have to learn to play properly. I see you have amassed quite a fortune, Sophia! Now I realize why your grandfather insisted upon using counters in place of money – one could all too easily acquire a liking for gambling!'

'Yes, indeed!' said her husband who enjoyed a flutter on the horses, but had no intention of allowing his wife to do so. 'Come, Delia, Elizabeth, and you, Francis. Send for our carriage, will you, m'boy?'

'Time you too were in bed, Sophia!' Aunt Georgie said as Mr Armitage and the Lamberhills were finally upon their way. 'I do hope you enjoyed the evening, Miss Challinor?'

Lavinia did not trouble to do more than a token stifling of a yawn.

'Most enjoyable!' she said vaguely. 'But I am quite exhausted and we must be up early tomorrow; the plumber is coming, is he not, Konrad?'

'I had forgotten!' said Konrad, his voice almost impercept-ibly slurred. Sophia, watching him, knew that she had succeeded – Konrad was fast becoming befuddled. A few more drinks and . . .

'I would like a glass of cordial. The room is so warm and I feel suddenly thirsty!' she said, as she led the way back into the room towards the table where stood the decanter. 'Would you not like a last nightcap, sir? Miss Challinor?'

'Certainly not!' Lavinia said. 'I am going to bed! Good-night, my dear,' she added as she lifted her face for Konrad's kiss.

'Sleep well, *mein kätzchen*!' Konrad replied, almost missing the proffered cheek as he swayed unsteadily.

'That will depend upon the chance I am given to do so!' Lavinia said coldly as she made to follow the aunts out of the room. 'I am convinced there are mice in the wainscoting. There was such a dreadful noise last night that I barely had any sleep at all.' With the aunts insisting – much to Lavinia's horror – that the noise more probably came from bats than mice, they disappeared up the stairs.

'A most congenial evening!' Konrad commented as he settled himself into one of the chairs. 'I find the Misses Calverley quite delightful. Small wonder you had so happy a childhood, Sophia!'

Sophia remained standing by the table, her eyes thoughtful as she watched Konrad stretch out his long legs and lean his head back against one of the cushions. In one hand, he held a half-empty glass of brandy; the other was tucked behind his fair head. He looked perfectly at home . . . and very much as if he might drop off to sleep at any moment.

I would be perfectly happy if we were a married couple and this had been our dinner party! she thought. Moreover, I could make him a deal happier than could Lavinia Challinor, for all her airs and graces. Since it seems Konrad cannot see her faults – and she has certainly not shown herself in a good light this evening – I will be acting for his good by liberating him of so tiresome a fiancée.

Having rid herself of any last remaining vestige of guilt, she walked over to the reclining man and put the brandy decanter on the coffin stool beside him.

'Most thoughtful of you!' Konrad said, smiling up at her. 'I really think I have drunk enough this evening, but what harm in another!'

Without warning, the warmth and seeming intimacy of Konrad's smile affected Sophia in a way quite strange to her. Her cheeks felt hot, her legs weak and there was a sinking sensation in the pit of her stomach. At one and the same time, she wanted to escape from the room, and yet she longed to smooth those fair curls from this man's forehead, lay her face against his, embrace him.

Was it possible she was, after all, falling in love? she asked herself as she stood there staring down at him. Or had she, too, had too much champagne, and her mind and body been affected? She drew in her breath sharply. It was better not to consider such a thing. It was marriage to Konrad and not love she was seeking. Tonight she had the perfect opportunity to carry out Mrs Groom's plan, and if she did not do so, it would forever be too late.

'I think I shall follow Miss Challinor's good example and retire,' she said lightly. 'Please don't get up, sir!' she added as Konrad attempted to rise to his feet. 'I hope you will sleep well!'

Only with an effort did she refrain from running from the room. As the door closed behind her, she hurried up the stairs to find Ada. The maid was dozing in the armchair, her mouth slightly open as she snored. On the bed lay Sophia's old white cotton nightgown, her warm *peignoire* beside it. There were freshly ironed sheets and pillowcases, the former neatly turned back, and on the floor, her velvet mules. Everything was as usual – and yet she felt as if someone else was observing it.

'Ada, wake up. I have something to tell you!'

With a sense of urgency, mingled with excitement, she roused the sleeping woman.

'It's of the utmost importance, Ada!' she said in a low voice. 'You must listen very carefully, and I warn you not to try to dissuade me, as I shall carry out my plan with or without your help.'

The woman rubbed her eyes and shook her head in perplexity as she tried to make sense of her mistress's words. The excited sparkle of the girl's eyes and the tenseness of her stance warned Ada that some hare-brained scheme was afoot.

'What plan, Miss Sophia? What's you a-scheming now?'

'I'm going to compromise the baron!' Sophia replied without hesitation. 'In an hour's time, I shall go to his bedroom, climb into his bed and . . . and kiss him.'

At last Ada was awake and galvanized onto her feet.

'Adone-do, Miss Sophia!' she cried aghast. 'You baint going

to do no such wicked thing! Whatsoever daft shenanigan will you be thinking on next!'

Ignoring these protests, Sophia took the maid by her arms and stared into her eyes.

'Pay attention, Ada, because this is what *you* are going to have to do!' she said.

CHAPTER SEVENTEEN

1889

The elaborate meal and excess of liquor had taken their toll upon Konrad. He lay on his back in the large feather bed, his slumber disturbed by strange dreams. An extraordinary fencing duel with Francis Lamberhill, fought in their nightshirts in the centre of the stage of the Staatsoper in Vienna was followed by a nightmare in which he was attempting to save Crown Prince Rudolf from drowning in Ortolans' river.

A brief period of wakefulness was followed by yet another dream in which he was lying in a bed when the door of his room opened. He could see nothing, for the room was in total darkness, but he heard the faint whisper of clothing as someone approached him. He realized it was a woman when the faint fragrance of lavender water reached him. He knew that the invisible visitor could not be Lavinia, and he felt a surge of excitement as soft, gentle hands reached out and touched his face.

Unaware that he was not dreaming, Konrad felt no surprise when, without speaking, his unknown visitor slipped into bed beside him. His heartbeat quickened as her lips touched his mouth. At first the kisses were tentative but as he drew this dream-lover into his arms, they became more ardent. The silence that prevailed was broken only by their hurried breathing.

The identity of the soft, warm body he was embracing was of little concern to him. He could feel his companion trembling and supposed her to be as stirred by desire as himself. His hands moved to her breasts and he felt her shudder as he touched her nipples. Her all-but-inaudible gasp broke the silence as her body tensed.

Afraid now that she was going to leave him as mysteriously as she had arrived, his arms tightened around her slim waist.

'Stay with me! You must not go! Stay here with me!' he murmured, moving his body so that she lay beneath him. He began once more to caress her. He sensed her response as he lifted her nightgown and his desire quickened. Silently cursing the alcohol which he now vaguely realized was seriously inhibiting him, he gently parted her legs, and renewed his caresses. Wishing desperately that his mind and body were not so hopelessly uncoordinated, Konrad tried to concentrate upon his one coherent instinct – to possess the soft vibrant woman now lying beneath him.

He was not sure how many minutes had passed when suddenly, without warning, she screamed.

'Help me, Ada! Ada, where are you?'

Her voice shocked him into full wakefulness – and a horrified awareness of who she was.

'Help me! Ada, Ada, where are you?'

Before Konrad had gathered his senses sufficiently to fathom how Sophia Calverley could possibly be here in his bedroom, *in his bed*, the door opened and he saw, silhouetted by her lamplight, the rotund figure of her maid. His head swimming, he sat perfectly still, watching as the girl beside him pushed back the bedclothes and, running across the room, threw herself into the servant's arms.

'Oh, Miss Sophia! Miss Sophia!' the woman wailed.

'Take me out of here, Ada! Thank goodness you heard me call! Oh, Ada, help me. I have been disgraced!'

No, this was not a dream, it was a nightmare, Konrad told himself as he reached for his dressing-gown and tried to climb out of bed. The contours of the room blurred and as his feet touched the floor, he all but fell on his face.

'Be damned if I've not drunk too much!' he muttered, shaking his head in an attempt to clear his vision. He was

still far from convinced that he was not caught up in a nightmare from which he would presently awake.

'Don't come near me!' Sophia called out as he made to
move towards her. 'How could you . . . when I trusted you
. . . you took advantage of my ignorance . . .'

Stupefied, Konrad stood watching in disbelief as, breaking
free from her maid's arms, Sophia rushed from the room.

Avoiding Konrad's bewildered gaze, Ada, recalling her
instructions, said reproachfully:

'Oh, sir, you shouldn't oughta a-done it;' and hastily
followed Sophia out of the room.

As the door closed behind her, Konrad stood swaying in
the centre of the floor. Feeling his way to his bed-table, he
fumbled for matches and lit his oil lamp. Staring down at the
rumpled sheets, he tried to recall the sequence of events. How
had the girl come to be in his room? Try as he might, he could
not remember the circumstances preceding the opening of the
door and the sound of her approach.

Slowly, he collapsed on to the bed and rested his aching
head in his hands. It was inconceivable that a young unmarried girl like Sophia Calverley would visit him of her own
accord, he reasoned – and for a purpose which could hardly
be mistaken! The memory of that soft, inviting body set his
blood racing once again; *but he had not taken what she offered,*
for surely he could not fail to remember it if he had!

With a feeling of dismay, Konrad realized that he could
be certain of nothing, for he had supposed he was dreaming
when she had come to his room. He had a hazy memory of
the two of them, earlier, alone together in the drawing-room.
He had been drinking brandy. He could remember quite
clearly thinking what an exceptionally attractive girl Sophia
was with those large hazel-green eyes and flame-coloured
hair; thinking that she deserved far better for a husband than
the pompous young Francis Lamberhill; thinking her a deal
better company than Lavinia.

The memory now of his betrothed was like a dash of cold

water. His head was beginning to clear, and soberly he reflected that Lavinia would undoubtedly hear of tonight's extraordinary events. How could he possibly explain them to her when he could not explain them to himself?

He picked up his gold watch from the bed-table and saw that it lacked only two hours to dawn. There was nothing to be done now, he decided. His head ached unbearably and common sense suggested he get back into bed and sleep off the night's excesses so that he had a clear head in the morning.

Konrad lay back on his pillows praying that if sleep should come, this time it would not be troubled by nightmares or by dreams.

Too excited to sleep, Sophia could only doze fitfully for the remainder of the night. Although in part triumphant that her plan had succeeded so well, she was hopelessly confused by the unexpected effect the experience had had upon her. When she had entered Konrad's bedroom, her courage had momentarily waned and she had been horribly afraid that he would guess her identity and challenge her. When neither happened, her courage had returned and she had slipped silently into bed beside him. When still he did not question her, she had faithfully followed Mrs Groom's instructions. However, from there on, events had ceased to go as planned. When she had put her lips to his and he had drawn her against him, fear had given way to a trembling excitement. Her shivering body had suddenly sprung to life, and she had been filled with a deep inexplicable yearning that was both pain and ecstasy.

She had tried in vain to concentrate her mind upon why she was there in Konrad's bed, but had thought only how firm and strong and warm his body felt; how astonishing the sensations his hands aroused as they touched her breasts; how tantalizing his mouth as he had kissed her neck, her shoulders, her lips. Her body had been on fire, consumed with longing, with a fierce, sweet expectancy. Her nerves were so tautly strung that when his fingers had touched her nipples, she had cried out with pleasure.

Laying her hot cheek against the cool linen pillow, Sophia recalled Mrs Groom's comment that some women enjoyed marital pleasures – and knew herself to be one of them. She did not feel 'despoiled', but exultant that not only would Ortolans be in her safe keeping when Konrad married her, but that she could share his bed and the euphoric sensations of his naked body lying beside hers. It did not worry her in the least that she was no longer a virgin; that she had actually permitted a man to caress her; not just to touch his lips to hers, but to feel his tongue searching her mouth. It was hard to believe that such extraordinary intimacies could give such pleasure. She could understand now why those who knew about them were embarrassed to describe them and girls like herself were left ignorant of how children were conceived.

So lost had she been by the rapture of the moment, she had had to force herself to remember that Ada was waiting outside the door. She had had to force herself to call for help, when all she had wanted to do was to remain where she was for ever! The sound of her own voice had shattered the silence – and broken the spell.

As dawn broke, Sophia stared out of her window at the river mist curling in over the lawn and, tired as she was, she was filled with a sense of well-being. Her courage had not failed her and she had won! Now there would be no Miss Lavinia Challinor to evict her from this room; to prevent her ever again seeing this view of the garden; of going down to breakfast with the aunts in the dining-room; of taking her place beneath the portrait of Grandmother. She would continue to sit in the library at her grandfather's desk; to write the weeks' events in *The Calverley Journal*. Ada, Cook, Annie, would continue to look after the household and Ortolans would remain unchanged. Dick could be told that he was not after all required to make any horrible alterations to the house; the aunts would not have to sort out all their personal possessions in order to remove to the east wing; the servants could settle down again and she, Sophia, would once more be the undisputed mistress of her home.

When Ada came in with her cup of hot chocolate, Sophia was still in her nightdress staring at the roof of the west wing where the rising early summer sun was turning to gold the sand-coloured Horsham slabs.

'Look at the house-martins feeding their babies, Ada!' she said, 'which reminds me, I must tell Dick to put a grating over the drawing-room chimney – the starlings are nesting there again.'

'Adone-do, Miss Sophia, you'll catch your death!' Ada said, tight-lipped. 'Now drink your chocolate this minute, afore it gets as cold as you are!'

Sophia laughed and flung her arms round the old woman.

'I couldn't possibly drink or eat anything, Ada!' she said. 'Tell me what is happening? Did you do as I asked?'

Ada nodded, her face a mask of anxiety as she put the tray down on the table. Her cap was awry on her grey hair, her apron straps were wrongly criss-crossed and her hands were trembling.

'I doant approve of this, not nohow!' she muttered close to tears. 'No good will come of it, Miss Sophia – mark my words!'

'*But you told Miss Challinor's maid what you saw?*' Sophia persisted, needing to be certain that her plan was proceeding.

'That I did, may God forgive us both, Miss Sophia!'

Sophia laughed.

'It's Miss Challinor's forgiveness we need!' she said. 'Not that I care a fig about her, any more than she cares about me or my aunts – or indeed, you, Ada. So stop fussing and tell me what she said.'

Ada gulped as she wrung her hands together.

'She didn't say naught, Miss Sophia. She looked that shocked with her mouth dropped open and no word a-comin' out! She went hot-foot up them stairs like a scalded cat . . .'

'. . . to tittle-tattle to her mistress!' Sophia concluded

triumphantly. 'Quick now, Ada, help me get dressed. Something is bound to happen soon. Is the baron up?'

'His manservant were tekkin him a big jug of coffee,' Ada said. 'He didn't say naught to me, but then he allus keeps hisself to hisself.'

'Only because he doesn't speak English!' Sophia explained as she struggled into her chemise. 'Now help me with this horrible corset, Ada. How I hate it!'

As soon as she was dressed, Sophia sent a reluctant Ada back downstairs to see if she could glean any further information. She was filled with impatience to have the final results of her plan concluded. Surely, she told herself, Miss Challinor would not leave? Would Konrad go with her? But that was unlikely if they had broken their engagement . . .

The minutes seemed to crawl by as, restlessly, Sophia paced the floor of her bedroom, pausing once in a while to look out of her window. Down in the yard, the grooms were taking the horses out for their morning exercise. Tommy, the bootboy, was carrying out a pail of scraps for the chickens. From the woods came the high-pitched squawk of a cock pheasant. One of the maids opened a window and shook out a quilt. Annie came out of the dairy carrying two pitchers of milk, and crossing the yard disappeared into the kitchen. One of the farm dogs emerged from the tack room and scattered the flock of white doves pecking amongst the cobbles, sending them into the air in a cloud before they settled in safety on the platforms of their dovecot.

It was like any other summer morning at Ortolans, Sophia thought – and yet it was not. She was viewing the scene with the eyes of a lover who had so nearly lost a beloved and had been reprieved. Where – oh, where – was Ada? What was Miss Challinor doing? And Konrad? Was he angry? Remorseful? Relieved? How would he greet her? Sophia's cheeks suddenly flamed at the memory of the previous night, and unconsciously, she touched her lips with her fingertips where his mouth had covered hers with kisses – those special kisses . . .

Downstairs in the library, Konrad's hands were fingering uneasily the worn leather cover of *The Calverley Journal*. His head throbbed and he wished very much that Lavinia would lower her voice which seemed to beat against his skull like gunshot.

'I am very sorry, my dear, but I am unable to give you any explanation,' he said truthfully in reply to her oft-repeated demand. 'I am not denying that I had had far too much to drink – quite unforgivable in a gentleman, I agree. I can only say again that I do not recall any of those events attributed to me – of feeling ill, crying out for assistance, hearing Sophia come into my room, inviting her into my bed. I remember nothing of it.'

Lavinia looked at Konrad's dark head and noted that, even when shamefaced, he was still excessively handsome. She did not doubt that he was speaking the truth, for he was never devious. On the contrary, he was inclined at times to be too straightforward when a white lie might have better served his purpose. Even now he did not deny that the girl had been *in his bed*! He would have done better to refute it. He did admit to being drunk, but, according to him, he had been far too inebriated to be able to comply with any amorous demands Sophia may have made upon him or that he may have wished to make upon her. Lavinia did not fully understand what he meant by the statement but she had no doubt he was telling the truth. Were her mother to learn of this, she would direct her instantly to break off her engagement.

Now that the first shock had passed and Lavinia's anger had abated, she realized that she was reluctant to do so. There were other husbands to be had – but few as attractive, amusing and good-natured as Konrad. Moreover, his family were extremely highly connected. As the Baroness Valschintzky, she would move in royal circles, and the Empress herself – a friend of Konrad's mama – would be attending the wedding which was to be held in the Augustinian church adjoining the Imperial Palace. Invitations would already have been sent to the eight hundred guests but for the death of the Crown Prince which, to Lavinia's annoyance, had meant a postponement of their wedding plans.

Treading firmly on her emotional reactions, Lavinia coolly assessed her position. The announcement of her engagement to Konrad had been a very public affair, bringing forth a spate of congratulations. Were she now to announce that she had changed her mind – for whatever trumped-up reason – there would be an immense amount of speculation and gossip, perhaps even requests for a true explanation from her family and friends. She had no wish to become the laughing stock of Viennese society if the truth were ever to be known. Might it not be better in every way to squash such a possibility at source?

Lavinia felt a surge of renewed anger towards Konrad for placing her in this humiliating position. She would not easily forgive him – a thought which led her once again to a less emotional but more practical outlook – her 'forgiveness' of this premarital lapse might greatly increase the power she had over Konrad in the future. She would have but to remind him how magnanimous she had been, to make him feel guilty were he ever to neglect or deceive her. In short, he would begin their married life heavily indebted to her for her broad-mindedness. As to the girl, Sophia . . .

Lavinia's thoughts took a sharp turn. Little Miss Calverley had left no one in doubt that she resented Konrad's claim to Ortolans – and even more, her place as future mistress of the house. Was it possible that the girl was not as innocent as she seemed? That she had planned this excursion to Konrad's room in order to achieve this very situation? Granted, Konrad should not have drunk himself into a state of stupidity – but he would not be the first gentleman to do so! It was, however, highly improbable that he would have had sufficient of his wits about him to persuade an *unwilling* girl to go alone to his room in the middle of the night! Suppose Sophia had screamed for help and woken her, Lavinia? The aunts? Even if Konrad did not respect the girl, he had sufficient respect for her, his fiancée, and for the two old dears whom he idolized, to ravage their niece under their own roof!

'I think you may have been tricked, Konrad,' she said quietly. 'Let us sit down and discuss the possibility. If what I suspect is the case, then I have misjudged you. You deserve my sympathy and cooperation, not my dismissal.'

Delighted to have Lavinia in less strident voice and happy to comply with anything which might bring this unfortunate incident to a conclusion, Konrad collapsed into a chair and turned to face his fiancée.

'So you see, my dear, there is little doubt that this was the girl's attempt to come between us,' Lavinia concluded her theorizing, 'and we must not allow her to do so, not merely for the sake of the love we share, but for our parents' sake. Just think how upset your poor mama would be! And, indeed, mine. Then we must think of the poor Misses Calverley. No, Konrad, we cannot allow it. Do you not agree?'

Konrad frowned.

'I think it unlikely – most unlikely – that a young girl like Sophia would take such a terrible risk, even if one allows that she was capable of devising such a scheme. She is very young and . . .'

'And determined, Konrad,' Lavinia said firmly.

Despite his wish not to do so, Konrad was obliged to agree that Sophia had been very determined in her resistance to Lavinia. 'It is very noble of you, Lavinia, to consider that I may not be entirely to blame. Nevertheless, I cannot but honour my obligations in the circumstances. Moreover, I am obliged to consider your reputation as well as Sophia's. Your maid . . . her maid . . .'

'They can be silenced!' Lavinia said quickly. 'Mariette will not have told anyone else – she was far too shocked! As to the Calverley maid – from all I have heard, she is totally devoted to the family. I have no doubt she too could be persuaded to keep her mouth shut. The aunts are still blissfully ignorant of the facts. Why then should you be obliged to save reputations that are not yet in danger?'

Konrad's head was spinning and throbbed unmercifully. Nonetheless, he could see the force of Lavinia's quite unexpected arguments. He had not, he told himself wryly, appreciated that she was so fond of him! As to Sophia – he had to admit that she might well be culpable. Her love for Ortolans was clear enough for a blind man to see. Nevertheless, it required a very great deal of courage, and cunning, to plan his downfall – if such she had.

He now found himself confused by vague memories of the hours – or was it only minutes? – when he had held Sophia's body in his arms.

With an effort, Konrad tried to forget the sudden surge of desire that was undermining his fear of what he might have done. Surely he could not in fact have ravaged her, for he knew himself quite incapable when he was intoxicated. If only he could remember, he thought desperately. If the girl had been a virgin and was no longer so . . . she must now believe herself ruined. Even if she had engineered her own seduction for her own ends as Lavinia suspected, the price she would have to pay was a heavy one if the truth became known and he did not marry her!

'You must speak to her, Konrad, tell her that we have discussed the matter and are agreed that it is best, in the circumstances, to overlook it. If it was indeed a trick, then she will be angry and disappointed, but it is a situation she has brought upon herself. There is nothing she can do to separate us if you do not allow her to blackmail you.'

'And if she is innocent? If I did persuade her to my room and took advantage of her?' Konrad argued.

With difficulty, Lavinia curbed her irritation, but cleverly, she concealed it.

'These things do happen from to time to time, my dear!' she said. 'Believe me, a year from now, she will in all probability be married to that Lamberhill boy, and the whole unfortunate incident will be forgotten. In the meanwhile, if you think it will compensate her, I shall raise no objection to her remaining here until we are married – provided, of course, that she never again behaves so foolishly, so wickedly. I understand from her aunts that Francis Lamberhill has proposed. If she is sensible, she should accept him. If she does not then we will arrange for them to remove to The Grange.'

Lavinia, it seemed, had worked out a solution to this whole shocking affair, Konrad thought with a surge of irritation as his fiancée left the room. He sat down heavily in the leather armchair and supported his head in his hands as he leant his elbows on the leather-topped desk. In a few moments, he must confront Sophia, who was being summoned to join him in the library. More than anything else, he needed a drink to help clear his thoughts, but he resisted the temptation. Brandy might add to his confusion!

One point at least seemed clear. If he had taken advantage of the girl, he was in honour bound to marry her – and he would do so, whatever Lavinia had to say about it. As an officer and a gentleman, he could do no less. Nor did the prospect appal him. It was the thought of the reactions of his mother, Lavinia and her mother, the Calverley aunts, which he found most distressing. How could he have got himself into this position? He was not a silly young *kadett* who lacked the experience to realize how much liquor he could hold without losing his senses!

Nevertheless, he had been senseless, and in such a state, he might well have wished to bed a pretty – and available – girl. The enigma remained as to how she had come to be in his bed. Could Lavinia be right in her somewhat brutal judgement of little Miss Calverley? Had Sophia deliberately tried to compromise him? Despite all the problems crowding in on him, he would have to admit that he found her daring intriguing. Deep in his heart, he believed she could have been capable of such a reprehensible scheme; but until he could be certain – and that might never be possible – he had no alternative but to give her the benefit of the doubt. She alone knew the truth – and if she were to confess that he had done no real harm to her, then he need feel under no further obligation to her. As Lavinia had said, her reputation would not be tarnished and she could marry Francis Lamberhill if that was her wish. He hoped it was not. The idea of her giving her beautiful body to such an ineffectual, effeminate young man grated in a manner Konrad could not understand.

Despite everything Lavinia had said and, indeed, the conviction with which she had stated her views, he was strangely unwilling to believe Sophia guilty. At the same time, if she were innocent, then *he* had been guilty of the worst possible offence against her. He must find out – if he could – where the truth lay, however unpalatable it might be.

Wearily, he tried to compose himself as Sophia came hurrying into the room.

Although there were dark shadows beneath her eyes, she looked astonishingly bright and colourful in a pink and white candy striped blouse tucked into a slim, tailored skirt. The tight frilled collar of the blouse framed her face. Her burnished red hair was plaited into a low loop, caught up by a large pink and white bow.

'You wanted to see me,' she said demurely as Konrad rose to his feet and pulled back a chair for her to be seated. His face was expressionless as he said quietly:

'Yes, we have to talk – about last night! I think I should begin with an apology – and since I have no excuse, I shall not seek to try to excuse my behaviour.' He avoided her eyes which looked unusually large and filled with expectancy as he continued. 'Only once before in my life have I been so inebriated that I cannot recall how I reached my bed. It is to my eternal shame that last night I disgraced myself for the second time.'

'I expect it was my grandfather's brandy,' Sophia said ingenuously. 'It is very strong and . . .'

'. . . and I partook too freely,' Konrad broke in. 'Now, since

I cannot conceive how you came to be in my . . . my room, perhaps you would explain.'

Sophia regarded him with the first suspicion of unease. Konrad's tone bordered on the accusing.

'But do you not remember? You were ill – you called out for someone to help you and I . . .' The well-rehearsed lies came out with conviction and by now, Sophia was almost believing them herself. 'I had been on the point of sleep when I thought I smelt smoke. Fire is such a hazard in old houses like Ortolans, so I was making a check of all the empty rooms.'

'You did not think to call a servant to do this for you?'

'Why should I?' Sophia retorted. 'They were all asleep and it was late.'

'I see! So you heard me call out and came into my room. Was I ill?'

'Well, no!' Sophia replied, her unease deepening at this interrogation. 'I came across to your bedside because you were moaning and . . .'

'Yet my man, who was in the adjoining room, heard nothing of this?'

Sophia had forgotten his manservant who she herself had allocated the bedroom adjoining Konrad's.

'Possibly he was sleeping soundly!' she improvised quickly.

Now Konrad knew she was not telling the truth. When his valet had come to his room to dress him this morning, he had questioned the man carefully, hoping that he might be able to throw some light on the previous night's events. His servant had retired early to bed, having been told by Konrad that he need not wait up for him. He had been woken by the noise his master had made some hours later when he had stumbled into his bedroom.

'I did wonder, Herr Baron, if I should come to your assistance but as you did not call out for me . . .'

'Quite so!' Konrad had reassured him. 'But later . . . did you hear nothing?'

His servant had indeed heard movements and whispered

voices on the landing. He had opened the communicating door and seeing Konrad asleep in his bed, had been sufficiently curious to open his own door leading on to the passageway. There he had seen 'the young lady and her maid'; had seen Sophia position Ada by the doorway and then go in to Konrad's bedroom.

'You have always instructed me, Herr Baron, that under such circumstances, I am never to intrude, so I returned to my bed!'

Confound the man, Konrad thought now. It was true he had always insisted upon total privacy when he had had an assignation with a female; but in this instance, his servant's interruption would have been most fortuitous. He did not doubt the man's word. There would be no advantage to him to lie, whereas Sophia . . .

'I see! *You* heard me but my *valet* did not. So you approached my bedside, and then?'

A deep rush of colour spread to Sophia's cheeks. She had not expected to be questioned on such a delicate subject. Biting her lip and lowering her eyes, she said defiantly:

'Then you pulled me down beside you and . . . and kissed me . . . and then . . . then it happened.'

Sophia's blushes lent authenticity to her professed innocence, and Konrad was momentarily confused. This was not the 'brazen hussy' Lavinia had described. He could not bring himself to question Sophia further although he would very much like to have known what 'it' meant. Almost as if she could read his thoughts, Sophia said quickly:

'I begged you to desist but you did not seem to hear me. I was afraid to call out for fear my aunts might hear me. I realized you had had too much to drink and were not responsible for your actions, but they would have been so fearfully shocked it might have killed them! Then I heard footsteps outside the room and suspecting it might be Ada come to search for me, I was able to call for help – only by then it was too late,' she concluded triumphantly.

This was yet another blatant untruth! Konrad realized. According to his valet, Ada had already been stationed outside the door and Sophia had been perfectly well aware of her presence there from the moment she entered his room. She could have called out to her maid for help at any time.

From the start, Konrad had been reluctant to believe Lavinia's wild suggestions that Sophia had deliberately planned to compromise him. He had been unwilling to think such a young, innocent girl capable of anything so dishonest, yet now he was obliged to admit that he knew only too well this other aspect of her character. Had he not admired that fiery determination; that courage; that forceful independence of spirit which had enabled her to manage his estates as if she had been a boy?

In a voice devoid of expression, he said quietly:

'Then we have to decide what is to be done now.'

Sophia's face brightened now that the subject of what had occurred in the bed was done with.

'It is surely not so terrible a disaster,' she proffered. 'We can be married quite quickly, can we not? I am sure my aunts would raise no objection. They are very fond of you. Truly, Konrad, I am not in the least angry with you; I realize you were not responsible for your behaviour. Anyway, I think we could be very happy together. As for Ortolans . . . well, you know that I can manage here alone if the need were to arise after we were married – if you had to go to your own country to see your estates, for example.'

Konrad met her earnest gaze with a growing sense of disappointment. This confident, ebullient young girl with her bright eager eyes and ready answers bore no resemblance to the professed victim of a cruel, drunken assault upon her innocent person. There had been no tears, no recriminations, no regrets for her lost virginity. If anything, her manner was exultant! He was in no doubt now that Lavinia had been right – Sophia had planned everything, even down to their ultimate marriage and her resumption of ownership of the house.

Embarrassing though he realized it might be for her, he determined to question her further.

'You are proving very tolerant of a man who has caused you the gravest injury!' he said, the gentleness of his tone lulling Sophia into a false sense of security. 'You do not hate me for what I did?'

Sophia looked genuinely surprised.

'But why should I hate you? I know you did not intend me any harm.'

'No, indeed, but I did not hurt you? Cause you pain?'

Now that she believed she had achieved her aims, Sophia felt she could afford to be generous. She beamed down at his white, anxious face.

'Indeed you did not! Since we are to be married, I will confess that I found your embraces very pleasurable. I had not known that kisses could be so enjoyable.'

'Kisses!' Konrad repeated sharply. 'And the rest of it . . .?'

Sophia blushed.

'You mean when you caressed me? Do you wish me to tell you that I enjoyed that, too? You know, Konrad, now that I have experienced marital bliss, I am astonished that no grown-up person will speak of it. It would be so simple to say that it is the most exciting and satisfying thing in the world to kiss and touch as we did. Delia and I had always supposed that it would be . . . well, undignified, unpleasant . . . something we would not want to do. We thought quite stupidly that . . .' She broke off, suddenly too embarrassed to tell her silent companion that she and Delia had supposed the mating of man and woman was akin to that of animals. 'Well, we supposed that after our wedding night, we would not want to do it again; but I shall be more than content to be your wife and share your bed!'

The ingenuousness of her declaration touched him only momentarily. He could think only that Sophia must be the first female ever to describe the taking of her virginity in such glowing terms. She had just confessed her ignorance of the act of love and might well be as ignorant of the existence of her maidenhead. From all he had heard from his various mistresses, that first invasion had been difficult, painful and entirely without pleasure.

It was ironic, he thought, that this young girl's very innocence had betrayed her guilt. Had she spoken of pain, of telltale signs of blood, of his use of force to overcome the resistance, he would have been convinced of his seduction of her, and unquestionably would have married her. Clearly she had planned to compromise him exactly as Lavinia suspected. He felt a momentary urge to pick Sophia up and put her over his knee and spank her; but he reminded himself that she was no child. She was eighteen years old and had deliberately, knowingly, schemed to compromise him to achieve her ends.

Wearily, he leaned back in his chair and forced himself to look into those bright, expectant eyes.

'I can only apologize once more for my behaviour,' he said. 'Fortunately, it does not seem that any great harm has come of it. You must realize, however, that I am in no position to marry you, Sophia, however successful a match you deem it might be. You appear to have forgotten that I am already betrothed.'

He turned away from the look of shock and astonishment on Sophia's face.

'But Miss Challinor . . . surely she . . . you cannot mean that . . . *what of my reputation?*'

The last part of the sentence was almost a wail. Despite the extreme gravity of the situation, Konrad nearly smiled.

'Miss Challinor is aware of what happened, and because of the circumstances, she has generously offered to overlook my unfortunate lapse,' he said gravely. 'As to your reputation, I have given it much thought and have decided your name is best protected if we behave as if last night's events never happened. Miss Challinor can rely absolutely upon the discretion of her maid, and it is to be hoped that you can rely upon the discretion of yours. Since we four are the only ones who know the truth, your reputation should, therefore, remain undamaged. If it is your intent to marry Mr Lamberhill, you could do so without his being any the wiser.'

Sophia was on her feet. Her eyes blazed.

'Marry Francis – *never*! Besides, he would know I was not a virgin. Ada says a man can always tell. I thought you were an honourable man. I thought you would admit the terrible wrong you did me and . . . and the very least you could do is marry me.'

Now Konrad rose to his feet.

'If I thought for one minute that your reputation was in jeopardy, I should indeed honour my obligations, Sophia. However, I am not convinced that you, I, Lavinia, or indeed, our relatives, should have our lives disrupted on so unlikely a possibility.' The look of shock on Sophia's face momentarily softened his tone. 'Come now, Sophia, your servants are exceptionally devoted to you and I am sure no word of last night's happenings – even if they knew of it – would pass their lips. Lavinia will certainly not speak of it and I . . . well, since it is very much to my discredit, there is no likelihood that I shall do so. Try to put it from your mind, as Miss Challinor and I intend to do.' He gave her an encouraging smile. 'If we can all forget it, perhaps we can resume our plans to share Ortolans. That is what you would like, is it not?'

Tears of mortification, anger and disappointment filled Sophia's eyes.

'You speak as if your . . . your offence was of no great importance!' she flared. 'You . . . you despoil me and then ask me to forget it. Suppose I don't choose to do so? Suppose I tell my aunts how disgracefully you behaved – you, a trusted guest in their house! Where would *your* reputation be then?'

Konrad's expression was phlegmatic.

'My dear child, you have not given enough thought to the consequences. It is your future happiness and not my own reputation which prompts me to suggest this course of action. As you so truly say, your aunts would be obliged to dismiss me from their lives. Their distress would be immense and they – you – your servants would certainly have to leave Ortolans for which I, ultimately, am responsible. I am sure that on reflection, you will agree that this is not what you want.'

Sophia could not trust herself to speak. She, who had been so certain of victory, must now acknowledge defeat. With one final furious look at Konrad, she turned and left the room.

As the heavy oak door slammed shut behind her, Konrad raised his hands in protest against this unbearable assault on his throbbing head.

CHAPTER EIGHTEEN

1889

Ada watched in silence as Sophia paced to and from the window, her fists clenched, her brows drawn down as the furious torrent of words poured from her.

'. . . and to think I believed him an *honourable* man! It's all *her* fault! She means to marry him whatever his faults. You would have thought she'd have more pride! I hate her! I hate him . . .'

As she paused for breath, Ada said ill-advisedly:

'I tole you no good would come of your trickery, Miss Sophia. Now . . .'

She got no further before Sophia rounded on her.

'It would have worked – if that Challinor woman really loved him. I don't think she cares one whit what . . . what happened between the baron and me. If I'd been her, I'd have killed him if I found out he'd . . . he'd done those things to someone else.' To Ada's consternation, Sophia, who so rarely cried except in anger, now burst into tears.

'I think I care far more about him than *she* does!' Sophia sobbed. 'I know the only reason I went to Konrad's room was to trick him into marrying me, but it all turned out so differently from the way I had planned.' She sniffed and blew her nose on the handkerchief Ada proffered with one hand whilst patting the soft curls with the other. 'I *liked* kissing him, Ada – and when he . . . when he touched me . . . I . . . oh, Ada, I almost forgot to call out to you! I didn't want it to stop. I think I may have fallen in love with him.' She choked on a sob before adding quickly: 'Don't you see, Ada, I'd make him

a far better wife than his fiancée ever could. It isn't just
Ortolans, any more. I *want* to be married to him. I *want* to
be his wife.'

Ada sighed.

'Only a minute ago, you was a-tellin' me you hated him!'

Now it was Sophia who sighed.

'Well, I do . . . at least, in one way. He said if I told my
aunts, we'd all have to leave Ortolans. Suppose *she* won't
allow us to stay? Oh, I wish I knew what they are doing now.
Will she just stay here as if . . . as if nothing had happened?'

'You should go downstairs and find out, Miss Sophia. It's
long past breakfast time and your aunts will be worrying as
to where you be.'

'No, no I won't go down . . . I can't!' Sophia said as she
jumped to her feet and hurried to look at her reflection in the
mirror. 'They will see I have been crying and . . . and I won't
give that Challinor female the satisfaction of seeing how utterly
devastated I am. You go, Ada. If they are having breakfast,
Adam may have heard what they're saying. Off you go and
hurry back and tell me!'

She waited in an agony of impatience until Ada returned.

'Her's leaving!' she announced dramatically. 'Her tole
the Misses Calverley she had had an urgent message from
her mother to say she was ill, and her was leaving directly.
The master – the baron, that is, is driving her hisself to the
station.'

'But he's coming back?' Sophia asked, her heart in her
mouth.

'He's a-going to stay on a day or two. Your aunts has sent
Adam to find me so's I can tell them if aught is amiss with
you.'

Sophia's face brightened.

'Then at least we are rid of *her* for the time being. Go
down again, Ada, and tell my aunts I'm indisposed. I need
time to think before I see the baron again. I don't care in the
least if *he* knows how devastated I am. Perhaps he'll think

better of . . . of abandoning me in this . . . this dishonourable fashion!'

Seeing that Ada was about to argue, Sophia shooed her out of the room, but not before the old woman had advised her that she had better undress and get back into bed lest her aunts decided to pay her a visit.

Reluctantly, Sophia undressed and climbed back between the sheets. If her aunts came in, she would feign sleep – and having had no sleep the night before, she did indeed need the rest; but she was far too overwrought even to close her eyes. The sun was streaming in through the open casements, and the sunbeams were dappling the end of her bed. It was, she thought, quite unbearable that so beautiful a day, which had begun with such promise, should be turning out to be the worst day of her whole life! The most awful part of it was the fear that Konrad might decide after all to turn them out of the house – or if he did not, Miss Challinor might insist upon it, and she and the aunts would not even have the east wing to live in.

By the time Ada reappeared, Sophia was struggling back into her day clothes.

'I have made up my mind – I shall not be intimidated by the baron. I shall go downstairs as if this was a perfectly ordinary day. I shall not allow him to see how . . . how upset I am!'

'And I've just tole your poor aunts as how you be sleepin'!' Ada bemoaned as, for the second time that day, she fastened Sophia's corset strings.

Sophia did not see Konrad until they all foregathered in the dining-room for luncheon. As if nothing untoward had happened, he chatted amiably to the aunts and, after a quick glance at Sophia's flushed imperious face, attempted to engage her in conversation. Her chin tilted a little too high, her tone of voice cold, Sophia made monosyllabic replies.

Admiration, pity and an unexpected tenderness mingled in Konrad's mind. In an attempt to re-establish their former relationship, he suggested they might ride together that afternoon since it was so beautiful a day.

'If that is your wish!' Sophia said. Although her voice was prim, she was unable to conceal the gleam of interest in her eyes.

The aunts regarded Sophia anxiously.

'Are you sure you are well enough?' Aunt Georgie enquired as she peered short-sightedly at her niece.

'Ada said—' began Aunt Nellie when Sophia broke in quickly: 'Oh, you know how Ada fusses, Aunt Nellie! I was quite simply still sleepy after our late night. I am quite recovered and the fresh air will do me good.'

Sophia was a very pretty girl, Konrad reflected as the meal progressed. It was surprising that Lavinia should not have shown any sign of jealousy! Obviously she had not considered Sophia a rival – possibly because he himself had always referred to the girl as if she were a child, and considered her as such until . . . until last night. Now that he considered it, Sophia was by far the more attractive of the two. He felt a sudden unexpected urge to reach out and touch her hand. Vague memories of last night's intimacies returned – the warmth and softness of her body; its slender firmness as she pressed herself against him. Her breath had been hot against his face as she opened her mouth for his kisses. How eager she had been for love – or so he had supposed! Was it possible she had feigned such passion? Had she really had no idea of the fire she had ignited? If he had indeed 'ravaged' her as she declared, why could he remember nothing of it when he recalled her kisses and caresses with such pleasure?

His mind still on this enigma, he did not break the silence as he and Sophia rode side by side in the direction of the river. Here, Konrad drew his horse to a halt as two white swans with a clutch of cygnets glided slowly downstream.

'It was at this very spot we first met, Sophia,' he said. 'I had no idea then that you were one of the three Miss Calverleys I had come to meet, still less that you were so deeply attached to your home – my home,' he added. As the quick colour stained her cheeks and a look of defiance blazed momentarily in her eyes, his innate good nature made him regret the remark. He said gently:

'I am beginning to understand what Ortolans means to you. Is it of any consolation to know that Lavinia has agreed that we should permit you and your aunts to continue living here until our marriage? Because of what happened . . .' his pause was only brief '. . . she feels it might be best if you and your aunts then remove permanently to The Grange.'

The look of horror on Sophia's face was unmistakable and he said quickly:

'I shall do my utmost to persuade her to my own point of view – namely that, since we are unlikely to spend a great deal of our time at Ortolans, it would be to our advantage to have the house occupied and for the estate to continue to be so carefully nurtured by you.'

'You mean we might be able to stay here always?' Sophia cried impulsively before she remembered that she had not the slightest intention of allowing this man to patronize her, however grateful she might feel for his intervention. 'I suppose you would like me to say that I am grateful to you – and Miss Challinor – for not immediately dismissing me as if . . . as if I were a wanton servant girl! Perhaps I should remind you that this situation has arisen because you chose, in your cups, to seduce me. Since you do not see fit to take the honourable step appropriate in the circumstances, the very least you can do is to abandon the idea of using this house as your English country residence. Why don't you both go away and leave my aunts and me here in peace. We were perfectly happy until *you* came!'

Konrad remained silent, uneasily aware that despite all the available evidence to the contrary, he might, just possibly, be guilty of having seduced Sophia. If only he could be completely certain that he had not. It was reassuring that even now it was the house she was laying claim to by way of compensation – not a restitution of her honour!

'Whether or not you will accept the fact that I, myself, have already become much attached to Ortolans is for you to decide,' he said gently. 'What you seem to have forgotten, Sophia, is that I, ultimately, am responsible for the Calverley estate and it is time I assumed those responsibilities. Your aunts are elderly and you . . . I have to assume you will soon marry, in which case you will go to live in your husband's home. It has become clear to me that Detcham needs its squire.'

All the same, he thought suddenly and irrelevantly, I hope Sophia does not rush off and marry the Lamberhill fellow. She deserves a more full-blooded male – and needs one to curb that headstrong element.

'Since Lavinia and I will be often in Austria or London, we may only spend a few months of the year here. You may continue your management in the meanwhile. Were you to override your . . . your objections to my future wife and become friendly with her, I would be better able to convince Lavinia that there is no real necessity for you ever to leave your home.'

So her future happiness was to be decided on Miss Challinor's whim, Sophia thought furiously. How blind this man must be if he imagined she could ever, *ever* be friends with his hateful fiancée. The only explanation for his attitude was that he believed her, Sophia, responsible for her own seduction; that somehow he had guessed that she had been trying to compromise him.

'When will you be married?' she asked coldly. 'My aunts said it would be in the autumn.'

Relieved by this turn in the conversation, Konrad relaxed.

'We return to Vienna next week and shall finalize a date when we do so. But for the dreadful death of my friend, Prince Rudolf, we would have had the ceremony this summer. Naturally, you and your aunts will receive an invitation. My relatives will be most interested to meet you once they realize we are distantly related.'

Konrad was far from sure Lavinia would agree to Sophia's

presence at their wedding. He had spoken impulsively and now he determined that in this instance, Lavinia should not exclude her, despite the magnanimous way she had decided to overlook his shocking behaviour. It was the last reaction he would have expected from her and he was still bewildered by it. He drew a deep sigh.

'Despite what transpired last night, I want us to remain friends, Sophia – good friends. I want it very much. We are already good companions, are we not? For both our sakes, can you try to forget last night?'

The softness of his voice weakened the hard shell Sophia had allowed to build itself around her heart. Although Konrad did not know it for certain, she knew only too well that he was in no way to blame for what had occurred in his bedroom. He was trying so hard to make the best of the predicament in which he found himself – and to put matters right.

'I will try!' she said, knowing as she spoke that she had no wish to forget anything that had passed between them – the feelings he had aroused when he kissed her, the strange new sensations of her body, the sheer miracle of what she now thought of as 'married bliss'. Despite all Ada's warnings, she did not feel in the least degraded by the loss of her virginity – on the contrary, she felt elated. Were it not for the fact that she had lost her battle to safeguard her occupation of Ortolans, she would have no regrets, other than that she could not be married to this man whose soft voice and gentle, smiling eyes could turn her knees to water. It was only because of Ortolans he must remain her enemy.

'Since I shall be leaving here tomorrow, let us enjoy our last ride together,' Konrad said, cheered by Sophia's seeming acquiescence. 'We must go first to the village – for I need to have a word with Dick who will be starting work next week. Afterwards we can have a canter up on the Downs if you would like it.'

But for the mention of Dick Pylbeam, Sophia would instantly have agreed, but at this reminder that alterations – Lavinia

Challinor's chosen alterations – were to begin next week, her heart instantly hardened.

'I am not quite so well recovered from my earlier indisposition as I had thought,' she said abruptly. 'As you know, I am well accustomed to riding on my own, so do go on to the village as you plan and I will make my own way home.'

Without waiting for his approval, she turned her mare's head and with a light touch of her whip, urged the startled Silver Mist into a furious canter back along the riverside and across the meadows towards home.

Delia Lamberhill had departed with her parents to Scotland for the annual August grouse shooting. Francis remained in Sussex and was a constant visitor at Ortolans. The aunts were using gentle persuasion as a means of encouraging Sophia to accept 'the poor young man's' proposal. Sophia was aware that Francis was so hopelessly in love with her he would agree to any condition she cared to name, even to the point of 'sharing' Ortolans with the Valschintzkys if this was what she wanted. The fact that he would not then be the master in his own home was, it seemed, no deterrent.

Sophia could not help but despise Francis for his weakness. Moreover, she did not think Lavinia would agree to *her* remaining at Ortolans, and certainly not if she, Sophia were married.

'Could we not at least discuss the possibility with Baron Valschintzky?' Francis had protested when she had pointed this out to him. Like many weak people, he was proving remarkably stubborn in his refusal to accept defeat. 'Can you not write to him, Sophia, and ask him if he will consider it?'

Sophia had not the slightest intention of doing so. The promised invitation to his wedding had duly arrived, giving the date as early December, the start of the Season in Vienna. There were still four months left in which somehow she would devise a plan by which she could prevent his marriage; but the summer days were passing, haymaking had finished and the corn and barley were standing high in the fields, and still she could think of no way to do so.

Of all unlikely people, it was little Annie Pylbeam who inadvertently provided Sophia not only with the possible means of achieving her aims, but with every hope of success.

'The poor child has got herself in the family way!' Ada said. 'I found her a-cryin' her eyes out in the broom cupboard. Her dad'll skin her alive and like as not, her mum'll show her the door. Happen you'll talk to her, Miss Sophia?'

Sophia was in the library, sitting at her grandfather's desk writing in *The Calverley Journal*.

> . . . Home Farm meadow yielded two stacks of hay – a record crop. Merrymore is delighted. Rogers caught Dick Weller poaching yet again and has warned him that next time, it will be the local constable and not I who passes sentence. I fined him two shillings and gave him six months to pay as I know his wife is expecting again and he is hard put to feed his family. He'd only taken two rabbits and a pheasant, but Rogers thinks me far too lenient . . .

She broke off as Ada pushed the weeping scullery-maid into the room.

'Ada tells me you are with child,' she said, as Annie dabbed at her eyes with the corner of her none-too-clean apron. 'How old are you now – fourteen?'

'Fifteen, miss – come Michaelmas!'

'And you are quite sure – about the baby, I mean?'

'Yes, miss. I didn't have no monthly fortnight after I done it and not next month neither – and I been sick in marnins . . .'

She dissolved once more into tears.

It was not the first time one of the Calverley servant girls had been in trouble, but the matter was usually resolved with a hurried wedding. On one such occasion, the bride had given birth the day after the wedding.

'So it's still quite early,' Sophia said as much to herself as to Annie. 'I suppose you've told the father?'

'Yes, miss, but Luke's afeared to tell his dad – Master Merrymore that be – him being only sixteen and 'prenticed to t' butcher. He says as how he carn't marry me nohow . . .'

Between her sobs, the girl gave a graphic description of the implacability of both sets of parents and her fears that she would end up in the workhouse.

'Nonsense, Annie,' Sophia said firmly. 'I'll talk to Luke's father, but first we must be certain you really are with child.'

'Oh, miss, I knows as 'ow I am. It were haymaking time and Luke an' me . . . he were that keen, miss, I let him tek liberties. It only happened twice, m'um – I mean, miss. I didn't think no harm would come of it. We was carried away, miss, not meaning no harm to no one, surelye.'

'Go down to the kitchen and tell Cook I said she's to give you a cup of tea. I shall make up my mind what is the best thing to do. Now stop crying, Annie. I'll think of some way to help you.'

Annie's tearful expressions of gratitude accompanied her out of the room.

Sophia returned to her desk, her eyes narrowed in concentration. She had little doubt that she could persuade Luke's father to agree, however reluctantly, to a wedding. She knew that he was anxious to increase his acreage and only last week, Mr Endicote had written to advise her that the trustees of the Howells' estate were anxious to sell off one of the farm holdings at The Grange. She had been contemplating buying in any event and now she could offer to lease the land to Merrymore. No, she reflected, she had no need to waste further thought on Annie. What she needed to consider was how she might apply Annie's circumstances to herself; for it had occurred to her, in a blinding flash of inspiration, that if *she* were with child Konrad Valschintzky would have no choice but to marry her.

Annie, she recalled, had said that she and the boy, Luke,

had 'only done it twice'. If this was the result, why could she, too, not be with child?

Sophia bit her lip as she sought to recall what else the girl had said – that she had missed two of her 'monthlies'. Who was to know that she, Sophia, had had no such irregularity? If she were questioned, she could quite simply lie if this was part of the process of conceiving or carrying a baby.

She drew a deep sigh. If only she were not so ignorant. Were there pitfalls of which she knew nothing? If so, she could keep a watchful eye on Annie.

Slowly, Sophia's frown turned to a look of excitement. She would write at once – this very afternoon – and tell Konrad she was to have his baby.

Would he believe it? He had doubted her story that he had persuaded her into his room on a pretext of illness and, even more so, that he had seduced her, but could no longer doubt the latter if he learned that it had resulted in a child. Annie seemed to know she was pregnant two months after she had allowed Luke to 'take liberties', as she had put it. It was now six weeks since she had lain with Konrad. *He must believe her!* she thought, her eyes now glowing as her thoughts raced onwards. She would make sure that he did – and that Miss Challinor would have no opportunity to cast any doubts. She had devised a perfect way to convince him.

Sophia wasted no time, and that afternoon she took Annie in the wagonette to Brighton. Seeing the brass plate of a doctor on a respectable looking house in The Drive as they passed through Hove, she dragged the terrified girl inside. Despite her own nervousness, Sophia boldly requested an examination for her young servant.

If the doctor was surprised by this request to examine a working-class girl of such obvious humble circumstances, he did not think of questioning her imperious young mistress, but took the tearful Annie into his surgery. A few minutes later, he emerged, leaving Annie to dress and compose herself whilst he rejoined Sophia.

As she expected, he at once confirmed Annie's fears.

'I am in dispute with the father of the baby,' Sophia vouch-safed her prepared story in casual tones. 'He refuses to make provision for the poor girl until he is assured she is pregnant. As I shall have to sack her, it seems only charitable to ensure she is not left destitute.'

Entirely satisfied by this story, the physician was not surprised when his visitor added:

'Would you be so good as to write me a note confirming your diagnosis?' Sophia spoke in as haughty a tone as any she had heard Lady Lamberhill use. 'Then I can settle your account immediately, sir, and I shall not have to trouble you again.'

Since the doctor was being paid for his time – and, contrary to the normal behaviour of the gentry, on the spot – he was more than happy to oblige.

'Kindly address your letter to "Miss Calverley"; and, since I have no wish for the unfortunate girl to become a subject of village gossip, would you be so good as to refer to her simply as "the patient"! There is no need to name her.'

No longer curious, the doctor wrote as requested.

As she and Annie drove home in silence, Sophia hugged the letter to her. The few brief lines were all she needed, she thought exultantly. After luncheon, she would deal with Luke's father and Annie's parents, and then, her conscience clear with regard to the unnecessary ordeal to which she had subjected the abject Annie, she would write to Konrad.

Dear Miss Calverley . . .

(That could apply to either of her aunts since she herself should correctly be addressed as Miss Sophia Calverley)

. . . I have today examined the patient and it is my considered opinion that she is pregnant. The girl is young, in good health and I see no reason for any complications with the birth which should very approximately, be early in March . . .

Sophia's letter to Konrad was less vaguely worded.

. . . I think you should know that I am carrying your child, which the enclosed letter will confirm. As I had been unwell recently, the aunts insisted that I should see a reliable doctor in Hove. Fortunately, with Ada's assistance, I was able to intercept his reply to my aunts so they are as yet unaware of my predicament and impending disgrace. I can do nothing now but pray that you will save me from the terrible consequences of that unfortunate lapse for which I was in no way responsible.

My poor aunts will have to be advised sooner or later and I fear the shock may kill them. I have contemplated forging an alternative reply from the doctor, making no mention of my condition, but I am afraid they might detect my handwriting.

I do not know which way to turn and am the more fearful remembering that on the last occasion I begged you to rectify the harm you did me, you did not feel obliged to do so.

I have now to subject my pride and ask you once again to save me, for the sake of your honour and your child, if not for me.

With an admixture of guilt, anxiety and above all, excitement, Sophia somehow managed to fill the days until at last she received Konrad's reply.

Though very brief, it contained all she wanted to read:

I shall be arriving at Ortolans a week from today. In the meanwhile, please keep the information you gave me entirely confidential. Above all, do not worry.

Sophia flung her arms round Ada's waist and waltzed her round her room.

'I've won, I've won!' she cried. 'He's coming back – the baron is coming back. I've won, Ada. Now Ortolans really will be mine!'

CHAPTER NINETEEN

1889

Konrad and Sophia were married in Detcham on 20 September.
The aunts had seen to it that the little church was ablaze with
flowers. The sun shone brilliantly, and everyone in the village
had gathered outside to throw flowers and rice at the bride
and groom. As Miss Longhurst, the vicar's daughter, thumped
out the Wedding March on the organ, Sophia and Konrad
came through the open doors into the sunshine. The children
shouted, waved flags, threw wild flowers; the women called
out good wishes; the men doffed their caps and wiped their
sweating brows. The church bells began their pealing.

Suddenly a nanny goat, which had broken loose from its
tether, came galloping across the graveyard, burst through
the crowd of well-wishers and skidded to a halt as it espied
Sophia's beautiful bouquet. There were screams from the
children and shouts of approval from the women who
deemed this a lucky omen. A young lad grabbed the trailing
chain.

Ada, still inside the church, saw none of this. She was
sobbing quietly whilst Elizabeth Lamberhill did her best to
comfort her.

'Come now, Ada,' she said quietly. 'This is the happiest of
days, and you should be rejoicing at the thought of the
wonderful life Miss Sophia has ahead of her.'

'Yes, m'um, I know, m'um!' Ada sniffed as she blew her
nose. 'But I justabout can't forget as how I found a dratted
bird in Miss Sophia's bedroom this morning.'

'That's ignorant superstition,' Elizabeth said firmly as she urged Ada out of the pew, 'and I hope you did not upset Miss Sophia with such nonsense.'

Ada had indeed treated the appearance of the robin with loud cries of calamity when she had wakened Sophia that morning. Though unaware of the events leading to the marriage, Ada was yet uneasy.

Sophia, plagued by moments of guilt and near panic at the enormity of her deception, had not confided in her faithful old servant. She knew only too well she would have received unrestrained disapproval from her, and she had no desire to have her last remnants of confidence undermined.

Whilst awaiting Konrad's return from Austria, she had spent long hours going from room to room of the house, from gardens to stables to woods to fields, telling herself repeatedly that her love for Ortolans – her need of it and its need of her – justified her actions. Once married, she had but to announce to Konrad that she had suffered a miscarriage and then – if he were anxious to have an heir – she would produce a real child for him.

Her feelings of guilt were exacerbated when Konrad returned to Ortolans. Making light of the embarrassment and extreme difficulties he had faced in Vienna at the cancellation of his wedding to Lavinia, he was gentle, affectionate and totally supportive to Sophia.

'You are not to worry about anything,' he had told her repeatedly. 'I shall invent some satisfactory reason for our sudden wedding to give your aunts. You can have the child in Austria, Sophia, so no one here will be aware that it is born only six months after our wedding. I will take care of everything. You have had more than enough to bear already. I shall never forgive myself for my failure to believe that I had harmed you in so nefarious a fashion; I still have no memory of it. Try to forgive me, Sophia. I swear I will do everything I can to make you happy. We will be married as soon as possible.'

Ada had sensed that this change of plan by the baron was not of his making, and she knew her young mistress was capable of having perpetrated further trickery. Sophia had been far too moody – downcast, silent, irritable one moment, and overexcited the next. Now she felt her unease compounded by the unlucky omen of the robin that morning.

With an effort, Ada pulled herself together and went out into the sunshine in time to see Konrad slipping his hand beneath Sophia's arm as they began the short walk down to the lychgate. Here the bride and groom paused for a further photograph. Konrad, his grey top hat tucked under one arm, stood staring down at Sophia who was wearing her grandmother's white, figured satin bridal gown and flowing Brussels lace veil; beside them were grouped their attendants – Delia and her two little sisters in pale blue satin, and her youngest brother in matching page's costume. It made a charming picture. The wedding guests, one or two of whom were Konrad's relations from Austria, were smiling as they exchanged expressions of admiration.

Only Francis Lamberhill was scowling. Until Valschintzky's return and the sudden announcement of his engagement to Sophia, he had stubbornly nursed the hope that she might marry him. He was far from convinced by Delia's romantic protestations that the couple were head over heels in love and that this was why they had rejected the more conventional long engagement in favour of an autumn wedding. Sophia had been staying in their London house, whilst Delia and his mother had helped her buy her trousseau. On several occasions, Francis had seen Sophia looking unnaturally thoughtful, almost downcast, and he had questioned whether she was quite as enamoured of the Austrian as Delia supposed. Today, however, he had no alternative but to face the fact that Sophia was lost to him for ever. She was now Baroness Valschintzky, and at the same time, Lady Calverley, for her new husband had the right to both titles. She looked radiant.

As far as the inhabitants of Detcham were concerned, Konrad was their new squire, and for all he was a foreigner in their eyes, he was young and handsome. Since his marriage to their own Miss Calverley from Ortolans meant that she and her aunts would be remaining in the big house, they were prepared to celebrate the wedding with all possible enthusiasm. They would shortly be making their way to Ortolans where there would be beer and food laid out on trestle tables on the lawns for them, and luncheon in the house for the gentry. The village band would play and without a doubt, there would be toffee apples and sweetmeats for the children. To crown it all, the sun was shining as brightly as if it was midsummer.

'How admirably you and the aunts have planned the day!' Konrad said to Sophia as they drove in their flower-bedecked carriage towards Ortolans. Even the two greys pulling the landau had white rosettes on their bridles. 'In every respect this is preferable to a big society wedding. It is perfect!'

Did he truly mean this or was he regretting the cancellation of his elaborate Viennese wedding to Miss Challinor, Sophia wondered? Was he secretly wishing that it was Lavinia and not herself who was his bride?

In point of fact, Konrad was congratulating himself on his escape from a marriage he had never really wanted. Lavinia had been particularly demanding and quite unsufferably forgiving since their return to Vienna. He had realized that she intended to exact her price for her forgiveness and that if he were not careful, he would find himself married to a domineering wife who constantly nagged him.

Sophia's letter had come as a severe shock – but on reflection, a welcome one. This time, Lavinia could not 'forgive' him since he had no alternative but to make an honest woman of the young girl he had, it seemed, deflowered. But for his mother's anger and disappointment, he had no reason to regret his timely escape from a tearful but irate Lavinia.

Fortunately for both him and Sophia, her dear old aunts looked upon his sudden return to Ortolans to claim their niece for his own as highly romantic. In a way it was, he decided, when he had placed the engagement ring on Sophia's finger, for she had looked both beautiful and desirable and he found himself cherishing the thought that she was carrying his child. He betook himself to London to await with impatience their wedding day.

'Your relations and friends are so . . . so elegant, Konrad!' Sophia was saying. 'We must seem like country bumpkins to them!'

Konrad's laughter drowned the clatter of the horses' hoofs.

'My darling Sophia, they are all quite charmed by your beauty, as indeed am I. No one could look less "a country bumpkin"!'

He took one of her hands and pressed a kiss into her palm.

Sophia's heart was beating so fiercely she dared not trust her voice. These past weeks since Konrad had returned from Austria had seemed like years. Her emotions had see-sawed from wild happiness to guilt each time he assured her that he believed they would be very happy together; that he was preparing a surprise for her; that he was busy planning their honeymoon. They were, he had informed her, to stay in the luxurious new Savoy Hotel in London for their wedding night, travelling next day on the boat train to Calais and thence on the Orient Express train overnight to Vienna. Since it was not practical for the aunts at their advanced age to host a big wedding reception at Ortolans, he had arranged a big ball to be held in his house in Vienna to which all his friends and relations would come. After a week – during which time he would conduct her round his beautiful city – he was taking her to Wachau to enjoy the peace and solitude of their schloss.

As far as Sophia could judge, Konrad was a man without doubt as to their future happiness. Sophia's spirits had soared – only to be undermined when he told her that he was having a little difficulty with his mother, from whom he had received a long letter.

'I am so sorry to tell you that Mama does not feel well enough to make the long journey to England, Sophia,' he told her. 'I think it is best to be honest and confess that she is angry with me for breaking with Lavinia. As you know, it was

Mama who arranged our betrothal and who was most anxious, as was Lady Challinor, for the match.'

When Sophia made no reply, he had taken her hand and held it reassuringly. 'I am quite confident this will all be forgotten when my mother meets you and discovers what a charming girl I am marrying. Moreover any prejudices she might have will be forgotten when she knows you are going to give her her first grandchild. Perhaps I should warn you that she has become somewhat of a recluse since my father died, and from time to time, she lives in a world of fantasy. She is quite convinced that you are only marrying me in order to become chatelaine of Ortolans – and I suppose I am the last person to criticize her since I myself was stupid enough once to suspect it! How cruel you must have thought me, Sophia!'

Sophia had been tormented at that moment by the need to confess. She longed to tell Konrad that he and his mother had been right to suspect her. She had tricked him and there would be no grandchild. But even he must realize that everything was different now; she loved him and would want to be married to him even if it were not for Ortolans. As to the child, she would be only too happy to provide him with a family if that's what he wanted.

Her uncertainty as to whether he loved her well enough to forgive her stayed her tongue. It was a risk she dared not take since she might lose both him and Ortolans for no better reason than to ease her conscience. Konrad had told her that he was not in the least distressed by the loss of Miss Challinor; that he cared very much for her, Sophia, but never once had he said he loved her, even though his manner was affectionate and his conversation filled with plans for their future happiness.

I will make him happy, Sophia thought as Ortolans came into sight. I will never let him regret this day. I will love, honour, obey him always.

As the carriage drew to a halt outside the iron-studded

front door, Konrad lifted her down and stood with his arm around her.

'Before everyone arrives, I have a little surprise for you, Sophia!' he said. 'I had thought first of giving you jewellery as a wedding gift but your aunts told me that you already have many lovely heirlooms that were your mother's and grandmother's. I thought of a pedigree white Arab, but I know you would never love it as you love Silver Mist. I was in quite a quandary until suddenly I thought of something I could give you that I truly believe will please you – namely, all that part of the Calverley estate which is not entailed.'

He smiled as Sophia gasped. 'I wish I could have given you Ortolans, my darling, but the lawyer tells me I do not have the right. Nevertheless, I want you to look upon the house as yours, at least until our son is born. I will not bore you now with details, but all those lands, cottages, farms which the Calverleys have acquired since the original entailment in the 1500s are yours, and the income from them is yours to do with as you please. I signed the necessary papers in Endicote's office yesterday morning.'

He was rewarded by the look of jubilation on his bride's face. Flinging her arms around him, Sophia cried breathlessly:

'Thank you, *thank you*, Konrad. Oh, I am so happy, so grateful! This is the most wonderful day of my life!'

Konrad kissed her tenderly.

'I, too, am happy,' he said in a low husky voice. It was several weeks since he had last seen her, and he had forgotten how immensely desirable Sophia could look when, as now, her eyes sparkled and her cheeks were flushed. 'And there will be even happier days to come,' he added softly. 'Soon we shall have a child to start a new generation of Calverleys. No matter the circumstances in which it was begotten, I cannot but rejoice at its advent.'

Appalled by this sudden unexpected reminder of her perfidy, Sophia's mood swung from euphoria to one of horror compounded by guilt.

I won't cry, I won't! she thought. He'll never know I have
not suffered a miscarriage. I'll have a child if it means so much
to him. Ada's just a cavelling old fool with her 'means doant
justify the ends!' Ortolans belongs to me now and this is truly
the happiest day of my life!

To her consternation – and to that of both Konrad and the
coachman – Sophia burst into tears.

It was Ada who, on her return from the church, managed
to bring her mistress to her senses. Sophia was lying face down
on the bed, repeating between sobs a defiant:

'It was all his fault. I had to do it, I had to do it! I wouldn't
have done it but for *her*!'

'You stop that cryin' this instant, Miss Sophia. No matter
what you done, you be married to the master now, surelye,
right or wrong!' she said, as she bathed Sophia's face in cold
water. 'The master be justabout the nicest gen'leman you could
get yourself, Miss Sophia, and he doant deserve you a-moanin'
and a-weepin' afore all his kinfolk like as how you's sorry
you wed him. Aint no use now a-cryin' over spilt milk.' She
began to straighten Sophia's crumpled veil and refasten it to
her red curls. 'Happen you was brave enough to go chasing
him the way you did, you got courage enough to tell him you
was just a-cryin' 'cos you was so happy,' she said more gently.
'And there's the mistresses – what'll they think if'n they sees
you sobbin' away as if'n you be at a burial, surelye! Adone-do,
Miss Sophia. Adone-do!'

For once Ada was right, Sophia thought. There was no
point in crying over spilt milk. As abruptly as it had deserted
her, Sophia's courage returned, and as she rejoined Konrad
downstairs, she was able to turn his consternation aside
with a smile and the excuse that she had been momentarily
overcome by the emotion of the day. Gradually, as the festive
drinks and buffet luncheon progressed, her happiness became
genuine. She found Konrad's cousins delightful and warmly
welcoming; his friends, mostly former fellow officers,
amusing and flattering. Konrad stood at all times proudly

at her side and when the time came for her to advise him that she was going to her room to change into her new russet velvet, going-away outfit with its intricate military frogged jacket, he whispered mischievously:

'You will look lovely in whatever you have chosen to wear, *meine liebchen*, even if it be those boy's breeches and shirt you wore the day I first met you!'

Suddenly, all Sophia's anxieties vanished together with the guilt. She and this tall, dark-eyed, sunny-natured man she had married were going to be happy together. She loved him – truly loved him, and he had given every indication that he loved her. His gift of parts of the Calverley estate was all the proof she needed.

Radiant in her tiny, high-crowned bowler, the veil turned back, Sophia's smile was unforced as she kissed each of the aunts goodbye.

'I forbid you to shed one single tear, Aunt Nellie!' she whispered as she kissed the soft, wrinkled cheek. 'I shall only be gone a few weeks.'

'You will send us postcards, won't you, dear!' pleaded Aunt Georgie.

'We are planning a special wedding album for you to show your children in years to come,' added Aunt Nellie.

Konrad, too, hugged the old ladies with genuine affection.

'I shall take good care of her!' he promised. 'And you are to take good care of yourselves. You are my favourite aunts, you know!'

Sophia had had no opportunity to tell them of Konrad's wonderful wedding gift to her. She would tell them in a letter, she decided, as the train taking them to London left Hassocks little station. Konrad's manservant and her two big travelling trunks were safely boarded, and Sophia sat comfortably beside her husband in a first-class carriage as they sped towards Victoria Station. Her honeymoon had begun.

The hotel was every bit as luxurious as had been reputed.

Not only did they have a large bedroom but an adjoining sitting-room and their own private bathroom. Moreover, there was an electric bell by which Sophia could summon the personal maid provided by the hotel; fires burned in both rooms, and at the turn of a switch, electric lights shone brightly in place of the gas mantles Sophia had become accustomed to in the Lamberhills' London house.

'Perhaps we shall be able to install electric lighting at Ortolans one day!' Sophia said, unable to resist playing with the switches.

Konrad, watching her, smiled at her simple delight.

'It could be some time before an electricity supply reaches country districts like Detcham,' he said. 'Now I expect you would like to change your clothes before we dine, so I will leave you for a little while.'

He crossed the room and carefully removing her hat, he laid it on the bed and then cupped her face in his hands.

'I think I like you best with your hair down!' he said smiling. 'Tonight I hope you will allow me to remove the pins. You have such beautiful hair, Sophia.'

Impulsively, she reached up and lifted her face to his.

'I love you very much!' she whispered. 'I am so happy, Konrad!'

'I am much relieved to hear you say so!' he replied seriously as he kissed her gently. 'I had wondered when you shed those tears after the wedding if you were perhaps regretting . . .'

'No, no, I regret nothing!' Sophia broke in. 'Only, perhaps, that I do not deserve so kind and generous a husband. Your wedding gift took me by surprise!'

Konrad was smiling again.

'That was my intention! As to you deserving a husband like myself, you deserve far better, Sophia. I wish now that I had led a more blameless existence, but looking back, I do not think I took life in the least seriously until . . . until that night when to my everlasting shame, I was overindulgent and behaved as no gentleman should. I can only assure you that from the moment when I came to my senses next morning, I have ceased to be a rakehell. My days as a libertine are over!'

Although he was smiling, Sophia could not. She longed to tell him that he was blameless, but all she dared voice was a cry from her heart:

'I beg you, let us forget that night. Let us never speak of it again!'

Although startled by her vehemence, Konrad was not surprised by it. He had not stopped reproaching himself since receiving her letter telling him she was with child. He should never have doubted her; or at very least, he should have given her the benefit of the doubt. Even though he knew Sophia had gone of her own accord to his bedroom, he should instantly have sent her away. In many ways, she was still a child, and the great surge of protectiveness he now felt towards her should have been uppermost that night.

Since it was not fitting for a lady to dine in the public rooms, they enjoyed a sumptuous private repast in the intimacy of their sitting-room, talking easily and companionably of the day's events as the waiters served their meal. Every once in a while, their eyes met and Konrad was enchanted by the delicate blush that came to Sophia's cheeks when he held her gaze. He wondered if her new aura of soft femininity was due to her condition. He sensed that she was not playing the coquette yet her every gesture and movement was provocative.

Although she had begged him not to speak of it, the memory, however hazy, of the night he had held her in his arms was vivid in his thoughts as he tried to curb his impatience for the meal to end. He drank very little, wanting on this, his wedding night, to be fully in possession of his senses. In all his past experience, he had never before felt such a profound desire for a woman.

Later that night, Sophia sat waiting in the big double bed, her beautiful hair tumbled about her shoulders, her eyes fastened upon Konrad as he came through the door from his dressing-room. He was wearing a dark blue dressing-gown thrown casually over white silk pyjamas – the first she had ever seen and which she thought most becoming. He switched off the electric lamp by the bedside and the room was lit only by the glow of the fire. Without hesitation he removed the dressing-gown and threw it over the back of a chair. As he undid the buttons of his pyjamas, Sophia's innate modesty required that she close her eyes, but she could not do so. She was mesmerized by the revelation of his strong, masculine frame. She had known what it was to touch that body but had never yet seen its unimaginable shape outlined by the firelight as he approached the bed.

Konrad knew a moment of intense happiness as he took Sophia in his arms and she melted into his embrace. Despite the thudding of his own heart, he felt the beat of hers, and her cheek was fiery hot where it touched his own.

'Sophia, my love, my own sweet wife!' he murmured, and heard her voice husky and muffled as she clung to him, saying:

'I love you. I love you!'

Konrad was well aware from conversations with his married friends that there existed many women who did not enjoy the physical aspects of marriage. Such men took their pleasures elsewhere, most often with their wives' unspoken but willing compliance. As he felt Sophia's body respond with uninhibited pleasure to his caresses, he realized that he was one of the most fortunate of men; that despite the reasons leading to his marriage, their life together would indeed be a real marriage.

He had been celibate for the past three months, a state of affairs unusual for him but which, strangely, had been of his own volition. With his mind full of memories of Sophia, he had lacked desire for other women. Now, on the point of possessing her, he was aware of a tumultuous joy as he realized that, astonishingly, he had fallen in love with this girl – this vibrant, exciting, passionate young woman who was his wife. However urgent his desire, he must not forget that she was carrying his child and he must therefore be gentle with her.

At the moment of consummation he heard Sophia's muffled

cry but, if he thought at all, it was to mistake it for one of pleasure and gratification. Almost immediately, without warning, the truth gradually reached his consciousness – her cry had been one of pain! The girl he still held in his arms had been a virgin. He had had to force his way into her and had hurt her.

For a chilling moment, he fought against the knowledge. It could not be true, for he had already violated her that night at Ortolans! Yet there was no gainsaying what had just occurred. It explained why he had remembered nothing of the event. It had not been his memory, blurred by brandy, which was at fault. *He had failed to recall his violation of her that night at Ortolans because it had never taken place!* There was no child! She had deceived him after all.

Sophia lay silent, her fists clenched at her side as, without warning, Konrad drew away from her. She was shocked into immobility. Her thoughts were in chaos and she was speechless. This, then, was 'married bliss'! This was what Mrs Groom had meant when she had spoken of a man's need to mate! After all their doubts, Delia and she had been wrong in assuming that humans must mate differently from animals. How naïve, ignorant, stupid they had been! Now that she herself knew the truth, it seemed ridiculous, impossible to have believed that the pleasure she had felt when Konrad had kissed, touched her that night she had first lain with him was the sum total of married intimacies. If only Konrad would speak! she thought as she lay rigid beside him.

Cold shivers of fear coursed through her body. Konrad must now know she was a virgin – had been a virgin, she corrected herself.

One of Ada's favourite proverbs sprang into her mind.

'*Gain gotten by a lie will burn one's fingers!*' and another more recent warning: '*Be sure your sins will find you out, Miss Sophia!*'

But she had not deliberately told a lie, she reminded herself. She had truly believed Konrad had taken away her chastity;

but *would he believe her?* His silence was far more difficult to bear than the soreness of her body.

Abruptly, Konrad sat up and switched on the light. Sophia lay with her head on the pillows, tears of embarrassment, mortification and fear sliding from beneath her closed lids.

'Open your eyes and look at me!' Konrad ordered, his voice harsh, 'and I don't want any lies. You cannot be with child. Answer me this minute. The very least you can do is tell me the truth.'

When she made no reply, he threw back the sheet and got out of bed. Pulling on his dressing-gown, he stared down at her, both hands clenched in tight fists at his side as he fought to keep control of himself.

Slowly, Sophia opened her eyes. From the tone of Konrad's voice, she knew that he was very, very angry. He was regarding her with an expression that was close to contempt. It was too late now that he knew the truth for another lie! Why, oh why, had her informant, Mrs Groom, not warned her that this could happen?

'You say nothing!' Konrad's voice was cold, accusing. 'Yet you had plenty to say when you called your maid for help, did you not? Tell me the truth, Sophia. You owe me that. I did not violate you that night. You tricked me into believing that I had – and I was too befogged to doubt you. Now – and I'm finding it singularly difficult to stomach – I discover that you have tricked me into marriage with this invention of a child. Have you no sense of honour, of decency, of right and wrong? I am not one of your playthings like that poor devil, Francis Lamberhill, manipulated to suit your will. Good God, Sophia, how dared you do this?'

Her continued silence and the sight of her white, shocked face momentarily confused him. Not ten minutes ago, he had believed himself desperately in love with his young wife. Now he was aware only of a sick disappointment that she had lied to him. Had she also been lying when she said she loved him? Was she really as amoral as she now seemed?

'You are seldom lost for words, Sophia, and I am not asking for but demanding an explanation,' he said.

Sophia hesitated. Perhaps, she thought, if she confessed everything, Konrad would forgive her and they could begin their marriage again. It was her only hope.

As Konrad listened to her halting confession, his heart hardened in proportion to the undermining of his pride. He was prepared to believe that Sophia's ignorance of the facts concerning the functions of her body was genuine. It was highly unlikely that her two elderly aunts would have spoken to their innocent young niece about such delicate subjects. Those few married women he had known intimately had confessed that they had gone to their marriage beds quite unaware of what lay in store for them! It was not this ignorance which so angered him – it was the reason behind her actions. On her own admission, she had wanted Ortolans – not him, but a house! Now he could not doubt the sincerity of her words when she said childishly:

'On my word of honour, Konrad, I truly thought we had done it.'

'And the baby – how do you suppose a child could be conceived in such a fashion?'

Sophia gulped, embarrassment once more engulfing her.

'When a man kisses a woman . . . the way you kissed me . . . I thought perhaps she might swallow a seed which grew into a baby.'

For a brief moment, his heart softened. Sophia must just now have been as greatly shocked as he – albeit for different reasons. Then his mind hardened yet again, and he regarded her with bitter, furious eyes.

'Even supposing such a thing were possible – which it is not – you had no other cause to think you had conceived. God alone knows how you obtained that letter from the physician to say that you had done so. There cannot have been a child resulting from that night, and you knew it. You lied to me – not once but many times!'

It was not only Konrad's loss of pride which affected him, but a genuine disappointment in the knowledge that he was not after all to be a father. Once he had recovered from the shock of learning Sophia was pregnant, he had found himself quite delighted at the prospect. He had never doubted her after reading the physician's letter to her aunt.

'That letter from the doctor? How came you by it? And don't lie again, Sophia. I intend to learn the truth – the whole truth.'

A direct and totally straightforward man himself, Konrad found it difficult to believe a young girl like Sophia Calverley could be so devious; and, he now told himself, so single-mindedly determined to gain her own ends. He could not tolerate the thought that he, thirteen years her senior, had allowed himself to be tricked by this . . . this child! She had used him – and the unfortunate Lavinia – without any consideration for their happiness. He could think of nothing by way of mitigation. This day of their wedding had been one of the happiest of his life and, ironically enough, he had remained on the very pinnacle of happiness until his discovery that she was a virgin! How many bridegrooms had there been whose happiness had been destroyed by finding the opposite! he reflected bitterly.

'If Francis Lamberhill had owned Ortolans, I suppose you would be lying in his bed now!' he said harshly.

At last Sophia found her voice.

'If it had been Francis, I could not have done what I did! I could not have loved him as I love you,' she said tearfully.

Konrad, his face a mask of bitterness, turned away and, with his back to Sophia, stared down with unseeing eyes into the fire.

'Love!' he echoed scornfully. 'You have no need to lie to me now, Sophia. If nothing else, at least let us have honesty between us at this juncture.'

Sophia, though still very frightened, could no longer see Konrad's angry face and began to recover her wits.

'Well, I tried to be honest when you first arrived at Ortolans. You knew from the start how much I loved the house; that it had been my home ever since I could remember – and that Aunt Georgie and Aunt Nellie had lived there all their lives. We were perfectly happy as we were, and you yourself said that I had managed the estate very well. It would not have been so dreadful if *you* had come to join us. It was that dreadful Miss Challinor! She wanted to change everything and you were going to let her. She didn't even love you, and you wouldn't listen when I tried to warn you about her . . .'

She got no further. Konrad said icily:

'You will please leave my former fiancée out of this discussion. It was not for you, Sophia, to judge her feelings for me – or, indeed mine for her. It was none of your business. I will concede you may have devised your scheme not only in your own interest but in what you believed to be that of your aunts. I suppose that is some small mitigation. I am in no doubt whatever that they, at least, are entirely innocent. I have become greatly attached to them both and I dread to think what low opinion they would have of their adored little niece if they were ever to learn of this. Nor, indeed, must my mother hear of it since it would afford her every opportunity to advise me that she warned me what you were about.'

That his autocratic, dogmatic parent should have been proved right was further fuel to the flame of Konrad's bitterness.

'Naturally, we can no longer expect our marriage to be happy, founded as it has been on a pack of lies and a mountain of deceit,' he said coldly. 'Nevertheless, for the time being, I insist that we maintain an illusion for the outside world that it is. Either you will agree to this condition or we shall live apart. The choice is yours, my dear. I cannot believe that your aunts would welcome the idea of a divorce.'

'A divorce!' Sophia echoed aghast. 'But . . . you cannot . . . we could not . . .'

'Anything is possible if you wish it hard enough,' Konrad broke in, his voice heavy with sarcasm. 'I think you yourself have proved that dictum to be well founded. Since divorce does not seem to appeal to you, we will continue as man and wife – but in name only. I have no wish to share my bed with a charlatan so I shall sleep in the other room. The couch will suffice.'

I don't care! I won't allow myself to care! Sophia thought. She had Ortolans – and that was all that mattered – or should have been. Now, more even than Ortolans, she wanted this man she had married to love her; to hold her in his arms, to kiss her, forgive her so that they could be happy again. There must be some way she could soften the implacable stance he had taken. If he was angry with her because there was no baby, she would willingly give him a child if that was what he wanted. She would sacrifice her rides on Silver Mist and endure the dreadful pains of childbirth Ada had so vividly described when her mother was confined. She had but to entice Konrad back to her bed, and however uncomfortable she might be feeling, allow him to enter her again and all would surely be well.

She held out her arms to him in appeal.

'Konrad, please – don't go like this. I beg you to forgive me. I know you don't believe it, but I do love you – I really do. I have told you how sorry I am and I swear I will never lie to you again. Can't you forget what is past?'

By now, Konrad had moved across the room, and he stood with one hand on the door, hesitating. Her immaturity struck him anew as he listened to her. She spoke as if she were a child who, having stolen a sweetmeat, could be quickly forgiven if she said she was sorry! Yet it was no child he was looking at. She was a vibrant, beautiful woman. Her large eyes were glistening with unshed tears. Her soft white shoulders looked somehow very vulnerable where he had accidentally torn the delicate lace of her nightgown in that moment of passion – which now seemed so long ago. He wanted to forgive her – yet he knew he could not. His pride would not allow it.

Ignoring her appeal, he turned silently and, leaving the room, closed the door behind him.

Sophia spent the remainder of her wedding night alone. For a short while, she enjoyed the luxury of tears, but gradually her self-pity gave way to resolve. Naturally Konrad was angry now – but once he recovered from the shock, he must surely relent. He had made no mention of cancelling their honeymoon plans and if they were to continue to cohabit, it should not be beyond her powers to think of a way to soften his opinion of her. He had frightened her with his use of the word 'divorce'. Although he had given her the deeds to some of the cottages and the land, Ortolans still belonged to him. Had he grounds for divorce? She did not know, but she had no intention of risking the possibility. She must regain his goodwill. Perhaps she could somehow convince him that she had been influenced by a third party to pretend there was a child – that she had never wanted to lie to him, had resisted doing so but been forced into it! But who might have done so? Ada? Konrad would not believe she could have been coerced by a servant. The aunts? No, that was inconceivable. Delia? But Konrad might question her and discover her in another lie! Mrs Groom? After all, she had truly been the one to suggest the compromising of Konrad, albeit not with the invention of a child. Mrs Groom would have known no virgin could conceive.

Sophia had still not resolved the difficulty when exhaustion overcame her. She fell asleep without once recalling that she had promised Konrad she would never again tell him a lie.

CHAPTER TWENTY

1889

Sophia could not remember a time in her life when she had been more unhappy than during the three weeks of her honeymoon in the beautiful, baroque city of Vienna. Its very light-hearted, spontaneous gaiety only highlighted her steadily decreasing confidence as day followed day with no change in Konrad's cold distancing of himself. Physically, he was never far away, playing the part of a devoted, adoring husband whenever they were in company. No one seeing them together on the evening of the big reception his family had arranged would have doubted that he adored her. Alone, he addressed no more than necessary words to her, and he continued to sleep in a separate bedroom.

Cleverly, he contrived not to be in her company during the day, stating that he had business matters to attend to and that one of his many female cousins would be only too delighted to show her the sights. Sophia was taken in a *fiaker* by Mitzi, a pert, flirtatious young married cousin, down the Ringstrasse, an avenue bordered by linden trees, now bare of their gold autumn leaves, to see the Hofburg Palace where the Emperor Franz Josef was in residence. Later, they went to the great Gothic cathedral of St Stephen's where, Mitzi informed her, thousands of Viennese were buried in the catacombs. In the afternoons, Mitzi took her shopping in Kärntnerstrasse and on another day, to luncheon at Sacher's Hotel where she insisted Sophia tasted the world-famous *Sachertorte*. All the while, Mitzi chattered in her open, friendly way, about Konrad, how handsome and amusing he was; how popular he had always been; how magnificently he rode a horse; how well he danced; how envious all Konrad's former girlfriends were of Sophia.

'Although no one is surprised that he preferred you to that other girl he so nearly married. None of Konrad's friends liked Lavinia and I positively disliked her. We were all agog with excitement when she broke off the engagement in so extraordinary a fashion – only a few months before their wedding, too!'

Seeing that she had Sophia's full attention, she continued:

'The baroness – Konrad's mama (she's my aunt, of course!) was absolutely *enragée*. Then, when we heard Konrad was to be married in England only a few weeks after he and Miss Challinor had parted company, the speculation was mountainous!' She giggled as she added confidentially: 'We all wondered whether some girl had caught him on the rebound – or, an even naughtier idea – that he had got a girl into trouble. Now, of course, everyone understands – Konrad's madly in love with you, and wasn't going to let anyone else have you. He himself told me you had another suitor who had been pursuing you for ages. No one is surprised any longer – not now we've all met you. You are so beautiful, Sophia, and so sweet!'

At least Konrad could not accuse her of failing to play her part of adoring wife in front of his friends and relatives, Sophia thought. Could he not see for himself how much happier they would both be if they stopped pretending? Surely now that she had made a full confession he could accept that everything she had done had proved to be for the best. As Mitzi had said, he was well rid of Lavinia Challinor and it simply was not fair of him to go on punishing her, Sophia, in this silly fashion. He was spoiling what could have been an exciting, enthralling honeymoon.

Although by now it was October, the sun still shone brilliantly in a sky dotted with tiny puffballs of white cloud as she and Mitzi drove the four kilometres through the outskirts

of the city towards the surrounding Weinerwald. Quashing
her private misgivings, Sophia allowed herself to be diverted
by Mitzi's cheerful prattle as she pointed out the impressive
sight of the Schloss Schönbrunn, the magnificent palace where
the Emperor lived when he was not at the Hofburg. Franz
Josef was approaching sixty years of age and, Mitzi confided,
people were saying he would never recover from the death of
his only son who, it was now known, had committed suicide
in his hunting lodge called Mayerling.

'When Konrad visited us last April, he would not talk about
Prince Rudolf's death,' Sophia said. 'He was obviously very
distressed by it as he knew the Prince quite well.'

Mitzi nodded as she directed the groom to take them to
Belvedere Palace. 'Rumour has it that Rudolf was not alone
– that there was a lady involved!' she whispered. 'You must
not tell Konrad I have told you but the latest rumour is that
the poor man's ghost, dressed in the uniform of a Hussar, has
been seen on horseback galloping through these woods; but
this is all too sad and I want you to enjoy yourself. In Vienna
we try always to be happy!'

If only it were possible, Sophia thought, suddenly and
unexpectedly close to tears as yet again, she realized how
happy she might have been had the circumstances of her
marriage to Konrad been different.

'The Emperor's nephew, the Archduke Franz Ferdinand,
lives here with his wife, the Duchess of Hohenburg,' Mitzi
informed her, unaware of Sophia's inner turmoil. 'He is now
heir to the throne. I fear he is not very popular. No one has
ever seen him smile and his heart is deaf to music – a sorry
deficiency as far as we music-loving Viennese are concerned.'

As they crossed the Danube on their way to the Prater
Gardens, Sophia commented on the unromantic grey colour
of the water.

'I had expected it to be blue as in the song composed by
your wonderful Johann Strauss!'

'A romantic notion – but untrue!' Mitzi replied with a laugh.

'Konrad tells me that tonight he is taking us all to the operetta *The Gypsy Baron*. You will enjoy it, I know, Sophia. There is so much still for you to do and see before you go to Wachau. I do hope you will enjoy it there. You must not allow Tanta Theresa to frighten you. She can be quite intimidating if you allow her. Of course, she dotes upon Konrad and spoils him quite dreadfully. Papa thinks it most rude of her – he is her brother, by the way – that she did not attend the reception. He said it was her way of showing Konrad that she was still cross with him for not marrying Miss Challinor who she had chosen for him! But all the rest of the family think Konrad has made a wonderful choice, so you must not mind about his mama, Sophia.'

Sophia had not been looking forward to meeting her mother-in-law and Mitzi's remarks added to her unease. Konrad was far from reassuring as they drove in his carriage out to Wachau. Silent for most of the journey, as the huge Gothic castle came into view, he said pointedly:

'I am relying upon you to play your part before Mama, Sophia, as I shall play mine in the presence of your aunts; and I would like you to refrain from mentioning to my mother that I presented part of the Calverley estate to you as a wedding gift.'

Sophia would like to have retorted that she did not see what business it was of his mother's how he distributed the Calverley estate, but not wishing to anger Konrad, she held her tongue.

The immensity of the schloss was intimidating, although Sophia could not deny its beauty. As the carriage drew to a halt, the huge double doors opened as if on cue, and servants in livery came hurrying towards them, their faces alight with pleasure as they stood in line to greet their master and bobbed curtsys or bowed to her. Familiar now with the greeting, she heard them calling *grüss Gott*, and shyly responded.

There was no such happy welcome from the Baroness Valschintzky. Dressed entirely in black, her grey hair concealed by a black lace cap, she reminded Sophia of a far larger version of her own Queen Victoria. Tall, upright, her full bosom high above her plump corsetted waist, the baroness stood in the hallway unsmiling as Konrad presented Sophia to her.

'You are later than I expected!' were her opening words as her dark eyes darted swiftly from Sophia's fur toque to the tips of her patent leather boots. She held out her hand to be kissed and then, ignoring Sophia, turned to her son with a distinct softening of her features.

'Konrad, my dear boy!' she said in faultless English. 'What a great pleasure to see you. You are looking tired.'

'Sophia and I have been keeping too late hours enjoying ourselves in Vienna, Mama,' Konrad replied, drawing Sophia against him and gazing at her with all the appearances of devotion. 'We were both so disappointed you were not well enough to attend the reception. It was a splendid occasion. I trust you are better now? You are looking well.'

'I have good days and bad!' the baroness replied, her face expressionless. 'Now I expect you would like to change from your travelling clothes. Dinner will be served in an hour's time. I have put you and . . .' there was the faintest pause before she said, '. . . and your wife in the turret guest room.'

Konrad looked momentarily taken aback but made no comment until, after a long walk down endless stone corridors, he stood aside to allow Sophia to precede him into a vast circular bedroom. Heavy tapestries covered the stone walls and thick brocade curtains concealed tall, thin, turret windows. Despite a wood fire burning in the grate, the room was very cold and Sophia shivered.

'I see our luggage has already been brought up!' Konrad remarked as he opened a door leading out of the room into another. He glanced inside and turned back to face Sophia.

'It would seem that Mama has assumed we shall be sharing the marital bed!' he said abruptly. 'There is no second bed in my dressing-room.'

Sophia felt her heartbeat quicken as her eyes went involuntarily

to the huge, curtained four-poster with its voluminous continental feather quilt. True to his word, Konrad had not shared
her bed since their wedding night, for in the Valschintzkys'
Viennese house, there had been a single bed in the adjoining
dressing-room. Now she felt a sudden surge of hope. Alone
in the darkness, they could be reconciled and this terrible
iciness would melt in a night of passionate love! She had
seduced him once and here was her opportunity to do so a
second time. She was momentarily disconcerted when Konrad
added:

'I would ask one of the servants to put in another bed for
me but I am unwilling to have them report my request to my
mother. No, we shall have to make the best of it.' He gave a
short, humourless laugh.

It would not be easy! he thought as he turned quickly away
from the sight of Sophia's face. The fact that he could not
forgive her did nothing to alleviate his physical longing for
her. Holding her in his arms when they danced, sitting beside
her in a carriage, her beauty and her proximity were a constant
torture to him. The prospect of sharing a bed with her was a
tantalizing and a bitter one, for he would not allow himself to
betray his need of her.

He stood still for a moment, staring down into her flushed
face.

'There is no need to look so concerned!' he said brutally.
'The bed is big enough – and I shall not touch you!'

Sophia opened her mouth as if she were about to speak,
but before she could do so, Konrad turned quickly on his heel
and disappeared into the dressing-room. She stared after him,
her spirits momentarily at such low ebb that she was close to
tears of frustration. Then slowly, her chin lifted and a look of
defiance flashed into her eyes. Although she could not be
certain, she sensed Konrad's need of her. There had been many
occasions in Vienna when she had caught him staring at her
with a particular look in his eyes that she had seen on their
wedding night. Once, at a ball, he had been dancing the waltz

with her and his arm had tightened around her waist, pressing her body close against his own. It had excited her, and as her breathing had quickened, so had his! The dance had ended and he had afterwards behaved as if nothing had happened, but Sophia's instincts told her that he was not as indifferent to her beauty as he cared to pretend. She was more than ever determined that, given this opportunity, she would make him want her too much to resist her later tonight.

It was not as if she had anything to lose, she told herself, as a young, rosy-cheeked Austrian maid came into the room and began to unpack her cabin trunk. Tonight she would look as beautiful as she could. She would do as Mrs Enid Groom had recommended, and force Konrad to desire her so fervently that he could no longer withhold his forgiveness.

As she allowed the smiling maid to dress her, Sophia wished the memory of Mrs Groom had not come into her mind, for with it came the unwelcome recollection of the warning that had accompanied her advice – *be very sure that you do not grow to love this man you intend to deceive.*

Why let this caution bother her now? Sophia asked herself as she opened her jewel case and handed the girl her diamond necklace to fasten round her throat. She was not in love with Konrad. All she wanted was to forget the past and lead a normal married life with a husband who was devoted to her. Surely it was not too much to ask of Konrad that now they were man and wife they could settle down and enjoy their married bliss!

'It is my pleasure to give Konrad all his favourite recipes when he is home,' the baroness said to Sophia as yet another large dish of rich food was carried in by one of the six servants in attendance. The dining-room was more like a hall, with high ceilings and heavy mahogany furniture, lavishly carved and cluttered with glass, china, candelabra and silver and brass ornaments. Despite the many candles, the room was filled with dark shadows and an icy draught whistled between the various doors. Huge portraits of the Hungarian Valschintzkys and the baroness's German ancestors decorated the stone walls. The baroness herself bore a remarkable likeness to her obese grandfather, whose portly frame was garbed in the uniform of a Prussian general.

'I have asked my chef to prepare a list for you of Konrad's preferred dishes,' the woman continued. 'I presume your English cooks will be able to produce them after a little practice.'

'I have developed a preference for English food, Mama!' Konrad said, irritated by his mother's implied suggestion that Sophia's servants could not feed him adequately. 'However, it was kind of you to think of it.' He glanced at Sophia who, he could not fail to notice, looked particularly lovely in an apple green tulle evening dress which accentuated the smallness of her waist. He recalled when he had last seen her in that same gown and at the memory of their wedding supper, he caught his breath. How her eyes had sparkled that night! How sweetly she had smiled at him, clung to his hand across the intimate table, promising with every movement and gesture the delights that were to come! Anger at his gullibility vied now with renewed desire for her, and he looked quickly away, reaching for his wine glass in an effort to divert his thoughts. He sensed that Sophia was watching him and as a further diversion, he pointed to one of the portraits on the wall behind his mother's high-backed chair.

'You may be interested to look at that picture, my dear,' he said. 'It is of my great-grandfather, Johann, who is a distant relative of yours. He was your grandfather, Richard Calverley's twin brother. Johann, although born a Calverley, adopted the name of Valschintzky.'

'It was through him that Konrad came eventually to inherit the Calverley title and estate,' the baroness stated. 'Such a pity there was no other heir! Konrad really has no need of property in England.'

Colour flooded Sophia's cheeks and she forgot her promise to Konrad not to speak of Ortolans.

'But it was Konrad who determined that the property has need of him,' she said pointedly. 'As he says, he inherited obligations as well as privileges and wealth! Detcham, our village, has always had a squire and although we were able to fulfil most of the duties whilst my aunts were younger, they are nearing eighty now and Konrad did not feel it right to leave local affairs to me.'

The baroness looked even more surprised than Konrad, but in no way disconcerted by this spirited outburst, she said smoothly:

'Doubtless your aunts were concerned lest the Calverley line should die out. It will be yours and Konrad's duty to provide heirs. Fortunately there is no dearth of Valschintzkys to continue *our* line. For the sake of your family, Sophia, we must hope that you will soon be *enceinte*.' Her use of the French expression did nothing to lessen Sophia's embarrassment. Her aunts would never have permitted such a discussion in front of the servants. Moreover, she wished that Konrad had not been reminded of the heir she had invented. He was scowling and silent and did not once glance in her direction.

It was quite late before the long, drawn-out meal finally ended.

'I have matters I wish to discuss with Konrad which you might find of little interest,' the baroness said to Sophia as she rose from the table. 'So by all means retire if you wish.'

It was not so much a suggestion as an order, Sophia thought as reluctantly she made her way up to the big bedroom. Konrad had not invited her to remain at his side – on the contrary, he had endorsed his mother's proposal. She felt disappointment and a rising anger at her mother-in-law. When she had stooped to kiss the baroness's cheek – a gesture she had felt obliged to make – the stern-faced woman had deliberately turned aside, merely inclining her head as Sophia bade her goodnight. What justification had she for being so cold and unfriendly? Sophia asked herself as her little maid, Anna, chattered away in a country dialect which Sophia could not understand. She could see by Anna's gestures that the girl was enthusing over her satin and lace nightgown and *peignoir*, and admiring of Sophia's waist-length hair as she brushed it meticulously.

'*Schön, schön!*' the girl kept repeating.

But what was the use of beautiful hair if Konrad either did not or would not admire it? What use the figure-hugging nightgown or her slim scented body beneath it if they could not excite him?

She climbed into the big bed and, despite the several warming pans which had been placed between the sheets, she shivered as she lay back against the pillows. How implacable had been this man she had married, she thought uneasily; how determined in his resolve since their wedding night never to allow any close intimacies. He had tipped the night attendant on the Orient Express to provide two single compartments in place of the double one he had previously booked; he had retired each night in Vienna to his dressing-room and breakfasted downstairs whilst she had been served a tray in bed; he had himself arranged for her to spend the days sightseeing or shopping with Mitzi, the evenings with groups of friends at the theatre, the opera, at concerts or dinner-parties. Somehow he had at all times successfully contrived that they were never alone.

Well, she would not be intimidated by Konrad's indifference, she thought defiantly. Sooner or later he would have to come to bed and would no longer be able to ignore her.

The maid put more logs on the fire, smiling over her shoulder at Sophia as she did so, muttering something about '*Herr Baron*' and '*später*' which Sophia knew meant 'later'. How much later? Blowing out the candle, she lay in the darkness waiting.

It was over an hour before she heard Konrad's footfall on the landing. The door opened softly, and from between her half-closed lids, Sophia saw his figure silhouetted by the light of his candle. Without glancing at the bed, he went straight to his dressing-room. Slowly, Sophia edged herself nearer to the centre of the bed. She had no intention of allowing him to hug the outside edge in order to leave a chasm between them.

As Konrad came back into the room, his candle extinguished, Sophia feigned sleep. He pulled back the clothes on his side of the bed and a moment later, she felt the warmth of his body touching hers. Instantly, he drew away. Sophia's excitement mounted as she struggled to control her breathing. Simulating a sleep-drugged sigh, she turned towards him and allowed her arm to fall across his chest. As his body tensed, she snuggled closer against him until there was no part of their bodies which was not in contact.

Konrad caught his breath, now acutely aware of the soft rounded curves of Sophia's breasts touching his arm, of her breath against his cheek, of the warm, sweet feminine scent of her body. He supposed she *was* asleep – yet the memory returned of the first time he had held her in his arms. She had tricked him then. Was this yet another trick?

Suddenly Konrad did not care. This was his wife and his desire for her was paramount. It was he, not Sophia, who had imposed the rule of celibacy between them, and if he now chose to ignore it, he would do so. Why should he deny himself when his need for her was so overwhelming?

Sophia herself was beyond pretence. For those few seconds whilst Konrad hesitated, she had been afraid he would leave the bed and find himself somewhere else to sleep. As he turned and grasped her in strong, unyielding arms, a barely audible cry burst from her lips. A moment later, his mouth found hers and he was kissing her, not tenderly but with a fierce, demanding passion that set her body on fire. She made no resistance when he lifted her arms above her head, and throwing back the bedclothes, covered her whole body with kisses. Then he was above her, a dark menacing shadow bearing down, forcing himself into her. Her body arched towards him and instinctively timed itself to his rhythm. Miraculously, this time there was no pain, she thought, only a surging need as they became one person, soaring together towards a single conclusion.

The silence that accompanied their lovemaking was broken as, simultaneously, Sophia gave an uncontrollable gasp of pleasure and Konrad gave a single cry before lying silent and motionless within her. Sophia's arms tightened around him and she pressed her burning cheeks against his shoulder. She was filled with joy, peace, and an overwhelming sense of relief that this miracle had happened. They were united again. Konrad had forgiven her at last and had allowed himself to love her; and she . . . she had finally discovered what her body had needed to make her feel complete. It was as if a veil had been lifted from her understanding. Despite Mrs Groom's warning, she loved this man who had just made her a part of himself; who had given her such indescribable pleasure. Her cheeks still flushed with the aftermath of passion, Sophia raised her face, needing only now to kiss him, to tell him what lay in her heart.

At the same moment, Konrad lifted himself from her and without a word, turned on his side, moving his body as far from Sophia's as the bed allowed.

He must speak to me, kiss me, at very least talk to me! Sophia thought. Surely what had just transpired had meant more to him than . . . than a momentary desire to mate . . . like an animal . . . like Merrymore's bull let loose with the herd? It cared nothing for the cow after the coupling, and it had ambled away with complete indifference. Did she, Konrad's wife, mean no more to him than this?

Tears of anger and mortification stung Sophia's eyes. She would not allow him to treat her in so humiliating a fashion! But what could she do? In a thousand years she would not plead with him. Nor, she decided, would she let him know how bitterly hurt, how cruelly disappointed she was.

Konrad lay wide awake beside her. The euphoria which had engulfed him during their lovemaking had given way to an acute depression. He was now convinced that Sophia had never been asleep; that she had intended the outcome to be as it was; that she had determined this way of enforcing his forgiveness. It was not the first time she had used her body to fulfil her aims. She had sensed his need of her and planned to use it to weaken his resolve. This suspicion increased his feeling of self-disgust. He had believed himself well in control of his emotions – and certainly well in control of his bodily demands, yet when temptation had been put in his path by this chit of a girl, he had succumbed as easily as a child to a sweetmeat, a moth to a flame.

Konrad's bitterness was not lessened by the knowledge that the restrictions he had put on their married life were of his own devising. It was he who had insisted that they should cohabit 'in name only'; he who had advocated separate bedrooms but who had failed to ensure that they did so this night! It was he who, rashly, had put the embargo on claiming his marital rights, and for three whole weeks had denied himself the pleasures of his wife's body.

It must never happen again, he told himself. He would find some other woman to satisfy his desires; some other woman . . . but who? Whilst in Vienna, he had paid a visit to his former mistress, a pretty blonde opera singer who in the past had attracted him and always managed to please him. On this last occasion, despite the fact that he had intimated in his note that she might expect him to spend most of the night with her, he had felt no stirring of desire. He had been obliged to make some excuse and leave early. There had also been the brunette – a married lady – who in the course of their acquaintance, had invited him to her house for what she laughingly called 'a little extramarital entertainment'. It was not the first time Konrad had spent an afternoon in her company for she was a pretty, amusing young woman who happily indulged her appetites with whoever took her fancy, as did so many of the bored aristocrats living in the city. Although he had managed to pleasure her – or so she had told him – the interlude had afforded *him* no pleasure at all, and he had known that whatever her former appeal, he would not visit her again.

It was, he now realized, Sophia's fault. She alone filled him with an insatiable desire which demanded satisfaction. There was something about her which, inexplicably, dimmed his lust for other women. Even when with his paramour, he had been thinking of Sophia, imagining her eyes, her mouth, her hair, her body. That he must deny himself what he wanted most in the world was proving a bitter pill to swallow.

He slept only fitfully and rose early. Sophia lay, her hair spread over the pillow, her face pale and vulnerable in sleep. Not yet nineteen years of age, she looked even younger – a child. He thought suddenly of the boy urchin by the river and for one long moment, he stood by the bed, fighting the desire to lean down and gather her in his arms. He knew he was on the verge of weakening, and pride surged back, hardening his heart. Sophia had admitted that she had tricked him into marriage in order to secure Ortolans for herself and her aunts. Well, she had achieved her ends! As his wife, Ortolans was still her home. He had given her what she'd wanted. Now he'd be damned if he was going to give her love as well!

CHAPTER TWENTY-ONE

1890

'You woant have no eyes to see with if'n you doant stop that scribbling, Miss Sophia,' Ada said, anxiously regarding her mistress's pale face and violet-ringed eyes. She had hoped when Sophia returned from her honeymoon that her pallor was due to pregnancy, but she knew now that this was not the case – nor likely to be! she thought grimly as she put down Sophia's supper tray and shuffled out of the room. Except for occasional short visits to Ortolans, the master was either in London or abroad, and when he was here at home, he never shared Miss Sophia's bed.

Sophia laid down her pen and straightened her aching back. Daylight was so soon gone on these cold February days, she thought as she turned down the smoking oil lamp. Ada was quite right – her eyes were very sore, but she was reluctant to abandon her work. The novel she was writing was the one sure way she could avoid thinking about the abyss of misery her life had become. She had been forced to accept that her relationship with Konrad had become a mere formality. When she did see him, his manner towards her was never more than icily polite.

When Konrad made it very clear during the remainder of their visit to his home in Wachau that there would be no repetition of their lovemaking, she had decided to try other means to provoke him. On their return to Vienna, she had set about flirting quite outrageously with several of his former fellow officers. Konrad had been furiously angry.

'I don't care personally who takes your fancy, Sophia, but

I will not allow you to make me a laughing stock. We made an agreement – to behave in public as a devoted married couple. I warn you – you will regret it if you continue with this ridiculous and unseemly behaviour!'

In the mistaken belief that she was succeeding in arousing his jealousy, Sophia had encouraged the attentions of a somewhat foppish but ardent young admirer. Konrad immediately cancelled all their social engagements and within the week, they were back in England. He despatched Sophia to Ortolans whilst he remained in town in the Calverley home in Sackville Street. He refused to say when they would see each other again and told her she could make whatever excuse she cared to invent to satisfy the aunts with regard to his absence from Ortolans and hers from Sackville Street.

For a few weeks, Sophia was content to be back in her beloved home and to be reunited with her aunts; but, however hard she tried, she could not keep Konrad from her thoughts. She missed his presence, his company, even the sound of his voice. Most of all, she missed him when she lay alone in bed at night. The effort to keep up a pretence that all was well between her and her husband became increasingly taxing. She knew she must find something to occupy her time lest she go quite mad with longing – and with the growing despair that the damage she had done to their marriage could never be put right. She prayed that she might conceive a child – her only hope of effecting a reconciliation – but it seemed as if in this, too, she was to remain unhappily frustrated.

Now, adding further to her distress, both her beloved aunts were seriously ill.

First Aunt Nellie had caught a bad cold at Christmas and a day later, Aunt Georgie was also confined to bed. By the New Year, their colds had turned to pneumonia. The physician advised Sophia that in the light of their age, she must not take their recovery for granted. Konrad, who was devoted to the two old ladies, had immediately obtained from St Thomas's Hospital two nurses from the Nightingale Training School –

kindly, efficient and competent women whose care was undoubtedly prolonging the aunts' lives. Although Sophia spent several hours a day in their sickroom, reading to them or, since it gave them so much pleasure, recalling episodes of her childhood years, the remaining hours of the day hung heavily on her hands. Konrad's visits were more frequent but always of short duration, and she had no idea what he did with his time in London. Delia, now engaged to her medical student, said she had seen Konrad at the opera one night and he told her he had just returned from Paris. Because everyone knew of the aunts' illness, no one was surprised by Sophia's absence from London.

'Aren't you lonely without him, Sophia?' Delia had enquired sympathetically.

'I'm never lonely at Ortolans!' she had replied, too proud to admit the truth to her best friend. Once it had been true, but it was no longer so.

That same pride prevented Sophia from visiting Mrs Enid Groom, although she was several times tempted to do so when she was riding in the direction of Newtimber. It was, after all, Mrs Groom who had once warned her that Konrad might hate her if ever he discovered that the marriage had been forced on him for her own purpose; that a loveless marriage could be a bitter burden for a woman to carry.

Love had been very far from her thoughts then! Now, apart from her anxious concern for her aunts, the thought of Konrad was an unending torment both for her body and her mind.

It was not until after the New Year that Sophia had found a means of escape. One evening, she had happened to glance at one of the novels much enjoyed by the aunts' two nurses. With nothing better to do, she had read one of them, and despite the simple, not very literary style, had been caught up in the story of a child from an orphanage who had become a millworker and, by a somewhat unlikely chain of events, ended up marrying the owner of the mill! Feeling the plot somewhat contrived, Sophia's imagination had worked out a more plausible one which, when she told it to the nurses, they instantly approved.

'You should write stories yourself, Lady Calverley!' one of them said.

'I have been reading *The Calverley Journal* you lent me, your ladyship,' said the other, 'and you do have a way with words – such lovely descriptions of the house and gardens!'

They pointed out that she could use a pen-name in the manner of Marian Evans who had become famous as George Eliot, if she did not wish others to know of her literary efforts.

At first Sophia had not taken the light-hearted suggestion seriously, but gradually the idea had taken hold of her. Delia, on one of her visits, was wildly encouraging.

'If you wrote a novel, Sophia, you could send it to Elizabeth's publisher friend, Mr Armitage. Would it not be quite splendid if you became famous?'

Fame was not the spur to Sophia's subsequent efforts. Once started, the writing of her story had become compulsive, her imagination transporting her to another world where she no longer counted the hours when she might see Konrad again. She never knew when he would appear and although she had long since ceased to believe that they would ever be reconciled, she clung stubbornly to the hope that on his next visit, he might soften towards her, even forgive her, or at very least, be tempted to share her bed! Surely, she told herself, she had been punished enough!

Meanwhile she poured out her emotions on paper, disguising her own identity and his in the characters of her hero and heroine. Delia, on learning that the first eight chapters were completed, insisted she should post them immediately to Mr Armitage. Better still, Delia said, she would herself deliver them to him without revealing Sophia's real name.

At the end of January, Delia forwarded the publisher's reply.

Dear 'Sidney Sale',

I have omitted the courtesy of the title, mister, since, after reading your manuscript, I question whether I may be addressing a female. Having said this, I hasten to add that I am most impressed by your unquestionable storytelling talent, so much so that I am prepared to offer you a contract to publish your finished novel on terms I think you will consider most favourable.

Miss Delia Lamberhill has explained your wish to remain anonymous – a wish I respect. However, there are one or two minor changes I would very much like to discuss with you. If you are able to come to London, we could take lunch together somewhere in privacy and I assure you that I would consider myself in honour bound not to reveal your true identity. Miss Lamberhill will confirm that I am to be trusted!

May I once again congratulate you on your novel which I have little doubt will be widely read. You have proved your ability to portray those all important ingredients of a novel – love, despair, joy, sorrow – in short, the gamut of human emotions.

I look forward with great eagerness to reading the second half of your book.

Sincerely yours,

Murray Armitage.

There was a postscript suggesting that if by chance Sophia might not wish to be recognized by Mr Armitage if she was known to him, he would ask his nephew, John, his most able junior assistant, to take his place.

Sophia said nothing to the aunts. Mercifully they were still ignorant of the rift between her and Konrad. In their presence, he pretended a deep affection for her and expressed elaborate regrets that duty prevented his spending more time at Ortolans. Despite their protests that Sophia should be with her husband in London or Austria, he assured them that it was his wish as well as Sophia's that she should remain with them until they had fully recovered.

In one way it was fortunate that the seriousness of their

illness had brought with it a certain confusion of mind, and the two ladies had only vague concepts of time. Occasionally, they expressed concern that they were responsible for keeping the happy couple apart but there were days on end when they even forgot Sophia was married. Sophia herself was happiest when Konrad's name was not mentioned for it brought only pain and a desperate longing to see him. In the daytime she busied herself as always in the affairs of the estate which Konrad, with seeming indifference, had told her she might continue to manage. She also supervised the replacement of the worn thatched roofs of the stables and outhouses with peg tiles. Nevertheless, it was all too easy to lie awake at night imagining Konrad in Vienna, enjoying the gaiety of the Season there. As Mitzi had said, he was immensely popular. He would never lack for invitations, or the attentions of females, and the aristocratic ladies in Vienna seemed to thrive on intrigues and affairs.

At night, Sophia slept so fitfully that often she would light her oil lamp and try to stem her longing for Konrad by writing a further few pages of her novel in one of the mounting number of exercise books.

Tomorrow, St Valentine's Day, it would be finished. By next week she could post it to Mr Armitage. The nurses had assured her that her absence in London for a day would probably not be noticed by the aunts who were now barely clinging to life. Sophia's only comfort was that each seemed as tiny and frail as the other, and that when the time came, they would go together and not be left grieving one for the other. She dared not think what she herself would do when they died – an inevitability she had finally faced but could not bear to contemplate. Would Konrad allow her to join him in London or return to Vienna with him? Would he demand that she visit his cold, haughty mother again? Well, she would do none of these unless he behaved more affectionately towards her. Nowadays, she realized, for her to be in Konrad's presence was almost more painful than living in his absence. She could always stay here at Ortolans and write another book, but he could not expect her – a girl of just nineteen – to live the life of a recluse. If it were not for Ortolans, she might demand a divorce. To be socially ostracized could not be as humiliating as being put in purdah by her husband.

She decided that for the time being, she would say nothing to Konrad about her novel. She would wait until the contract was signed, then put it before him to read, for it now occurred to her that he could not fail to be impressed by her achievement and as a consequence, he could no longer treat her with contempt.

It was, however, another month before Sophia caught the train to London to keep her appointment with Mr Armitage's nephew at Brown's Hotel. She had been sitting in the foyer some ten minutes before a tall, pleasant young man approached her and introduced himself.

'You must forgive me for keeping you waiting, Miss Sale!' he said with a pleasing smile and a marked American accent. 'I noticed you the moment you came into the hotel, but I must confess that I was not expecting someone so . . . so young, if you will forgive the comment. I had expected a mature lady of middle age!'

Returning his smile, Sophia replied:

'And I had assumed you would be English.'

'Which indeed I am! My father emigrated to California in the early sixties and I grew up there. My mother is American.'

With easy good manners, he led Sophia to a comfortable armchair in a quiet corner of the lounge, and seated himself opposite her.

He was overlarge to be considered elegant, Sophia thought as she studied her companion covertly, although the clothes covering his tall, broad-shouldered frame were well tailored if a trifle loose-fitting. His thick blond hair framed a rugged open face, the features of which were irregular but redeemed by a ready engaging smile.

'I have arranged a table for one o'clock luncheon,' he said.

'I hope that is agreeable to you? My uncle and I both applaud your modern approach to dining in public. For it to be improper for ladies to do so has always seemed such an absurd convention since they may appear at the theatre and opera and other public places. Between now and luncheon, we can talk about your book. It is quite astonishingly good, Miss Sale! My uncle was on tenterhooks until you signed the contract he sent to you.'

His friendly smile put Sophia at ease.

'I am interested in your adjective "astonishing"!' she said. 'Is it because a woman is not supposed to write as well as a man?'

Her companion shook his head vehemently.

'On the contrary, I doubt if any mere male could have written your book, Miss Sale. Only a woman could have so expressed another's feelings. It is just that . . . forgive me if yet again I am being too personal . . . that you are so very young – I mean, to have experienced so much. My uncle described your writing as "from the heart", which I take to mean "from experience".'

He watched with curiosity the colour staining Sophia's cheeks, and realized that he had inadvertently hit upon the truth. He must learn to be more reticent, he reproached himself. He hoped very much that he had not given offence, for in all his twenty-eight years, he had never yet been so instantly attracted to a girl. He hoped, too, that she was not a married woman. His uncle had instructed him to address her as 'Miss Sale', and wait for her to correct him. His curiosity had trebled now that he had met her, and he waited anxiously for her to speak.

'I have a friend – a married friend!' Sophia proffered. 'She is somewhat older than I and has had an unhappy life. I have to some extent drawn on her experience of life.'

Somehow, he did not believe her, although he pretended to do so.

'Your explanation leads me to the reason for our meeting,'

he said. 'My uncle wishes me to make it quite clear that he is prepared to publish your novel as it is – without alteration. However, he feels that given the opportunity to do so, you might wish to improve certain aspects of it.'

Seeing that he had Sophia's full attention, he continued:

'Whilst your description of the life of your heroine, Cecilia, in the duke's home, is entirely believable, her earlier years in the East End slums of London would appear to have been drawn from Charles Dickens's works rather than from first-hand knowledge.' He smiled in the most friendly manner as he added: 'Having met you, Miss Sale, I appreciate that you are most unlikely to have first-hand knowledge of the sordid side of London. I hesitate to suggest that you might wish to be so enlightened. However, since the rest of your book has such splendid veracity, my uncle wished me to advise you that the sister of our go-between, a Miss Elizabeth Lamberhill, does a great deal of work for London's destitute girls.'

'Elizabeth!' Sophia echoed unguardedly. 'Delia did once mention it to me.'

'Miss Lamberhill's parents do not approve of her association with such people,' John Armitage said gently. 'Many of these girls she assists are "fallen women" before they reach the age of fourteen. In any event, my uncle has not spoken of your book to Miss Lamberhill as he respects your request for anonymity. It is for you to decide if you wish to do so. He thinks Miss Lamberhill could greatly assist you in regard to your early chapters.'

'Then you . . . your uncle . . . think my novel worth this extra care and detail?' Sophia commented thoughtfully.

'Without the slightest doubt, Miss Sale. He considers your style will greatly appeal to those ladies of leisure who prefer a novel such as yours to more erudite tomes!'

Sophia had only written the story because it had filled the lonely evening hours and enabled her to lose herself in make-believe. She had not been seeking literary recognition, fame, money. It was warmly satisfying to be told that as a novelist she could succeed. For the first time in many months, she felt excited, almost happy. Her face broke into a smile as she said:

'You are very kind, Mr Armitage. I will be guided by you and your father, and take advice from Miss Lamberhill. I must confess that I drew much of Cecilia's early life from my imagination as well as from Mr Dickens!'

John Armitage insisted upon ordering a bottle of champagne to celebrate the occasion, and their luncheon was a long drawn-out, pleasant meal at which neither was lost for conversation. He told Sophia about his home in San Francisco where his father had founded his shipping company. His two elder brothers had followed their father into the business, but he had been interested only in books. Since he had no talent for writing, he had decided to become a publisher, and after majoring in English and Literature at college, he had come to England to learn the ropes from his uncle.

It seemed suddenly to Sophia as if she and her companion had been long acquainted. For the most part, they discussed books, and John was newly impressed by her intellectuality. He considered her very well educated compared with her counterparts in the States. American girls of his acquaintance could be amusing and good company, but were usually quite predictable. They lacked Sophia's mystery. He was intrigued by the suspicion that the heroine of the author's novel voiced her own attitudes and feelings.

Before Sophia departed for Victoria Station to catch her train back to Sussex, he discovered that she was married – a disappointment, but a fact which no longer surprised him. Although she had only once referred briefly to her husband, he was convinced the marriage was not a happy one. If Sophia's novel was indeed autobiographical, then her husband neither loved her nor cared that she was unhappy.

As he stood on the platform watching her train depart, he determined that before long he would see her again.

For once it was not the absent Konrad who was on Sophia's mind as her cab driver deposited her at the front door of

Ortolans. The effects of the champagne and her young publisher's complimentary remarks were still in the forefront of her mind, and she did not notice Konrad's tweed ulster on the hallstand. As she removed her own coat, hat and gloves, and handed them to the waiting parlour-maid, she was startled by his voice.

'Will you join me in the library, my dear!' he said, his voice cold despite the affectionate mode of address which he had used for the benefit of the servant. 'I have been awaiting you all afternoon.'

As always, Sophia's heart beat faster at the sight of this man. It had been several weeks since his last visit and he had given her no advance warning of this one. Questions raced through her mind. Had he come only to see the aunts? How long would he be staying? Would he notice the new smart brown and white tailor-made dress and brown velvet hat she had worn to impress her publisher? Had he, by some miracle, decided that he missed her?

Konrad had indeed noticed her appearance, and was made even more uneasy by it. He had certainly not expected Sophia to be absent when he arrived in time for luncheon. As far as he was aware, Sophia never left Ortolans unless it were to go shopping in Detcham! All Ada would tell him was that her mistress had gone to London – to London, of all places! He had been convinced that Ada knew very well who Sophia was visiting but had pretended ignorance. The woman was a bad liar and his suspicions were aroused. Whilst he awaited Sophia's return with growing impatience, he wondered who she could be visiting that she had felt it necessary to warn her maid not to reveal her whereabouts.

'I must compliment you upon your appearance, Sophia,' he said, his voice heavy with sarcasm. 'Ada tells me you have been in London. May I ask what you have been doing? You had a luncheon appointment, I understand.'

Sophia was beset by a variety of emotions. Konrad's voice held a strongly accusing note – as if she had no right to go to London if she so wished! *He* did not tell her where he spent *his* time – or with whom! At the same time, her heart was beating even faster at the thought that he sounded jealous – as if he suspected that she had a secret assignment with another man! She was on the point of telling him that yes, she had indeed lunched with a charming American publisher who was most anxious to see her again; but now she decided that this was not the moment to tell Konrad about her novel. Let him wonder how she occupied her time! Let him have a taste of his own medicine!

'Well, do you intend to answer me or not?' Konrad asked sharply, his unease increased still further by her hesitation. When her eyes blazed and her chin came up in that look of defiance, she was at her most beautiful, her most desirable. It was all he could do to refrain from crushing her in his arms.

'I cannot see that it is of any concern of yours, Konrad, but since you seem to think it is, I was taking lunch with Delia.'

Now it was Konrad's eyes which flashed and narrowed with anger.

'How strange that I should have travelled on the train from London with the Lamberhills this morning, and that Delia should have made no mention of your luncheon appointment. As I recall, she told me she would shortly be visiting you here since she had not seen you for over a month!'

Sophia was unable to prevent the blush that suffused her cheeks. She had told Konrad a lie – but only a harmless one. That she was innocent of any wrongdoing did not help her now that he had caught her in yet another deceit.

'Doubtless it was naïve of me to believe that you had given up the practice of lying to me,' he said bitingly. 'However, as you say, what you do is no concern of mine; but let me warn you, Sophia, I will not be cuckolded. If you are considering taking a lover, think twice before you do so. If I should so much as hear your name linked with that of another man, I should not hesitate to divorce you!'

'Are you then faithful to me?' Sophia asked defiantly. 'Do you live a life of celibacy, Konrad, that gives you the right to demand it of me? Were you and I married – truly married – you would not have to doubt my faithfulness. Perhaps you still think me ignorant of such matters but I am not. I am well aware that a divorce may be obtained by a man whose wife denies him his marital rights; and that no such law applies to a woman. It is a man-made law, Konrad, and I, a woman, do not see the justice in it. When you are a real husband to me, then only shall I consider myself under an obligation to be a faithful wife to you.'

Sophia had had no intention of making this speech but the words poured from her in almost literal repetition of the words in her novel when her heroine, Cecilia, had been unjustly accused of adultery. At the time she wrote the scene, Sophia had researched the subject, never suspecting that she might use her knowledge in real life.

Konrad stared at her in astonishment. Then his anger flared to equal her own.

'You have chosen in your homily to forget that we are married only because you tricked me into it. Can you wonder that I do not find any pleasure in behaving as a true husband?'

Although Sophia's anger was now cooling, she was not prepared to accept less than the truth.

'At your schloss in Wachau – that night . . . you took great pleasure in "behaving as a husband". Or were you just taking advantage of the fact that your mother had put us in a double bed? It was the only time she actually acknowledged that I was your wife!' she added bitterly.

For one long moment Konrad was effectively silenced. It was true that he had been unable to deny himself the unimaginable pleasure of his wife's body; true, too, that his mother had been no more than icily polite to Sophia and treated her more like an unwelcome guest than a daughter-in-law. Uppermost in his thoughts, however, was not the past but the present. Sophia had all but admitted that she felt justified in doing whatever she pleased – and that could mean a lover! The thought of her lying in another man's arms was intolerable. His face was now white with anger as he took a step towards her and caught hold of her arms.

'I demand an answer, Sophia. Have you been unfaithful to me?'

As Konrad's anger mounted, Sophia's decreased. Joy filled her heart at the thought that he cared enough about her to be jealous. On the other hand, he might only be prompted by pride. Joy now gave way to despair.

'No, I have not been unfaithful!' she said bitterly, 'though I am sure you will not believe me when I tell you so.'

She tried to pull away from his grasp, afraid lest he see the tears stinging her eyes.

'Confound it! How am I supposed to know if I can believe you or not!' Konrad shouted. 'Let me repeat my warning, Sophia. If you take a lover, I shall divorce you – and you will lose your precious Ortolans once and for all.'

'So you are now blackmailing me!' Sophia flared. 'Surely even you would not stoop so low as to rob me of my home. You know what Ortolans means to me. I'd rather die than leave it!'

'Exactly, Sophia!' Konrad said, his bitterness exacerbated by her reminder that it was the house and not her husband she feared to lose. 'So I suggest that you don't forget my warning, or that you are my wife, Sophia – mine, do you hear me? And I shall not allow you to behave like a wanton, a whore!'

As Sophia's arm lifted to strike out against his insult, Konrad ceased his fight to control himself. Of all the women in the world, his wife was the one he least wanted to desire. Yet she was the one whose image haunted him, who dimmed the attractions of other females, whose very existence brought him again and again to her side.

As he caught her elbow, he pulled her roughly against him, imprisoning her as he felt her resistance. It inflamed him still further and he brought his mouth down on hers, uncaring that he bruised her lips with his kisses. Sophia's moment of rebellion was shortlived as the urge to melt into his arms became too strong. Her body relaxed against him. He held her fiercely, his hands hurting her as his hold upon her tightened. His face was flushed and his eyes were brilliant as they gazed into hers with an expression she could not mistake. This was lust, not love! The thought was unbearable and she could not withhold the scalding tears which finally spilled on to her cheeks.

'No, Konrad, no . . . please, no . . . !' she whispered.

As if her voice had broken the spell, Konrad released her. His voice held a bitter coldness as he said scathingly:

'So even you have the decency to baulk at leaving your lover's arms for mine so soon after he has pleasured you!'

He released her arms and, turning abruptly, walked over to the fireplace where he stood with his back to her. 'How very inconvenient for you that I should have chosen this afternoon to come home!' he said cruelly. 'However, it was not you I came to see. Unlike you, it would seem, *I* am concerned for the aunts. According to the physician their condition has seriously deteriorated. I shall therefore prolong my visit, and I have informed the servants accordingly.'

Not trusting herself to speak, Sophia merely nodded and with as much dignity as she could muster, she turned on her heel and left the room. She went straight to the sickroom where the day nurse informed her that both the aunts were asleep but that they were no worse than when Sophia had left for London that morning. Reassured that there was no immediate danger, Sophia went to her bedroom. Ada was awaiting her.

'Seeing as how the master was home, I've told Cook to make something special for dinner,' she said as she helped Sophia out of her dress. 'And I've ironed your mauve taffeta, Miss Sophia, seeing as how you'll be wanting to wear something pretty tonight.'

Sophia's immediate instinct was to say that she did not care in the least what she wore. But her pride was now resurfacing. At very least, Konrad's violent, jealous reaction was an indication that he cared – even if it was only for his reputation. If it hurt him to imagine she looked radiant because she had come from the arms of another man, it was just retribution for the hurt he inflicted upon her, so why not look her most beautiful? Her most attractive? She wanted him to be as unhappy as she was.

Sophia's random supposition proved to be an arrow well on target. Seated opposite her at the dinner table, Konrad was unable to ignore his wife's appearance. The softly swelling curve of her bosom was accentuated by the tightness of her bodice. The frilled edges of the V-shaped neckline barely concealed her white breasts between which glowed an amethyst pendant. Her hair, tied back in a loose chignon, shone a deep chestnut red in the lamplight. Her eyes, violet-shadowed, looked enormous.

Unaware of what he was eating, Konrad became more and more convinced that Sophia had been with a lover. But who? Was that miserable puppy, Francis Lamberhill, in London? If not he, who else? As far as he knew, Sophia had neither entertained nor been to any entertainments since their return from Vienna, and today was the first time – that he knew of! – that she had been to London.

It was all too easy, he reflected, for a man to fall head over heels in love with Sophia. His fellow officers, his relatives, his Austrian friends had been admiring and envious. Not only was she beautiful, but she had a damnable air of innocence about her which only he knew to be simulated. *He* knew how sensuous she really was when she was aroused! *He* knew how she used her body to seduce a man into gaining her own ends; *he* knew that she had found their lovemaking highly pleasurable. It was only too likely that she had now found someone else to pleasure her.

Sophia retired as soon as the meal was over. Konrad remained downstairs, morose, thoughtful and unable to dull his suspicions with the aid of his after-dinner brandy. He was still quite sober when he dismissed the servants for the night and went upstairs. A light was burning in the sickroom and he opened the door softly. The night nurse rose to her feet and put her finger to her lips.

'I did not want to distress her ladyship, sir,' she said in a whisper, 'but I do not think either of the patients will last the week. They are so frail, poor dear ladies! I doubt if either of them weighs more than five stone now. Her ladyship is so devoted, I dread to think what effect it will have upon her when they pass away; but then I dare say you will be taking her ladyship back to town with you – and that will be a blessing!'

No, not London, Konrad thought as he went to his room. In London, Sophia would have access to her unknown lover! Nevertheless, he could not leave her here alone. The damnable fact was that he could not trust her. His own experience in the past gave him an insight into the mind and feelings of young, healthy women bored and unsatisfied by their husbands.

All evening long Konrad had been fighting against the urge to make love to his wife. By now he had talked himself into believing that he had every excuse for doing so. When his valet finally left him, he put on his dressing-gown, and taking his oil-lamp, went down the passage to Sophia's bedroom.

As in all old houses, the floorboards creaked and the dark corners seemed alive with shadows. Inconsequentially, as he passed the door which opened on to the unused stairway to one of the attics, he recalled the story the aunts had told him of one of the Calverley ancestors who had died when falling down those stairs. According to family legend, the man had been an illegitimate half-breed who had tried to claim the Calverley title and estates, and was suspected of having murdered their father's cousin, William. Fortunately the blackguard had met with an untimely end at the foot of the attic stairway, and one of the servants, who held a grudge against him, was thought to have engineered his death. The aunts took a childlike, mischievous delight in relating this story to Konrad and constantly corrected each other in the telling of it. Sophia, who had read the story many times in *The Calverley Journal* and had been intrigued by this tale of a black sheep in the family, insisted it was Ortolans and not the old caretaker who had killed the fellow.

Sophia! Konrad's lips formed her name as he paused outside her door. For better or for worse, she was his wife and he had every right to enter her room. It was she who had brought about their marriage. Let her submit to the consequences.

Sophia feigned sleep as she heard Konrad close the door behind him and approach the bed. Her heart was beating rapidly and she held her breath as he stood staring down at her by the light of his oil-lamp. He turned down the wick and she let out her breath in a long, shuddering sigh as he climbed in beside her. She was consumed by conflicting emotions. She wanted him . . . and she wanted him to want her . . . but not like this; not without love. Whatever reason had prompted him to come to her room, she was in no doubt it did not derive from affection.

Sophia wished she had the strength and the will to resist him, but as his arms drew her fiercely against him, she had neither. Her hunger matched his and she gave up the effort to pretend indifference. What vestige of pride remained was lost in the vortex of feeling that eradicated all other thought than that she loved him, belonged to him, and this was the only way she could express what she felt.

As in the big bed in the schloss at Wachau, Konrad departed in silence after he had withdrawn from her. He did not relight his lamp, and in the morning, at breakfast, he behaved as if the night had been no different from any other. Perhaps fortunately for Sophia, she was called by the nurse to the sickroom. Aunt Georgie was having difficulty breathing and it was necessary to send word to the physician. Aunt Nellie appeared to be in a coma, unaware of her sister's struggle for breath as Sophia sat holding the old lady's hand.

Konrad appeared briefly with the physician. The doctor put his stethoscope to Aunt Nellie's heart and shook his head. There was, he told them, nothing more he could do. He had given instructions to the nurse to increase the ammonia and senega stimulant for the heart. He knew of no other way to prolong the old ladies' lives, which were now in the hands of God.

'They have had a long and happy life, Lady Calverley,' he said as Sophia followed him out to his carriage. 'I will call in again later today. Meanwhile, please try and get some rest. You look quite exhausted.'

Konrad was waiting for her in the hall. Unexpectedly, he put his arm round her shoulders.

'I am very sorry, Sophia. Try to be consoled by the thought that neither of the aunts is aware the other is failing. For that we must be thankful.'

His voice was gentle and there was no doubting his sincerity as he added: 'I love them, too, you know, and I share your grief.'

Somehow Sophia managed to control her voice as she looked up and met his sympathetic eyes.

'Thank you for pretending to them . . . that all was well between us!' she said in a low, husky voice. 'They were so anxious for me to . . . to find a husband before they died. You put their minds at rest, and I am grateful!'

He kept his arm around her a moment longer. Then, as one of the footmen came into the hall, his arm fell to his side and he walked away in the direction of the library. Sophia's gaze followed him, but he did not look back.

CHAPTER TWENTY-TWO

1890

The aunts' funeral was a moving occasion. Not only were Sophia, Konrad and the staff in deep mourning, but the entire village attended the simple service. Many of the old villagers, who had been contemporaries of the aunts and knew them as children, were in tears. Curtains were drawn in cottage windows and many doors had black crêpe bows pinned to them. The church bells tolled from sunrise to sunset.

Sophia's grief was so intense that she was beyond tears. Although it was almost three months to the day since the aunts had last been seen downstairs, she missed their presence everywhere. As she wandered from room to room, a weeping Ada close behind her, she felt that Ortolans, too, was grieving.

Aware of her emotion and saddened on his own account, Konrad suggested they go to London where at least there would not be so many reminders; but Sophia refused to leave. Kind and considerate though he had been these past weeks, the rift between them remained, and she did not feel able to explain to him that in its own strange way, the house was trying to comfort her. The aunts would always be a part of it – of its history, its permanence. So long as it remained standing, their spirits would live on in the very walls and floors and ceilings; in the gardens which they had so loved; in the library where she had carefully placed their favourite bedtime books. She had not yet been able to list their deaths in *The Calverley Journal*.

In his genuine desire to console Sophia, Konrad had set aside his own jealous suspicions that Sophia might have a lover in London and decided that the time had come when they should both put the past behind them and try to make a new start to their marriage. Now, when Sophia clung to Ortolans, making its importance yet again obvious to him, the conciliatory words he might have said remained unspoken. Nevertheless, he did not have the heart to leave her here alone, and he remained for the time being, occupying her thoughts as best he could with estate affairs. He discussed with her the advantages of doing away with the pump in the kitchen and having a running water supply installed; of planting a beech wood on the high ground beyond the ten-acre lambing field. He insisted she accompany him on an inspection of all the cottages in the village and list the more urgent repairs that were required.

Early in April, however, he received a summons to Hungary where there had been some kind of uprising among his estate workers.

'I will try not to be away too long,' he said. 'A week or two at most.'

Sophia, unaware of how dependent she had become on his company, was bereft after he had gone. Following an unexpected visit from Delia, she allowed herself to be persuaded to go to London for a few days.

'You can stay with us, dearest,' Delia said, 'and pay that promised visit to Elizabeth. She asked me only the other day when she might expect you.'

It would be a diversion if she could renew interest in her novel, Sophia thought, as two days later, she made her way to the tiny house in Walton Street rented by Elizabeth Lamberhill. Although the little dolls' house had but two small rooms on each of three floors, Sophia felt far more at home here than in the Lamberhills' big London house.

Elizabeth had two young girls to attend to her needs, and a daily cook, who was helping her mistress to train them. Tall, dark and far from unattractive, Elizabeth's lifestyle was a revelation to Sophia. Already in her mid-thirties, Elizabeth was very modern in her outlook and had a total disregard for many of the social conventions which she deemed old-fashioned.

'Had my parents seen fit to give me the same excellent education they insisted upon for my brothers,' she informed Sophia, 'I would have become a barrister. Do you not agree with me that it is ridiculous that such an occupation is barred to women? However, since this profession is not open to me, I do what I can to defend the most helpless members of our vice-ridden society. Mr Murray Armitage has told me about your novel and I am most anxious to assist in every way possible. People in our circle, especially women, should know what is going on around them. Most, like you, Sophia, are so protected from the seamier side of life that they spend their whole lives in total ignorance of what goes on beneath their noses!'

Their friendship developed rapidly, and Sophia's interest in Elizabeth's work went beyond research for her book. Listening to her new friend's accounts of her daily occupation, she was able temporarily to forget Konrad's absence and the terrible sorrow caused by her aunts' deaths.

'Naturally, I have not told either Mr Armitage or his nephew who you really are, Sophia!' Elizabeth said with her customary frankness. 'I expect you know that Murray is a widower. He would like me to marry him, but I am not prepared to give up my independence.'

She put an arm round Sophia's shoulders and after only a moment's hesitation, added: 'Now that we have become so intimate, I shall trust you with a confidence. For the past two years, Murray has been my lover. It is an arrangement which suits me very well and we are, of course, very discreet. Have I shocked you?'

'No, no, of course not! Well, just a little, perhaps!' Sophia added with an apologetic smile. 'I think on reflection that I am more surprised by your daring than by the . . . the fact.'

Elizabeth nodded.

'But you would not have been surprised if I had been a man and had taken a mistress. There lies the unfairness of life for us females. My poor Murray was shocked when I first suggested the notion! But he is a very broad-minded man and we are harming no one. We suit one another very well, and he never interferes with what I do. He is, by the way, a most generous contributor to my Refuge for Girls in Lambeth. He tells me his nephew is head over heels in love with you, but I told him it was a hopeless quest since you were happily married to one of the best-looking men in London!'

This unintentional irony pierced through the armour in which Sophia had encased her heart since the day of the funeral. Without warning, she burst into tears. When she recovered her composure, she heard herself confessing the history of her unhappy marriage to Elizabeth. Far from sounding shocked, the older woman's comment was indicative of her feminist outlook.

'So typical of a man!' she said sighing. 'They may be unfaithful as and how it suits them, but woe betide the wife who steps out of line. Whatever good you may have to say about your husband, I suspect he is no less hypocritical than other men. In the course of my work I have discovered salons, houses, secret rooms where men with the best of reputations indulge all manner of sexual appetites as and when they please. Even the most famous and principled of men – including ordained members of the Church! – visit such places. I would be greatly surprised if your Konrad is faithful to you. If I were in your shoes, Sophia, I would establish your right to a life of your own. Murray tells me you have the making of an excellent novelist. If John can be of assistance or guidance to you, why not let your friendship with him develop? If your husband leaves you alone so much, you have every reason to establish your own circle of friends apart from his. Would he object, do you think?'

'I wish I could say that he would mind very much – but I fear that is not the case,' Sophia replied unhappily.

To distract Sophia who seemed close to tears again, Elizabeth told her of the cruelty and vice surrounding the children of the poor, explaining that these were far more harmful to them than the extremes of poverty they endured.

'From the age of five,' she told a horrified Sophia, 'their parents oblige them to work, to beg, to pick pockets, to steal. Many are beaten, savagely ill-treated or simply thrown out on to the streets. Incest, prostitution, paedophilia are rife!'

Elizabeth was obliged to explain the meaning of these words to Sophia who now realized why Mr Armitage thought the impoverished child, Cecilia, in her novel, was quite unrealistic, suffering at worst hunger and cold!

'Stay here in London and I will take you to my Refuge to meet some of these girls,' Elizabeth promised. 'They are the fortunate ones. The hundreds I cannot rescue go to the poor-houses where they are half-starved; but most are destined to death, prostitution, prison, or torture at the hands of their parents. They deserve a better life, Sophia, and given the chance, these children can live decent, good lives. The two girls who work for me I am training to be housemaids. Once they have reached a certain standard, I find them jobs and take on two more girls. This might be a more realistic method by which your heroine finds her way into the house of a duke! I very much doubt he would have taken Cecilia – almost certainly verminous and probably foul-mouthed – into his service, however pretty your heroine might be beneath the layers of grime!'

Encouraged by Elizabeth – and since there was little else she could do by way of diversion during the period of mourning – Sophia decided to remain in London until Konrad's return from Hungary, and revise her book. Unwilling to impose any longer on the Lamberhills' hospitality – and depressed by Francis's woebegone face and reproachful glances – she moved into her own house in Sackville Street. Here, in solitude, she could concentrate upon her novel.

After visiting the slums with Elizabeth, who gave her all

the background material she needed, Sophia began the task
of rewriting the early chapters of her book. Some of the material Sophia felt might be too distressing for her readers, and
she left the selection of these passages to John Armitage, with
whom she now took luncheon regularly at Elizabeth's house
in Walton Street.

'To use his own Americanism, John is quite crazy about
you, Sophia,' Elizabeth confided. 'He told Murray that you
were the first girl he had met who he would have liked to
marry, and that you have many interests in common.'

Sophia smiled uneasily.

'We do have an amusing time together. John is the first
American I have known and I suspect that it is quite usual
for young men like him to flirt. I do not take him seriously
when he pays me extravagant compliments!'

Elizabeth did not return her smile.

'I know that you are in love with your husband and therefore believe you can keep your admirer at arm's length; but
sometimes when a marriage is going through a difficult patch,
a woman can be tempted to seek consolation elsewhere. I
would not want to be responsible were you to become too
deeply involved with John and put your marriage at risk!'

'You have no need to worry, dearest Elizabeth!' Sophia said.
'I am quite able to control my emotions. Besides, as you have
yourself said, I am still in love with Konrad.'

Sophia spoke with a conviction that belied her true
feelings.

She had been telling herself that her luncheons with John
were entirely a matter of business, but she knew very well
that they were not. Not only was the American very personable, he was frankly adoring and his uncritical admiration did
much to restore her self-confidence. She had not realized before
how greatly Konrad's rejection of her as a woman had affected
her. She did not doubt that her attraction for John Armitage
was partly of a physical nature. He never lost the opportunity
to touch her hand, her arm, her shoulder, and as their friendship

ripened, told her frankly that he could not sleep at night for thinking about her, wanting her. That he now knew her true identity seemed to make no difference.

'Come away with me, Sophia! You must know I am madly in love with you! Why will you not let your husband divorce you so that I can marry you!' he said in pretended jocular fashion, but she was in little doubt that he meant what he said.

Aware that Sophia spent all her evenings alone at Sackville Street and that this was not good for her, Elizabeth arranged a small dinner party at her house to which both Murray and John were invited. Sophia looked forward to the occasion. Her luncheons with John were so often curtailed by his need to be elsewhere for a business appointment. Moreover, it would be lovely to be able to wear one of her pretty evening gowns again and to enjoy John's repartee.

Innocent of any wrong intent – as she believed herself to be – Sophia dressed herself with particular care; but as she glanced at John across Elizabeth's small dining-table, she knew that she wanted him to think her desirable; that she wanted to feel feminine and beautiful, if for no other reason than to dispute Konrad's opinion that she was neither.

Throughout the excellent meal Elizabeth provided, Sophia engaged in conversation with Mr Murray Armitage. She enjoyed their discourse and although she considered him to be quite old, she could understand why Elizabeth had succumbed to his charm. She hoped that by concentrating her attention upon him, both he and Elizabeth would realize that she was not seriously interested in John. The fact that whenever she turned her head, it was to find John staring at her and that she was excited by his undisguised admiration, only increased her determination to pretend her indifference.

Elizabeth was not deceived. As a woman, she realized how much attention Sophia had paid to her toilette – with quite devastating effect! – and John was making no attempt to hide his admiration. She wished now that she had not suggested the dinner party. Matters were made worse when soon after they had repaired to the drawing-room, one of the maids announced that there was a policeman at the back door who wished urgently to speak to her. It transpired that one of Elizabeth's girls had been badly beaten and raped by her father. The man had discovered his daughter's whereabouts at Elizabeth's Refuge for Girls, dragged her home and assaulted her. The police had been alerted by neighbours to the girl's screams and when they had calmed her sufficiently to discover what had happened, she had begged them to fetch Elizabeth.

'I shall have to leave you,' Elizabeth said to her guests when she had explained the situation. 'This girl trusts me and perhaps I can persuade her to go to the hospital since the police seem unable to do so. She is quite badly injured.'

Murray Armitage rose to his feet.

'I shall accompany you, my dear!' he said. 'I will not have you going to that insalubrious district unescorted at this time of night! John, dear boy, would you be so good as to take Sophia home? I will tell my coachman to call a hansom.'

'Must we end this pleasant evening so precipitately, Sophia?' John said as, ten minutes later, the hired cab left Walton Street. 'We could drive round the park, could we not?'

Gently, he took her hand in his, and giving Sophia no more than a moment's time for hesitation, leaned forward and instructed the coachman to take them to Hyde Park and drive around for a while.

'We've hardly spoken to each other all evening!' John said. 'I am eaten up with jealousy at the attention you have paid to my uncle. Am I right in supposing you have been deliberately avoiding me?'

'Perhaps!' Sophia answered, aware that her heart was beating abnormally fast. 'I was anxious that your uncle . . . Elizabeth . . . should not suppose that . . . that there is more to our relationship than mere friendship.'

'But there is more . . . much more!' John's voice was husky with emotion. 'You must know how I feel about you! I meant what I said the other day, Sophia – come away with me! Leave your husband . . . let him divorce you. I will take you to America – to a new life. It is not as if you have anything to keep you here in England. I love you, Sophia. I'll make you happy.'

The warmth, the proximity of his body was, for a moment, all Sophia could think about. It was so long since Konrad had made love to her . . . and then it had not been from love but to establish his right as her husband! As John's arm drew her against him and his mouth covered her with kisses, it was like balm to her wounded heart. At the same time, his words, so passionately spoken, were infinitely disturbing – *leave Konrad . . . divorce . . . a new life in America . . .*

She pulled herself away from his embrace.

'John, you don't understand. I could not leave my husband. He owns Ortolans and even though my beloved aunts are no longer there, it is my home. I'm sorry . . . I should not have let you think . . .'

'Your voice says one thing, but your body tells me something else,' John broke in as he pulled her back into his arms. 'You want me to make love to you . . . you want me to kiss you, hold you. You cannot deny it!'

As once again he covered her face with kisses, Sophia allowed herself to respond to the undeniable truth of his words; but even as she returned his kisses, she realized quite lucidly that it was not John she wanted. He was but an antidote to her longing for Konrad – *his* mouth, *his* hands, *his* body.

'John, I'm sorry! Let me go, I beg you. You have to understand . . . I may not be happily married, but I am still in love with my husband. I should not have allowed you to think otherwise!'

Her companion seemed undisturbed as his hands dropped to his sides.

'I have never thought otherwise, Sophia. I have after all read your book! But equally I am aware that your husband does not need you as I do. If he did, he could not bear to be parted from you even for one night, let alone for weeks on end.'

Seeing the expression of pain in her eyes, he took her hand in his and said gently:

'I did not mean to hurt you, Sophia, but sooner or later, you will have to decide whether the life you lead is really making you happy. I want you to know that no matter how long I might have to wait, I am here on the sidelines hoping. I'm convinced I could make you happy. You would like California – the climate is quite perfect – and if it is a country house you prefer, I will build one for you every bit as beautiful as your home in Sussex. And—' he said with a smile as he opened her hand and pressed a kiss into the palm '—I shall never leave you – even for one night!'

He did not try to touch Sophia again but ordered the coachman to drive them to Sackville Street. He sat beside her in a friendly, companionable way which did much to reassure her that despite his declaration, they could still remain friends. As the driver turned the horse's head into Piccadilly, Sophia knew that her life would be diminished were she never to see John again.

She did not in her heart believe that after its unfortunate start, her relationship with Konrad could ever be put right. Clearly he would never again trust her, and, so it seemed, without trust, love could not flourish. John, however, held no such prejudices against her. He was charming, well-bred, intelligent – and wealthy. He had offered her a new life in America where the scandal of a divorce would barely touch her. Here in England, she would become an outcast of society, and although Konrad had made her financially independent by the gift of some of the Calverley lands and cottages, her chances of making a good second marriage would be minimal.

Why should I even consider such a thing! Sophia thought. If I cannot be happily married to the man I love, then I could not be happy with anyone! I would not want to marry another man – not even John, who would make such a good husband and who adores me!

'I am sorry, John, but I can never be more to you than a friend,' she said as the hansom drew up outside her house. 'I hope that in time, I shall be reconciled with Konrad – and that hope sustains me. Were it not for Konrad . . .'

'I know, my darling Sophia, and I bow to your wishes; but I, too, have a hope for the future. I feel in my heart that one day, somehow, sometime, you and I will be far more to each other than friends. There is something between us that convinces me we belong together.'

He opened the door and lifted her down from the cab. He was smiling once more as he put his arms around her and, with great tenderness, kissed her goodnight.

For the third time, Konrad rang the bell to summon Ada. He was standing in the main bedroom where Sophia's night attire lay on the big bed which had been neatly turned down. It was approaching midnight.

'You are quite certain your mistress did not intend to stay the night with Miss Lamberhill?' he questioned the old woman. There was something about the way Ada avoided looking at him directly which added to his unease.

Ada was well aware that Sophia had been seeing a great deal of the young American gentleman who, Sophia had told her, was a publisher. The very fact that her mistress talked so little about him had made Ada suspicious. It was the first time that she could recall Sophia not 'tumbling over herself' with descriptions of her activities, plans, her likes and dislikes. In Ada's opinion there could be only one reason for this unusual reticence. 'Miss Sophia's up to no good,' she told herself, 'and hers a-feared her old Ada would try to stop her misbehaving.'

Now, here was the master home unexpectedly and wanting to know why Miss Sophia was not at Ortolans; why she had come to London: what she had been doing.

During the two hours Konrad had been home, he had been too keyed up to sit still, and his feet had eventually brought him to Sophia's bedroom. It was not that he intended to find fault with her for dining with Elizabeth Lamberhill – a harmless enough occupation – but that now he knew she was in London, he could not curb his impatience to see her. He had made up his mind, whilst in Europe, that he would on his return be reconciled with her. She had been constantly in his mind, day and night, and he no longer tried to pretend that he did not love her. He did not want to go abroad again without her, and he wanted them to be able to enjoy the pleasures of London and Ortolans side by side. Believing that he would have to wait one further day to see her, he had planned to leave for Ortolans at dawn. On finding her in residence in London, he had tried to settle down to await her return.

'Yes, sir, I mean no, sir!' Ada faltered. 'I mean, it's usually luncheon she takes with Miss Lamberhill, and then hers back in time for supper.'

Was the old woman telling the truth? Konrad asked himself as she shuffled once more out of the room. And what possible reason was there why Sophia should have taken to seeing Elizabeth Lamberhill on so regular a basis? It was not even as if they were of an age. It was the sister, Delia, who was Sophia's friend.

He paused by the window, drawing back the heavy drapes so that he could look down the lamplit road to see if his wife was coming. Several carriages had driven by already and each time, his heart had quickened its beat as he had imagined Sophia coming upstairs, opening the door and seeing him. He would hold out his arms and . . .

The sound of horses' hoofs on the bricked road accompanied the sight of a hansom cab turning into Sackville Street from Piccadilly. The driver was in no hurry and the old horse was allowed to amble its way towards the house. With a rush of excitement, Konrad saw it draw to a halt outside the front door. Wishing to surprise Sophia, he let the curtain fall almost into place, and eager for his first glimpse of her, he continued to watch the cab.

A tall young man emerged from the far side, his silk scarf and gloves startlingly white in contrast to his black evening coat and top hat. Whilst the driver remained seated, the man opened the near door and lifted Sophia down beside him. There was no doubting that it *was* Sophia. The hood of her evening coat was turned back and he could see the bright flame of her hair.

Konrad observed with a numbing sense of shock as Sophia's escort placed his hands on her upper arms and drew her towards him and kissed her. If there were words, Konrad was too far away to detect them. Then Sophia broke free and with a wave of her hand, came hurrying up the steps and rang the bell.

The butler had already opened the front door before Konrad reached the hall. Dismissing him, Konrad took Sophia's arm in an unyielding grip and hurried her into the drawing-room. On her face was a look that combined both shock and joy and, as he stared down at her unsmiling, an expression of uncertainty.

'Obviously you were not expecting me, so I assume my letter telling you of my return has not preceded me.'

Only the coldness of Konrad's voice kept Sophia from allowing her happiness in seeing him to reveal itself.

'I suppose that you posted it to Ortolans, presuming me there,' she said. 'I have been in London this past month. Have you eaten, Konrad?'

Ignoring her question, Konrad said:

'Ada tells me you were dining with Miss Lamberhill. I cannot think that your aunts would have approved of you encouraging your servants to lie, Sophia!'

Sophia gasped and her temper flared.

'It was not a lie! I *was* dining with Elizabeth. Since you seem to doubt my word, you may ask Elizabeth to . . .'

'To give you an alibi, Sophia?' Konrad's voice was bitter. He looked quickly away from her flushed cheeks and blazing eyes. 'You may as well know, I was watching your arrival

from the window. I saw you with your paramour, Sophia, so
there is no point in lying to me further!'

Sophia was appalled, yet a tiny part of her was exultant.
Konrad must love her a little to be so jealous. The time had
surely come to explain everything – to tell him about her book
and how she had come to meet John Armitage; even that John
was in love with her, but that she did not return that love;
that she loved only him, Konrad.

As her explanation began to unfold, she watched eagerly
for Konrad's reaction. His face was turned away from her and
she was unable to see the expressions on his face, first of
longing as he tried to believe her; then of growing doubt.

'So you have written a book and this Mr Armitage is going
to publish it. A likely story, Sophia!'

'Konrad, I can show you the contract – it is down at
Ortolans – and the publisher's letters. Why don't you believe
me? They will confirm everything I have told you. I came to
London because Elizabeth Lamberhill offered to give me the
background material I needed. I stayed on because Mr
Armitage offered to help me with my revisions and—'

'That is enough, Sophia. I have no wish to hear any more!'
Konrad broke in, but now Sophia would not be silenced.

'But you shall hear it!' she cried. 'It is the truth, Konrad,
and I have done nothing of which I am ashamed. I did not
know that Mr Armitage was going to fall in love with me. I
did not encourage him. I am not trying to hide from you the
fact that I enjoy his company; that I was flattered by his
admiration. It is nice, you know, to feel loved!' she ended
bitterly.

Konrad was shocked into momentary silence. He could
recall with great clarity his meeting with Armitage last year
at Ortolans when Elizabeth Lamberhill had brought him with
her family to a dinner party. He had supposed at the time
that the fellow was Elizabeth's admirer – perhaps lover. He
remembered the man as being at the very least in his fifties
– and it had been a *young* man he had seen just now with

Sophia . . . tall, upright, and bearing no resemblance to the somewhat portly gentleman he had met. Yet Sophia would have him believe she had been dining quite innocently with her publisher!

So this was another falsehood! he told himself. Was this story of a novel still another fabrication? Since Sophia had felt obliged to lie, it could only be to get herself out of trouble, and therefore she must be guilty. Much as he might wish to think otherwise, he had the evidence of his own eyes to condemn her.

'It is past midnight and I am going to bed,' he said abruptly.

Sophia took a step towards him.

'But Konrad, you cannot leave me like this. It is not fair. You . . .'

'You can do the rest of your explaining in the morning,' Konrad interrupted her, his disappointment so great that he could not bear to continue the conversation nor look at that beautiful, young face so deceptively innocent.

'Goodnight, Sophia!' he said abruptly as he strode out of the room.

For several minutes, Sophia stood staring at the doorway, hoping, praying that Konrad would return. Then her chin lifted. Elizabeth was right – he would never forget that she had cheated him into marriage; never trust her. There was no hope for them. If only . . . if only she did not love him. Even now when she hated him, she still loved him.

'Marry me, Sophia. I will make you happy!' John's words flashed into her mind. Perhaps, after all, she should accept defeat and say yes to the man who did love her.

Although Sophia was not a late riser, Konrad left the house before she went down to breakfast. He was on his way to Essex Street to visit the publishing firm of Armitage & Company. He was obliged to wait half an hour before Mr Armitage's secretary arrived and informed him that the publisher was not expected until after luncheon, but that if the matter was urgent, Konrad might find him at the Carlton.

Konrad took a cab to Pall Mall and entered the portals of the club. Fortuitously, he had himself become a member during his engagement to Lavinia whose uncle had offered to put his name up. He walked into the lounge and glanced at the predominantly bald heads buried in copies of *The Times*. Suddenly, by the window, he espied the man he was seeking.

'Mr Armitage? I wonder if you remember me – Konrad Valschintzky, or Calverley, if you prefer. We met last summer at Ortolans.'

Murray Armitage rose to his feet, regarding his companion with interest. A singularly handsome man, without a doubt, he thought, and very much the aristocrat.

'But of course I remember you, though I don't think I've seen you here before, Calverley. May I order coffee for you – a drink?'

Konrad shook his head. He was feeling far from elated at being proved right – the man was at very least fifty! – and bitterly disappointed that his suspicions had been confirmed. *This was not the young man who had escorted his wife home last night!*

'Thank you, sir, but no! I'm on my way out. I thought I would have a quick word – about my . . . my wife's book!'

Murray Armitage smiled.

'Ah, so you finally know about it! Sophia wanted to surprise you. Yes, we are delighted with her novel. She shows great talent. We hope to publish it in the spring.'

'Then doubtless we shall be seeing more of each other!' Konrad said politely. 'I must tell her that I ran into you.'

'Do give her my kind regards!' Mr Armitage said, wondering if Calverley knew anything of his wife's friendship with his nephew. Under the circumstances, he thought, it might be better not to refer to John. As Konrad excused himself and walked away, he watched his visitor speculatively. He had the feeling that this young man was not very pleased by his wife's hidden talents . . . or even particularly interested in them. From everything John had told him, Valschintzky treated his wife abominably, neglecting her and spending a great deal of his time abroad. Another woman? he wondered. The hasty, unexpected marriage to little Sophia Calverley and the broken engagement to the Challinor girl had surprised them all; the Lamberhills had talked of little else at the time. It looked as if the age-old adage, Marry in haste, Repent at leisure, was proving all too true! Poor John – head over heels in love with a married woman who, according to Elizabeth, was still in love with her husband.

'Quite the makings of a good plot!' the publisher thought, before his natural kindness obliged him to reproach himself for considering the heartaches of these young people's lives in such materialistic terms.

Konrad walked home, taking as long as he could to do so. He was unaware of the soft June sunshine warming his face; of the congestion of traffic as carriages, carts, horse buses, wagons jostled for space; of the flower girl trying to sell him a bunch of violets. He was lost in thought as he pondered what next he would say to Sophia. Long ago he had told her that if ever he discovered she had cuckolded him, he would divorce her. Their marriage had become a farce – and yet . . .

Konrad's thoughts turned briefly to the comely young widow with the country house in Leicestershire who had been trying for so long to entice him there for a discreet liaison. He had several times been tempted to enjoy what she offered, but his experiences in Vienna had taught him that no other woman would erase Sophia from his mind. She was the only one who could assuage his desires. This hold she had upon him was quite maddening – the greater because he could not explain it except by that imponderable word, love! One did not love a woman, however beautiful, who lied, cheated, deceived, betrayed. One despised such a person.

Now that he knew the depth of his wife's perfidy, he could not allow his marriage to continue. There was no alternative to divorce – yet his mind shrank from such a step. It was not, he reflected, as if he had evidence of her adultery. It was just possible that she had been enjoying a flirtation with this unknown lover. Since it was not Murray Armitage, who *was* the fellow? He hadn't the slightest idea. He both wanted and did not want to know the man's name. Like it or not, he had to find out. Ada, who quite possibly knew the truth, would not tell him; nor would his pride allow him to question the servants, nor indeed Elizabeth Lamberhill, who Sophia was obviously using as a cover. He could, if he wished, hire a private investigator – someone discreet who would report his findings only to him. The idea was abhorrent and yet, he thought, in fairness to Sophia, it was perhaps only right to have proof of his suspicion before reaching any irredeemable decision about their future.

It did not occur to Konrad, who had no reason to contemplate the possibility, that there might be a second Mr Armitage; that had he allowed Sophia to complete her explanation of her activities, this would have become apparent. It was not until it was far too late and he learned the truth that he would blame himself for having been too ready to jump to the worst conclusions. Having assumed her guilt, he therefore gave her no benefit of any doubt; no time to explain her association with young John Armitage of whose existence he was ignorant.

By the time Konrad reached Sackville Street, his mind was made up. He would go up to Leicestershire and attempt to forget Sophia whilst he had her followed. He would let her know that he was going to be away for at least three weeks. This would, ostensibly, allow her time to complete her book but also, if such was her intention, to see her lover again. Dependent upon the intelligence he received from the investigator, he would then decide if they might both be happier were they to have a divorce.

CHAPTER TWENTY-THREE

1890

Konrad departed that morning as soon as his valet had packed. He allowed no time for further conversation with Sophia other than to tell her he would be away for at least three weeks. Sophia did not go round to Walton Street to see Elizabeth, but took to her bed suffering an unexpected attack of nausea. For some days now she had been feeling far from well. She was sleeping badly and not eating enough. Ada, unaccustomed to seeing her mistress ill, nagged Sophia to see a physician. She was full of tales about members of her family who had died from this or that complaint because they had not been able to afford the services of a doctor, and had failed to take the right medicines.

'If'n you doant see the doctor, Miss Sophia, I'll be telling the master when he gets back. 'Tis his duty, no matter what, to see you does so. I reckon as 'ow he must be blind if he didn't notice you be lookin' ill. Happen he still thinks you be fretting for the poor dear Misses Calverley.'

'Then he has a strange way of showing it!' Sophia flared. 'It is less than three months since . . . since we buried my aunts and yet he leaves me alone once more.'

Ada said thoughtfully:

'The master were weepin' when they put the coffins to rest! I never did 'spect a big strong man as was once a soldier to show his feelings thataway. "Ada!" he says to me arterwards, "Ada, you are to do everything you can to console your mistress. I wish I could be a-takin' her to London with me. T'aint good for her stayin' here in this house with its mem'ries."

He were that worrit about you, Miss Sophia, and that's a fact!'

'Then he did not remain worried for long, did he!' Sophia said emphatically.

Ada, of course, knew nothing of last night's exchange between her and Konrad, for she had felt far too distressed to speak of it when Ada put her to bed. The old woman was adamant in her belief that Konrad was a good man who loved his wife – for all he was forever leaving her alone. Elizabeth, however, was insistent that he was neither good nor loving.

'It is quite intolerable!' she commented when Sophia related the events two days later. 'Perhaps I should not be telling you this, Sophia, but that female, Clare Fullard, lives in Leicestershire. She's a widow and a merry one at that! Everyone knows that she has determined to marry again as soon as she can catch a husband – and she has set her cap at your Konrad. Mama was in a box adjoining hers at the opera and told me the Fullard woman was flirting quite outrageously with your husband. Mama was quite shocked . . . but then she would be. Of course, that was before your poor dear aunts—'

She broke off to put her arm round Sophia's shoulders.

'Ada is quite right – you do look ill!' she said. 'What you need, my dear, is a holiday. I will take you away for a week to the seaside. Murray – Mr Armitage – has a villa in Rottingdean. It is quite isolated and he and John make use of it when they have a great deal of reading to do. It looks over the sea and is very healthy. I know Murray would permit us to go there.'

Sophia's mood of deep depression now gave way to one of defiance. By what right did Konrad pursue an affair with some other woman whilst condemning her for having an affair with John? Perhaps it was to salve his own conscience that he was so determined to believe ill of her. The least he could have done was to give her the benefit of any doubt; but he had jumped to a wrong conclusion and it suited him to stick stubbornly to it.

In one way, she would be pleased to get away from London, from Sackville Street; go to the seaside with Elizabeth and forget for a little while how angry and unhappy she was. Slowly but surely, Konrad was destroying all her pleasures. She could not even be happy at Ortolans any more. He wanted to hurt her! And she was allowing herself to be hurt when she could be in the company of someone like John who wanted only to make her happy! Perhaps John would be at the villa. If he knew she was going, he would unquestionably arrange to be there.

She glanced at Elizabeth uneasily. This woman was her kind, devoted friend and despite her own unconventional relationship with Mr Armitage, was unlikely to condone a serious liaison between John and herself. It was different for Elizabeth – she was not a married woman and as she had once said to Sophia, she and Murray harmed no one. Were she, Sophia, to agree to take John as a lover, it would endanger her marriage, and hurt – if not Konrad – then his pride! But he deserved to be hurt, punished, as he was punishing her. Was it fair to John? Would it add to those hopes he persisted in maintaining that she would ultimately leave Konrad and marry him?

Whilst gratefully accepting Elizabeth's invitation to go with her to Rottingdean, Sophia said nothing of her intention of telling John of their plans. She would leave the decision to him as to whether he wished to pay a visit to the villa whilst they were there.

As Sophia had known deep down that he would, John made immediate arrangements to arrive 'unexpectedly' at the villa for the weekend.

At first, Sophia feared that she might not be feeling well enough to enjoy the holiday. Before she and Elizabeth departed, however, her nerves quietened and she found herself looking forward to it. Only one of Elizabeth's young servant girls, her cook and Ada were to accompany them.

'We will spend the first few days very quietly to give you

time to recuperate, Sophia,' Elizabeth suggested as they made their final preparations. 'We will take the train to Brighton and it is an easy coach ride to Rottingdean from there.'

Sophia tried not to think about Konrad as she recalled that in all possibility, he was even now enjoying the favours of the 'merry widow'. As far as her plans to see John were concerned, since Konrad believed her guilty she might as well give him cause to do so. By the sound of it, he intended to put an end to their marriage whatever she did or said.

Four days at the tiny remote seaside village of Rottingdean did much to restore Sophia's health – and to a lesser extent her spirits. The weather was perfect, and she and Elizabeth went for long walks along the beach and took picnics up on the Downs. Hearing the larks, watching the sheep with their half-grown lambs, Sophia felt a nostalgic longing for Ortolans. If she were one of those larks, she could be hovering over her beloved home which could not be more than ten miles away! Despite Elizabeth's companionship, there were moments when loneliness engulfed her and she was close to tears.

John Armitage arrived in time for lunch on Saturday. He came armed with a huge bunch of white roses which he had purchased in Brighton, and some delicious *marrons glacés* which he had acquired from Fortnums. As always, he was well turned out in a checked Norfolk jacket and knickerbockers.

Elizabeth voiced her surprise.

'Your uncle did not tell me you would be joining us for the weekend,' she said. She did not miss the quick glance that passed between him and Sophia, and her uneasiness increased.

'I do hope you have no objection, Miss Lamberhill. The weather is so good that it seemed a shame to waste it in London. I cannot tell you how hot and stuffy it is in the City.'

John's arrival and his acceptance by Elizabeth calmed Sophia's nervous reaction to his appearance. He seemed well in command of the situation and happy to be there. Perhaps his most important asset, she thought, was his bright, cheery mood. That afternoon, he accompanied them down to the edge of the sea and without any ado, removed his spats, shoes and socks, and paddled in the water. Before long, Sophia was doing likewise and Elizabeth laughingly accused them of behaving like children.

'It's good sometimes to be young and silly – and happy!' John said as they walked home. 'I shall always remember today. It has been tremendous fun – or as you English say, really jolly!'

'It's far too long since I heard you laugh like that, Sophia!' Elizabeth remarked as they went upstairs to rest before changing for dinner. 'John is good for you, my dear,' she added thoughtfully.

Sophia nodded. She had enjoyed the afternoon, not least, perhaps, because she had not thought of Konrad and what he might be doing with his time. It had been impossible for her not to notice John's admiring glances; to feel the pressure of his hand when he held her arm; to sense his awareness of her. Even whilst he talked and laughed, there was a look in his eyes which she could not mistake. She had been unexpectedly moved by the sight of this leviathan of a man kneeling in the wet sand as he attempted with great tenderness to dry her bare feet with his silk handkerchief. If only *she* could fall in love with *him*, she thought! If only he could help her forget Konrad for more than an afternoon!

'You be all of a fidget, Miss Sophia!' Ada complained as Sophia tried to rub some colour into her pale cheeks as she dressed for dinner. 'That foreign gentleman didn't ought to have kept you out so long by the sea. The master would be that puckered if he knew.'

'Well, he doesn't know, Ada – and even if he did, I doubt very much if he would care.'

'Adone-do, Miss Sophia!' Ada said in a shocked voice. 'He's your husband lest you've forgot it.'

'Forgotten it!' Sophia echoed bitterly, her chin high. 'It's about time I did, Ada, whatever you may think!'

'You baint up to no good, surelye, Miss Sophia!' Ada said

shortly as she laid down Sophia's hairbrush with an angry thud. 'For better nor worse, you said in church, and seem' as how your poor dear aunts isn't here to 'vise you, I'm a-tellin' you, you'll be sorry if'n you meks it worse.'

Despite Ada's obtuseness, Sophia was aware of her maid's intended warning, and was angered by it. She would not have Ada – no matter how old and faithful a servant – tell her what she could and could not do.

'I suggest you mind your own business, and I'll mind mine!' she said, and before Ada could reply, she hurried out of the room.

Because Ada had so closely echoed her own misgivings, Sophia was defiant. She had a right to happiness, and why should it not be John who was the provider? Elizabeth had a lover! Many married women had lovers! Clare Whatever-her-name was had Konrad for a lover! Why should she not let John be hers?

Elizabeth called to her as she was about to go downstairs. As Sophia went into her bedroom, Elizabeth turned from her dressing-table stool to regard her.

'Sit down a moment, my dear. I have something I wish to say to you.'

As Sophia reluctantly sat down on the side of the bed, Elizabeth drew a deep sigh.

'You look very beautiful, Sophia – and John will unquestionably find you so. There is no need to look so defensive – I am not about to berate you for arranging this rendezvous behind my back, although there was no need. I am your friend, my dear, and it is as such I speak.'

She paused briefly to fasten a jewelled comb in her upswept hair.

'I am concerned for your future. I know that John makes you happy – I have seen that for myself this afternoon. He loves you and you are in need of love. I should have had the foresight to realize that this could happen and I regret now that I encouraged you to make such a close friend of him.'

She saw the heightened colour in Sophia's cheeks, but she was too fond of her to baulk now at voicing her fears.

'It is not from any moral conviction that I am warning you against taking John as a lover, which I suspect you may be about to do. It is because I think I know your character very well by now. You are not a person who can do things by halves. Once your mind is made up, you put your whole heart into it; but Sophia, have you thought how impossible this will be? You are still in love with your husband. Naturally, because he has behaved so badly towards you, you are very vulnerable and it must seem very tempting to accept the love of another man. But where can this lead? You will find yourself unable to keep a love affair casual – it is not in your nature. You and John will see more and more of each other, and with each dangerous assignation, put your marriage to Konrad at serious risk. Is that what you want?'

Sophia met Elizabeth's steady gaze, her own eyes flashing.

'I cannot see that my marriage could be in any worse state than it already is!' she flared. 'Konrad believes me guilty of adultery, so I might as well be hung for a sheep as for a lamb.'

'So you are prepared to risk Konrad divorcing you,' Elizabeth said quietly. 'Does this mean that you can contemplate marriage to John?'

'John loves me. He wants to marry me!'

'My dear child, I am well aware of that. You, however, are not in love with him. Attracted to him, maybe, but physical passion is not enough.'

'I respect him, I admire him. I . . . might grow to love him . . .'

Elizabeth nodded.

'You could indeed! He is a charming man and if you truly believe you could be happy with him . . .'

'I could not be less so than I am living with a husband who does not care whether I am alive or dead!' Sophia broke in. More quietly, she added: 'I know you are only trying to help me sort out my feelings, Elizabeth. It is so confusing. If only John were not an American!' Seeing Elizabeth's puzzled expression, she attempted a smile. 'I do not know if I could bear the thought of living in California . . . of leaving Ortolans and perhaps never seeing my home again. As for Konrad, he does not deserve any consideration. There are times when I come close to hating him!'

'My dear, there is a very thin dividing line between love and hate!' Elizabeth said. 'You alone can decide how to manage your life – I have no right to interfere. All I seek to do is caution you before you allow your relationship with John to go further. I fear for that impulsive nature of yours.'

Sophia rose to her feet and crossed the room to Elizabeth's side.

'You are my good friend, Elizabeth, and I know you love me and mean well, but I don't think even you realize how . . . how terribly lonely and unhappy I have been since my marriage. If I do take John for a lover, it will not be because of the physical pleasure this might bring me – it will be from a need to be loved, wanted; to feel desirable, a woman. If John is willing to take me on those terms, why should I not agree?'

Elizabeth put her arms round Sophia and held her in a warm embrace.

'That is for you to decide, dearest. Naturally, I will do everything I can to protect you if it becomes necessary. I sense that your mind is already made up. I hope you will be happy, Sophia – and John, too. He is a good man.'

As again and again during dinner Sophia's eyes met John's ardent gaze, her last doubts vanished. Elizabeth was right, she thought – her mind was made up; it had been so since she had advised John that she would be spending the week here in Rottingdean and would not be averse to his joining her at the weekend. Had there been no ulterior motive at the back of her mind, she would have told Elizabeth that he was coming! Elizabeth's fears for the future had worried her only momentarily. Why must she concern herself with tomorrow? It had never been in her nature to do so. She had lived too often in the future of late, thinking what she would do, say 'when

Konrad returned from abroad'; how he would behave towards her; whether the post boy would bring a letter from him tomorrow, the next day, the next. Since her wedding night, she had been waiting for the future. Now she was going to live for today.

Elizabeth retired immediately after the evening meal. John sat himself beside Sophia on the tiny chintz-covered sofa, and took her hand in his.

'I love you so much, Sophia!' he said. 'I don't think I have ever been in love before. I've certainly never met a girl I wanted to marry. I have tried since our last meeting to imagine the kind of man your husband is, but none of it adds up. How can he leave you alone so often? I know females are supposed not to need men's company . . . have the same desires, I mean, but surely every woman likes to be loved? Wanted? Does he not know this?'

'I don't want to talk about him,' Sophia said quickly. 'I want to forget him, John – at least for tonight. I want . . .'

'I know what you want!' John said huskily, as without hesitation, he gathered her into his arms.

His kisses were different from Konrad's, Sophia thought – far more gentle and caring. Perhaps this was the difference between a man prompted by lust and a man prompted by love? If it were so, then Konrad did not . . . could not love her. Only on their wedding night had he kissed her in this fashion – as if seeking to give her pleasure rather than taking his own.

'Don't think about him!' John whispered against her ear. 'I am here, Sophia, and I love you. I want you to marry me. I need you. I love you.'

His strong muscular body was pressing against hers and her own responded. Thoughts of Konrad receded as John's urgent hands reached for the tiny pearl buttons of her dress.

'Not here – not like this!' Sophia murmured. 'Our rooms adjoin, John, and there is only my maid's room in our passage. Be very quiet when you open my door, and then Ada, who is somewhat deaf, will not hear you.'

For once, Sophia thought, she would undress herself. If she did not summon Ada when she went upstairs, the likelihood was that the old woman would doze on undisturbed.

The door of Ada's bedroom was ajar. Sophia peered in and with a feeling of relief, saw that she had been right – the maid was asleep. Gently closing the door, she moved silently into her own room. Her heart was beating hurriedly as she struggled with the unfamiliar fastenings of her dress. She had not realized how dependent she was on Ada's help.

At last she was naked, and picking up the nightdress Ada had laid out on the bed, she pulled it over her head and hurriedly climbed between the sheets. Once John came into the room, she would turn down the oil-lamp, she decided, suddenly shy and ill at ease. In the past ten minutes, she had had no time to reflect upon what she was about to do. Now, as she awaited the man who was about to become her lover, she tried to distract her mind by gazing round the little room. It seemed tiny after her big bedroom in London, although the feather bed in which she lay was large and comfortable.

Perhaps she would turn the lamp out now, she thought. It would be less embarrassing if the room was in darkness and John could not see from her face how nervous she was. It was so unlike her to be afraid – she who had had the courage to walk into Konrad's bedroom that fateful night at Ortolans and climb uninvited into his bed! How ignorant, how stupid she had been!

Turning on her side, Sophia reached for her oil-lamp and it was then she saw the picture frames. Ada must have packed them, for *she* most certainly had not! One was a delightful daguerreotype of Aunt Nellie and Aunt Georgie, sitting side by side in the garden at Ortolans outside the arbour. Both were smiling as they looked directly into the lens. They seemed to be looking at her, Sophia, their lips slightly parted as if they were about to speak.

Sophia closed her eyes in an effort to wipe their image from her thoughts. She did not wish to remember them now, at this moment, when she was about to break one of the ten commandments in which they believed so fervently. How unhappy, how distressed they would be if they knew . . .

Sophia opened her eyes which were drawn involuntarily to the second frame. This time she saw herself and Konrad – a well-focused, black and white photograph taken on their wedding day. Konrad had his arm around her and was gazing down into her eyes. On her face was a radiant smile. In the background was the beautiful south aspect of Ortolans, its casements reflecting the afternoon sunshine; a cluster of white doves on the uneven slabs of the roof; the big, iron-studded oak door opened wide in welcome to their guests.

Angry tears filled Sophia's eyes. She was in no doubt that Ada had placed these here deliberately whilst she had been at dinner, intending to remind her of the life she was trying so hard to forget; of the innate goodness of her beloved aunts; of the husband she was trying to forget; of the love that they had once so briefly enjoyed. Ada could not have known that she, Sophia, had lost all hope of finding happiness with Konrad; but she did know of Sophia's love for Ortolans. There would always be Ortolans, and it would always be her spiritual home. No matter how wonderful the life John painted of California and its perpetual sunshine, of the house he would build for them, of the escape marriage to him offered her, she could not abandon her home, perhaps never to see it again.

'My dearest girl!' John said as he came to her bedside and discovered her weeping. 'If the prospect of my being here causes you so much distress, then I must leave you at once. I cannot bear the thought of making you unhappy.'

With an effort, Sophia choked back her tears and reached out to take her would-be lover's hand.

'I thought it would be . . . all right!' she whispered. 'I wanted it to be so. I really did, John!' She drew a deep breath. 'Once – a long time ago – I deceived Konrad and I have lived to regret it every day of my life since. I want above all to be honest with you. You know already that I do not love you in the way you would like, but I have grown very, *very* fond of you, and I am happy in your company.'

As his hand tightened about hers, she said quickly: 'What we intended to do tonight, it might have given us pleasure, happiness of a kind, but only momentarily, John. If we were to enjoy a liaison, it could only complicate both our lives still further. I could never leave Konrad, never leave my home. *I could never marry you.*'

For a moment, John was silent, his sense of loss overwhelming. Then he said:

'I know you do not love me – you have never pretended to do so – but I truly believe you could grow to do so in time. You say you will never leave your husband . . . and I believe you, but suppose he were to leave you, Sophia? I do not wish to hurt you, but Elizabeth told me that he has threatened divorce. She is devoted to you and felt it her duty to caution me lest inadvertently I was responsible for further complicating your life. You had wandered off for a few moments in search of seashells, but were not absent long enough for her to elaborate. I learned of your husband's threat to divorce you, but I do not understand on what grounds. However, if this were to happen, surely he would not allow you to continue to live in what, after all, is his home, is it not? Would you then marry me?'

It was several minutes before Sophia could bring herself to speak. She had put to the very back of her mind Elizabeth's warning that Konrad might divorce her if she gave him reason to do so. Whether she married John or not, she would have to leave Ortolans. The risk was too great, the prospect unbearable, and all too real. Konrad would allow her no choice.

'I don't know . . . what I would do if I was forced to leave my home,' she said truthfully.

'Then there is still hope for me,' John replied quickly. 'Believe me, Sophia, I want far more than an occasional illicit night with you. I, too, have principles and I do not care for the thought of making love to another man's wife behind his back.

In our case . . . knowing that your husband does not begin
to love you, need you, respect you as I do . . . I would have
taken what he values so little. Not, however, against your will,
so please do not cry any more, my darling. You have nothing
with which to reproach yourself, and I was wrong to be so
precipitate. I love you – and I will wait for you.'

He kissed her with great tenderness and for a moment,
Sophia clung to him. It would be so easy – so very easy – to
lose herself in his embrace; to take the comfort he offered; to
use him to satisfy her own need for love. But she liked him
too much to do that.

For a long time after he had left her, she lay awake deeply
regretting that she had allowed him to go, yet paradoxically,
immensely relieved that she had done so. Next door, Ada
Pylbeam lay awake, congratulating herself on the success of
her cunning ruse to protect the young girl who meant more
to her than anyone else in the world; and, moreover, who the
dear late Misses Calverley had so trustingly placed in her care.

CHAPTER TWENTY-FOUR

1890

On Sophia's return to London, with Konrad still absent, she decided to take Ada's advice – now reinforced by Elizabeth – to see a physician. She was once again feeling far from well, and the benefit of her brief seaside holiday seemed to have been shortlived. The doctor's diagnosis came as a deep shock for she had never once suspected what might be wrong. She was with child.

'I would hazard a guess that you have been pregnant for some three months, Lady Calverley!' the physician said. 'Your baby should therefore arrive some time before Christmas. My congratulations!'

Elizabeth was the first to be told the news. Looking at Sophia's pale face, she said gently:

'Aren't you pleased, dearest Sophia? Your Konrad will undoubtedly be delighted. You told me he wanted a son. Now the pair of you will be reconciled, and that is what you really want, is it not?'

Remembering the night in March when Konrad had come unasked to her bedroom at Ortolans, Sophia was in no doubt that this was the occasion when she had conceived the child she carried. If Elizabeth was right and this child was to lead to a reconciliation with her husband, then she would welcome her condition with all her heart.

With still several days to go before she could expect Konrad's return, Sophia's hopes began to rise. She cancelled her luncheon appointment with Elizabeth and paid a visit to the new, fashionable hairdresser in Bond Street to have her hair restyled.

She bought a new Worth gown, and the day before Konrad's arrival, she filled the house with flowers to match her festive mood. Ada, knowing nothing of the reason, was astonished by this transformation, and attributed it to the bottle of medicine the physician had given Sophia to lessen her nausea.

Not without difficulty, but knowing that it must be done, Sophia wrote a note to John, informing him of her condition and hoping that he would agree that in all the circumstances, they should not see each other again – at least for a while. When they did meet again, it could only be as friends. In any event, she concluded, she would almost certainly be going back to Ortolans to await the birth of her child. She hoped very much that eventually John would find happiness with someone else.

Feeling far happier when this letter was despatched, Sophia settled down to wait with growing impatience for Konrad's return.

When Konrad finally came through the front door of Sackville Street, he at once noticed the change in Sophia as she greeted him in the hallway. Her beauty, her air of excitement, however, gave him no pleasure. He handed his ulster, gloves and hat to the butler, and told Sophia he was going upstairs to change his clothes. Apparently unabashed by his perfunctory tone, Sophia informed him that she had news of some considerable importance to convey to him, and that she would await him in the drawing-room.

Nothing could be more important to him than the contents of the letter he had received in Leicestershire, Konrad told himself as he went to his room. It was the report from the private investigator.

The evidence it contained was damning – but inconclusive. Lady Calverley had been regularly taking lunch with Miss Elizabeth Lamberhill – and a gentleman who called himself Mr John Armitage – on occasions at Miss Lamberhill's house in Walton Street. Lady Calverley was also known to Mr Armitage's coachman as 'Miss Sale'. On two occasions, the couple had been seen to drive together to Green Park where they had walked arm in arm before parting company and leaving in opposite directions. It had not been possible to gain access to the house of Miss Elizabeth Lamberhill in Walton Street. Whether adultery had taken place there was a matter only for speculation, but Miss Lamberhill's own reputation was in doubt. She had twice been observed going to the house of Mr Armitage senior unaccompanied by a chaperon and spending the night there.

Sophia's other visits to Elizabeth, to various shops, to a physician in Harley Street were also listed, but it appeared she had not been in Mr Armitage's company on these occasions.

The most damning evidence came at the end of the report. Sophia had spent a week by the sea with Miss Lamberhill at the Sussex village of Rottingdean in a house belonging to Mr Murray Armitage. Mr John Armitage had joined them for a weekend where he had been observed disporting himself with Lady Calverley on the seashore. The couple had been laughing, splashing water at one another and appeared to be enjoying themselves. It had not been possible to gain access to the house to observe the bedroom arrangements, but Mr Armitage and the lady were alone together late at night for a period of an hour in one of the downstairs rooms, and were seen to embrace and to kiss one another in an affectionate manner. All three subjects had returned to London together by train on the Monday morning where Mr Armitage was seen to kiss Lady Calverley's hand on parting. Four bunches of red roses purchased by Mr Armitage had been delivered on different occasions to Sackville Street during the period of observation. The bouquets had contained no card.

At least he now knew the identity of Sophia's escort, Konrad thought grimly. Immediately upon receiving the investigator's report, he had bade farewell to Mrs Clare Fullard and hastened back to London. Before going to Sackville Street, he had called for the second time on Armitage & Company in Essex Street. There he had learned from the doorman that there was indeed a Mr John Armitage, nephew of the publisher – a 'very personable young American gentleman' – according to his informant.

Tight-lipped, Konrad descended the stairs, his brows furrowed in thought. *No conclusive evidence* . . . The investigator's words seemed to imply that although there had been adultery, it could not be proved. They mirrored his own beliefs. Sophia had been consoling herself with 'the personable American', using her novel as pretext for meeting him. It confirmed his belief that she was capable of any deviousness to obtain what she wanted . . . and to think that he had felt uncomfortably guilty whilst consoling himself with the rapacious Leicestershire widow!

Recalling Sophia's flushed pretty face as she had greeted him so fulsomely in the hallway, her colourful new gown, the bloom on her cheeks, he was in no real doubt that Mr John Armitage was her lover. She portrayed all the telltale signs of a woman in love!

'Well, Sophia, I understand you wish to speak to me on a matter of importance?' he greeted her as the footman closed the door behind him and they were alone. 'I also have something of importance to discuss with you, but first let me hear what you have to say.'

Sophia's heart beat more rapidly. Konrad's tone was far from encouraging. She busied her hands rearranging the big bowl of roses on the sofa table. Watching her touch the flowers – her lover's? – Konrad's scowl deepened.

'I was obliged to visit a physician whilst you were away,' she said. 'I had not been very well, you see. His diagnosis was . . . is . . . I do hope you will be pleased, Konrad – I am to have a child.'

Konrad swung round from the window, his mouth agape. This was news he had not anticipated. A child! If it was true . . . if it was *his* child . . . His cheeks paled as his mind raced with speculations. He had not lain with Sophia for weeks, months! If she was carrying a child, it could not be his. It could, therefore, only be her lover's.

He felt a swift, primitive urge to lift his hand and strike her. How innocent she looked, how young and appealing!

His hand dropped to his side and a cold despair replaced the heat of his anger as he said in a cool, emotionless voice: 'Do you take me for a complete fool, Sophia? Or do you imagine I am ignorant about these things? For pity's sake, let us be done with pretence. Let me save you the trouble of inventing any further lies. I should tell you that I happen to know that you have a lover.'

'But that is not true, Konrad! If you mean . . .'

'You deny it?' he interrupted furiously. 'Do you also deny that you have been continuing to meet Armitage – John Armitage – at Elizabeth Lamberhill's house? That you went to Rottingdean with him?'

Sophia gasped. How could he know about her holiday? Had he been questioning Ada? Elizabeth would not have told him. It was not fair that he should always assume the worst. He *must* understand:

'Konrad, please listen to me. It is true that I have been lunching with John Armitage. He is the nephew of Mr Murray Armitage, the publisher, whom you've met. It is true that John came to Rottingdean to spend the weekend with Elizabeth Lamberhill and me. John is in love with me. I told you that the night he drove me home. He wants me to allow you to divorce me and go to America with him as his wife. It is also true that I have told him I cannot do as he wishes because, in spite of everything that has happened, I love you. Lastly, Konrad, I have *not* been unfaithful to you – although I admit I once came close to doing so.'

Konrad, who had listened to Sophia's words in silence, now turned to face her.

'Not only do you lie, but you do so most plausibly. I am supposed to believe that this fellow – this Armitage – loves you, spends the weekend with you, but you, nobly, reject his advances and remain faithful to me, the husband you do love! I am also supposed to believe that you are with child, and that I am responsible! For once your powers of fabrication fail you, Sophia. I have been away since April and the one night we did sleep under the same roof, we did not cohabit. You underrate my intelligence, my dear.'

He walked over to her and stood staring down into her shocked face.

'Quite frankly, I am wondering if there *is* a child. It would not be the first time you have fabricated an offspring to suit your own ends.'

Sophia's mouth tightened.

'For what purpose, Konrad? You know very well that last time I had no alternative but to invent a child. You would never have married me otherwise.'

Konrad's dark eyes were filled with bitterness.

'Oh, I understood your motives, Sophia. You wanted Ortolans at any cost! Is this any different? You were aware I suspected you of having a lover and were afraid that if I divorced you, you would lose your precious home. You worked it all out, didn't you, Sophia? It was essential for you to be reconciled with me and what better way than to tell me you are about to give me the son and heir I want!'

Sophia caught her breath.

'It is no invention, Konrad. The physician will confirm . . .' she broke off, remembering with a sick feeling in the pit of her stomach that she had used the word of a physician once before.

With a feeling of utter helplessness, she said quietly: 'I know you find it difficult to believe anything I say, but even if you doubt everything else, you *must* believe that I love you!'

'*Love me!*' Konrad echoed scornfully. 'I doubt that you have ever loved anyone but yourself, Sophia – yourself and that house of yours. You will go to any lengths to keep it, won't you? Even to the point of trying to convince me I am the father of another man's child!'

'You insult me!' Sophia cried, her eyes blazing. 'I have never denied that Ortolans was far more to me than just my home. I do love it . . . I always will, and I don't know how I would survive if the haven it has always been were denied me. Nevertheless, my love for you is greater, although clearly you don't intend to believe it. If you were to read my book, Konrad – read between the lines – you might learn far more about me than you now know. It is the story of my life with you very thinly disguised. My heroine, Cecilia, speaks for me, and her love for the duke she tricked into marriage is no different than mine for you.'

If only he *would* read it, she thought despairingly, but she knew that he would not. It was too late. Konrad was determined not to trust her – and without trust, there could never be love. It was not altogether his fault. The damage had been done initially by her. If only she had some way of proving that the child inside her was his!

'This baby *is* yours, Konrad,' she said in a small, clear voice. 'I am sorry that you do not believe me. I am sorry, too, that you do not believe me when I tell you that John Armitage was never my lover. No matter how low your opinion of me, I would not have stooped to asking you to father another man's child simply to save my reputation.'

She sounded convincing, Konrad thought, but then Sophia had always sounded convincing when she lied. He could not – and did not – believe her.

'Perhaps not to save your reputation, Sophia!' he said grimly. 'But to ensure that you could remain at Ortolans. I warned you long ago that if ever I found out you had been unfaithful to me, I would divorce you, and so on the point of discovery, you could do nothing else but pretend the child was mine.'

His face was a mask of bitterness as he turned away from her and stared out of the window with unseeing eyes. For a moment, he felt suddenly unsure of himself. Did he really wish for a divorce? Perhaps never to see Sophia again? Suppose he was misjudging her, and the child *was* his? He had only her word for it. He had made love to her but once since their honeymoon, and although the memory of the completeness of their union that night at Ortolans had remained a tantalizing, unforgettable memory, the coincidence was too narrow for belief. The odds were that the child was another man's.

His heart hardened.

'There was a time when I was sufficiently in love with you to give you the benefit of the doubt – more fool I! That time is past, Sophia. I will not have another man's bastard hoisted on my shoulders, do you understand? I shall commence divorce proceedings immediately. As for Ortolans, you have exactly one month from today to remove yourself and your possessions. Have I made myself clear?'

Two angry spots of colour now stained Sophia's pale cheeks.

'You cannot divorce me. You have no grounds!' she cried. 'You have no right to turn me out of my home. I won't go!'

'Oh, but you will, my dear. I shall close the house – Rogers can look after the estate, and if he is not capable, I shall find someone who is. Ortolans is no longer your concern. You will be out a month from today or I shall have to have you ignominiously evicted – and I am sure you don't want that happening in Detcham!'

There was a hardness in Konrad's tone Sophia had never heard before and she was unsure how to deal with the situation which seemed suddenly to be quite out of her control.

'If you mean to carry out this . . . this threat . . .' she said hesitantly, 'what is to happen to me?'

'I really don't care, Sophia. I suggest you go to your lover. If Armitage is a gentleman, presumably he will honour his obligations to you, poor devil. Just as I did when you first told *me* you were pregnant.' He turned once more to face her. 'Our marriage was a farce from the beginning – and the sooner we bring it to an end the better. That is all I have to say to you, Sophia. Now, if you will excuse me . . .'

He walked out of the room, closing the door with an ominous crash behind him.

Sophia's heart was thudding furiously and her hands and legs were shaking. She drew a long, deep breath and the threatening nausea slowly receded.

He cannot do this to me – he cannot! she thought. The child was his, and she was innocent of any wrongdoing. There must be a way to prove that innocence. He could not be allowed to divorce her – to have her thrown out of Ortolans like some errant serving girl! One month's notice Konrad had given her and . . . she thought with rising anger . . . the worst of references!

One thing she would not do, she decided, was plead further with Konrad who appeared to be beyond reasoning. She would go to Elizabeth, who was so much more worldly-wise than herself. Elizabeth would tell her if she were really in any danger.

Elizabeth received Sophia's near hysterical account of events with growing anxiety.

'I am familiar with the laws relating to my slum children, such few as exist!' she said, 'but I must confess I know nothing about the laws concerning marriage or divorce. You should see Mr Endicote as soon as possible, Sophia, if you truly believe Konrad means to do as he has said.'

She paused whilst one of her young maids brought in some tea, but once they were alone again, she added:

'Konrad is right in one respect, Sophia. It has not been a happy marriage. Have you thought that it might be best if you were to separate? You are very young – only twenty, are you not? I have no doubt that if you were free, John would marry you. However discreetly managed, divorce carries a fearful stigma and you would be socially ostracized in England, whereas if you were to go to America with John, the scandal would in all probability not touch you.'

A little colour returned to Sophia's cheeks as she said vehemently:

'You are forgetting the baby, Elizabeth. If it were to be a boy, he would be heir to the Calverley title and estate. It is his birthright, and he should be brought up in Ortolans as I was.'

Elizabeth bit back the words that sprang to her mind – namely that in time Konrad might decide to acknowledge his son, if such it were to be, who in any event would bear the surname of Calverley. Even if Sophia were ultimately to marry John, the divorce would almost certainly not take place until after the birth. But this would not guarantee a place at her child's side for Sophia.

'You must see Mr Endicote first thing tomorrow, Sophia!' she said. 'We both know that whatever is in that document Konrad was waving at you, it cannot contain proof of your guilt. Frankly, I am deeply shocked that he should have stooped so low as to have you followed by a common investigator! Now try to relax, dearest. It is not good for you in your state of health to be so *énervée*. My maid can go round to Sackville Street and ask Ada to pack a few nightclothes for you. I will not allow you to go back and face further argument from Konrad. You shall stay the night with me.'

No, she could not bear to see Konrad again today, Sophia thought as she allowed Elizabeth to put her to bed in the tiny spare room. She wished very much that she could weep, but the tears which might have brought relief would not come. She felt as shattered as she had when the physician had told her that her aunts were dying. If Konrad were within his rights, she would lose for ever both the man she loved – and Ortolans. The prospect was unbearable and had she not felt so ill, she would have gone immediately to Mr Endicote.

As her spirits revived the following morning, Sophia waited with growing impatience for the afternoon to come. Mr Endicote, his clerk had informed her, was occupied with a client and would not be disengaged until after luncheon.

When finally she and Elizabeth, who had cancelled her own appointments to offer what support she could, were seated in the lawyer's office, she received a further shock.

'I am extremely sorry, Lady Calverley, but I find myself unable to offer you advice. Your . . . er, husband came to see me this morning and it would be most unethical for me to act for both parties in a dispute between you.'

'But you are my lawyer!' Sophia protested. 'You have always been our family lawyer. This is ridiculous!'

The elderly man shuffled the papers on his desk with a look of discomfort on his face. He had served the two late Misses

Calverley for many years and had known Sophia since she was a small child.

'I am really deeply sorry, Lady Calverley, but your husband, Sir Konrad, is also a Calverley and I was unaware when he approached me this morning that you would . . . er, would be contesting his decisions.'

'But I am unjustly accused!' Sophia cried, jumping to her feet. 'Of course I shall contest a divorce. I have a right to defend myself!'

Mr Endicote also rose to his feet.

'But of course, Lady Calverley! That is why I suggest – if I may do so – that you see Mr Levensaler of Messrs Lewin and Levensaler. He is an excellent lawyer who makes a speciality of handling divorce cases. In many ways, he is probably better qualified than I to help you. May I give you a letter of introduction?'

In the cab taking them round to Gray's Inn, Sophia said bitterly: 'It is clear I cannot hold out much hope of Konrad thinking better of such cruel behaviour. He wasted no time in commencing legal proceedings. If it takes my last penny, Elizabeth, I shall fight him.'

Sophia's 'last penny' seemed to preoccupy Mr Levensaler when she was finally seated opposite the portly figure of the divorce lawyer.

'May I ask if you have . . . er, funds of your own, Lady Calverley? Although you may not be the guilty party, it could be a long time before you were able to recoup the cost of legal action. We might have to engage the services of a barrister and my own fees . . .'

'I have a small income of my own from the cottages and lands my husband gave me when we were married,' Sophia broke in. 'Besides which, my father left me a considerable sum of money, which legacy I am entitled to claim on my twenty-first birthday. Your fees will therefore be met, Mr Levensaler, as you appear to be in some doubt!'

At once, the lawyer's tone became more obsequious, for

which Sophia liked him even less; but she put aside her personal antipathy and said brusquely:

'May we now get down to the matter in hand, sir? My husband intends to divorce me for acts of adultery I have not committed. I am with child, his child, which he intends to disown – and he has given me one month to vacate my home.'

Slowly, painstakingly, the lawyer prised the details from her. He became increasingly uneasy. His attractive young client had undoubtedly lain herself open to suspicion by her behaviour. The American, Armitage, would not be considered a reliable witness since he was the supposed lover and must defend the lady's reputation as well as his own. Miss Lamberhill seemed a sensible young woman unlikely to be flustered under cross-examination but, on her own admittance, she had left the couple alone and could not swear on oath that adultery had not taken place on the night in Rottingdean. The maid, Ada, knew nothing according to Lady Calverley, and would be quite unable to withstand a court ordeal. The husband was a titled gentleman of unblemished reputation whose duties had frequently taken him abroad, thus leaving his pretty young wife alone – and subject to temptation. There was little doubt who the court would favour. The wife was far too attractive and impetuous judging from the several dangerous admissions she had already made to him. Honesty was by no means always the best policy!

'So what is my position?' Sophia demanded. 'Mr Endicote told me you specialized in such cases. What exactly can I do?'

'I would very much like to see the investigator's report, Lady Calverley, so that I can be sure of the evidence against you. Please do not upset yourself – I am not doubting your innocence. However, this I can tell you, your home belongs to your husband, and he is within his rights to close it down and ask you to leave, quite regardless of your marital status. As far as the divorce is concerned, of course we can defend any action your husband takes against you. I should warn you however, that for people of your . . . er, background, the case would undoubtedly arouse publicity of the most unwelcome kind. Even if you were to be proved innocent, and I can see no way to guarantee that at this point, you – and indeed, your husband – would suffer a great deal from the scandal. It would cause less stir were you not to contest the case. Mud does stick, and very often, the innocent . . .'

'I am not concerned with scandal!' Sophia broke in, her eyes blazing. 'I am innocent and Konrad should be made to acknowledge it! And there is the child – *it is his*. He shall not disclaim it!'

Privately, Mr Levensaler was wondering for the first time if indeed his client was as innocent as she professed. She really was quite remarkably attractive, very obviously of gentle birth and good intelligence, and it did seem most unlikely that a husband of only nine months should be contemplating casting her out on no more than suspicion. Then there was the child – perhaps not, as she vouchsafed, his offspring! There could be no proof in such matters. Supposing the husband were able to prove adultery, the legal action he was taking was quite understandable and there would be very severe doubts cast on the child's parentage.

'I will, of course, act for you, Lady Calverley,' he reiterated. 'However, nothing can be done until you are notified by your husband's lawyer that he intends to pursue this course of action, in which case, you must at once notify me. In the meanwhile, I can only advise you to reconsider the possibility of a reconciliation, if this is at all possible. It might be of great benefit if you can remain together at least until after the birth of your child. I am sure I have no need to tell you that you should not in any circumstances see Mr Armitage or communicate with him.'

'But he is my publisher – or at least, his uncle is and John is my editor!' Sophia protested.

'Then you must deal only with the uncle – and never without someone else present to witness that Mr John Armitage is *not* present. Do you understand, Lady Calverley?'

'Oh, I understand very well, sir!' Sophia cried. 'You dare not say it to my face but you think my husband will succeed in this dispute. Have the courage to admit it!'

The lawyer stood up.

'The fact that I may consider your situation very precarious, Lady Calverley, would not alter my willingness to act for you,' he said not without a certain dignity. 'Please do get in touch with me as soon as you have reached a decision about your immediate future. I shall, of course, need to know where I can contact you.'

'I shall be at Ortolans House in Sussex for the next few weeks, unless I am obliged to leave sooner,' Sophia said bitterly as she picked up her gloves. 'If you have further advice for me after you have reflected upon my position, please write to me there!'

Sophia was silent on the return to Walton Street, and it was Elizabeth who reopened the subject. She was deeply disturbed and not a little guilty at the thought that it was she who had encouraged Sophia's friendship with John; who had, furthermore, not raised any objections when he had joined them on holiday in Rottingdean.

'What will you do, Sophia?' she asked. 'Where will you go? When you leave Ortolans, I mean. You are most welcome to stay here with me – or at least until the baby is born. Then, alas, there would simply not be the room!'

'I don't know what I shall do!' Sophia said, close now to tears at the realization that she really was obliged to leave Ortolans. The prospect was quite intolerable. Maybe Konrad would relent! Maybe she could yet think of a way to persuade him as to her innocence. Perhaps tomorrow, when she felt calmer, she would return to Sackville Street and talk to him. He, too, might be calmer.

'Can't you buy a house in London near me?' Elizabeth suggested. 'You could assist me with my work and at least I would be nearby to look after you!'

'It is too soon to think about it!' Sophia prevaricated. 'First

I must go back to Sackville Street and see Konrad. That horrible Mr Levensaler may be right and I should see if Konrad will change his mind. Please don't worry!'

Elizabeth worried nonetheless. After Sophia had retired to bed, she wrote a long letter to Murray Armitage, telling him in strictest confidence of the events. She left it to his discretion as to whether he would advise John of the situation. He, poor boy, would inevitably be dragged into the case if there were a divorce – and in the meanwhile, he must be told not to try to get in touch with Sophia.

To Sophia's growing apprehension, Konrad was not at Sackville Street. He had, so Ada informed her, gone to his club.

'He said as how you'd be going back to Ortolans and I was to go with you, but not the other servants, Miss Sophia!' Ada related. 'They's to stay on here.' She looked at Sophia anxiously. 'Baint he a-coming with us, Miss Sophia?'

'Apparently not!' Sophia said more sharply than she had intended. Since Konrad had made it obvious that he had no intention of seeing her again, she knew her hopes of a reconciliation were useless. Sooner or later, she would have to tell Ada everything – but for the present, she could not bring herself to cope with Ada's distress as well as her own.

'Get my things packed right away, Ada,' she said. 'And tell Phipps he's to have the coach at the door at midday. He can drive us down and return as soon as the horses are rested.'

For the first time in her life, Sophia felt no lifting of her spirits when she had returned to Ortolans. Although Ada had alerted Cook and all was made ready for her, the big house seemed to echo with memories . . . of her aunts who she missed unbearably; of Konrad; of their meeting by the river; of her wedding day. Although it was still her dearly loved home, without Konrad at her side it was barren, empty, lonely beyond bearing. Perhaps it knew that she was soon to leave it for ever, she thought fancifully as she wandered from room to room. It was as if its very heart had stopped beating.

Two days after her return, a letter arrived for her from

John. It was imperative, he wrote, that she should know he loved her deeply and wanted to marry her. If it suited her purpose, he would be happy to take her to America to begin a new life there. Ignoring Mr Levensaler's advice not to communicate with John, she wrote back:

> You are forgetting that I am carrying Konrad's child! That alone prohibits any future for us, John. Besides – I have never misled you about this – I love my husband. In spite of everything, I still love him.

John replied by return of post.

> I know about the child. It can have my name, Sophia. I will love it because it is a part of you. As to your love for Valschintzky, I am not frightened by it. In time you will learn to love me. Even if you do not, I shan't mind. I want to marry you; to have the right to call you my wife; to love you as you deserve.

Remembering his open, frank face, the devotion shining from his eyes, Sophia felt suddenly a hundred years older than he. He had never been in love before and like so many young men, he had succumbed to the temptation of a married woman whose inaccessibility enhanced the excitement of a liaison. He had told her many times that he found most young girls quite boring. The fact that she loved her husband was an added challenge and one he seemingly felt confident he could meet. She could tell him, if he would listen, that it was not enough for one partner in a marriage to love, if the other did not! His letter continued:

> I know it would not be the same for us as it was between you and Valschintzky. But I am prepared to take the risk, Sophia, and you need someone to take care of you – and your child.

Perhaps marriage to John some day in the future might be possible, Sophia wrote back, weakened by his reminder that it was not only her future she had now to consider.

> It is not a decision which we should rush into. It is enough that I have already once made a terrible mess of my life. I have no wish now to ruin yours!

There was another reason. Deep down inside her, she still hoped that Konrad might change his mind. Deliberately she had left the manuscript of her book on the bedtable for him to read – and perhaps at this eleventh hour, understand. Surely he would see that it was so obviously autobiographical; that this was the reason she had needed a pseudonym.

For the next few days, she moved like an automaton around the house. Whenever she could, she escaped into the garden, cut dead heads off the rose bushes, pulled weeds from the flowerbeds, gathered lavender heads as she had once done for her aunts for the lavender bags they liked to put in their clothes drawers and in the linen cupboard. Although she never allowed Ada to see her do so, each morning found her in the driveway watching for the arrival of the postboy from the village. Every time there was the sound of carriage wheels in the drive, she hurried to a window to see if it might be Konrad.

Ada was not deceived. She had been looking after her mistress for close on fourteen years, and when she took in the breakfast tray each morning, she was quick to see the signs of Sophia's tears. Her heart hardened towards her master who until now had had her sympathy. She could not understand how he could inflict such heartbreak on his wife. She knew about the coming child and could not understand how he could behave as if he were not the father. She, Ada, could have told him that her young mistress was innocent of any wrongdoing with Mr Armitage. Sophia had thought her asleep that night at the seaside, but she had heard, with her ear to the wall, how they had talked until the American gentleman had left. Perhaps, she thought, this after all was where Sophia's future happiness lay. Nevertheless, she watched as avidly as her mistress for the postman, or even better, for the master himself to come home.

Although there was no word from Konrad, the postboy delivered a letter from John's uncle. He was, he informed her, shortly leaving for America for a visit to his brother and sister-in-law. If Sophia had not already made other arrangements, would she care to consider an extended visit to California. John's parents would be delighted to see her and would make her very welcome. Such a visit, he emphasized, would not commit her in any way to a future relationship with John, and since John himself would be remaining in England, the courts could not put a significant interpretation upon such a holiday. Sophia, after all, was his author and an important one he wished to nurture. He hoped she might consider writing another book in the new environment which could not fail to be a stimulant.

The letter was closely followed by one from Elizabeth.

I hope so much you will accede to Murray's plan. He tells me John's parents are charming and would genuinely love to have you. If there is to be a scandal as the lawyer warned, then you would be far away from it. You could have your child in peace and where wagging tongues cannot hurt you.

She added that she had gone to Sackville Street in the hope of finding Konrad there so that she could speak for Sophia's innocence. Alas, she had been instructed by the butler that his master had departed for Austria only a day after Sophia had left for Ortolans, and had left no word as to when he might be expected back!

It was the moment when Sophia finally accepted that Konrad's carriage would not be coming up the drive; that he had no intention ever of seeing her again.

CHAPTER TWENTY-FIVE

1890

Sophia's immediate reaction was to reject Mr Armitage's proposal – gratefully but without further ado. It was totally against her nature to 'run away and hide' as if she were indeed guilty. But gradually it dawned on her that this could be an answer to her immediate problem – where to go when physically she must leave Ortolans. Her pride would not permit her to remain here until Konrad took the undignified step of having his wife evicted! It seemed obvious now that he had presented Mr Endicote with the necessary instructions and removed himself as far away as possible until the divorce was accomplished. He would be no more anxious than she to be questioned by their friends as to why, since the aunts were no longer there to require her presence in the country, she and Konrad were living apart; why, if it was necessary for him to go to Austria, she had not accompanied him; why he was not here at Ortolans with her.

She delayed her reply to her kind publisher and wrote instead to Mr Levensaler. Would her absence abroad in any way jeopardize her defence? she questioned.

On the contrary, Mr Levensaler replied. There would be inevitable delays if she had to return to England and any delay would be to her advantage. Since Sir Konrad had gone abroad himself, technically deserting her, he could hardly claim desertion against her. For her to accept the offer of a place of refuge was a natural enough step to take in the light of her financial state. The sum she had indicated as her income from those lands and properties which she owned was certainly insufficient to keep her in the proper manner for a lady of her consequence. She was, therefore, partially dependent upon the charity of friends. He could advise her by cablegram if he needed to get in touch with her. If she should decide to go, would she be so good as to take the time to call in at his office and sign a statement of the facts she had given him at their last meeting. He had not, he ended, had notification from Mr Endicote that Sir Konrad had commenced proceedings against her.

For a further day, Sophia allowed herself to hope that perhaps after all, Konrad was reconsidering his attitude. That last lingering hope was dashed when Rogers asked to see her. Cap in hand, the bailiff stood in the library looking bewildered.

'Lawyer's written to ask if'n I'm prepared to manage on my own,' he said. 'He said as how you and the master would not be living here no more for time being and if'n I didn't see as how I could manage, I was to tell him, so's he could employ someone what was.'

Shuffling his feet, he said awkwardly:

'You didn't say nothing to me yesterday, your ladyship – about you leavin', I mean.'

Sophia drew a deep breath.

'No, I wasn't sure myself, Rogers,' she said. 'As it happens, the master has gone abroad and I shall shortly be going, too. I'll write at once to Mr Endicote and tell him I am quite sure you will manage very well. I am confident that you will.'

The man hesitated.

'T'won't be the same without you, your ladyship. Ortolans ain't never been closed – not in my lifetime anyroad.'

'The master may decide to open the house again one day,' Sophia said in a false bright tone. 'I shall be leaving two weeks from now, but I don't think Ortolans will be shut immediately. In the meanwhile, just carry on as usual. I will keep you informed if there is any change in plan.'

She herself received a letter from Mr Endicote the following day. He had been instructed by Konrad to tell her that the indoor servants were to be dismissed with a month's pay, with the exception of Albert who was to remain as caretaker. The outdoor servants were to remain and were to be paid as usual by Rogers.

Konrad could at least have undertaken the giving of these instructions himself, Sophia thought bitterly. Obviously he did not trust *her* to carry them out unless ordered to do so by Mr Endicote! Since she was no longer to be mistress of her home, it was not for her to make arrangements for her absence. As Rogers had said, Ortolans had never been closed and it was beyond bearing now to think of it shuttered, shrouded in dust sheets, abandoned.

Dry-eyed, anguished, Sophia wandered about the house, tormented by the thought that in fourteen days' time she must leave. Where would she go? How could she bear it? Now Mr Armitage's suggestion that she go with him to America took hold. She must get away – far, far away. Ortolans, which had once proved a sanctuary in her unhappiness, was now a torment – a constant reminder that *it* had been the reason why she had told the wicked lies she had believed necessary to safeguard her presence here, but which now led to her leaving it for ever. It was those lies which had prompted Konrad's mistrust and which ultimately made any love between them impossible.

Knowing that the time for vacillation was past, Sophia took the carriage into Lewes, from which post office she sent a telegram to Mr Armitage telling him she would be pleased to travel with him and would he be so good as to book a passage for her.

Tomorrow, Sophia decided, she would start packing. The telegram had been despatched and the decision made. There could be no going back. Later that evening, she went into the library where *The Calverley Journal* lay open, untouched these past weeks. Someone else could write of her departure. She could not bring herself to do so. With tears stinging her eyes, she recalled that there had been an ancestor who, like herself, had used evil means to secure the house for himself. He, too, had come to a dreadful end. Was it possible that Ortolans was now trying to punish *her*?

Ada looked anxiously at her mistress's white face when she came in search of Sophia.

'Do *you* think the house is trying to punish me, Ada?' she asked.

Ada looked shocked.

'You'm fanciful on account of your condition, Miss Sophia!' she said as she tried to encourage her mistress to eat the food she had brought into the library on a tray. 'You'll harm that little mite of yourn if'n you allows yourself to think such things, surelye!'

Sophia drew a deep sigh.

'I know I should be thinking of the baby now,' she said. 'That is why I have decided to go away, Ada. I have written to Mr Murray Armitage telling him that the decision is made – I shall travel out to America with him and stay with his family until after the baby is born.'

It was the first Ada had heard of the possibility, and now she gasped.

'Adone-do, Miss Sophia! This be another of your nonsensical ideas. I'll not listen to suchlike, not nohow!'

'The telegram has been sent, Ada,' Sophia said gently. 'You must try to understand – I don't want to go, but sooner or later I shall have to. I cannot bear the thought of being put in the humiliating position where I have to be turned out of my . . . my home, for that is what my husband has threatened to do if I do not leave of my own accord!'

Close now to tears, she put her arms round the old woman and hugged her.

'I'd take you with me, dearest Ada, but you would not be happy in a foreign country. American ways would be different from yours. Perhaps after the divorce I will come back to England and you can come and look after me again if you want. Please don't cry, Ada! I know you will miss me . . . but it is time you were thinking of retirement anyway. I have written to Mr Endicote telling him you are to have the freehold of Rose Cottage in the High Street. You can start that little wool shop you always said you wanted to keep you occupied in your old age. Mr Endicote will see to everything for you . . . and I shall write to you!'

'Oh, Miss Sophia, you knows as how I carn't read!' Ada sobbed.

'But your niece's little girl has learned to read at school – you told me so. She will read my letters to you – and write back to me. Perhaps she will even teach you to read and write, Ada. I may not be away for very long.'

Ada mopped at her eyes with her apron.

'What will happen to the house, to Ortolans?' she asked.

Sophia bit her lip.

'That is for Sir Konrad to decide. One day, if I do not have need of the income, I shall return to him the land and the other cottages he gave me. You and I both know, Ada, that I acquired them on false pretences. Until he decides what he wishes to do with this house, the servants who are not remaining in London are to be dismissed. Your brother, Albert, is to stay on at the lodge to look after the horses and act as caretaker. Silver Mist is to go to Miss Delia over at Newtimber, and it will be up to the master to do what he wishes about the other horses.'

'So 'tis all decided!' Ada said, mopping at her eyes. In a choked voice, she added: 'I do hope as how it's for the best, Miss Sophia. I do hope so, surelye!'

'I am certain it will be,' Sophia said as firmly as she could. 'I shall go to London tomorrow to make arrangements for my journey with Mr Armitage, and see my lawyer. Then we must begin the packing, Ada. There is so little time left and such a great deal to do!'

Mr Levensaler was impressed with the written statement Sophia signed in his office. It was comprehensive and concise,

and devoid of the flowery exaggerations so often employed
by females.

'I happen to be an author!' Sophia informed him, momentarily enjoying his hurried apology for having sounded somewhat patronizing.

Her visit to Mr Armitage was less brief. He would, he
informed her, send a carriage to Ortolans to collect her at
midday to take her to Brighton. He would travel directly there
from London.

'We shall then take the train to Southampton where I have
booked passages on a liner,' he said. Anxiously regarding her
pale face, he added paternally:

'My dear child, this may all be a trifle precipitate and I
shall not blame you if you tell me that you are reconsidering
my proposition. John's parents are unknown to you and
although I have no doubt whatever that you will like them,
the prospect of living with strangers must be a little daunting,
to say the least.'

As Sophia nodded, he continued:

'You must realize, my dear, that like Elizabeth, I feel it is
my duty to be of assistance to you. I, after all, had the
opportunity to discourage John when first he told me that
he was in love with you. It was my duty to do so and I
failed in that duty. I am therefore in part responsible for
what has transpired as a result of your friendship with John.
There is, however, another reason why I am encouraging
you to go to America. I have high hopes for you as a novelist,
as you know. These coming months whilst you await the
birth of your child will afford the perfect opportunity for
you to write your next book. It could also be therapeutic
for you.'

He smiled disarmingly and regarded her sympathetically
over the rim of his spectacles.

'I have always believed that there should be a special relationship between a publisher and his authors – an intimacy that
permits each to understand the other. On reading your last book,

I was immediately aware that it was autobiographical – and the writing of it probably helped you over a difficult patch in your marriage. Now it may help you again to pour out your present conflicts on paper. It *can* clear the mind. John tells me you are still in love with this husband of yours!'

Not far from tears, Sophia nodded.

'Then, for your sake, my dear, if not for poor John's, I shall hope for a reconciliation. I also want you to know that because I have booked your passage to America, you do not have to be on that boat if you change your mind about leaving England. I shall assume that you will be accompanying me but even at the eleventh hour, you may alter that decision. If I do not see you at Brighton railway station, I shall know the reason!'

'You are very kind – but my mind is made up, Mr Armitage. To be honest with you, the fact is that if I have to leave my home, then it is best for me to be as far from Ortolans as I can. If I were to set up home in London, I think I would be forever finding excuses to return to Detcham. I love my home very dearly and since there is to be a break, I am obliged to make it a clean one.'

Having said her farewells to Elizabeth in Walton Street, Sophia returned home. She had known that poor Ada would be as devastated as herself by this painful parting and discovering her in tears, she forced herself to sound practical and unemotional. They must start at once, she said, to sort the contents of each room of the house – a mammoth task which would keep them both well occupied.

'Apart from the clothes I shall take with me, everything else that is mine must be put in trunks and boxes until I make up my mind how they should be disposed,' she instructed the old woman. 'We must make haste, for there are only seven days left to complete the task.'

Her statement brought Sophia perilously close to changing her mind. To hear herself saying that she would be leaving Ortolans for ever in a week's time made the reality unbearable.

Hurriedly she told Ada that they would start at once to sort the contents of each room, for the old woman's grief at the thought of their impending parting was almost as hard to bear as her own.

Sophia finally decided to leave the attics untouched. They contained for the most part family heirlooms – pictures, boxes full of daguerreotypes, the aunts' butterfly and moth collections, a trunk full of letters and papers which must have belonged to her parents and grandparents for some were dated a hundred years previously. This last she labelled with her name, hoping that one day it could be sent to her, not just for her interest but for her child's. The room in which she and Delia had their 'secret den' she could not bring herself to disturb.

So the days passed. Each post brought a letter from John – but still no word from Konrad. John's were full of anxiety that she might change her mind, and reassurances that his parents would make her welcome.

I was deeply concerned by your last letter. Reading between the lines, I felt you were beset by doubts. I do understand that your husband has given you no alternative but to leave your home, but you must not allow yourself to believe that this is 'the end of the world'. A whole new start to life awaits you, Sophia, and I pray most earnestly that one day, you will allow me to be part of it.

The letter, like all those preceding it, ended with declarations of love, and promises of happiness for their future. It was a future Sophia somehow could not imagine. It was as if her mind did not wish to function beyond the next task.

When the packing was almost completed, she spent the last afternoon writing letters. One was to Mr Endicote, advising him of her intention to return the deeds of the Calverley lands and cottages to Konrad. One was to Elizabeth telling her that there were parcels of clothing for her to collect for her waifs next time she was down at Lamberhill Court. The third – and most difficult of all – was to Konrad.

I am guilty of only one thing. I did trick you into marriage because Ortolans was so important to me – and to the aunts. I know you do not believe it, but long before our wedding day, I discovered how much I truly loved you. The vows I spoke I meant with all my heart. I do not expect it to be of any importance to you now but I have never been unfaithful to you.

I have instructed Mr Endicote to make over the deeds of Rose Cottage which I have given to Ada. The other land and cottages are to be returned to you in due course. Were Ortolans mine, I would be giving back the house, too. It has been in the family for over three hundred years, and despite my love for it, it was never rightfully mine.

Since I have been back here, I have realized that I should have told you about my book far sooner than I did, and you would have understood why it was desirable for me in those early days to have had those meetings with John – and condoned them. You would not then have assumed me guilty of having a liaison with him.

If it was your intention to punish me for those iniquities of which I am guilty by forcing me to leave my home, be consoled that you have achieved your purpose, for alas I cannot believe there could ever come a time when I cease to need either you or Ortolans.

Perhaps one day you will find it in your heart to forgive me and to remember me more kindly.

Ada could post the letters in the village after she, Sophia, had departed, she thought as she sealed the envelopes and carefully placed a penny stamp on each of them.

She had no way of knowing that before departing for Austria,

Konrad's valet had inadvertently packed the manuscript of Sophia's book in his master's valise.

Despite the sun streaming in through the casements, Sophia shivered. Her bedroom looked cold and bare without its familiar ornaments. Trunks and boxes were piled by the open door; sheets of tissue paper littered the bed which Ada had stripped of its coverings.

She glanced at her fob watch. In half an hour's time, the carriage would be here. Gathering up her hopsack mantle, gloves and narrow-brimmed grey straw hat, she said to Ada:

'I think that is everything, but check the cupboard once again, Ada. I am uncertain if we emptied the hat shelf!'

She was doing everything possible to keep Ada occupied since, when the old servant was not weeping, she was sniffing, and Sophia knew she was liable to break down completely at the moment of parting.

'Lor lummy!' exclaimed Ada as she withdrew a brown paper parcel, 'These be your winter drawers, Miss Sophia. Whatever be they doing up there!'

Despite the tension that had prevailed since she had awoken that morning, Sophia smiled.

'They had best go up to the attic, Ada,' she said. 'There's room in the Noah's Ark trunk. I am going to say goodbye to Cook.'

Time was beginning to run out, she thought, as she made her way downstairs. She decided to go first to the stables to say goodbye to Albert and to her beloved little mare. Delia would take good care of Silver Mist, she consoled herself, as she hugged the animal's soft muzzle against her cheek.

Sophia was on her way back to the house from the stables when she realized that, intent as she had been upon leaving no trace of herself visible at Ortolans, she had yet forgotten to check that there were none of her possessions in the store-room in the cellars.

The cellars were cold, but dry. The stairs from the kitchen quarters led down to the still-room beneath. Here were stored Cook's preserves, home-made cordials, buckets full of eggs preserved in waterglass, and shelf upon shelf of bottled fruit. From this room another door led to the vault containing the barrels of ale, casks of cider and all the wine racks. The bottles were covered with dust, the maids never being allowed there lest they disturbed the wines. Yet another door led to the coal bunkers, fed by a chute from the backyard; and at the furthest end, directly below the library, was the storeroom.

Sophia had always loved it when the aunts had brought her as a child to visit this room. It was like a museum, for here were packed all her father's effects, sent by ship from India after his death – an engraved, silver-handled sword in its leather sheath; a topee; a brass Buddha; a large statue, sculpted in copper, of some Indian goddess; a set of musical instruments which looked like a sitar, a kind of violin, and a number of tribal drums.

What would Konrad do with these curios, Sophia thought, as now she held up her oil-lamp and peered at the cluttered shelves. Memories of the past flooded her mind. She could almost hear the aunts' gentle voices as they explained to the wide-eyed child she had once been. '*Your father so admired Indian culture . . .*' '*. . . he bought that Buddha in Nepal, dear.*'

How greatly she missed them both, Sophia thought with an ache in her throat. How greatly she longed to have them here beside her! If only she were a child again – Aunt Georgie saying: 'Come along, my precious, it's time for tea!' and Aunt Nellie: 'Cook has baked your favourite cinnamon cake, Sophia!'

With an effort, Sophia attempted to push such sentimental memories away. She should be glad the aunts were not here to see her go; to know that she was facing the disgrace of divorce; that she had lied, cheated, deceived the man they had both loved.

Quickly, Sophia turned her thoughts to the present.

On one of the topmost shelves was a huge, stuffed elephant's foot and next to it, a small wooden object which she instantly recognized. It was the little carved wooden horse which had been her favourite plaything as a child. It must be all of ten years, she reflected, since she had last set eyes on it, and now it took on a meaning of great sentimental significance. Not only would it remind her of her happy childhood with her aunts, but it was a link with past Calverleys that she could pass on to her own child.

Unfortunately, it was just out of her reach. Sophia set down the oil-lamp and searched around her for a box or chair to stand on. Seeing there was none, she pulled towards her a dented, brass-topped table. Although it wobbled precariously, she was determined not to abandon the toy which she had decided on impulse to take with her in her hand luggage. Carefully, she hitched up her long skirts and climbed on to the table.

The thin, spindly legs might have supported Sophia's weight had she stood still, but now she reached above her to push the heavy elephant's foot to one side. The horse was a finger-tip's length away and she leaned sideways to grasp it.

The tabletop stood only a few feet above the stone floor, but as it collapsed, flinging Sophia backwards, her head hit the edge of a big, iron strongbox. The brass tray clattered to a halt near the door.

As silence fell once more, Sophia's body lay motionless in the shadows, but the oil-lamp continued to cast its light on the shelves above. In the gently flickering flame, it seemed as if the inscrutable face of the brass Buddha was smiling. Far away in the distance, Detcham Church clock gave warning that it was now a quarter to twelve.

The carriage, hired by Mr Armitage, stood in the driveway. The coachman, cap in hand, was loading Sophia's trunks on to the roof, aided by Albert. Ada, with apron flapping, ran from room to room calling her mistress. Scarlet in the face from her exertions, she made her way once more to the kitchen.

'You certain sure you not seed Miss Sophia?' she panted. 'She tole me she were a-coming to bid you goodbye!'

'No, Ada, I told you twice already, I haven't seen the mistress since I took the tray with her hot chocolate up to her bedroom soon after ten. Anyroads, I've been busy in t'wash house this past hour.'

'She ain't nowhere to be found!' Ada moaned. 'Coachman said as how they must be on their way by midday sharp.'

'Best look round the house again,' Cook said. 'I'll come with you.'

The two women went once more from room to room. Since Cook was afraid to go up to the attics, believing them to be haunted, Ada went up on her own. She did not expect to find her mistress there.

'Happen Miss Sophia be outdoors somewheres,' Cook said finally as they returned to the hall to inform the coachman that they had not yet found his passenger.

'The mistress were down in stables not long since,' said Albert. 'She bid me goodbye and then I seed her a-huggin' and a-kissin' Silver Mist.'

Ada gave a sigh of relief.

'Reckon she's still there,' she said. 'Miss Sophia never did pay no count to time!' She trundled off in the direction of the stable yard.

When she returned ten minutes later, the colour had left her face and she looked far older than her years.

'She b'aint there! She b'aint nowhere!' she gasped, and burst into tears.

Cook put a comforting arm around her shoulders.

'A body can't just disappear!' she said practically. 'Albert, you go look in the sheds, and in that there arbour, and in the barns and haylofts, too.' She bent to whisper in Ada's ear so that the coachman could not overhear her: 'Happen Miss Sophia's changed her mind and is hiding herself till carriage is gone!'

For a moment, Ada's spirits lifted. Then she pointed to

Sophia's coat, gloves and hat on the hall chair, the hand luggage neatly placed beside it.

'I'll make us all a cup of tea!' Cook said. 'Happen the coachman could do with one, and I know I could.'

She bustled off to the kitchen, but by the time she returned, so, too, had Albert. He announced breathlessly that he had seen no sign of the mistress.

Ada's tears began to flow again. The coachman finished his tea and said firmly that it was now a quarter of an hour past twelve and he wouldn't guarantee to reach Brighton on time, as he had been ordered, if they didn't leave at once.

'You can wait a little longer,' Cook said firmly. 'You go have another look round, Albert, and if you see any of the gardeners or farm lads or that there woodcutter, you set them a-looking, too.'

Ada's sobs quietened as she listened in growing horror to Cook's orders.

'Ain't no way Miss Sophia's lost herself!' she said. 'She knows her way round every inch of this place blindfold.'

'You can't be sure what's happened, Ada,' Cook said pessimistically. 'Happen she's had an accident, fer all us knows.'

Ada's panic returned.

'What accident? Miss Sophia weren't riding that horse of hern and she knowed very well carriage were a-coming at midday. She were in her travelling clothes. She wouldn't go no walks far out, not nohow.'

'I'm sorry, ladies, but I can't wait no longer!' the coachman said stepping forward. 'Gentleman as employed me said as how I was to get to Brighton punctual-like, seein' as how he were catching the train to Southampton what wouldn't wait. I'll not get my fare if'n he goes off afore I gits there.'

Not even the offer by Cook of a pint of ale would detain him longer.

'Good riddance, I say,' said Cook when the man had unloaded Sophia's trunks from the carriage and disappeared down the driveway. 'Happen Miss Sophia has come to her senses, Ada! Just to think of the poor child going off on her ownsome to them foreign parts fair turns my stomach!' She flapped her apron in disapproval before adding dolefully: 'Whatever would the Misses Calverley have said! You mark my words, Ada, Miss Sophia'll come out of hiding now carriage has gone, just you see.'

For a further half-hour, Ada continued to hope that Cook would be proved right, though in her bones she did not believe that Sophia, whose nature she knew as surely as she knew her own name, would be hiding. Even as a child her Miss Sophia had never lacked daring, and, 'if it needed courage to confess she had changed her mind going to Americky with that there Mr Armitage', she told Cook, 'she'd have come right out and said so.'

By two o'clock, Cook was less sure of herself. Although fond of her mistress, she was not as closely attached to Sophia as was Ada, and now her sense of the dramatic came to the fore.

'Happen poor Miss Sophia couldn't face life no more,' she said to a trembling Ada. 'Happen like that girl from Edburton, she's thrown herself in the river! You recall, Ada, t'were ten years or more ago. She were in family way and . . .'

'Hush this minute!' Ada broke in. 'I'll not listen to such talk, not nohow!'

But Cook had sown the seeds of doubt and Ada realized the necessity to pull herself together. She sent Albert down to the village to bring back a search party. She herself went round the house once more. It did not cross her mind to go down to the cellars.

To her relief, Rogers, the bailiff whose existence she had quite forgotten in her flurry, arrived before Albert returned with twenty volunteers. Glad to have the responsibility at least partially removed from her shoulders, Ada informed the man that her ladyship had vanished.

There was not a worker on the estate or a single villager who had not known Sophia since she was a tiny girl. Under the bailiff's instruction, they were sent in small groups to search the woods, the riverbanks, the fields, every hut and barn in the vicinity, and the footpaths. Cook and Ada made still another fruitless search of the house, even looking in wardrobes and chests and under the beds – as if Sophia were a child and might be playing hide-and-seek.

It was close on four o'clock when the bailiff announced that he had thought of sending Albert to Newtimber in the hope that Sir Richard or Lady Lamberhill might be in residence; but one of the village girls who went daily to Lamberhill Court as a kitchen maid had announced that all the family were in London.

''Tis the master we should be sending for,' he stated. 'And Constable Green. We can't be certain her ladyship hasn't been kidnapped.'

Ada tried to gather her wits about her. Loyalty to Sophia would not allow her to reveal any details of her mistress's private life. It was not for the likes of the bailiff – or indeed, Constable Green – to know that the master and mistress were about to be divorced, she told herself grimly.

'I'll go with Albert to London, explain to the master what-all is a-happening!' she said, forgetting her aching legs and general exhaustion. 'If'n I goos this minute, us'll be back soon after midnight.'

It was growing dark when, four hours later, the butler let Ada into the hall at Sackville Street. Sir Konrad, he reminded her, was in Austria. He had no knowledge of when the master might be expected to return.

For a moment Ada was close to collapse. How could she have forgotten? How *could* she? Who was there now to turn to? Suddenly she remembered Sophia's new friend, Miss Elizabeth Lamberhill. Sophia had told her of the good works this capable lady was doing and how fine a friend she had proved to be. *She* were the one what got Miss Sophia mixed up with them there Armitages in the first place, Ada told herself sourly.

Within half an hour, Ada was in Elizabeth's house,

obediently sipping the glass of brandy that had been pushed into her hands.

'We will go together to Mr John Armitage's house,' Elizabeth said. 'It is possible he has had word from his uncle of your mistress's whereabouts. Are you feeling well enough to go out and hire a cab, Ada?'

They encountered John on the pavement outside his home, about to leave for his club.

'I can tell you nothing more than you already know, Elizabeth,' he said with a worried frown. 'My uncle contacted me from Brighton. He had been afraid that Sophia might change her mind, and when the coachman told him she was missing at the appointed time of departure, he assumed she must have done so.'

'Beggin' your pardon, sir, Miss Lamberhill, if'n Miss Sophia had changed her mind, she'd have told me, surelye,' Ada said emphatically. 'Her weren't one to hide herself away, not even if'n she were a-doing some mischief! Her were all packed up and ready to leave. Something's happened to her – I just knows it, surelye!'

Avoiding Ada's stricken face, Elizabeth and John looked at each other with the same thought going through their minds – a thought very similar to that of the cook. Could Sophia have been so depressed and unhappy that she had decided to end her life? Might she now be in the river that flowed through the bottom of Home Field?

John was horrified.

'Perhaps we should send a telegram to Valschintzky,' he said. 'He is still her husband and he should be informed.'

Elizabeth regarded him bitterly.

'I think he forfeited those rights!' she said. 'He has treated Sophia cruelly, to say the very least. However, perhaps he *should* be told. Meanwhile, I will go back to Ortolans with Ada.'

'I shall come with you!' John said urgently, but Elizabeth gave him a warning glance.

'It might not be wise for you to go to Detcham, John,' she

said pointedly. 'Besides, for all we know, Sophia may by now have returned.'

'But where from, Miss Lamberhill?' Ada said tearfully. 'Miss Sophia's plumb vanished from the face of this earth. I doan't think we'll ever set eyes on the poor little mite agin.'

'Nonsense!' said Elizabeth briskly. 'Your mistress is a very kind and lovely person, Ada, as I'm sure I don't have to tell you. For one thing, she has the baby to think about, and for another, she would know how worried and unhappy we would be if she . . . disappeared. It is not in her nature to do anything so unkind, so hurtful, as you very well know.'

It was not until they were alone together in Mr Armitage's comfortable barouche, on their way down the London to Brighton road, that Ada, in tears once more, disputed Elizabeth's last remark.

'She did do something wrong, surelye!' she sobbed. 'I told her t'was wrong and she knowed it herself . . . but she didn't want Miss Challinor a-spoilin' all their lives. She tricked the master, Miss Lamberhill, and God knows it, same as He knows everything. This is His vengeance, like Vicar says. "Be sure your sins will find you out!" Vicar says from pulpit. "The vengeance of the Lord is upon you!"'

'The vicar was not referring to Miss Sophia!' Elizabeth said firmly. Silently, she offered up a prayer that Ada would take her word for it. 'You wait and see, my dear, we may well find your mistress at home, safe and sound.'

CHAPTER TWENTY-SIX

1890

The manuscript of Sophia's novel lay undiscovered amongst Konrad's papers for two long weeks. He had had but one idea – to make the most of all the many dissipations so readily to hand in Vienna and thus put his wife from his mind. They had not proved to be the distractions he had anticipated. Sophia was constantly in his thoughts.

Despite everything he had said to Sophia at the time, he had recognized the fact that the child – if indeed there was one – could be his. If it *were* so, was he still prepared to end his marriage? Mr Endicote had warned him that he had no actual proof of guilt and that the court would have to decide on circumstantial evidence alone. The old man had actually pleaded with him to reconsider so drastic a step, warning him of the consequences to the Calverley good name. In all the three hundred years of its family history, no scandal had ever been attached to it. Did Konrad, he asked, not think he should give Sophia the benefit of the doubt – for doubts there must be! To close Ortolans was one thing, but divorce – that was a far more serious matter.

One evening two weeks after his arrival in Vienna, seeing no point in yet a further fruitless search for entertainment, but unable to settle to answering the letters awaiting his attention on his desk, Konrad caught sight of the manuscript of Sophia's novel. How it had come to be there caused him only a moment's curiosity. Sophia's large sprawling script was instantly recognizable. Konrad drew a deep sigh as he pushed the manuscript away from him with a feeling of irritation.

This ridiculous idea of hers to write a novel had been instrumental in bringing Armitage into her life, he reminded himself – a fact that he deeply resented. Furthermore, now that he came to consider the matter, if Sophia's warning that he would find her story autobiographical had any validity, he would object most strongly to the book's publication.

Perhaps it was his duty to read it, he thought. Unless Sophia had made a second copy, it could not yet be in the process of printing and there was still time to stop its publication. Despite Sophia's use of a pseudonym, there were people like Elizabeth Lamberhill who might reveal Sophia's true identity, and he had no wish to become a laughing stock in society.

Fighting his reluctance to do so, Konrad sat down at his desk and began to leaf through the first few pages. His immediate reaction was that this was no literary masterpiece; and that despite Sophia's use of a male pseudonym, this was clearly a book written by a woman for females. Nevertheless, the story held his attention, and when his valet came into the room to enquire whether there was anything further he required, Konrad dismissed him saying that he would not require the man's services again that evening, and returned impatiently to the novel.

Deep into the night, Konrad read – and reread – the passages that he now recognized as being thinly disguised autobiography. One passage stood out above all others: the heroine, Cecilia – in reality Sophia – had deceived the hero, a duke, by pretending that she was to have his child. The duke – a parody of himself, Konrad realized – had believed the lies and proposed marriage.

For the fourth time, Konrad reread the ensuing paragraph:

> I long to confess the truth, but I am afraid to do so, for of a certainty my beloved will no longer wish to marry me. I dare not take the chance . . .

Yet another passage was almost as revealing.

Today I am to be married and I want only one thing . . . his love!

Cecilia's nocturnal seduction of her duke varied only in the slightest degree to Sophia's visit to him, Konrad. He suspected that there had been some woman in Sophia's life, not unlike the actress in her story, who had prompted her to use her beauty to achieve her ends. It was not important now. All that mattered to him was that Sophia genuinely regretted that she had married him under false pretences; that she *had* loved him on the day she made her vows; that despite his rejection of her, her love had never faltered. She had been right in assuming that if he read her novel, he would guess the extent of that love; of her guilt, her suffering. His pride had prevented him even trying to understand her behaviour. If he had been gentle with her instead of angry; willing to listen, to forgive . . .

Long before he reached the end of Sophia's novel, Konrad was convinced that he must prevent the publication of this book and even more importantly, return immediately to Ortolans to see her. There were still two days to go before he had ordered the house to be closed. To waste even a moment's time seemed unforgivable. He could not bear to think of Sophia there, on the point of leaving the house she loved, alone and unhappy, and, he no longer doubted, carrying his child!

Despite the lateness of the hour, he woke his valet and instructed him to pack. Within the hour, he was on his way to the station. It was not until he was finally on the train to England that he found time to read the concluding chapters of *Cecilia*. He turned the pages with a growing sense of unease which deepened still further as he came to the last few lines.

. . . If she were to die, Cecilia thought, her poor child might never see the light of day, but Peregrine would be free . . . free to marry the beautiful Countess Arborfield . . . (*Lavinia?*)

. . . who had proved her love for him so long ago. Now she, too, could prove her love for her husband by setting him free.

Cecilia removed her bonnet and cloak, and with a look of joy shining through her tears, she slipped quietly into the murky water of the Thames.

As the train crossed the border from Austria into France and rattled on through the early hours of the morning, Konrad tried to convince himself that this melodramatic ending was pure fiction. Sophia had once said to him that she would rather die than leave Ortolans, but he had not taken the declaration seriously. Much as she loved Ortolans, he refused to believe that she would put an end to her life rather than be parted from it! No house could ever be worth such a sacrifice. Nor indeed, would Sophia, like her heroine, destroy the life of her unborn child. She had far too much courage to take such a way of escape.

Nevertheless, it was some while before Konrad regained his equilibrium. *Cecilia* was a story of fiction, not a diary, for all the similarities to his life and Sophia's that it contained. It had sufficed to enlighten him that she truly loved him; that the child was his and that he had been far too hasty and prejudiced in his judgement of her.

When Konrad reached England, he set off immediately to Ortolans. He could not wait now to hold Sophia in his arms; to tell her that he could see how it had been his mistrust which had undermined their relationship; that he should have acknowledged her confession, forgiven her, accepted that she loved him, and put the past behind them.

The scene that met Konrad's eyes as he approached the drive leading to Ortolans instantly destroyed his newly acquired serenity and filled him once more with a deep sense of foreboding.

It was now twenty-four hours since Sophia had disappeared. Men, women and even children were spread out across the fields, beating with sticks and pitchforks in the long grass and in the hedgerows. Everywhere Konrad looked, there were figures searching. He ordered his driver to halt as he recognized his bailiff climbing out of a ditch by the side of the lodge.

'What's amiss, Rogers?' he asked.

'Oh, sir, I'm that glad to see you,' the bailiff said, wishing fervently that he was not the one to have to tell the master the bad news. He removed his cap and wiped his forehead with the back of his hand.

'Well, out with it, man. You look as if you've seen a ghost!'

'Yes, sir! No, sir! I mean to say . . . it's Miss Sophia, sir. No-one has seen her since midday yesterday. We've all been a-searching since dawn. There's a dozen men, two of 'em in boats, searching the river. Keeper's got twenty lads in woods. The whole village 'as turned out – but nobody ain't seen sight nor sound of her ladyship.'

His heart in his mouth, Konrad drove up to the house and strode into the hall. Ada was in one of the hall chairs having an attack of the vapours. Cook and two of the village women were trying to revive her. They stood back as Konrad approached.

'Pull yourself together, Ada!' Konrad said in a harsh voice. 'I want to know what has happened – everything, you understand? *Everything*. The rest of you please leave us.'

It was some minutes before Ada recovered sufficiently to reply coherently to Konrad's questions. Convinced now that Sophia was dead, she saw no reason to withhold the fact that Sophia had been on the point of departing to America with the elder of the two Mr Armitages.

'Leastways, that was what Miss Sophia led me to believe!' she ended, the tears flowing freely once more. 'Mayhap she dursn't tell me what she really intended, knowing I'd stop her if I could, surelye. Oh, sir, her were that unhappy, I think she's drowned herself in that there river!'

'Fiddlesticks!' Konrad all but shouted with a conviction he was very far from feeling. The ending of Sophia's book was now uppermost in his mind. 'It is quite clear to me from what you have said that your mistress has met with some kind of accident.'

'That is exactly what I told Ada!' Elizabeth said as she came through from the kitchen where she had been organizing beer, tea and sandwiches for the searchers. She was as surprised to see Konrad as was he to see her.

'I came down with Ada last night,' she explained. 'I am so glad you are here, Konrad. The whole of Detcham has been searching for Sophia since sunrise. Your bailiff has been organizing them most efficiently. I am sure Sophia will be found unharmed, perhaps locked in some shed or outbuilding . . .'

Her voice trailed into silence as she saw by the look on Konrad's face that her tone had lacked conviction.

This was not the time for personal confrontation, Konrad thought as he looked away from Elizabeth Lamberhill's handsome face. He believed her to be – with her modern, feminist outlook – responsible for Sophia's association with John Armitage. It was, after all, common knowledge in the family that she was Murray Armitage's mistress! But he did not intend to waste precious time discussing past events. All that mattered was that Sophia should be found.

'Sophia left these letters for Ada to post,' Elizabeth said quietly. 'I hope you will forgive me for opening them. I thought they might have provided us with some clue as to . . . as to Sophia's intentions. I am afraid they do not!'

In silence, Konrad took them from her, and walking to the window, hurriedly scanned them. The one addressed to himself brought a lump to his throat and a resurgence of his wild fear that, despite the child, she had decided to end her life. With an effort he forced himself to think coolly and logically.

'I would have expected someone to have come upon my wife by now if she had been trapped outside,' he said, his tone brusque. 'I shall search the house.'

'I done that, sir, over and over again!' said Ada, recovering herself now that her master was back in charge. 'And Miss

Lamberhill came with me this morning – we was in every room – and in the attics, too, sir! And Cook and me—'

'It will not hurt to look again,' Konrad interrupted fiercely. 'I shall begin at the top and work my way down.'

His mood became increasingly apprehensive as he ransacked first the attics and then the bedrooms. Seeing the dustsheets covering the furniture in Sophia's bedroom, the bare mantelpiece and bookshelves, he could no longer doubt that she had intended to leave Ortolans for good. Despite his orders, his threats to close the house, he had not believed she would do so. It had been more important to her than anything else in the world, and she had admitted it. Once again, her words came back into his mind:

'I would rather die than leave Ortolans!'

Could it really have come to that? Was she even now beneath the surface of the river where the searchers could not find her?

With a sense of unbearable horror, Konrad hurried downstairs and went into the library. On the big leather-topped desk, *The Calverley Journal* lay open. Only with an effort could he bring himself to read the final page which might record Sophia's last thoughts before . . . before . . .

To his surprise, the entry was dated several weeks earlier.

Today Cook bottled forty-two pounds of gooseberries which is a record. We had to rearrange the shelves in the still-room as there was not space enough beside the rhubarb. We shall be harvesting the currants soon if this good weather continues.

There was no further entry, and he closed the book gently. There was no clue here as to Sophia's possible whereabouts . . . unless . . . unless . . .

'Ada!' he shouted as he ran back to the hall. 'Ada, where are you? Did you search downstairs – the still-room, the storeroom, the cellars?'

By the expression on the old woman's face, he knew that she had not.

'Weren't nothing as belongs to Miss Sophia down there, sir!' she mumbled. 'Theys things mostly as belonged to 'er father, and she said as how we was only to pack what were hers . . .'

Konrad did not stop to hear more, but hurriedly lit the oil-lamp standing on the hall table, before making his way to the passage leading both to the kitchen quarters and to the cellars. The door, against all rules, was unlocked. The still-room door was also unlocked. On one of the shelves facing him stood rows of big jars containing the bottled fruit to which Sophia had referred in the journal. There was no corner where Sophia could be concealed. He glanced at the door of the wine vault, his hopes gradually receding. Common sense told him that there was no logical reason why Sophia, upon the point of leaving Ortolans, should have come down here.

He noticed suddenly that the door leading out of the still-room was unlocked and ajar. Someone had been down here and not locked the doors behind them! Going into the room, he set his lamp down on one of the wine racks and began peering behind the big casks of ale. Despite the absurdity of his actions, he was determined not to leave one foot of space unexamined.

As Konrad reached up to brush aside a dusty, clinging cobweb, he heard a muffled cry. He stood perfectly still, holding his breath. For a moment, there was complete silence; then the noise came again. His head turned towards the sound. It seemed to him to come from the storeroom beyond the coal cellar.

'Pray God it is Sophia!' he whispered aloud, then hurrying to the door, he began to shout her name. 'Sophia, is it you? Are you in there? Sophia?'

Stumbling over a heap of coal, he swung open the door of the storeroom. The first thing to catch his eye was the brass tabletop near his feet. Then he saw Sophia. She was lying on her side just inside the door, her arms stretched out towards him. Her eyes were open – staring at him. As he flung himself down beside her, quite suddenly, she smiled.

'I am . . . so very, very . . . pleased to see you, Konrad!' she whispered. Her lips were swollen with thirst and her voice was indistinct.

Tears sprang to Konrad's eyes as with infinite tenderness, he put his arms around her.

'I was trying to reach the little horse . . . I fell . . . I called and called . . .'

'Don't try to talk, my dearest. Everything is all right now!' Konrad broke in, but as he lifted Sophia gently from the ground, she said:

'I thought I heard footsteps above me in the library . . . yesterday, I think it was. Oh, Konrad, I'm so happy you're here!' Then her eyes closed and she lapsed into unconsciousness again.

The Buddha and the Indian goddess watched with their inscrutable gaze as Konrad, believing himself too late to save her, gathered the limp body of his wife into his arms.

Sophia was severely concussed, but although it was three weeks before she was fully recovered, she was well enough to spend long hours with Konrad at her bedside. He talked endlessly about their coming child which, mercifully, had been unharmed by her accident. He was determined she would have a son who resembled her, but Sophia wanted a little girl with Konrad's large dark eyes and endearing smile! She insisted upon keeping the little wooden horse by her bedside for without it, she told him, she might never have fallen in the cellar and by the time Konrad returned, she would have been on her way to America. She might even have married John Armitage and lived a lifetime of regrets, whereas since she and Konrad had been reconciled, each day was a perfect idyll.

Sometimes Konrad chose to think that it was Fate which had brought him back to England in time to save Sophia's life – for the physician had declared that she would not have survived another day; sometimes he would declare with a smile that it had been the will of the brass Buddha.

Sophia knew different. As she awaited with joyful impatience for the birth of their child, she knew that it was the house, Ortolans, which had made up its mind it would not allow her to go away.

CHAPTER TWENTY-SEVEN

Extracts from The Calverley Journal *1890–1950*

20 DECEMBER, 1890. *Sophia was safely delivered of our son, who we shall name Thomas Karl Richard Calverley. Sophia and the baby are in excellent health. I have marked the occasion by giving all our estate workers a holiday, and the villagers are to celebrate with a barn dance in the newly completed village hall, for which I am supplying the beverages. There will be some sore heads in church on Sunday!*

1 FEBRUARY, 1891. *Thomas's christening. Our tenants have presented Thomas with a beautiful oak cradle, carved by old Jim Pylbeam – a charming gesture.*

15 APRIL, 1891. *Mama arrived yesterday and will be visiting us for two weeks. She is enchanted by the baby who, she insists, looks exactly like me at that age! Tomorrow, two of Elizabeth Lamberhill's girls arrive to be trained by Ada as nursery maids. Jim Pylbeam's eldest, Harry, is currently converting the big attic room into a bedroom for them.*

29 SEPTEMBER, 1891. *Sophia and I took Thomas to the Harvest Festival. He was very good and did not cry once.*

18 DECEMBER, 1891. *We leave tomorrow for Vienna where we will spend Christmas with Mama. Thomas is coming with us. In two days' time, he will be a year old.*

14 MARCH, 1892. *We were obliged to have Silver Mist put down – she was thirty-two. Sophia is heartbroken although it is some time since she has been able to ride as she is expecting our second child in September. I shall buy Thomas a pony at the spring horse sales next week.*

20 SEPTEMBER, 1892. *This morning we became parents of identical twin sons. We shall call them Frank and Henry. Thomas is very excited. Since he cannot make up his mind which baby shall be given his wooden horse, he has decided to keep it for himself! Sophia is tired but otherwise has come through the ordeal very well.*

14 FEBRUARY, 1893. *We attended Ada's funeral. Sophia is grief-stricken, but the poor woman's death was a merciful release for she had been in great pain these past few months. Thomas asked me this morning when can he go to visit her in Heaven. He is such a sturdy, lovable, good-natured little chap. We must take care not to spoil him.*

SPRING, 1895. *Dreyfus has been found guilty of treason which I find hard to believe. I met the fellow in France on several occasions and liked him very much. I have written to his wife who has appealed for support in clearing his name. I fear there is little I can do.*

1 AUGUST, 1896. *Work has started on dredging the river to clear the bullrushes and silt. I have employed extra men from Newtimber. The weather is hot and as a consequence the water level is low.*

22 MAY, 1897. *Our first daughter arrived at midnight. We shall call her Victoria for the Queen. The physician assures us Sophia will be well enough recovered to attend Her Majesty's Diamond Jubilee celebrations in June.*

15 DECEMBER, 1897. *The old document from Queen Elizabeth granting a baronetcy to the first Sir Richard Calverley has been hung in the drawing-room beside the fireplace. The elegant maple frame was made for us by Jim, and it looks very good against the dark walls.*

12 SEPTEMBER, 1898. *News of the dreadful murder of our poor Empress of Austria reached us today. I can conceive of no reason, political or otherwise, for this senseless outrage. Mama, who was a close friend, is distraught. Sophia and I leave for Vienna tomorrow and shall remain until the funeral. We shall not take the children although Sophia hates to be parted from them even for a few days. They will be quite safe with Nurse, and the new governess is most reliable.*

12 JANUARY, 1899. *Our fourth son, William, was christened today. We have named him after Sophia's grandfather.*

1 MAY, 1899. *Ada's old bedroom is being converted into a bathroom. Happily the men are able to hide the pipes below the floorboards as they are unsightly. Sophia has decided upon green and white tiles for the walls which will look pleasing with the carved mahogany surround to the bath and basin. We will have a tasselled curtain over the doorway to the water closet which will afford extra privacy.*

10 OCTOBER, 1899. *We are at war against the Boers in South Africa. Thomas talks of little else and is determined to join the Army when he is old enough. I have allowed him to keep by his bedside his grandfather's sword which he discovered in the cellar.*

4 FEBRUARY, 1901. *Sophia and I attended our late Queen's funeral – a solemn but moving occasion. The British manage such ceremonies so well.*

MAY DAY, 1901. *We have a second daughter, Louise Eleanor. Jim and Harry Pylbeam have completed the conversion of the two attic rooms for Nurse and are about to start work enlarging the day nursery by knocking down the wall between it and Nurse's old sitting-room. Jones has completed the plumbing and even Nurse will have running water in her room.*

3 JUNE, 1901. *John Armitage and his wife – a delightful Boston girl – took lunch with us today. Sophia has asked Armitage to stand as godfather to Louise. 'My rival', as I call him, looks like the successful publisher he has become – bald and rotund! A pleasant fellow, however. He insists that I am to blame because Sophia is not a famous novelist and assures me that had she not been so happily married to me, she might have written another book. I countered with the argument that motherhood has usurped all her creativity! She dotes upon our children – and upon me!*

JUNE, 1902. *For once the vicar's sermon did not send me to sleep. An interesting précis of the Boer War, but I doubt if many members of his simple-minded congregation were much the wiser. They were nevertheless pleased to celebrate the end of this tiresome war.*

9 AUGUST, 1902. *Yet another impressive ceremony! Sophia and I were present in the Abbey when Edward VII was crowned. The Lamberhills gave a magnificent celebration ball. As usual, my beloved wife outshone all others. Much as we enjoyed our week in London, we are both, as always, more than content to be back here at Ortolans.*

12 JULY, 1903. *I leave tomorrow for my homeland of Austria to offer such comfort as I can to Mama. Both Mitzi and her husband, an equerry to King Alexander of Serbia, were*

murdered when a party of conspirators broke into the palace and assassinated the King and Queen. I shall forbid Mama to go to Mitzi's funeral. There is too much unrest in that turbulent state. Poor little Mitzi cannot have been other than an innocent party; she was as disinterested in politics as is my Sophia.

28 APRIL, 1906. A letter arrived today from John Armitage telling us of his parents' narrow escape from death during the recent horrifying earthquake in San Francisco. Their town house, from which they had removed the previous day to their home in the country, was destroyed by fire. He tells us that the whole city was devastated and confirms the newspaper reports that thousands have perished.

1 APRIL, 1907. Enlargement of Ortolans. The kitchens are being updated and a magnificent new stove is being installed. Quarry tiles are to be laid on the floor as the old stones were so uneven. An extension is being added beyond the drawing-room, with windows looking towards the rose garden. We are using wood from Bluebell Wood which has been stored since coppicing five winters past. Sophia has given me a billiard table as a birthday present, which will look very handsome in the centre of the room.

10 MARCH, 1908. My fiftieth birthday and, I suspect, a few more grey hairs! Sophia has arranged a birthday dinner and Thomas has obtained leave from Sandhurst. He seems to be greatly enjoying life at the Military College. Frank and Henry have sent birthday greetings from Eton. Their house-master says he still cannot tell them apart. Even Sophia and I sometimes get them confused.

OCTOBER, 1908. Perhaps I am growing old, but I am appre-hensive about my country's annexation of Bosnia and

Herzegovina. It can only create further unrest in the Balkans, and Russia will not like it.

6 MAY, 1910. *We were saddened by the news that our dear King Edward died today.*

20 MAY, 1910. *We decided not to go to London for the King's funeral as the weather is too hot and Sophia has been unwell with a summer ailment.*

10 MARCH, 1912. *Frank has decided to become a mountaineer in preference to becoming an explorer having read the splendid news that Captain Amundsen reached the South Pole last December. Still no news of Scott's expedition. Frank and Henry have determined to climb Mount Everest!*

15 MARCH, 1912. *The miners have been on strike this past fortnight. I have ordered Rogers to see that wood is delivered to anyone in the village who is suffering from lack of coal. Let us hope it will end soon. The weather is bitter.*

15 APRIL, 1912. *We are doubly shocked. Not only has that magnificent new liner, the* Titanic, *gone down in the North Atlantic, but Armitage and his wife and children are not among the survivors. What a terrible tragedy!*

6 JUNE, 1912. *I journeyed to Kingston-upon-Thames in our new Rolls-Royce motor car to meet with Mr Sopwith, and I am greatly impressed by the flying machines he is building. If I can overcome Sophia's fears that it might be too dangerous, I shall buy the boys a biplane which they can fly from the fields at Shoreham. However, I have first to install a generator so that we can dispense with the oil-lamps and enjoy electric lights. Although Sophia fears that*

they will give a harsher illumination, she has agreed that it will be a great saving in time and that the air will be purer.

FEBRUARY, 1913. *News has arrived that Scott's party have all perished. There are as yet no details.*

4 APRIL, 1913. *The men started work today erecting the telegraph poles which will run in a straight line across Home Farm Field through Bluebell Wood and up past the river to the house. The children are very excited and they have drawn lots as to who will be the first to use the apparatus. We are also arranging for old Dr Knight to be connected as we so often require his services for poor little Louise who suffers so frequently from the croup.*

28 JUNE, 1914. *Archduke Franz Ferdinand and the duchess, his wife, have been assassinated at Sarajevo by a Bosnian serb. I do not doubt that von Hotsendorf, our Chief of General Staff, will welcome this excuse for military action against the agitators in Bosnia and Croatia. On my last visit to Vienna, he spoke most vehemently to me on the subject. Regardless of the Archduke's unpopularity, his death is an outrage my country cannot tolerate, and I suspect that war is now inevitable.*

3 AUGUST, 1914. *The situation is serious indeed. Last week my country declared war against Serbia; two days ago Germany declared war against Russia, and I have just learned that Germany has declared war against France. I see no way that this country can avoid being drawn into the conflict. Pray God I may be wrong. It would be intolerable to think that my adopted country could become the enemy of my native land. Although I am now a citizen of this great British Empire, I cannot disregard my loyalties to my homeland.*

4 AUGUST, 1914. *The very worst has happened. The Germans have invaded Belgium as a consequence of which Great Britain is now at war with Germany. Sophia can think of little else but that we have three sons old enough to participate. I fear for them too, but I cannot bring myself to think of my country as their enemy.*

12 AUGUST, 1914. *Great Britain has now declared war on Austria-Hungary.*

1 OCTOBER, 1914. *Thomas has been given a commission and is home on embarkation leave. Frank and Henry have joined the Royal Flying Corps. They look upon firing at German pilots with rifles at close range as 'great sport'. Sophia and I try not to let our sons see how fearful we are for them. The girls are envious, and Victoria has announced that she is going to become a VAD. Thank goodness William is still at Eton!*

10 DECEMBER, 1914. *Today we laid the body of our thirteen-year-old daughter, Louise, to rest in the family vault. Sophia is inconsolable. The twins have been granted compassionate leave and are doing their best to comfort us although they too are heartbroken.*

MAY, 1915. *The war is dragging on and the casualty lists are horrifying. I have released six of the staff who wish to volunteer for service in France. Italy has now declared war on my country.*

9 NOVEMBER, 1915. *Yesterday they requisitioned our horses who are needed by the cavalry. But with Albert and Phipps joining up, perhaps it is as well. Sophia was very distressed and will not go near the empty stables.*

JANUARY, 1916. *We have evacuated Gallipoli. It was an absolute disaster with great loss of life.*

1 JULY, 1916. *Thomas was Killed in Action on the Somme whilst saving the life of one of his men. He is to be awarded the Military Cross for extreme bravery under fire. I am proud of this decoration but bereft by the loss of our eldest son.*

MARCH, 1917. *News is reaching us of a revolt by the peoples of Russia against their royal family. They have suffered terrible military defeats with an estimated four million of their soldiers killed. It seems the combination of humiliation, hunger and mistrust have brought about the abdication of the Tsar. The Government has offered sanctuary to him and his family.*

6 APRIL, 1917. *The United States of America has declared war on Germany. Their troops are desperately needed in France where the fighting continues adding to the ever-lengthening casualty lists. Let us hope the American troops will arrive soon to reinforce our armies. With so many dead we have no more young men to fill the gaps in the ranks. Dangerous as their aerial expeditions might be, I thank God that Frank and Henry are not having to face the horrors of trench warfare.*

MAY DAY, 1917. *Frank was married today in Detcham Church to Mary Amelia Buckhurst. Mary will live with us until after the war when they plan to build a house in Newtimber.*

In Sophia's handwriting was a single entry . . .

17 JUNE, 1917. *My beloved Konrad was killed in a German air raid on London.*

There is a gap in the journal until Sophia resumes:

3 NOVEMBER, 1938. *Today Basil's little daughter, Georgina, my first great-grandchild was born.*

This new young life has given me new hope for the future and I have found the strength to reopen The Calverley Journal *which I had not had the heart to do since I recorded the death of my beloved Konrad over two decades ago. There are moments when I am glad that he did not live to old age as I have done and suffered my grief at the loss of so many loved ones – our darling Frank who was shot down by a hun while on a troop-spotting mission over Arras in May 1918; Henry's tragic death in a mid-air collision with a German aeroplane on the day the war ended; the death of our youngest son William at the age of twenty from peritonitis and of Arthur, the young grandson Konrad never knew, in the Siege of Madrid during the Spanish Civil War.*

There have been happy events – the birth of Frank's identical twins, Basil and Arthur; Victoria's marriage to Reginald, a fine young stockbroker, whose company Konrad would much have enjoyed as Reginald is an excellent shot and a keen fisherman; Basil's subsequent marriage to the American girl Patricia, who nursed him when he was wounded in Zaragossa.

They have not been easy years here at Ortolans. Our family has become impoverished as a result of the devastating repercussions on the London Stock Market from the Wall Street Crash in 1929. We have only been able to stay on here thanks to Mr Endicote's clever sales of the cottages, farms and properties in Detcham. I have become accustomed to managing with so few staff. So many of them never came back to domestic work after the war, but those of the Pylbeam family who survived the horrors in France have remained loyal.

So much has remained unrecorded: the death of our dear King George V; the twins' participation in the war against the Fascists in Spain; the invasion of Konrad's homeland by Herr Hitler's National Socialist armies; Victoria and Reginald's emigration to Australia; and of course, in '36, we were deeply shocked by the scandal attaching to the Crown. I listened on our wireless set with the staff to Edward's abdication speech, but although I have a certain sympathy for him, I strongly disapprove of his abrogation of his duty to his country. His brother Bertie showed great courage when he broadcast to the nation, overcoming his speech impediment with determination and fortitude. Everybody was most impressed.

I would not have thought it possible that I could survive these past twenty years without the support of my beloved husband; but I feel he is never far away from me here at Ortolans and the memories of our life together sustain me. I have my grandson Basil, the new baby and my home to comfort me in my old age. It is hard to believe that I shall be sixty-eight next year. Somehow we manage to run the house with only a handful of servants. Anna and Egon, the German Jewish refugees, cope very well in the kitchen. Wilkins, the chauffeur, takes care of the Delage. We have never replaced the horses after they were requisitioned for war service, and the stables are empty. Perhaps I will buy a pony for little Georgina in a year or two's time.

3 SEPTEMBER, 1939. We have declared war on Germany. It is hard to accept the sacrifice of all those hundreds of thousands of young lives such a short while ago. 'The war to end all wars' has been in vain. I am thankful that my dear Konrad cannot know that the two countries he so loved are once again enemies, and that many of his countrymen have joined the ranks of Hitler's National Socialists.

OCTOBER, 1939. Basil has joined up and been posted abroad. Patricia has volunteered for the Women's Auxiliary Air Force.

Ada's great-great-niece is coming to help me take care of the baby.

25 JUNE, 1940. *The French have surrendered and the whole of Europe is now in German hands. Thank God we saved so many of our troops at Dunkirk. We are all preparing for invasion. Bonfires have been built on the Downs, one of which we can see on a clear day, to be lit as soon as the enemy is spotted. Patricia wishes me to go to her family in the United States, but I could never leave Ortolans and shall die here if I have to.*

1941. *The weekly meat ration has now been reduced to one shilling a week. Jones is very good about letting Anna have offal when he gets it. He's so pleased to have the pheasants and rabbits Wilkins shoots in Bluebell Wood for his customers. We are so much luckier than the city dwellers. The air-raids seem to be getting worse, and when I see and hear the hundreds of German bombers passing overhead on their way to London, I realize how much worse the bombardment is in this war than in the last. A bomb dropped last week in one of Green's meadows. Thank God it missed Detcham. Poor Mr Hicks has lost two sons at sea, and the Pylbeams have lost a son in Tobruk.*

6 DECEMBER, 1941. *The Japanese have attacked Pearl Harbour and the Americans have declared war. Mr Churchill has said we have a long fight ahead before we can hope to achieve victory.*

1 MARCH, 1942. *Patricia has received notification from the War Office that Basil was taken prisoner when the Japanese overran Singapore. We pray for his safety.*

NOVEMBER, 1942. *Patricia was home on leave for Georgina's fourth birthday. Anna managed to save enough butter to*

*make the child a beautiful cake. How sad to think that
Basil is missing his little daughter's development. She is a
sweet child. We have had only one card from him sent
through the Red Cross. Patricia's family have been sending
regular food parcels to him (and to us), but we do not know
if he has received them. Patricia has heard that conditions
are very bad in the Japanese camps.*

*1943. Last winter I slipped on the stone steps leading down
from the terrace and broke my hip. Such a silly thing to
do! Since then I have been quite ill with pneumonia, and I
think Dr Knight is surprised by my recovery. I am quite
determined to live to see the end of this war and Basil's
safe return to Ortolans.*

*8 MAY, 1945. The war in Europe is over at last and Mr
Churchill tells us that it is only a matter of time before
we shall defeat the Japanese. How I wish my Konrad was
here to celebrate VE day. Peace in Europe was his dearest
dream.*

*2 SEPTEMBER, 1945. Due to the new American atomic bomb,
the Japanese have surrendered and the world is once more
at peace. The entire household has attended a thanksgiving
service in Detcham. Many were in tears. Patricia and I
prayed for news of Basil.*

*JANUARY, 1946. Basil is home at last. Although he is still
very ill we thank God for his safe return. Despite the care
he received in hospital, he is very thin and frail. Patricia
and Georgina are his devoted nurses. Dr Knight says the
peace and quiet here at Ortolans will aid his recovery.*

*1 JUNE, 1947. Basil has made arrangements for the old
generator to be dismantled and we are to be connected to
the mains supply next week. At long last he is beginning to*

take an interest in life again and is so much better in every way.

NOVEMBER, 1948. *Georgina's tenth birthday. How quickly the years are passing! Dr Knight has told Patricia she must not give up hope of having another child. Basil's health is much improved and he is as anxious as I for a son to carry on the family name.*

OCTOBER, 1949. *We have all been ill with the influenza. Patricia and I are over the worst, but they have removed my darling Georgina to hospital as it seems she is allergic to the new antibiotics. Basil, too, is very ill, but he will not leave the house. He says a hospital would bring back memories of the hundreds who died in hospital when tragically their release had come too late.*

20 OCTOBER, 1949. *Georgina died in hospital last night, a fortnight before her eleventh birthday. Basil is very weak.*

4 NOVEMBER, 1949. *Despite all Dr Knight's efforts, Basil passed away in the early hours of yesterday morning. His heart had been weakened by the terrible privations during those years in the prison camp and proved unequal to the struggle. The vicar has exhorted me not to lose my faith in the ultimate goodness of the Almighty, but I find it very hard to reconcile myself to God's will. He has taken all my loved ones. Patricia tries to console me with her conviction that the child she is carrying will be a boy. If she is wrong, then one of the oldest baronetcies in England will die out now my dearest Basil has passed on.*

10 JANUARY, 1950. *It is with great joy that I record the birth of Simon Konrad Calverley, a strong healthy baby weighing eight and a half pounds. Dear Patricia has assured me she will never return to her homeland except to visit*

her family, and this darling child will be brought up to fulfil his heritage.

21 MARCH, 1950. *Baby Simon was christened today on this, my seventy-ninth birthday. I rejoice in his baptism and in the renewal of my Faith, for I found myself able to say once more, 'God's Will be done'.*

PART THREE

1986–88

CHAPTER TWENTY-EIGHT

1986

'Thank you very much, Sir Simon. I think that about wraps it up. And thank you, Joanne!'

Emma Foster nodded to Pete, her cameraman, who turned to his assistant and together they started dismantling the spotlights focused on Emma's interviewee – a not very attractive young woman in her early thirties with a bad complexion and heavy dark-rimmed spectacles. However, she had had plenty to say in reply to Emma's questions and clearly was a worthy candidate for her *Women in Financial Careers* programme.

Emma was thoroughly satisfied with the interview which had gone far more easily than she had dared to hope. According to Simon Calverley, the high-powered merchant banker who employed Joanne, his assistant had proved herself well beyond the written assessment that had prompted him to choose her in preference to the alternative candidate for the job – a young man. He had used such terms as 'totally reliable', 'dedicated', 'single-minded' – needless to say, in the same tones of surprise so often used by men when referring to their female employees. The interview would lend weight to the theme she was pursuing, Emma decided – namely, that women in top positions had always to prove themselves, whereas a man was assumed to be capable until he proved he was not!

Hopefully Derek, her programme editor, would be pleased, Emma thought as she slipped on her jacket and picked up her notes board.

'If you have no further need of me, I should be getting back to my desk, Simon!'

Joanne's boss nodded and the woman hurriedly left the conference room where the interview had taken place. As Emma turned towards the door, Simon Calverley intercepted her.

'May I take you somewhere for dinner tonight?' he asked in voice pitched low enough for Pete not to overhear. Concentrated upon the job in hand as Emma had been, she had not noticed the intent way in which he had been observing her throughout the interview. His personal interest now came as a surprise – and not a welcome one. He was too good-looking, she thought; too self-assured, too attractive to be her choice of escort. If she accepted invitations from men at all – and she seldom did so nowadays – they had to be unattractive enough for her to guarantee her disinterest in them as men. She had determined three years ago, when she had finally broken off her relationship with Paul, that there would be no more emotional involvements, that never again would she allow a man to distract her from her work.

'The trouble with you women is that you can't keep your emotions separate from your intellect!' Derek had said after the break-up with Paul. 'In your heart of hearts, you knew perfectly well he was no good – yet you convinced yourself that the sex side of it was love. If you can't sleep with a fellow without getting emotionally involved, then steer clear of the ones who attract you. That's my advice, darling.'

Emma had taken that advice. Derek was not only her boss but her friend, and one she knew she could trust absolutely. In his early forties, he had had a great deal more experience of life. Twice divorced and now living with an attractive model of Emma's own age, he was more a father-figure than a man friend. Lucy, Emma's flatmate, called him her guru and in a way, he was. From the start, he had encouraged her to confide in him and she had come to depend on his sympathetic and sensible advice.

She glanced quickly at the man who had invited her out and decided that he was altogether far too attractive to be 'safe'. When he had smiled at her from those unusual green eyes, his mouth lifting at the corners, she had felt her body respond to his physical magnetism. Tall, perfectly proportioned, he moved his long legs with an athlete's rhythmic grace. She liked, too, the way his fair hair tended to curl at the nape of his neck. It might have looked effeminate, but for the strong face with its long, straight nose and firm jaw, now tilted a little to one side as he awaited her answer. The thought flashed through her mind that he would look as perfect without his clothes – a perfectly cut City suit which hung easily from broad, straight shoulders.

Conscious of the fact that she had been assessing Sir Simon Calverley on a purely sexual basis, Emma reminded herself sharply that she couldn't afford any diversions. Her career in television was and must remain the number one priority if she were to achieve her ultimate aim – to be a producer. Derek had said that it was only a matter of time; that meanwhile she was gaining useful experience and as soon as he could, he would recommend her for promotion.

'I'm sorry, but I have to correlate my notes tonight. Thanks again for setting up the interview, Sir Simon.'

Her tone of voice was dismissive, but she had underrated Simon Calverley's determination. It had taken him less than an hour, he was reflecting, for him to fall totally under this girl's spell. She was quite astonishingly attractive – a heart-shaped face framed by light brown hair cut in a neat, geometric style; large brown eyes; small nose and wide, curved mouth above a somewhat square cut, stubborn little chin. Her figure was perfectly proportioned, but not obviously defined beneath the concealing full skirt and shaggy long loosely knit pullover. Very much a 'media' young woman, he judged – probably in her late twenties or early thirties, educated, intelligent and capable, but the veneer was very occasionally obvious, as for example when Joanne had corrected her 'Mister Calverley' to 'Sir Simon Calverley'. She had actually blushed! He, of course, had quickly put her at ease saying that there was no reason why she should have been aware of the title, at which point she had argued with astonishing vehemence against herself, saying that she should have done her research more thoroughly. He had been intrigued – and now he persisted:

'Some other night, Miss Foster? You name your next free evening and I'll fit in with it.'

'Ready to go, Emma!' said the cameraman coming towards them. Emma hesitated. After all, it was a bit stupid to turn down what would clearly be a good dinner simply because she'd made a rule never to date a man she might fancy! She was no teenager who couldn't cope if he did make a pass! Moreover, she could always cancel an appointment at the last minute if she changed her mind about going out with him.

'I could probably manage next Wednesday,' she said with a pretence of studying her Filofax. In fact, she had no evening dates before then.

'I have your work number,' Simon said quickly. 'I'll ring you Tuesday to confirm time and place.'

There was a half-smile on his face as he escorted her to the lift and Emma, conscious once again of its attraction, tightened her mouth. He was probably married anyway, she told herself. Men of his age usually were – or else they were gay, or divorced with three children! Even if he were not, men with titles were no more her scene than were merchant bankers. Her world was television, directors, producers, technicians, cameramen, writers. She would have nothing in common with this man and she had been a fool to accept his invitation.

That evening, however, as Emma settled down in front of the television set with her usual supper tray and a pile of notes to try and put together an outline script, she felt the customary mood of depression take hold of her. As her flatmate, Lucy, so often said, she could not become a lonely old spinster at her age! Night after night spent alone in the flat was not on – she was getting into a rut which, said Lucy, she would soon not be able to get out of. Lucy, herself, was never without a date and shared her evenings between three different boyfriends.

Sometimes she was out all night and she was certainly away every weekend. Emma supposed she probably slept with one or other of the young men who drifted in and out of the flat they shared in Shepherd's Bush. Lucy temped for a living and although she seemed to be able to earn quite large sums of money, she did not want the responsibility of owning her own place.

Two years ago, when Paul had finally moved out, Lucy had answered Emma's advertisement for a flat-sharer and they had managed to get along fairly well despite the differences in their characters. Lucy had no set aim in life and liked to drift from one job to another or from one man to another, whereas Emma had been very much a 'one-man-woman', and certainly a 'one-job-woman', and had put all her energies and resources into making a success of both aspects of her life.

How mistaken she had been in the first, in Paul, she thought with a bitterness which she was still not fully able to master. In fact, the break-up of their affair had been the best possible thing and Derek had been delighted. He'd taken her out to dinner, encouraged her to talk her heart out and behaved much as a beloved parent might have done. Not that he looked anywhere near old enough to be her father. Despite the fact that there was a liberal sprinkling of grey hairs amongst the dark brown, he was fanatical about keeping fit and his short, somewhat stocky build was enhanced by the very latest designer gear. One of his dictums was that people often judged others by their appearance and that to be well turned out indicated a willingness to pay attention to detail. Emma always looked stunning, he told her, and he'd been impressed by her appearance when he first interviewed her.

There was no doubt that Derek was a very attractive man – and worldly-wise. After Paul's casual indifference – unless they were in bed – Derek's fatherly concern for her had been an enormous consolation. It was not as if she had her own parents to turn to. Eight years ago her father, a brilliant scientist, had been invited to work on the space research programme in the States and her mother, a talented biologist, had gone with him. At the time, Emma had wanted to accompany them but, after a year at a crammers, she had finally managed to obtain high enough A level grades to get a place at Bristol University, and her parents were adamant that she should not forgo this further step in the education that they had planned for her.

At first she had been bitterly disappointed and wondered how she would manage without them; but by dint of hard slogging she had scraped through her exams and then she had met Paul. Perhaps because of him, she had ceased to be single-minded about her work and had only achieved a third. Her parents had been unable to conceal their disappointment which Emma could understand. Her elder sister, Rosalind, had been a gifted student and, with little effort, had obtained a double first. Clearly, Rosalind had been destined to follow in their mother's footsteps until tragedy had struck, and she had been killed in an automobile accident in the States shortly after she had gone to live with their parents. Emma, who had loved and revered her clever sister all her life, had desperately wanted to go to the funeral, but her parents had not wanted her to interrupt the much-needed revision she was currently engaged on that week before her finals.

Somehow, her plan to visit them after she had acquired her indifferent degree had become indefinitely postponed. They had been too busy to come to England and knowing their disappointment at her failure to get a good degree, she had felt reluctant to face them. They had been unenthusiastic when she wrote of her plans to work in television and she did not feel strong enough to confront them with the argument that she would infinitely prefer to be top in her chosen profession than have a third-rate job connected with the sciences at which they – and Rosalind – had excelled.

So the years had slipped by with only an irregular exchange of letters. She determined that when she did finally make the trip, she would have some positive achievement to offer them as some small compensation for the loss of their other daughter for whom they had had such high hopes. For a while, her attempts to get work in television had met with depressing failure, but then the job of production assistant in Derek's team became vacant and when she had been chosen from twenty other applicants, she had jumped at the chance to begin her career. It had been the right decision. It was only two years before Derek had taken her on as his researcher when he had vetoed the renewal of poor Eloise's contract.

Emma preferred not to remember her predecessor, a plump, plain girl not unlike the one she had been interviewing today. Eloise was highly efficient and had been with Derek for years but, as Derek said, their personalities didn't 'click' and he found working with Emma a lot more productive. Eloise had been quite disturbingly vitriolic about her dismissal.

'You think he wants you because you're more efficient than I am. Well, think again, Emma Foster. You flutter your eyelashes at him and wear those see-through shirts and play hard to get and he's fallen for it. I've seen the way he looks at you! Just wait till he gets tired of you and sends you packing – and he will if you don't sleep with him. But perhaps that's what you mean to do – you're certainly ambitious enough not to let a few morals stand in your way . . .'

Emma had had to push Eloise out of the room for she was fast becoming hysterical. Fortunately Derek, who had heard most of it, had come in and told her not to give Eloise another thought.

'The poor woman has been hopelessly in love with me for years!' he said reassuringly. 'Naturally, she was jealous of you – you're a very attractive girl – and she, poor thing, is the proverbial woman scorned. You've got brains as well as looks, Emma, and that's what interests me – brains and talent.'

Those words had been very comforting. She had never considered herself as 'brainy'. Rosalind had been the clever one. It had been of little consolation to her to know that people considered her the prettier of the two sisters nor that she was attractive to the opposite sex and that if she wanted any favours, she could usually get them; but she wanted a career and not via a stream of casting couches. As Derek had said, being attractive helped smooth a lot of rough edges, but it couldn't get you to the top if you lacked ability.

Paul – the drama student she had met at Bristol – had been a distraction to her otherwise single-minded purpose. She had fallen hopelessly in love with him, and not even the slow revelation of his feckless, weak, amoral nature had been sufficient to release her from her bondage to him. Perhaps Derek was right and it had been a sexual bondage. Whatever its content, she had forgiven Paul again and again – for stealing money from her; for being unfaithful to her; for taking the drugs he had sworn to give up; for not turning up on time; for not telephoning when he had promised to do so; for letting her down; most of all, for not seeming to care enough about her to realize that he was breaking her heart.

At the time, Derek had offered her a week's holiday to get over it, but she had preferred to work, knowing that the less time she had to think about Paul the better. Gradually, the work itself had taken his place, absorbing all mental and physical energies, and Derek had promised that next year when her contract came up for renewal he would use his influence to get her promoted to the more senior job of assistant producer. No man – certainly not Sir Simon Calverley – was going to put that prospect in jeopardy.

On the morning of the following Wednesday, Emma made up her mind she would have a last-minute migraine and instruct Lucy to tell her date when he arrived that she could not after all go out to dinner with him. By the time she had finished work and got back to her flat, she was not only exhausted but very late. Derek had wanted her to discuss a new documentary with him over a drink and the session had taken longer than she had expected. Outside the flat was a gleaming navy-blue Porsche, and inside was Simon Calverley, comfortably seated in one of the armchairs, enjoying a drink.

'Least I could do, pal!' Lucy whispered as with a wink, she shoved a large whisky into Emma's hand. Simon rose to his feet and said easily:

'Your kind friend has been entertaining me!'

'I'm dreadfully sorry!' Emma apologized. 'I was working and—'

'Calm down. There's no hurry. I've booked for eight-thirty, but we can eat any time. Now you look as if you could do with that drink!'

'I'll be happy to hold the fort whilst you change, darling!' Lucy said. 'Simon and I have discovered mutual friends in Sussex so we really aren't boring each other!'

Simon laughed and Emma felt the tension leave her body. As she went off to shower and change, she reflected that she had possibly misjudged this man, supposing that, since he was a banker, he would be stuffy, pompous, and probably not endowed with a sense of humour. It was silly to typecast people when really their jobs were not necessarily indicative of their natures. Remembering the Porsche, however, she had been right in assuming that he would turn out to be moneyed as well as titled!

He took her to an unpretentious but expensive French restaurant just off the King's Road, recommended various dishes which proved to be very much to her taste, and chose excellent wines. The meal was long-drawn out because, somewhat to Emma's surprise, they did a great deal of talking, first about her and her job, and then about Simon Calverley's family home in Sussex. It was, she soon realized, by way of being an obsession with him. There was a special note in his voice when he mentioned the house which, had it applied to a woman, would have betrayed a deep, abiding love.

'Ortolans first came into our family in the 1500s,' he told her. 'Queen Elizabeth gave a parcel of land and a title to a young man who had distinguished himself on the high seas.' He smiled disarmingly. 'Records don't relate what deeds of bravery warranted the award, but I suspect it was an act of piracy which embellished the Queen's coffers! In any event, this fellow, Richard Calverley, decided to build a house on the land he'd been given and bring his young wife down from Yorkshire where he had been born and settle in Sussex. Calverleys have lived there ever since. Interestingly enough, I still have the old deed granting the baronetcy to him.'

Emma was genuinely fascinated.

'A year ago, we did a programme on the theme of domestic work today as compared with the drudgery of domestic work in the past. Someone else did the modern kitchens – dishwashers, food mixers – that kind of thing; and I was responsible for the "as-it-used-to-be" part of the documentary. Of course, I went to the obvious places like the Brighton Pavilion where they have that magnificent exhibition of a Georgian kitchen, but I also visited a number of old houses round the country where, despite the modernization, one could still see what drudgery it must have been in olden days. Derek was very pleased because we had a crop of letters from viewers saying they had never really appreciated how lucky they were! We did a repeat last summer.'

Simon looked at the glowing face of his dinner companion and was intrigued by the transformation that took place whenever Emma spoke of her work. When she was not thus animated, her expression was somehow guarded, speculative – almost, he thought, as if she were protecting herself from a verbal attack! He was pleased with himself as the evening wore on for having broken down that reserve and seen glimpses of what he took to be the real girl behind the image she chose to portray.

By the time they were drinking coffee, he had learned that Emma's parents lived in the States; that she shared her flat with the effervescent Lucy; that her career was the most important thing in her life; that she was twenty-eight years old; that she valued her independence and – not least – the absence of a man in her life. She had volunteered no information whatever about past boyfriends although he was in no doubt that such an attractive girl must have had several. Emma, like himself, had grown up in a permissive age when the old-fashioned ideas had all but disappeared. He himself had led a fairly colourful existence, although he had never been specifically trendy except for a brief period at university. He had gone straight into Steinfeld Galt, the merchant bank of which he was now a director, where long-haired, kaftan-wearing employees were not exactly acceptable! Emma had laughed when he had made this comment.

'So you knew from the start that this was what you wanted to do with your life,' she said, and was surprised when Simon shook his head.

'On the contrary, my career has only ever been a means to an end. I needed money, you see, and since I had a degree in maths and economics, merchant banking was the obvious place to make it.' Seeing her expression, he added: 'I haven't been chasing the silver dollar in order to enjoy The Good Life, although it would be silly to pretend that I don't love owning my Porsche and renting a fairly decent flat in Brunswick Square. But I don't hanker after yachts or holidays in Barbados or any of the usual status symbols. I need the money to restore Ortolans. There was a time when the Calverleys were very well heeled. They even owned Detcham, the village, and hundreds of acres of land. These were gradually sold off post the First and Second World Wars when the family fortunes declined.'

Sensing Emma's interest, he continued:

'My father died before I was born and my mother, an American, soon after. My grandparents were already dead, and I was brought up by my great-grandmother, a fantastic old lady who by then was living in the east wing of the house. We'd been crippled by death duties and when the Labour government shoved such a huge tax on unearned income – which is what my family had survived on – we had to sell everything but the house and four acres of garden. Fortunately, my great-grandmother had set up an educational covenant for

me and so I had a decent schooling, but the house slowly
went into a state of decay. There simply wasn't the cash to
do the necessary repairs – and these old houses are always in
need of repair, let alone cash for overall restoration. Gradually,
I'm getting Ortolans back into shape and one day, I hope to
be able to retire and live there, get married, raise a family. If
I don't, the Calverleys will die out with me.'

Emma had very firmly resolved that this date with Simon
Calverley was to be a one-off meeting – one she would in no
case repeat, but now that resolve weakened. Perhaps it was
the brandy, she thought, on top of the wines. When Simon
suggested that she might like to pay a visit to his house the
following weekend, her 'no' was half-hearted and when, as
he dropped her at the front door of her flat, he repeated the
invitation, she heard herself agreeing to go.

'I'll pick you up at around eleven on Saturday morning,'
he said, making no attempt to kiss her, but retaining hold of
her hand. 'It's a fairly quick run down there. If you didn't
want to stay over the weekend, there's an excellent train service
from Hassocks. Bring plenty of warm clothes. If the weather's
cold, the place can be like a barn!'

Lucy was agog with enthusiasm when next evening, she
questioned Emma about her 'new boyfriend'.

'A Porsche, a title and a fantastic mansion in Sussex – what
more can you want, darling, and he's fabulously good-looking.
I'm green with envy!'

'Well, you can stop thinking what I know you are thinking!'
Emma said firmly, 'Once and for all, Lucy, I am not looking
for a husband and I am not looking for a lover. A friend,
perhaps, but there it has to stay. Anyway, it's pretty obvious
Simon must already have a girlfriend. He isn't married and
he definitely isn't gay, so it stands to reason there's someone
in his life.'

'All's fair in love and war!' Lucy giggled. 'You're quite
bonkers, Emma. Eligible bachelors don't grow on trees. Snap
him up – that's what I say!'

'Lucy, for heaven's sake – I've only met the wretched man twice! It's his house I am interested in – not him.'

'Tell that to the marines!' Lucy said, tossing her long fair hair and disappearing into the tiny kitchen to heat up a pizza for her supper.

For some reason Emma did not try to define, she did not tell Derek about her weekend plans. When he invited her to *Starlight Express*, for which he had managed to obtain complimentary tickets on the Saturday night, she found herself muttering a distinct lie about a previous date with Lucy.

'Put her off, Emma!' he said frowning. 'Tell her it's work. It's damned hard to get seats for *Starlight Express*, and you'd enjoy the show.'

Emma knew Derek did not mean to make it sound like an order, but it was sometimes difficult to distinguish between their daily working relationship and off-duty occasions. His manner was always proprietorial, which, after all, was only to be expected, Emma realized, since he was her boss. If someone else from a different department needed a helping hand, they naturally asked Derek if they could 'borrow' her, and stupid as it might seem, it always pleased her when he refused, saying he could not spare her – even if it did make her sound like a piece of office furniture.

'I really can't, Derek!' she said now. 'I'm sorry!'

Derek could look pretty intimidating at times, she thought as she went out of his office to find her cameraman. He had very clear blue eyes which could turn steely when he was angry – and he could be extremely temperamental, especially if he had had a few drinks. He did drink quite heavily but not, so far as Emma knew, to excess. He could drink three double whiskies to her single and still retain that sharp, incisive thinking which made him so successful a producer. From time to time, he would disappear to Champneys to lose a stone and lay off the alcohol.

Emma was aware that not everyone hit it off with Derek. He could be intolerant of inefficiency. She had heard him called vain, autocratic, self-opinionated and ruthless – but she felt the criticisms were unfair. He could be – and frequently was – extremely critical if he thought her work did not meet the required standards. He reminded her of her father whose favourite expression had always been: 'You could do better if you tried harder, Emma!' At such times, Emma was always painfully aware that she had tried her hardest, but simply lacked what was needed to meet the high standards required of her.

There was no denying Derek's vanity, but Emma felt this small weakness was justified by his ability, which no one questioned. An Australian by birth, he had come to England as a journalist, found his way into television and quickly made his way to the top. Although not known to the public by face, his programmes were household words. *In Our Times* was but one of his many successes with a particular appeal to female audiences. Much of the criticism levelled against Derek was, she felt, prompted by jealousy. A lot of people envied his ability and resented his success; but she knew the side of Derek unconnected with his work; knew how sensitive he was, how kind, how supportive, asking only dedication to her work in return. It was typical of Lucy to say that Derek 'fancied her rotten' and was simply biding his time. He had never once propositioned her and in any event, he had his steady girl-friend. In a way, she reflected, it was silly of her not to have told Derek about Simon, but she had not felt in need of the caution he would undoubtedly have advised – to steer clear of a man she found so physically attractive – since she had already made up her mind not to get involved. Nevertheless the fact that she had skirted round the truth made her uneasy.

On the Friday evening whilst she was drying her newly washed hair, Lucy put her head round the door.

'Just off to Stringfellow's!' she announced. 'Expect me when you see me!'

There was a frown on Emma's face as she switched off her hairdrier.

'Lucy, do me a favour. If by any chance you should bump into Derek, will you bear me out that you and I have a date tomorrow night? I don't suppose you will but – just in case . . .?'

Lucy's small round face took on an exaggerated expression of disapproval.

'Naughty, naughty!' she said brightly. 'Who's been telling porkies then?' She laughed and then shook her head. 'Anyone would think that boss of yours owned you, Emma. Why on earth didn't you tell him you were off for a dirty weekend with the best-looking man in London!'

'Because I'm not off for "a dirty weekend" and I don't think Simon Calverley is all *that* good-looking. Anyway, I just don't want Derek getting any mistaken ideas that I'm becoming involved. He's always emphasizing the fact that I'm single-minded about my work and don't get sidetracked like so many other girls do.'

Lucy shrugged. 'Darling, you've told me all that crap before. If a man wants you to be single-minded, you can bet it's about him! Now I must fly, I'll be late. See you in the morning!'

The trouble with Lucy, Emma thought, as she picked up the case notes she would have to work on tonight since she would not have time to go through them tomorrow, was her conviction that everything was sex orientated. Perhaps to the kind of men with whom Lucy associated – and, indeed to Lucy herself – sex was all-important. She herself could do very well without it – and had for the past three years. As Derek had so often said, she was a career woman, and unless a man contributed in some way to that career, he simply did not come into the equation. Being well turned out, having verbal flirtations or exchanging dirty stories with Pete or one of the technicians was no more than a convenient way of ensuring that they liked her. She knew only too well how obstructive such chaps could be when they disliked the women they had to obey. As Derek so truly said, a clever woman could always get her own way if she was charming as well as attractive; that obvious feminism antagonized men. After Paul, she had tended to be a bit brittle and blatantly cynical, and it had been Derek who, in the nicest possible way, had straightened her out.

'We aren't all shits, you know, Emma. Keep your femininity – it's a valuable asset!'

Tomorrow, she reflected as she picked up her pen, was in many ways going to be a complete waste of time, and time was a commodity she was always short of. On the other hand, the weekends could be pretty dreary, more especially if Lucy were away which, as often as not, she was. It was difficult to enjoy the telly since she now found it difficult to view a programme without mentally editing it! The novels she had consumed as a young girl no longer interested her as invariably they had heroines whose only aim in life was to find love; and there was a limit to the number of autobiographies about women achievers. Most were about men, and the Florence Nightingales, Amy Johnsons and Vera Brittains had achieved against entirely different odds to those facing her in her career.

Although Emma loved London and would not want to live anywhere but near the studio, she had spent most of her childhood at a boarding school in the country in a remote corner of Hertfordshire. In the spring and autumn especially, she longed for the sight and smell of trees and flowers, of hay drying in the sun, and bonfires. Simon Calverley's house in Sussex sounded interesting and it would do her good to get out of town, breathe some fresh air and discover exactly what this man did with his spare time. It was difficult to imagine the dark-suited, conventionally dressed man-about-town in country gear. In all probability, he belonged to the green-welly brigade and wore immaculately tailored tweeds and a Barbour!

Realizing that it was now eight o'clock and that she had done no work at all, Emma firmly put Simon Calverley and his house out of her mind, and settled down to her notes for *Women in Financial Careers*.

CHAPTER TWENTY-NINE

1986

At Emma's first sight of Ortolans, the house was bathed in a hazy autumn sunshine. Its contours were distorted by a vast tarpaulin covering one of the wings.

'I'm having that part of the roof repaired,' Simon explained as he switched off the car engine. He unfolded his long legs from beneath the dashboard and with quick easy strides, came round to open the passenger door and helped Emma out. His arm still lightly supporting her elbow, he gazed upwards at the large stone slabs that made up the roof.

'They call it Horsham slab because that's where the stone is quarried,' he explained. 'Imagine it surviving all these years! Unfortunately, the supporting timbers have been eaten away by woodworm and Rentokil said they were too damaged to carry the weight safely. So we're having to have new timbers put in before we can replace the slabs!'

'But it's beautiful!' Emma gasped, and realizing that this might sound as if she had not expected it, she added quickly: 'I'd not imagined the house to be so large . . . so old! You'd told me it was beamed and had mullioned windows, but I suppose I had not conceived such . . . such a perfect example of Elizabethan architecture. It's lovely, Simon.'

He was smiling with obvious pleasure at her halting attempts to express her admiration.

'I suppose a lot of people might see Ortolans as a tumble-down old ruin,' he said disparagingly. 'In a way, it is; but later on I'll show you a picture of my home as it used to be before the war. Of course, you have to like old houses really to appreciate its charm.'

Emma gazed at the gentle curves of the roof, the weathered pattern of the oak beams and warm red brick of the front façade with its sheltering L-shaped wings and, for a moment, had the fantasy that it was holding out its arms as if to embrace its visitors. Then she smiled at her whimsy. Simon was no visitor. He belonged here. If the house was welcoming anyone, it would be him, one of the Calverleys who had lived here for so many generations.

She glanced at him, seeing him suddenly in a new light. Gone was the dark-suited merchant banker. Here was the squire, fair-haired, green-eyed, handsome, very much the titled aristocrat, unassuming in faded blue jeans and a black polo-necked sweater with a gaping hole in one elbow. As he assisted Emma from the car, a piece of wool unravelled from the ribbing caught in the buckle of her belt. He gave a very boyish grin.

'Don't tell me, I ought to get it mended. It's a favourite, I'm afraid, and I can't bring myself to chuck it away!'

Emma returned his smile.

'Seems you have a distinct leaning towards things old!' she said. 'I really love the pale grey colour of those oak beams.'

Simon grimaced.

'There'll be no beams left if Tom doesn't get those creepers cut back. Trouble is, he's a bit old for ladders. I expect I'll end up doing the job myself!'

Old Tom, he explained as he pushed open the heavy oak door, was the ancient family retainer who came in from the village to 'keep an eye on the garden'.

'He's one of the Pylbeams who have lived in Detcham as long as we have,' Simon said. 'In the old days, nearly all our servants were Pylbeams and those who weren't, were builders. Tom's the only one still "in service" as he puts it. He's great-uncle to my architect, Roddy, who you'll meet this afternoon – a good chap, and damned good at his job!'

He kicked aside a pile of cardboard cartons littering the floor of the dark, dusty hall and grinned.

Those fabulous green eyes all but disappear when he smiles! Emma thought irrelevantly, conscious once more of the immediate effect it had upon her. Telling herself that the sinking sensation in the pit of her stomach was due to her skipping breakfast, she forced her thoughts back to what Simon was saying.

'Hazel seems to think the only cleaning she need do is in the rooms that are habitable. She's the unmarried mum who does – or is supposed to do – for me! She has the attic flat for herself and her three-year-old – a little girl called Vicky. Frankly, I sometimes wonder why I let Hazel stay on. She never does any real work!'

As if on cue, a young girl with pink dyed hair came wandering into the hall, a cigarette dangling from one hand, a small child clinging to the other.

'Whatcha!' she greeted her employer. 'Thought I heard the car. For God's sake, Vicky, let go of my hand. She seems to be going through a ghastly clinging stage!' she added to Emma as if she had known her all her life.

'This is Emma Foster – Hazel and Vicky!' Simon said. 'I hope you've got some lunch for us, Hazel? And the fire lit in the drawing-room as I asked!'

'Yea, no problem!' the girl said nodding. It was her standard affirmative, Simon explained later. 'Want some coffee?'

The child now stood staring up at Emma with huge, liquid black eyes. Her skin was a deep golden brown and she was quite remarkably beautiful, Emma thought – or might have been but for a runny nose and a nasty sore on one side of her mouth.

As her mother dragged her back towards what Emma supposed were the kitchen quarters, Simon said:

'The father was a Singalese – a university student of very good family. Needless to say, his family hotfooted him smartly back to Sri Lanka when they found out he'd got Hazel pregnant. Her parents turned her out once they realized the child was coloured. The Job Centre sent her to me when I said I wanted a live-in housekeeper – and frankly I was silly enough to take her on. That was three years ago and I haven't had the heart to turn her out – because of the kid, I suppose!'

He opened the door on Emma's left. Her eyes widened in admiration as he drew her inside the room. A log fire blazed in the huge stone fireplace. Sunshine poured through the leaded light windows and gleamed on some of the most beautiful antique furniture she had ever seen. Big comfortable armchairs had been newly covered in a primrose yellow linen which seemed to tone perfectly with the dark oak beams. On the wide polished oak floorboards were scattered some faded, but still beautiful, Persian rugs.

'Like it?' Simon asked with a pleased grin at the obvious approval on Emma's face. 'This and my bedroom are the only rooms I have so far been able to decorate and furnish as I want. It seems to be taking a lifetime, but gradually, Ortolans is returning to its former glory.'

'I'm beginning to understand why it's so important to you!' Emma said.

Simon nodded.

'It's been my ambition to restore it – ever since my great-grandmother died when I was fifteen. She was in her nineties and nearly blind, but her mind was as clear as crystal. She had a fantastic memory, and when she read passages to me from a kind of family diary that has passed down the generations, she would elaborate with all kinds of fascinating anecdotes. The morning she died, she virtually handed over the house to me. "You're only young," she said, "but old enough to understand that the safe keeping of this house will very soon now lie in your hands. Take care of it – and Ortolans will take care of you. It has always looked after those who love it".'

He glanced at Emma with an apologetic smile.

'That isn't quite as fanciful as it sounds. There have been many incidents in the past when the house has saved the family from disaster, or saved a marriage. Great-Gran swore that it saved hers – and she and my great-grandfather were totally devoted.'

'Is that her portrait?' Emma asked with genuine interest as she pointed to a large oil painting at the far end of the room.

Simon nodded.

'That was done shortly after the birth of my grandfather. She would have been about twenty-one at the time. She was quite a beauty, with green eyes, flaming red hair and a volatile nature to go with it! I adored her. We lived in one wing which was all we could afford to maintain. In one way, it was all the more fun for me. I was always allowed to invite my school friends in the holidays and we had the run of the house without fear of doing much damage. Of course, we ran wild in the gardens, too. Great-Gran never fussed – except about manners. We had to be punctual for meals and be – well – moderately clean!'

So he had inherited those fantastic green eyes from his great-grandmother! Emma thought as she listened with growing interest. Not only was his story unusual, but he himself seemed quite another person than the dark-suited, impeccably dressed banker who, with his able personal assistant, juggled hundreds of thousands of pounds of other people's cash as if it were Monopoly money.

'Let's go out while the sun is still shining,' he said. 'I'd like to show you the old stables – and then we can walk down through the field to the river. There aren't many fish in it now, but Great-Gran said it used to be full of trout before the days of pollution.'

'You mean acid rain?' Emma asked as they went out to the hall to put on their wellingtons.

'Not just that. There's a soap factory a few miles upriver and despite all our protests and the regulations, every now and again they discharge waste into it. You should do a programme one of these days on conservation. Maybe with a bit more publicity, people will really start caring about the way we are destroying our world.'

'I'll talk to my boss about it,' Emma said. 'At present I don't have much say in the type of documentary we choose to do, although Derek does let me spout ideas from time to time.'

As they went out through a door on to a brick path which led to a cobbled courtyard, Hazel appeared from another doorway.

'If you're going for a walk, can Vicky go with you? I'll get on better without her under my feet!'

Simon shrugged his shoulders in a gesture of resignation.

'Hope you don't mind!' he said to Emma. 'I feel sorry for the kid – no one to play with. When I'm down for the weekend, I usually let her tag along. She's not much trouble.'

It quickly became clear to Emma that this man had yet a further unexpected facet to his nature – he was obviously child-orientated. The little girl adored him and clung to his hand with a permanent expression of joy. She spoke very little when Simon pointed out to her a passing bird and gave its name, but nodded as if the information were of the utmost importance to her.

'Seems to remember most of what I tell her!' Simon said as they walked along an overgrown brick path past the tumble-down stable block towards a gate into the field. He picked a twig from a tree and handed it to the child.

'What's that, Vicky?' he asked. 'Do you know?'

'Mulberry!' said Vicky without hesitation. Emma, who had not known the answer, was amused when Simon nodded approvingly.

'She's quite bright for her age,' he said in a low voice as the little girl ran ahead of them. 'Not that it will get her far. Hazel couldn't be less interested. I sometimes wonder why she did not have the child adopted. Her idea of bringing up her offspring is to sit it in front of the telly!'

'Perhaps Hazel didn't realize what it would be like,' Emma suggested. 'A small baby asleep in a cot is a very different thing to a toddler demanding time and attention. And Hazel is very young still, isn't she? I expect she wants a bit more out of life than domestic work and minding Vicky.'

Simon gave her a quick glance.

'You mean a career of some sort? I doubt it. Hazel couldn't manage even one O level. From what she tells me, she was always truant from school, left when she was fifteen and got a job in Lewes in a supermarket. That was where she met Vicky's father. He was a university student and was studying English and Economics. I don't think he realized quite how brainless poor Hazel was . . . or perhaps he didn't care. We know he came from a very wealthy Singalese family and could afford to give Hazel the good time she wanted. I don't suppose for one moment he ever considered marrying her. She hoped he would. Anyway, her parents would have nothing to do with him – colour prejudice, I'm afraid – and when Vicky arrived, all golden brown, that was it. Out she had to go.'

'Hazel's quite pretty – in a way,' Emma said. 'Perhaps she'll find a husband to take on her and the child. It happens.'

Vicky's return made further mention of her impossible and the conversation turned to birds, first the kingfishers which nested every year in the riverbank; and then to the ortolans, from whom the house had derived its name, but which were now no longer to be seen in the fields. Far from being bored – as Emma had told Lucy she anticipated – the morning passed quickly, and immediately after lunch Roddy, the architect, arrived. He was a pleasant, unpretentious young man with sandy hair and eyebrows, and somewhat dreamy blue eyes, and Simon seemed to set great store by him. When he disappeared to the library to discuss something with Simon, Emma was left to browse through *The Calverley Journal* – a document she found fascinating. Almost reluctantly, she put it down when the two men returned, Roddy to say a polite goodbye and Simon to say that Hazel would be bringing in tea.

'If you are still determined to go back to London, Roddy says he can give you a lift into Hassocks,' he said. 'However, I hope you won't rush off. There's lots more to show you!'

'Then I'll stay on,' Emma said without hesitation. 'I do have work to do – but for once, it can wait!'

Simon looked pleased.

'I'll tell Hazel to get the fire lit in the spare room – we've no central heating as yet, although it's on the agenda, isn't it, Roddy! These old houses can get incredibly cold on autumn nights – and positively arctic in the winter. At least I do have an electric blanket for female guests!'

So he has other women down here! Emma thought as he disappeared with the departing Roddy. Not that that should surprise her. Obviously she was not his only girlfriend – even if that were the right description for her since she had no intention of allowing this friendship to develop. Nevertheless, her curiosity was aroused, and by the time they had finished supper – a spaghetti bolognese proudly produced by Simon himself – they were on sufficiently relaxed terms for Emma to steer the conversation to a more personal level.

'With so many family traditions to uphold, I presume you don't intend to let the Calverley name die out!' she said. She was curled up, her feet tucked beneath her, in one of the outsize armchairs, a glass of Cointreau in one hand, the other supporting an old photograph album on her lap. Simon, opposite her, had his feet stretched out towards the cheerful flames of a large log fire.

'It would be a pity – and poor Great-Gran would turn in her grave – if I didn't produce an heir!' He smiled. 'To be serious, I shall get married one of these days. For the present, I'm too busy trying to earn the cash to do what I want with Ortolans. I suppose if the right girl came along . . . but she'd have to fall in love with this house as well as with me! And want kids, of course. As a matter of fact, I suppose I might have got married if Cilla . . .' He broke off as if suddenly aware that he was talking to a comparative stranger. Then he added: 'Cilia's an extremely nice girl. We've known each other for donkey's years – since we were at university. I suppose there was a time when we both thought we might get married; but Cilia's a "town" person – adores London and all that goes with life in a big city. A weekend down here is about as much as she can stand! She's in business – lives in a mews cottage, all tubs and hanging baskets, and runs a gift shop full of trendy presents in the Fulham Road.'

He looked at Emma curiously.

'I've told you about me – now what about you? Why aren't you married, Emma Foster? I am sure there has been no lack of candidates?'

Although Emma would not have believed that she could talk to anyone but Lucy or Derek about Paul, she now found herself doing so – and with far more candour than she intended when she began.

'I suppose – being wise with hindsight – I always knew Paul was no good,' she heard herself saying. 'I was so much in love with him, I just didn't want to see the rotten side of him. He was my first Big Affair and for ages, I went on forgiving him in the ridiculous hope that he really didn't mean to be such a . . . a bastard. And he was such a plausible liar! Whilst I . . . I was naïve to a degree and about as gullible as they come. Anyway, he walked out and that was that. It was a godsend, really. He stood between me and what I most want – to succeed in my career. I've been very lucky – having an understanding boss like Derek. You must meet him some time, Simon. I think you'd like him!'

Even as she heard herself speak, Emma realized that the two men had nothing whatever in common. Derek was most certainly not country-minded, although he had a house in Gerrards Cross where he spent most weekends. Not that he spent his time tramping over fields with gumboots and gun dogs! The house would be filled with weekend guests – writers, directors, actors and their various appendages. He believed in entertaining 'people who mattered' and did so in lavish style – good food, unlimited champagne, caterers to do the work. He was always inviting Emma to go down to these parties but first because of Paul and, after Paul, because she felt too emotionally drained to cope with so many strangers, she had so far declined. No, she thought, Derek and Simon would not automatically be friends . . . which really was of no significance since she did not intend to get involved with Simon Calverley, nice as he had turned out to be.

Simon, who had been watching Emma's expressive face with growing interest as she talked, was aware of the tightening of her mouth, the stiffening of her body as she said firmly:

'By this time next year, I hope to be an assistant producer. It's what I want more than anything in the world and nothing – absolutely nothing – is going to stand in my way.'

'So we have one thing in common – a burning ambition!' he said with a lightness of tone that belied the seriousness of his voice. 'I to restore my home and you to further your career!'

Emma nodded. If Simon had ideas about her, he would now know exactly where he stood. Somehow she did not think he would be prepared to hang around in the wings waiting for the few odd occasions she could spare him! In any event, it sounded as if he already had a girlfriend.

'Tell me more about Cilla,' she said. 'Is her shop her ambition?'

'No, I wouldn't say it was,' Simon replied. 'It's more a means to earn a living. When I first met her, she was set on being an interior designer . . . but I suppose she just didn't have the necessary flair. Of course, like most women, she wants to get married.'

It was on the tip of Emma's tongue to ask: 'Married to you, Simon?' but she bit back the words. This man was still a virtual stranger and it was not for her to be interested in his love-life.

Simon remained silent, consumed once more by the familiar feeling of guilt that always overcame him when he thought of Cilla. They had had an on-off affair for over five years. In the beginning, they had shared a flat and got along very well – particularly in bed. Sex had been very much the overriding factor in their lives, but gradually the relationship had deteriorated. Cilia had become increasingly possessive – started to talk about marriage which by then he'd realized could never be on the cards. In a way it was the house which had come between them. Cilia resented the time he spent at Ortolans but equally, he had resented her rejection of anything to do with the country. She had frequently infuriated him by her totally illogical statement that even the weather was worse at Detcham than in London! Finally, they had agreed to part company. He'd moved out of the Fulham flat into another in Brunswick Square. Inevitably, they had missed the regularity of the sexual side of their relationship and although they had kept their individual flats, Cilia often spent the night with him. He suspected that she still hoped that one day they might get together again, but too lazy – or was it selfish? – to tackle the future, he had allowed things to drift. There had been a brief interlude when she had found herself another boyfriend, but it had not worked out and once again, against his better judgement, he'd allowed their relationship to be renewed.

Glancing at Emma, realizing how much he had been looking forward to this third meeting with her, he knew that he must make the break with Cilia final. He had not loved her. He knew that now. He had never felt with Cilla this affinity he had shared all day with the girl sitting opposite him. He had the oddest impression that Emma belonged exactly where she now was, her hair gleaming in the firelight, partially concealing her profile, long legs in tight-fitting jeans tucked beneath her, the outline of her breasts just discernible beneath the shaggy black and white sweater. He felt a sudden urgent desire to touch her, take her in his arms, make love to her. Despite all her talk about the importance of her career, she was essentially feminine. Obviously she had been badly hurt by this Paul fellow she'd spoken of so bitterly, but that unhappy affair had ended several years ago. Her life now from all accounts was an emotional void – and he wanted to fill it. Nevertheless, he decided, it would be a mistake to try to rush things. He was not interested in a casual relationship – and if things were to develop between them, they must first be friends. He had no wish to discover when it was too late – as he had with Cilia – that he and Emma had nothing in common.

'Tell me more about Roddy Pylbeam,' she said now. 'Is he a qualified architect?'

'Just! He's still only twenty-six. His father's a builder. He wanted Roddy in the business with him as soon as he left school, but Roddy was bright and got a grant enabling him to get to college. He'd always wanted to do architecture, but with a view to specializing in the restoration of old buildings. That's why Roddy takes such an interest in this place. Frankly, I think he'd be up here lending his expertise even if I couldn't pay his fees, which thank God, I now can. He goes to endless trouble finding old beams or tiles or hinges – whatever we need to keep the repairs in period. In due course, I shall have to try and find someone with the same kind of know-how to help me with the garden. Tom does his best but he's so rheumaticky, poor old chap, he only comes up when the weather's fine.'

'I may know someone who could help,' Emma said. 'I interviewed three girls a few months ago. They'd completed a course in horticulture and had started up a business doing landscape gardening. They were having a bit of difficulty getting work because as soon as someone answered their advertisement and discovered they were girls, the assumption followed that they weren't up to doing men's work. In fact, they were all extremely capable. Maybe they would come and blitz the garden for you at cut rates!'

'I may take you up on that,' Simon said with genuine enthusiasm. 'As you know from your interview with Joanne, I'm all for equality of the sexes – although I suppose I'm old-fashioned about mothers with children staying at home to look after them . . . at least whilst they're young.'

'I agree,' Emma said vehemently, remembering how little she and her sister had seen of their mother during their childhood. 'That's why I don't intend to have children. As far as I am concerned, my career is more important to me than anything else and I'm not prepared to abandon it for the sake of having children.'

Simon regarded her speculatively.

'You say that now – but what about ten years from now? Surely you'd want kids eventually?'

Emma shrugged.

'I suppose I might. It depends how exacting my job would be by then. If – as I hope – I'm in Derek's shoes, there's no way I could cope with kids.'

'You could get a nanny or an au pair. Lots of women do. Or don't you want to be tied to a husband, either?'

'No, I don't!' Emma said without hesitation.

'Not even if he were a liberal-minded sort of chap who didn't object to your career? Perhaps even encouraged it?'

This time, Emma did not hesitate. She sensed that Simon's tone of voice did not intend to elicit a flippant reply – that he really wanted to know how she thought. Half of her resented this intrusion into her personal feelings. The other half felt irrationally excited. She told herself that it would be stupid to deny that there was a strong sexual attraction between them. She was aware of him in a way she had not been aware of any man since Paul. It was astonishing, she reflected, that without Simon having made the slightest physical approach, she was nevertheless vividly conscious of his masculine magnetism. Had she been Lucy, she thought wryly, she would have been in bed with him by now! Yet for all his reticence, she knew he found her attractive; knew from the way he looked at her, the way he was trying to reach into her thoughts, her innermost feelings.

'Anyone who says they will never do this or that is talking nonsense!' she prevaricated. 'Personally, I don't think about the future. I've quite enough on my plate worrying about the present. Which reminds me, I really must not be too late back tomorrow – I do have work to do and Derek can be pretty devastating if he thinks I've been wasting my time!'

'So your boss is a slave driver?'

Emma returned Simon's smile.

'Oh, not really! He just wants me to produce my best – and

so do I. They usually pick men for this job and there are dozens – as well as girls – waiting for the chance to step in if I fail. So even if I wanted to slack off, I couldn't afford to. As Derek says, you've got to be single-minded if you want to be a success.'

'Sounds a fairly ruthless sort of chap!' Simon murmured. Emma jumped to her boss's defence.

'One has to be a bit ruthless. Derek started from nothing so he knows how hard it is. Maybe it was easy for you – you started with certain privileges that could open doors for you. Well, Derek opened the door for me and I'm not going to let the opportunity to do what I want – be what I want – slip through my fingers.'

'So you are a bit ruthless, too!' The remark was voiced humorously, but there was no smile on Emma's face as she replied:

'No, I'm not ruthless but I am determined to succeed. I've worked hard to get this far, and I intend to go a lot further. I mean to succeed. If necessary, I will be ruthless. Derek maintains you should never keep staff who aren't efficient simply because you feel sorry for them. He says it's bound to reflect on your work.'

Simon nodded.

'It's a dog-eat-dog world out there, isn't it?' he said. 'It was different in the good old days. Great-Gran used to talk a lot about the old family retainers – in the days of upstairs, downstairs. It was a Calverley tradition – had been since the year dot – never to sack one of the staff simply because they were getting old, weren't as efficient as they used to be. They'd be found other jobs if they couldn't cope, or they'd be pensioned off. Great-Gran's old maid – another Pylbeam needless to say! – was given a little shop in the village. In those days, money wasn't a problem – and certainly not a *raison d'être*, and of course, if one footman left, there were plenty of others to replace him! I don't think Great-Gran ever understood the changes that took place after the war. I can remember her saying: "I simply don't understand why young people don't enjoy domestic service these days. Our servants were part of the family. We took care of each other!"'

'And you are still carrying on the old tradition!' Emma said quietly. 'Keeping on old Tom, for instance.'

'Well, I suppose so,' Simon acknowledged. 'I'm not so sure I'd feel the same responsibility for the unfortunate Hazel. She's not a Detcham girl, of course. Few of the people now living in the village are the old families. I must show you some pictures of Detcham as it was pre-First World War – if it would interest you!'

'It would – very much!' Emma said, rising abruptly to her feet. 'I think I'll turn in now, if it's OK with you. Must be the country air making me sleepy!'

Simon was disappointed, but endeavoured not to show it.

'Tomorrow's another day!' he said as he went to open the door for her. 'If the weather's fine, we might walk down to the village. I could show you the old church – and the family vault!'

Contradicting the forecast, the weather was appalling. It rained solidly from breakfast to tea when Simon drove Emma back to London. Despite the persistent downpour, it had been fun, Emma reflected as they reached the suburbs. In the morning, she had volunteered to help him clean the panelling in the library and dust and polish the hundreds of leather-bound books which lined one wall. The room had slowly but surely come to life. Hazel had once more foisted the child on them, but Vicky had been little trouble, sitting happily in front of the log fire playing with an old wooden horse on wheels which Simon had found in the attic. Hazel cooked a passable Sunday lunch which the four of them ate in the big, old-fashioned kitchen, after which Simon had refused Emma's further offer of help with the panelling. Instead, they had sat on the floor in the drawing-room leafing through the several hundred pages of *The Calverley Journal*. It had surprised Emma how frequently Ortolans was mentioned – almost as if the house had been a member of the family! She was, she reflected, now able to understand Simon's unusual single-minded ambition to restore it whatever the sacrifices he had to make.

'Oh, I don't spend all my ill-gotten gains on the place!' he said when she voiced her thoughts. 'I'm reasonably self-indulgent. Which brings me to the coming week, Emma. Will you have dinner with me again?'

Emma felt a surge of pleasure. The request must mean Simon had enjoyed the weekend as much as she. If he had expected 'any funny stuff' – as Lucy had so eloquently expressed it – he had certainly given no indication of it and she, Emma, liked him the better for it.

'I'd love to!' she answered simply.

'Wednesday be OK?'

Wednesday, she said, would be fine.

Derek, however, had other plans. Somewhat to her surprise, he'd listened in silence when she told him over a pub lunch a half-truth – namely that she had spent Sunday with Simon at Ortolans – and then told her she was wasting her time.

'These yuppies are all the same!' he said. 'This one's a bit smarter than most – that's all – pretending he's interested in the house when all he's really interested in is getting you into bed. I suppose you – silly child that you are! – are impressed by his title.'

'That isn't true, Derek – any more than it's true that he wants me to sleep with him. He genuinely loves that house. If you saw it, you'd understand why. Anyway, Simon's . . .'

He cut her short and switched the conversation to an interview he wanted her to do with a woman who'd just got the job of head chef at one of the big hotels.

'It's set up for three o'clock tomorrow afternoon,' he said. 'I rather gather she's a younger edition of Fanny Craddock! Should be interesting.'

Emma felt her stomach knot with the customary pang of foreboding. Cooking was one of the least of her accomplishments and supposing she could not think up any interesting questions to put to this woman? Supposing the woman gabbled recipes which she failed to note correctly and some wretched viewer ruined a dinner party as a result of her failure?

Emma caught herself up sharply. She was being absurd, she thought. It was high time she managed to control the automatic feeling of inadequacy when she felt her abilities put to the test. She had had the same physical fear of failure as long as she could remember, before exams, before the opening of her school reports, always dreading her father's inevitable comment, 'This isn't good enough, Emma. Rosalind was top of her class . . .' She felt the same dread now when she handed in her research notes to Derek, fearing that he might say: 'Really Emma, you could do better than this . . .' The fact that he seldom did so had not cured this legacy from her childhood.

As always the interview went well enough. The woman was interesting, especially in her long fight to get to the top of a profession that was so much a male preserve. Emma worked on her outline script on Tuesday evening revising and rewriting her notes until she felt she had produced her best possible work, and left it on Derek's desk the following morning. He did not call her in to discuss it until four o'clock.

'It simply won't do, Emma!' he said, not so much crossly as sadly. 'You're capable of a hell of a lot better than this.' He pushed her notes back across his desk towards her. 'The info's OK – it's the way you've presented it. Don't look so het-up, honey. It'll come right. We'll go through them together this evening. I'll be free around six.'

Emma was shocked. She had thought he would be pleased with her efforts. She herself had been pleased. It was nice of Derek to offer to help her get it right, but what about her dinner with Simon?

'Couldn't we do it this afternoon, Derek?' she asked. 'Remember I told you Simon had asked me out? Or tomorrow morning? I could—'

'Look, Emma, this isn't a bit like you!' Derek interrupted, his tone of voice still quiet, but with an underlying note of criticism she rarely heard from him. 'I thought work came first with you. It's one of the things I most admire about you – your dedication. In any event, I'm tied up this afternoon and tomorrow, so it's this evening or not at all. It's up to you, my dear.'

'Of course, I'll stay on as long as necessary,' Emma said. 'I'm sorry you don't like my treatment, Derek. I honestly thought it had gone well.'

'We'll soon have it right!' Derek said, standing up and putting his arm around her shoulders. 'We've all got to slip up once in a while, for God's sake. Don't be so tough on yourself.'

Emma telephoned Simon at his office.

'I'm sorry it's so last minute,' she said genuinely. 'Something important has come up and I'm afraid I'll have to work late.'

'I'm disappointed, naturally, but not defeated. Tomorrow night, Emma? Or Friday?'

'Better make it Friday – in case I botch it again!' Emma said, feeling as if a weight had been taken off her shoulders. She went back to her desk with a smile on her face. Derek could not be more wrong in his judgement of Simon. She really would have to get the two of them to meet so Derek could see for himself what a thoroughly nice person Simon was.

It was nearly ten o'clock before she was free to return to her flat. A huge vase of flowers stood on the kitchen table, a note propped beside them saying: *Looking forward to Friday. S.*

Nearby was another note from Lucy:

Cor! Snap him up before I do. That is one nice guy!

Emma buried her face in the fragrant yellow roses before picking up the vase and carrying it to her own room to place beside her bed.

CHAPTER THIRTY

1987

'I'd be a hypocrite if I congratulated you, Emma. Frankly –
and I have to say it – I think you are making a big mistake!'

Emma felt her body tense. One half of her had expected
this reaction from Derek when she told him she was unoffi-
cially engaged to Simon, and that they would be getting married
at the end of February; the other half had hoped that he would
be glad for her sake that she was so happy. Derek's approval
was important. She had sensed an inexplicable coldness in
their relationship these past few weeks and been uncomfortably aware that he had become quite critical of her work. He
blamed Simon who, he maintained, was distracting her,
diverting her concentration, pushing her work into second
place.

'I know you don't believe me, Derek, but my marrying
Simon isn't going to interfere in any way at all with my job
here. Simon knows how I feel about my career and he has
accepted that he will have to take second place. I'm keeping
my flat on in case you need me to work late or to make an
early start, so nothing is going to change – nothing! And that's
a promise!'

Derek looked far from convinced.

'I just hope you can keep that promise, Emma. You've a
great future ahead of you and I'd hate to see you chuck it all
away. Frankly, I thought you had more sense than to fall for
some guy's spiel about "taking second place". You're so bloody
gullible, Emma. First Paul – and now Simon. You believe what
you want to believe.'

Emma felt her cheeks burn.

'You can't put Simon in the same league as Paul. You'd realize that if you would only meet him. It's really quite absurd – I've known Simon for two whole months and in all that time, I haven't been able to get the two of you – the two most important men in my life – together.'

'Frankly, my dear, I'd been hoping this "affair" would wear itself out. It seems I misjudged the situation.' Unexpectedly, he smiled. 'I'm sorry if I sound discouraging. You're a very special person, Emma, and I've always taken a personal interest in you, as you know. It's a bit of a shock, that's all. Marriage is a hell of a big step, and I should know, I've taken that step twice and I know the pitfalls. Why the hell can't you settle for an affair, Emma? It's not like you to be old-fashioned. Sleep with this chap if you must, but for pity's sake, don't marry him.'

'I'm not being old-fashioned – neither of us are. It's just that we both believe we've met the right partner. We realized it that second visit I made to Ortolans.'

Emma's face softened at the memory of that weekend. With only two weeks to go before Christmas, Simon had suddenly taken it into his head to decorate part of the house – for the child, he had maintained – but in the end, it had been she and Simon who had had such delight in transforming the place. They'd tacked holly on all the beams, cut the top off a small fir tree and found a box full of old Christmas tree candles in the attic – little tin holders with real miniature wax candles, tinsel and even a fairy to go on top of the tree. Vicky had watched them wide-eyed, whilst Hazel complained about the muddy footprints they made in the hall. Finally, Simon had disappeared into the garden and returned half an hour later with some mistletoe. 'I remembered it growing on an ancient old apple tree down by the ha-ha,' he'd said, before hanging it triumphantly from the elongated carved boss joining the beams in the centre of the high ceiling in the hall, and then kissing her.

Emma felt her body stir at the memory of that first kiss.

Despite the interested gaze of the child, it had been so much more than an 'under-the-mistletoe' embrace demanded. It was the moment they had both acknowledged their need for each other. Inevitably, Simon had come to her room that night and their lovemaking had been in every way perfect. Astonished at the force of her feelings, Emma had realized that she had never known this depth of pleasure with Paul; that a physical union could be so complete. Driving back to London that Sunday evening, Simon had told her he loved her, and although she had delayed another week before telling him she loved him, she had known then that she would do so.

She looked now at Derek's disapproving expression and her heart sank. She had intended to ask him for leave, a week in the middle of January to fly out to Florida with Simon to introduce him to her parents, and two weeks at the end of February for their honeymoon. She was due the time off so Derek could not refuse her request, but at the same time, she did not want to heighten his suspicion that she was losing interest in her job. Maybe she would postpone the trip to America and take Simon to meet her parents in the summer. The last thing she wanted was to upset Derek.

Somehow, she had the feeling her parents would not be particularly disappointed. Each had written individually to say that Simon sounded a very nice young man and that they had no objection to her marrying him, but each felt she was making a big mistake in getting married on so short an acquaintance. Her father had written:

> Besides Emma, you should not be taking on the added responsibilities of a wife at this juncture of your career. Surely now that you are on the point of promotion, as you intimated in your last letter, you should be giving your job all your attention. You are still very young and have ample time to get married after your contract has been renewed and you are established.

In a way, Emma could see her father's comments made sense, but for the first time in her life, she was really, truly in love. She wanted to be Simon's wife. She wanted to belong to him, not only physically, but in the traditional sense. Simon wanted it too.

It irked Emma that Derek should be taking the same line as her parents. In a way Derek's approval was more important than her father's or her mother's, from whom, she now realized, she had been alienated for a long while. She was desperately anxious for Derek to meet Simon and see for himself what a wonderful, caring, intelligent man he was.

Simon, too, was just as anxious to meet 'the boss man', as he called Derek, and was puzzled by Derek's inability to meet any date Emma had suggested so that they could be introduced. 'Reckon he's afraid I'm going to steal his glamorous researcher!' Simon had said finally, and Emma had agreed.

'Since I'm going to marry Simon next month,' she said now, 'I really do feel you should meet him, Derek. He'd soon re-assure you. He understands how I feel about my job – my career! If I thought marriage to him would undermine my career, I wouldn't have agreed to it.'

Derek's expression did not change.

'We'll just have to see, won't we? Now we've already wasted enough time this morning. Let's get down to work. I want you to go up to Scotland tomorrow . . .'

Simon was sympathetic when he called round at the flat that evening.

'Give the fellow time – he'll come round!' he said, adding with a sideways grin at Lucy: 'I'm the one who should be jealous, not your boss!'

Lucy returned the grin.

'Small wonder if his nose is out of joint. Emma has sat at his feet and worshipped for years. Mind you, he's quite some-thing, is our Derek. Women seem to fall for him and I'll grant he's attractive – if you go for older men, that is. Emma won't have it but I've always believed he's nursing a secret yen for her and has been biding his time till he's certain of making the grade.'

'That's nonsense – and you know it, Lucy. Derek's never tried anything like that. He's been a wonderful friend – my best friend, if you want the truth . . . the one person whose friendship and advice I could always depend on. Besides, he knows how I feel about Simon!'

'Well, these gurus can be quite dangerous!' Simon laughed, putting his arm round Emma's shoulders. 'So watch it, my girl. I don't mind sharing you with your career, but I won't share you with another man!'

'Looks like you'll have to,' Lucy said. 'Derek rules Emma's life!'

'Lucy, you're stirring it deliberately,' Emma reproached her. 'Simon will soon begin to think he's got real reason to be jealous. You're also very unfair to Derek. I owe him one hell of a lot. I think he's clever, amusing and extremely talented, but there it ends. I happen to be in love with Simon!'

'There now, Lucy. Put that in your pipe and smoke it!' Simon said, dropping a kiss on Emma's head. 'Corny as it may sound to your sophisticated little ears, now Emma and I have found each other, nothing and no one is ever going to part us.'

Lucy gathered up the empty coffee mugs and put them in the sink.

'Divorce rate is one in three – or is it two!' she murmured with pretended seriousness.

'Give us a chance – we aren't married yet!' Simon countered.

A week later, Emma moved into Brunswick Square. Derek kept her inordinately busy during the day, but she and Simon treasured the domestic intimacy of their evenings together and their weekend visits to Ortolans where they made preparations for their wedding which was to take place in Detcham Church. When Mrs Foster wrote to say that they would be unable to attend as Emma's father was booked to go into hospital for a heart bypass operation, Simon at once suggested they must postpone the wedding date. At first, he was unable to comprehend Emma's reaction that they should do no such thing.

'My parents and I have never been close – as you were to your great-grandmother,' she endeavoured to explain. 'It was my sister, Rosalind, they really cared about. They wouldn't even let me go to Ros's funeral because it might interrupt my finals. I don't mean to sound bitter, but they've been abroad for eight long years and never made any attempt to come and see me. The few times I've suggested I visit them, one or other of them has had an important conference or lecture tour or whatever, that coincided with my holiday dates. I honestly don't think they'll mind missing our wedding. They hate "functions" – or anything that isn't directly tied up with their jobs.'

Finally, she and Simon had agreed on a quiet ceremony with only a few guests – business colleagues, neighbours, and of course, the entire Pylbeam family. Derek agreed to act the parental role and give Emma away, 'reluctantly, though!' he'd told her, 'seeing I don't approve of you rushing into marriage like this, as well you know!'

Little Vicky was Emma's bridesmaid and Lucy, her maid of honour. Derek, looking impeccable in morning suit and grey topper, with members of the studio, helped to fill Emma's side of the aisle, together with several of her former school and university friends with whom, over the years, she had kept in touch by letter.

The weekend before the wedding, Derek went down for the day to attend the rehearsal and, for the first time, to meet Simon. To Emma's intense relief, he could not have been more charming, admiring the house, showing a genuine interest in its history and presenting Simon and Emma with a very beautiful set of antique decanters as a wedding present. After he had taken the train back to London, Emma had caught Simon chuckling to himself at some private joke.

'It's just that I'd built up such a completely wrong impression of the chap!' he admitted when Emma had persuaded him to share the joke. 'Either I thought of him as a kind of modern Don Juan, or, in my less jealous moments, as a tyrant, a martinet with Svengali-type power over you. In fact I think he's genuinely very fond of you, darling, and really does mean to help you up in the world. All the same, Lucy's right when she says he's very possessive about you – you know, darling, that business about "*my* Emma is going places!"'

Emma laughed.

'That's just his way!' she said, her happiness brimming over because the two most important men in her life had at last met and liked each other. 'Anyway, Derek will be giving me to you in his official capacity next weekend, so there can be no doubt who I'll belong to, can there?'

'You'll be *my* Emma, until death us do part!' Simon said huskily.

The wedding took place on the following Saturday afternoon, a cold but sunny day. Derek had given Emma the Friday off to complete her packing and Friday night, she, Simon and Lucy drove down to Ortolans where Vicky was in a fever of excitement as Hazel laid out her bridesmaid dress. Emma had had made for her a charming replica of an Elizabethan child's velvet frock with a wide lace collar and matching Juliet cap. Partly to please Simon, but also because she herself thought it so beautiful, Emma wore a simple cream silk wedding-dress in a style copied from Great-Grandmother Sophia's beautiful old wedding-gown which she had found stored in a trunk in one of the attics.

'Not even my beloved Great-Gran could have looked more beautiful than you, my darling!' Simon said as finally, suitcases packed and locked, they prepared to set off on their honeymoon. Emma paused to put her arms round Simon and say:

'I'm so happy, darling, I don't think I've ever been as happy as I am at this moment and I know I could never be happier!'

Simon had booked a beautiful double room in the Rhodania Hotel at the Swiss resort of Crans. Since it was to be a winter honeymoon, he'd suggested they should take the opportunity to go skiing. Although Emma was only a moderate skier, Simon was black run standard and a real enthusiast. It was high season, the sun shone brilliantly and there was plenty of perfect powder snow. They skied all day and made love all night, the champagne air and their never-ending need for one another making both possible.

'Although I'm sure I'll be exhausted by the time we get back,' Emma said, her naked body stretched out beside Simon's in the large comfortable double bed. 'Derek said there'd be a backlog of work and I was to prepare myself for a busy few weeks. You won't mind, will you, darling?'

'Of course I'll mind! I shall resent every moment I'm not with you,' Simon said, drawing her back into his arms. 'I love you so very much, Emma. It seems to get worse and worse – or should I say more and more?'

'Better and better!' Emma whispered as her body ignited once more beneath his caressing hands. 'We're so lucky, Simon – to have found each other!'

'Poor people!' Simon murmured. 'Poor all the chaps in the world who aren't married to you!'

They were barely five minutes back in Simon's flat in London before the phone rang. It was Lucy.

'Welcome home, lovebirds. No broken bones, I trust?'

'No, we're fine – and thanks for the flowers. I presume they're from you?'

'Not exactly. Derek asked me to buy some for him – didn't trust Interflora to deliver over the weekend. Which brings me to the other reason for the call – he wants you in early Monday morning. Something about a documentary you're to do with him about the Royals. Said it was important.'

Emma put down the phone and went through to the living-room where Simon was leafing through his mail. There were several parcels – belated wedding gifts, he suggested, and pushing them towards her, he said:

'You open them, darling!' He lifted a strand of hair from her forehead and stared down at her.

'I just can't get over how beautiful you are,' he said. 'Perhaps it's because I'm now wearing rose-coloured spectacles. Because I'm in love with you, I can see only the good points, not the bad.'

Emma returned his kiss.

'And what are the bad ones?' she enquired.

'Oh, your nose isn't straight and your mouth is too big and your left ear sticks out and you've got a mole on your right breast and you'll never, ever learn to do a jump turn in deep snow!'

Abandoning the plan to unpack, they made love instead, after which they went out to dinner to a Spanish restaurant where they ate paella and drank a great deal of red wine.

'If it isn't snowing or blowing a force ten gale, we'll go down to Ortolans next weekend,' Simon said when finally, exhausted, they fell into bed. 'I'll give Roddy a ring and tell him to fix up a meeting with the plumber and kitchen people. I've learned how important hot water is to you, my girl, and our bathroom at Ortolans is number one priority. The kitchen is number two. Hazel does nothing but complain, and although you won't be in it a great deal, you should be the one to choose the design. I've stopped thinking of Ortolans as "my" house. Now it's "ours"!'

Emma felt a warm glow of happiness. She had everything in life she wanted, she thought – the man she loved, the career she loved, a home she loved. It was strange how quickly Ortolans had begun to feel like home – hers as well as Simon's. This week, if there was time, she'd get some brochures on bathrooms and kitchens – perhaps drop into some shops and see what was available. Whatever she chose, it must be in keeping with the antiquity of the old house. She'd ask Derek for the name of the firm who had modernized his house in Gerrards Cross a year or two ago.

The thought of Derek reminded her of the studio and the job they were to do on Monday. It sounded exciting, important. Maybe this would be her chance to prove herself. It was a long while since she'd worked alongside her boss. He would be able to see for himself how much more authoritative she was; how much better organized; how quickly and easily she could now deal with on-the-spot problems. Life, or Fate, was being so good to her, perhaps this would be the year she'd finally get to be an assistant producer. She must not be too late to bed tomorrow night – be fresh and alert for Monday morning. Although Derek had not begrudged her time off for her honeymoon, he'd obviously been afraid she would return in no mood to put her nose back to the grindstone. Now was her chance to show him that she had meant what she had said – her career was not going to suffer at the expense of her marriage. At least she was on the pill now and there could be no unfortunate accident with an unwanted baby! One day, of course, she and Simon would think about starting a family. For the present, she was only twenty-eight and she did not have to worry about leaving it too late to have children. As she had pointed out to Simon, lots of women nowadays were waiting until they were nearing forty! At first, he'd argued that this would be leaving it too long, but he'd finally seen her point about waiting till she was established. Then she could take time off to have a baby and still be sure of getting her job back afterwards.

'If that's what you still wanted,' Simon had agreed. 'But by then, you might feel you'd had enough of it all and be happy to retire to a life of leisure. I'm told women who have previously been violently opposed to becoming mothers, often go broody when they give birth.'

'There are also plenty of others who have children and then become violently opposed to motherhood!' Emma had replied. 'And don't look so worried, darling. I promise I'll give you that son and heir one day.'

'And we'll end up with five girls!' Simon had laughed. 'Did you know that identical twins run in my family? I think I'd rather like two identical little Emmas running round Ortolans.'

'Heaven forbid! I'll settle for two little Simons – when and if the time comes!'

In the meanwhile, she thought, she wanted nothing but Simon and her job – and there was little enough time once she was back at work to share with Simon. Fortunately, he liked to play squash twice a week with one of his colleagues, and she had persuaded him not to cancel this long-standing arrangement just because he had got himself married! It would give her the chance to get through her paperwork . . . or some of it. He also liked to go swimming and have the occasional workout at a gym. In the summer, he played golf and tennis, and one of his plans for Ortolans was to have the old croquet lawn surfaced so that they could give tennis parties.

Emma had finally met his previous girlfriend, Cilla, at the wedding. She was a petite, attractive brunette with a size eight, model-girl figure. Emma could well understand why Simon had been so attracted to her. She was colourful without being ostentatious – the kind of girl who turned heads when she went into a restaurant. Very self-assured, voluble, she was also highly strung, talking in a high-pitched, excited little voice and laughing a great deal. Her manner towards Simon was intimate but without being possessive; towards Emma, openly envious.

'So you're the girl who Simon's been raving about!' she'd said, her small hand with its long, silver-painted nails grasping Simon's arm as she smiled up at him. 'I can see why, now I've met you. He certainly never raved about me although *I* was always madly in love with *you*, wasn't I, darling! Ah, well, so long as you're both happy!' She had turned her small dark head towards Emma. 'Be warned, my dear, if you don't look after him properly, I'll be in the wings waiting to pick up the pieces. Eligible, good-looking guys like Simon don't grow on trees!'

'She always talks in that flippant way,' Simon had said later. 'She reminds me a bit of your Lucy. Unlike you, my darling, poor Cilla doesn't seem to know what she wants out of life. For a while, she thought it was me, but as I told you, we simply didn't hit it off. I don't really worry about her – there are always plenty of boyfriends around.'

With a feeling of relief, Emma had realized that she had no more reason to be jealous of Cilia than Simon had of Derek.

On her first day back at work, Emma discovered that, as usual, Lucy had got her wires crossed. The documentary was not to be about a member of the royal family and Derek would not be accompanying her.

'You're to do an interview at two-thirty this afternoon,' Derek informed her. 'Lady Mary Compton, aged fifty odd; married to the late Lord Compton; the daughter of an earl, and now enjoying life as a jobbing gardener at Hever Castle in Kent.'

'Is that the angle you want me to take – riches to rags?' Emma asked.

Derek grinned.

'Far from it. I understand Lady Mary is rolling in it. Does it because she used to visit the former owners, the Astors, as a child and fell in love with the garden. Could make an interesting story – one day wheeling a barrow load of manure and the next in a privileged place in Westminster Abbey for Prince Andrew's wedding. Probably plants roses wearing a tiara!'

He laughed and put an arm affectionately round Emma's shoulders.

'You're looking fantastic, darling! Smashing tan. Honeymoon a success, I take it?'

'Two hundred per cent!' Emma replied. 'I'm just so lucky, Derek. Now you've finally got to know Simon, you understand why I'm so mad about him!'

Derek removed his arm and returned to his desk.

'He's certainly a very good-looking bloke, but I can't exactly claim to *know* him, can I? I mean, we didn't get the chance to do much chatting at the wedding, did we? Anyway, he's your worry – not mine. All I'm concerned about is that he proves himself as tolerant as you say he is.'

Emma felt a moment of irritation.

'I've told you a dozen times, Derek – Simon understands about my job here.'

'OK, OK, calm down! Now let's get back to work. I'm quite pleased with the way this *Women of Today* series is going. Our viewing figures were up again last week, but we've still a long way to go. So off you go, darling, and see what you can get out of Lady Mary!'

The interview went surprisingly well. Emma took an immediate liking to the older woman who, despite her baggy, muddied corduroy slacks and man's Harris tweed jacket, still managed to look remarkably aristocratic. She was both articulate and photogenic. It seemed she had always secretly longed to work with the soil but had been prevented by her background. She had been conventionally educated, been presented and more or less pushed into a 'suitable' marriage by her father – the autocratic old earl. Lord Compton had been an MP and, as his wife, Lady Mary had never had the freedom to indulge her obsessive love of gardening. Soon after her husband's death, she had applied for the job at Hever – not using her title – and talked herself into the vacant post. She was now perfectly happy and did not miss her old way of life one little bit. Her only regret was that she had not had the courage to stand up to her parents thirty years earlier.

'It's the reason I've agreed to participate in this film you are making, my dear,' she explained to Emma. 'I want to get it across to any young girl starting out in life that the most important thing is to be doing a job you really want to do. Girls these days should not let anything sidetrack them – least of all marriage. I was married to a good man and I have three wonderful children – but I was always a wife, a mother – never myself until now.'

Later that evening, recounting her day's activities to Simon, he remarked that although Lady Mary was obviously a very interesting person, she was undoubtedly an eccentric.

'Hardly typical of the *Woman of Today*, darling!'

'Maybe not typical,' Emma argued, 'but her philosophies

are relevant. You could apply them to me, for instance. I couldn't be happy doing anything other than the job I'm in. My parents hoped that I'd make the grade in one of the professions like my sister, who was very clever. They were bitterly disappointed when it became obvious I lacked the ability; but Derek has no doubt that I can get to the top if I work hard, and I'm happy in what I'm doing. I would have been utterly unfulfilled as a doctor or a solicitor or working in finance like your girl, Joanne. And I certainly couldn't bear being the wife of an MP and having to live my own life through my husband's!'

Simon grinned.

'I agree that doesn't sound like you, my darling! All the same, life can't have been all that bad for your Lady Mary. She liked her husband and adored her children. Doesn't sound as if she was particularly unhappy.'

'But that isn't what she was saying, Simon – that she was unhappy. She was saying she was unfulfilled. That's different!'

'How do you know she wouldn't have felt just as "unfulfilled" if she'd become a gardener when she left school and never married or had children?'

'You're assuming every woman wants a husband and kids,' Emma argued. 'It's a typically male attitude. There are plenty of bachelors who remain unmarried and no one thinks it odd.'

Simon shrugged.

'I suppose you've got a point there. Time for the nine o'clock news, darling. I want to catch the latest on the Zeebrugge disaster. It's pretty grim, isn't it?'

He switched on the television and sat down in one of the chairs, pulling Emma on to his lap.

'Love you!' he said, kissing her as pictures of the stricken ferry filled the screen.

'Love you, too!' Emma said, glad to be physically as well as mentally close to Simon again. Despite her concern for the survivors of the disaster, her concentration was marred by Simon's comments. Their dispute – for it could not have been called an argument – disturbed her. It seemed to indicate a very conventional – almost old-fashioned – side to Simon she had been unaware of. He had always professed to believe absolutely in the equality of the sexes – and yet she had sensed just now that not far below the surface, he believed all women were incomplete if they were not wives and mothers.

The following evening added to her unease. As on the previous night, he was back at the flat before her. He was laying out glasses and bottles.

'I've asked the Keelings round for drinks, darling,' he said, holding a bowl of ice to one side as he kissed her. 'They'll be here about eight-thirty. Then I thought we'd go round to Domenico's for a meal.'

Emma put down her briefcase.

'Darling, you should have asked me first!' she said. Simon swung round to look at her.

'How could I? I only ran into Philip in the office this morning. If I'd thought of it yesterday, I would have told you.'

'You could have rung me at the studio – warned me!' Emma said.

Simon's green eyes darkened.

'You're not suggesting I need your permission to invite my friends to a drink?' he asked bitingly.

'Don't be such an idiot, Simon!' Emma's voice was sharp. It had been a long day and she was not feeling her best. 'It's just that I've a mass of work to do tonight and like it or not, it's got to be on Derek's desk by ten tomorrow.'

'For God's sake, Emma, you've already done a ten-hour day! How was I supposed to know you'd be bringing more work home? Anyway, I can't put them off. They moved a few weeks ago and I don't have their new address.'

'Then I'll just have to get through this lot later tonight!' Emma said, pushing past Simon and walking into the bedroom. In a way, she could see Simon's point of view – he had every right to invite friends back to his flat for a drink if he chose to do so. Perhaps in future, if she had work to do, she should go back to Shepherd's Bush. Lucy was always out and she could work there in peace. It wouldn't hurt either of them to sleep apart occasionally. It was the only compromise she could think of.

Emma had met the Keelings several times before their wedding and liked both of them. Tonight, however, she was in no mood to be sociable. Once or twice she stopped listening to the exchange of chit-chat and thought about the work she had to do. Simon noticed her silence and mistook the reason for it. As soon as they left, he turned to Emma and said furiously:

'If that was your puerile way of getting back at me, it was damned rude!' he said. 'You hardly said a word to either of them!'

'That isn't true, Simon!' Emma flared back. 'It was all very well for the three of you, knocking back the alcohol and getting "ever-so-jolly". With one glass of wine and a tiring day behind me, it wasn't so easy for me. Anyway, I don't want to talk about it. I've got to get down to work.'

Simon looked at her aghast.

'But it's nearly midnight, Emma. You look exhausted. Surely it can wait till tomorrow!'

'No, it can't!' Emma snapped back. 'I thought I told you earlier, it's important!'

Simon's expression was now contrite.

'I really am sorry, Emma. I suppose it was pretty thought-less of me. I'm just not used to sharing my life and it simply didn't occur to me you might be busy.'

Emma ran into his open arms.

'I'm sorry, too – for being so touchy.'

'You get on with your work. I'll clear up this mess and make you a nice big mug of coffee. I just wish I could help you, darling.'

'I'll be OK!' Emma said. 'Stop fussing and go to bed, Simon. No point two of us being tired in the morning!'

Somewhat to Emma's surprise, Derek instantly noted the shadows beneath her eyes.

'Burning the midnight oil, obviously. Tell that fellow of yours to control himself. He can have his oats at the weekend!' he said crudely. It was a remark Emma did not intend to pass on to Simon.

The remainder of the week was moderately quiet and Emma found herself looking forward to the weekend. Simon had had a call from Roddy to say that the meeting with the plumber and the kitchen planners was set for ten-thirty.

'We'll go down Friday night,' he said. 'Then we can have a lie-in on Saturday morning before they arrive.'

At four-thirty on Friday afternoon, Derek called Emma into his office.

'Great news!' he said, lighting one of his innumerable small cigars. 'Phyllis Farraday has agreed to an interview. She's the woman who's written that fantastic book about elephants. Remember how she followed a herd for five years – almost became one of them?'

Emma nodded. She had read the book and was eager to see the film which had followed and was already breaking box-office records in the States.

'Heathrow, one-thirty tomorrow!' Derek said. 'She's doing a two-hour stopover between flights. She'll give you half an hour after the press conference they're setting up. One hell of a *Woman of Today,* eh, darling?'

'We'll incorporate her with some other women who are involved with animals!' Emma said. 'I'm not sure, but I think there's a female vet at Whipsnade or somewhere like that – operates on lions, cheetahs . . .' She broke off, realizing suddenly that Derek had said tomorrow. She had arranged to go down to Ortolans tonight with Simon.

'Something wrong?' Derek asked. 'No problems, I hope?'

'No, it's OK – fine. I'll take Pete, of course, and maybe Tim for the lighting and someone for sound – I'll organize it.'

'Ritchie wanted the job, but I stuck out for you, Emma,' Derek was saying. 'I think you'll do it well. By the way, I liked the script for Lady Mary very much.'

'I'll get off right away to the library and mug up on Farraday this evening,' Emma said. She was immensely excited to be given the job in preference to Richard Ritchie, who like herself, was also hoping to become an assistant producer. It was good of Derek to give her this chance to prove herself capable.

She could barely contain her excitement as she opened the door of the flat.

'It's a wonderful opportunity for me, Simon,' she ended her story. 'I should be through by two, and with a lift back to town in the BBC car, I'll be able to get to Victoria by three – catch a train down and be with you by four. I'll ring you from the station. OK, darling?'

Simon, who had remained silent, his face expressionless, now said very quietly:

'No, it isn't OK, Emma. You seem to be forgetting we have an appointment tomorrow morning.'

Emma's mouth dropped open. She had forgotten.

'Oh God! The plumber!' she gasped.

'*And* the kitchen fitter *and* Roddy! Have you no idea how bloody difficult it's been for Roddy – a) to get either of them there on a Saturday morning, and b) to get them there together? For heaven's sake, Emma, give that boss of yours a call and tell him to send this Ritchie fellow instead.'

The colour rushed to Emma's cheeks.

'Are you out of your mind, Simon? This is a big chance for me. If you think I'm going to mess it up just for a . . . a plumber . . . I'm sorry, sorry I forgot, but that's all there is to it. Count me out. You see the wretched plumber and whoever. You choose what you like – I don't care. I'll go along with whatever you want.'

For one long moment, Simon stood staring down at her, his green eyes narrowed speculatively. Then he turned, zipped up his case and, without a further word, disappeared through the front door, closing it with ominous quietness behind him.

CHAPTER THIRTY-ONE

1987

It was six o'clock before Emma finished work. She went back to the flat in Shepherd's Bush. Lucy was washing her hair. Emma poured herself a large gin and tonic and sank on to a chair in the kitchen. Lucy came through from the bathroom, her head wrapped in a towel. She eyed Emma's glass and said with a grin:

'Good idea, Em! I'll keep you company. What brings you here, by the way?'

'It's been one hell of a day!' Emma said, avoiding the question. 'I've a splitting headache. I suppose I should be taking two Panadol instead of this!'

She emptied her glass and poured herself a second drink. Lucy raised her eyebrows.

'Your precious Derek been nagging you?' she asked succinctly. 'And why are you here – not Brunswick Square?' she persisted.

Emma frowned.

'Because Simon's gone down to Sussex and here is nearer. As for Derek, I haven't seen him, as a matter of fact.'

'OK, OK!' Lucy broke in. 'Something has upset you, though, so if it isn't the boss, what is it?'

Emma bit her lip.

'It's not just one thing. If you really want to know, I'm thoroughly fed up. The Farraday woman's plane was delayed two hours. As a consequence, my interview with her was cut to about five minutes and frankly, it's hardly worth writing up. Derek is going to be livid. I called back at the studio to explain things but he'd already left, so I've got that bad news hanging over till Monday. I'm sure he'll try to make out it was my fault.'

'Don't be such an idiot!' Lucy said, rubbing her hair vigorously. 'You don't control British Airways, for heaven's sake!'

Emma drew a deep sigh.

'I suppose you're right. But it's been such a wasted day, Lucy. I might just as well have gone down to Ortolans last night.'

'I thought you were going this afternoon, after the interview,' Lucy said, eyeing Emma's drawn face surreptitiously.

'I was! But with it being so late, I decided I might as well stay the night here and maybe, if I feel like it, go down to Ortolans for the day tomorrow!'

'Won't Simon be expecting you this evening?' Lucy asked.

Emma felt a sudden urge to burst into tears. The alternative was to break something, but it really wasn't fair to vent her feelings on the innocent Lucy.

Keeping a tight control of herself, she told Lucy in a few short sentences of the row she had had with Simon; how *he* felt she was letting him down; how *she* felt he was being totally unreasonable in thinking she had any choice.

'He knows how important my work is to me. I've told him a dozen times. He agreed I should put my career first. Damn it, Lucy, all this just because he has the plumber coming! What the hell's importance does a bathroom have! Simon's going back on his word – and I don't like it.'

Lucy shrugged.

'Have a heart, Emma! You've only been married three weeks. Naturally, he wants you with him. Anyway, from the sound of it, the interview was a total waste of time.'

'So what has that got to do with it?' Emma flared. 'How was I to know that ruddy plane would be delayed? Besides, it's the principle that matters. Just because I'm married to Simon, I don't have to kowtow to his every whim.'

'For heaven's sake, Emma! There are times when you drive

me up the wall! If I were in your shoes, I wouldn't give a damn about this stupid job of yours. It's becoming an obsession. It's not even as if you need to work. Why in God's name don't you chuck the whole thing, tell Derek to stuff it? Anyone would think you weren't in love with your husband. If you must work, get yourself some part-time job that won't interfere with your marriage.'

Two angry spots of colour suffused Emma's cheeks.

'I don't want some footling part-time job!' she shouted. 'This is my career, Lucy, not a meaningless method of filling in time. I want to get somewhere – I *mean* to get somewhere – and Derek says . . .'

'To hell with Derek. I'm sick and tired of his name,' Lucy interrupted with rare bluntness. 'I've never said so before – and it's none of my business – but I've seen you night after night, slogging away, denying yourself any fun, wasting the best years of your life. Simon's offered you a way out, and you're waffling on about your footling career, which, frankly, strikes me as being more of a headache than a pleasure. It's not even as if you enjoy what you are doing.'

'That's a lie!' Emma said quietly. She was now pale and Lucy feared she might be on the point of tears.

'Sorry I blasted off, duckie,' she said gently. 'It's just that I think you and Simon are bloody lucky to have found each other and I hate to see things go wrong. As you say, you've got your own life to lead. So it's up to you, Em. In your shoes, I'd pack a bag and get the next train down to Sussex.'

'Well, you're not me and anyway, all my gear is at Simon's flat. Besides . . .' Emma added in a more moderate voice '. . . it's been pouring all day and I'd need my waterproofs and wellies.'

'Can't you call round at the flat first and collect them on your way to the station?' Lucy suggested.

Emma hesitated.

'I could, but I'm not going to. Why should I? Let Simon stew for a bit. He's the one who walked out. If he'd phoned and apologized, we could have made it up.'

Lucy screwed up her nose.

'But apologized for what, Em? You were the one who let him down, so to speak – although I know you couldn't help it,' she added quickly.

'Let's not talk about it. You going out, Lucy?'

'Um – a disco with Jimmy. I'd better get a move on. Sure you're OK, Em?'

'I'm fine! Sorry to rant on at you, Lucy. Not one of my good days, I'm afraid.'

The gin was beginning to take effect and, feeling calmer, Emma went to her own room and drew out the pathetically few notes she had made. Perhaps if she were to augment the new material with passages from Ms Farraday's book, she could yet salvage the interview. Derek wouldn't know what was new and what wasn't! Perhaps she could arrange a meeting with the woman's publishers – get some anecdotes from the editor who, presumably, must have been in contact with her author during the production of the book. At least Pete had some good pictures – and the library would have something on African elephants. Perhaps, after all, she could build up a half-hour slot of which Derek would approve.

Simon dropped a piece of ice into the tumbler and added a generous dollop of whisky. Cilla had asked for 'a double' and he was only too happy to oblige her. He had driven back from Ortolans at lunchtime and spent the rest of the day alone at the flat growing steadily more depressed when Emma showed no sign of returning after her interview. When, shortly after six, Cilla telephoned him to ask if she might come round and see him on a matter of some urgency, he had readily agreed. He had no wish to do any more soul-searching about the row he had had with Emma. He knew she had not caught the train to Ortolans as she had originally intended. The plan had been that she would telephone him at Ortolans when her interview ended to say which train she would be on; but Hazel, who had promised on pain of death to ring him if Emma did call, had remained ominously silent. Emma would not know, therefore, that he had returned to London. Stupidly, he now realized, he had been certain she would telephone and on hearing he was back to London, would realize he was trying to make amends. It now seemed that she was in no hurry for a reconciliation and had other plans. Quite possibly, the boss man had taken her out to dinner!

'My God, Cilia, you're absolutely soaked!' he said now as he pushed the whisky tumbler into her hand.

'Hardly surprising, darling. It's raining bathwater and I couldn't get a taxi. There *would* be a deluge the one day I didn't take a brolly to work. God, what a life!'

Simon looked at his former girlfriend with a mixture of emotions. It was strange how he could still see that Cilla was an amazingly attractive young woman, immensely sexy with that low-cut shirt and tight-fitting skirt, yet not feel any stirring of desire for her. Not even the conjuring up of past sessions, when they had devoured each other in the big double bed, could arouse any longing to recapture those earthy pleasures. It was Emma's body he now craved. Sex for its own sake now seemed a paltry thing compared with sex as an expression of the love he felt for Emma. He felt sorry for Cilia whose current lover was middle-aged, inclined to be pompous and often bored her. She did not love him, but allowed the relationship to continue because, as she put it, he was 'good in bed'.

'Take your shoes and tights off – you can dry them by the fire,' he suggested. 'And stop looking as if you have the weight of the world on your shoulders!'

Cilla's face lightened momentarily into an uneasy smile.

'Feels like I have!' she murmured. 'Look, Simon, I really ought not to be bothering you like this. You've only just got back from your honeymoon. Where's Emma, by the way?'

'Working!' Simon said vaguely. 'Here, give me your shoes, woman!'

Cilla allowed Simon to remove her shoes and with a swift,

graceful movement, stood up and drew down her tights. As he put them in front of the electric fire, she flopped once more onto the sofa. Regarding her downcast face, Simon said encouragingly:

'You said on the phone you were in trouble – and if I can help, you know I will. We're old friends, Cilla – and that is what friends are for. What trouble?'

'Financial!' Cilia said after only a short pause. 'It's the usual cash-flow problem. The bank won't increase my over-draft and one of my major creditors is threatening to take me to court. I need five thousand, Simon. If I can't raise it – well, I suppose I'm going to have to shut up shop.'

'But I thought Nick-Nacks was doing so well!' Simon said, sitting down beside her and putting an arm comfortingly round her shoulders. 'You told me you had one hell of a good Christmas and that . . .'

'And then nothing, Simon. We did very badly in the January sales and in February, whilst you were on your honeymoon, another gift shop sprang up overnight like a mushroom four doors up from us – where the luggage shop used to be. It's right opposite the bus stop and people on their way to me see their window first. I'm sure this is the reason we've been doing so badly. I sent one of my sales assistants to suss out the place and she came back saying it was chock-a-block with customers. What's more, they are selling the same sort of things we are – and cheaper.'

'I see!' Simon looked thoughtfully into the fire. 'You know I'll lend you the five thousand, Cilla – that goes without saying. But do you want to put more money into the business if it isn't going to be profitable? It doesn't make good sense.'

Cilia turned to look at him, her eyes now bright and excited.

'If I can weather the next few weeks, I can turn the tide,' she said eagerly. 'I've found a new supplier – they've some fabulous natural wood toys for kids and they'll let me have them immediately, and Simon, they're almost half the price of Gait's. These people do bits and pieces for kitchens too, which means if I open up the basement I could really extend. Smarties, the new place, has nothing to compare.'

Simon nodded. Five thousand wasn't such a vast sum of money and he'd recently negotiated a large bank loan, partly to finance his share dealings, but mainly to cover the costs of restoring Ortolans. After the kitchen and bathroom, the next project – to renew the lead surrounds to all the old square-paned casements – would begin later in the summer. His investments had been moving up sharply – so sharply, in fact, that he had decided to add considerably to his portfolio. The profit he had made from his share dealings more than paid the interest on the overdraft, and since their living expenses were moderate, he reckoned he'd be able eventually to finance Roddy's estimated bill for complete restoration of Ortolans – an amount in the order of £200,000. With the way things were going, he saw no reason why he should not lend Cilia the five thousand she needed to keep her afloat.

'Naturally, I'll pay interest at current rates!' Cilia was saying. 'I should be able to pay back the capital in full within a year. Needless to say, I did try the bank but they simply won't play.'

Simon nodded.

'You've no assets to back a loan!' he said. 'Whereas it's been easy for me to borrow with Ortolans as security. Look, Cilia, I know you wouldn't be asking me for cash if you weren't reasonably sure you can make a go of it, so give me a week to get the five thousand off deposit and it's yours for a year!'

It was a generous gesture as Simon knew he could make it earn far more for him on the money market, but Cilia had, after all, been his girlfriend for five years. He knew very well that she had always hoped he'd end up marrying her despite his frank denials of the possibility. Nevertheless, he felt guilty for having taken up five years of her life simply because the relationship suited him. Now there was Emma, and he'd packed up Cilia without a qualm. The loan would ease his conscience; show he was not entirely heartless.

Cilla's expression changed from the downcast to the ecstatic. She flung her arms round Simon's neck and hugged him.

'You're a darling and I love you and I shall be eternally grateful to you!' she cried, planting excited kisses all over his face.

Neither heard the door open or were aware that Emma was standing, open-mouthed, watching them.

After Lucy had left her alone, Emma had gone to her room and for an hour, struggled to make something of the all-too-few notes she had taken at the airport. Her mind had not been fully concentrated on the task. Lucy had put her head round the door and announced that she was going out. The front door slammed and then there was silence. Slowly, it dawned on Emma that she was being exceedingly stupid; that it was entirely her own fault she was feeling lonely and miserable. It was still only eight-thirty and if she were to get a move on now, she could catch a train to Hassocks that would get her there before ten. Simon could meet her and they would be in Detcham by ten-fifteen. They would make up the quarrel and the entire weekend would not be wasted.

Hesitating only a few moments longer, she had gone to the telephone and dialled the Ortolans number. Hazel had answered. Simon, she informed Emma, had returned to London after lunch and planned to drive down again with Emma as soon as she returned from work.

Emma's depression vanished as she telephoned immediately for a minicab. Simon had given up his Saturday afternoon to come back to London to be with her – a gesture she really appreciated, knowing how he valued his time at Ortolans.

Her heart was singing with happiness as the cab drove her through the empty streets and deposited her in Brunswick Square. It was so late now, she supposed Simon had given up hope of her returning there. Emma smiled as she planned to surprise him. She would let herself in quietly, tell him how sorry she was to have messed up his day and he would apologize for walking out on her last night and . . .

She stared in total disbelief at the couple embracing on the sofa. This was a nightmare – she was dreaming! she thought stupidly. How could Simon . . . Cilia, his old girlfriend . . . kissing . . . ! Her eyes took in the shoes and tights lying on the floor. There was every indication that the two of them were – or had been – making love.

As Simon extricated himself from Cilia's arms, he heard Emma's horrified gasp and looking up, realized immediately what she was thinking. He rose hurriedly to his feet and approached her.

'Darling, don't look so shocked. It's all perfectly innocent, I assure you!'

Cilla straightened her skirt as she, too, stood up.

'I was just thanking Simon for being such a wonderful friend,' she said. 'I came round to ask him to lend me some money and . . .'

Emma was attempting to twist herself free of Simon's grasp on her arm.

'I'd really prefer it if you would leave, Cilla!' she said sharply. 'I know this used to be Simon's flat, but it happens to be mine, too, now that I'm his wife. I am married to him, you know.'

'Emma, that's enough!' Simon said equally sharply. 'You're jumping to absurd conclusions. What Cilia just told you is the truth, so stop behaving like an idiot.'

'It's time I left anyway, Simon,' Cilia said, crossing to the fire to retrieve her shoes and tights. 'These are dry now!' She disappeared into the bathroom and, turning to face Emma, Simon said:

'Come on darling, be sensible. I know it must have looked a bit odd but truly, Cilla turned up out of the blue. She's in financial trouble and wanted my help. She didn't know you weren't going to be here when she arrived. As a matter of fact, she only telephoned me on the off-chance as she had supposed I'd be at Ortolans, and that's exactly where I would have been if I hadn't missed you so much.'

Emma twisted away and walked across to the window. She did not turn her head as Cilia came in briefly to say goodbye. Declining Simon's offer to phone for a taxi, Cilla shot a last anxious look at Emma's rigid back, and shrugging helplessly, let herself out of the apartment.

Suddenly, Simon's sense of humour resurfaced, and he put a placating hand on Emma's shoulder.

'Look, darling, you'd see the funny side if you weren't so determined to act like someone in one of the soaps.' He grinned. 'I'm really not another JR! So stop behaving like a jealous little idiot! Come and sit down and I'll get you a drink!'

Perhaps she was behaving stupidly, Emma thought as, unexpectedly, tears stung her eyes. It really had been a ghastly day – and more than anything in the world, she wanted to believe Simon. She couldn't bear the thought that he was wishing he had never married her and that he was back with Cilia who was probably far more accommodating than herself!

As she turned into his open arms, the tears rolled down. Between bouts of blowing her nose and sniffing, she tried to tell him about the abortive day she had had and how upset she had been at their quarrel.

'I do love you, Simon. I simply couldn't stand seeing Cilia kissing you as if . . . as if . . . you were still lovers. It all looked so . . . so domesticated – her shoes and tights by the fire and . . . well, she looked as if she belonged here!'

Simon stopped the flow of words with kisses which, as Emma responded, became increasingly ardent. They fell backwards onto the sofa closely entwined, and made love with a fierce impatience that was different, and in its way, reassuring and completely satisfying. When he had recovered his breath, Simon said disarmingly:

'Now you can't be in any doubt that I was not unfaithful to you with Cilia. My case rests, m'lud – or should I say m'lady?'

Emma smiled.

'You've given me an idea, Simon. I could do a *Women of Today* documentary about women judges. I suppose there are some. I shall have to do some research.'

'Don't you ever think about anything but work?' Simon asked, his tone light but with a hint of seriousness behind it which Emma missed.

'Yes, I do, I think about you and us and our future,' she said. 'I love you, Simon, and I want us to be happy. We've only been living together for two months but already we've had our first quarrel.'

'Misunderstanding!' Simon corrected her. 'Look, when you agreed to the meeting with Roddy and Co., I naturally took it for granted you wouldn't be working. It didn't occur to me you might be "on call" at a weekend. After all, darling, I'm not in your line of business and I don't know the routine.'

Emma sat up and smoothed her hair out of her eyes.

'It doesn't happen very often, honestly, Simon!' she said. 'And never on a Sunday! I'm not really supposed to work at weekends – but when Derek first interviewed me for the job, I said I'd be available whenever he wanted me. You know how pessimistic he was when he heard about you. He's convinced you are going to divert me.'

'Sounds as if he doesn't know you all that well, my love!' Simon said with a barely perceptible hint of sarcasm. 'I'd say you were totally dedicated, and no mere male could put a spanner in the works.'

They both laughed and then, her face serious once more, Emma said:

'I can't be any different, Simon. I know you were disappointed about this morning, but that interview really was too good an opportunity to miss – or should have been if that wretched plane had been on time.'

'Forget it, my love,' Simon said. 'You win some, you lose some. Let's have a bath and go to bed. We can go down to Ortolans first thing in the morning . . . come back after supper. That'll give us a good long day.'

'Whatever you want, darling,' Emma said reaching up her face to kiss him.

'All I want is you!' Simon said.

It went through his mind at that moment that he might have said: 'All I want is *all* of you!' but that would not have been fair. Emma had been perfectly straight with him from the start. Her career came first. He had thought he could accept it. There was no doubt that she was in love with him and women in love were usually pretty single-minded, malleable, often taking on their men's views even if sometimes they were quite contrary to those they had held before. Emma had said firmly: 'No marriage, no kids – not until I'm really established', so he had prepared himself to wait – or thought he had. Now he was so desperately in love with her that he found himself resenting anything which diverted her thoughts from him! Her job, her boss, the time she spent working. It was selfish and he knew he must curb that possessiveness . . . give Emma her head. He just wished he did not suddenly feel so insecure. He was not accustomed to the feeling. As far as the women in his past were concerned, he had always been well in control of the relationships and been the one to lay down the rules.

He was reminded suddenly of the French proverb: '*Il y a toujours l'un qui baise, et l'autre qui tend la joue!*' So, now it was he who kissed and Emma who offered her cheek. Somehow he must adapt to this change of role – but it was not going to be easy. Perhaps he had been browsing too often in *The Calverley Journal* where the men's wishes invariably came foremost in their women's lives.

Thinking of the journal reminded Simon of Ortolans. He'd been fortunate in getting hold of Roddy on Friday night who had assured him that the morning would not be wasted. The kitchen design firm could still do all the necessary measuring and the plumber could do his preliminary assessment of the central heating requirements. Whilst the two men were there, he, Roddy, would try to arrange another tripartite meeting in the near future.

'Sure you want to go to Ortolans tomorrow, darling?' he asked Emma as she emerged from the bathroom in his towelling robe. 'You're not too exhausted?'

Emma put her arms round his neck and leant her wet cheek against his.

'Of course we'll go. And I love you very, very much and I'm truly sorry I was so stupid about Cilla. What's wrong with her, anyway?'

Simon dropped a kiss on top of her head.

'Money worries. I'm lending her five thousand. You don't mind, do you?'

Emma looked astonished.

'Why should I? It's your money, Simon. Just so long as you don't decide to rekindle old fires!'

'Put that out of your mind. I was never in love with Cilla, although there was a time, I suppose, when I thought I was. Falling in love with you has straightened me out on that once and for all. I've never been really in love before. Believe it or not, you're the first!'

'As you are for me!' Emma said huskily. 'I was obsessed by Paul. I was in love with what I wanted him to be – not with what he really was. Derek maintains that love is just another word for obsession – that they're one and the same, and that love is just a pretty name for sexual attraction.'

Simon frowned.

'He seems to have got sex on the brain,' he said thoughtfully. 'If you hadn't told me he'd never once tried it on, I'd have said he had more than a working interest in you. Personally, I fail to see how he can have you around day after day and not lust after you – I would!' He laughed but the smile did not linger very long in his eyes. 'Better watch your step, Emma. One of these days he may decide to show his hand.'

Emma laughed.

'You've got rose-coloured spectacles on. Derek doesn't even notice me – I'm no more than a member of his staff. Besides, he's got a live-in girlfriend.'

'Glad to hear it!' Simon said, kissing her again. 'I can tell you one thing, darling, if he ever so much as lays a finger on you, he'll be in big trouble. There'd be no more Emma Calverley dancing attendance upon him, and you'd better tell him I said so!'

Emma laughed.

'Now who's being an idiot. You've far less cause to be jealous of poor Derek than I have of Cilia. After all, she was your girlfriend – and there's never been anything like that between Derek and me. In addition to being my boss, we really are "just good friends!"'

'But he's a good-looking chap – if you like the type!' Simon said, grinning. 'Besides, I'm not sure if I believe in platonic friendships. He's just a shade too possessive about you for my liking!'

'Just because he referred to me as "my girl" when he told you to take care of me at our wedding! Anyway, I am "his girl" at work.' Kissing Simon before she gently detached herself from his arms, she added: 'Ours is a sort of father/daughter relationship and I trust him absolutely. He's a really nice guy, Simon, and I want you to like him.'

'OK, so I'll do my best, but do me a favour, darling. Tell him you're *my* girl now.'

'No, I'm not!' Emma said, kissing him again. 'I'm your wife! And it's my wifely duty to advise you that the bathwater will soon be stone cold!'

'So what!' said Simon as he pushed her gently back amongst the sofa cushions and made love to her again.

CHAPTER THIRTY-TWO

1987

Hazel was out in the scullery washing the lunch dishes. Vicky sat on the floor in front of the old Aga playing with some coloured counters Simon had found in the drawer of a tallboy. He, Emma and Roddy were sitting at the long, scrubbed kitchen table drinking coffee.

'My grandad would have fifty fits if he could see me now!' Roddy was saying, his blue eyes twinkling as he addressed his remarks to Emma. 'His aunt, my Great-Great-Aunt Ada, was nursemaid to Simon's great-grandmother; and Great-Uncle Tom, who started as bootboy, is still working as gardener. Nearly everyone in that branch of the family was in service to the Calverleys in the days of The Great Divide.'

Seeing Emma's puzzled expression, he laughed.

'Upstairs, downstairs – and ne'er the twain did mix. Now here I am drinking and eating at the same table as the squire himself, not to mention the fact that the said squire is dining in the kitchen!'

Simon grinned.

'I suppose we should thank the war for bringing some sense into our class system. At least those with brains like you, Roddy, were given the chance to improve your lot. I reckon your grammar school education was every bit as good as mine at Eton and you swanned through the exams. Your grandfather didn't have those opportunities.'

Emma listened to the interchange with interest. It was the first time she had really heard Roddy talk about himself. He and Simon were usually too caught up in their plans for

Ortolans. Roddy's voice was accentless with no hint of the
Sussex vowel sounds she had heard in Tom's voice. His freckled
face was open and his manners faultless. She would not have
known that he did not come from a monied background,
whereas Hazel spoke with a marked cockney accent and she
had but to open her mouth to betray her origins. Little Vicky,
curiously, spoke with two accents – her mother's and, when
replying to Simon, his intonations. The child was clearly bright.
It would be a pity if her mother did not encourage her to do
well at school. Hazel had apparently left at the earliest opportunity without one O level to her credit.

'You might like to meet my grandfather one day, Emma,'
Roddy said. 'He's steeped in Ortolans's history. In a funny sort
of way, the house and the Calverleys are as much his family
as his own. I expect you've already read *The Calverley Journal*?
It's a fascinating document. Unfortunately, it only begins in
the 1700s and I would love to have known more about
Ortolans's origins.'

'Roddy thinks one of his ancestors may have built the
house,' Simon explained. 'That's why he takes such an interest
in it.'

'Always was fascinated by it, even as a kid!' Roddy said
grinning. 'I used to bike up here from the village and shin up
the old walnut tree when no one was around and just sit there
looking at the house. You would suppose it always looks the
same, but it doesn't. In the winter, it seems to huddle into
itself like some old person who feels the cold and wraps their
arms around themselves to trap the warmth inside. In the
spring and summer, it opens its arms and seems to expand,
as if it were filling its lungs with air and delighting in the
garden as it returns to life. I suppose I must have been a
fanciful kid. Still am, at heart! When Simon and I are working
on the house, I imagine I can hear it sighing with satisfaction
as we repair the damages of age – give it a heart transplant,
inject new life into it.'

'No need to look so sheepish when you say that, Roddy – I

feel the same,' Simon said. 'I think Emma has begun to feel it, too.'

Emma nodded.

'Perhaps it isn't so fanciful. After all, no one thinks it odd if you talk about a house being haunted, having a sinister or oppressive atmosphere; so why can't Ortolans have an aura of its own – a happy, loving, caring spirit. I love it here.'

Simon reached for her hand and squeezed it.

'I'm so glad you feel like that, darling. After all, one day it's going to be our home – where we spend our lives, day in and day out. It's the reason I want you to choose the curtains and colours and kitchen units and all that kind of thing. Interior décor is not really my scene although I always know what I like and don't like.'

He broke off as Vicky abandoned her toys and climbed on to his lap. For once, her face was moderately clean. Hazel had tied her straight black hair back from her forehead in a tiny pony-tail and she looked enchanting.

'So what mischief have you been up to today, madam?' he asked, rocking her gently on his knee.

The child's huge dark eyes crinkled into a smile.

'Notta mischef!' she murmured.

'Oh, yes you are!' Simon teased. 'Your mummy said you wouldn't go to bed last night when you were told. That was naughty!'

'Not norty!' the little girl replied. 'Vicky see Simon!'

Simon turned his face away from the child and said in an undertone:

'It's all a bit tricky. I think the poor kid sees me as a kind of father figure. Apparently she'd been told by Hazel I'd be coming down yesterday evening and was still watching for my car from the window when it was time for her to have her bath. Trouble is, she's too young to explain things to, and Hazel hasn't a great deal of patience with her at the best of times.'

'I suppose one has to make allowances,' Roddy said. 'Being

a mum at that age can't be much fun. All the same, I wish she wouldn't smack her so often. Half the time, the child doesn't realize she's doing wrong.'

He broke off, clapping his hand to his forehead.

'I clean forgot to tell you, Simon. Old Burchell has had a stroke. Mrs B wanted me to tell you. They decided against hospital which the poor old boy would loathe and anyway, he's not expected to recover. I thought you should know.'

Simon set the child down on the floor and rose immediately to his feet.

'I'll go down right away and see him,' he said. He declined Emma's offer to go with him. 'You stay and chat to Roddy. I won't be long.'

After he had departed, Roddy said:

'Burchell used to be the family chauffeur – in the days when the late Lady Calverley could still afford one! Simon's so good about things like this – it's a kind of tradition to look after old retainers. It goes back to the days when the head of the family was also the squire of the village. Nowadays, there is hardly anyone left in Detcham who remembers those days. My family, the Burchells and one or two of the farmers hereabouts talk of "the good old days" and still come to Simon for advice if they've a problem.'

'The class divisions were even more unfair than they are today,' Emma said. 'The poor had no chance of becoming rich, however hard they worked. Did your family never resent the disparity?'

Roddy grinned.

'I don't honestly think they did. They accepted it as the natural way of life. Besides, the Calverleys were always good to their servants and tenants. It'll mean a great deal to old Burchell and his wife, that Simon is taking time to visit them. He's a thoroughly good chap is Simon.'

Emma smiled.

'I know! And he thinks the world of you, Roddy. He has a great respect for what you are doing for Ortolans.'

'I suppose it's as much my pleasure as his!' Roddy said thoughtfully. 'I hate to see a beautiful old building like this decaying. Of course, it's a valuable asset and worth preserving, but Simon isn't doing it for the money. I expect you know that without me telling you.'

Emma nodded.

'I feel a bit guilty about yesterday, Roddy. I believe you went to a great deal of trouble to get the meeting organized. I'm really sorry.'

'Simon explained how important your work is. You were doing an interview, weren't you? Someone famous?'

Emma nodded again, this time unable to admit to Roddy that it had all turned out to be a total waste of time. She was about to tell him about her work when Hazel appeared.

'Can I have a word?' she said, addressing Emma. 'If you're not doing anything important, I mean?'

'I want to take some measurements in the attics,' Roddy said, rising to his feet. 'I'll see you later. When Simon gets back, will you tell him where I am?'

As he disappeared, Hazel sat down at the table.

'It's about Vicky, you know,' she said, lighting one of the cigarettes she seemed to chain-smoke. 'Well, actually it's about next weekend . . .'

She regarded Emma speculatively.

'There's a "do" at the White Horse next Saturday. I've been asked to go but I can't, can I? Not with her . . .' She pointed her cigarette at Vicky. 'Bloody well tied, I am – can't have no fun with her on my hands morning, noon and night. Sticks in my gullet, sometimes.'

She drew on her cigarette and blew out a cloud of smoke.

'You don't know what it's like!' she said accusingly. 'You can please yourself what you do. Your lot's got everything, a husband, money, decent clothes. I'm not saying Simon doesn't give me a fair wage but take my word for it, it doesn't go far these days – what with the kid's clothes and all, and the family allowance is a joke! And my fags cost an arm and a leg.'

She stubbed out her cigarette and drew a deep sigh.

'I get right fed up sometimes!' she said confidentially. 'Not seeing no one and not having no fun. I thought . . . maybe . . . maybe you'd not mind babysitting next Saturday – if you're coming down, you know? I mean, it isn't as if she's much trouble – not once I've got her to bed. I'd really like to go to this disco – just this once!'

Emma felt a mixture of compassion and irritation. She wished Hazel would not always refer to little Vicky as 'she' or 'her' – as if the child were an object rather than a person. She thought, also, that Hazel should have made this request when Simon was here. He, after all, was her employer. At the same time, she knew that he would not refuse it. He was much too kind-hearted, and she herself felt sorry for Hazel. It couldn't be much fun, as Roddy had said, being only twenty years old and finding herself a virtual prisoner.

'We haven't discussed next weekend, but we will almost certainly be down,' she said. 'If we are – and I'll have to talk to Simon before I promise anything – then certainly I'll baby-sit for you.'

'Great! That's great! Thanks a lot!' Hazel said, her face lighting up. She glanced briefly at Vicky. 'She's not a bad kid, really. Looks just like her father, though, rotten sod! Said he'd think about marriage once he'd finished his studies – but he'd no more intention of it than flying to the moon. Your Simon said Alwis came from a really high-class family and wouldn't have been allowed to marry me even if he'd wanted. Didn't know these coloured chaps had high-class families! I mean, we sort of look down on them in this country, don't we? My mum and dad wouldn't hear of me keeping the baby once they heard she was coloured, poor little devil. Oh, well, that's water under the bridge. Sometimes I think it might have been best if I'd had her adopted.'

'I'm sure you don't mean that, Hazel!' Emma said. 'Vicky is such a beautiful little girl. It'll get easier as she gets older.'

'Bloody well hope so!' Hazel said, pushing back her chair. 'I don't want to be cooped up here all my life.'

'Don't you like it here?' Emma asked. 'It's such a lovely house – and a wonderful place for Vicky to grow up.'

'That's as may be,' Hazel said darkly. 'You try living without a bloke!'

I have tried, Emma thought, and at times she had been very lonely and, after that wild affair with Paul, very sexually frustrated. But then she had not been tied to a child. She had been free to accept invitations to a drink, to dinner, the theatre. She had been free to go to a wine bar or a cinema with Lucy on the few occasions when Lucy was not otherwise engaged – and to attend office parties with Derek as standby escort if she needed one.

'You going to give up your job now you're married?'

Hazel's question took her unawares.

'Certainly not!' she replied instantly. 'I love my work and it would take a lot more than marriage to make me give up four years of slogging away to become a producer. No, of course I'm not going to give up my career.'

Hazel grinned.

'OK, keep your hair on. I just thought that with Simon being so mad about children, you might decide to start a family, you know? After all, you're not exactly young, are you? I mean, you must be getting on for thirty!'

It was not meant to be cheeky, Emma realized, but nevertheless she felt more than a trifle irritated. In cool tones, she said:

'I know Simon is fond of your Vicky, but I would not say he was "mad about children", as you put it. Now I'm sure you've lots to do, Hazel. Don't let me keep you gossiping.'

Hazel shrugged indifferently.

'Oh well, you should know!' she said as she lit another cigarette. 'OK to leave Vicky here with you? She's not in the way, is she?'

'No, leave her by all means!' Emma replied. The child was now standing on a chair by the window staring out at the empty drive.

She's watching for Simon, Emma thought, as Hazel went through to the scullery. She felt a sudden aching sympathy for the little girl. Remembering her own childhood and how she had longed for her parents' love and approval, she knew what Vicky was missing. Like her own mother, Hazel was not the kind who cuddled and kissed a child. Emma was both amused and touched when Simon's Porsche braked in the driveway and like a flash, Vicky was off her chair and running into the hall to greet him.

When he came into the kitchen, Vicky was sitting ecstatically astride his shoulders. With some difficulty, he bent his head and kissed Emma.

'Sorry to be so long, darling. I'm afraid old Burchell is on the way out and Mrs B knows it. We were discussing his funeral, of all things. I'll have to go, of course. She'll arrange it for a Saturday so I'll be here. Is that OK with you?'

Emma nodded. She did not feel it was the right moment to remind him of yesterday and add the proviso that she would only be at Ortolans if Derek did not have work for her. Instead, she told him about Hazel's request to her to babysit the following weekend.

'It's OK by me,' Simon said equably. 'You're no trouble, are you, my love!' He swung the child into the air and lowered her, squealing with delight, on to the floor. 'Hope you weren't too bored, darling?'

'On the contrary, Roddy was talking about "the good old days". What a nice person he is, Simon. When I first met him, I didn't think he was particularly attractive, but he grows on you. He's got a devastating smile. Some girl is going to fall head over heels one of these days.'

'But not you!' Simon said, a half-smile softening the sharpness of his tone. 'I warn you, darling, I'm the jealous type. I don't want you being attracted to anyone but me!'

Ignoring the child who was once again playing with the box of counters, he drew Emma against him and kissed her fiercely.

'I can't help being jealous. You're so damned attractive. You've got what my darling Great-Gran used to call "sex-appeal" and I know only too well what effect you have on the male sex. Let's go upstairs and make love,' he added in a low tone Vicky could not hear.

Emma had been on the point of complying when Roddy returned.

'I hate to tell you this, Simon, but there's death-watch beetle up in the new attic rafters. We knew about the woodworm, of course, but we'll have to notify Rentokil. The whole house will have to be fumigated again. At least you're under guarantee so it won't cost you. The beetle is definitely active although I have to admit it's a very small infestation and could easily have been missed.'

Simon looked sheepish.

'I don't think it was their oversight,' he said. 'Since they treated the house last year, I bought some old cupboards at an auction and stored them up there. If they have been infested, it has probably spread.'

'I'll get on to Rentokil tomorrow,' Roddy promised. He smiled at Emma. 'We get these setbacks from time to time. It's inevitable with old houses like this. I know we're going to have trouble with the central heating pipes. You can't chop holes in wattle and daub, or in panelling, without ruining it. We'll probably have to box them in.'

'See what we're up against, darling!' Simon said to Emma. 'Thanks be to God, my investments are flourishing and I can meet the bills, especially now the bank has increased my loan. Since house prices have escalated, they were more than happy to take the deeds of Ortolans as security.'

'I should hope so,' Roddy said dourly. 'When it's all finished, this place will be worth a bomb – and it's my bet house prices will continue rising. Not that you'd want to sell, Simon, but it's good to know you're not throwing good money after bad. Every penny you borrow to spend on this place is more than justified financially.'

'I couldn't afford to get into debt when I was at Bristol,' Emma said as they walked through to the drawing-room, the child following like a puppy at their heels. 'I didn't get the full grant, so my parents made it up and I had to manage on that. The habit of keeping in the black stuck when I started earning.'

'A reasonable maxim at one time,' Simon acknowledged. 'It's very different now. If you borrow from the bank at – call it 10 per cent to make the mathematics easy – and can make the money earn 15, you'd be crazy not to do it.'

Emma laughed.

'Yes, if you have the know-how to do that,' she said. 'I haven't got a clue about stocks and shares and to be honest, I don't think I want to. I'm not really a gambler. The most I put on a horse is a pound each way and then it has to be a cert!'

'There's no such thing as a "cert", Emma,' Simon said with a smile. 'The best one can do is take an educated guess. It's the same with stocks and shares. It was a reasonable certainty you'd make money if you were allocated shares in British Airways when the Government sold them off last month – but if they had been undersubscribed, you *could* have lost money.'

'Interesting as this talk on high finance might be, I shall have to be on my way,' Roddy said with his engaging smile. 'See you next weekend, I hope.'

With his departure, Vicky came to stand by Simon's knees.

'Read a story, please?' she asked her dark eyes lifted hopefully to his.

'Well, I was going to look at the Sunday paper!' Simon said with a sigh. 'However, since you asked so nicely, I tell you what I'll do. I'll show you the picture albums, shall I?'

He grinned at Emma.

'For some reason I have failed to fathom, she adores the old family photograph albums.'

Emma leant back against the cushions, listening whilst Simon entertained the child. It struck her that he was getting as much enjoyment as Vicky from the exploration of the worn leather albums.

'This is Silver Mist, Great-Grandmother Sophia's very own pony,' he was saying. 'She was very, very old when she died. This is Great-Gran when she was a little girl – not much older than you. Now in the picture, her hair looks dark like yours, because they did not have coloured pictures in those days, but her hair was red – a beautiful coppery red; and she had green eyes.'

'Which one? Which one?' Vicky asked, stabbing her finger at another picture.

'Ah! Now you have me, Vicky. One is Great-Great-Great-Aunt Georgie, and one is Great-Great-Great-Aunt Nellie, but nobody could tell them apart because they looked exactly like each other. Let's call this one Nellie and this one Georgie, shall we? I don't think they would mind if we've got it wrong!'

He had a natural way with the little girl which explained the child's devotion to him, Emma thought. He would make a good father one day. Had Hazel been right in her supposition that Simon was 'mad about children'? It was unusual for a man to have such strong paternal feelings, especially as he had his own career and his precious Ortolans to occupy his time. More probably Hazel's little daughter was simply a novelty, someone who amused him for an hour or two.

Watching him as he cuddled the child, she felt a deep surge of love for him. She loved his strong, masterful manner when he made love to her – in one way dominant but at the same time ensuring that she, too, was free to express herself as she wished, without inhibitions. Afterwards, he would lie with her in his arms, her face against his shoulder, and talk of the love they shared and the wonderful future they had to look forward to now that they had been lucky enough to find each other.

When Hazel came in to collect Vicky for her tea, Emma looked at Simon questioningly.

'You put a proposition to me after lunch. Is this a good moment to take you up on it?'

Simon drew her to her feet.

'Too true it is, my darling!' He kissed her fiercely and the familiar flame of desire took hold of them. 'Upstairs, right now!' he murmured. 'Otherwise I shall make love to you here and now. God, how I want you, Emma!'

They made love in the huge four-poster which had once belonged to Simon's great-grandmother, Sophia, and her beloved husband, Konrad. Simon had bought a king-size duvet and now told Emma with a smile that he had done so in anticipation of sharing the marital bed with the woman he loved.

'Of course, I didn't know then that it was going to be you,' he said. 'I didn't even know you existed. Just imagine, Emma, if you had not decided to interview Joanne, or if I had not been sufficiently curious to sit in and listen, we might never have met.'

'I don't believe that!' Emma said quietly. 'I feel as if we are fulfilling our destiny, Simon. Does that sound as if I've been reading too many Barbara Cartlands? You know, don't you, that I love you . . . very, very much! I think I always will!'

'And I shall always love you!' Simon said, taking her once more into his arms. 'You know, darling, I used to dread Sunday evenings – having to drive back to London, leave Ortolans. Now, although I don't want to go back to town, at least I'll have you with me. Maybe we could stay on tonight. What do you think? If we got up early, we could be in London by nine. It would give us another night here. It seems to have been such a short visit this weekend.'

Emma knew he had not intended to make it sound like a reproach but she was instantly conscious of the fact that it was because of her commitments that they had not come down on Saturday. It was on the tip of her tongue to remind Simon that he need not have come back to London on Saturday, but she bit back the words.

'Provided I'm in the studio by nine, it should be OK,' she said. 'But I'll have to call in at the flat first – my flat. I left all my papers there. I really shouldn't be late, darling – especially with yesterday being such a fiasco.'

Derek's unspoken name lingered in the air between them. This time it was Simon who bit back his words.

'We'll leave at seven – that should give us plenty of time, even if the traffic's bad,' he said. 'Coming for a bath, darling? With a bit of luck, I'll get the old gas geyser to function. I can't wait to get this awful plumbing replaced. Imagine what it must have been like in the old days, Emma. Great-Gran used to have a tin bath as a child and the servants had to carry cans of hot water upstairs to fill it. Thank God for mod cons!'

Derek was forgotten as they went with arms linked to the drafty old bathroom and Simon managed, with patience, to fill the old, cast-iron bath with sufficient water to cover both of them.

'I reckon by the summer, we'll have this house fit to live in!' he said as with lazy contentment, he sponged warm water over Emma's shoulders. 'It mightn't be a bad idea to think of commuting. London's such hell in the hot weather. We could drive in to Hassocks and catch an early train. How does the idea strike you, darling?'

Emma's idyll came to an abrupt end. One moment, she was wonderfully and perfectly at ease with the world, happy as she had never been in her life before – and never more in love with Simon with whom she felt totally united. Now, not even the warmth of the water could prevent a cold shiver encompassing her body. Surely, she thought, Simon realized that there could be no question of her commuting. Sometimes, it was eight or nine at night before she could leave the studio. Sometimes, if she had to travel to the Midlands or the north or down to the West Country, she and the crew would leave in the early hours. London was central for most places, and her job could take her anywhere in the country at any time. Simon knew that. It was simply not fair to put a proposition to her to which he knew she could not agree.

Looking up at his open, questioning gaze, she could only assume that he had spoken without thought; that he had forgotten the importance to her of her career. She knew that she ought to speak out now, before the whole subject became too complicated, explain that it was not for herself that she wanted success; explain her passionate longing to be able to write and tell her parents that they had no need to be disappointed in her any longer; that she was in a position of importance, authority, responsibility, someone worthy of their respect. But Simon might not understand, and she could not bring herself to spoil this moment of closeness. Weakly, she said:

'We'll think about it, darling. Summer's a long way off, isn't it!'

It was a prevarication that all too soon she was going to regret.

CHAPTER THIRTY-THREE

1987

'I suppose it might work! Can't say I'm frightfully impressed, Emma!'

Derek's voice was more than a little doubtful as he leafed through Emma's hurriedly written synopsis. Fortunately, he had been late in to work and Emma had had time to get hold of some excellent footage of elephants from the archives before he arrived and called her into his office.

'Frankly, it all looks a bit rushed – as if you haven't put much time into it!'

Emma felt the familiar onset of queasiness and her palms felt damp.

'Derek, I told you, I only had Ms Faraday to myself for ten short minutes. There was no way she was going to miss her connection just to talk to me. She's one of the few people I know who wasn't in the slightest degree interested in publicity. All she cared about was preserving her animals. I did try to get it across to her that a TV programme could rouse a very large number of ordinary people to take an interest, but she seems to think her book and the film will do that anyway.'

'OK, OK, don't let's make a thing of it. Had a nice weekend? You're looking good.'

Although Derek had frequently made similar personal remarks in the past, there was something in his tone which, to Emma's intense discomfort, made her blush. It was Lucy's fault, she told herself as she ran a hand unconsciously through her hair. She seemed determined to believe that Derek had more than a boss's interest in her – or, as she put it, a 'thing' about her. It was so ridiculous. If Derek had ever nurtured any designs upon her, it would have been obvious long ago. She had been pretty vulnerable after the break-up with Paul and there had been times when Derek had put his arms round her and she'd cried like a kid on his shoulder. He had often given her a hug or kissed her, but then he was a tactile kind of person. None of that stiff-upper-lip English reserve about him, which was one of the reasons she had always found it so easy to confide in him. She'd told him things about Paul she would not even have told a battered wives' counsellor! Nothing could be more unlikely that now, when he knew she was crazy about her new husband, he would step out of line. He was her good friend in the truest sense of the word – and she needed his support.

'You're looking good yourself, Derek!' she said easily. 'New tie?'

He nodded as he shouted to Marie, his secretary, who was in the adjoining room.

'Bring us some coffee, will you, Marie. Black for me, white for Emma! And give Graham a bell – tell him I don't want to see him until eleven.'

As the girl went out, he turned back to Emma.

'Pull a chair up and we'll see if we can tart this up a bit. I don't want any lowering of standards – not when the programme is doing so well. It's your reputation as well as mine, Emma, that's at risk, and as you know, I've been plugging the high ratings whenever there's a chance. I can't think why, but it's as important to me that you get your new contract as it is to you. You're my pupil, when all's said and done, and I shall take some of the credit when you're made an assistant producer.'

Emma felt a surge of excitement course through her. Derek had said 'when', not 'if', and so much depended upon his goodwill.

'You should have *all* of the credit,' she said with genuine warmth. 'I was completely green when you took me in hand. You taught me everything I know.'

Derek's somewhat full lips parted in a gratified smile as he lit one of his cigarillos.

'To be honest, Emma, I have been wondering of late if you really did appreciate what I've been trying to do for you. Oh, I know you used to, before you married this chap, Calverley. Since then, well . . . frankly, I wouldn't be all that surprised if you decided to chuck in your hand.'

Emma's eyes flashed.

'How can you think that?' she said. 'You're the one person who really does understand what my future here means to me. My marrying Simon hasn't changed anything. I told you that.'

Derek put a hand on hers.

'Well, of course you did, darling, but a blind man could see how crazy you are about your husband – and when women think they're in love, common sense can all too easily fly out of the window. After all, my dear, Calverley is rich. You don't *need* the job now.'

'But I want it!' Emma cried. 'Of course I love Simon, but I love my work, too. Simon knows perfectly well how import-ant it is to me, and he knows perfectly well that he's got to wait for a family.'

Derek nodded.

'So long as you're on the pill and there aren't any slip-ups.'

'There won't be!' Emma said quickly.

'I'm pleased you said that, Emma. I have been a bit worried. Tell you what, we'll go out for lunch somewhere and celebrate. I'll take you to a slap-up meal at the Connaught. How about that?'

'It sounds fine – but I'm really not dressed for a smart hotel!' Nor, thought Emma, did she want to go out for a prolonged lunch. On the other hand, she did not want to upset Derek by a refusal. 'What about work, Derek? I really ought to get down to this.' She tapped the notes in front of them.

'You can catch up this evening,' Derek said. 'Frankly, Emma, I had a lousy weekend. If there's one thing I really hate it's my Sunday-a-month access to my kids. It's an ordeal for all of us – and of course, there's always a scene when I take them back to their mother. It doesn't matter what alimony I give her, she always wants more. However . . . that's not your worry. My mistake was ever getting married and having kids. Between you and me, I never did like mine. Not the paternal type, I'm afraid!'

Emma was reminded suddenly of Simon, his fair head bent over Vicky's dark one, patiently explaining the pictures in the photograph album to her. Obviously Derek had never enjoyed the same communion with his children.

'So, if you're going to feel embarrassed about your clothes, we'll go to Francesco's instead of the Connaught – not that you need be self-conscious, darling. Even in jeans you look absolutely stunning. You've got a fantastic figure. You ought to be in front of the camera, not behind it! I'm more a "boobs-and-bums" than a "legs" man but you've got the lot, Emma.'

It was a typical Derek remark – one which dear Lucy might all too easily misinterpret but which epitomized the kind of comment which was meaningless in the free and easy atmosphere of the studio.

'This is a silly conversation!' she said, smiling. 'It's nice to know you approve, but I'm your researcher and how I look doesn't come into the equation.'

Derek gave a mock sigh and lifted both hands, waving them in a theatrical gesture of pacification.

'I know, I know! But don't blame me if once in a while I regret it. A mouse may look at a cat, may he not?'

Emma's laugh was genuine.

'You're hardly a mouse, Derek – and I'm certainly not a cat! Now for goodness sake, let's be sensible. It's almost eleven and you're seeing Graham at any moment whereas I must get back to work.'

'True! I'll see you at one o'clock, Emma. Off you go, girl.'

Emma had barely returned to her own desk before Simon telephoned. 'Just wanted to tell you I love you!' he said. 'Hope I'm not interrupting anything?'

'No, of course not, darling. I love you, too.'

'Don't be late back if you can avoid it,' Simon was saying. 'I've just realized that it's five months, one week, three days and ten minutes since we met and I thought we should celebrate . . . go to Le Bijou's tonight – the place where we had our first date and I fell in love with you.'

'You've got it wrong, darling,' Emma said glancing at her watch. 'It's five months, one week, three days and twenty minutes since we met. Having said that, we'll certainly celebrate. I love you.'

'I love you, too!' Simon answered and rang off.

She would have to be sparing about the meal she chose with Derek, Emma thought, and go easy on the wine. Without consciously doing so, she had refrained from telling Simon she was lunching with her boss. Likewise, she did not talk of Simon to him. This reticence had sprung from an instinctive wish to keep the two men in separate compartments of her life. She wanted Derek to feel that as far as her job was concerned, she might never have been married.

Fortunately, she had cleared her desk by Friday afternoon and Derek found no last-minute trips to spoil the weekend. As she and Simon drove down to Ortolans, stopping *en route* at The Red Lion in Handcross for a quick supper, Simon was in excellent spirits.

'The weather forecast's really good, darling!' he said as they neared Detcham. 'If you like the idea, we could nip into Brighton tomorrow. We could even take Vicky with us – go on the pier. I used to love it when I was a kid. Old as she was, Great-Gran used to take me on the pier every Easter holidays – and to the Aquarium.'

'I thought you planned on stripping the wallpaper in the gallery.'

Simon turned the car off the main road and headed towards Henfield.

'I did! But we can do that on a rainy day. It's just an idea, Emma. I thought it might be fun.'

'I'll go along with it!' Emma said, 'but don't forget we're babysitting for Hazel anyway. I suppose if we take Vicky off her hands, she'll have some time to prepare for her "do".'

Simon laughed.

'Heaven alone knows who she's got in tow – someone she's picked up in Detcham, I suppose. Roddy said he saw Hazel a week or two ago chatting up a long-haired youth on a motor-bike.'

'I thought it was all flat-tops and geometrics that was fashionable these days,' Emma remarked. 'Though come to think of it, one of our technicians has a ponytail!'

Simon grinned.

'We seem to be the last bastion of conventional dressing in the City. Which reminds me, darling, it's been a good day for me – my shares have rocketed.'

Emma did her best for the next ten minutes to understand what he was talking about, but she was little the wiser by the time they turned into the driveway to Ortolans. Lights were burning in the downstairs windows and the smell of woodsmoke drifted towards them as they climbed out of the car. With a bag in each hand, Simon stood still, sniffing the night air.

'Home!' he said softly. 'There's nowhere in the world like it. I think we'll have to get a dog, darling, or two dogs. We've always had gun dogs in the family, although Great-Gran had a King Charles which she adored. I wonder if Hazel would cope – we certainly couldn't have a dog in town.'

'It would be company for little Vicky!' Emma agreed as they went into the house. 'If you can afford it, Simon, an increase in Hazel's wage might convince her it was a good idea. She was complaining last weekend that she was short of cash!'

They could hear from the sitting-room attached to the kitchen – once the domain of the resident family cook – the sound of the television which Hazel seemed always to prefer at maximum volume. It sounded like the concluding music of *The Colbys* or *Dynasty*.

'Goodness knows how she'd hear Vicky cry out over that row!' Simon said. 'I offered to have the telly put upstairs in her flat but she says she prefers to sit down here after the kid's in bed. Nearer the kettle for those endless cups of coffee she drinks, I suppose.'

'Be glad it's only coffee!' Emma said laughing as she removed her jacket. 'She could be rifling your cellar – all those priceless old vintage clarets or whatever you keep stored down there!'

'No, she couldn't!' Simon said, putting his arms round her. 'I keep the cellar very firmly locked. Which reminds me, darling, we finished the brandy last weekend. I'll nip down and get another bottle whilst I think of it. We'll have a nightcap.'

By the time she had consumed the large drink Simon gave her, Emma was half asleep. It seemed a very long time since she had gone off to work that morning. Now that she lived in Brunswick Square, it meant she had to leave three-quarters of an hour earlier than when she had lived in Shepherd's Bush. At her third yawn, Simon pulled her to her feet and half-carried her across the room. The old stairs creaked as they went upstairs and when Emma commented, Simon laughingly told her it was the family ghost.

'None of the family believed he existed!' he told her as they undressed. 'But the servants did. It was one of those bits of folklore that went back years and years. A pretender to the Calverley title called Daniel, a half-caste Indian, had bumped off the real heir and was about to marry his widow. He fell down the attic stairs and broke his neck. Thereafter, he was supposed to haunt the place! Great-Gran didn't believe in the ghostly Daniel, but she always insisted Ortolans had a spirit – a benign one. If you read *The Calverley Journal*, you'll see how this so-called spirit pushed over the table she was standing on and prevented her running away from the man she loved, my great-grandfather, Konrad.'

'I'll opt for the benign spirit!' Emma said sleepily. 'Can't say I fancy being bumped off by a Red Indian!'

'He was a very attractive fellow, from all accounts, and

women found him irresistible!' Simon murmured as he reached for her body beneath the large duvet.

'One irresistible man at a time is quite enough for me,' Emma answered, feeling the first familiar wave of desire pervade her. 'Kiss me, oh, Daniel, my beloved. Hold me. Love me. Take me!'

'Idiot – who I love to distraction!' Simon whispered, and needed no second bidding to carry out her request.

Brighton was crowded with visitors, attracted by the fine weather. Despite the difficulty of parking, the jostling of the day trippers and the queuing, Simon, Emma and Vicky thoroughly enjoyed their day. Vicky was given rides on everything mobile and they ended up watching the dolphin show in the Aquarium. By the time they returned home, the child was exhausted.

'Reckon you won't have much trouble with her tonight!' Hazel said as she greeted them. Clearly, she had used her afternoon to transform herself. She had brushed her hair into a spiky pink halo. Her eyes were heavily outlined and her lashes dark with mascara. Her lips were painted black and her nails varnished to match. A miniskirt, barely covering her thighs, showed long, not very shapely legs in fishnet tights. Emma could do no more than give a kindly nod when Hazel asked if she looked 'OK'.

When her escort called for her on his motorbike an hour later, Simon and Emma were unable to assess his attraction for Hazel as his head was encased in the obligatory crash helmet and he did no more than blare his horn, remaining seated all the while. With a promise not to be too late back, Hazel climbed up behind him and they roared off down the drive.

'Ah well, what it is to be young!' Simon said as he and Emma sat down in the kitchen to the casserole supper Hazel had left for them.

'You should know!' Emma rejoined, her voice teasing. 'You've behaved like a five-year-old all day. I still think you enjoyed the helter-skelter far more than Vicky!'

'And who was goggle-eyed at the dolphins!' Simon rejoined. 'It was fun, darling, wasn't it?'

Emma nodded.

'And a real treat for Vicky. She was very good, although she did give me a heart attack when she disappeared whilst I was in the loo. I kept thinking of those ghastly NSPCC statistics about child abusers.'

'It's a hell of a world for kids to grow up in these days.'

'Which is one reason why people are thinking twice about becoming parents,' Emma said. 'It's a responsibility I for one am not ready to take on, even if . . . if I were free to do so.'

Simon put down his knife and fork and leant across the table.

'You could be free – if that's what you wanted,' he said. 'One thing I am not short of is money, and anyway, your earnings are just lumped on to mine for tax purposes, and most of what you earn will be whittled away. You could chuck the job in – if you wanted to, Emma.'

'But I don't want to!' Emma's voice was sharper than she had intended. 'OK, so I needed the money I earned to support myself before we got married, but that isn't why I worked. I enjoy what I do, and I'd hate to give it up.'

Simon nodded, his face now averted from hers as he toyed with his food.

'I suppose it was silly of me to bring up the subject. It's just that today . . . in Brighton . . . watching you walking hand in hand with Vicky . . . it put the thought in my mind that she could be our child, our daughter, and for a moment, I wished it was true. I think you'd make a good mother – you're so gentle and . . . and good with her. I'm sorry, darling. I didn't mean to be controversial!'

'It isn't that!' Emma said, trying to sort out her emotions. 'It's just that you make me feel . . . well, guilty, I suppose. And it isn't fair. When you asked me to marry you, I told you that part of me belonged to my work and that if you couldn't accept that, I'd have to say "no". It isn't I who have changed our agreement – it's you!'

Simon let out his breath.

'That's fair enough. I accept what you say. I'm not going back on anything, Emma. I merely hoped that perhaps you might have begun to change your mind. I know that in a way I've changed. I had no yardstick by which to measure my love for you. I suppose sex was fairly high on my agenda – still is! But it's grown to be so much more, Emma. I want to be part of you, to know that you are a part of me – that we belong absolutely. Sometimes I have the feeling that I only have little bits of you – the bits you want to give me. There is the professional Emma I can't share . . .' He broke off and gave a short, awkward laugh. 'I sound as if I've been drinking. I'm not even sure if what I have said makes any sense. One thing I do know is that it is wrong for couples to be too possessive. They should allow each other breathing space and enrich each other's lives – not curtail them.'

'If you really believe that, Simon, you must understand why I don't want to give up my career to have a child. One day I will, but not now; not when I'm about to reach my goal. Please try to understand, darling!'

Simon pushed his plate to one side and leant back in his chair, a half-smile on his face as he said:

'I know I married a career woman, but Em, you're not the kind of dedicated female we have at Steinfelds. Joanne, who you interviewed, is just one of them. They're a pretty ruthless bunch. People don't matter to them. They'll stab their best friend in the back if it will advance them. People are there to be used for their own ends. No doubt they will succeed because they are totally single-minded in their determination to do so. One can admire them, but not like them. In some ways, I feel sorry for women like Joanne. They'll get to the top and suddenly, they won't be young any longer and what will they have – no husband to care for them in their old age, no children, few real friends who will last the course. I realize that, being female, they've probably had to work harder than their male counterparts to get where they want, but subjugating their femininity has turned them into ruthless predators. I simply can't see you as one of them, Emma. I don't want to see you as one of them. They're all neurotic, lonely, unhappy, for all their success.'

'You can't *know* that,' Emma argued. 'You may think they are, but do *they* think so? Joanne sounded highly satisfied with her life. She earns a fantastic salary, she loves her work and she's more or less her own boss. She didn't strike me as being in the least neurotic!'

'Believe me, she is! So is Gaynor who you haven't met. She's married – or was before her husband divorced her. She had three abortions in three years because taking maternity leave didn't fit in with her plans. She reckoned – probably quite rightly – that whoever stood in for her would stay in the job and she might not get her contract renewed. She kept the job but not her husband.'

'Sounds as if she was rather stupid!' Emma said. 'Why didn't she go on the pill after the first mishap?'

'Because, according to Joanne, she had high blood pressure – which I can well believe. If the husband hadn't divorced her, she'd probably have had a lot more abortions. Now she's universally disliked because she hasn't a decent word to say to anyone and she can't keep her secretaries for more than six months at a time. If she gets much more neurotic, she'll get the push. It's on the cards now.'

'So she loses all along the line!' Emma said. 'Well, I may not be Joanne or the wretched Gaynor, but I *am* dedicated to my job. I'm sorry if you are disappointed, Simon.'

'Emma, don't! It was never my intention to make an issue of this. I just opened my big mouth and said what I was thinking – that it would be nice if we had a kid like Vicky. It's been a lovely day – don't let's spoil it. Tell you what, let's listen to the news on Hazel's telly whilst I brew some coffee. I want to hear the debate on what the Government's likely to do about putting sanctions on Japan. It's high time they did something about the balance of trade figures. It'll affect the market in a big way if Mrs Thatcher wins out.'

Simon seemed able to put the subject of her career out of his mind, but Emma could not. Long after they had gone to bed and he was asleep, she stayed awake, perturbed by the lingering feeling of resentment that would not be banished. Tired as she was, it was in the early hours of the morning before she finally fell into an uneasy sleep. When she awoke several hours later, it was to find Simon standing by the bedside with a tray.

'Thought you might like breakfast in bed for a treat!' he said. 'Hope you can cope with it, darling. Hazel's cooked you egg, bacon, toast and fresh coffee! I've already had mine.'

Emma sat up, rubbing her eyes, the misgivings of the night before totally forgotten as she noted the napkin folded over Simon's arm like a waiter's.

'Would madam like her tray on her lap?' he enquired, balancing it precariously on one hand.

She felt a rush of tenderness as she took in the slightly ridiculous figure of her husband. There was something very endearing in his appearance. He looked like an overgrown schoolboy, fair hair tousled, long bare legs protruding beneath a well-worn silk dressing-gown which barely reached his knees. There was a slight, fair stubble on his chin and a look of smug satisfaction in his green eyes. He seemed unaware of the fact that his dressing-gown was inside out as, with a grand gesture, he flourished the napkin which had been folded over his arm, and tried ineffectually to lay it across her lap.

'Darling, you'll drop it!' Emma laughed. 'You are an idiot – but I love you – and thanks for the treat.'

As she took the tray from him, he sat down on the edge of the bed and leant over to kiss her.

'I'm sure the lady of the manor should not be kissing the butler, or floor waiter or whatever!' she said, endeavouring not to knock over the coffee pot as she returned his kiss.

'Hazel's in good form. Seems she enjoyed herself last night!' Simon commented. 'She wants to see you in due course – probably to thank you.'

Although Hazel did express her thanks when an hour later Emma went down to the kitchen, she had something else on her mind.

'Gary says there's a darts match in The Plough this evening and he'll take me along if you say I can go.' She busied herself lighting a cigarette, thus avoiding Emma's eyes. 'I know it's a bit of a cheek – well, asking you to baby-mind two nights in a row but . . . well, I'd really like to go. I mean, seeing as how Simon said you'd be staying on tonight and driving back in the morning like last week, you know? Of course, if you'd rather not . . .'

Emma hesitated. In one way, it was – as Hazel put it – a bit of a cheek, and yet it really wasn't going to inconvenience them.

'Wouldn't have asked 'cepting those as don't ask, don't get, and as Gary said, you can always say "no"!' Hazel smiled disarmingly.

'That's OK with me – if Simon agrees!' Emma replied. 'Who is this Gary? Is he a local boy? Does Simon know the family?'

Hazel shook her head.

'Doubt it! He's from London. We met in The White Horse a week or two ago when I was doing the weekly shop. Fancies me, he does. He come down special from London last night and says he'll stay on if I can meet him again this evening.'

'I'll talk to Simon,' Emma said, touched by the girl's obvious excitement.

Simon raised no objection.

'It's OK by me, darling. Vicky's no trouble at night.'

They spent the afternoon stripping wallpaper, much to the delight of the child who happily tore the loose pieces within her reach. Hazel, clearly grateful for the opportunity to see more of her new boyfriend, was surprisingly helpful and cheerfully sang the words of all the pop songs which blared from her radio as she wielded her scraper.

'It may be physically exhausting but it's mentally relaxing,' Simon said as they collapsed that evening onto the sofa.

'It was fun!' Emma said. 'I really enjoyed it. The gallery looks twice the size without that gloomy Victorian paper.'

'Great-Great-Great Aunts Nellie and Georgie were responsible for that!' Simon said with a smile. 'It was very fashionable at the time and according to Great-Gran, the aunts thought themselves very modern and daring when they had it papered.' He yawned and put his arm round Emma's shoulders. 'We're going to have to be up at dawn,' he said. 'Shall we have an early night?'

Emma had not the slightest difficulty falling asleep, her head resting as always in the hollow of Simon's shoulder, his arm across her waist. She was unaware how long she had been sleeping when she was woken by Vicky's screams. She waited a minute or two for them to stop, but there was no sound of Hazel's footsteps in the attic flat above their room and Vicky's yells continued. Emma shook Simon into wakefulness.

'One or other of us ought to go and see what's wrong!' she said. 'I'd go, but Vicky's more used to you.'

Simon was already pulling on his dressing-gown. He glanced at his watch before hurrying to the door.

'It's four o'clock!' he said. 'Hazel must be back!'

But she was not. Simon returned with the child in his arms, his face furious.

'The bed has not been slept in. God knows what she's up to! Hush, Vicky, Mummy will be back soon.'

Emma peered at the child's flushed cheeks.

'I don't think there's anything wrong with her,' she said. 'It was probably a bad dream. I'll go down and warm up some milk.'

It was the best part of an hour before they were able to coax Vicky back to bed. Hazel had still not returned. Simon was very angry.

'I don't like it when people take advantage of a kindness,' he said. 'If she ever does this again, I'll get rid of her, child or no child!'

But would he? Emma wondered. Hazel was one thing but Vicky another. Simon was too kind-hearted to turn them on to the street, although theoretically, the council was obliged to house them if they were made homeless. The difficulty lay in the fact that there were so few houses available and they would almost certainly have to spend some time in a bed and breakfast establishment before accommodation was found for them. As Simon had once remarked, he sometimes felt guilty having Ortolans all to himself when there were so many homeless people.

'I'll make a cup of tea,' Emma said. 'I'm too wide awake to go back to bed.'

'I'll come down to the kitchen with you – it'll be warmer there,' Simon said.

By half-past five, Hazel had still not returned and they went back to bed but not to sleep. It occurred to Emma that Hazel was cutting it fine if she had decided to stay out all night. She and Simon were leaving at seven. Simon must have had the same concern, for he said:

'I suppose we shouldn't condemn Hazel until we hear what she has to say. She may have had an accident on that lethal-looking motorbike of her boyfriend's.'

They abandoned any attempt to catch a little more sleep and Simon went off to shave whilst Emma got dressed and went down to make some breakfast. She was beginning to grow seriously worried. Derek was holding a staff conference at nine-fifteen and she herself could not afford to be late. If Simon were to remain with Vicky until Hazel did return, she would have to catch a train.

'I'd better phone the station and get the train times!' she said, handing him a cup of coffee as he came into the kitchen. 'We'll have to wake Vicky. We can't leave her here on her own so she'll have to come in the car to Hassocks.'

Simon paused in the act of drinking from his cup.

'But darling, you know the Porsche is insured for one driver only. I'll drive it up and you can get a taxi into the station later.'

Emma frowned.

'I wasn't thinking of driving,' she said. 'I'm talking about taking an early train up to Victoria.'

Now Simon looked puzzled.

'But you can't leave until Hazel gets back. Someone has to stay and organize Vicky.'

'But not me, Simon!' Emma said quickly. 'I have to be at work by nine-fifteen and that's all there is to it.'

'Emma, this is an emergency and your boss will have to accept it. I can't possibly stay. I have one of our most prestigious clients coming to see me at nine-thirty. There's no way I can get in touch with him and change the time – he's flying in from Geneva and going straight to the bank.'

'Darling, you'll just have to arrange for someone else to see him,' Emma said, her voice quiet but emphatic. 'I can't ring Derek. He simply wouldn't understand. I'm terribly sorry!'

For a moment, anger flared in Simon's eyes, but then he put down his cup and walked round the table to put an arm round Emma's shoulders.

'I know it's a bloody nuisance to say the least, but it's really a woman's forte to cope with a kid of Vicky's age. God knows where Hazel is or when she'll be back but I'm not suggesting you stay here all day. You could ring whoever is supposed to cope in such circumstances – social service or the health visitor or whoever, and get them to make suitable arrangements for the child.'

'I don't see why you can't do that just as easily as I could,' Emma said as anxiety took hold of her. She knew without any doubt what Derek's reactions would be if she failed to turn up on time. 'Why should you assume that it is my responsibility rather than yours to stay with Vicky just because I'm a woman? You're very good with her – and she's used to you. I'm sorry, darling, but I can't afford to miss this conference – it could be very important, and since it will certainly concern me, I've got to be there. That's all there is to it.'

'Well, I don't accept that your blasted conference is half as important as my meeting with my client. There's a hell of a lot of money at stake – big money, Emma. I'm talking in hundreds of thousands, and I'm the one who handles this chap's portfolio. *I have to be there.*'

Emma did not reply. She walked through to the hall and lifted the telephone with a trembling hand.

'Send a taxi straight away to Ortolans, will you?' she said. 'To go to Hassocks station. Yes, as soon as you can.'

Simon was now standing in the doorway of the kitchen watching her.

'I shall catch the next train up – thank God there are plenty of them!' Emma said. 'I'm sorry, Simon, but we might as well get this settled once and for all. I happen to believe that my career is as important as yours. You seem to be old-fashioned enough to think that because I'm a woman and you're a man, your interests come first. Well, not to me. I'm sorry, but that's all there is to it.'

'I see!' Simon's voice was ominously quiet. 'Well, let me tell you something, Emma. I think you are egotistical, selfish, irrational and – if you want the truth – absurdly paranoid about this stupid career of yours. You're obsessed with this nonsense about women's rights! You're as ridiculous as those Greenham Common females.'

'And you, Simon, are a typical male chauvinist pain in the neck!'

Each regarded the other in furious indignation and with an emotion close to hatred, which contrasted violently with the love they had so recently shared. Neither noticed Hazel as she sidled into the room.

'Sorry if I've cut it a bit fine!' she muttered.

As far as the lovers were concerned, her return was five minutes too late.

CHAPTER THIRTY-FOUR

1987

Simon did not speak until they reached the outskirts of London. The traffic was unusually heavy and he pulled into the kerb outside Clapham South tube station.

'You'll be quicker going by tube,' he said, adding sarcastically: 'Can't have you late into work, can we?'

Without a word, Emma climbed out of the Porsche and joined the throng of people hurrying down the stairs. Her anger at the unfairness of the situation Simon had placed her in was cooling, and although she still believed herself totally in the right in maintaining that it was not up to her to remain with Vicky, she was deeply disturbed by the implications of their argument. Here she was, a wife of less than two months and already beginning to doubt that she should ever have committed herself to a marriage which clearly was not going to work. The thought kept going through her mind that Derek had warned her not to count on the promises Simon had made with such ease.

'You're a bit touchy this morning, darling!' Derek said after the conference. 'Nothing wrong, I hope?'

Suddenly, Emma found herself recounting the story of Hazel's absence and its repercussions. She did not wish to be disloyal to Simon by discussing their private life with Derek, but she badly needed his reassurance. He gave it unstintingly: 'You might as well start your marriage as you mean to go on,' he said. 'There are bound to be hiccups to start with and you've got to remember that Simon is not one of us – I mean, he's wrapped up in the financial world and probably hasn't got a clue about the importance of the media. People like him look on telly as a bit of entertainment whereas we know the enormous influence it has on people's lives. Take your *Women of Today* series. It's opening the doors for thousands and thousands of women whose lives may be radically changed by what they see other women doing. It broadens their vision; lets them see they can compete with men and succeed. It's important work you're doing, Emma.'

Emma looked at his sympathetic face and gave an uneasy sigh.

'Simon rarely looks at the telly – although he never misses the sporting programmes and, of course, he likes to watch the news. My father wouldn't have one in the house. He maintained it was a dreadful waste of time, although he has come round to admitting that it can be of some educational benefit. I don't think he or my mother believe that the work I'm doing has any real value. Simon doesn't think so either. I wish you could talk to him, Derek, really explain how important it can be.'

Derek lit a cigarillo and regarded her thoughtfully as he blew a cloud of smoke into the air.

'I could try, but it might not be easy to convince him. Tell you what, darling, I'll invite you both down one weekend – as soon as the weather improves a bit. Do you both good and I can raise the subject without being too obvious. As a matter of fact, I've some good news for you. I think I've been able to swing it with Jonnie and by the summer you should be an assistant producer! I wasn't going to tell you until the contract was ready for signing, but perhaps it will cheer you up.'

Impulsively, Emma got to her feet and hugged him, her face radiant.

'I'm speechless, Derek, except to say that I'm tremendously grateful. I just don't know what to say.'

Derek put his arm round her waist and squeezed it.

'Don't go berserk just yet,' he cautioned. 'These things can go wrong and I wouldn't want you to be disappointed if they did. Maybe I shouldn't have spoken about it . . .'

'Oh, no, I'm glad you did!' Emma interrupted, removing herself from Derek's embrace. 'Quite apart from anything else, when I tell Simon, it might help him to view my job here with . . . well, with a bit more respect.'

'Let's hope so!' Derek replied, his tone lacking conviction. 'Meanwhile, darling, don't hesitate to confide in your old pal any time you feel the need. That's what friends are for, and I don't have to tell you, I've a very special interest in you. You're a special sort of girl!'

Her mood immensely lightened, Emma decided that she would telephone Simon – not to apologize since she did not feel she had been in the wrong, but to let him know that thanks to his driving skills, she had arrived on time for the conference and that she had some wonderful news to tell him.

Simon, his secretary informed her, was lunching with a client and she was uncertain when he would be back at his desk. Since Emma herself had an interview that afternoon, she did not telephone again.

Simon, too, was in a better frame of mind. His client had decided to increase his investments by 50 per cent and had approved the suggestions for the portfolio Simon had proposed. It was nearly four by the time he was back in his office and his secretary handed him several messages. One informed him that Emma had telephoned – a gesture he took to be one of reconciliation. He was greatly relieved, for their argument this morning had left him feeling more than a trifle uneasy. The second message was from a client and the third from Cilia asking him to phone her.

He dialled her number, which he knew by heart, from his outside line.

'Thanks to you, I'm over the hump!' she said in her bright, high voice. 'Reckon I owe you a lunch, Simon. Bring Emma if you want.'

'I doubt that she'd be free,' Simon said, 'but I'd enjoy it. Glad things are going better.'

They chatted for a minute or two about the shop and then Cilla said:

'How're things at Ortolans? I suppose you still go down at weekends?'

'Everything's fine there,' Simon replied, 'except that I'm having trouble with Hazel.' He outlined briefly Hazel's failure to return at a reasonable hour from her outing.

'Sex rearing its ugly head!' Cilia said with her tinkling laugh. 'The trouble with you, Simon, is that you're too weak. Hazel isn't your responsibility. I should get rid of her if I were you, but then I've told you that a dozen times and you never listen to me!'

'OK, so you're probably right!' Simon acknowledged. 'I dare say Emma will suggest the same thing. She's not as attached to the child as I am.'

'Not the maternal type?' Cilia's tone was only half questioning. 'I presumed when you two decided to get hitched, the idea would be to have children. What other reason, for heaven's sake?'

'I happen to be very much in love with Emma!' Simon said quietly. 'I didn't just want an affair.'

'Makes it easier when you split up, though!' Cilia's voice was matter-of-fact. 'We did it pretty painlessly, didn't we, darling?'

'Well, Emma and I don't intend to "split up",' Simon said quickly. 'Now let's fix this lunch date, Cilia – if you really want to go through with it. I'm pretty tied up this week.'

'How about next Wednesday? And do bring Emma if you can!'

'I'll ask her,' Simon promised, but he knew already that she would not ask Derek for time off to lunch in the City.

'And get rid of that useless girl at Ortolans!' Cilia added as a parting shot as she put down the phone.

Was he being weak in allowing Hazel to stay on at Ortolans, he asked himself on his way home. The arrangement had suited him surprisingly well in the past. It was only recently she had become restless . . . but that had nothing to do with this morning's débâcle . . . unless Cilla was right and Hazel, seeing how close he and Emma were, had suddenly woken up to the fact that she was missing out. Maybe the girl would be better off in a council flat where she would not be so isolated as she was at Ortolans. Maybe it would be better for Vicky, too, to have other young children to play with. If he made an effort, he ought to be able to find someone in Detcham who would come up on a daily basis to keep the house clean and cook at weekends. Emma would probably welcome the idea.

Surprisingly, it was Emma who dissuaded him from dismissing Hazel. He had been back in the flat less than half an hour before she arrived home and went straight into his open arms.

'I'm sorry I shouted at you this morning,' she said when he stopped kissing her. 'But the conference was important, Simon, and after it was over, Derek gave me some wonderful news. I shall shortly be an assistant producer – almost for sure. I'm not supposed to know but he was nice enough to tell me seeing I was a bit depressed – about us, I mean. I suppose I was somewhat quiet for me, and being Derek, he'd noticed it. Isn't it splendid, Simon? I'm so thrilled.'

'Congratulations!' Simon said, wishing he could feel more pleased. 'When will you know for certain?'

'Oh, I expect I'll have to go for an interview with Jonnie Copeland, the head of our department – Features and Documentaries. I'm not 100 per cent sure, of course, but Derek wouldn't have told me, knowing what it means to me, if it wasn't pretty much of a certainty. And darling, he wants us both to go down for a weekend to his house in Gerrards Cross so that he can get to know you better. I've never been, believe it or not. I suppose I felt I might be a fish out of water – he knows so many famous people and they, of course, all know each other. But if you were there, it would be different.'

She was too excited to notice the lack of enthusiasm in Simon's face as he moved away to pour them both a drink, or to notice his look of relief when she added: 'Not that it'll be for some time. Derek wants us to go down when the weather is nice so that we can swim in his pool and enjoy the barbecue. His weekend parties are pretty upmarket from what I've heard and it's quite an honour to be invited!'

In which case, Emma will almost certainly get advance notice, Simon thought, and he could devise some watertight excuse not to go. The prospect of a whole weekend with a crowd of people he did not know and with whom he had nothing in common did not appeal to him, quite apart from the fact that Derek Meadows was not the type of man he cared to have as a friend. He had tried to rationalize his antipathy to the man, accepting that jealousy might well lie at the root of it. Meadows talked in an amusing enough way and was clearly intelligent, yet underlying the entertaining monologue was a hint of aggression, as if he were challenging those who listened to disagree with him. Simon suspected that if anyone did so, he might show himself in a very different light! Emma, of course, would not hear a word against him.

With an effort, Simon now pretended an enthusiasm for Emma's pending promotion, which delighted her.

'I'm so glad you're pleased for me, darling!' she said. 'I was afraid you'd worry about my getting even more deeply involved than I am already.'

She moved away from him and sat down on the sofa, her face now serious.

'You've no idea how difficult it is for anyone to make headway in the BBC. I know one girl who's been there twelve years and is still where she started, earning a mere £9,000 a year. As a temp she could be earning twice that, or more! I've been so lucky. You see, in the end it's a matter of who you know rather than what you know, and when Derek made me his researcher, I knew I was in with a chance – provided I didn't blot my copybook. That's why I can't afford to let anything affect my work. If Derek thought it was doing so, that would be enough to kibosh any hope of promotion.' She gave a deep sigh. 'You do understand, don't you, Simon?'

Simon nodded, but his eyes were uneasy. This, however, was not the moment to discuss such a subject. He was far too deeply in love with her to want to risk a further rift in their relationship. Instead, he broached the subject of Hazel who, he told Emma, he had decided must go now that she had proved her unreliability.

Emma listened quietly as Simon expressed his views and then said:

'I was pretty angry with her this morning, but it was her first lapse. She must have been very well aware how we both felt, and I think it's unlikely she will ever do such a thing again. She is still very young, Simon, and I suppose that since Vicky was born she has never had a chance to go out and have a good time. In her own way, she does her best for the child, and it can't be easy. Half of me feels so sorry for her, trapped the way she is. Besides, darling, it won't be easy to find someone willing to do weekend work and although I can cook, it's lovely to go down and find fires lit and a meal waiting!'

Simon nodded.

'We'll have a talk with her on Saturday, and for the time being, no more babysitting on a Sunday night! Maybe she'll want to leave anyway. I'm pretty sure she'd get a council flat in due course, although she wouldn't be able to get a job where she could have Vicky with her. Detcham hasn't got around to providing crèches for unmarried mums and I doubt if Hazel would find it much fun managing on social security handouts. She's quite hopeless about money.'

It had already occurred to Hazel that she was financially far better off living in her rent-free flat at Ortolans, with her light, heat and food provided and a tempting weekly wage, than she would be if she were dependent on the State. She was suitably repentant the following weekend, and begged to be allowed to stay. Her boyfriend had gone back to London, she told Emma, so she wouldn't be needing to leave Vicky at night.

'You'd think I'd have had more sense than to let him have

it off!' she said bitterly. 'They're all the same, wanting what they can't have and no time for you when you give in. Scalp hunters – that's what they are. Want to be able to boast to their pals they can make it with any girl they want. I should've known better at my age!'

Emma was saddened by her cynicism although not surprised by it. Hazel, as an unmarried mum, was particularly vulnerable.

The weekend – and those following – not only passed without mishap, but were richly rewarding. Work on the installation of the new kitchen units began and the plumber with two assistants started work on the central heating system. The weather took a sudden turn for the better and almost overnight, the garden was ablaze with spring bulbs and early blossom. Simon's friends, Philip and Joan, came down one Sunday to lunch which they were able to eat sitting out on the terrace. The following weekend, they were invited to dine with their neighbours, the Finden-Reids, at The Grange. Their three sons were childhood friends of Simon's. The eldest, Greville, was a stockbroker like his father and unmarried, and at Simon's suggestion, Lucy was invited down for the weekend so that she could go with them to the dinner party.

Lucy thoroughly enjoyed herself and was filled with envy.

'You're the only one of my friends who has ended up with the lot!' she said to Emma. 'Handsome, adoring husband, gorgeous weekend home, no money worries, some super friends and no in-laws!'

'In a way, I'm sorry Simon has no close relatives living,' Emma said with a smile. 'He did have a sister, you know, who was twelve years older than he. She died of influenza in the same epidemic which killed his father. Apparently she had red hair, green eyes like Simon's and the same fiery spirit as the great-grandmother he adored. I think that it is as much in her memory as to please himself that Simon is so determined to restore the house to its former glory. I can understand how he feels – I'm beginning to love the place myself. In a strange kind of way, it seems to reach out and claim me. When I come down here, I feel as if I've come home.'

'Well, I simply can't understand why you don't chuck up the job and move down here,' Lucy said. 'Why work if you haven't got to?'

Emma looked at Lucy's cheerful face with a frown on her own.

'Don't start that again!' she said sharply. 'If you think for one minute I'd give up my job just when I'm getting where I want, you're very much mistaken.'

'OK, keep your hair on!' Lucy said grinning. 'But this promotion Derek promised you has been a long time promised and an even longer time a-coming. I suppose it *is* going to materialize?'

Secretly, Emma had been wondering the same thing but she did not like to question Derek who was particularly pre-occupied. According to Pete who always seemed to be *au fait* with every bit of gossip circulating the studio, rumour had it that Derek had had a bust-up with his girlfriend who had walked out on him, severely damaging his ego. For several weeks, he barely spoke to Emma and then, quite suddenly, he seemed to recover his spirits. He was arranging a big weekend house-party for the beginning of June, he told her. He was inviting Jonnie Copeland, and if Emma put on her best bib and tucker and charmed him, it could be the turning-point.

'Of course, you can bring your better half along with you if you want, Emma,' he said, 'but if I were you, I think I'd play down the "married" angle. It's up to you, naturally, but Jonnie's like me – he prefers his staff uninvolved.'

Emma did not see how Simon's presence could be anything but an advantage. Everybody liked him and he was invariably a good mixer. Besides, she needed his support. Although this was to be a social occasion, she would be on trial. Jonnie Copeland might have a fair idea of her written capabilities, but he knew nothing of her as a person. In a way, it would be much the same as attending oral interviews following written exams. She would be nervous, and Simon's presence would lend her confidence. It went without saying that she would go looking her most attractive because it was silly not to make use of any asset one had, but if she was to impress Jonnie as to her suitability to cope with her own programme, what mattered was that she should show herself as poised and intelligent, and able to get on well with important people. She was oddly disturbed when she mentioned the invitation to Simon and without hesitation, he said:

'You'll have to count me out, darling. I'm playing golf on that Saturday. I forgot to tell you about it.'

'Surely you can put that off,' Emma pleaded. 'This could be a very important weekend for me, Simon.'

He gave her a quick, searching look.

'I'm sure you can carry it off without me hanging around,' he said. 'No doubt Meadows will look after you.'

'What's that supposed to mean?' Emma asked sharply.

For a moment Simon remained silent, his eyes thoughtful. Then he crossed the room and put his arm round her shoulders.

'I honestly don't know!' he said slowly, 'but it worries me that you are so dependent upon him. It's an instinct, if you like, but I don't trust Meadows's motives. It seems to me that he set out to become your Svengali and he has succeeded. He says "jump" and you jump. Anyone would think you couldn't cope without him.'

'Well, of course I could!' Emma said defensively. 'You don't understand what it's like in my business. If I was difficult or uncooperative or argumentative, how long do you think Derek would have put up with me? Of course I do what he wants.'

'I'd still like to know why he takes such an interest in you, Emma. You can call me a cynic if you want, but I don't believe people like Meadows do anything for anyone without hope of gaining something for themselves. It wouldn't surprise me one bit to hear he fancies you rotten and one of these days he's going to capitalize on his investment!'

'That's crazy!' Emma was really angry now. 'It just shows how little you know about Derek. He's got a live-in girlfriend he adores and . . .'

She broke off, suddenly remembering Pete's 'reliable' rumour that Derek's woman had walked out on him. It was only a rumour – and Derek had said nothing to her. Perhaps it was unlikely that he would have done so, seeing that his ego must be badly damaged. As a rule, Derek was the one who walked out. He'd left each of his wives for another woman.

'This is a ridiculous conversation,' she said in a stilted voice. 'It is also insulting to me. You are inferring that it's my body and not my talent that Derek is interested in. Obviously, you don't think I have any talent worth nurturing. Well, you are entitled to your opinion and I don't intend to have an argument with you about Derek. As far as the weekend is concerned, I'll go on my own. When I get back on Sunday I'll let you know if he tried to make it with me!'

She wished the last remark unsaid when she saw the look on Simon's face, but at the same time, she bitterly resented his implication that Derek had only been helping her career along because he fancied her.

Inevitably, as the weekend approached, there was a growing tension between Emma and Simon, aggravated by the fact that both avoided the subject. Emma took a long lunch hour on Friday to have her hair cut and blow-dried, but if Simon noticed it when she got home, he pretended not to do so. She made no comment when he brought his golf clubs in from the boot of the car and spent the evening polishing them and sorting out his collection of tees, markers and golf balls. That night they did not make love, each pretending to the other that they had fallen asleep until, finally, a genuine fatigue had overcome them.

On the Saturday morning, Simon drove Emma to the station to catch her train to Gerrards Cross. He was unaware of the fact that she had declined to go down by car with Derek the previous evening.

'Ring me tomorrow if you need collecting,' Simon said, giving her a brief kiss as she picked up her suitcase.

'I'll probably get a lift back to town,' Emma answered. 'Enjoy your golf!'

As she sat down in the crowded carriage, she felt a sudden unexpected urge to jump out of the train and cancel the weekend. The coolness between her and Simon had taken the edge off her excitement. He should be here with her, she thought with a return of her former resentment, or else driving with her down to Gerrards Cross. This was business, not pleasure, and no matter how dull his banking friends might be, she would have supported him had their positions been reversed.

As the train moved out of the station, she found herself wondering about Jonnie Copeland. She had seen him around the studio on many occasions – a tall, grey, long-haired man with Dennis Taylor spectacles who looked more like a professor than a television VIP. Although he had always nodded at her vaguely when she said good morning, she doubted if he had any idea who she was although, according to Derek, he was by now well aware of her name and familiar with all her *Women of Today* documentaries.

It was only a short taxi-ride from Gerrards Cross station to the big, white house in a smart residential avenue where Derek spent his weekends. Cars were parked in the road as well as in the driveway, indicating that a sizeable number of lunch guests had already arrived. From the terrace at the rear of the house drifted the sound of voices and laughter. A manservant came out of the front door and took her case as she paid off her taxi.

'Mr Meadows is on the terrace and would like you to join him there,' he said. 'If you will give me your name, I will show you first to your room.'

He was obviously imported for the occasion, Emma thought as he led the way upstairs with all the aplomb of an old-fashioned butler. Clearly Derek was giving this party in style.

She ran a comb quickly through her hair, touched up her lipstick and made her own way downstairs. Derek came hurrying towards her as she went out on to the terrace.

'At last!' he said, kissing both hands in a theatrical gesture which made her smile. 'Champagne, darling? You're looking great!'

He took two glasses from a passing, white-coated waiter and tucking an arm through hers, led her towards a group of people.

'This gorgeous girl is Emma Foster, my most brilliant researcher who is every bit as clever as she is pretty. Darling, meet my dear friends . . .' and he reeled off a string of names which Emma desperately tried to memorize. One or two of the men gave her approving glances, the women cast quick calculating eyes over her clothes – a white linen jacket over a black and white spotted dress. Emma knew that she looked smart without being flashy and the wide white belt and short straight skirt showed off her slim figure and long legs.

Derek kept his arm securely in hers and after a few moments, drew her away from the group.

'Clever girl not to bring your better half,' he murmured. 'I'll take you over to Jonnie in a minute or two, but first I must tell you how stunning you look. You're quite a girl, Emma!'

'Thanks for the compliments!' Emma replied, laughing. Gently she removed her arm from his. She was sure he did not intend to give an appearance of possessiveness but at the same time, she did not particularly want everyone thinking she was Derek's new girlfriend. Recognizing a face in a group at the far end of the terrace, she said casually:

'I must go over and have a word with Sandy Burrows or she'll think I'm cutting her. Shout when you want me, Derek!'

'Don't be long, honey!' Derek replied, adding in a pseudo-American accent, ''cos I'll sure as hell miss you!' He bowed in an exaggerated gesture of farewell and reached for another glass of champagne from a passing waiter.

As Emma walked over to the tall, fair girl who was a PA to the producer of one of the lunchtime magazine programmes, she realized that Derek must be a good many drinks ahead of her. His face was flushed and she noticed with surprise that he was not 100 per cent steady as he walked over to greet some new arrivals. Usually he could hold his liquor and seemed well able to drink quite heavily without it affecting him unduly. She had only once seen him the worse for wear – at a Christmas party when he'd become embarrassingly drunk and made lewd suggestions to one of the juniors in Make-up. The men were amused but the girl wasn't sure how to react. It had been all talk and no do, but Emma had not cared to see him make a fool of himself.

Now, she did not see Derek again until the buffet was served by the caterers in the dining-room. There were forty or so for lunch, seven of whom, including herself, were house guests. Jonnie, who was one of the seven, seemed heavily engrossed in his female companion, a busty young pop singer half his age wearing little more than an inch or two of white leather mini-skirt and a low-necked, sleeveless T-shirt so tightly stretched across her chest that it looked as if her nipples might thrust through the material at any moment. Emma had still not had a chance to talk to him, and Derek, appearing at her elbow with a plate of food which she did not want, said in a low voice:

'No point trying to chat up Jonnie now, darling. He's got other things on his mind. He'll disappear upstairs with Martina after lunch, and if I know him, he'll lose interest once he's had it off. Good grief, Emma, you'd think he'd have more taste. *Chacun à son goût*, I suppose. Don't go for tarts myself. I like a touch of class.'

'Damn good film that!' a man said picking up the wrong end of the conversation. 'Not that I'm sold on Glenda Jackson. You a film star, Miss er . . . er . . .'

'Foster!' Emma said, laughing. 'Emma Foster, and I'm certainly not a film star. I work at the BBC. I'm one of Derek's researchers!'

'Are you now! Good old Derek – he likes his surroundings to be decorative. Good party, don't you think? Splendid lunch. Don't think I've seen you here before, have I?'

'It's my first visit,' Emma said, wondering how soon she could extricate herself from this boring companion. 'I normally spend my weekends in Sussex with my husband.'

'Oh, you're married then,' the young man said as if the news disappointed him. 'Just my luck! I was going to ask you if you had a free evening next week – go out to dinner or something.'

As he moved away, Emma felt a sudden aching need for Simon. At the same time, she knew that these were the kind of people in whom he would have no interest. Apart from the unknown pop singer, everyone here was in fact someone of importance in the industry. Even the young man with his clichés and clumsy approach to her she had recognized as being a presenter on *Saturday Sportsview*. Derek only invited people who 'mattered'; whom he could use. They were clever, talented and should not be judged by Simon's conventional standards. It was irritating that, for no reason at all, she was now viewing them through his eyes, critically, whereas in fact, she was one of them.

Unaware of the reason why, she went out on to the terrace in search of Derek. He seemed to have sobered up and immediately put his arm round her shoulders.

'You haven't said what you think of the house, the garden!' he said. 'I hope you approve?'

'Indeed, I do!' Emma answered at once. It was not Ortolans – but then no house could ever match up to that. This was a modern building – a little pretentious perhaps but inoffensive to the eye and luxurious enough to be indicative of Derek's financial status. Knowing his background, she could understand why he wanted to own a house like this in the Home Counties where his surroundings suggested respectability as well as wealth. He professed to despise the so-called upper classes and yet wished to be accepted on equal terms by them.

'You'll never get anywhere in this life hobnobbing with nonentities!' he'd said to her in the days after she had split up with Paul. 'He wasn't an asset, darling – he was a millstone.' Emma had sometimes wondered if the only reason he had reconciled himself to Simon was because of the Calverley title. She was surprised that he had not as yet introduced her to anyone as 'Lady Calverley'. Instead, he had persisted in using her maiden name.

Gradually, the luncheon guests dispersed and by half-past three, they had all departed, leaving Derek, Emma and two couples alone on the terrace. One of the men was a producer with a quiet, unassuming wife, middle-aged like himself but who Emma liked. They had five children and these, she told Emma, had occupied her life; she had never had a career. The other couple, unmarried, were both pop music promoters and clearly Derek had determined upon working with them on a documentary about their new band which had become an overnight sensation. He talked with great persuasiveness about this scheme whilst Emma was chatting to her maternally minded neighbour. Martina reappeared in time for drinks which were served by a manservant at six o'clock. Jonnie, she announced, was having a nap before dinner. Knowing that there would almost certainly be wines served with the meal, Emma decided to decline the aperitif Derek was urging on her and repair belatedly to her room to have a shower and change her clothes.

Her room was comfortable with a large, modern divan, built-in wardrobe and a choice of books on her bedside table. The bed was large enough for two, and as she lay down on it in the voluminous towelling bathrobe provided by her host, she felt a renewed longing for Simon. If he had been here, they would almost certainly have made love before dinner, she reflected with a smile. The thought was followed by one of resentment that he had chosen not to accompany her. It was true she did not need an escort, but it would all be a lot more fun had he been here.

Dinner, served in the spacious dining-room at eight-thirty, was a convivial affair with excellent food and a wide choice of wines. Derek, Emma decided, had selected his house guests very skilfully. Martina had been seated opposite Jonnie where her admirer could gaze down the low-cut *décolletage* of her silver sequinned gown to his heart's content whilst Derek, on her left, engaged her in conversation. Emma was seated on Jonnie's right and when she was able to distract his attention, was free to interest him in herself. Naturally, she did not raise the subject of her promotion, but she believed she was able to talk intelligently about the various programmes she mentioned, including her own. Once or twice, she caught Derek's eye and he nodded approvingly as if to indicate that she was making a good impression on his boss. The erudite producer on her other side was charming and interested in Ortolans.

'I have an elderly grandfather who used to live not far from Detcham,' he told her. 'He was the youngest son of a family by the name of Lamberhill who owned one of the houses nearby. He's now in his nineties and lives in a nursing home, and like a lot of very old people, he rambles on about the past which he recalls better than the present. I've often heard him talk about old Lady Calverley – Aunt Sophia, he calls her, although they were not in fact related. He said the house was really beautiful in its heyday, but became somewhat dere-lict after the war.'

Martina's sudden shrill laughter interrupted their conversation.

'Come on Derek, I adore them and Jonnie does, too, don't you, honey!'

Jonnie nodded and turned to Emma.

'One thing about Derek – you can trust him to get quality stuff. Buys them in Sweden, I gather.'

As everyone rose to leave the room, Emma noticed the producer glance at his wife, who said:

'I think we'll turn in, Derek. I can't keep my eyes open and Peter always falls asleep in films.'

So it was to be a film show, Emma thought as Derek led the way out of the house and across the garden to a large, brick building she had assumed was a garage. It had been skilfully converted into a projection room. A giant screen, five feet by five, covered one wall; a video box was mounted in the ceiling, access to which was obtained via a neat wrought-iron spiral staircase. At the far end, facing the screen, were several comfortable sofas, beside which was a well-stocked bar. Whilst Jonnie and Martina seated themselves on one sofa and Emma sat down on another, Derek poured drinks before selecting a video from a cabinet behind the bar and, mounting the staircase, placed it in the projector. Turning out the lights, he came down to seat himself beside her.

'Think you'll enjoy this if you haven't already seen it,' he said in a low voice as the credits appeared on the screen against a backdrop of a desert at sunset. 'Wonderful photography!'

The dialogue was in Swedish and there were no English subtitles so it was several minutes before Emma was able to fathom the storyline. It seemed to her to be a cross between *Lawrence of Arabia* and *Ashanti*. A young white girl appeared to be trying to escape from an evil slave trader and in ever-diminishing *déshabillé*, was struggling alone in the sand-dunes when out of the sunset rode an incredibly handsome, macho-looking sheik on a white Arab horse. Although as Derek had promised, the photography was superb, the story struck her as somewhat ridiculous and her attention wandered. Beside her, Derek was lounging in a relaxed position and now he put an arm round her shoulders and said in a low voice:

'It hots up in a minute. Want another drink, darling?'

She felt his leg pressing against hers and wondered if it was accidental. On the sofa to her right, Martina was curled up beside Jonnie, her face nuzzling his neck. Emma declined the drink and Derek edged his body closer. She became aware of the combination of conflicting odours of eau de Cologne and sweat. Involuntarily, she turned her head aside, disliking the intimacy and wondering how she could indicate tactfully that Derek's proximity was far from welcome.

The girl in the film had by now been transported to a tent where the muscular sheik was slowly removing her clothes. Having exposed her naked body, he equally slowly divested himself of his own garments and Martina gave a little squeal of delight as the camera focused and lingered on his full-frontal nudity.

Now Emma realized what exactly she had let herself in for – a blue movie. Naturally, she had heard about them but had never been interested enough to see one. Pornography in any form had never appealed to her, not because she was prudish about such things but because she could only feel pity for the inadequacies which prompted people to seek titillation in order to enjoy their sex lives.

It astonished her that Derek, twice married and very much a man of the world, should be one of them. Suddenly she found herself wondering if it had been his failure to satisfy his wives which had prompted his divorces. She brushed the thought aside as irrelevant. In any case she was far more concerned as to how to deal with Derek's fumblings. To protest even in a low voice when the other couple were clearly locked in an amorous embrace could embarrass everyone. Slowly, she edged away from him and on the pretext of wanting to tuck her legs beneath her for comfort, succeeded in obliging him to remove his hand from her thigh.

The love scene on the five-feet-high screen was becoming steadily more explicit. The only dialogue – if such it could be called – consisted of highly exaggerated gasps and groans as the two lovers became entangled in ever-more unlikely contortions.

Emma felt a wild desire to laugh at the absurdity of the scene. Had Simon been with her, she would have given way to the need to do so but now, without warning, Derek's hand reached towards her breast. With a feeling of disgust tinged with astonishment that Derek could have been aroused by such nonsense, she uncurled her legs and stood up, pretending a vast yawn.

'Simply can't keep my eyes open!' she murmured. 'Too much wine at dinner, I suspect. Don't get up, Derek, I'll find my way back to the house.'

Despite her request, he rose at once and gripped her arm. 'You can't leave yet!' It was almost an order which he quickly softened by a change of tone. 'Come on, honey, you can't leave now. The best's yet to come. I'll get you a drink. Whisky? Brandy? Or how about a liqueur?'

'No, honestly, I've had enough. See you in the morning, OK?'

In the darkness she could not see the expression in Derek's eyes, but she could decipher the scowl on his face as he released her arm and said in a furious tone:

'Fuck you, Emma, I thought you had more sense!'

As Emma found her way back to the house which was still ablaze with lights, she realized she was trembling although the night air was balmy and she had no reason to feel cold. She was far from sure what the second of Derek's cryptic remarks had meant. 'Sense' did not come into the argument. Had he, perhaps, meant 'sophistication'? He knew perfectly well that she was in love with Simon and couldn't, after all these years, have known so little about her that he supposed she'd enjoy 'a bit on the side'. As to the film, lots of women disliked pornography in books, let alone portrayed on a life-size screen! What exactly had he been expecting?

She felt a sudden irrational sense of betrayal. How could Derek, who knew her better than anyone else in the world – even Simon – have believed that she might be susceptible to what Lucy would have called 'a bit on the side'? Derek *knew* how much she loved Simon; knew that she wasn't and never had been interested in casual sex. Could he really have misjudged her so badly? Had he thought that her coming here for the weekend without her husband was an indication that she was available?

Emma felt an absurd desire to weep. It not only galled but upset her to think that Lucy might have been right all along and that Derek secretly fancied her and had been biding his time to show his hand. It belittled not only her but Derek . . . and even more importantly, it would affect their future relationship. Derek was not the kind of man who cared to have his ego pricked! Perhaps he'd felt the need to convince Jonnie Copeland that he could make it with a woman, too. Jonnie must have heard that Derek's model had walked out on him and Derek's ego had taken a knock. All she could hope for now was that in the morning, he would have forgotten all about the incident. Unwilling to accept the alternatives, she now convinced herself that he had had a great deal more to drink than she had realized and had not been fully conscious of the fact that it was she, Emma, his researcher, he had been propositioning.

The uneasiness of her thoughts did not prevent Emma falling asleep almost as soon as her head touched the pillow. She had been up early that morning in order to clean the flat and leave a casserole ready for Simon's supper, and for an hour, she slept soundly. It was therefore several minutes after she awoke before she realized that she was not alone; that someone was sitting on the edge of her bed – and that it was not Simon.

Before she could clear her thoughts, she was aware of a moist, brandy-smelling mouth pressing against her own; of two hands gripping her arms, imprisoning her, and then a voice – Derek's voice – saying:

'Don't be frightened, honey. It's only me!'

Emma had never been more frightened in her life.

CHAPTER THIRTY-FIVE

1987

'You can't tell me you don't want it . . .' Derek's voice was so slurred his words were all but indistinguishable '. . . you've been asking for it all evening.'

Emma might have protested at the absurdity of the accusation had Derek not been so drunk. She tried to fend off his hands which were tugging at the bedclothes she had pulled up to her neck.

'Go to bed, Derek!' she said in as calm a voice as she could muster. 'We'll talk in the morning.'

Derek was wearing a dressing-gown over his pyjamas and he was now struggling to divest himself of his clothing. The button fastening his pyjama trousers had caught in a loose thread and he was trying to undo it, his sight hampered by his stomach which protruded over the waistband as he bent forward.

Inconsequentially, the thought struck her that she had not expected Derek, the health fanatic, to have a middle-aged spread; he was always so well-tailored! He seemed suddenly faintly ridiculous and her fear of him lessened.

She sat up and saw with relief that there was a telephone on the bed-table which in an emergency she could reach; but she hoped she could keep control of the situation.

'Derek, please go to bed. For your information, I don't want you in mine. I have no intention of being unfaithful to my husband and certainly not with you!'

The gratuitous smile on his face became an ugly grimace.

'Should have told me that before you got here!' he said,

abandoning his attempt to remove his trousers and falling on top of her. 'Didn't think you were a cock-teaser, darling. 'Course you want me . . . and I'm going to give you what you want right now.'

'Get off me this minute. You disgust me, if you want to know the truth. I don't have to put up with this.'

She twisted away from him as he reached for her breasts and attempted to kiss her. Pushing his hands away, she managed to scramble out of bed. As he tried to follow her, she picked up the bedside lamp and raised it above her head.

'If you touch me again, I'll hit you!' she said. 'Now get out of my room.'

He collapsed back on to the bed and stared up at her, his eyes trying to focus on her in the darkness.

'Don't understand you!' he said. 'Why the hell offload that poncey husband of yours if you didn't fancy sleeping with me? Why the hell d'you think I asked you to stay the weekend? First it's the "come-on" and then the "lay off me". What the hell *do* you want?'

No longer afraid that he was going to force himself on her, Emma's rising hysteria cooled. *Was* this all her fault? Should she have realized that Derek might take it for granted she had come without Simon in order to sleep with him?

'You know why I came down here – to meet Jonnie Copeland!' she said coldly. 'You said if I made a good impression, he'd get a move on and sign the contract.'

'Fuck the contract!' Derek said in a perfectly clear voice. 'I can get that signed any day I want. I'm the one you need to make a good impression on. You play ball with me and I play ball with you, OK?' His voice suddenly took on a wheedling tone. 'Come on, honey, don't be so old-fashioned. What's a lay these days! Bet that husband of yours has a sheila or two hidden away. Besides, how'd he ever know?' He gave a drunken giggle.

Emma was too shocked by Derek's implied threat to argue about Simon. White-faced, she stared into his half-closed, bloodshot eyes.

'Are you blackmailing me, Derek? Either I sleep with you or you kibosh my contract?'

He gave a leering smile.

'Put it that way if you want, darling. I see it as doing each other a good turn. You like me, don't you? You come to Daddy – tell me all your troubles and Daddy sorts them out for you. Well, Daddy has had his eye on you for some time. Always knew we'd make it in the end. Don't tell me you didn't know it was on the cards.'

'I didn't know!' Emma said. 'If I'd known . . .'

'So what would you have done, eh?' Derek's voice was scornful. 'Think you could have got yourself as good a job elsewhere? No way, darling! You're nothing special where work's concerned, believe me. Your talents lie elsewhere and I'll tell you what they are – that fabulous figure and sexy smile. Turn a chap on any time you want, can't you? Oh, we all know you're choosy – don't hand it round on a plate like some of the girls. Keep it for the ones that matter, don't you? Well, it's time you realized I matter, Miss High-and-Mighty. Time you thought of putting a little bit of nooky my way – *if you want that contract*. Think about it, darling.'

Emma shivered as she walked over to the door and opened it.

'I don't need to think about it, Derek. You can keep your contract – and the new job. Find yourself another researcher who can bear the thought of going to bed with you. Now get out of my room, or I swear to God I'll go to court and say you tried to rape me.'

Derek was not so drunk as to be unaware that short of raping Emma, he was not going to get what he wanted. Frustrated, humiliated and furiously angry, he half fell off the bed, and grabbing his dressing-gown and pyjama top, stumbled his way to the door.

'Stupid little bitch,' he said. 'Time you realized which side your bread was buttered. And don't expect me to give you a reference. You've just put the lid on your career, my girl, and

I can tell you one thing – you'll be bored as hell working as a canteen assistant – because that's the only job you're likely to get. I'll see to that!'

Emma did not go back to sleep after Derek had gone and she had locked her bedroom door behind him. She sat hugging her pillow for comfort until six o'clock when she washed, dressed and telephoned for a taxi to take her to the station. No one in the house heard her leave. She was obliged to wait until eight o'clock before she could catch a train to London. When finally she let herself into the flat, she did not go in to the bedroom where Simon was still asleep. She sat in the kitchen drinking coffee until he appeared, bleary-eyed, by which time she was once more in control of her emotions.

'What in heaven's name are you doing here?' he said staring at her as if he could not believe his eyes.

'I live here, don't I?' Emma replied flippantly. 'The coffee's cold. I'll make some more.'

She turned away to fill the kettle as Simon stepped forward to kiss her. For the moment, she did not want his sympathy and she turned her head away.

'The party was proving to be a rotten waste of time!' she said, putting grains in the coffee pot. 'Masses of booze, blue movies for entertainment and everyone but me drunk to the eyeballs. Not really my scene!'

Simon ran his hands through his hair. He realized at once that there was more to this than Emma was allowing him to know but, other than to take her in his arms, he could think of no way to break down the invisible barrier she was putting between them.

'You look exhausted!' he said. 'You feeling OK, darling?'

She handed him his cup of coffee and sat down at the opposite end of the table.

'As a matter of fact, I'm pissed off!' she said, knowing that Simon would dislike her swearing. 'I suppose I should have listened to you – and Lucy. Derek's the dregs. I must be a hell of a lot more naïve than I thought – trusting him, I mean. Have you ever seen a blue movie, Simon?'

Taken aback by the question, he nodded.

'A client of mine – Dutch, actually – always brought a batch over from Holland on his business trips. I suppose I'm a bit square but frankly, I found them off-putting. Once you know what sex is all about, there's not much that's new, is there? Except the varied perversions and I don't go for those. What was it – three in a bed or something?'

'No – lifesize oral sex and it was enough to put you off for life!' Emma managed a parody of a smile. 'Not that the movies were the big surprise. It was Derek. Seems he thought I'd be willing to sleep with him. Needless to say, I disillusioned him and . . . we had a row and I've quit – packed in my job.'

Simon gave a huge grin.

'Bully for you, darling!' he said. 'If it took a blue movie and Derek trying to bed you to get you to resign, God bless them both! I can't tell you how pleased I am!'

The look on Emma's face kept him in his chair.

'Thanks a million!' she said in a cold, harsh voice. 'I suppose I was silly to expect you to feel sorry I'd ruined my chances for the new contract.'

'I don't see why,' Simon argued. 'Derek might not continue to employ you as a researcher, but surely an assistant producer's job comes under somebody else's department?'

Emma regarded him helplessly.

'Well, of course, but you don't imagine Derek's going to take my resignation lying down, do you? People will wonder why I've resigned and he'll set about convincing everyone he prompted my resignation because I wasn't up to the work. He can't officially prevent someone else employing me, but behind the scenes he can do a lot of damage.'

Simon reached across the table and tried to take her hands but she would not allow him to do so.

'Of course I'm sorry – for you, I mean!' he said awkwardly. 'I know it was important to you; but don't you see, darling, it's all going to work out for the best – once you get over the disappointment. There's just no need for you to work now you're my wife. We can live at Ortolans and I'll commute; and there are a hundred and one really important things for you to do down there. You know what these workmen are like if there's no one to keep an eye on them, and Roddy simply can't take time to supervise them. Someone will have to be there when they do the rewiring; say where the switches and sockets have to go – that kind of thing; and you can have your own car and nip into Brighton or up to London and choose materials for curtains and . . . it'll make all the difference you being there.'

'It isn't going to make any difference, Simon,' Emma said, her face expressionless. 'You see, I've no intention of retiring from work as you seem to think.' There was no way she would consider writing to tell her parents what had happened until she could add the fact that she had moved elsewhere as a step up the ladder. 'I'm going to get another job – and that's all there is to it!' she added quietly.

With an effort, Simon quelled his own feelings of disappointment. He had spoken, he now realized, too impulsively, without forethought. He should have realized how upset Emma must be and waited for a suitable moment before proffering suggestions for an alternative to her career! He sensed that she was not far from tears and said:

'It's still early. We could be down at Ortolans by lunchtime if you'd like to go, darling. I told Philip yesterday that I'd lunch with him, but I can easily put it off.' He glanced at the sun streaming through the kitchen window and added: 'It's really too nice a day to spend in town. What do you think?'

Emma sensed that Simon was trying to be kind; take her mind off her troubles. It would be lovely down at Ortolans. They could lunch in the garden and Simon could finish making the swing he had begun for Vicky last weekend.

'OK! I'll give Hazel a ring and warn her we're coming after

all,' she said. 'She can probably find something in the deep freeze for us to eat.'

There was no reply to her telephone call, but assuming Hazel was sleeping in, Emma changed into her jeans and shortly after midday, they were on their way down the M23, the Porsche eating up the miles on the comparatively traffic-free road. There was no sign of Hazel as they reached Ortolans an hour later, but Vicky was sitting on the sunny terrace playing with one of her dolls.

'Mum's not feeling well!' she told them as she jumped up to hug first Simon and then Emma. 'I'm all by myself!'

'Not any more!' said Simon lifting the child on to his shoulders as Emma went upstairs to see what was the matter with Hazel.

She was lying in bed in a room littered with clothing, Vicky's toys, empty coffee mugs and full ashtrays. She gave a wan grin as she noticed Emma's glance around her.

'Sorry about the mess!' she said. 'Wasn't expecting visitors!'

'Vicky says you aren't well!' Emma said. 'You do look a bit pale, Hazel. What's wrong? Do you need a doctor?'

Hazel grimaced.

'Heaven forbid! I've seen enough of them for the time being, thank you very much. Be a dear and pass me a fag. There should be some on the dressing-table.'

'Do you think you should be smoking? – if you're ill, I mean . . .' Emma said tentatively, but Hazel interrupted.

'I'm not ill – just bloody sore!' she said, taking the packet of Silk Cut from Emma and lighting a cigarette. 'No need to tell Simon, but you might as well know, I had an abortion yesterday.'

As Emma gasped, her expression became defensive.

'It's not a crime, you know! Anyway, I didn't have no alternative, did I? One kid's bad enough. I wasn't going to have two!'

Emma sat down weakly on the end of the bed.

'Did you go alone, Hazel? You should have had someone with you. Was it . . . awful?'

Hazel grimaced.

'It wasn't exactly fun, if you want to know. I suppose the worst part was dragging Vicky back home afterwards and getting her to bed.'

'You mean, you took Vicky with you?'

'Well, what the hell else was I to do?' Hazel said aggressively. 'I shoved her in the supermarket crèche. Of course, you're not supposed to leave a kid all day unless you've booked them in beforehand, but I wasn't to know that, was I? So the rotten sods fined me. I'd only got twenty quid on me so they had to settle for that, or else keep the kid all night! By that time, she was screaming the place down so they let me go. Vicky cried all the way back in the train and I damn nearly chucked her out of the window I was that fed up. Then we had to wait for a bus to get back here as I'd no money for a taxi. So it isn't surprising I'm not feeling up to much today, is it?'

Emma felt a mixture of pity and exasperation.

'I know accidents happen,' she said gently, 'but surely you know how to protect yourself, Hazel. Aren't you on the pill?'

Hazel stubbed out her cigarette and lay back on the pillow.

'Didn't seem much point – me living in this out-of-the-way dump, you know? Not much chance of having any fun. That fellow Gary didn't want to know me after he'd got what he wanted . . . scarpered off back to London and I never saw him again. Wasn't his kid, though. I was just unlucky. Funny when you think about it – bloke came here in a van a few weeks ago wanting to know if he could clean the windows.' She gave a sudden grin which for a moment, made her look like a child. 'Bit of all right, he was! Took Vicky and me for a spin in his van and forked out for lunch at a pub and came back here for a cuppa. I didn't think it would come to anything – not doing it just the once, you know? Suppose I should have known better with my luck!'

'Did you tell him – about being pregnant?' Emma asked.

'For heaven's sake, of course I didn't. He was married, see? Anyway, I haven't seen him again. Don't know as I much want to. No future in it if they're married, is there? Suppose now you're here, you'll want some lunch!'

'No, you stay put. I'll fix something for all of us,' Emma said. 'I did try to telephone, but there was no reply. I'm sorry, Hazel. You must have had a bad time!'

'Well, it's over now, thank God!' Hazel said. As Emma moved towards the door, she added: 'No point telling Simon. I mean, he's that crazy about Vicky he might just think I oughtn't to have got rid of it. I dunno! Men don't realize what it means being tied to kids, do they? They think it's natural for us to want them. When I first came here, he kept telling me how lucky I was to have such a beautiful, healthy baby, you know? I s'pose he meant well, but it used to get my goat!'

Clearly Hazel knew Simon better than she did, Emma thought when later that night she recounted in strict confidence the true nature of Hazel's 'indisposition'. She would not have told him the facts had she not been so certain that he would understand Hazel's dilemma.

'Abortion seems such a drastic way out of trouble!' he said. 'I'm not against it for medical reasons – but to destroy a healthy life, especially when there are so many hundreds of couples wanting to adopt a baby . . . If Hazel didn't want another – and I understand that – why couldn't she carry it full term and have it adopted?'

'I wonder if you'd say that if you were the one who had to do the carrying, go through the pain of childbirth and then give your baby away.'

Simon looked thoughtful.

'Perhaps not! I don't know how I'd feel. All I do know is that I don't think I could bear it if you were carrying my child and . . . well, got rid of it!'

'You'd rather I had it – a child I didn't want and therefore quite likely would not love – just so *you* could have it?'

'I don't know. I suppose the answer to that is, yes, I would. *I'd* love it – if it was yours. We could get a nanny to look after it. Lots of people do.'

'Well at least I'll know what to do if I get pregnant,' Emma said. 'However, there's no fear of that since I'm on the pill.'

For a moment, Simon was silent. Then he said quietly:

'You don't think this might be a good time to have a child?', his voice tentative. 'I mean whilst you are between jobs? If you had a baby and a nanny to look after it, you could go back to work whenever you wanted.'

'But Simon, I thought we had agreed not to start a family for a good many years,' Emma protested, her heart sinking as she realized that his agreement had only ever been superficial. 'I am only twenty-eight so there's masses of time. Why the sudden hurry?'

Simon turned away so that she could not see his face. His voice was carefully controlled as he said:

'I suppose it's partly because we're married and because I love you so much, and because I look at Vicky and think how nice it would be if we had the Ortolans nursery full again. Maybe it's tied up with this restoration we're doing. I've been browsing through *The Calverley Journal* with Roddy to find bits of information that are helpful to him – when the roof was last repaired; when the conservatory was built – that kind of thing; and of course, in between the house bits are family bits – births and deaths of babies; the children's progress – and so forth. The dynasty angle has probably hit my subconscious. Am I talking complete nonsense?'

'No!' Emma said quietly. 'It makes sense – but it also makes me feel guilty because I can't share your feelings. Maybe you married the wrong woman. Maybe you should have picked an earth-mother type who'd have been only too happy to fill the nursery for you!'

'Heaven forbid!' Simon said, forcing a laugh as he came round the table to put his arms round Emma. 'I fell in love with you, my darling, and I certainly don't fancy the idea of being married to an earth mother!' He kissed her with an unaccustomed ferocity. 'One thing I am quite, quite sure of is that you belong here at Ortolans, *with me*. How that disgusting little chap, Meadows, had the nerve to proposition you, I'll never know. I don't like to think of what I'll do to him if I ever run into the little creep.'

Emma laughed for the first time that day with genuine amusement.

'Derek may be a creep, but he isn't little!' she said. 'He has a paunch which hangs over his pyjama bottoms. It reminded me of one of those weightlifters on telly! As to his having the nerve – he was drunk. He probably won't remember a thing about last night. Right now, he's probably wondering why I disappeared. So let's forget him, Simon. I'd rather not have to think about him!'

Still less talk about him, Emma thought as, arm in arm, she and Simon went upstairs to bed. Although Derek had been very drunk, he had made himself perfectly clear – those past promises of helping her to get her own programme had never been more than a carrot to dangle in front of her nose; he did *not* think her particularly talented and his terms were quite simply the casting couch – if she slept with him, he'd help her up the ladder; if she refused, she was out. Not even Simon – least of all Simon – must know how deeply humiliated she felt. Derek had convinced her that she was good at her work – not brilliant perhaps, but by dint of hard work, her capability and reliability, she'd get where she wanted. Her initial fear of failure had all but vanished. She had truly believed she was good at her work – really good. Now, in one unpleasant incident, he had undermined that slowly acquired confidence. Somehow, she decided as Simon climbed into bed beside her, she was going to show Derek that he had underrated her; show Simon, too, that she did still have a career that mattered. Derek might blackball her at the BBC but there were other channels – and she did have a few contacts. Tomorrow, when she got back to London, she would get on the telephone and see if she could find an opening – anywhere, any job – where she could start again.

As the weeks went by with no positive replies to the numerous phone calls and letters she wrote, Emma's hopes waned. She had one unpleasant telephone call from Derek threatening to have her sued for breach of her contract, but her threat to countersue for sexual harassment was obviously effective as she heard nothing more from him and her P45 was sent on to her by the accounts department without comment.

'You should have stayed on and fought it out!' Lucy said when Emma stopped by the flat one evening. 'Why should you lose your job because of the way that sex maniac behaved! I'm surprised at you, Emma. I always thought you were a fighter! You could have asked for a transfer to another department.'

Emma sighed.

'I resigned on the spur of the moment. Anyway I didn't fancy having to see Derek face to face – and wherever I might have been transferred, I'd have been bound to run into him. I hate that man, Lucy. If it wasn't for Simon, I might well have put in a complaint about him. What really gets my goat is the fact that I believed him when he said he'd help me get the new contract. I still mean to become an assistant producer! Sooner or later something will come up.'

'What's happening to the *Women of Today* series?' Lucy asked curiously.

Emma shrugged.

'I had a pub lunch with Pete last week and apparently Derek's got a new assistant. Pete says she's a pain in the neck but Derek's "helping her to settle in" – and I can imagine what that means. I gather she's attractive!'

Although she managed to convince Lucy that she was not particularly bothered, Emma became more and more depressed. Only too well aware that Simon would have liked her to abandon her career plans, she kept her feelings to herself and quickly changed the subject whenever he referred to her work – usually when the post arrived with a further letter telling her there were no vacancies at the moment. Although they never quarrelled, there had grown up an indefinable coolness between them. She knew he was seeing Cilla who was once again in financial difficulties. The rational side of her realized that he would have been unlikely to tell her about their lunches if he had started up anything with Cilia. Occasionally she longed to challenge him about his need to concern himself with his ex-girlfriend's affairs, but her pride would not allow her to do so.

When there was still no sign of a job for her by the middle of July, Simon suggested they make the long-overdue visit to her parents. Although part of her longed to be reunited with them, she wanted it to be at her moment of achievement – not at her moment of failure. She told Simon that her parents were planning a visit to England which, in fact, was the truth. She did not, however, tell him that she had written back to say that she and Simon were going to be abroad at the time of their proposed visit and that she would let them know a more suitable date.

In August, Simon took two weeks' holiday and they went down to Ortolans. The weather was beautiful and despite her anxiety for her future, Emma's depression lifted and she really enjoyed herself. With Vicky shadowing them, they ate most of their meals out of doors and left the workmen, who were installing the central heating, the run of the house. Most of the day they spent gardening – driving to nearby garden centres to choose bedding plants, which were ridiculously expensive, being already in full bloom.

'I know it's extravagant!' Simon said as they completed the planting of a colourful row of petunias along the brick path leading to the arbour. 'But it does look lovely. One begins to see how splendid the garden must have been in the old days. Great-Gran said that when she was a child, they had six gardeners. Imagine!'

Roddy, who had stopped by to check that the workmen were not doing any structural damage to the house, flopped down into one of the rattan chairs outside the arbour and said with a grin:

'Those gardeners would turn in their graves if they could see this now. A lot of those men and boys who worked here were my ancestors, Emma. I remember old Tom telling me that he had a fourteen-year apprenticeship under the head gardener before he was allowed to cut the straight hedges and then he had to wait for the head gardener, his uncle, to die before he was allowed to do the topiary.'

Emma returned his smile.

'I suppose that means I ought not to have tried to trim the yew hedge this afternoon!'

'You've made a lovely job of it, darling!' Simon broke in, 'and don't you discourage her, Roddy. She was just beginning to enjoy herself!'

It was perfectly true, Emma thought as one sunny day followed another. She found gardening very relaxing. Vicky, with a tiny plastic wheelbarrow of her own, helped to collect the rubbish, and whilst Simon trundled the big barrow down to the dump near the ha-ha, Vicky trundled hers with a look of serious importance on her face. Like all of them, she had tanned and was now an even deeper gold than her natural colouring. Hazel was not pleased.

'No hope of passing her off as white the way she looks!' she complained. 'Grows more and more like her dad every day – as if I wanted reminding of the bastard!'

There was very little affection between mother and daughter, and Simon worried about it.

'Hazel's so sharp-tempered with her!' he said to Emma. 'I'm sure she slaps her when we aren't around. Perhaps it will be better when she goes to nursery school next year. Hazel says they're full up at the moment and won't take Vicky until she's four.'

Despite the fine weather, Hazel seldom came out of doors

and when she was not cleaning the house or preparing meals, she was either chatting up the workmen or sitting in front of the television set. She took the men endless mugs of tea or coffee and confided in Emma that she 'fancied the tall, blond one'! Unfortunately, he did not seem to return her interest.

'Perhaps there'll be a decent bloke amongst the electricians!' she said, not without a certain wistfulness. 'I could do with a break!'

With the weather so good and the obvious need for her presence, Emma agreed not to return on the Monday morning to London with Simon when his holiday ended, but to stay at Ortolans for a few days.

'Provided nothing comes up!' she said cautiously, referring to her job applications. 'If there's a letter with a TV logo on it, will you ring me immediately, Simon?'

Simon gave his promise and went back to London on his own with mixed feelings. He knew Emma was secretly fretting about her failure to get work and felt a certain amount of sympathy for her. At the same time, she did seem so much happier and more relaxed when she was at Ortolans. It was almost as if the house was managing to exert its influence on her. She looked completely at home, humming to herself as she matched up curtain materials with carpet samples or told one of the workmen to move a radiator more centrally under a window. She had a natural sense of colour and form and he approved all her choices and decisions which seemed so right for the house. Roddy adored her – and so, too, did little Vicky. It was to Emma the child ran if she fell and grazed her knee or toppled off the swing and bumped her head. It was Emma who had to read her stories before bedtime. Emma might not want a child of her own, but she could not hide the fact that she was a natural mother.

As the summer wore on, his hopes that Emma would finally settle down and forget her career looked as if they might be fulfilled. Not only were there no offers – or offers of the calibre Emma would consider – but she had taken to staying on at

Ortolans after a weekend until the Wednesday when she would join him at the flat. On those nights, they went out to dinner, either alone or with friends – and occasionally to a theatre or the opera which they both loved. On the Friday evening, they would drive down to Sussex and enjoy the long weekend together. The coolness which had grown up between them vanished and if anything, their lovemaking was more frequent and ardent than it had ever been. They were truly lovers again.

Hazel, too, was better-tempered, having found herself a regular boyfriend amongst the three electricians who were undertaking the mammoth task of rewiring the entire house. On the strict understanding that she would never again fail to return at night, Emma was once again babysitting for her on a Saturday so that she could make the most of her day off.

Lulled into a false sense of security, Simon was aghast when on the last Thursday in August, Emma did not go up to London, but went instead to Southampton for an interview with Southern Television. She had not told him of the tentative offer she had received, so the shock was all the greater when she telephoned him from Ortolans that night. She was all but incoherent with excitement.

'I've got it, Simon! I've got a job – and it's everything I ever wanted. I'm to be an assistant producer. And guess what, darling, there were five of us up for interview and my new boss never even bothered to see the other four! Right away she said I was exactly the person she was looking for and had all the right experience and provided I was willing to live in the area, the job was mine.' Without waiting for Simon's comment, she continued breathlessly: 'So I shall sell my share of my flat – Lucy's probably got a friend who'll take it on – and get myself a bedsit or something in Southampton. I had a look in some estate agents and accommodation is miles cheaper than in London so I may even get a small flat there. Of course, I'll need a car – to get home at weekends. Isn't it wonderful? I just can't believe my luck – and I can't wait to tell Pete so he can pass it on to Derek. I'll bet Derek's been wallowing in the fact that I've not got another job. Now he'll know I can manage perfectly well – better even – without him!'

There was a pause before Simon replied carefully:

'Of course I'm pleased for you, darling. But . . . well, Southampton – I mean it's miles away. We shan't be able to see each other except at weekends.'

'Well, we don't anyway!' Emma said cheerfully. 'And I shan't have to work on a Saturday – not unless I go abroad. I might get a chance to do research overseas – Europe, the Far East, wherever there's a good story. I may even get to America to see my parents again! I'm just so thrilled.'

Simon tried to subdue his bitter disappointment, but no matter how hard he struggled to be pleased for Emma, he could not understand how she could have accepted a job which would virtually mean they lived apart for the larger part of their lives. The thought festered as it struck him that Emma could not be as much in love with him as she professed since she was choosing to live miles away from him.

His greeting when he arrived at Ortolans on Friday evening was perfunctory and although Emma longed to raise the subject of her new job, she realized that Simon was tired and decided that it was best left until morning. Whether or not by design, he did not attempt to make love to her that night and in the morning, he rose and left the house before Emma was awake. With Hazel and Vicky at the lunch table, the subject was once more avoided and in the afternoon, Simon disappeared somewhere on the estate with Roddy. That evening, they entertained the Finden-Reids to an informal supper and when Emma retired to bed at midnight, Simon remained in the drawing-room, ostensibly writing up *The Calverley Journal,* which, he said in a firm voice, was too long overdue and could not be left until morning.

On Sunday morning, Emma determined that she and Simon would discuss her new job, however unpalatable he found it.

For one thing, she would have to go down to Southampton the following week to look for digs. For another, she must make up her mind whether to dispose of her half of the Shepherd's Bush flat. Not least, she wanted to put an end to Simon's chilly silence which she considered thoroughly childish as well as unnecessary.

'Simon, I need to talk to you,' she said firmly at the breakfast table. 'Let's take our coffee into the drawing-room!'

As he followed her into the room, she closed the door behind him and stood with her back to it, staring at his closed face.

'About Southampton . . .' she said tentatively. 'It's important to me, Simon, and I want you to understand. I've waited all summer for a job like this. Don't you see, darling, it's what Derek always promised, but never produced – and I've got it entirely on my own merit. It'll mean . . .'

'It'll mean I have a wife I might – just *might* see on occasional weekends!' Simon broke in in a cold, accusing voice. 'Damn it, Emma, we are supposed to be married! You said you could be abroad for three weeks at a time; what sort of marriage is that? You can't seriously expect me to be happy about it!'

Emma's cheeks flushed a deep pink.

'I don't see why not! I don't see why we have to live in each other's pockets.'

Simon bit his lip.

'Maybe we don't have to, but usually when people are in love, that's what they want to do!' he said. 'I happen to be in love with you, Emma. Believe it or not, I like being with my wife. I don't see enough of you as it is.'

Emma made a move towards him, but Simon ignored her outstretched hand.

'Darling, don't be old-fashioned!' she pleaded. 'It's not as if we can't trust each other. Apart from not wanting to, I'll be far too busy to even notice another man!'

Simon did not return her smile.

'The possibility of us being unfaithful to each other has got nothing to do with it. I just don't fancy us living apart!' he said quietly.

'Then if you feel so strongly about it, you chuck up your job and come down to live in Southampton with me!' Emma said facetiously. 'Seriously, Simon, why should I be the one to have to give up my career for you? You aren't going to give up yours for me, are you?'

'Well, I couldn't – even if I wanted to. You know very well I couldn't get a similar job anywhere else but in the City – and we need the money I make.'

'Oh yes, of course, for Ortolans!' Emma flared. 'I should have thought you'd got enough by now, Simon.'

'Well, if it's of any interest, I haven't! Doing up a place like this is a huge drain on resources. If you want to know, I've a fairly mammoth bank loan and I may need to negotiate an even bigger one.'

'All the more reason why I should be earning too!' Emma said triumphantly. 'They're paying me 25 per cent more than I would have got with the Beeb. I'll be able to contribute my share of household expenses and . . .'

'We don't need it!' Simon interrupted fiercely.

Emma gave him a withering glance and walked across to the window. Simon looked after her with an expression which was not far from hatred. Why, when everything was going so splendidly, did Emma have to ruin it all by taking on a job miles from anywhere? The very least she could have done would be to consult him first before accepting the offer. It seemed she had fully committed herself without the slightest consideration for his opinion. Women were impossible, he thought as he walked to the far end of the drawing-room to pour himself a drink. Cilla was little better. She'd used half the money he'd lent her to redesign the interior of her shop before waiting to see if her new stock was going to uplift her sales. She should have asked his advice, instead of which she'd made no mention of it until she was once again on the verge of insolvency. By the look of it, Cilla would have to go into voluntary liquidation and he could say goodbye to the cash he'd lent her.

Feeling both angry and deeply depressed, he made a last appeal to Emma who was standing with her back towards him.

'Please don't take this job,' he said quietly. 'I really don't want to lose you.'

Emma turned and regarded his downcast face with mixed feelings, the strongest of which was resentment. Simon was being entirely selfish. Had he any consideration for her, he would be opening a bottle of champagne to celebrate her good fortune. Instead, he was doing his damnedest to make her feel guilty.

'I've already accepted the offer,' she said defiantly, 'and even if I hadn't, I wouldn't change my mind. Why should I? You knew when you asked me to marry you that I had a career I intended to pursue. It's you who've changed – not me!'

'I thought you were happy here at Ortolans this summer,' Simon said, tight-lipped.

'So I was – up to a point. It's been a nice break. And I do care about the house, Simon – really care. But I want this job and nothing – no one – is going to stop me doing it to the very best of my ability. And it has nothing to do with my being your wife. It doesn't make me love you any the less. It seems to me that you are the one who's short on the loving. If you really cared about my happiness, you'd be pleased for me.'

'I am pleased for you – but I'm not going to pretend I'm pleased for myself. We're supposed to be a team, Emma. The least you could have done was consult me first!'

Two spots of pink coloured Emma's cheeks.

'Ask your permission, I suppose that means! And you would have said "no" – so what was the point? I may be your wife, Simon, but I'm not one of your employees to be told what I can and cannot do. Since you feel so strongly that I'm failing

in my duty to you . . .' her voice was heavy with sarcasm
'. . . then you'd better do some thinking and decide whether
you would prefer to trade me in for someone else. Let me
know when you've made up your mind!'

It was a challenge Emma had not really intended to make
but Simon, too, was too strung up to think before he spoke.

'My mind is already made up. If you can't put our marriage
before this job, it seems to me it isn't really a marriage at all,
and we might as well admit that we've made a mistake.'

Shocked, but still on the crest of anger, Emma said coldly:
'You mean, *you* made a mistake, Simon. You wanted a
chatelaine for Ortolans, not a woman with the ability to think
and act and achieve in her own right. Well, perhaps it's best
for both of us if we do go our own ways. I don't start my
new job for two weeks. I shall go back to my own flat in the
meanwhile. Thank God I had the foresight not to get rid of
it when I married you.'

It was, of course, a ridiculous suggestion. The very last thing
she wanted was to be parted from Simon. Despite what she
had said, she did not believe for one minute that their marriage
was a mistake. Their summer together had been perfect and
they were far more in love than they had been the day they'd
got married. But there was a principle at stake and Simon was
being ridiculously old-fashioned about the whole business.
Hundreds of women nowadays had demanding jobs which
took them away from home, and they managed. That woman
judge she had interviewed had a home and children, and was
frequently away on the circuit. There was that woman in ICI
who spent half the year in Europe whose husband had a busy
medical practice in London. There was that woman music
critic who traipsed round the world attending the great operatic
performances and her husband was a stockbroker. They all
had husbands who were prepared to tolerate their wives'
careers – and there must be thousands more like them. Why
did Simon have to be the one man who did not – or would
not – appreciate his wife's need for independence? Even if she

had not yet made her way to the top like those successful women she had interviewed, she had a right to try to get there. Even if Simon didn't believe she was brilliant, an achiever, talented – and she was even prepared to grant him the point – he could still have offered his support. Love – the real thing – should not be possessive, she told herself. Love meant understanding, tolerance. If she could manage to explain this to Simon . . . but he had turned away and was standing with his arms leaning on the mantelpiece staring down into the unlit fire.

All that afternoon she waited for him to argue with her, plead with her to rethink her decision to separate. He did neither. They drove back to London in silence, and as soon as they reached Brunswick Square, Simon announced that he was going out for a drink.

Only as he was going out of the door did he stop and really look at her.

'If you change your mind, you know where to find me,' he said in a voice devoid of emotion. 'If you don't, good luck with the job!'

Emma stood staring after him, tears of mortification warring with the steady hardening of her heart.

CHAPTER THIRTY-SIX

1987

'If you want the truth, Emma, I think you are out of your tiny little mind!' Lucy said, regarding her friend's pale, drawn face. 'OK, so this new job is everything you have ever wanted – and you can't be sure about that! It's what you said when you got the contract with Derek. Surely you miss Simon – and Ortolans? You were so mad about your precious house.'

'It's not "my precious house",' said Emma tartly. 'It's Simon's and what he does with his life is no concern of mine now.'

It was what Emma wanted to believe, but there were all too many unexpected moments when she would find herself aching for the feel of Simon's arms around her; when she had to fight against her need to be with him. She still had a key to the Brunswick Square flat and the urge to go there in the hope of seeing Simon was constantly with her. She was glad when she moved down to Southampton and could no longer be tempted to jump into a passing taxi and give Simon's address. Distance, however, did nothing to bar the use of the telephone. She would sometimes sit for minutes at a time, her hand poised to pick up the instrument and dial his number, the longing to hear his voice so acute that it was like a physical pain. Was Lucy right after all and she the fool to be putting her marriage second to her career?

It was a question Emma asked herself many times, arriving always at the same answer; it was not a matter of putting her marriage second; it was a matter of whether the marriage should ever have taken place. There could be no doubt that she loved Simon, but much as she wanted to do so, she could no longer believe that he loved her. If he did, he should understand her need for a career, even if her work took her away from him for part of their lives. He was being entirely selfish, demanding that she put her needs second to his. He was not even prepared to talk it over – reach a compromise. He had not once tried to get in touch with her. If it was pride which prompted his silence, then she, too, had her pride. However much she wanted to do so, she would not ring him. She determined that he would have to be the one to make the first move; to show a willingness to compromise. She would not allow herself to give way to her longing to hear his voice.

Nevertheless, there were moments when she found herself wondering not only how Simon was, but how Hazel was coping; how the work was progressing at Ortolans; and if little Vicky was well. Had the plumbers finished the second bathroom? Had the men finished releading the window lights? Were the builders taking proper care of the coat-of-arms in the oriel window over the front door? Had Harrods delivered the new dishwasher which Hazel had been so impatiently awaiting?

Again and again, Emma reminded herself that none of these things were her concern now; that as far as her marriage was concerned, it was Simon's chauvinistic attitude which had brought about their separation. It was now three weeks since she had cleared her belongings from Brunswick Square, and still there had been no letter, no telephone call from him – only silence. Added to which, Lucy reported that she had seen him with Cilia in Lincoln's Inn Fields where she was temping as secretary to a lawyer. It was pointless to care. Her marriage was over, finished; something which belonged to the past. She and Simon belonged to the one-in-four statistics for failed marriages. Love had not, in the end, proved enough to sustain a relationship where the partners' interests were basically opposed. Their basic differences, in the beginning, had been obscured by the euphoria of falling in love and discovering one another. They did not, after all, love one another enough to make the necessary sacrifices – Simon, to allow her to be her own woman; she, to give up her ambitions to please him.

Fortunately, her new job was proving even more exciting than she had anticipated. Her boss, a woman, was charming as well as highly efficient and seemed perfectly willing to give Emma the kind of responsibility she craved. In her fifties, with grown-up children, she was particularly sympathetic in her attitude to Emma's personal dilemma . . . the problem of juggling husband and career. She had found the same difficulties and ended up divorced.

'Some men can cope, others can't,' she said. 'It's a pity you married the wrong sort! But you're still young, Emma, my dear, and very attractive. You'll make new friends!'

'I don't want another man in my life!' Emma had replied. 'I don't want to be possessed body and soul!'

Her new job as assistant producer on a magazine programme kept her fully occupied doing the absorbing, creative work she had always wanted. Every day was different and her first week had flown by. Only the evenings spent in the room she rented in a small family hotel had been desperately lonely. She had immersed herself in a good novel, written a letter to her parents telling them of her change of job, and watched TV; but tired though she was, sleep did not come quickly when she turned out the light. It was then she most missed Simon and she knew it would be some time before her body became accustomed once more to the absence of a lover.

With nothing planned for the weekend, Emma decided on the spur of the moment to catch a train to London. The weather had turned considerably colder and she needed warmer clothes than she had packed for Southampton. Lucy was shocked by her pallor and obvious loss of weight.

'For pity's sake, Em, stop being so stubborn and give Simon a ring!' she said. 'I'm sure he's only waiting for a word from you. After all, you've made your point – you've taken the job. Maybe he has come around to accepting it.'

Momentarily, Emma was tempted. If Simon *had* reconciled

himself to the idea of her working in Southampton, they could start again; see each other every weekend. Almost as much as she missed him, she missed those long beautiful days at Ortolans. She really wanted to see how the restoration was progressing. She'd like to see Roddy, Hazel, Vicky . . .

'Even if you're right, it wouldn't work, Lucy!' she said. 'Sooner or later Simon would start putting pressure on me to pack in the job. He wants a full-time wife, not a career girl. In a way, I don't blame him. He does, after all, have a family dynasty to carry on. I'm just not ready to settle down and become a housewife – and that's all there is to it. Really, I'd rather not talk about it. Tell me what you've been up to.'

Emma was almost pleased to be on the train back to Southampton. Although Simon had not spent much time at the Shepherd's Bush flat, she found it far more difficult there to put him out of her mind than she did in an environment where they had never been together. Her job continued to be interesting and time-consuming, and since she put all her energies into it, she was producing good work and her new boss was delighted.

'You showed initiative with that centenarian,' she said at the end of Emma's first month. 'I was impressed by the way you ferreted out the fact that the old biddy had once been in service to the Queen Mum. It was a nice little touch to coincide with the review of the Queen Mum's biography, and you handled it well. Now have a look at this which arrived this morning. It's a booklet published yesterday by NACRO – the National Association for the Care and Resettlement of Offenders. If you think there's a human interest story in it, see if you can get an interview with Vivien Stern, the director; and maybe interview a few prisoners on parole. Seems they can't get jobs because of their convictions, and there's even greater discrimination by employers against female convicts. It could take a few days, but you've got a flat in town, haven't you?'

With three days in which to achieve her objective, and the

usual expense account to cover costs, Emma decided to cheer herself up. She rang Lucy and together they went to Molton Brown to have their hair cut, restyled and blow-dried.

'You look *really* great!' Lucy said admiringly as they left the hairdressers. 'We ought to be going out somewhere. Shall I ring Andy? He'll rustle up a friend. We could go to a club or something!'

She swept aside Emma's half-hearted protests. Although Emma did occasionally go out for a drink with other members of the team, and had once been invited back to her boss's house for a meal, her evenings were as lonely and uneventful as they had ever been and now, suddenly, she felt like being young, frivolous, responsive to the stimulus of male company.

The unknown Andy's choice of a blind date turned out to be a young man in his mid-twenties who worked in a literary agency. With dark hair, deep set brown eyes and a ready sense of humour, he was far from unattractive. He made Emma laugh – something she realized she had not done for a very long while. He was attentive – and made no attempt to hide the fact that he, in turn, found her attractive. Emma knew it would not take much encouragement from her for them to end up in bed together. Although she had never in her life before contemplated a one-night stand, as her escort pressed himself against her whilst they danced, she felt her own body responding. She wanted someone to make love to her – to hold her, caress her, satisfy that primitive hunger which, in the past, Simon had so often aroused. Above all, she wanted someone to help her forget Simon – and how much she still loved him.

Weakly, she agreed with Lucy that they should invite the two men back to the flat. She knew that Lucy would disappear with Andy into her own room and that she was making it almost impossible for her, Emma, to cry off at this stage of the night. As she poured a drink for her guest, she was reminded suddenly of Derek – of his voice slurred by alcohol – accusing her of being a cock-teaser. Tonight, perhaps, that accusation

would be fair for she knew in that same moment that it was
not this young man's lovemaking she craved; it was Simon
she needed . . . and no one else could assuage that need.

Her companion took her volte-face with remarkably good
grace.

'You don't have to tell me – you're carrying a torch for
someone else!' he said with unusual perception.

Emma felt tears stinging her eyes.

'I'll get over it!' she said. 'I just need time. Thanks for being
so nice about it. Maybe we can keep in touch . . . some other
time . . .'

They exchanged telephone numbers, but as Emma let him out
into the deserted streets, she knew that she would not ring him
when she was next in town. He was too nice – and too young
– to be used by her, for that was what she would have been
doing – using him as a temporary replacement for the husband
she still wanted, but who did not want her on her terms.

For the next two days, Emma threw herself into her work
and spent the evenings writing up her copy. The subject-matter
absorbed her thoughts for until now, she had never realized
the misery some women endured, many of whom had drifted
into crime for no better reason than that they'd fallen in love
with men already involved. One young girl, no older than
Hazel and with a child of Vicky's age, admitted openly to
Emma that she was going back to live with the man who'd
lured her into the drug scene; that not even the grim prospects
for her child could deter her. Hazel might be in the same boat
now but for Simon's offer of a job, Emma thought. The fates
of these girls lay in the hands of the men they fell in love
with. Unlike herself, they had no independent lives of their
own; no ambition, no hope.

Emma was still writing up her notes late on Thursday night
when Lucy returned from a date.

'Hell of a wind out there!' she said, trying to smooth her
new hairstyle back into shape. 'For heaven's sake, Emma, pack
it in – you look exhausted!'

Emma stretched her arms above her head to relieve her aching back. She had been so engrossed in what she was writing that she had not noticed the wind. The window-frames of the old converted building were not well fitted and there was a whistling noise as the draughts blew through the crevices.

'I've just about finished what I wanted to do. Want some coffee, Lucy?'

Lucy shook her head.

'I'm off to bed. Can't keep my eyes open. See you!'

Tired as she was, Emma could not get to sleep. Her mind was too activated by the things she had heard and seen that day. She had no doubt as to how she would slant her programme. People like that young girl must be helped, or there was no hope for them or for society who suffered from their crimes. It was so easy to imagine Hazel in her shoes and thoughts of Hazel inevitably brought with them memories of Ortolans, of misty summer mornings walking down to the river with Simon, of little Vicky kicking off her tiny trainers and dancing over the dew-covered grass, delighting in her small footprints; of winter evenings when Hazel lit the fire in the drawing-room and smoke from the apple logs would curl up from the old chimney disturbing the starlings who had nested there earlier in the year. The memories crowded in – Roddy's cheerful grin, Hazel's endless cigarettes, Vicky's giggles – and finally, when Emma could no longer keep them at bay, memories of Simon's quiet smile, his green eyes alight with enthusiasm as he planned some new renovation to his beloved house; of his strong arms encircling her, the feel of his mouth on hers.

It seemed to Emma that no sooner had she fallen asleep than she was woken by the wind which had intensified. The window-frames were rattling alarmingly. She decided to give up any further attempt to sleep, and to get up and make herself a cup of coffee. She pressed the switch on her bedside light and found that they were in the middle of an electricity failure.

With the aid of her torch, she went through to the kitchen, found a box of candles and achieved sufficient light to boil a saucepan of water on the gas stove. Lucy appeared, tousle-headed and bleary eyed.

'Hell of a din!' she murmured as Emma poured out a second cup of coffee. 'Woke me up! What's the time, Em?'

'It's nearly dawn!' Emma said. She crossed to the window and looked out on the empty street.

'Come and look at these trees, Lucy!' she said. 'They're bent almost double. It's quite a storm!'

'It wasn't forecast!' Lucy said as she joined Emma at the window. She gasped as a slate from the roof of the house opposite crashed into the street.

'Good thing no one was walking underneath!' she said. 'Don't think I'd like to be on the top floor of a high-rise block in this, would you?'

Surprised by the force of the gale, but not unduly frightened, Lucy and Emma decided that sleep was impossible. For a while, they talked of Emma's job, of the unspeakable Derek and the humiliation she had suffered that dreadful night at his house when he had told her that her so-called talent was a pipe dream. 'Now all my belief in myself has been restored,' Emma said. 'My boss couldn't be nicer or more encouraging, and since she's a married woman – or was! – I don't have to worry about her interest in my feminine charms!'

Lucy's hilarious account of how she had been propositioned by a lesbian for whom she had worked briefly as a temp led them back to a discussion about sex.

'It's obvious that you and Simon hit it off in bed,' Lucy commented. 'Don't you miss that side of things, Em? How can you contemplate a life of abstinence – or will you take lovers *when* you can spare the time?'

Emma smiled.

'There's no need to be sarcastic. OK, so I'm dedicated to my work, but I do get time off. If I wanted to have a casual affair, there's nothing to stop me.'

Lucy looked at her searchingly.

'*If* you wanted . . .' she repeated, 'but you needn't tell me, you're still crazy about Simon. Unlike me, you're a one-man woman, Em. Are you two going to get a divorce?'

'I suppose so! We haven't discussed it,' Emma admitted. 'I haven't spoken to Simon since . . . since the night I left the flat to come back here.'

Their conversation was interrupted by a sound like a car backfiring. Lucy went to the window and gave a shout.

'It's that plane tree at the top of the street!' she shouted in an awestruck voice. 'It's flat on the ground, Em. There's a whirlwind out there. Come and look!'

Leaves, a dustbin lid, part of a cardboard box and a For Sale board littered the road. The wind had increased in severity and Emma felt a moment's fear as the rubbish went bowling down the street.

'It's one hell of a storm!' she said. 'At this rate, no one's going to get to work tomorrow!'

'Today!' Lucy corrected her. 'I'm hungry, Em. I'm going to make some toast. Why don't you bring in your radio? We might catch some early news to go with our breakfast. Shame about the electricity or we could have watched *Breakfast Time*.'

'I couldn't eat anything,' Emma said. 'I'm going to have a hot bath whilst the going's good. At least we've got gas and the old Ascot will be working.'

She returned to the kitchen in time to hear the seven o'clock news. It seemed that London and the south of England had been suffering the worst storm in recorded history. The winds had reached hurricane force, but were beginning to abate. In the meanwhile, listeners were advised not to travel unless it was absolutely essential. Hundreds of roads were blocked, as were the south coast railway lines. The words 'disaster' and 'devastation' accompanied most of the newscaster's comments. Houses, hotels, ships had been wrecked; there was news of countless trees down in the London parks and of terrible damage in places like Kew Gardens. The entire city was blacked out, bringing back memories of the blitz. The storm had raged from Cornwall to East Anglia with wind speeds registered in places of 110 mph.

Emma and Lucy stared at one another in growing horror as they waited for the promised newsflashes giving further details as the radio station received them. Telephone lines in many of the Home Counties were down and communications were disrupted. Helicopters were to be sent up to assess the extent of the damage.

By eight o'clock, Emma was in no doubt that the situation was far, far worse than she and Lucy had imagined. Uppermost in her mind now was the thought that Ortolans had been in the path of the storm. If the wind had brought down the big walnut tree to the west of the house, it could have done untold damage. Outside the flat, rain was now washing the debris into the drains, many of which were becoming blocked. The wind was calmer and occasionally someone would venture out in waterproofs. There were no cars although in the distance, she caught the sound of a police siren and once or twice, the sound of ambulances. Someone on the radio was talking about a woman who had forecast a hurricane but been ridiculed by the Met Office. It was expected that the failure of the Met to forecast the storm would be referred today to the Home Secretary. Lives had been lost.

'I'm going to see if I can get through to Hazel!' Emma said with a growing sense of unease about the fate of Ortolans. Sussex seemed to have been one of the counties badly affected.

Although their telephone was working, Ortolans – or lines to the south – gave the out-of-order signal.

'Why not give Simon a ring,' Lucy suggested, seeing the expression of anxiety on Emma's face. 'Maybe he has managed to get through to a neighbour.'

Emma stood poised with the telephone in her hand. Simon would not yet have gone to work – if he was going in to the office. He might have news . . . yet Ortolans was not really her concern any more. He might well ask what the hell it had to do with her! Fearing a rebuff she put down the phone.

'No point!' she said, her voice sharp with inexplicable pain. 'It's really none of my business!'

'OK, OK, have it your own way!' Lucy said cheerfully. She peered out once more into the street which was no longer deserted. A few stalwart individuals were making their way in the direction of the Underground.

'Think I'll try and get in to work!' she announced, adding with a grin: 'There's a smashing bloke in the accounts depart-ment who said he'd take me out to lunch . . . don't want to miss the opportunity in case he doesn't ask again!'

Emma telephoned NACRO and after several abortive attempts, managed to get through. There was no question of keeping the appointment at Holloway Prison, she was told. It would have to be postponed, anyway until Monday. She made yet another cup of coffee and put a call through to Pete at the studio. They had been good friends as well as teammates, and with the studio so close, perhaps they might meet for lunch. It would help to pass the day which was now so much wasted time.

Pete was in the cutting-room but thanks to the telephone operator who remembered Emma, she was finally put through. He sounded delighted to hear from her and they arranged to meet at the usual pub for a quick lunch at one.

She still had the rest of the morning to occupy herself, she thought as she set about tidying the flat. Lucy's nature was such that she left everything where it fell. There was no way Emma could do any hoovering since the electricity was still off. However, shortly after ten o'clock, the lights came on. Emma went through to the sitting-room and switched on the television. Immediately the screen was filled with horrifying pictures of the storm damage. The scenes of the Kent and Sussex countryside were far worse than anything she had imagined listening to the radio. Inevitably, her mind returned to Ortolans. There seemed little chance that Detcham had been spared the terrible devastation. Perhaps, after all, she might risk a telephone call to Simon and put her mind at rest. This was no time for personal animosities.

There was no answer from the Brunswick Square flat, so Emma assumed that Simon, like many others, had managed somehow to struggle in to work. For once, his secretary did not answer the phone, but Simon himself came on the line. His voice was cool, remote as he said:

'Hope I didn't keep you waiting. Things are pretty hectic here at the moment.'

'Sorry to disturb you,' Emma said awkwardly. 'I just wanted to know if you'd had any news about Ortolans. I thought you might have tried to get down there. I did try to ring Hazel but the line is out of order.'

Simon's tone sounded a little warmer as he replied:

'That's right! However, I did finally manage to speak to Mrs Moneywell at the post office in Detcham. I gather the situation is grim.'

'Will you be going down after work this evening?'

'No way! The roads are blocked and there are no trains. I'd have tried to get down today somehow or other, but we've a bit of a crisis on here and I can't leave the office.'

Emma paused, searching for words.

'I'm in London for the weekend – at the flat!' she said. 'If you do get any news, will you ring me?'

'Sure!' Somehow even in that one word, Simon sounded surprised. 'I'm hoping Mrs Moneywell will ring through once someone has got up to the house. She said the farmers were out with chainsaws trying to clear the lanes, and the vicar and PC Porter were doing the rounds on foot checking on the old people. I just hope to goodness poor Hazel and little Vicky are OK. It must have been pretty scary for them alone in the house.'

'Maybe Hazel had the sense to take Vicky down to the cellars!' Emma said reassuringly. 'Well, I won't keep you, Simon. You sound busy.'

'Very, but thanks for the call. Perhaps . . .' he hesitated and then continued in a firmer tone '. . . perhaps we could meet up some time and have a drink.'

'Fine! Don't forget to let me know if you have any news.'

'I'll do that. Thanks again for ringing.'

As Emma replaced the receiver, she realized that her hands were clammy and that they were trembling. This was ridiculous, she told herself. She and Simon were adults, not silly teenagers beset with tensions and tantrums. Why shouldn't they be friends? They had not seen or spoken to each other for six weeks – although it seemed a great deal longer – and she ought to be able to talk to him, have lunch or a drink with him, without getting into this state!

She continued to watch the television screen until it was time to make her way on foot to her rendezvous with Pete. He greeted her with his usual wide-mouthed grin and a huge bear hug.

'Wonderful to see you, duckie! You look gorgeous, as always. I thought you'd forgotten your old chums at the Beeb – not a peep out of you!'

Emma laughed as they went inside.

'I'm not very often in London – and anyway, if I came to the studio, I might run into Derek – and that is something I can do without!'

Pete grinned. 'Dirty Derek has been consoling himself with your successor – she's obviously more accommodating than you were, darling!'

Having found seats at one of the tables, he fetched ploughman's lunches and beers from the bar, and rejoined her.

'I ran into that flatmate of yours, Lucy, a couple of weeks ago. She told me you'd got a smashing new job in Southampton. Good on you, as our Derek would say!'

'Don't mention that man again!' Emma said, laughing. For a few minutes they talked about her work and then, inevitably, the conversation turned to the storm.

'It's bad enough here in London, but a hell of a lot worse

in the country,' Pete said. 'I've elderly parents living in Burgess Hill and I'm going down to see if they're OK as soon as I can get away this afternoon.'

'But the roads are blocked and there are no trains!' Emma said.

'They've been clearing the main roads since dawn and I reckon I can get through on my motorbike. No problem! What about your husband's house in Sussex?'

It was on the tip of Emma's tongue to tell Pete that she and Simon had separated and that Ortolans was therefore no longer her concern; but her mind went to a more urgent consideration. If Pete could get as far as Burgess Hill, surely it should be possible to get from there to Detcham?

'Don't see why not!' Pete said with his usual optimism. 'Where there's a will there's a way . . . you can certainly hitch a lift with me if you can cope with riding pillion.'

It was a crazy idea, Emma thought as Pete went on to tell her that he hoped to get away around four. Even if she did manage to reach Ortolans, what could she do, other than to ascertain that Hazel and Vicky were OK; lend a little moral support? If nothing else, she could ascertain the damage to Ortolans and, hopefully, put her mind at rest if it were not too serious. What else was she to do with her weekend? Lucy would almost certainly arrange an evening date with her newest accountant friend – or if not, with Andy. She, Emma, had nothing whatever to do this evening, or for the next two days. There was little chance of her getting a train back to Southampton and nothing to tempt her back there.

'It'll be dark by the time we get to your home, Pete,' she said tentatively.

'So OK, you stay the night with us, and on Saturday, I'll try to get you to this Detcham place. They'll have cleared more roads by then. Mum will make you really welcome. She loves visitors.'

By the time Pete was due back at work, Emma's mind was

made up – crazy as it was, she would go. If the worst came to the worst and she couldn't get through to Detcham, she could return to London with Pete on Sunday.

For some reason Emma could not explain to herself, she decided not to tell Lucy where she was going – merely that she was meeting someone from the studio and might not be back that night. There was no justifiable reason for withholding the truth from Lucy – and yet she was reluctant to admit that Ortolans could still tug so fiercely on her heartstrings. Lucy would be bound to assume that it was Simon, not the house, she was hoping to see and this was simply not the case. Her brief conversation with Simon this morning had changed nothing. The fact that his voice could still leave her feeling weak with longing was a physical reaction that was only to be expected.

As it was still raining, Emma decided to wear her ski outfit which she hoped would keep her both warm and dry on Pete's bike. Unpacking it from its cardboard box where she had stored it since her honeymoon, she felt a deep wave of nostalgia. They had been so very happy! So passionately in love! So full of hope for the future! *She* had not changed. It was Simon who had found it impossible to keep the promises he had made those weeks in Crans.

It was only a little after four-thirty when Pete collected Emma at the flat.

'Thought you might have changed your mind!' he said as he handed her a crash helmet and fastened the strap under her chin. 'Off we go then – for better or for worse.'

The journey south, which Pete had said normally took him an hour and a half, now lasted three times as long. Although council workers, the Army and civilian volunteers had been struggling to clear the roads, in some places there were diversions; in others only single-lane traffic was possible and there were inevitable delays. As they left the suburbs, Emma was shocked by the huge areas of Forestry Commission woodlands flattened like matchsticks; at the sight of a row of poplars which looked as if a giant had lopped off the tops. In places, huge oaks had been torn out of the ground, their roots left pointing up to the sky, the great bowls in the earth they had occupied already filled with rainwater.

'Looks like a scene from one of those First World War films!' Pete said, his voice awestruck, when they stopped for a cup of tea. As they neared Burgess Hill, he became more anxious for his parents. It was nearly dark when they pulled up in a quiet housing estate devoid of street lighting, outside a small semi-detached house. A tarpaulin covered part of the roof. The remains of the garden fences of both houses were strewn across the flower beds.

Pete's parents came to the door and stared at their rain-drenched figures at first in dismay and then with delight. They were ushered into the small sitting-room and despite their wet clothes, made to sit in front of the blazing fire.

'Seems silly to be burning coal with all this wood knocking about!' said the old man. 'We'll all be burning logs this winter by the look of it.'

They were remarkably cheerful, despite the fact that they'd also lost a chimney and their precious greenhouse, and were happily recalling the wartime days of the London Blitz when they had been living in North Cross.

'There's the same spirit amongst folk as was there in those days,' Pete's mother said to Emma. 'All our neighbours have been out helping each other – and bartering, too.' She turned to Pete. 'Your dad's got a nice leg of lamb from next door – their deep freeze being on the blink with no electricity – and we let them have a bag of coal seeing as how they didn't get their usual supply today. Mind you, we were quite frightened in the night, but once morning came and we knew we'd survived – well, it's a matter of everyone turning to to do their best, isn't it, my dear!'

An hour and a half later, they sat down to a delicious lamb stew, miraculously conjured up by Pete's stalwart mother and cooked on the camping stove his father had brought in from the shed. They ate by candlelight and listened to the news on the portable radio. It now seemed as if the storm had been officially designated as a hurricane, but as Pete said, it was just as well the Met hadn't warned them it was on the way or they might all have been a lot more frightened.

His father, to Emma's surprise, knew Detcham and could remember playing cricket on the village green as a young lad. He even recalled a very regal old titled lady driving down in an old-fashioned pony and trap to present the winning team with a trophy.

'That must have been my husband's great-grandmother!' Emma said. 'There was a time when his family owned Detcham and some of the old people still talk of her as "the squire's lady".'

'Emma's married to the present Sir Simon Calverley!' Pete announced. 'Not that she looked much like a "squire's lady" on the back of my bike!'

'Well, fancy that!' his mother said, her cheeks pink with pleasure. 'So that's why you're so determined to get there tomorrow, dear! Kent got it worse even than Sussex, so let's hope your house isn't too bad.'

Emma's hopes of finding Ortolans intact were fast fading. As she tried to relax in the comfortable bed Pete's mother provided for her, her imagination continued to work overtime. When finally she did sleep, it was only to suffer further anxiety in her dreams. She was in the back of an ambulance with – of all people – Derek Meadows. The siren was screaming and she was aware of a terrible sense of urgency.

Suddenly, she knew that the tyres were crunching on the gravel drive leading to Ortolans.

'It's time you faced a few facts, Emma!' Derek said in a sneering voice. 'Your precious house is a ruin.'

She was about to argue with him when the back doors of the ambulance were opened by unseen hands. There in front of her eyes was all that was left of Ortolans, a great pile of debris. Horsham slabs were sticking up from a mound of plaster, on top of which oak beams lay criss-crossing one another like so much firewood.

'We'll be using them for logs this winter!' Derek said in matter-of-fact tones. 'I'll see if there's a chainsaw in the first aid kit!'

As he rummaged beneath one of the beds, Emma saw two men in orange council clothing approaching from behind the rubble. They were carrying a stretcher, on which lay a body covered by a white sheet.

'No need to tell you who *that* is!' Derek said, grabbing hold of Emma's arm, his face distorted by an ugly leer as he added: 'You should have listened to me, darling. If you'd slept with me, you wouldn't be going to his funeral now, would you?'

Tears were streaming down Emma's face and forming huge puddles at her feet. She wanted to protest – to tell Derek that he was mistaken; that this wasn't Ortolans; that the man on the stretcher was not who he believed him to be. The scream was still lodged in her throat as one of the stretcher-bearers leant forward and drew back the sheet. The scream tore from her body, mercifully waking her from the nightmare as she gazed down and saw that indeed, the face of the dead man was Simon's.

CHAPTER THIRTY-SEVEN

1987

Simon had no need to leave his car to realize that there was no possible way in which he could manoeuvre the Porsche past the two-hundred-year-old oak tree lying diagonally across the entrance to Ortolans's drive. Its four-feet-diameter trunk would have to be cut into smaller sections before even a tractor could drag them to one side.

He parked the car as best he could on the damp verge, knowing that whatever had happened to Ortolans, he must get back to London tomorrow for work on Monday. Mrs Moneywell had not returned his telephone call and this morning, he had discovered that the whole of the Detcham area was without a telephone service. None of the men working in gangs on the approach roads to Detcham could tell him what damage had been done to Ortolans. The larger roads were taking priority over the lanes in the hope of easing the traffic congestion, they explained.

Stepping over smaller branches and a telegraph pole that had been snapped halfway up its length, Simon became aware that the wind was getting up again. The rain was still falling and a damp, grey curtain of water obscured any early view of the house. Silently, he prayed that Ortolans was still standing.

Emma's call had surprised him. Thinking about it last evening, he had reached the conclusion that she, too, must care about Ortolans even if she no longer cared about him! The maddening thing was that *he* still loved *her*. He had not expected that she would walk out on him. When he'd left the flat that Sunday to go off for a drink and cool down, he had genuinely expected to find Emma still there on his return. He had never intended his challenge to be taken so literally. There was no denying that a problem existed, but somehow they should have been able to sort it out. Emma, it seemed, was not prepared to consider a compromise. She had jumped to the conclusion that he wanted her to give up her career when all he had wanted was for her to find some other job which would not mean her living all week in Southampton, of all places. There must be other jobs going. All it had needed was a bit of patience, but she had packed her belongings and gone, without even leaving a note. Nor had she telephoned him the next day. It was obvious that she intended their separation to be final and that her love for him had never been deep enough for her to make the slightest sacrifice. He was not only desperately hurt but angry. He still found it impossible to reconcile the memories of the love they had shared with her betrayal of all they had meant to each other. When finally she had telephoned him, it had been only to ask about Ortolans. At least she had sounded really concerned about the house and her love for it was genuine!

Simon had tried to forget Emma. Cilla had come back into his life, though not his flat, demanding his time and assistance. Her business affairs had finally reached the point of insolvency and she had had to go into voluntary liquidation. He had accompanied her to several meetings with the liquidation accountant she was employing and had spent endless hours with her discussing the alternative possibility to going bankrupt. At best, it looked as if she would be able to pay her creditors ten pence in the pound – and that was without repaying his loan to her. Suitably contrite, Cilla had alternated between tears and relief that she had finally ceased banging her head against a brick wall. As a consequence, Simon was either mopping her tears, or taking her out for a drink or a meal to celebrate the end of her business career.

'I'm simply not a career woman – that's the trouble!' Cilla

had said. 'I suppose at heart I'm hopelessly old-fashioned. I want a rich husband who will keep me in idleness for the rest of my life!'

Simon had not been able to bring himself to tell her that he and Emma had split up because, unlike Cilia, Emma was very much a career woman. He merely said she was tied up in a job in Southampton, and changed the subject, ignoring Cilia's expression of surprise. At least she had not belaboured the subject and she had filled some of the hours of loneliness which Emma's absence entailed.

Here he was, thinking of Emma yet again, Simon reproached himself as he neared the house. Ortolans was all that mattered to him now – and little Vicky. He was going to miss the child when Hazel finally packed her bags. Hazel had become increasingly restless since Emma had stopped coming to the house.

'She was good company, you know? And nice about the kid. It's just not the same!'

'It's exactly the same – the same as it was before I got married!' Simon had rejoined more sharply than he had intended.

'Well, I got used to her. I liked her! You gonna have a quickie?' Seeing the shocked look on Simon's face, she grinned. 'Divorce, I mean. I'm not a tart. Be a fool if you let her go. I think she's smashing!' Hazel had the last word.

Simon now had Ortolans in view. He paused, his heart beating unbearably fast as he saw the great walnut tree lying at an angle of forty-five degrees, its branches smothering the west wing of the house, obscuring part of the old roof. The roots had been torn from the soil, lifting great mounds of turf and all the new shrubs he and Emma had planted. The magnolia tree had been blown across the front of the house and was half-blocking the door. At least the main chimney was still intact, he thought as he saw smoke curling up from the stack – and Hazel must be alive to have lit the fire!

He pushed his way past the tangled branches of magnolia and opened the heavy oak, iron-studded door. A small shadow came darting towards him and Vicky flung herself into his arms.

'We had a great big huge enormous great big wind!' she told him breathlessly, 'and I was frightened and it was dark and I couldn't open Mum's door and so I cried.'

Simon's arms tightened protectively around her.

'There's no need to be frightened any more,' he said gently.

'I went downstairs and slept in your big bed,' Vicky said. 'Mum couldn't find me and she was very, very cross and she smacked me, and do you know, a huge great big enormous tree came through my window and it's sleeping in my bed!'

Simon gazed down at the bright innocent eyes with a sense of horror. Had the child not found her way downstairs . . . had she remained in her bed, she might have been killed.

'Where's Mummy?' he asked sharply.

'In the kitchen with Roddy and Emma and they're talking boring things and I was going upstairs to get my toys and you came.'

Simon halted, staring along the passageway leading to the kitchen quarters. Emma . . . here . . . but how? He had come as soon as the roads were passable. How had she possibly got here? Why had she come?

He walked slowly down the passage and opened the kitchen door.

The Aga was throwing out a welcome heat and the scrubbed pine kitchen table was laid for lunch. A tantalizing smell came from a game casserole simmering on the hotplate.

'Thought as how you'd turn up,' Hazel said as Simon appeared in the doorway. 'Just in time for lunch!'

The questions about Vicky and the danger she had been in died on Simon's lips as he stared at Emma. She was staring at him.

'Don't look so stunned!' she said. 'The house is OK, isn't it, Roddy?'

Roddy stood up and walked round the table.

'Could have been one hell of a lot worse!' he said with his

usual grin. 'Those old slabs stood up to the weight of the walnut so the roof's sound. Part of the west wall has a gaping hole between the beams where the wattle and daub was knocked out, and Vicky's bedroom window and the ones below have gone. That's about the worst of it. We've been lucky!'

Simon put Vicky down on her feet and sat down in an empty chair. Stupidly, he felt like bawling his head off. He was home . . . this was home . . . and Ortolans, despite all his worries, had survived.

'Quite an item to put in *The Calverley Journal*,' Emma said, sensing that he needed time before he could get control of his emotions. 'I tried to telephone you when I arrived . . . but nothing's working. Roddy says they've even had to get the village pump going. Because of the electricity failure, the main water supply pumps won't work. We're using the pump in the stable yard.'

'Given us some idea what it must have been like in the old days!' Roddy said.

'Drudgery, that's what!' said Hazel. 'Didn't half give me a turn when I woke up. Slept through the storm myself. Nearly had a fit when I went into Vicky's room and saw the tree lying across her bed! Of course, the telly's not working and I'm going to miss *Bob's Full House* and *Casualty*. Emma says she's got telly in London. It's bloody well not fair!'

'For pity's sake, Hazel!' Roddy protested with unusual sharpness. 'How can you possibly complain about going without television when the whole of the south of England is in a state of emergency? People have been killed, for God's sake, and injured, and there's men out there in this ghastly weather struggling to get things working again . . . essential things like heat and light and water. What about the sick folk in hospitals . . . and the old people who haven't got a warm Aga to sit by? And all *you* care about is your telly!'

Hazel did not look particularly abashed.

'Keep your hair on!' she said as she stubbed out her cigarette

and went to look at the stew. 'I only meant it was going to
be a pretty boring evening!'

Simon looked across the table at Emma.

'Talking of this evening, will you be going back to town?'
he asked. 'I gather some trains are running, but only from
Purley. Balcombe Forest was decimated and the Haywards
Heath area is pretty bad.'

Was he suggesting he did not want her down here? Emma
wondered, wishing suddenly that she had not turned up uninvited. At the same time, she was in little doubt that it was as
well she had arrived when she did. Simon would have found
Hazel's latest boyfriend installed in her flat. It was because
Hazel had been in bed with the chap on Thursday night that
she had locked her door and the terrified child had been unable
to get in.

'For God's sake, don't let on to Simon!' Hazel had begged
her. 'I'd really get it in the neck. Not that I much care if I do
lose my job. I'm fed up living here. Promise you won't tell
him. He's said I can have a fortnight's holiday at the end of
the month and Spence has promised to take me to Spain.
Costa del Sol, we're going . . . Torremolinos. I've got lots of
brochures – I'll show you.'

It was not the moment to sit around browsing through
holiday brochures, Emma had pointed out. Simon would
almost certainly be down and they would all need lunch. Hazel
said there was nothing to cook – she had not been able to
get out to do the weekend shopping on Friday. There was
only the pheasants Simon had brought back from a shoot at
the Finden-Reids a fortnight ago. Emma sent her down to the
cellar to fetch them and reluctantly, Hazel got back to work,
her mouth a sulky droop because Emma had sent her boyfriend packing.

For the few hours prior to Simon's arrival, it had seemed
to Emma as if she had never left Ortolans, that she was once
again mistress of the house. Little Vicky was pathetically
pleased to see her and had said wistfully:

'Mum said you might never come back. Don't go away again, will you?'

She should not have come, Emma thought once more as Hazel began dishing up the lunch. Simon was ignoring her and was clearly embarrassed by her presence. Hazel was still sulking and it was Roddy who kept the conversation going; he who told Simon that Emma had appeared on the back of a motorbike, of all things, having had a hazardous ride from Burgess Hill.

'I'd spent the night there,' she heard herself explaining. 'Pete had offered to bring me over here to see how you'd all fared. It seemed like a good idea.'

Simon did not comment. Perhaps he thought Pete was the new man in her life! Feeling strangely embarrassed, Emma announced that Pete would be picking her up after lunch tomorrow to take her back to London.

'I assumed it would be OK for me to stay here tonight,' she added, her embarrassment increasing when Simon glanced quickly at her with a questioning gaze.

She was grateful when Roddy once more took over the conversation. While he discussed the hurricane with Simon, she toyed with the food on her plate, wishing herself back in London in the impersonal surroundings of her flat. Why had she acted so impulsively? she asked herself. It was unlike her not to think a situation through to its obvious conclusion. She should have anticipated Simon's likely presence here and his reactions to her behaviour. She had not told him she was going to attempt to get down to Ortolans with Pete; had not asked his approval or considered that he might have no wish to see her. His casual invitation on the telephone to 'have a drink sometime' might not have meant he was considering putting their former relationship on terms of casual friendship – such as he had with Cilia! And what would she have done if he – unaware she was here – had arrived with Cilia or a new girlfriend?

Immediately lunch was over, Simon and Roddy disappeared

out of doors to begin the mammoth task of clearing the worst of the storm damage. Simon did not ask her to join them and so she and Vicky spent the afternoon moving the child's toys and clothes into the old nursery. Hazel remained in the kitchen reading old magazines. It was almost dark when the two men stopped work and came in for tea. Roddy announced that he would have to be making his way back to Detcham.

'Great to see you again, Emma,' he said with real warmth in his voice. 'We've missed you, you know . . . all of us!'

As Simon went out to the hall to see him off, Emma pondered whether Roddy's last remark had had a special significance. Had he been meaning to let her know that Simon, too, had missed her? Well, *she* had missed Simon – but it did not alter the situation. In the end, it was up to him to accept her on her terms. They were behaving like strangers, she thought. Simon's manner was entirely formal as he offered her a drink and enquired politely about her new job. Hazel managed to produce omelettes and cheese for supper which they had in the kitchen, after which she put Vicky to bed in the old nursery and announced that she was going up to her room to listen to the radio. Simon and Emma went through to the drawing-room where he threw some more logs on the fire.

'I expect you're pretty tired. You and Roddy had quite a day!' Emma said in an attempt to make conversation. 'He's such a nice person. It's strange he hasn't got himself a girlfriend.'

Simon looked up from his mug of coffee.

'Oh, but he has! Of course you wouldn't know, but since we split up, he's got himself engaged to a Lewes girl.'

Emma bit her lip.

'I wish I'd known – I'd have congratulated him. Is she nice?'

'Yes, very! They're getting married next summer and I've told Roddy he can use Ortolans for the reception. Her father came from Detcham so her parents are quite happy for their daughter to be married in Detcham Church. I hate to think of that lovely lychgate smashed beyond repair, but at least the church itself has survived. Roddy says the graveyard is a mass of fallen yews, and the Calverley vault is obscured by branches.'

There was a brief pause before he added: 'Why exactly did you come down, Emma? You're the last person I expected to find here!'

'I was worried about the house,' she replied quickly, 'and Pete said he was going to make sure his parents were all right in Burgess Hill . . . and the appointment I had was cancelled because of the storm, so I just thought I'd make sure everything was OK.'

She was conscious of Simon's eyes searching her face and turned quickly away. That questioning look when he narrowed those unusual green eyes, and the way he had of tilting his head a little to one side when he was unsure of something, never failed to touch some inner core no one else had aroused . . . a kind of tenderness that was almost maternal. It was absurd to consider Simon, so tall, strong, athletic, as someone capable of a little-boy-lost look – and yet she felt the familiar need to reach out and lay a reassuring hand on his arm.

Quickly, she quashed the urge. Simon's physical attraction for her had never been in question but was irrelevant to their compatibility. The last thing in the world she wanted at this moment was to reawaken the old need for _him_, yet with the firelight flickering on his face, his fair hair tousled, his head half turned towards her, there was an expectancy about him which in the old days, she would have responded to at once and it would have taken no more than a smile from her before they would be going, arms around one another, to bed.

Damn it, I won't think this way! Emma told herself fiercely. Abruptly, she said:

'I've made up a bed for myself in the small spare room. Hazel's put a hot-water bottle in so it shouldn't be damp.'

That, she thought, should put any ideas out of Simon's head.

It was some moments before he spoke. When he did so, it was to say:

'So it *was* the house you came to see! Just for a moment, I wondered if . . . if you'd missed me as much as I've missed you.'

It wasn't fair! Emma thought as the colour rushed to her cheeks. It simply wasn't fair to make this kind of emotional appeal to her. Yet deep down she knew a heady sense of relief that Simon still cared about her. She had felt so mortified by his seeming indifference. She decided that the time had come for complete honesty. She would not prevaricate.

'Of course I've missed you. There have been a dozen and one times when I wanted to telephone you, write to you. At weekends, I'd think about you here at Ortolans and remember the things we did together and I could hardly bear it. I even wondered if there might be a way in which we could sort things out so that I didn't have to live without you. But there isn't a way, Simon, and if you're honest you'll admit it. I was right to go when I did.'

He did not try to touch her but there was no need. His voice was husky with emotion as he said urgently:

'So you do still love me! You want me, don't you, Emma . . . as much as I want you!'

Emma put her hand to her mouth.

'Please, Simon, don't let's confuse the issues. I haven't changed my mind about the future – and I'm sorry if my coming here today led you to believe that I had.'

Now he reached over and caught her with an unfamiliar roughness in his arms.

'To hell with the future! I want you . . . desperately!'

He kissed her with a passion that found an immediate response in her body. Her legs, arms, stomach were weak with longing as she pressed herself even closer to him. But her mind remained apart.

'This will only make it more difficult for us!' she whispered. 'Don't you understand? It's been hard enough learning to live without you without renewing all the old memories!'

He seemed not to be listening . . . or else did not wish to

hear her words of caution. His hands were reaching beneath her warm pullover, closing over her breasts, bringing them instantly to life. She could feel his body hardening as she strained against him. Together, they rolled off the sofa on to the thick fireside rug, and now Simon began once more to kiss her, silencing her murmured protests.

'You want me to make love to you. Say it, Emma! You want me, don't you?'

With a cry that was partly one of defeat, Emma wound her arms round Simon's neck and closing her eyes, surrendered herself totally to the familiar thrills of pleasure, of urgency, of excitement which he had always been able to arouse in her. In their sexual unity, there had never been any doubt as to their total compatibility. Her body belonged to Simon, and his to her.

Even after they had reached the summit together, Simon would not release his hold on her. He lay beside her, one hand caressing her hair.

'You are so beautiful, Emma. When I came into the kitchen this morning and saw you sitting there, it was like that first time I ever saw you. I knew then that I had to have you with me, that you belonged to me.'

Emma could not spoil the intimacy of the moment by voicing the protest that rose to her lips. Did Simon really not understand that she only belonged to herself? Physically they were perfectly united, but mentally they could never be reconciled.

There was no question now of Emma sleeping alone in the spare room. Simon carried her upstairs to the big four-poster and made love to her again. In the morning, when they woke, they made love a third time after which Simon went down to the kitchen to make a pot of tea. Returning to their room, he drew back the curtains and turned to smile at her.

'Because of you, I can look out there at that . . . that devastated garden and still be happy!' he said. 'Do you know, darling, I never thought the day could come when I would

love something or someone more than I love this house? I'd
rather lose Ortolans than you!'

Emma felt her throat constrict. Simon looked so earnest,
so young, so happy, but far from making *her* happy, his
compliment could only sadden her.

As he came to sit on the side of the bed, nearly spilling the
tea he had poured out for her as he bent to kiss her, something
in her expression wiped the smile from his face.

'What's wrong, Emma? You're not regretting last night . . .
this morning . . .?'

Emma put down her teacup and taking one of Simon's
hands in her own, held it to her cheek.

'I do love you!' she said in a low voice. 'Please believe that
because it's true, Simon. I love you very, very much. But I have
to go back . . . to Southampton, my job. It's everything I ever
wanted. It's something I can do . . . and do well. I don't want
to give it up – not even for you, for Ortolans, for all the
wonderful things we share.'

Gently, Simon pulled his hand away and his face was devoid
of expression as he said:

'It would be a lie if I said I wasn't hoping you might have
changed your mind. I suppose it was stupid of me to hope
that you would. When you were talking to me after supper
about your job, you looked so . . . I don't know . . . fulfilled.
I can't pretend to understand it. I believe you really do love
me or I wouldn't be saying all this – but I honestly don't understand why a career means so much more to you than . . . than
us. What is it you are trying to prove? That Meadows was
wrong and that you do have talent? If that's the case, are you
really prepared to let that . . . that bastard ruin our lives? I
don't suppose he gives a damn what you are doing!'

Emma's mouth tightened.

'Probably not – and I couldn't care less what Derek thinks.
I care what I think about myself. Ever since I was a small child,
I've hated failing at anything. I wanted to be someone . . .
someone who, if I met them, I would respect.'

'And you wouldn't respect yourself if you were my wife, mother of our children?'

Emma's cheeks flushed.

'I didn't say that. Why can't you understand, Simon? I want to be more than somebody's wife, somebody's mother. I want to be recognized for myself . . . my abilities. I want to know that I can achieve.'

'Haven't you already done that? I presume there aren't that many assistant producers knocking around the country?'

'In a few years' time, I could become a fully-fledged producer, Simon. It's what I want to do . . . to be.'

Simon stood up and walked over to the window once more.

'If you won't give up your job, is that any reason why we shouldn't go on seeing each other?'

'As friends? Or as lovers?'

'Both!' said Simon.

Emma bit her lip.

'I'd like us to be friends, Simon – if it were possible. As lovers . . . well, there would be too many emotional ties, wouldn't there? We are neither of us capable of a casual relationship as the past twenty-four hours have proved. You'd need more from me . . . more than I could give, and I think it would all end as it did last time – you feeling resentful about my work commitments and me feeling guilty because I'd let you down.'

Simon's face twisted into a wry smile.

'Strange, isn't it? It's usually the male in a relationship who's the one to back off when he sees his freedom about to be curtailed.'

Emma felt close to tears.

'It sounds as if I don't really love you.'

'Perhaps you do, darling – but just not enough!' Simon said quietly.

He returned to the bed and put his arms round her. This time there was no element of passion in his embrace.

'Don't worry about it. I'm not sorry you came down. It's

cleared the air and I was feeling bitter before about the way it all ended. We don't have to get divorced, do we? Let's try to be friends. Let's keep in touch.'

Unable to speak for the threatening tears, Emma nodded.

'And darling, no going back on a motorbike in this weather. I've left the Porsche at the end of the drive, so if we leave directly after lunch and go via Burgess Hill, we'll be there in time to tell this chap of yours you're having a lift with me.'

When the time came for them to leave, Emma was once more on the brink of tears. Vicky was being forcibly restrained by Hazel, howling that they mustn't go away without her; that the great big wind might come back and blow her away. The child was almost hysterical and was only quietened when Hazel gave her a sharp slap and told her to 'stop being such a silly little sod!' She did not look as if she believed Simon when he promised her faithfully that he would be down next weekend without fail.

'Any hope of you coming up from Southampton?' Simon asked as later that afternoon he dropped her at the Shepherd's Bush flat. 'If the trains are running properly again, you should be able to get straight through to Brighton and I could meet you there.'

'I don't know what I'll be doing,' Emma said truthfully, 'but I'll come if I can – give you and Roddy a hand with the clearing up. I'll ring you, shall I?'

Simon would not go in for a drink, but Lucy had seen the Porsche from the window. She was grinning broadly as Emma let herself in.

'So *that's* what you were up to! You're a dark horse, Emma Calverley, if I do say so! All on again, is it?'

'No, it's not!' Emma snapped. 'We're just friends, that's all!'

'Huh – just good friends! Goodness, Em, you're not talking to the press for heaven's sake.'

'Lucy, I told you, we're friends and that's all there is to it. Now drop it, will you? I'm exhausted. I'm going to have a bath and go to bed.'

She knew that Lucy was far from convinced, but she was too tired to pursue the subject. She was certain of only one thing – that it would be better if she did not go to Ortolans the following weekend. She and Simon would once more end up in bed, a state of affairs which solved nothing. For one of the few times in her life, she accepted Lucy's offer of a sleeping pill. Tomorrow she needed her wits about her to handle the Holloway interview. Sleep was the only way she could think of to clear her mind of the sight of the distress on Simon's face; the sound of Vicky's screams and the even more worrying sound of Hazel's hand slapping the little girl's thin wrist.

The interview the following morning went well, and she was back at the flat by lunchtime. There was a message on the kitchen table from Lucy which threw her into a state of confusion.

Your mum phoned. She's staying at the Inn on the Park and wants you to ring. Sounds urgent . . .

Emma sat down on one of the kitchen chairs aware that her hands were trembling. This was the last thing in the world she expected. Why had her mother not let her know she was coming? Perhaps she had tried to reach her at Southampton? Why was she in England? Had something happened to her father?

Part of her felt the same childish excitement she had known at boarding school when her parents had turned up unannounced for an exeat. At the same time, she was not prepared for the searching questions she was sure her mother would ask. Obviously, Lucy had told her that she was in London so she could not avoid a meeting. After eight years, would they be strangers to one another? Perhaps, in a way, they had always been strangers! Nevertheless she would see her. She must!

With an effort she steadied herself and dialled the number. Her mother's voice sounded calm and unemotional as she explained that she had been asked at the eleventh hour to step into the shoes of some eminent biologist who was ill, and read a paper at Edinburgh University. She had broken her journey to Scotland expressly to see her daughter, and would be flying back to the States direct from Edinburgh.

An hour later Emma walked through the swing doors of the big London hotel and glanced round the spacious foyer. Almost at once, a tall woman, with beautifully coiffed hair and smartly dressed in a pale grey dress and jacket, came towards her and kissed her on both cheeks.

'My dear child, you haven't changed at all!' Her voice had a marked American accent which momentarily confused Emma as her mother led her through to the cocktail lounge. There were one or two businessmen at the far end of the room, but the bar was almost deserted.

'I thought we could be quiet here. Your friend told me you have to go back to work this evening, so I know our time together is short. We must make the most of it. A drink, my dear, or coffee?' It was almost as if she sensed Emma's nervousness and talked easily about the hurricane until the coffee had been served. She then turned with searching brown eyes which, Emma thought incongruously, were remarkably like her own.

'Now, my dear, I want to hear all about you. When I called your home a cockney-sounding girl said you didn't live there any more. I tried your studio in Southampton and they'd never heard of Lady Calverley. So then I called your friend at your old apartment.'

'I use my maiden name at work,' Emma said. 'I'm sorry you had difficulty getting hold of me. In fact, I'm not often in London.' She hoped to avoid further questions about Hazel's bland announcement that she and Simon no longer lived together. Her hopes, however, were dashed as her mother said with a directness Emma had forgotten:

'Your father and I suspected that something of the sort must have happened when you wrote to tell us you had moved

to Southampton to be near your new job. We had thought
you were so much in love with your husband. Did you rush
into marriage too quickly, Emma? You had only known him
a short while and your father and I did warn you to wait.'

Emma's mouth tightened imperceptibly.

'I expect you were right,' she said curtly. 'Simon resents my
career because it takes me away from home. He doesn't admit
it, but if the truth be told, he'd like me to settle down and
have half a dozen children.'

'A not unnatural desire!' her mother said wryly. 'If you love
the man, how come you don't want the same thing?' She was
unprepared for the look of blank astonishment, coupled with
anger, that twisted Emma's countenance.

'You – *you* say that! You were the one – you and father
– who were so determined I should make something of my
life. You wanted me to be a success like Rosalind. Now . . .
now that I'm actually getting somewhere . . . *now* you say I
should throw it all up in order to have children!'

For a moment, her mother did not speak. There was both
distress and surprise in her voice as she said gently:

'My dear, it was never a question of either/or. It's true that
I was very anxious for you to have an interesting life beyond
that of marriage and children. All I wanted for you and my
poor Rosalind was that you should both be happy.'

She broke off and, somewhat to Emma's surprise, beckoned
to the barman to bring her a vodka and tonic. Although Emma
very rarely drank in the afternoon, she accepted a glass of
wine. For once, she did not trouble to try to conceal the fact
that her hands were trembling. Her mother took possession
of one of them and held it firmly between her own. They were
cool and her grasp was surprisingly firm.

'You were too young when your father and I went to the
States for us to have become friends, my dear, as can happen
between mothers and daughters when their girls grow up.
You're a woman now, Emma, and I think it's important that
you should understand why I felt it so desirable for you to

have an alternative to love.' She paused briefly. 'When I married your father, he was eighteen years older than I and already someone of consequence in the scientific world. I knew he loved me and I thought he needed me. It was only after I had had you two girls that I realized his work was really his whole life. I loved him far too much to consider leaving him for a man who could give me more affection, devotion, more of his time. Fortunately, I had achieved a double first at Cambridge and I was able to get a good job at Guy's. We could afford a nanny and later, to send you to good boarding schools. It was very soon obvious that Rosalind had inherited her father's brain but you – you were more like I used to be – someone who had to slog hard to achieve. I could see that you might be as vulnerable as I once was – and marriage at the end of the day is such a gamble. I believe the statistics give one in three failing these days!' She gave a wry smile. 'So I was determined you would have a career to fall back on – as I did.'

She broke off to take a sip of her drink whilst Emma attempted to marshal her thoughts.

'And Father thought the same way?' she asked finally.

'Oh, no, my dear. Your father has always lived on a different plane. He simply cannot understand why ordinary human beings are so stupid! He expects them to grasp facts as easily as he does. That's why he gets so impatient when people fail to meet him on his own level. It's one of the reasons he had such a good rapport with your sister. Young though she was, he could see that one day, she would make as brilliant a scientist as himself. Rosalind never had to work the way you did. You had to do it the hard way. There was a time when we were both afraid you'd never get to university.'

Emma's voice was brittle as she said:

'There was a time when I thought so, too! Well, I did get there and I have got the career you wanted for me, Mother . . . and, so it would seem, the broken marriage you anticipated. Well, I may not have achieved your eminence, but I love my work and I'm really getting somewhere at last. It was a good thing you and Father did push me.'

Her mother regarded her uneasily.

'Then you are happy? When you came into the foyer and I caught sight of you, I was afraid . . . I've often felt guilty, you know, leaving you on your own at such a tender age; but your father came first and I really did think you'd join us in the States when you'd finished college – as Ros did. Maybe if we'd met Simon, I could have warned you that he was the wrong man for you.'

'He wasn't the "wrong man",' Emma said fiercely. 'At least, not in the way you mean. I loved him – I still love him. It's just that he won't understand that I want a life other than as his wife and mother of his children. I told him before we were married, and he agreed I should keep my independence. Now he's gone back on it. He says he needs me with him.'

'That's sounds a very old-fashioned attitude. In the States, it's unusual for a married woman not to have a job. I thought that was the norm over here, too. If there are children, they go into organized nurseries.'

For the first time Emma smiled.

'I'm afraid we're not quite so advanced over here, Mother. Hazel – our housekeeper – can't get her child into a nursery until she's four! But that isn't the point. Simon would be agreeable to my having a nanny and we could easily afford one. He simply doesn't like me giving my career priority. I suppose he *is* old-fashioned. Perhaps it's not surprising. He was brought up by his great-grandmother.'

Her mother's face looked suddenly much older – vulnerable.

'It's ironic, isn't it, that I would have given my right arm to have your father feel that way about me!' she said softly. 'Of course, I'm totally committed to my work and I enjoy it immensely but—' she released Emma's hand and gave an almost imperceptible shrug of her shoulders, '—but it was only ever second best. I don't know your husband, Emma, besides which, I have no right to offer maternal advice having failed in motherly concern for so many years. Nevertheless, you are my daughter and your happiness is important to me; therefore I feel I must caution you. Don't throw love away too lightly. It's not easily come by in this world we live in. Now let's talk of other things. Tell me more about this amazing house you described so vividly in your letters, and about your work.'

It was as if her mother had closed the door on any further intimacies, Emma thought. For the remaining hours of their time together, they had to search for general topics of conversation, and had it not been for her mother's astonishing revelation about her marriage, Emma would have felt as distanced from her as she had felt when she was a child. They kissed perfunctorily when Emma had to leave to catch her train back to Southampton.

Her carriage was almost empty and there was little to distract Emma's thoughts as she tried to analyse her emotions. In some indefinable way, she felt cheated. So much of her own ambition to succeed had been built upon her desire to emulate her mother and achieve what she had believed to be her parents' aspirations. They had become her own. Now during the course of the afternoon, those beliefs had been undermined. At the same time, she realized that there had been a time – perhaps in the days when she had met Paul – when if she had met Simon first she would willingly have abandoned all thoughts of a career. She might even have been content – as she had been last summer – pottering happily at Ortolans with no calls upon her intelligence or creativity. Now, it was different! Under Derek's influence, she had learned to welcome a challenge; to research with meticulous care; to develop her intellect. Her new job had given her increased responsibility and Simon had no right to deprive her of this mental stimulus. Love, she thought, should not be possessive; Simon should encourage her potential, not inhibit it. It was not she who, as her mother had put it, was 'throwing love away too lightly'. It was Simon who was unwilling to compromise.

Fortunately, she was kept inordinately busy for the next two days and it was not until late on Tuesday night she found time to read the morning paper.

UK shares plunge after Wall Street 'meltdown', said the front page headline. In the canteen at lunch, she had heard someone talking about the stock market collapsing the previous day, but she had not paid much attention. Clearly this was serious. Further down the page there were comparisons to the 1929 Wall Street Crash when thousands of people had been ruined and many had jumped out of skyscrapers in despair. It seemed now as if the situation in England was comparable. Every sector of the market had been affected and every share in the 100 Share Index had registered a double-figure loss.

Emma had never understood how the stock market worked, or indeed knew what it was exactly that Simon did in his merchant bank. She was aware, however, that he bought and sold shares and she wondered if he, too, had been adversely affected.

On the spur of the moment, she dialled the number of his flat.

'Emma! You are the last person I expected. You've just caught me. Is it urgent?' As if aware he must have sounded somewhat abrupt, Simon added in an apologetic tone: 'Sorry if I sounded a bit curt. It's been a ghastly day!'

'I won't keep you,' Emma said quickly. 'It's just that I was reading today's paper, and wondered whether this stock-market business is affecting you personally, Simon?'

His laugh was devoid of humour.

'Too true it is; me, and hundreds of others! I don't want to bore you with the details but the fact is, I've been dabbling in quite a big way and this . . . this catastrophe has come like a bolt out of the blue. No one is buying and I don't blame them.'

'Surely if you sit it out, things will improve eventually,' Emma said. There was a brief pause before Simon replied.

'I can't afford to sit it out, Emma. I took out options, you see, and a hefty bank loan to finance it all. I saw my bank manager today and he won't extend or increase the loan. There are too many people in the same boat.'

Emma heard the anxiety in his voice.

'So what's likely to happen?' she asked. 'Will you lose a great deal of money?'

'Far worse than that!' Simon answered in a flat voice. 'I agreed to put up Ortolans as security against the loan. If I can't find some way to meet my obligations very shortly, I'll be bankrupt – and sooner or later the bank will foreclose.'

'You mean they'll sell Ortolans so that you can repay the loan?' Emma gasped.

'I'm afraid so. At the moment, I can't see any other alternative.'

'Oh, Simon, I'm so sorry!' Emma was deeply shocked. 'Look, I've got five thousand in my savings account. Would that help?'

'Darling!' Simon's voice was husky with tenderness. 'It's wonderful of you to offer – and I'll never forget that you did; but that's a tiny drop in the ocean. I need half a million to get me out of this mess.'

'Your flat . . . my flat . . .' Emma said. 'We could sell the leases . . .'

'I don't own Brunswick Square. I rent it from a colleague who went out to the States. Emma, don't worry about this! I'll sort it out somehow. Things may improve. You can be sure of one thing – I won't let Ortolans go without a fight!'

Things did not improve. Emma scanned the papers before she went to work and asked anyone she ran into who might understand the situation for their opinions. Several times she telephoned Simon only to be told by his secretary that he was out, in a meeting, or in conference. Someone in the studio told her that President Reagan was trying to 'calm the market's fears'. On Thursday there was reference in one of the papers to a rally in world markets, but by Friday, the *Financial Times* Share Index had dropped to its lowest level since January.

At six o'clock on Friday evening, she managed to get hold of Simon.

'I'm catching the nine-thirty train from Southampton,' she said. 'Will you meet me at Brighton, Simon?'

'Too true, I will. Bless you, darling!'

'Are things any better?' she ventured.

His voice was quite calm as he replied quietly:

"Fraid not. In fact, to be honest about it, I very much doubt if they could possibly be any worse!'

CHAPTER THIRTY-EIGHT

1987

When Emma's train pulled in to Brighton station, she could see no sign of Simon. A moment later, she caught sight of Roddy at the ticket barrier.

'Hi, Emma! Simon asked me to meet you!' he said as he took her overnight bag from her.

For once his cheerful face was unsmiling. The moment they were settled in his Granada, he explained his presence.

'I'm afraid there's something of a hiatus at Ortolans. Simon did try to ring you, but you'd obviously left.'

'You mean, he was going to ask me not to come?'

'I suppose that was the idea. However, I think it's good you're here, Emma. Everything seems to be going wrong!'

Emma glanced at Roddy uneasily as he turned the car on to the London Road. She waited for him to continue.

'Hazel's done a bunk!' he said quietly. 'Minus the child!'

'But when . . . how . . . you mean Hazel's left Vicky at Ortolans?'

Roddy nodded.

'Simon got down early this morning and found Vicky locked in her bedroom, crying. There was a note on the kitchen table from Hazel. As you know, she was due to go on holiday with the new boyfriend on Friday night – with the kid, of course. Seems she had a last-minute change of mind – or else she'd been planning it for weeks. Anyway, she shot off to Gatwick and presumably is now somewhere on the Costa.'

'So what would have happened to Vicky if Simon had not come down this morning and found her!'

'Exactly! Simon was beside himself – rang up the airport to try to get hold of Hazel but she'd left on the two o'clock flight. He's been trying all morning to get hold of a social worker, but it's the weekend and, when I left to collect you, he was getting precisely nowhere.'

'Hazel's gone for two weeks,' Emma said slowly. 'Vicky will have to go into a children's home until she gets back.'

There was a brief silence from Roddy before he said:

'She isn't coming back. Vicky doesn't know that, of course, but Hazel made it clear in her note to Simon. She wants the child adopted.'

Emma gasped.

'But she was fond of Vicky . . . in her own way. I can't believe this!'

'Simon doesn't think she'll change her mind. Hazel was quite positive. She and the boyfriend are going to Australia to start a new life there.'

'But they'd need visas, work permits . . .'

'Oh, I don't think they're going to bother about those kind of niceties. They intend to go as tourists and "disappear".'

'I don't understand it,' Emma repeated. 'Why didn't she take Vicky with her?'

'Probably because the child would make it more difficult for them to do their disappearing act. I suppose the authorities will trace Hazel eventually. They'll have to if Vicky is to be adopted. Otherwise, the kid will have to spend her life in an institution – or else be brought up by foster-parents.'

Emma had a momentary vision of the little girl's large dark eyes gazing into hers with total trust; of the heartbreak Hazel's selfishness was going to bring the four-year-old.

'Simon must be feeling pretty agonized,' she said as much to herself as to Roddy. 'He adores Vicky!'

'Poor chap has quite enough on his plate without this!' Roddy replied. 'As you probably know, he lost every penny he had in this financial crash. Despite all his efforts, he's going to have to sell Ortolans. There are no other options!'

Emma covered her mouth with her hand.

'I can't bear it if that's true,' she cried. 'Surely—'

'No, he was telling me this morning before I came to meet you. It isn't a matter of a few thousand, Emma. The bank is certain to foreclose.'

'Oh, Roddy – isn't there anything – anything at all we can do?'

She knew it was a silly question, but surprisingly, Roddy answered it.

'I could put up some money . . . and I gather you already offered to do the same – but it's nowhere near enough, Emma. What I have been able to suggest, to raise immediate capital, is that Simon allows me to sell the oak panelling in the library. I've an American client who'd buy it like a shot and have it shipped back to the States. It's a drop in the ocean, of course – and Simon is reluctant to do it. He says if Ortolans has to go, it might as well be sold intact. I can't help feeling that if he can pay his more immediate creditors, he could buy time – and something might crop up to stave off the worst. I'm afraid he's mentally given up hope. Perhaps you can cheer him up, Emma. He's pretty low. In a way, it's good this business about Hazel has given him something else to think about!'

Emma was deeply shocked. She had realized that things were bad – but never once had she realized how bad. It was inconceivable that Simon should lose Ortolans . . . as unbelievable as Hazel abandoning Vicky to institutional care for the rest of her childhood.

Simon greeted Emma tight-lipped and with a deep frown furrowing his forehead.

'I hoped when I heard the car that it might be the social worker,' he said. 'Sorry you've walked into this mess, Emma. I did try to stop you but—'

'I'm glad I'm here,' Emma broke in. 'Where's Vicky?'

For a moment, the grim expression on Simon's face lightened.

'Cooking lunch, so she tells me. We'd better go back to the kitchen and see what kind of mess she's making!'

Vicky was standing on one of the kitchen chairs, a tea towel tied round her waist, the sleeves of her pink jersey rolled up and her face and arms covered in flour. In the bowl in front of her was a glutinous lump of dough.

'I'm making a cake!' she announced as Emma bent to kiss her floury cheek. 'We're going to bake it in the Aga, aren't we?' she added cheerfully, looking up trustingly at Simon.

He nodded as he lifted the kettle off the hotplate and made three mugs of coffee.

'She doesn't seem much bothered about her mother not being here!' he said in an undertone. 'It's beyond me how Hazel could have gone off like that. I got down here at nine-thirty and found Vicky locked in her room. She'd eaten a tube of Smarties and a Mars Bar which I gather "Mum" had left on her bed for breakfast. She was a bit tearful at first but eventually she informed me that Hazel had told her she was going away for a few days and that I'd be coming down to look after her; so the poor kid was waiting for me.'

'No luck with the social worker, then?' Roddy said. 'I suppose we could ring the police – or the NSPCC.'

'I don't want a policeman – or policewoman, come to that – dragging Vicky off and frightening the wits out of her.' Simon's glance rested momentarily on the child's dark head with a look of great tenderness. 'She'll have to go, of course, but I'm hoping it can be to foster-parents. She's led such a solitary life here I can't see her settling in a children's home.'

'Would you like me to see what I can do?' Emma volunteered. 'I can be quite authoritative on the telephone! Someone will have to do something!'

Simon looked at her gratefully.

'You'll find the relevant telephone numbers by the phone in the library. Vicky's got to be found a home before midday tomorrow and that's all there is to it. Things are pretty frantic at work and there's absolutely no way I can take time off.'

Emma nodded. Thanks to the information Roddy had given her, she knew how pressing Simon's affairs must be.

After several abortive attempts to get through to anyone in authority, Emma finally managed to talk to a social worker from a different area. It seemed she was doing her best to reach the woman who should be handling the problem, Emma was told, but so far without success.

'Do try not to worry, Lady Calverley,' she said in a falsely bright tone. 'If the worst comes to the worst, you can always take the child down and leave her at the police station. They'll have to find somewhere for her if only on a temporary basis.'

Emma felt angry and upset. This was Vicky they had been discussing as if she were an unwanted parcel no one knew where to deliver. Even allowing for the fact that the social services were dealing on a daily basis with such emergencies, she could not accept the impersonal attitude to the child's feelings. Vicky was such a loving little girl – and she had never before been parted from her mother. It was impossible to imagine how Hazel's defection would affect her – but it could only be worsened if she were moved from one lot of strangers to another.

'I wish I could offer to help,' Roddy said when she returned to the kitchen to relay the news. 'My mother has only just come out of hospital after a hip replacement operation – and there's no way she could cope. I just can't think of anyone else.'

'In the good old days,' Simon said with a wry smile, 'Great-Gran would have known a dozen or more women in the village who would have taken Vicky under their wing. Come to that, Great-Gran would probably have kept her here and let the servants look after her. I suppose there's no point trying to trace Hazel's parents seeing we already know they are racially prejudiced and won't acknowledge their granddaughter.'

It was on the tip of Emma's tongue to suggest that Simon might consider employing a nanny to take care of Vicky at Ortolans – but with the house about to be sold and Simon himself being bankrupt, the idea remained unspoken.

Vicky had tired of her cake-making and came to sit on

Emma's lap, her small fingers and face leaving white marks all over Emma's blue sweater. Emma's heart filled with pity. A four-year-old had no defences, and as far as she could see, the child was going to have to face some very unhappy experiences. Emma was unaware that Simon was staring at her thoughtfully as she rocked the little girl in her arms.

It was not until they had managed to scrape together some lunch, using tins of corned beef and oven chips for a make-shift meal, that Simon broached the subject of Ortolans. Emma had put Vicky down for a rest and left her happily reading some storybooks. Outside it was raining heavily and Simon lit the drawing-room fire.

'I'm putting Ortolans on the market on Monday!' he said abruptly as he lent forward to poke one of the logs that threatened to fall out of the fire. 'The estate agents wanted me to put it up for auction, but I've refused. I want to know who will be living here. If I don't like them, I'd take a lower price from people I did like!'

Emma was shocked.

'Must it be done so . . . so quickly?' she said hesitantly. 'Roddy was telling me in the car that he had a rich American who was interested in buying the panelling.'

Simon gave a shrug.

'So he's been saying!' He glanced at Roddy and then gave a deep sigh. 'I did speak to the bank manager, Roddy – and he said he thought they could give me a few more months. But what's the point? Stocks have collapsed so quickly and they aren't going to get back to where they were for a long time. We have been living in a fool's paradise, and in retrospect, we should have realized this would happen. I was so anxious to get on with the renovations, I took a gamble when I should have known better – and I lost. That's all there is to it.'

'You gambled once – and lost,' Emma said quietly. 'Isn't it worth another gamble? This time, you have nothing to lose – and if you did play for time as Roddy suggests, things might get better despite your predictions.'

Simon turned to glance at her briefly over his shoulder.

'Maybe I just wasn't meant to carry on the Calverley dynasty,' he said. 'It's crazy, when you stop to think about it – one man living here in this huge house for no better reason than that my ancestors have always lived here.'

'That isn't the only reason!' Emma flared. 'You love the house – it's the most important thing in the world to you. You'd be lost without it!'

There was a moment's silence before Simon said:

'There was a time when I would have agreed with you, but in the last resort, a house is only "bricks and mortar". People are what matter . . . and I've learned that the hard way.'

Emma caught her breath. Was it possible he was referring to their relationship? Was he trying to tell her in a roundabout way that if she was not willing to share Ortolans with him, he did not care whether it remained his home or not?

'No, Simon, Ortolans is not some ordinary house. Your great-grandmother left it to you in trust and you have a duty to it. You've no more right to walk out on it than Hazel had to walk out on Vicky!'

'Selling up to meet my debts is not "walking out on it"!' Simon said in a hard voice that betrayed his inner emotions.

'You're abandoning it before it's absolutely imperative to do so!' Emma argued, aware that she was trembling. 'Roddy says the panelling is worth a hell of a lot of money.'

'It's linenfold – and some of it is quite beautifully carved!' Roddy interposed. 'My client won't be concerned with the price – we can pretty well ask what we want!'

Emma reached out impulsively and laid her hand persuasively on Simon's arm. She was about to plead with him when the phone rang. Simon rose immediately to answer it. He came back within minutes.

'They've located the social worker. She'll be here in ten minutes.'

'To do what?' Emma asked anxiously.

'I don't know!' Simon answered. 'We'll have to wait and see.'

The social worker was a junior, still under training. She was young, unmarried and, she confessed, inexperienced with children. When Simon said he wanted Vicky placed immediately with foster-parents, she looked astonished.

'I don't think we can do that. We have to have the child assessed and then she's introduced to the foster-parents on a trial basis . . . and if it works out and they get on all right, we can arrange something permanent.'

She got out a pad of paper from her shoulder-bag and looked anxiously from Simon to Roddy and then at Emma.

'I need some details,' she said.

Roddy excused himself, announcing that he was going to have another look at the panelling and perhaps take some Instamatic pictures. 'In case you change your mind and decide to sell,' he said tentatively.

Simon shrugged.

'Do what you want, Roddy. I really don't care!' he said dismissively as he turned back to the social worker. Emma remained quietly in the background as he started to relate Hazel's history. She could see that he was growing steadily more impatient as the questioning continued.

'Surely Vicky's place of birth is irrelevant at this moment. What matters is where she is to go now,' he said finally. 'One of us will need to prepare her.'

'Yes, well, she'll have to go to the children's home, Sir Simon. We won't be able to do anything before Monday . . . and I'm afraid it could be a long time before we can place her with foster-parents. There aren't nearly enough of them, you see. And with the little girl being of mixed race . . . well, that makes it more difficult. White people don't want them because they see them as coloured and the coloured people don't want them because they're white. Children like this little girl don't really belong to either culture.'

'That's ridiculous!' Emma burst out. 'Vicky has never even met her father. She's like any other little English child. She's very intelligent and she has a sweet nature. She'd be no trouble. It's not as if she is used to having a lot of attention.'

'Then she should settle down in the home!' the social worker said with infuriating complacency. 'It's the ones that have got mother complexes who give all the trouble.'

'I thought you said you had not had much experience dealing with children!' Simon said sharply.

'Well, no, I haven't, but the books say—'

'This isn't really good enough!' Simon interrupted with unaccustomed rudeness. It indicated to Emma how upset he was. 'I shall want to be kept informed as to what is being done with Vicky.'

'But you're not a relative, Sir Simon, and—'

'I'm her unofficial guardian!' Simon broke in again. 'Please make it quite clear to your superior that I shall concern myself with the child's future.'

There were a few more questions to be answered before Emma, at Simon's request, went up to Vicky's room to break the news to her that she would be going to stay in a big house with a lot of other children to play with.

Vicky burst into tears.

'I want to stay here, with you!' she sobbed, clinging to Emma's arm.

'Darling, I can't stay here and look after you,' Emma said, stroking the dark head. 'I have to go to work – and so does Simon.'

'You stayed before!' Vicky's voice, husky with tears, was painfully factual.

'Yes, I did – last summer. But I have a job to go to now.'

'Why can't you stay 'til Mum gets back from her holiday?'

Now Emma's eyes filled with tears.

'Vicky, try to understand. We none of us know how long Mummy will be gone. It might be a long, long holiday and . . . you'll like having other children to play with. There'll be lots of toys and you can take Teddy and your dolls and . . .'

'And Simon's horse?' asked Vicky, grasping the small carved

animal and releasing her hold on Emma to hug it against her flat little chest.

'Yes, of course, I'm sure Simon will let you take it. Come on now, let's pack up your things, shall we? We'll choose some of your prettiest dresses . . . and your nighties and dressing-gown.'

For a short while, Vicky was interested in their shared activity, but as Emma took her downstairs, she was crying again. As she caught sight of Simon, she flung herself into his arms, sobbing incoherently.

'I want to stay here in this house with you!' she said over and over again.

Somehow, Simon and Emma managed to get her out to the social worker's car. The girl found a packet of Polo mints in the glove compartment and looked somewhat peeved when Vicky dashed them out of her hand.

'Now now, Vicky, that's very naughty!' she reproved her. 'Your uncle and auntie said you were a good girl!'

With no idea who her uncle and auntie were supposed to be, Vicky burst into a fresh storm of weeping. Simon buckled her into the back seat and, not trusting himself to speak, gave her a last hug and left Emma on her own to wave until the social worker and the now hysterical child had disappeared down the drive from view.

Simon was in the drawing-room, pouring himself a stiff whisky when Emma rejoined him.

'That was a damn sight worse than taking one's dog to the vet to have it put down!' he said gruffly. 'I feel like . . . like a murderer!'

Impulsively, Emma went across the room and put her hand on his arm.

'I know – I feel the same. How could Hazel do this to her?' she said. 'I wish . . . I just wish . . .'

Abruptly, Simon put down his glass and placed one hand beneath Emma's chin, lifting her face so that he was staring directly into her eyes.

'So what do you wish, Emma – that we could have kept her? Don't you realize I've been thinking the same thing for the past four hours! Well, we can't – and even if *you* were free to take care of her, it won't be long before there'll be no home for you or Vicky to live in. I faced that fact as I listened to that incompetent girl nattering on about Vicky's future. I've had to face a hell of a lot of facts lately and I don't much like any of them. I think I've lost just about everything that matters to me!'

It was on the tip of Emma's tongue to tell him that he was wrong if he thought he had lost her love. She did still love him. That was a fact *she* had had to face these past two months; but Roddy chose that moment to burst into the room. His face was as flushed with excitement as theirs were pale with distress.

'I've found something quite extraordinary,' he said. 'Come on, hurry, both of you. I can't wait to show you. You must come and look right away.'

He hurried ahead of them into the library.

'I was taking photos,' he said, his voice breathless, 'to send to the American – that is, if you agreed, Simon. Then I thought I would see if it was possible to remove one of the panels – thinking we might be able to airmail it to him so that he could see how exquisite the carving is. I decided to see if I could prise out the wooden pegs without damaging them and believe it or not, they were quite loose. I suspect the wood has shrunk since you had the central heating installed! Now see what's behind it . . . it's a painting of some sort; maybe part of a fresco, I think. God knows how long it's been there. The panelling is Tudor.'

Simon bent forward with a look of intense curiosity on his face.

'You can't see much. Sure it's not just daubs of paint, Roddy? Can you take another panel away so we can get a better idea?'

With infinite pains, Roddy managed to dislodge the pegs from one of the panels close to the floor. They did not come away so easily and he was obliged to split one of them so that it could be withdrawn in two pieces. When finally he was able to lift out the section of panelling, they were no longer in any doubt that a painting of some considerable size lay behind the carved oak wall covering. This time, the colour of the paint was predominantly green with a clearly defined trunk of a tree.

'This is fascinating!' Emma said. 'I don't think you should touch any more of it, Roddy. That painting has to be four hundred or so years old.'

'Emma's right!' Roddy said. 'We need an expert down here, Simon. No hope of getting anyone on a Saturday afternoon. The British Museum, the V & A, the National Gallery . . . they won't have anyone on duty who can deal with this kind of thing. My God, I wonder how big the whole thing is. See this white bit here . . . I'm pretty sure it's a seagull. If it is and if it is in proportion, the picture must be huge!'

'Let's go and have that drink and decide what to do!' Simon spoke for the first time. 'I'll get out *The Calverley Journal*. Maybe there's something in those early pages which will give us an idea of what the library walls were like before the painting was done.'

'I doubt it!' Emma said reluctantly. 'The journal starts in the 1700s. Roddy says the panelling is much older.'

Although they spent an hour looking through the yellowed pages of the journal, there was no entry referring to the installation of the panelling.

'It will almost certainly have been done by one of your ancestors, Roddy, they were master carpenters; but of course, they won't have left any written record!'

'The likes of the Pylbeams couldn't read or write in those days!' Roddy said grinning, '. . . except to sign their names, and as often as not, that was done with a cross.' Suddenly, he clapped his hand to his forehead. 'I've just thought of something,' he said. 'Or rather, of someone. I know an old chap in Lewes – he's retired now – who used to work in the Fine Arts department of Sotheby's. He spent all his life doing valuations of old paintings. I can probably get hold of his telephone number from directory enquiries. If he's there, I'm sure he'll come over and give us an opinion – and be pleased to do it. I might have to pick him up. Shall I try and contact him? He's an extremely knowledgeable old boy.'

Mr Wilderness arrived two hours later, still wearing a baggy pair of gardening trousers and an ancient tweed jacket. This delightful old man who, Emma thought, must be at least eighty, arrived in a battered old Morris, his white hair forming a neat frill round a shining bald pate. He wore a tiny pair of gold-rimmed spectacles and beamed at each of them in turn.

'This all sounds very exciting . . . very exciting indeed!' he said. 'Sir Simon Calverley, isn't it? I came here once in the twenties . . . to value the family portraits for insurance purposes. Beautiful house! Charming lady! Charming!'

'That must have been my great-grandmother, Lady Sophia Calverley,' Simon said as he led the old man towards the library. 'I must apologize for calling you away from your garden at the weekend, but Mr Pylbeam thinks he might have discovered something really important.'

'So the young man said, so he said!' Mr Wilderness muttered. He seemed to have a habit of repeating the end of his sentences. He removed his spectacles and replaced them with another pair before carefully mounting the library steps Roddy had left in place. Instinctively, Simon clasped the old man's legs to steady him as he bent precariously forward to look short-sightedly at the portion of exposed painting.

'Remarkable – truly remarkable!' He turned to beam at Simon. 'It's certainly very old – very old indeed. Artists made their own paints in those days. The practice declined after the sixteenth century when oil paints proved to be more versatile for large-scale works. Difficult to tell the exact age . . .' He inspected the exposed lower section. 'It's in magnificent condition – magnificent. This is most exciting! I'd need to see more . . . quite a bit more . . . before I can make any judgements but . . . would it be possible to remove more panels?'

Simon turned to Roddy who said immediately:

'Each of the panels is tapered on four sides and these fit into narrow grooves in a framework of stiles and rails. They're fastened to the house beams by oak pegs. So far, I've not had too much difficulty removing them, but the panels are very valuable, Mr Wilderness, as I'm sure I don't need to tell you.' He looked enquiringly at Simon. 'How do you feel about it, Simon? It's your decision.'

'Curiosity is getting the better of common sense!' Simon said with a grin. 'Let's have a couple more out at the far end of the wall and see if the painting goes right across.'

It was the best part of an hour before Roddy finally lifted away the bottom right-hand corner and stood back for Mr Wilderness to view what was undoubtedly an area of green grass. There was a sprawling black daub at the bottom which seemed to fascinate the old man.

'The artist's signature – yes, indeed, his signature!' he muttered. 'Done in paint, so it's not very clear – not clear at all. Let me see now – an M, yes, an M, followed by an "I" . . . I can't make it out. A capital "D", though, and the "A" is quite clear . . . Darwin . . . no, it can't be . . . this is too much . . . it is, though. Yes, it is, there's no mistake!' He had turned quite white and as Emma hurried forward to offer him a chair, he collapsed into it. He appeared to be speechless and was breathing heavily.

'Are you all right, sir?' Simon asked. 'Can I get you something . . . a little brandy?'

The colour was returning to Mr Wilderness's face and he recovered his voice to decline the offer of a drink.

'I'm quite well, my boy . . . quite well. It was such a shock, you see. Of course, I may be wrong . . . very wrong, and I would not want you to be disappointed, no, indeed. Nevertheless, the signature appears to be that of Michael Darwin.'

Now it was the turn of the other three to be shocked.

'You don't mean *the* Michael Darwin?' Emma gasped. She

had seen the great man's portrait of the Duke of Buckingham in the National Gallery, and his even more famous painting of Charles I.

Simon was the first to recover his composure.

'If you are right, sir, then this painting – or is it a fresco? – could be of great importance . . . in the art world, I mean, and we ought not to be risking any damage to it!'

'Absolutely, my boy. If I am right . . . and I must emphasize that it is *if* . . . then this could be of *international* importance. But I should explain that, despite the signature, it is very unlikely indeed that Darwin would have done this. He's a portrait painter, not a landscape artist. Landscapes, such as this would appear to be, did not become fashionable until much later although Darwin did a lot of religious frescoes in Florence and Rome. Let me see now, his dates . . . If my memory doesn't fail me, he was born in this country in the late sixteenth century and died in Italy some eighty years later. He studied over there as a young man and was middle-aged before his portrait of Louis XIII's little sister, Henrietta Maria, brought him renown. It was shortly after that he was invited to the English Court to paint the King.'

'So if he did do this—' Roddy said, pointing to the wall '—it must have been when he returned to England. But why this wall . . . why here at Ortolans? And why, if he was so famous, was it covered by the panels? It doesn't make sense.'

Mr Wilderness took off his spectacles and wiped them with a large white handkerchief.

'That's one of the reasons why I am advising extreme caution . . . yes, great caution. We must not jump to conclusions. There are experts who will advise us. It is surprising what they can tell us these days with so many modern aids – the date of the paints the artist used – that kind of thing. Darwin's life will be very well documented and we will know exactly how long he was in this country. We shall simply have to wait and see if this really is his work.'

He stood up and walked back to the painting, scrutinizing

it yet again with minute care. When he turned once more to face them, he said quietly:

'If this is Darwin's work . . . and there is a certain amateurish quality about it which leads me to suppose it might be a very early work, then it is of inestimable value, Sir Simon. It is probably the most valuable painting I have ever been asked to look at. I doubt very much whether a value could be put upon it. If it is a genuine Darwin, then this must be the most exciting moment I have experienced in all my eighty-one years!'

There were tears in his eyes as Emma gently took his arm and led him back to the drawing-room.

'I'm going to make us all a nice hot cup of tea!' she said. 'I'm sure you could do with one, Mr Wilderness.'

Simon followed her into the kitchen.

'I was going to suggest champagne!' he said as he stood in the doorway watching her set out a tea tray. 'But perhaps that's a bit premature. Do you think the old boy knows what he's talking about?'

'Yes, I do!' Emma said. She looked across the room at Simon and added:

'You may think this absurd, but I don't have any doubt about the picture. I believe with all my heart that it will turn out to be authentic. Your great-grandmother often referred in the journal to the spirit of Ortolans . . . the power the house had to affect the lives of the people who lived in it and loved it. Don't you see, Simon? If Mr Wilderness proves to be right and the painting is worth millions, you won't have to sell Ortolans. You can stay here for ever . . .'

She broke off as Simon caught hold of her hands and gripped them tightly in his.

'I realize that – and I ought to be on my knees thanking God. I suppose I am, in a way; but the future doesn't seem to have any point any more – not without you.' His voice was husky as he added: 'I'm still very much in love with you, Emma!'

'And I've never stopped loving you,' Emma said, but there

was the hint of reproach in her voice as she added: 'I only left because you gave me no alternative – give up my job or our marriage was over.'

'I know, I know! I was angry, hurt, because your work seemed to matter more to you than I did. There were dozens of occasions when I regretted my stupidity. I want you back, darling – on whatever terms. If I can only have you with me at weekends, then so be it. I'm not going to lose you again.'

For one long moment, Emma gave way to the urgent longing to be reunited with him. She responded with all her heart to his kisses, allowing her body to melt in his embrace. It would be so terribly easy to give in now that Simon had withdrawn his objections to her career. But how long would that last? How long would it be before he would resent her leaving when the weekends were over? Before he wanted to start a family? Before she herself was feeling guilty again because she could not be the kind of wife he wanted?

Slowly, she drew back from his arms.

'Simon, I want you to be completely honest about this – it's important. You said it was OK with you if I keep my job with TV South – but it isn't what you really want, is it? If I was willing to pack it in, you'd jump at it!'

He paused only momentarily, his green eyes thoughtful.

'Yes, I would!' He drew a deep breath and then said: 'What I don't understand, darling, is why you can't get a job nearer here or London. I know it might mean waiting for the right thing to come along, but wouldn't it be worth it? Southampton's such a hell of a long way off.'

Emma bit her lip.

'Simon, you simply don't understand. I can't go back to the Beeb – Derek would scotch any application; and as you know, I failed to get anywhere in Thames. Apart from Southampton, there's Yorkshire, Norwich, Leeds, Bristol, Plymouth . . . all even further away than my present job.'

'I see! Then couldn't you switch to radio? What are those stations Hazel is always tuned in to? Radio Mercury, Radio

Sussex? Either Crawley, or Brighton would be ideal, wouldn't they?'

Emma felt close to tears. Simon really hadn't any idea about the media. She didn't *want* to work in radio – it was a totally different ball game and she'd have to start all over again at the bottom of the ladder. She tried haltingly to explain and could see that Simon was halfway to understanding, but it altered nothing. When she ceased talking, he said quietly:

'It seems an awful shame, doesn't it? Our not being able to live together like other couples.'

Emma hardened her heart against the look of distress on his face. She knew she was right in her supposition that Simon was basically opposed to her new job and had only given way under pressure. Sooner or later, his resentment would surface and their relationship would deteriorate.

'I'm so sorry, Simon!' she said, the cry coming from the depths of her heart. 'I wish I could be different. I wish I could be what you want – but I have a brain – of sorts! – that needs the stimulus of challenge. I need to use my talents, such as they are. It's all my fault – I should never have agreed to marry you – I'm the wrong sort of wife for you.'

'That's not true!' Simon's voice was filled with conviction. 'I love you, Emma, and you say you love me, so surely we can work it out somehow. At least say you'll give it a try!'

More than anything in the world, Emma wanted to say yes, wanted to share Simon's conviction that it could work. She had still not come to terms with the facts revealed in that brief unexpected meeting with her mother. Even now, she found it difficult to believe that there was no need – nor ever had been – to prove herself; that all her mother had ever wanted was for her to be happy! Part of her could accept that there was no onus upon her now to succeed for someone else; but the habit had become so ingrained that she still needed to prove to herself that she was capable, talented. She needed this degree of intellectual stimulus to survive.

Deeply confused, she said weakly:

'May I think about it, Simon? I haven't had a chance yet to tell you, but I shall be away for a couple of weeks. We're doing a two-part programme about the Brook Hospital for Animals, a charity that provides veterinary care for horses and donkeys in the Middle East. I'm to go with a film crew to Egypt, Alexandria, and then on to Luxor where they have clinics.'

She turned away from the look of dismay on Simon's face.

'Naturally, I jumped at the chance to go abroad when my producer offered me the job. I didn't realize then that . . . that we'd be seeing each other again and . . .'

'. . . and even if you had, you'd still have wanted to go!' Simon broke in. 'I understand how you feel. It was silly of me to hope . . . to think . . . well, that's about it, then, isn't it? You're probably right.'

With difficulty, he managed a wry smile.

'Send me a postcard, darling, or better still, ring me when you get back to England.'

'Oh, I will!' Emma cried, close to tears once more. 'I'll want to know about the fresco . . . and what's happening to Vicky and . . . well, everything!' she ended lamely.

Simon released her hands and turned away so that Emma could not see the extent of his pain. Clearly she was unable to understand that he could no longer feel excited by the fresco, or indeed, the complete turnabout it would mean for his financial situation and the future of Ortolans. Without her, Ortolans would never again be the home he wanted. It would always be missing that one vital ingredient – love.

CHAPTER THIRTY-NINE

1988

'Let's break for ten minutes, Carol!' Simon said to the middle-aged woman who was standing in the doorway of the library at Ortolans, her clipboard clasped against her chest.

The employment agent gave him a sympathetic smile as she saw the look of discouragement on his face.

'I'm sure one of the candidates will turn out to be suitable!' she said bracingly. 'There are still four to come. Ring the bell when you're ready to tackle the next one.'

As she left the room, Simon leant back in his chair and tried to relax. The big, leather-topped desk was all but invisible beneath a covering of letters, bills, pamphlets, brochures, and, of course, the neat pile of CVs provided by the efficient Carol. When he had first got in touch with the agency, she had reacted to his request as if to a demand to supply him with the Angel Gabriel!

'A secretary, yes! A personal assistant, yes. A publicity agent, yes. A history graduate, yes . . . but all four rolled into one, Sir Simon . . .'

Simon almost smiled as she had added:

'And although your house is very beautiful – unique, in fact – Detcham is a little off the map, and as you so rightly say, whoever we find for you must be prepared to live in.'

Finally, she had come up with eight 'possibles' – or what she had termed as possible. Simon had not found one among the four he had so far interviewed who would begin to fill his requirements. At least he had found a woman with a car who was prepared to travel in every day from Brighton and who would take on all the secretarial work. Looking at his desk, she had revealed a sense of humour when she told him that if he was seriously offering her the job, she had better start on Monday. She, at least, would cope with the paperwork; but there was so much more to be dealt with.

Simon's gaze turned to the magnificent fresco now fully revealed since the last of the panelling had been removed by experts. He still found it hard to believe that he owned a painting by one of the most famous artists in the world. At Mr Wilderness's suggestion, the old man had contacted a friend in the Institute for the Conservation of Historic Works of Art. They had verified the signature as being that of Michael Darwin and had declared it to be the earliest of the artist's known works. Another expert had come down from the V & A who had not only enthused about the painting, but about the house and some of the family antiques.

It was after the latter visit that the discovery of the fresco hit the media. Not only Ortolans but the whole of Detcham village had been deluged by reporters from newspapers and the television companies. Simon was forced to apply for a week's leave. There were decisions of moment to be made and at Mr Wilderness's suggestion, a meeting was arranged at Ortolans comprising Roddy and himself, the expert from the Institute for the Conservation of Historic Works of Art, the enthusiastic lady from the V & A and a newcomer, a knowledgeable gentleman from English Heritage. Also present, as a quiet spectator, had been Simon's bank manager.

Simon smiled, remembering that gathering round the kitchen table at Ortolans with mugs of instant coffee provided by a discreet Roddy – so very different from one of the impressive board meetings at the bank, but, as it turned out, of far greater financial significance. The value of his house was immeasurable, so it now seemed, and the spectre of bankruptcy banished. The fresco, although it could have been removed by modern techniques, was to remain in place, an integral part of the house where it had reposed in almost perfect condition for

four hundred years. It was mooted that Ortolans be opened
to the public; not only the library but the drawing-room,
dining-room, hall, main staircase, the beautiful gallery with
its oriel window, the main bedroom with the 1920s green tiled
bathroom, were all to be on show to visitors. The east wing
and the attic flat were to be retained by Simon for his own
use. It was further suggested that the stables would make
ideal offices and that Roddy should also draw up plans for
the conversion of one of the outbuildings to public
conveniences.

Simon had had several further meetings with the man from
English Heritage who, using *The Calverley Journal* as a guide,
suggested plans to revert the old walled vegetable garden to
the herb garden created for Simon's ancestor, Eleanor
Calverley. He had also suggested that a replica of the
Elizabethan knot garden be re-formed below the terrace.
Roddy, bless him, had found a highly efficient firm of landscape gardeners who were already transforming the grounds.
He, Simon, had put his foot down at the suggestion of a
souvenir shop inside Ortolans but had accepted that leaflets
and postcards could be sold at the lodge gate where the
entrance money would be taken.

The bank manager, now falling over himself to be helpful,
had agreed to provide all the necessary finance until the newly
formed charity – Friends of Michael Darwin Society – had
sufficient funds to cover expenses. Money was already pouring
in from art lovers all over the world. Simon had been obliged
to resign from Steinfelds and give his full time to supervising
and organizing the whole enterprise. The trouble now was
that even working fourteen hours a day, and with a competent
woman coping with the domestic side of affairs, he could not
keep pace with the work. His newly engaged secretary would
at least answer the ever-ringing telephone and the daily inrush
of mail, he thought, but there was so much else to be done.

Just for a moment Simon felt a nostalgic longing for the days
when there had been only Roddy, Hazel and poor little Vicky

in the house, and the weekends had been long leisurely days spent in or out of doors on small tasks of their choosing.

He had long since trained himself not to remember the days and nights when Emma had been with him at Ortolans. She had been to the Middle East and to the Falklands since that day they'd discovered the fresco and he had seen her only once briefly last Christmas when he'd been allowed to have Vicky for the weekend. Fortunately, he had had little time for regrets. For months now, there had been little to differentiate between Ortolans and Piccadilly Circus, he thought ruefully. Only at night, when the visiting experts, builders, society organizers, reporters and the rest of the related paparazzi had departed, did he feel Ortolans once more belonged to him; was trying to encourage him to allow it its period of glory! It had been left to him to decide how often the house was opened to the public, and once everything was finally organized and running smoothly, he might yet again find peace in this, his home.

There was a knock on the door and Carol Aldridge came in, accompanied by a florid-faced, portly woman in her mid-fifties.

'Miss Priscilla Hanworth!' Carol said, seating herself in a chair by the window whilst Simon waved the woman into the vacant chair opposite him. He shuffled through his papers and found Miss Hanworth's curriculum vitae. On paper, anyway, she sounded highly efficient.

Too efficient, he thought after a moment or two's conversation. She knew everything, could do anything, had, so it seemed, had experience in a multitude of not dissimilar jobs . . . secretarial, organization, accounting, fund-raising, marshalling people in groups. Carol was looking at him hopefully. He forced himself to ask some further questions.

'Yes, Sir Simon, I am an excellent driver . . . no, I have no encumbrances and would be happy to live in . . . yes, I would be happy with the salary offered . . . yes, I would be prepared to take my annual holiday in the winter when there would not be so many visitors.'

Simon dismissed her, but beckoned to Carol to stay.

'I agree Miss Hanworth seems ideal!' he said reluctantly. 'I know this probably sounds crazy to you after all the hard work you've put in, but the fact is, I just wish the good lady wasn't quite so perfect! I have a strong suspicion she will be organizing me if I'm not careful! She has a very domineering personality.'

Carol grinned.

'I know what you mean – but she does seem ideal in so many ways, and I'm sure you can keep her under control.'

'I suppose so!' Simon acknowledged. 'Put her on the short-list, Carol, and I'll see the others in case I find someone I like a bit better.'

He wasted no time on the next applicant – a girl in her twenties who was about to get married. Her husband would commute to London, she told him, where he had a good job in an advertising firm, but would naturally want to share the attic flat with her. Carol had shown her the flat and she had liked it very much. They were not planning to start a family for at least ten years by which time they hoped to buy a house.

'If mortgages get cheaper, they might buy one far sooner than that!' Simon said to Carol as the girl left the room. 'I want someone I can count on to be permanent.'

'Like Miss Hanworth!' Carol said with a smile.

The next applicant, she told him, had decided whilst awaiting her interview that the house had an eerie atmosphere and that she could neither live in nor work in it.

'Said she was psychic and felt vibes!' Carol added despairingly. 'I really am sorry, Sir Simon. She seemed so sensible at both my interviews with her. However, there is one more, a man, ex-army officer, a retired major who has been a quartermaster, so he prides himself on his organizing abilities. He has excellent references from his commanding officer. He seems a decent sort of chap, so let's hold thumbs. I'll make us some coffee while you interview him.'

'Is he worth the effort?' Simon asked. 'I have a nasty feeling I'm destined to employ the perfect Miss Hanworth.'

'You never know,' Carol replied and gave him an encouraging smile as she left the room.

She genuinely hoped that the major would turn out to be the perfect person for the job. If she had not been happily married, she thought as she walked down the passage towards the kitchen, she would have applied for the job herself! Sir Simon was really dishy – gorgeous green eyes, sexy smile, fabulous long legs and narrow hips. He was the epitome of the English aristocrat but with that understated elegance went a disarming natural friendliness. No wonder she was happy to give up her Saturday to accommodate him with these interviews!

She opened the kitchen door to find Sir Simon's architect, Roddy Pylbeam, sitting at the table with an attractive young woman who was cuddling a small girl. The child regarded her with solemn dark eyes.

'You haven't come to take me back, have you?' she asked in an anxious voice.

'No, Vicky, this is Mrs Aldridge who is trying to find someone to help Simon with his busy work!' Roddy broke in, rising to his feet. 'We're just going down to the stables to see the new dovecot, aren't we, Vicky!'

'I can go, can't I, Emma?' the child said. 'I don't have to go back till tomorrow, do I?'

As Roddy and Vicky left the room, Emma indicated one of the empty chairs.

'Vicky lives in a children's home – hence all the references to "going back". Roddy and I have just collected her and brought her here for the weekend. She used to live here, you see, and she and Simon are very attached to each other. Vicky was the former housekeeper's daughter. My name's Emma, by the way!'

'Mine's Carol. Smoke?'

Emma shook her head.

'I'm trying to give it up!' Carol said. 'Fourth attempt! I'll do it one of these days. What a lovely little girl. Is she a foreigner?'

'No, English, but her father was Singalese.'

Carol nodded.

'That explains it. Sir Simon never mentioned the child – but then he doesn't talk much about his private life. I know he was married – but I gather his wife left him. I can't think why. She must have been off her noddle! I've had quite a lot to do with him these past weeks, and he strikes me as utterly charming. Have you known him long?'

Realizing that the woman had no idea who she really was, Emma felt it would be less embarrassing for them both if she did not enlighten her.

'Several years!' she said vaguely. 'Roddy tells me you've been trying to get appropriate staff for Ortolans.'

Carol nodded.

'Yes, I have – but this time I'm hoping to fix Sir Simon up with a PA and I can tell you, it ain't easy!' She elaborated the qualifications required of this particular member of the staff. 'As you can imagine, the job has quite a bit of responsibility attached to it. Sir Simon needs someone with exceptional organizing ability, imagination, the ability to get on with everyone – members of the public, cleaners, secretary, visiting officials – the lot . . . not to mention Sir Simon himself. And they've got to live in. Not everyone wants to be buried in the depths of the country. Where do you live, Emma?'

'Southampton. It's near my job, you see.'

'Which is?' Carol prompted as she went to put on the kettle and prepare a tray.

Emma leant back in her chair and endeavoured to explain the duties of an assistant television producer. Carol, whose task it was to extract information from job applicants, sat down opposite her and listened with professional interest, occasionally asking a pertinent question.

'I've never had anything to do with the media world,' she said when Emma had concluded her account. 'Mostly, I deal with domestic staff, and some secretarial. This finding a PA for Sir Simon is a one-off. I nearly didn't undertake it because

I guessed it was going to be tricky – but the man himself was so charming, I couldn't refuse. You know, Emma, listening to you talk, it struck me that it was just my luck – finding someone who was tailor-made for this job but who doesn't want it.' She grinned. 'Now why couldn't you have been jobless, then I could have sent you in for an interview. You've got all the perfect qualifications! I suppose I couldn't tempt you into a change? What's your salary, by the way – although you don't have to answer that!'

'I'm getting twenty-five thousand, but . . .'

'I know, you love your job!' Carol broke in with a smile. 'Pity! I'm sure I could have bumped up the salary Sir Simon's offering. He's rolling in it now, you know. Roddy, the architect, was telling me that, before they found the fresco, Sir Simon was on the point of having to sell up. He said it would have broken the poor man's heart – the house having been in the family for donkey's years! Ah, there's his bell! Must mean the interview is over.' She rose quickly, spooned coffee grains into a jug, and turned to smile at Emma as she poured boiling water on to them. 'Hold thumbs Sir Simon has approved the major.' She paused as she lifted the tray. 'Do you know, for once in my life, I don't gave a damn about my commission. I just want to see that nice man happy. Know what I mean?'

Emma nodded as she rose to her feet and took the tray from Carol's hands.

'I'll take it!' she said quietly. 'I think . . . I hope he'll be pleased to see me.'

Ignoring the look of astonishment on Carol Aldridge's face, she edged open the door with her foot and carried the tray into the passage. Automatically, she adjusted her step to avoid the uneven dip in the old flagstone outside the pantry. She noticed that there was a new push-button telephone in the niche outside the dining-room door where once the old brass gong had hung. Emma smiled, remembering how exasperated Simon had been when Hazel, with every good intention, had tried to clean it with caustic soda and so pitted its surface that it had had to be thrown away. Ever after, Hazel had used it as a convenient place to put an ashtray and long after she had gone, Emma had found one of her half-smoked cigarettes stubbed out in a corner.

She paused as the library door opened and a grey-haired man with a military moustache came out.

'Just want a quick word with Mrs Aldridge,' he said as he held the door open for her. 'Hope you have better luck than I did!' he added in a whisper. 'Get malaria, you see. He wants someone healthy!'

As he walked past her, Emma took a step forward. She could see Simon now. His elbows were on the big, leather-topped desk, his hands covering his forehead. His whole bearing was one of dejection.

She should have told him that she was coming to Ortolans today, she thought. Roddy had phoned her to say that Simon was to be allowed to have Vicky for the weekend and suggested that she might want to see the child. Simon, he had informed her, would be tied up for a large part of Saturday doing interviews; and he, Roddy, had volunteered to collect the child and keep her occupied whilst Simon was busy. She'd be doing everyone a favour and it would be a lovely surprise for Vicky.

That, at least, had proved the case, she thought, remembering the little girl's rapturous welcome; but would Simon resent her unannounced intrusion? These past long weeks, months, there had been no letter, no telephone call from him! Suddenly she felt unbearably nervous, wondering if he would be pleased to see her, if . . .

At that moment Simon became aware that he was not alone. He looked up and stared in disbelief at the silent figure standing in the doorway.

'Good God, Emma!' he said. 'What are you doing here?'

She gave a tentative smile as she returned his gaze.

'Hello, Simon!' she said. 'I've come to apply for the job!'

EPILOGUE

May 1989

'Simon, look!' Emma said pointing. 'The swallows are back!'

Simon kept his arm around her shoulders as he glanced up to see the small dark shadows darting in and out of the eaves, looking for last year's nesting sites. It was a perfect May morning and the warm sunshine had only just lifted the carpet of dew from the freshly cut lawns. From their lounge chair by the arbour, they could see the massed bunches of pale mauve wisteria covering the south wall of the house. On the roof, two pairs of doves, a brilliant white in the bright sun, were strutting to and fro in a mating dance. Already, to Vicky's delight, there were two hen birds nesting in the new dovecot.

Simon's arm tightened around Emma's shoulders and his voice was husky as he said:

'It frightens me sometimes to think that but for the merest chance, you might not have been here with me!'

'You don't really believe that, darling!' Emma replied quickly. 'Quite apart from Carol putting the idea into my head that I'd infinitely prefer this job to the one I had, I'm sure Roddy was determined to see us together again!' She smiled, remembering how forceful Roddy had been in his persuasions that they should keep her visit to Ortolans a surprise; how when she had protested that Simon must be asked first if it was all right for her to spend the day there, he'd insisted that there was no need – Simon wouldn't mind one way or the other.

At the time, she had been piqued – no, hurt – to think that Simon had so quickly adapted to their separation and, seemingly, was not missing her as much as she had been missing him! It had been easier on her pride to convince herself that Vicky was the only one who mattered. Roddy refused to take any credit for their ultimate reconciliation.

'Oh, you'd have got together sooner or later!' he'd said. 'It was only a matter of time! Besides, it was as obvious to me as to Carol that you were tailor-made for the job. That's why I insisted you should come on the Saturday rather than the Sunday. Telling you I needed you to help look after Vicky was just a ruse.'

Emma smiled, remembering how difficult Simon had found it at first to believe she really did want the job. He'd been afraid it was a spur-of-the-moment decision – one she might later regret. It had not been easy to explain her sudden change of heart.

Now that she'd got where she wanted in her career, it didn't seem to matter any more, she'd told him. Perhaps she had simply needed to prove she could reach her goal; prove to herself that she had the ability; that in the end it was the getting there and not the being there that mattered. She had admitted that, crazy as it sounded, she'd tried very hard not to love him, that she'd wanted to be free to go her own way.

'And you don't feel that any more?' Simon had persisted.

Her way was now his way, she'd told him. When Carol had pointed out that someone else would be living in the house helping to run Ortolans, she'd realized that her career in television was not the most important thing in the world to her; that all she wanted now was to work here, beside him.

Only then had Simon taken her in his arms.

Now, with their hands tightly linked, they were savouring this quiet hour alone together. Vicky had gone down to the woods with the young girl who Carol had engaged for them to look after her.

'The swallows don't seem to mind all the visitors,' Simon commented. 'I wish I could say the same. I suppose I'll get used to the invasion of our privacy!'

Emma laughed.

'It's only twice a week, darling. Actually, I enjoy being a guide. The people who come are so interested and enthusiastic. A lot of them are connoisseurs.'

'I suppose I could always wear my oldest clothes – and pretend to be one of the gardeners!' Simon said smiling.

'You can't blame them for wanting to meet one of the genuine Calverleys!' Emma teased. 'Anyway, if you really get bored being stared at, I'll say you are writing your memoirs. That sounds suitably impressive!'

'It's just what I should be doing,' Simon said with mock self-reproach. 'Or at least, writing up *The Calverley Journal*. There's such a lot to go in it. We don't want to leave it so long we forget.'

'You must include the changes in the village,' Emma said. 'It's astonishing how much prosperity the fresco has brought to the parish – the post office snowed under with postcards; the grocers now a flourishing tea-room; the pub having an extension built . . . The repercussions have been endless.'

Last year, news of the discovery of a Michael Darwin painting at Ortolans had hit the headlines in most of the national newspapers. It had been on all the television channels, and when the house was finally ready to be opened to the public at Easter, Emma's former boss in Southampton had filmed an exclusive documentary which had done much to soften the fact of Emma's sudden resignation from her job. It had also brought in a vast number of donations for the Friends of Michael Darwin charity.

Emma lay back with her head against the soft cushions of the new garden swing seat she and Simon had chosen together in Brighton. It was a strange feeling – having so much money they never had to consider the cost of anything Ortolans needed and which took their fancy. Perhaps one day, she thought, she would grow accustomed to being rich!

Throughout the autumn and winter, they had received innumerable visitors, many of them foreign connoisseurs who had flown to England especially to have a preview of the hitherto undiscovered work of the great artist. Hosting these visits, together with supervision of the builders, decorators and gardeners, had kept Simon and Emma fully employed throughout the year.

At Christmas, Emma's parents had come to stay for three weeks. The visit had been an unqualified success. Simon and her father had spent hours debating the state of the world's finances and had discovered a mutual interest in chess. Emma and her mother, although never really close, had found comfort in talking about Rosalind and the childhood treats they had shared when they had been taken to the Science Museum, the Zoo, the Planetarium or the V & A. Somehow, Emma had forgotten the good times and she could remember Rosalind now without pain.

Much as she and Simon had enjoyed this successful reunion, they had welcomed the return of their privacy, so soon to be lost. Now that the house was open to the public, on this, one of their treasured Sundays 'off-duty', they were savouring the rare chance of a lazy day alone together. Both were therefore reluctant to see the visitor whose unexpected arrival the housekeeper now came to announce.

'I'll go and see who it is – explain that it's our day off,' Emma said.

In the hallway stood a professorial-looking gentleman who said he had come from Brighton, and very much wanted to see the painting. He had already seen it twice in the company of other paying visitors but for reasons he would later explain, he wished to see it again and to have a word with Sir Simon. He appeared so earnest that Emma agreed to call Simon in from the garden.

Apologizing to Simon for disturbing him on a Sunday, he said:

'I am compiling a book on the history of Sussex, and for the past two months, I have been doing some research in Detcham – a most interesting and historic little village.' He paused before continuing: 'I am particularly curious about the Pylbeam family. I thought you might be interested to know, Sir Simon, that there is little doubt a man called Thomas Pylbeam – a master carpenter – built this house. I have here his family tree – with some conspicuous gaps, of course – but those early years seem fairly well authenticated. I wonder if it would interest you to look at it? You see, I think it may well have a relevance to the Darwin painting.'

Both Emma's and Simon's curiosity was now aroused.

'I am intrigued to hear more,' Simon said, leading the way into the library. 'Do sit down, sir!'

The historian seated himself and, encouraged by Simon, continued to expand his theory.

'Thomas Pylbeam had a wife and eight surviving children. It would be natural in those days for the sons to follow their father in his trade, so we can assume that "John" and "Tom" helped build this house. I suddenly recalled last week when I was drawing the family tree that these two names were on the painting. I checked with last year's newspaper cuttings which I had kept and indeed, it was reported that they were. Now, if I am right – and this can only be an educated guess, you understand – then we might assume that the experts are wrong in thinking that Darwin painted these people before he left London. I believe he painted the Pylbeam family at the time Master Thomas Pylbeam was building the house. This ties in with the experts' theory that the self-made paints Darwin used could only have been applied to *wet* plaster. Darwin would have been about fifteen or sixteen years old at that time . . . he reached Italy in his seventeenth year, having left home against his father's wishes. He might – and almost certainly did – have travelled to the coast via Detcham and remained here at Ortolans for a few days. Do you agree he might well have painted that lovely scene to amuse himself and the builders?'

All three stood up and went across to the painting. The woman in the pink dress with three small children grouped around her was unnamed, but beneath the sturdy figure beside her was the name Thomas. The lad on the south bank of the Thames was called Tom, and the boy holding out his cap to receive a coin from the soldier on horseback was John.

'I cannot identify the man on the ramparts of the Tower!' the historian said; 'Possibly one of the other workmen? There were Armitages, Greens, Hicks in Detcham at that time. Hicks was a master mason so he would have been involved in the building of Ortolans. It rather looks as if Darwin only named the Pylbeams – possibly because he was indebted to them for some reason.'

'These are Roddy's ancestors!' Simon said. 'I must go and telephone him at once. If you are right, this painting is as much a part of his family history as of mine. Roddy, my architect, is a Pylbeam, you see. You'll stay for a while, won't you, sir?'

With Roddy's arrival, the four of them talked until finally the visitor departed, promising to come again when he had a draft manuscript to show them.

'When your book is published, we shall certainly put it on sale!' Simon promised as he accompanied his visitor to his car.

It was some while before Emma could quieten Vicky who she discovered hiding in a cupboard under the staircase. The child had been afraid their visitor was a social worker come to take her back to the children's home.

'She'll get over the fear eventually!' Simon reassured Emma as Vicky's young nanny came to collect her to take her to bed.

Hazel, they now knew for certain, was never coming back. Simon had received a letter from her from Spain.

Spence and me have had a smashing time here. By the time you get this, we'll be on the plane to Ostralia. I hope Vicky isnt being to much of a noosance. Give her my love. I hope she gets herself a decent Mum and Dad. Time the state did sumthing for her. I did try to look after her but I guess I'm not cut out for the job.

I hope the house is OK and you've found someone to cook and that for you. You was decent to me and the kid but I couldn't take no more. I was going barmy on my own. Spence is a good bloke and I'm sticking with him becos we hit it off real well. He's given me a smashing braselet to make up for leaving the kid. Please tell Vick I did my best but can't do no more.

Give Emma my love if she's around. I think she makes you a smashing wife and she can cook and all.

Yours faithfully,

Hazel.

PS Will you sign what papers come about Vicky? I want her adopted. Her birth sertificit is in my cupboard on the shelf.

Simon had employed a first-class lawyer in an attempt to get the courts to agree to their adopting Vicky. It wasn't going to be easy and could, the lawyer said, be a very long while before they could achieve this goal – if indeed, they were ever able to do so. Meanwhile, they had been accepted as foster-parents, and last summer a radiant Vicky had been retrieved from the children's home and returned to live with them. She rarely mentioned Hazel, and when Simon or Emma did so, she showed no sign of distress and seemed unconcerned as to when her mother might return from her prolonged 'holiday'.

The day after the historian's visit, Roddy produced a faded, dog-eared charcoal drawing which, he explained, had been pasted into the back of the big family Bible he had inherited from his grandfather. Within days, it was verified as a Michael Darwin and thus proved the historian's theory that the Ortolans painting had been done when the house was being built. In the 1500s, with the young Darwin's fame still in the far distant future, no one would have thought to prevent the covering of the painting with the panelling ordered by the first of the Ortolans Calverleys. Only the Pylbeams, and perhaps the master mason, would have been there to regret that so delightful a scene would be hidden from other eyes for close on four hundred years.

'What would you have done, Emma, if the painting had been valueless?' Simon said as he unlocked the front door in preparation for the first of the day's stream of visitors who would soon be arriving.

'Well, my darling, if you had been in no position to keep me, I would have had to stay in my job and keep you!'

She was laughing as she darted swiftly through the door leading into the garden. Simon caught up with her as she collapsed breathless on to a chair in the arbour.

'That's enough of that!' he said as, without the slightest regard for her dignity, he tipped her out of the chair.

As Vicky came towards them, her arms filled with the bluebells she so loved to pick, there was a questioning look in her large, dark eyes. She regarded them solemnly as they wrestled like children on the lawn.

'What are you doing?' she asked. 'Are you fighting?'

'No, sweetheart, we're loving!' Simon said, and the bluebells scattered around them as he drew the child down into the circle of their embrace.

THE END

Love. Passion. War.
Family. Secrets. History.

Stunning timeless classics from the bestselling
novelist Claire Lorrimer.

Available in paperback and ebook.